THE TIME MUSEUM

THIS BOOK IS DEDICATED TO ABBY DENSON

A very special thanks to all the people who helped make
this book happen: Abby Denson, Brian Stone, Dan Loux,
Patsy Loux, Alexandra Graudins, Yuuko Koyama,
Seth Fishman, The Gernert Company, and Mark Siegel
and everyone at First Second Books.

THE TIME MUSEUM

Matthew Loux

First Second

New York

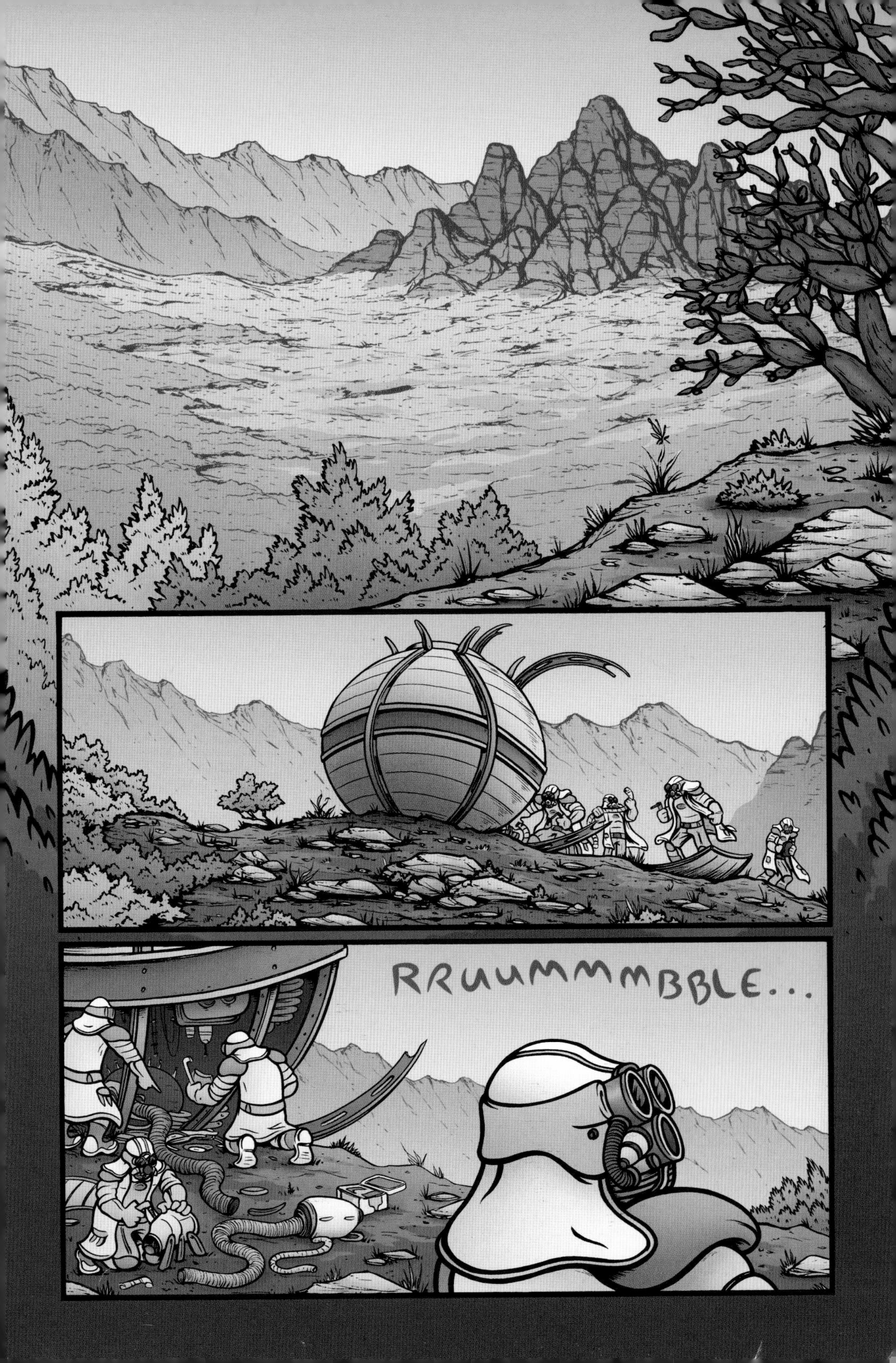
RRUUMMMBBLE...

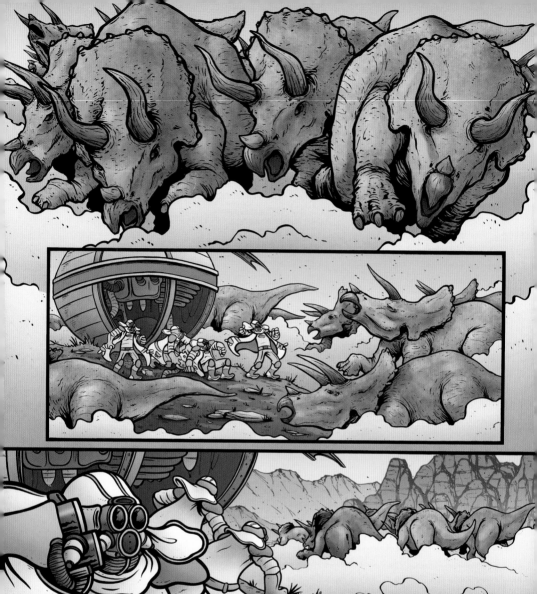

I WONDER IF THEY KNOW SOMEHOW...

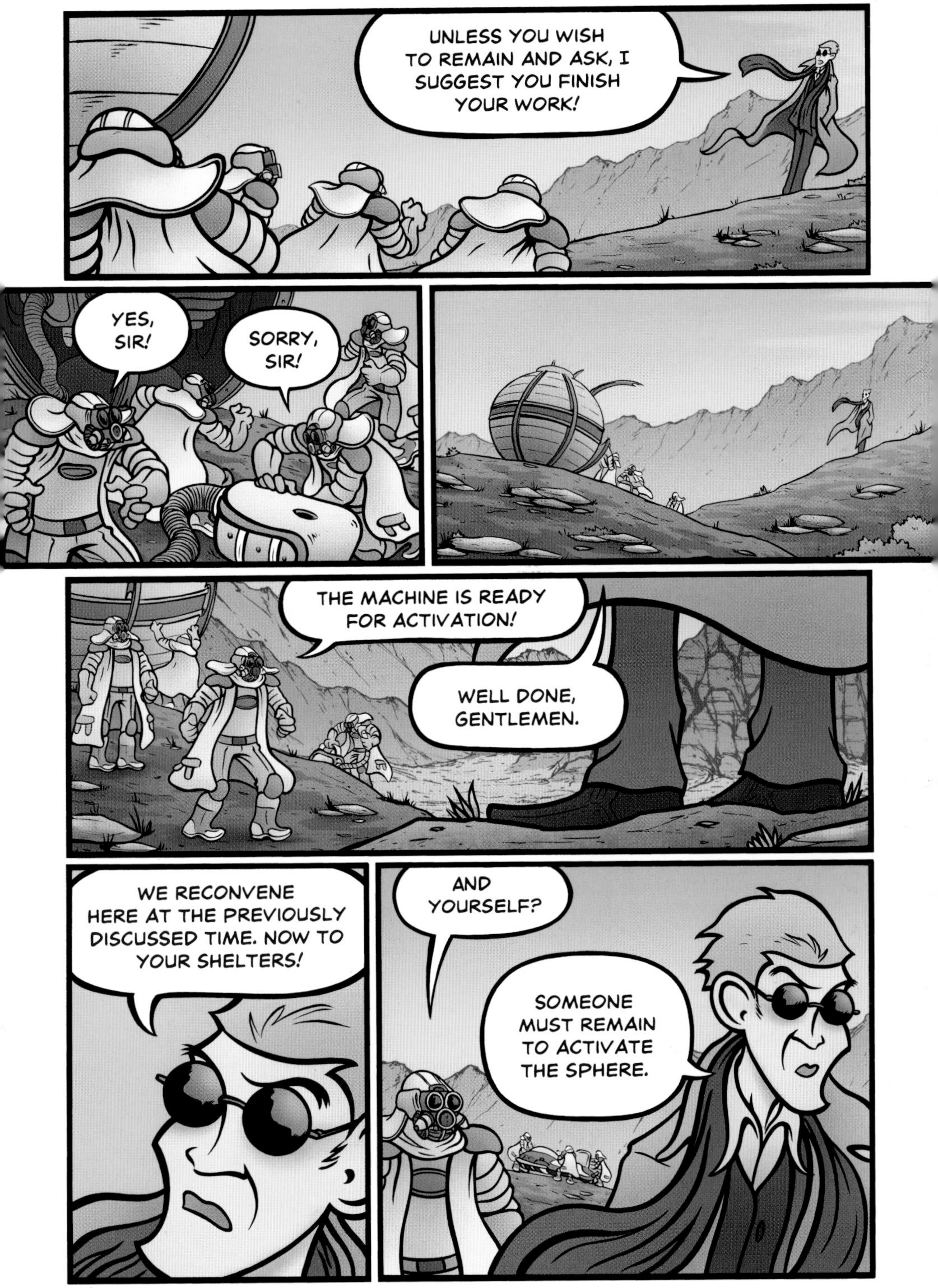
UNLESS YOU WISH TO REMAIN AND ASK, I SUGGEST YOU FINISH YOUR WORK!
YES, SIR!
SORRY, SIR!
THE MACHINE IS READY FOR ACTIVATION!
WELL DONE, GENTLEMEN.
WE RECONVENE HERE AT THE PREVIOUSLY DISCUSSED TIME. NOW TO YOUR SHELTERS!
AND YOURSELF?
SOMEONE MUST REMAIN TO ACTIVATE THE SPHERE.

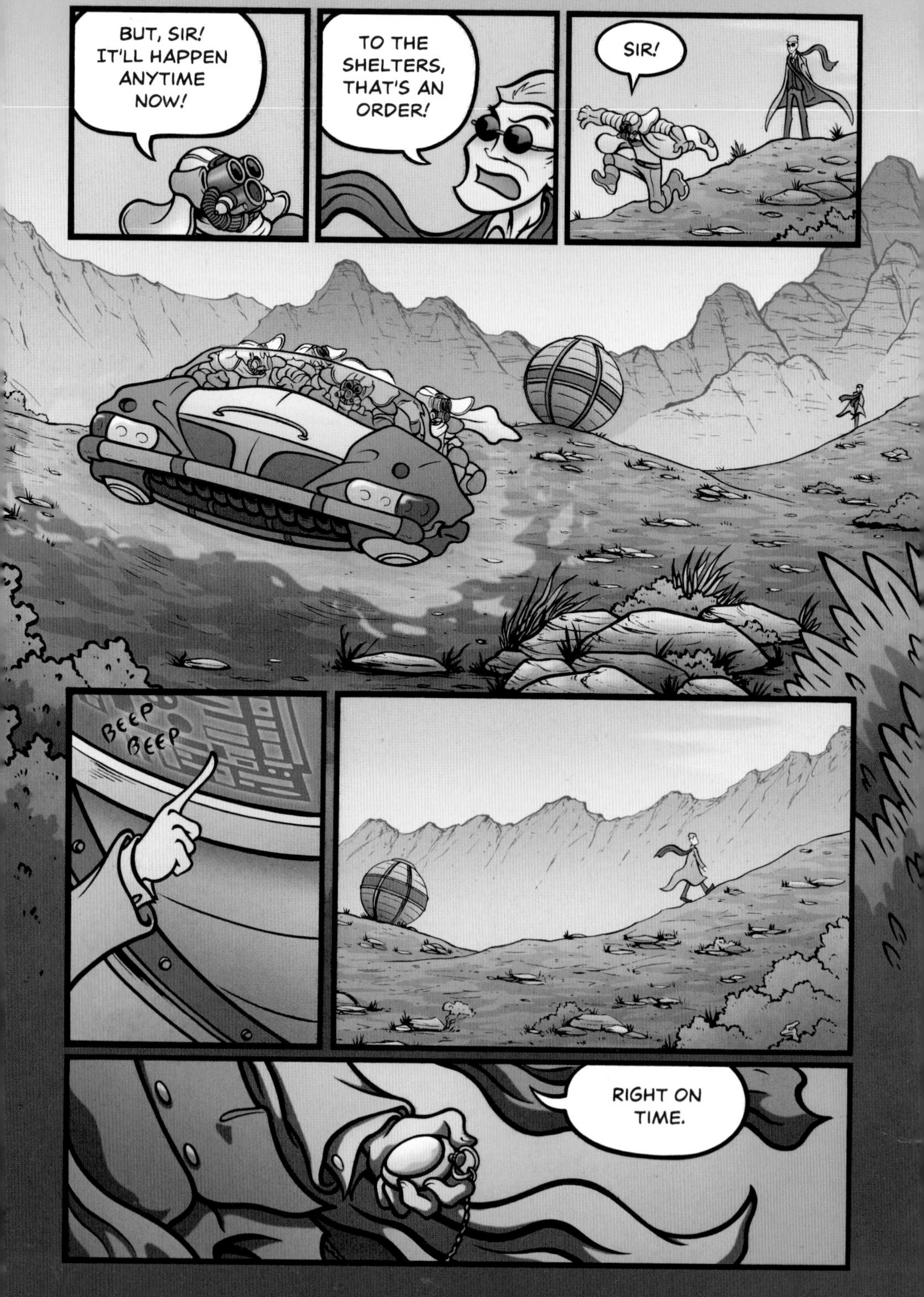
BUT, SIR! IT'LL HAPPEN ANYTIME NOW!
TO THE SHELTERS, THAT'S AN ORDER!
SIR!
BEEP BEEP
RIGHT ON TIME.

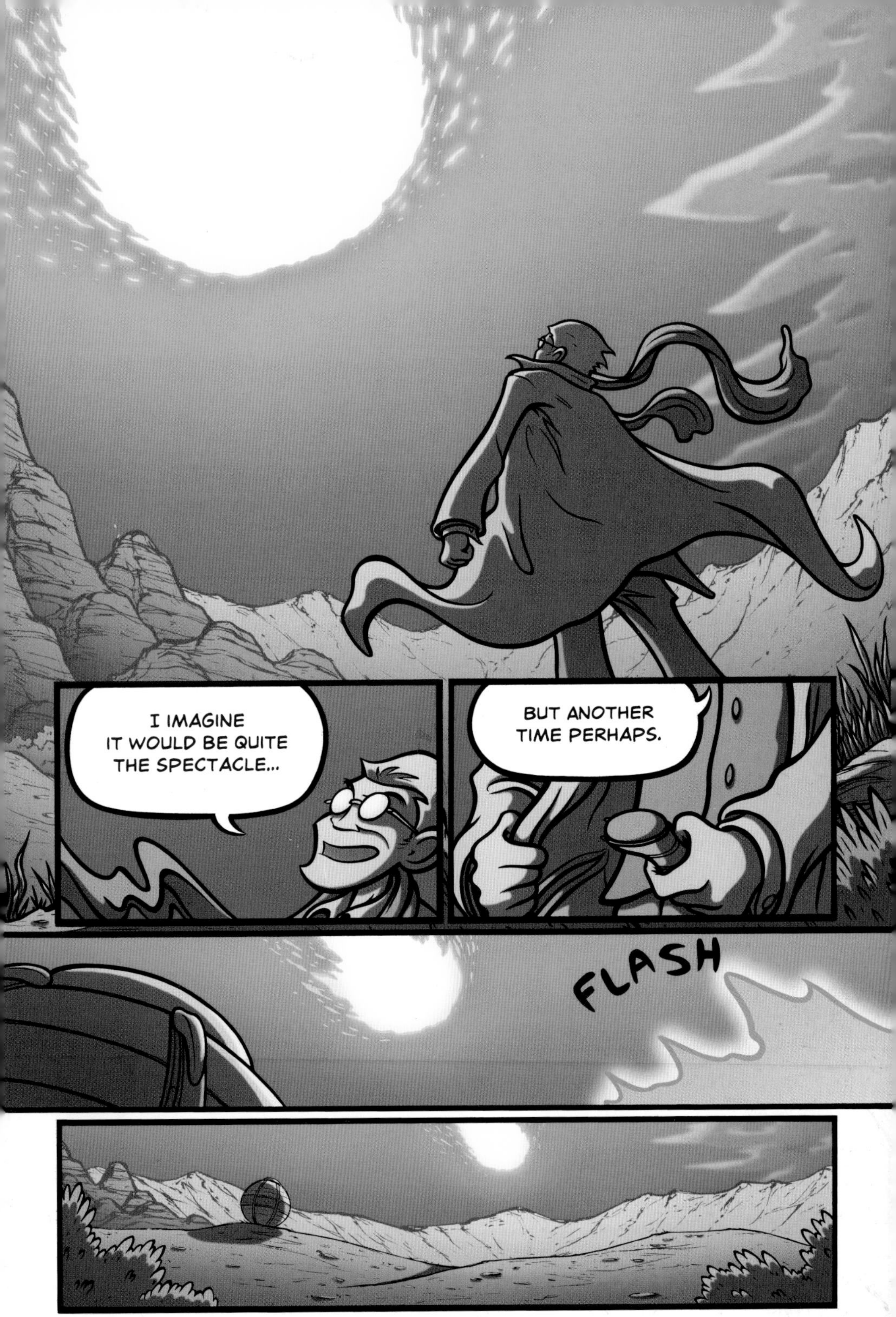
I IMAGINE IT WOULD BE QUITE THE SPECTACLE...
BUT ANOTHER TIME PERHAPS.
FLASH

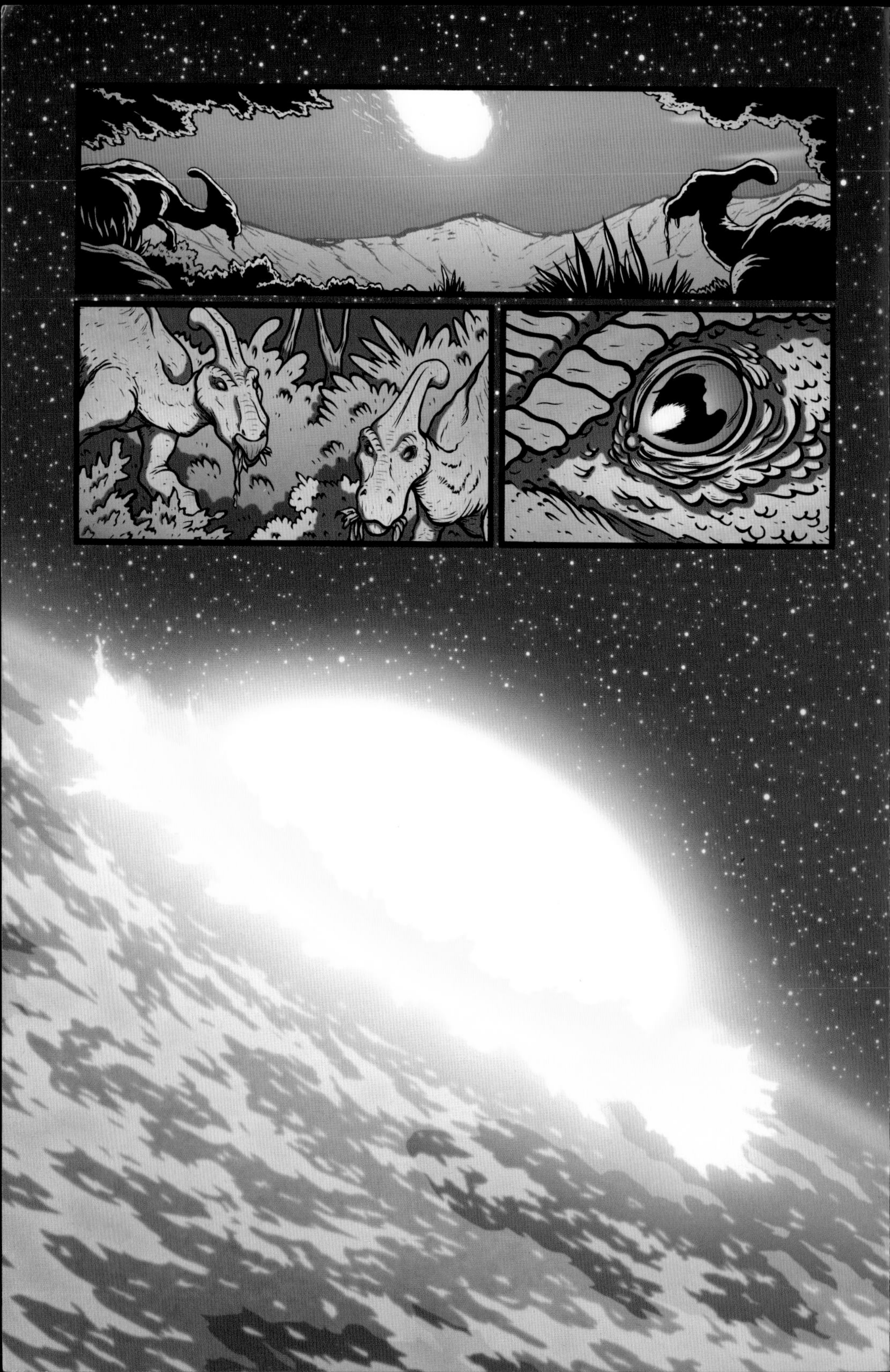

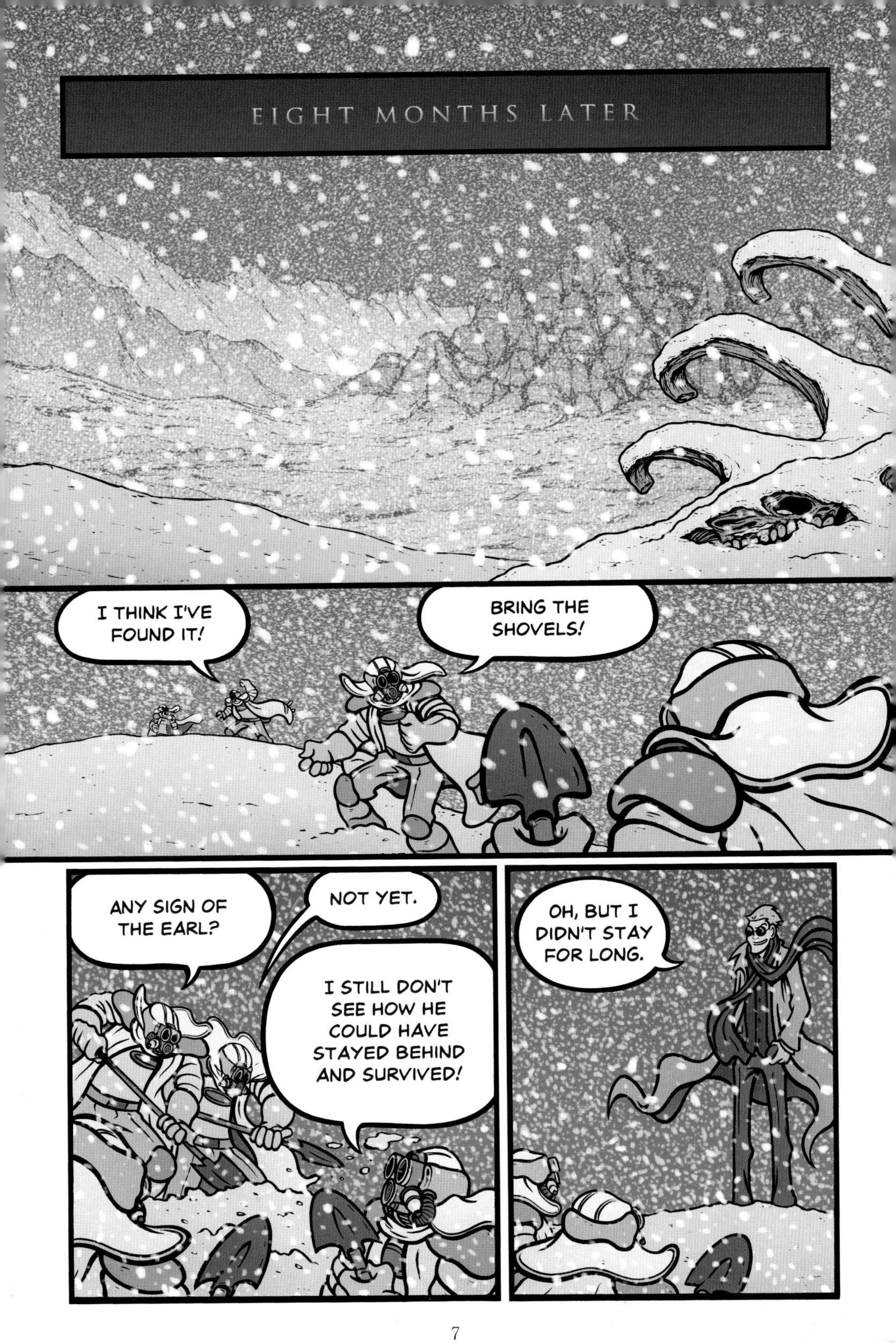
EIGHT MONTHS LATER
I THINK I'VE FOUND IT!
BRING THE SHOVELS!
ANY SIGN OF THE EARL?
NOT YET.
I STILL DON'T SEE HOW HE COULD HAVE STAYED BEHIND AND SURVIVED!
OH, BUT I DIDN'T STAY FOR LONG.

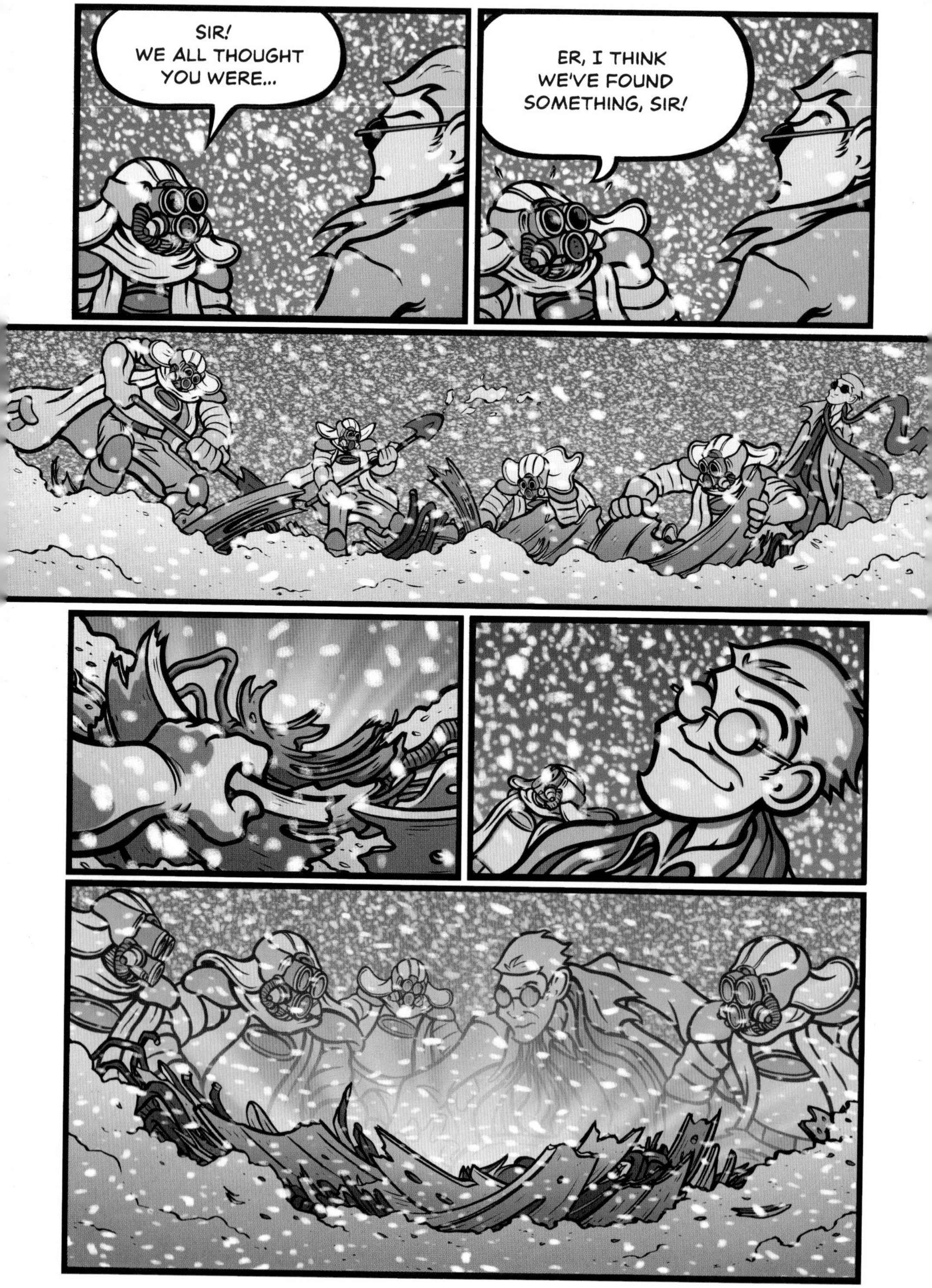
SIR! WE ALL THOUGHT YOU WERE...
ER, I THINK WE'VE FOUND SOMETHING, SIR!

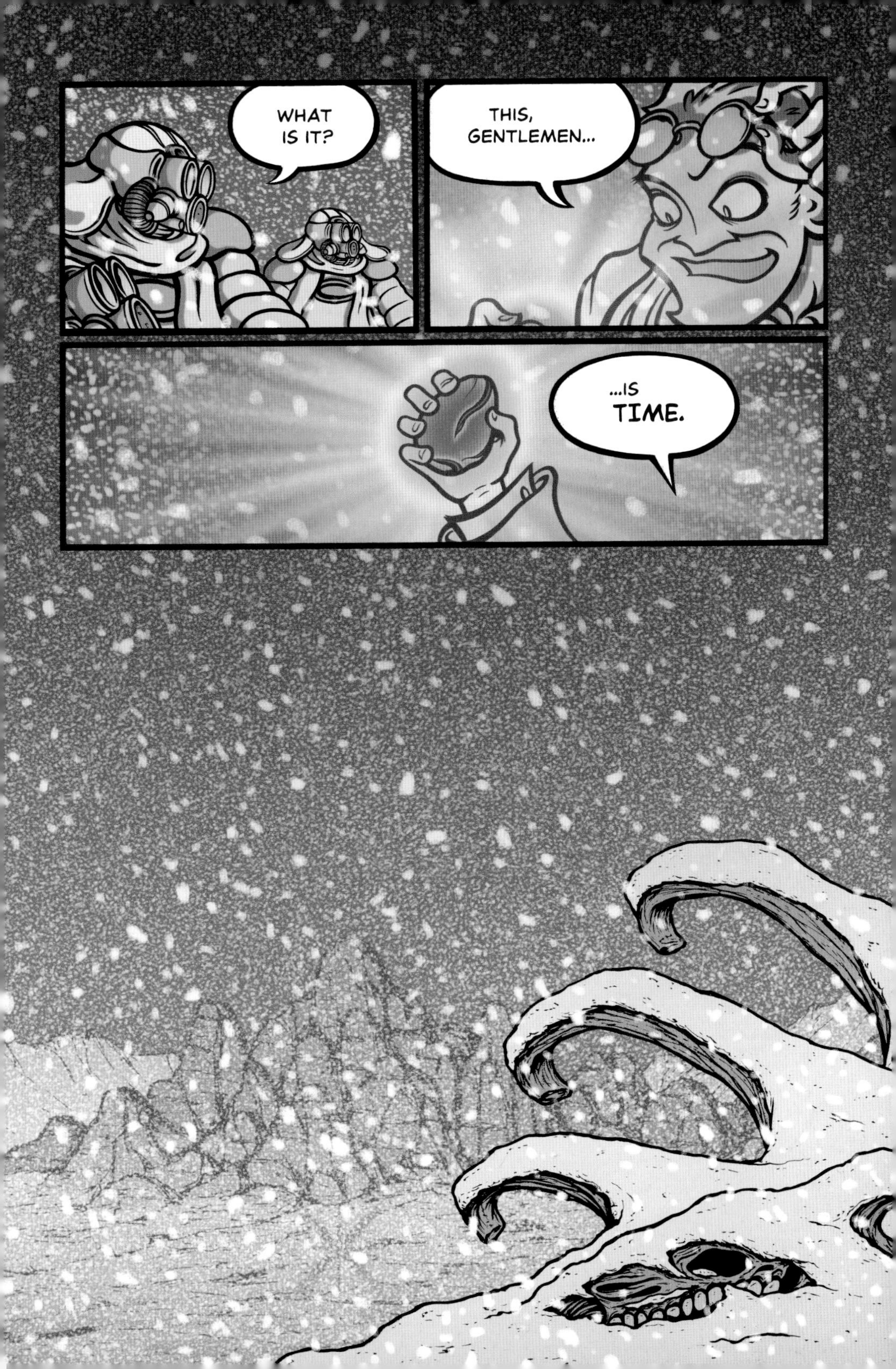
WHAT IS IT?
THIS, GENTLEMEN...
...IS TIME.

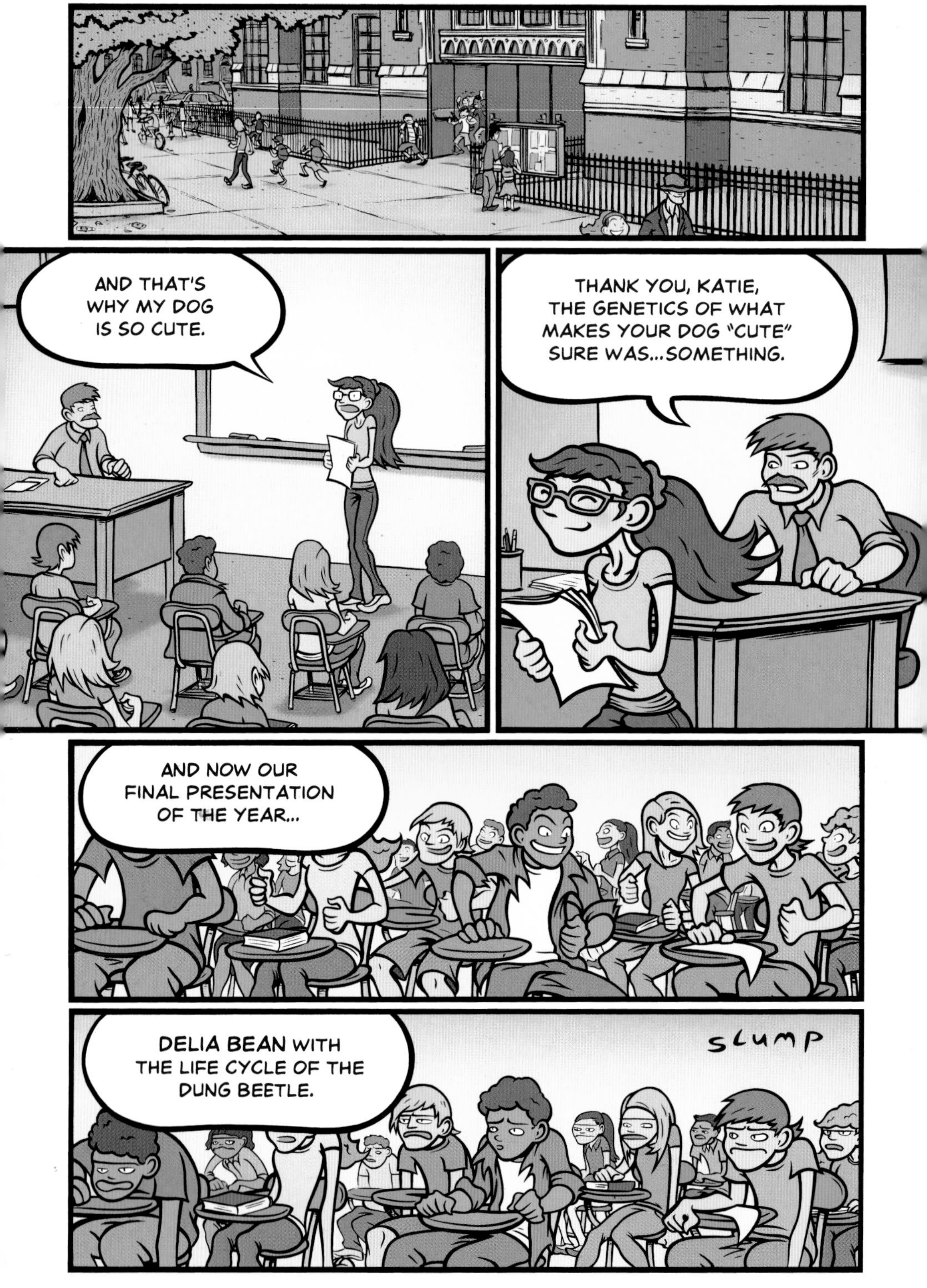
AND THAT'S WHY MY DOG IS SO CUTE.
THANK YOU, KATIE, THE GENETICS OF WHAT MAKES YOUR DOG "CUTE" SURE WAS...SOMETHING.
AND NOW OUR FINAL PRESENTATION OF THE YEAR...
DELIA BEAN WITH THE LIFE CYCLE OF THE DUNG BEETLE.
SLUMP

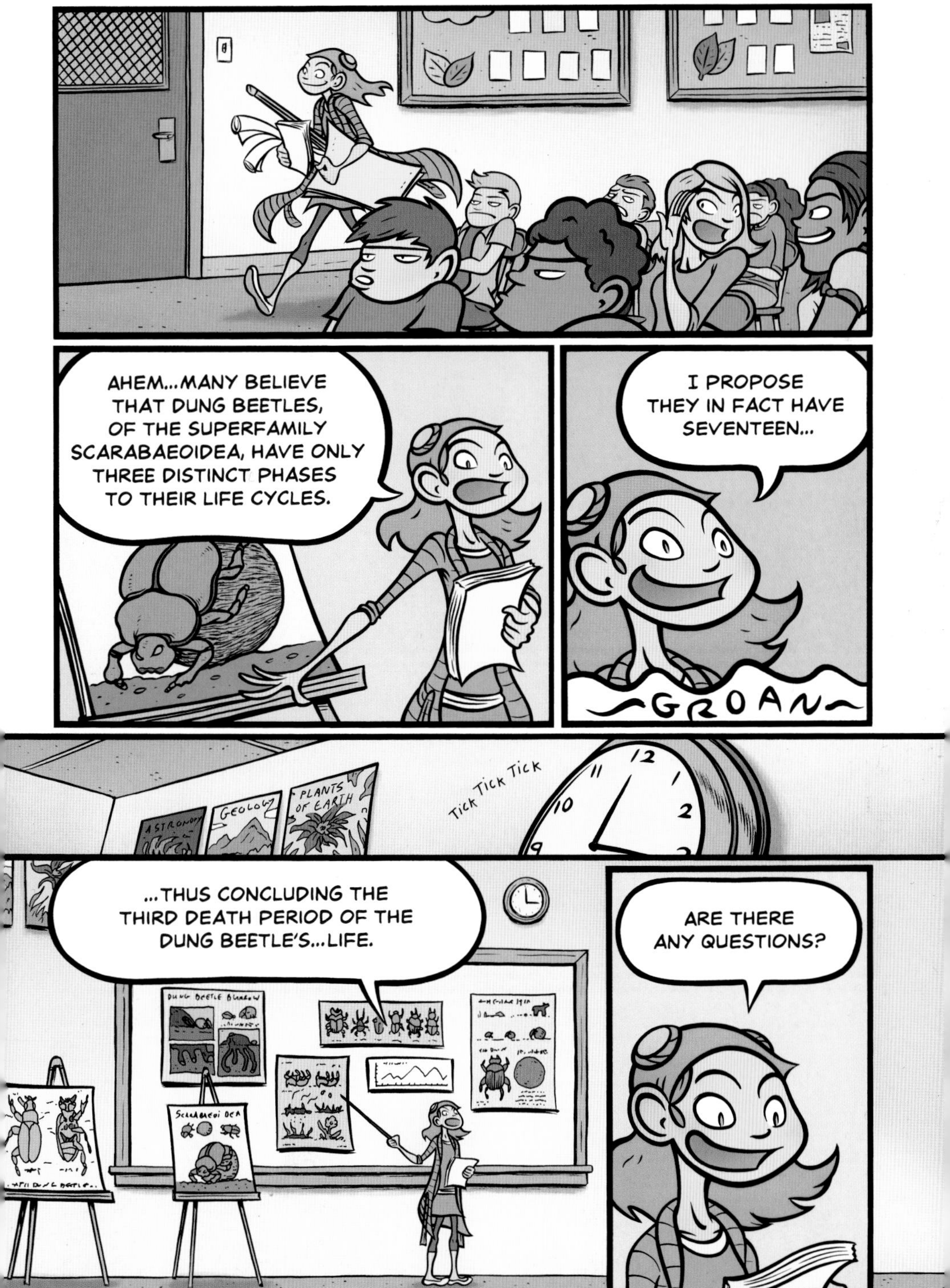
AHEM...MANY BELIEVE THAT DUNG BEETLES, OF THE SUPERFAMILY SCARABAEOIDEA, HAVE ONLY THREE DISTINCT PHASES TO THEIR LIFE CYCLES.
I PROPOSE THEY IN FACT HAVE SEVENTEEN...
GROAN
GEOLOGY
PLANTS OF EARTH
Tick Tick Tick
...THUS CONCLUDING THE THIRD DEATH PERIOD OF THE DUNG BEETLE'S...LIFE.
ARE THERE ANY QUESTIONS?

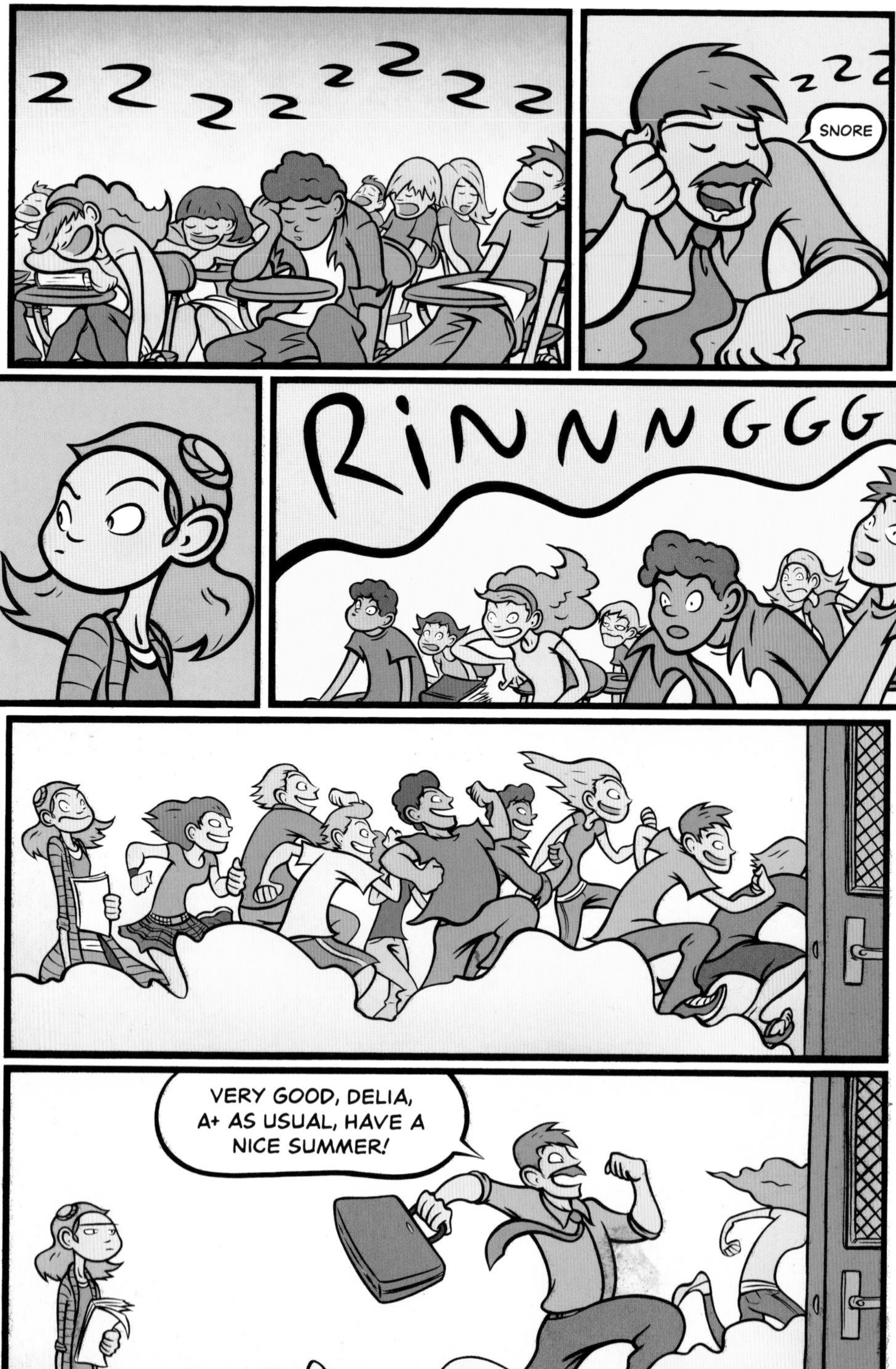

ZZZZZZZZZ
SNORE
RINNNGGGG
VERY GOOD, DELIA, A+ AS USUAL, HAVE A NICE SUMMER!

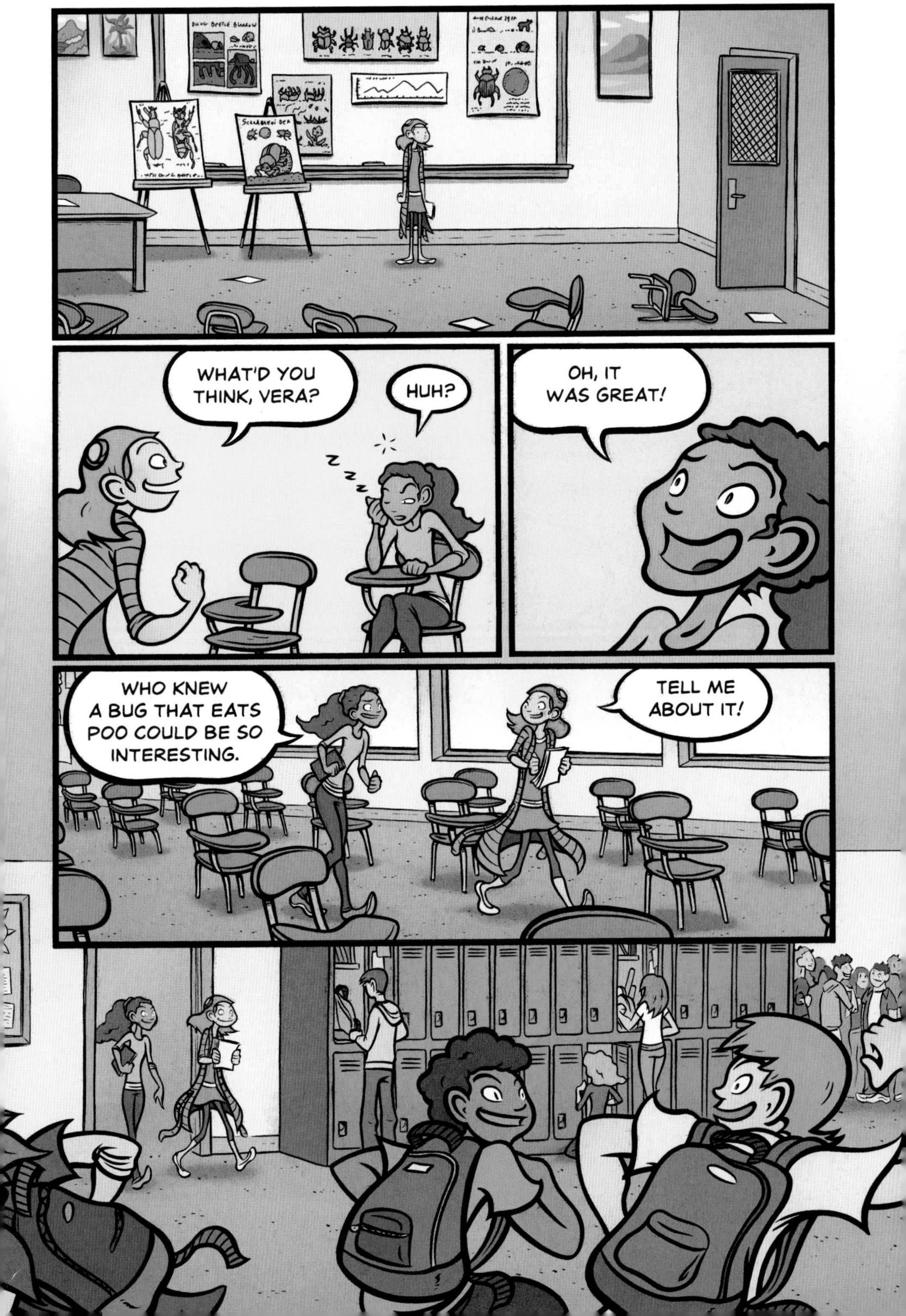
WHAT'D YOU THINK, VERA?
HUH?
OH, IT WAS GREAT!
WHO KNEW A BUG THAT EATS POO COULD BE SO INTERESTING.
TELL ME ABOUT IT!

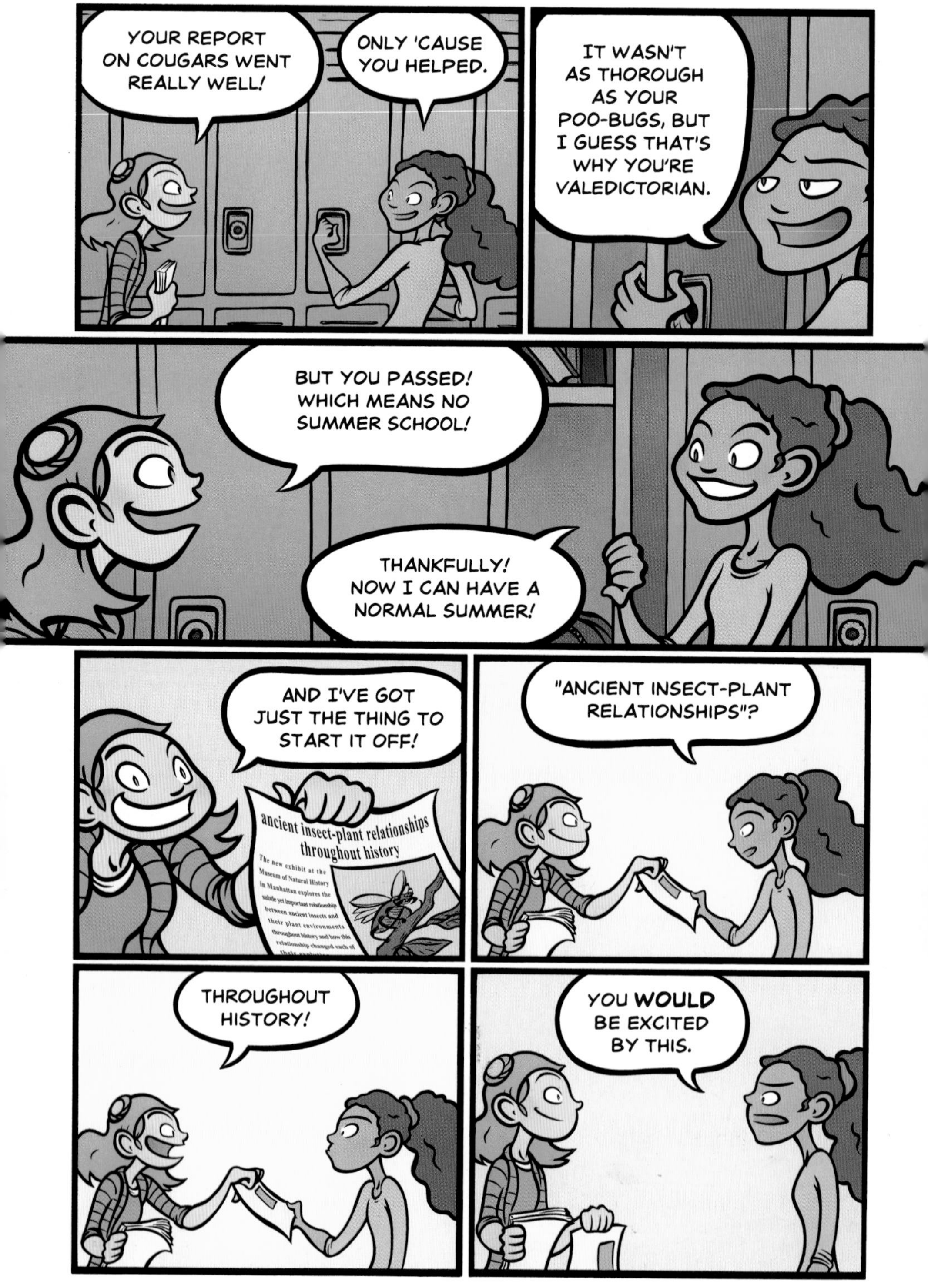
YOUR REPORT ON COUGARS WENT REALLY WELL!
ONLY 'CAUSE YOU HELPED.
IT WASN'T AS THOROUGH AS YOUR POO-BUGS, BUT I GUESS THAT'S WHY YOU'RE VALEDICTORIAN.
BUT YOU PASSED! WHICH MEANS NO SUMMER SCHOOL!
THANKFULLY! NOW I CAN HAVE A NORMAL SUMMER!
AND I'VE GOT JUST THE THING TO START IT OFF!
ancient insect-plant relationships throughout history
The new exhibit at the Museum of Natural History in Manhattan explores the subtle yet important relationship between ancient insects and their plant environments throughout history and how this relationship changed each of
"ANCIENT INSECT-PLANT RELATIONSHIPS"?
THROUGHOUT HISTORY!
YOU **WOULD** BE EXCITED BY THIS.

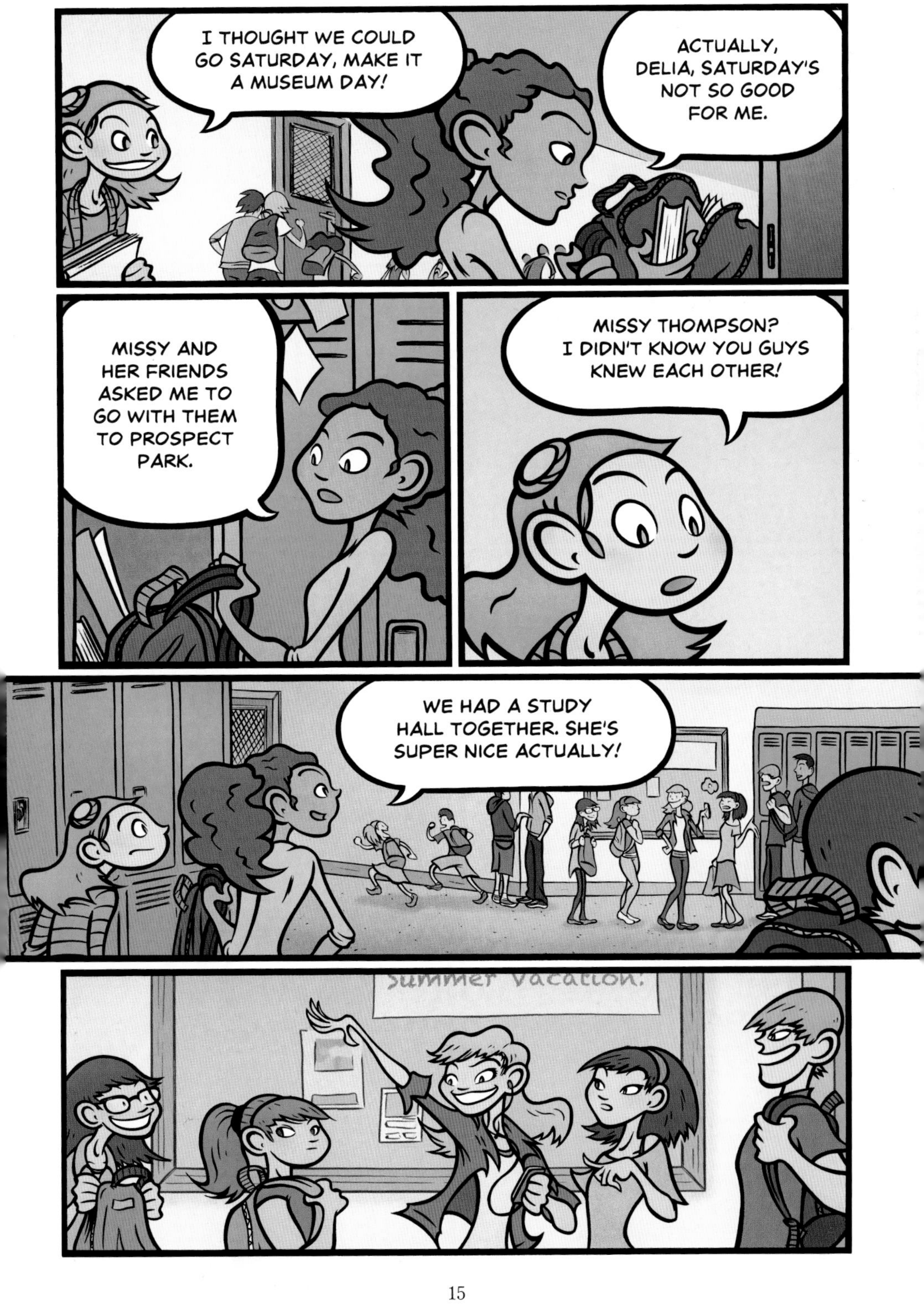
I THOUGHT WE COULD GO SATURDAY, MAKE IT A MUSEUM DAY!
ACTUALLY, DELIA, SATURDAY'S NOT SO GOOD FOR ME.
MISSY AND HER FRIENDS ASKED ME TO GO WITH THEM TO PROSPECT PARK.
MISSY THOMPSON? I DIDN'T KNOW YOU GUYS KNEW EACH OTHER!
WE HAD A STUDY HALL TOGETHER. SHE'S SUPER NICE ACTUALLY!
Summer Vacation!

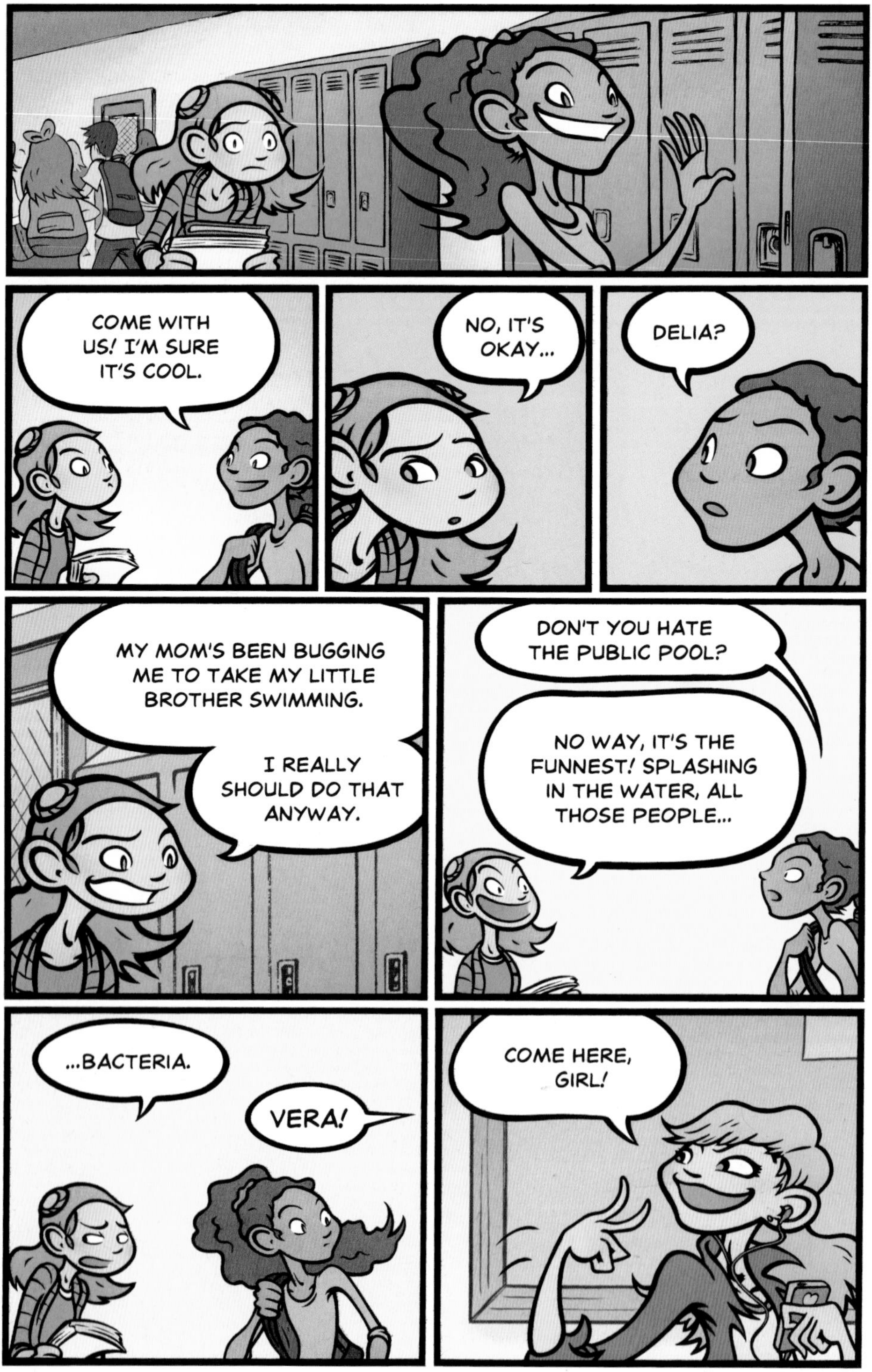
COME WITH US! I'M SURE IT'S COOL.
NO, IT'S OKAY...
DELIA?
MY MOM'S BEEN BUGGING ME TO TAKE MY LITTLE BROTHER SWIMMING.
I REALLY SHOULD DO THAT ANYWAY.
DON'T YOU HATE THE PUBLIC POOL?
NO WAY, IT'S THE FUNNEST! SPLASHING IN THE WATER, ALL THOSE PEOPLE...
...BACTERIA.
VERA!
COME HERE, GIRL!

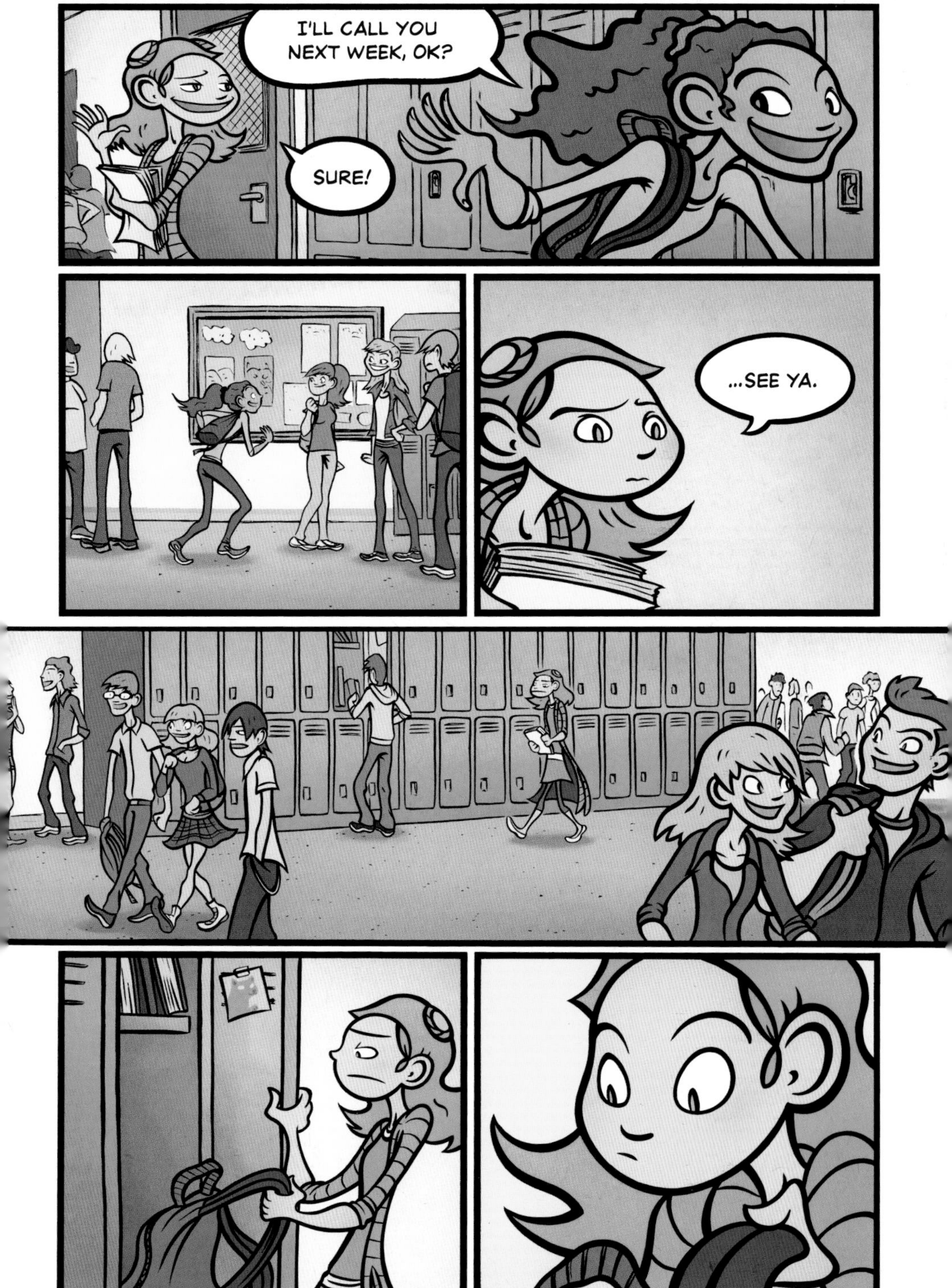
I'LL CALL YOU NEXT WEEK, OK?
SURE!
...SEE YA.

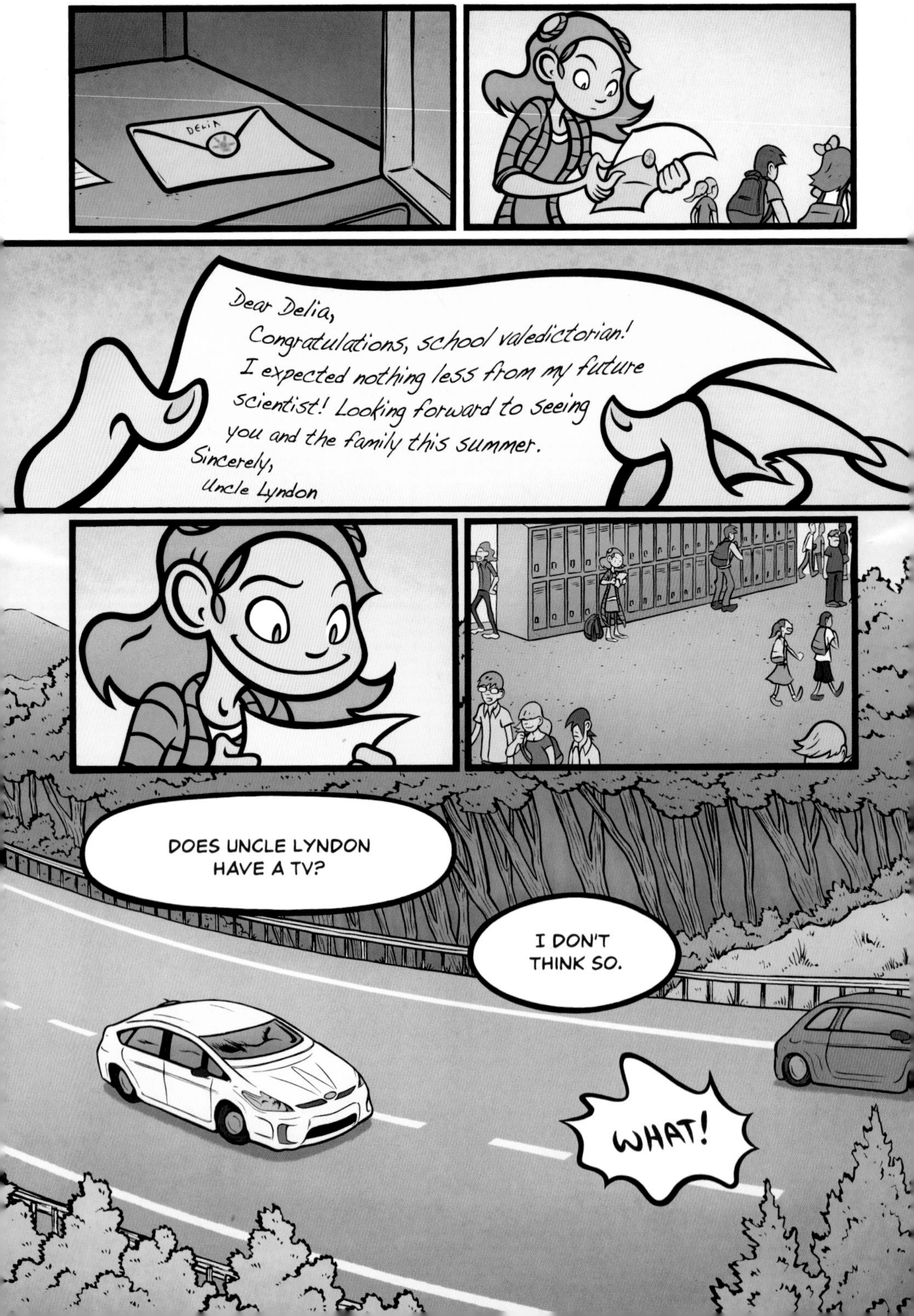
DELIA
Dear Delia,
Congratulations, school valedictorian! I expected nothing less from my future scientist! Looking forward to seeing you and the family this summer.
Sincerely,
Uncle Lyndon
DOES UNCLE LYNDON HAVE A TV?
I DON'T THINK SO.
WHAT!

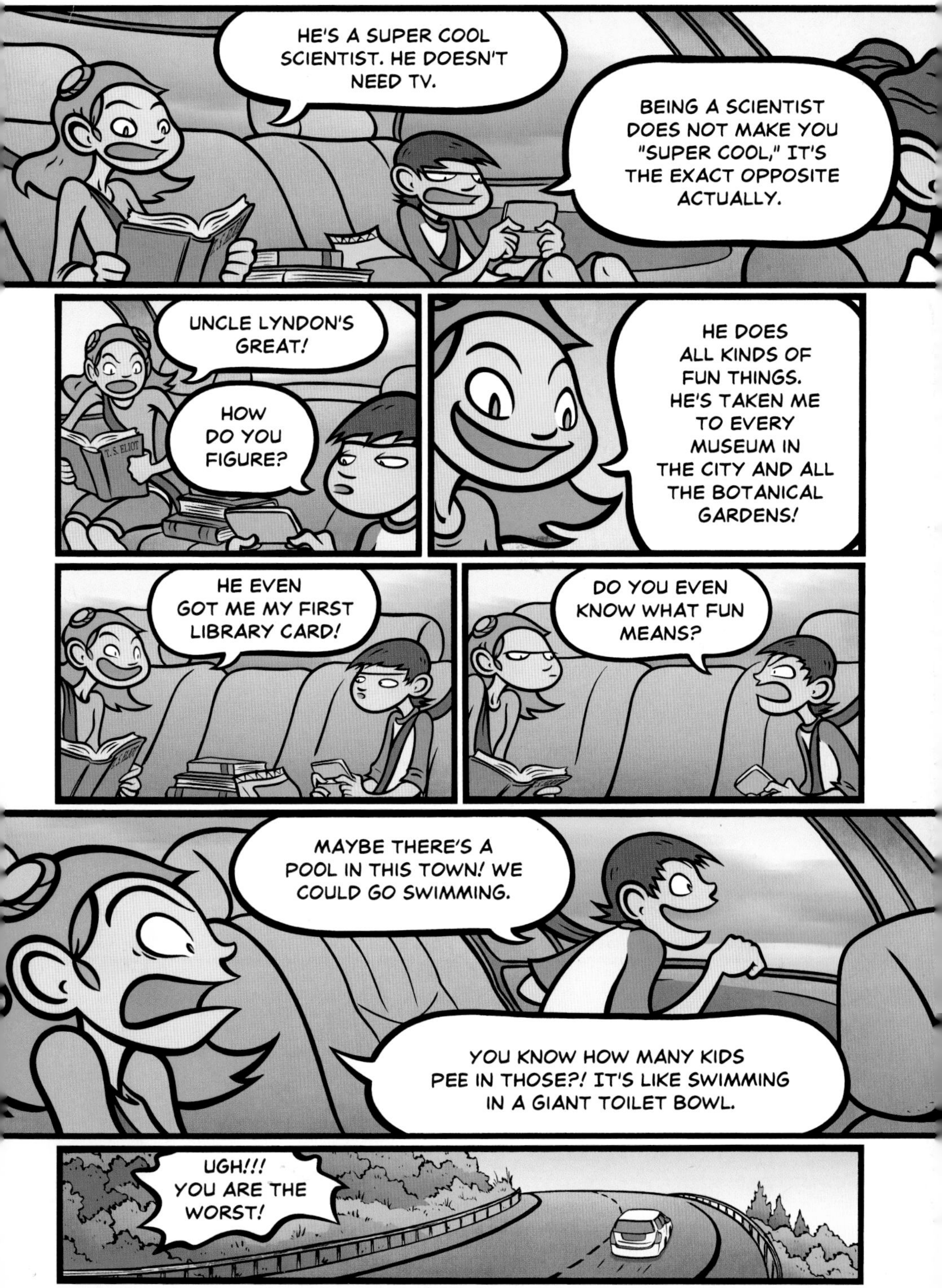
HE'S A SUPER COOL SCIENTIST. HE DOESN'T NEED TV.
BEING A SCIENTIST DOES NOT MAKE YOU "SUPER COOL," IT'S THE EXACT OPPOSITE ACTUALLY.
UNCLE LYNDON'S GREAT!
HOW DO YOU FIGURE?
T. S. ELIOT
HE DOES ALL KINDS OF FUN THINGS. HE'S TAKEN ME TO EVERY MUSEUM IN THE CITY AND ALL THE BOTANICAL GARDENS!
HE EVEN GOT ME MY FIRST LIBRARY CARD!
DO YOU EVEN KNOW WHAT FUN MEANS?
MAYBE THERE'S A POOL IN THIS TOWN! WE COULD GO SWIMMING.
YOU KNOW HOW MANY KIDS PEE IN THOSE?! IT'S LIKE SWIMMING IN A GIANT TOILET BOWL.
UGH!!! YOU ARE THE WORST!

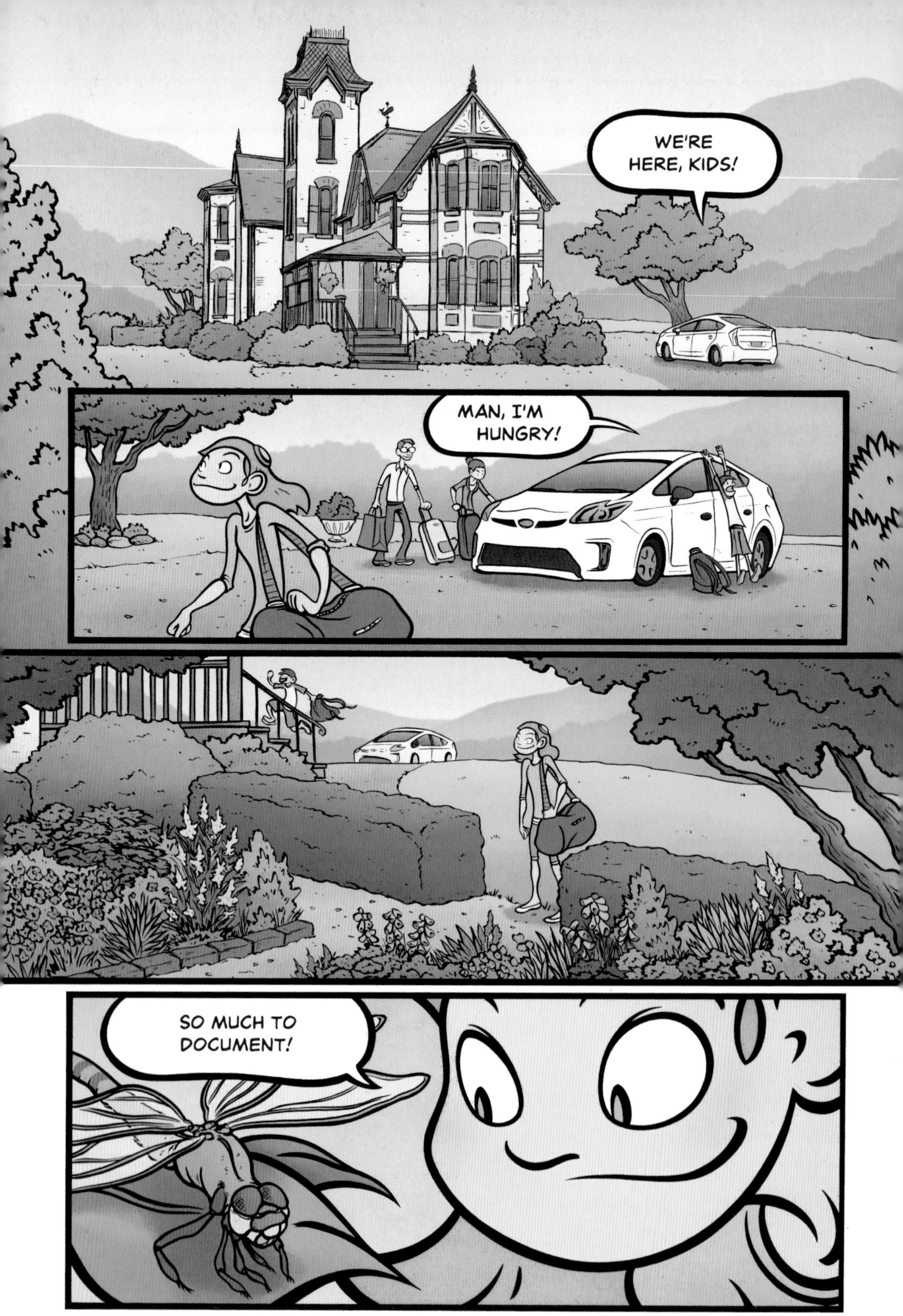
WE'RE HERE, KIDS!
MAN, I'M HUNGRY!
SO MUCH TO DOCUMENT!

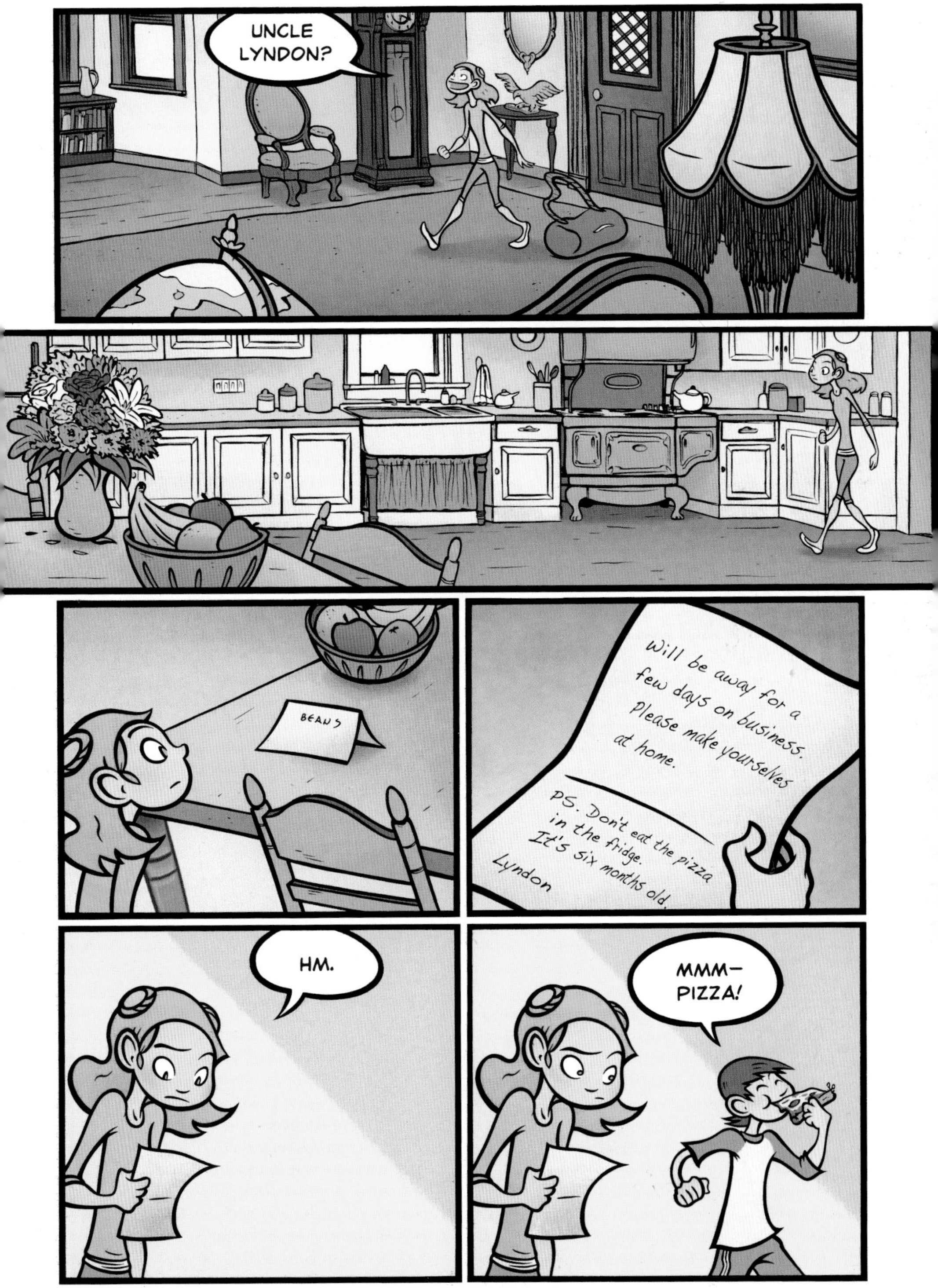
UNCLE LYNDON?
BEANS
Will be away for a few days on business. Please make yourselves at home.
PS. Don't eat the pizza in the fridge. It's six months old.
Lyndon
HM.
MMM— PIZZA!

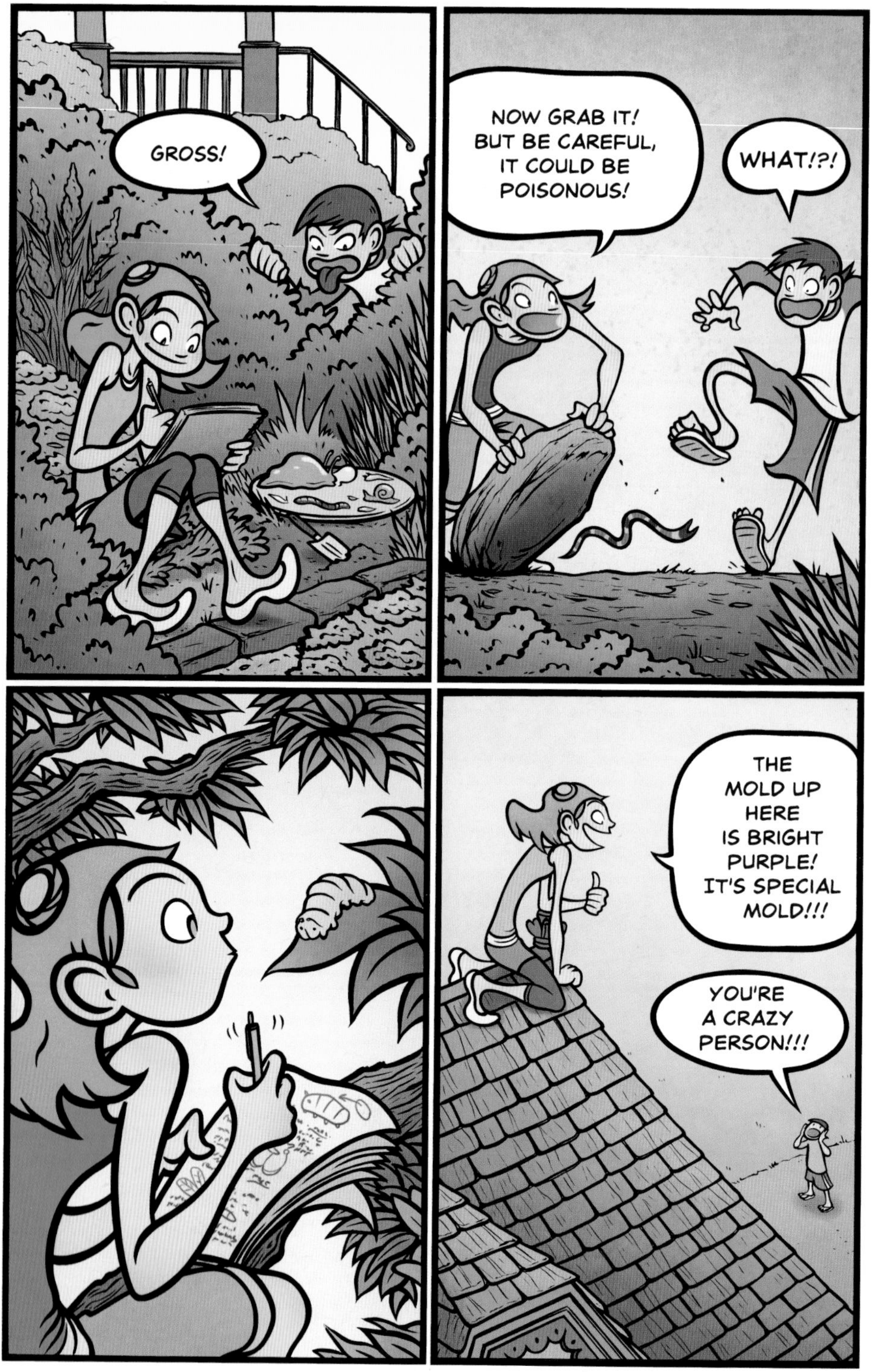
GROSS!
NOW GRAB IT! BUT BE CAREFUL, IT COULD BE POISONOUS!
WHAT!?!
THE MOLD UP HERE IS BRIGHT PURPLE! IT'S SPECIAL MOLD!!!
YOU'RE A CRAZY PERSON!!!

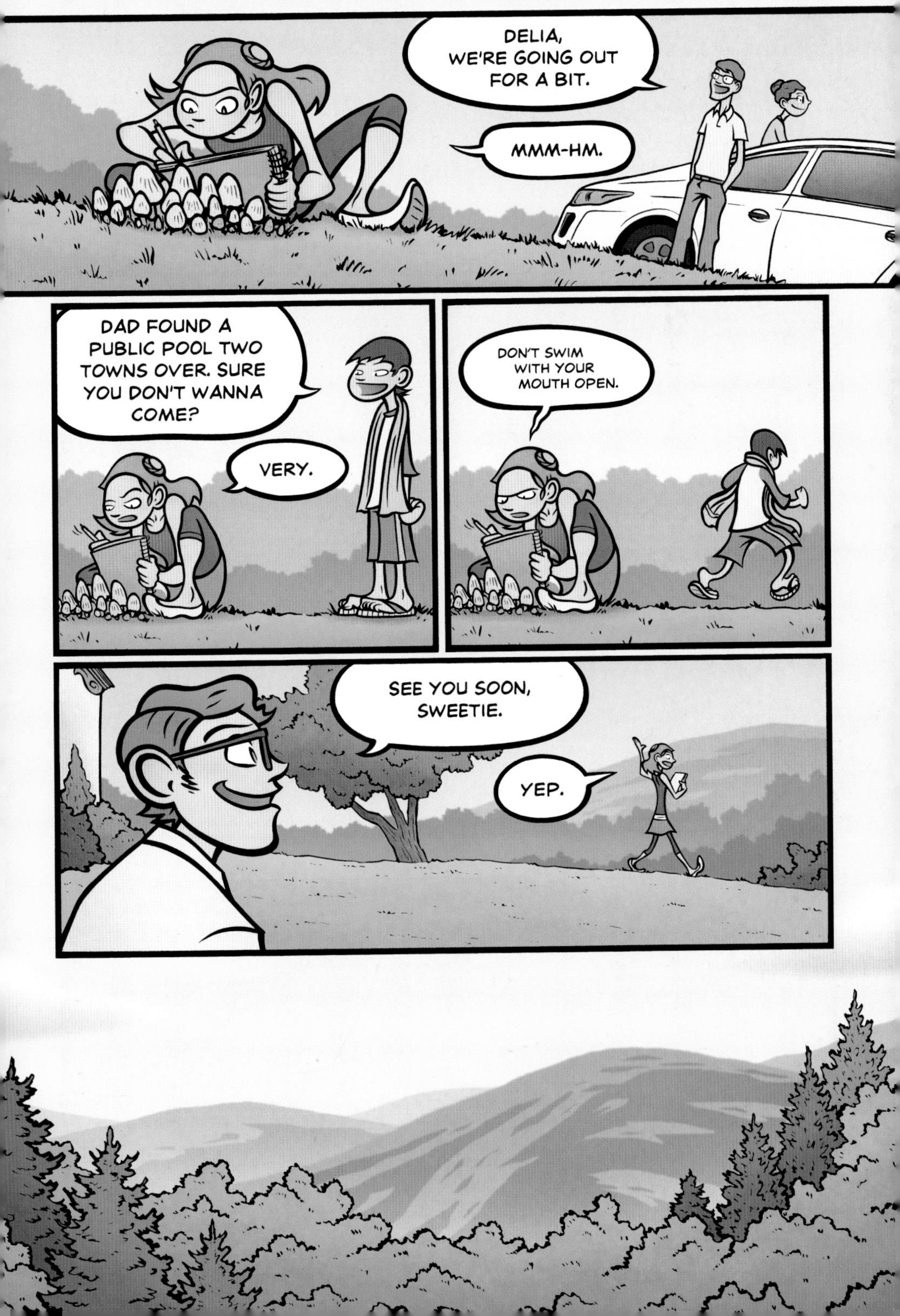
DELIA, WE'RE GOING OUT FOR A BIT.
MMM-HM.
DAD FOUND A PUBLIC POOL TWO TOWNS OVER. SURE YOU DON'T WANNA COME?
VERY.
DON'T SWIM WITH YOUR MOUTH OPEN.
SEE YOU SOON, SWEETIE.
YEP.

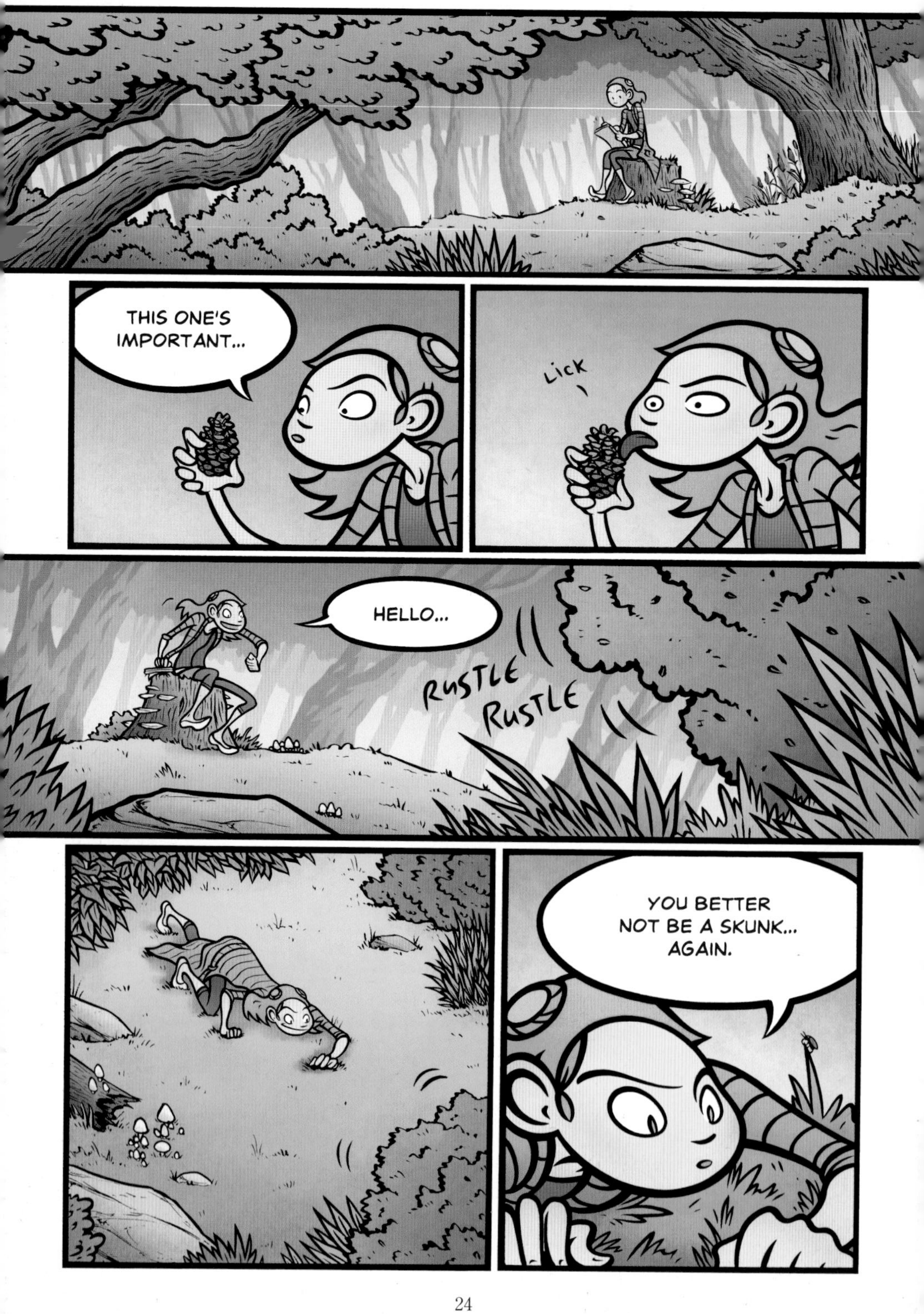

THIS ONE'S IMPORTANT...
LICK
HELLO...
RUSTLE
RUSTLE
YOU BETTER NOT BE A SKUNK... AGAIN.

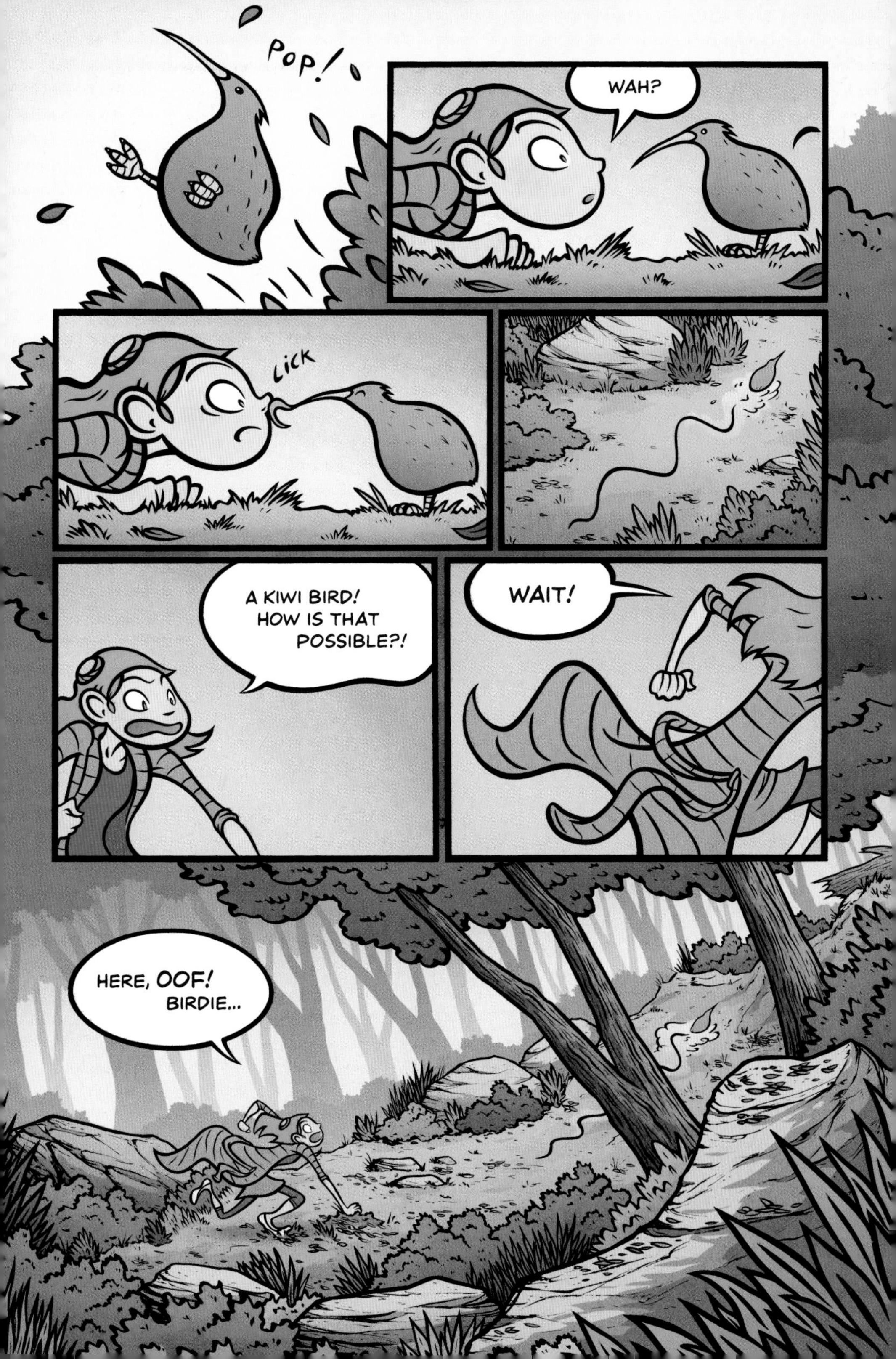
POP!
WAH?
LICK
A KIWI BIRD! HOW IS THAT POSSIBLE?!
WAIT!
HERE, OOF! BIRDIE...

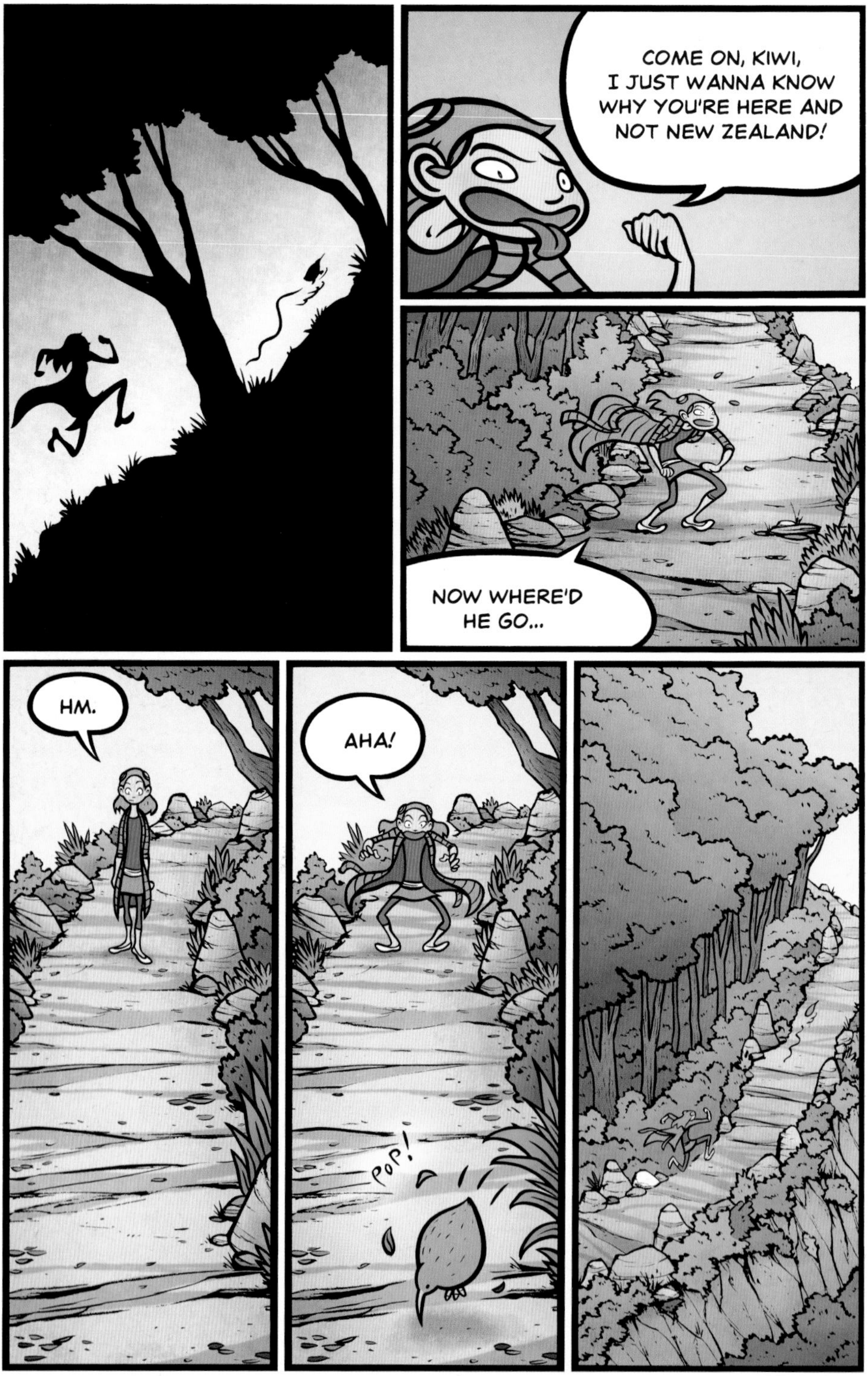
COME ON, KIWI, I JUST WANNA KNOW WHY YOU'RE HERE AND NOT NEW ZEALAND!
NOW WHERE'D HE GO...
HM.
AHA!
POP!

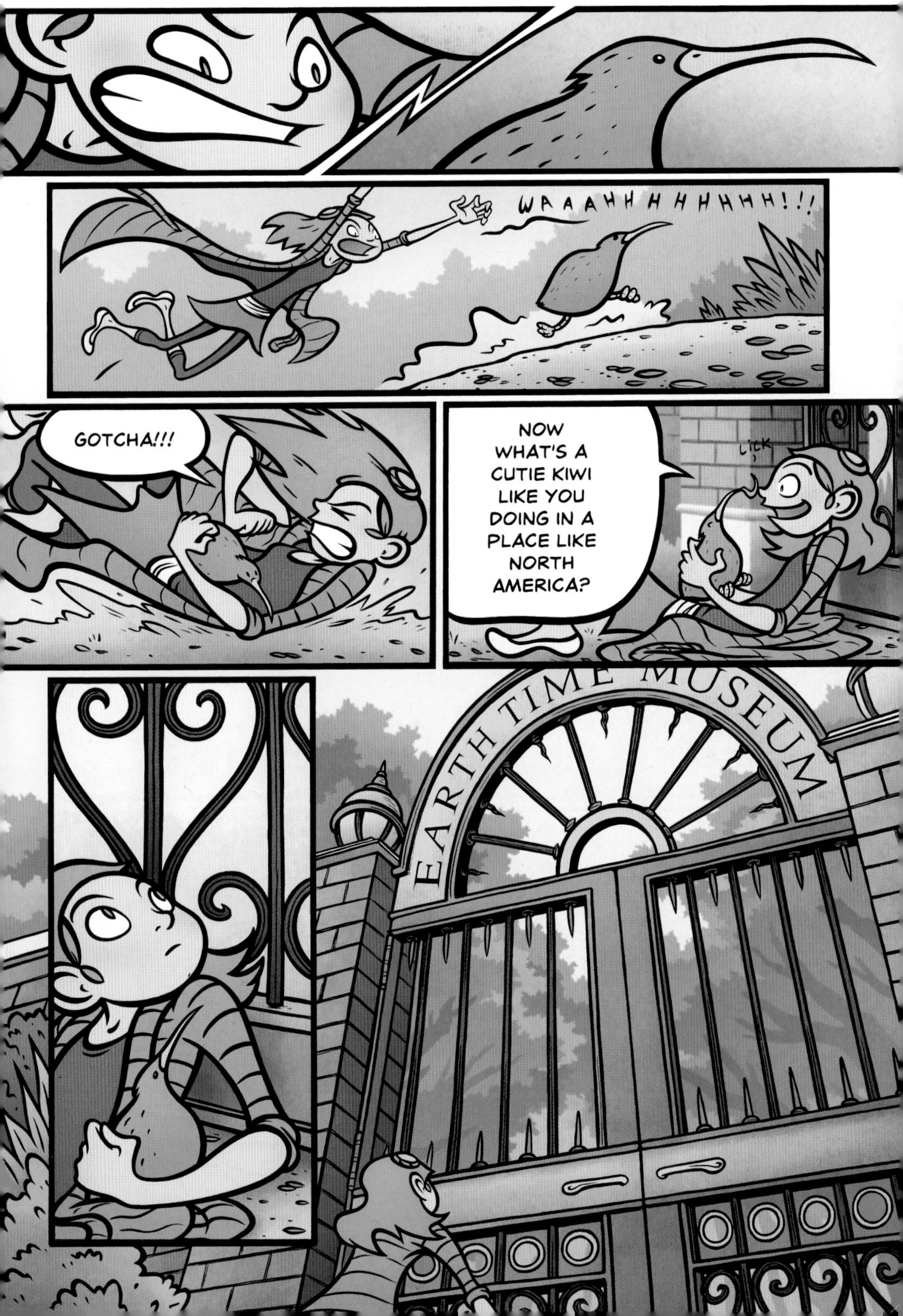
WAAAHHHHHHHH!!!
GOTCHA!!!
LICK
NOW WHAT'S A CUTIE KIWI LIKE YOU DOING IN A PLACE LIKE NORTH AMERICA?
EARTH TIME MUSEUM

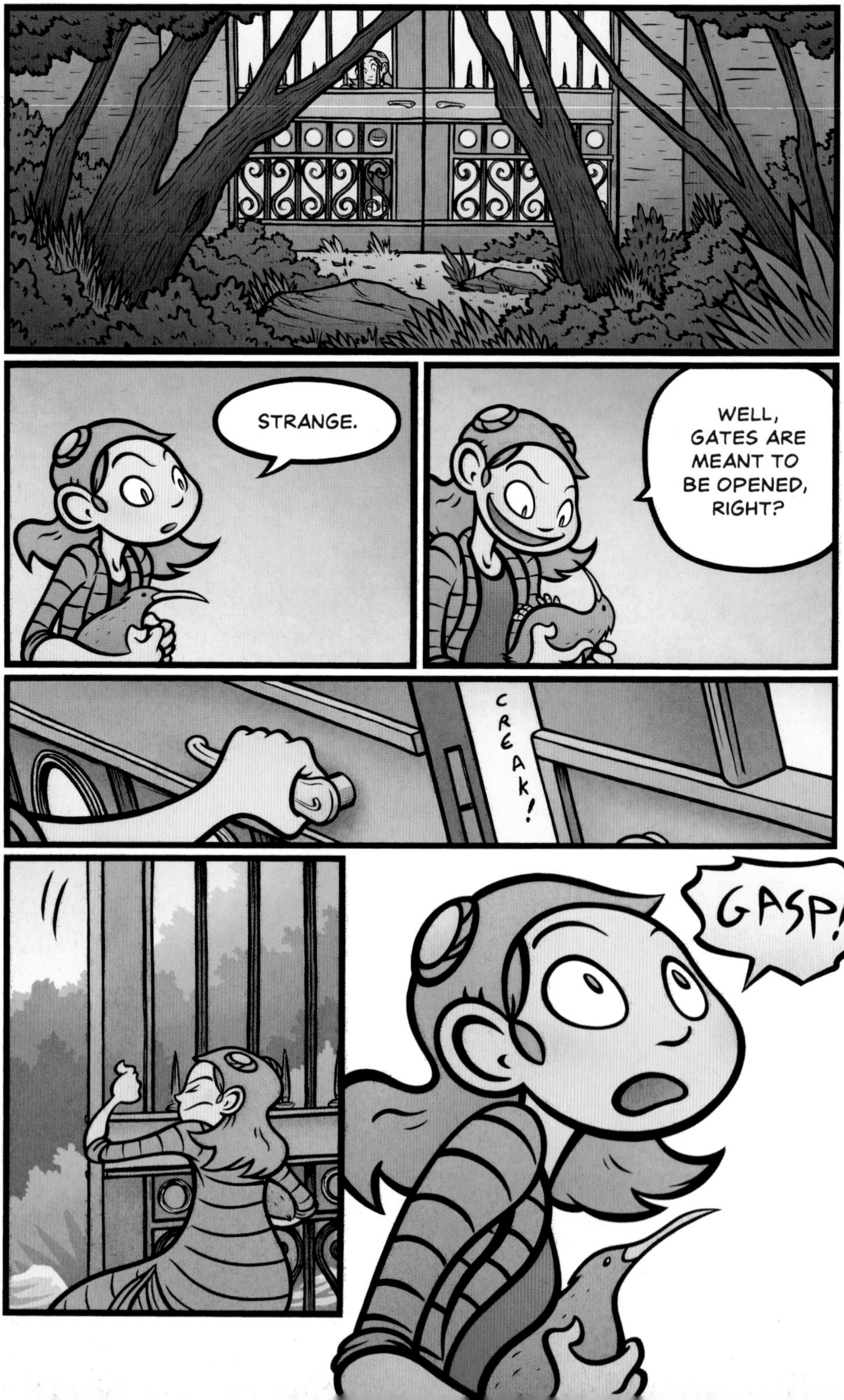
STRANGE.
WELL, GATES ARE MEANT TO BE OPENED, RIGHT?
CREAK!
GASP!

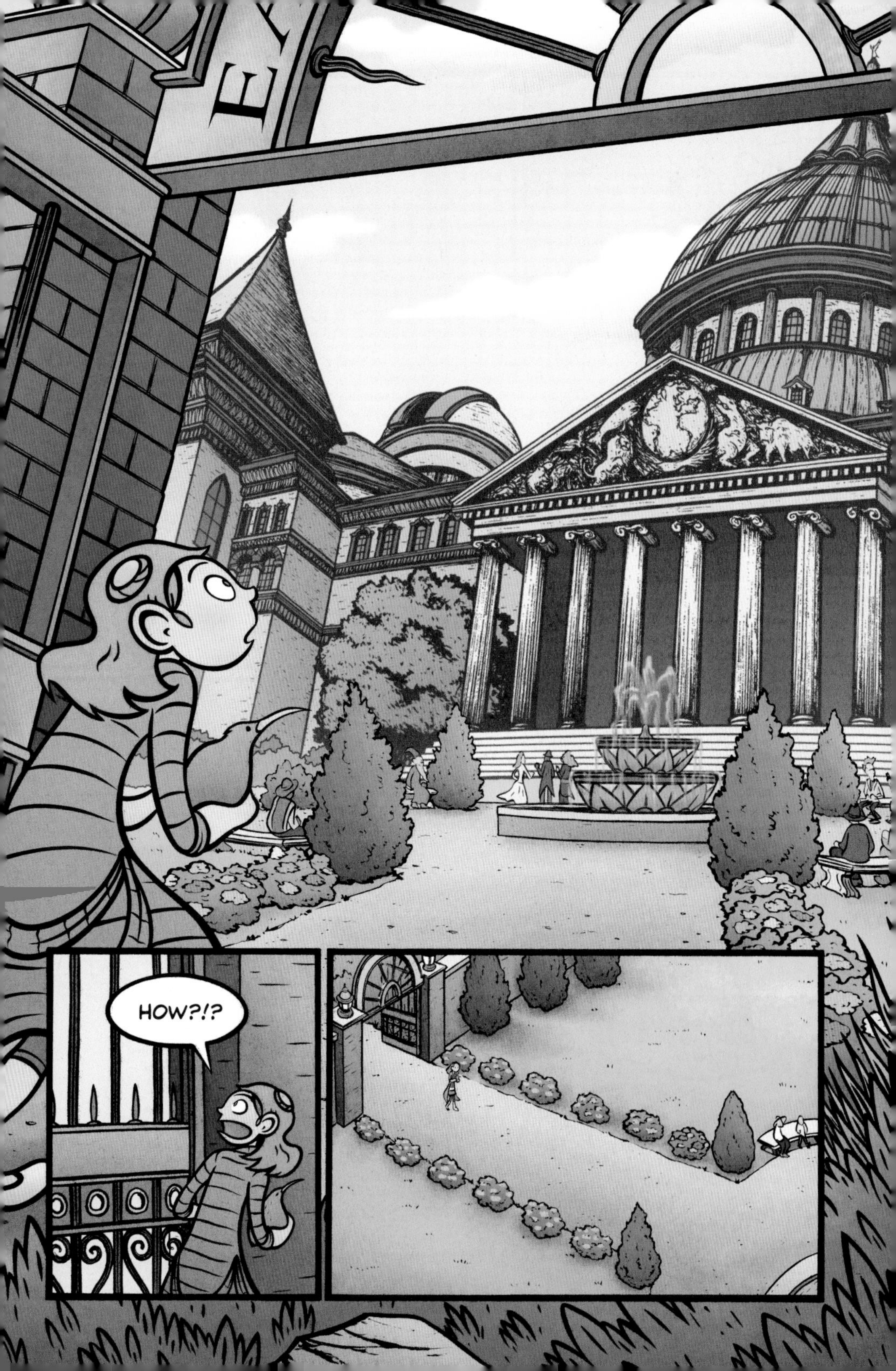
HOW?!?

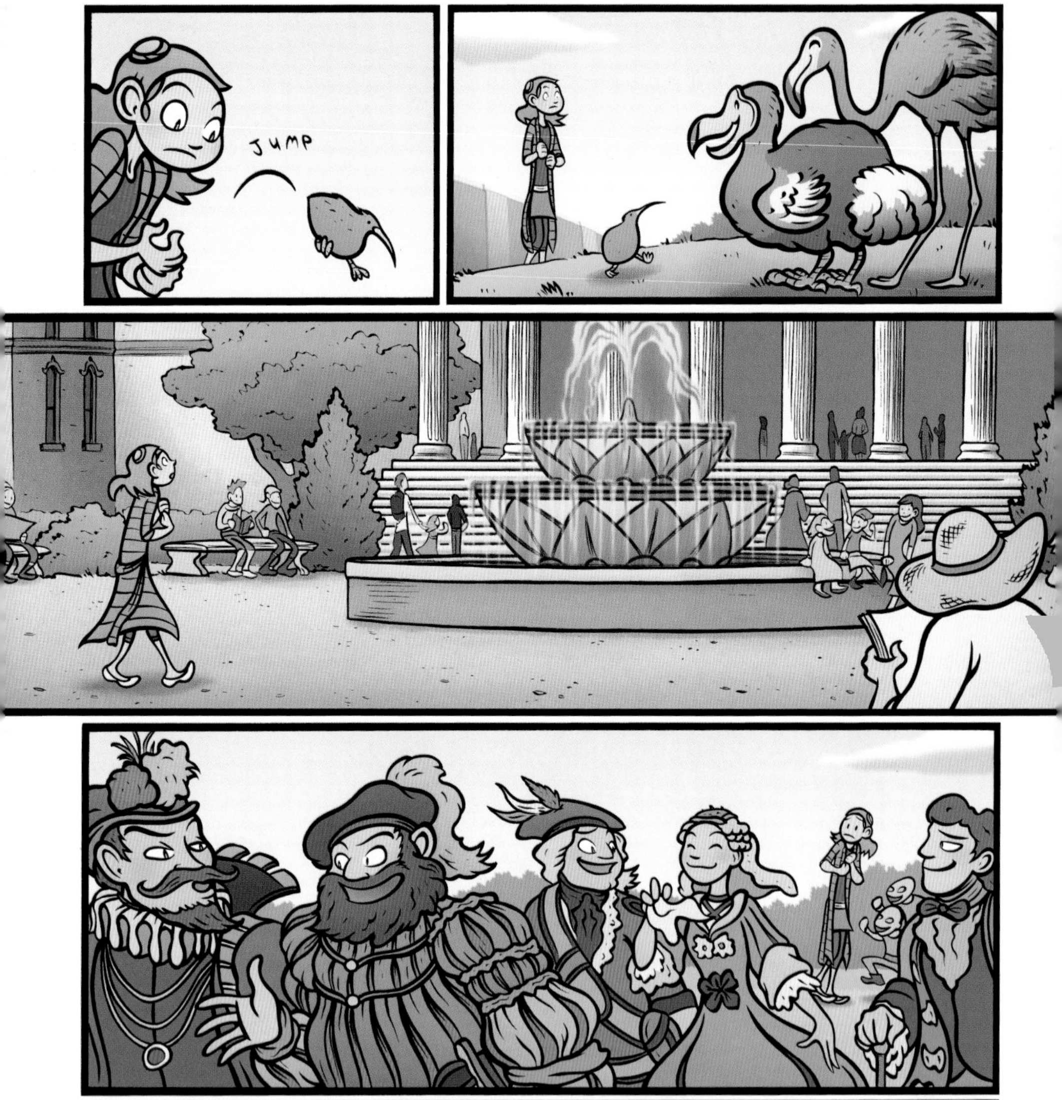
JUMP
SORRY?

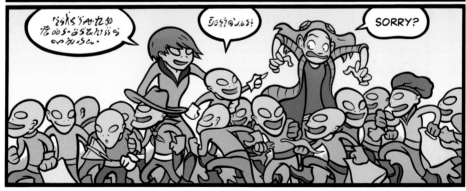

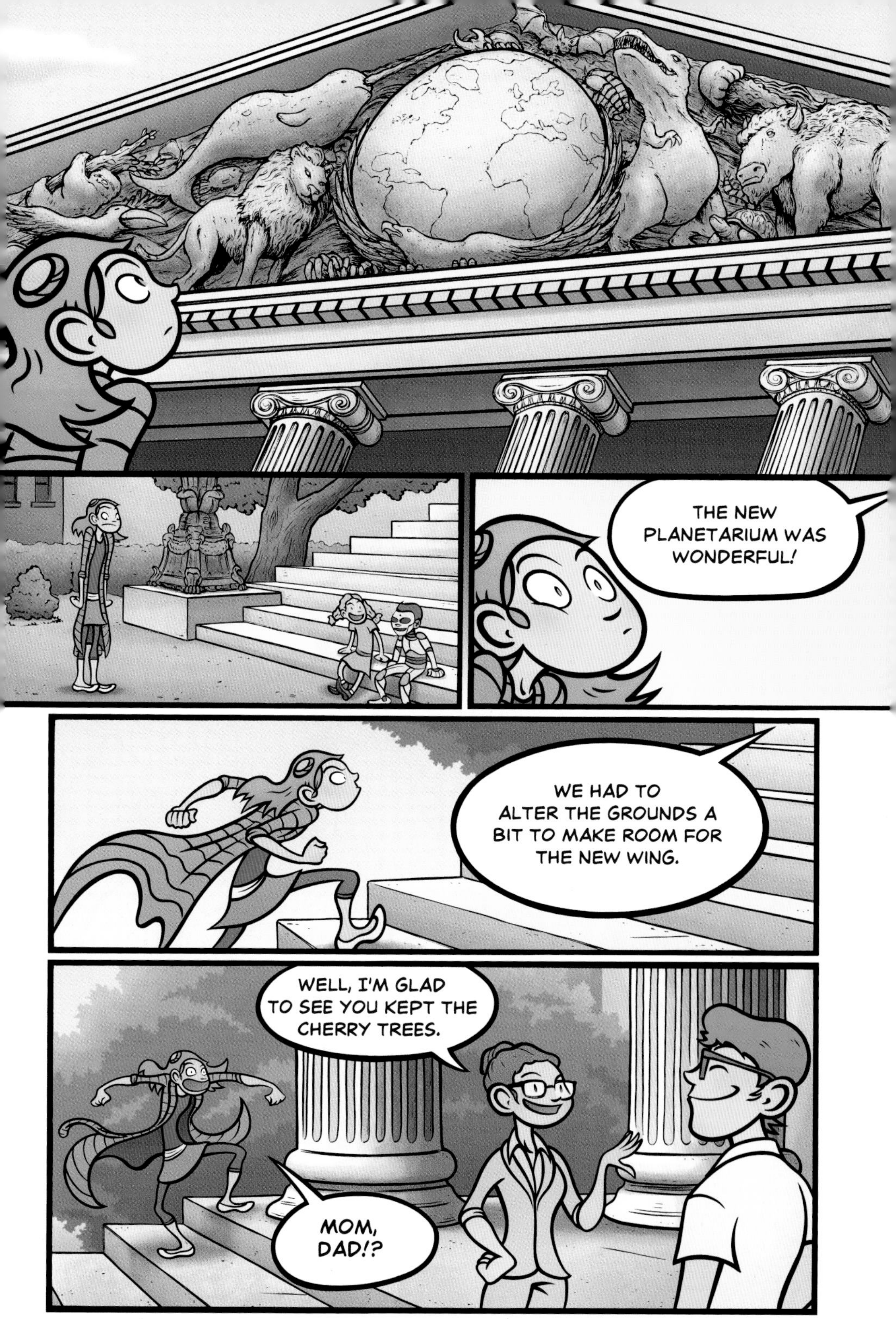
THE NEW PLANETARIUM WAS WONDERFUL!
WE HAD TO ALTER THE GROUNDS A BIT TO MAKE ROOM FOR THE NEW WING.
WELL, I'M GLAD TO SEE YOU KEPT THE CHERRY TREES.
MOM, DAD!?

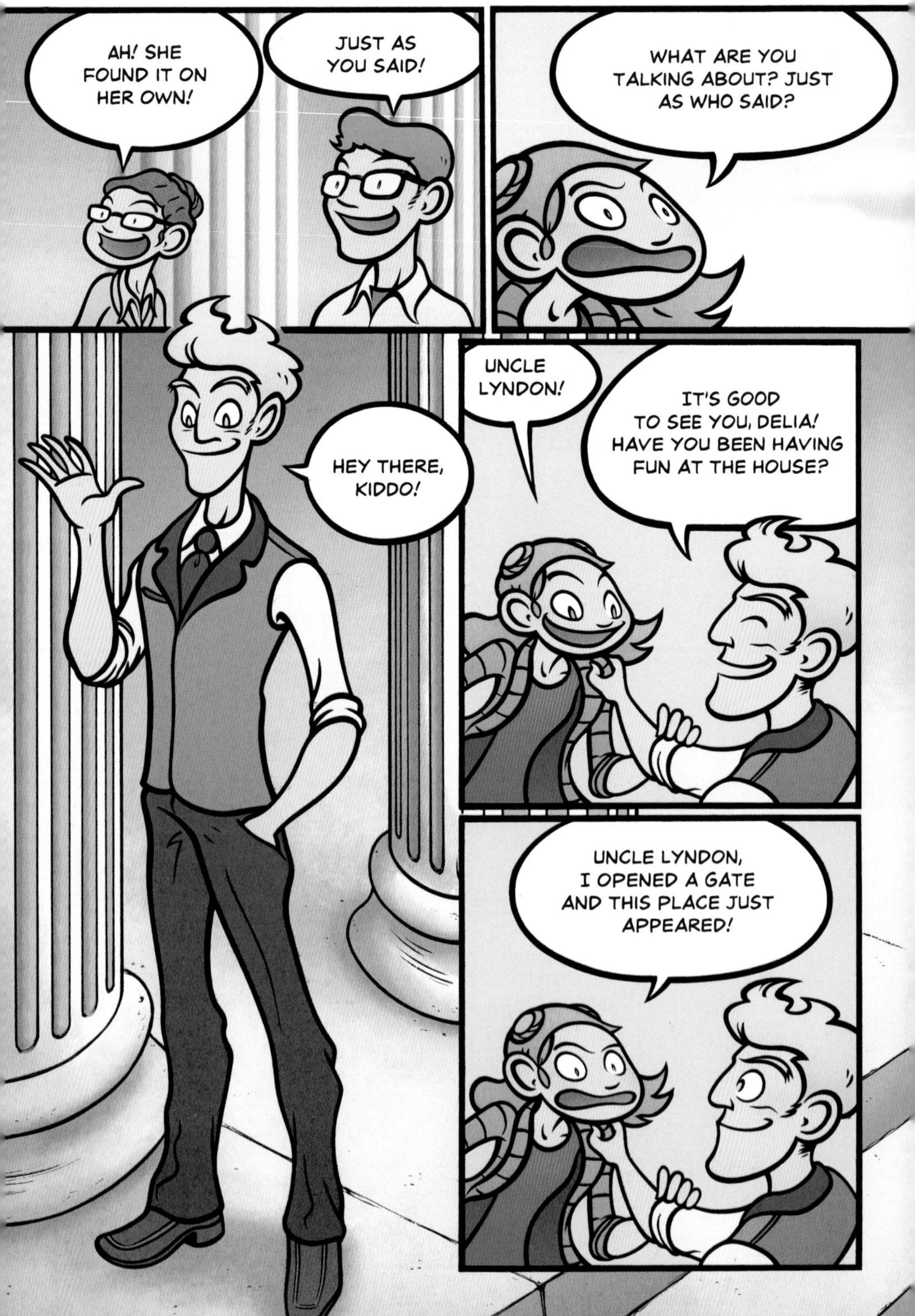
AH! SHE FOUND IT ON HER OWN!
JUST AS YOU SAID!
WHAT ARE YOU TALKING ABOUT? JUST AS WHO SAID?
HEY THERE, KIDDO!
UNCLE LYNDON!
IT'S GOOD TO SEE YOU, DELIA! HAVE YOU BEEN HAVING FUN AT THE HOUSE?
UNCLE LYNDON, I OPENED A GATE AND THIS PLACE JUST APPEARED!

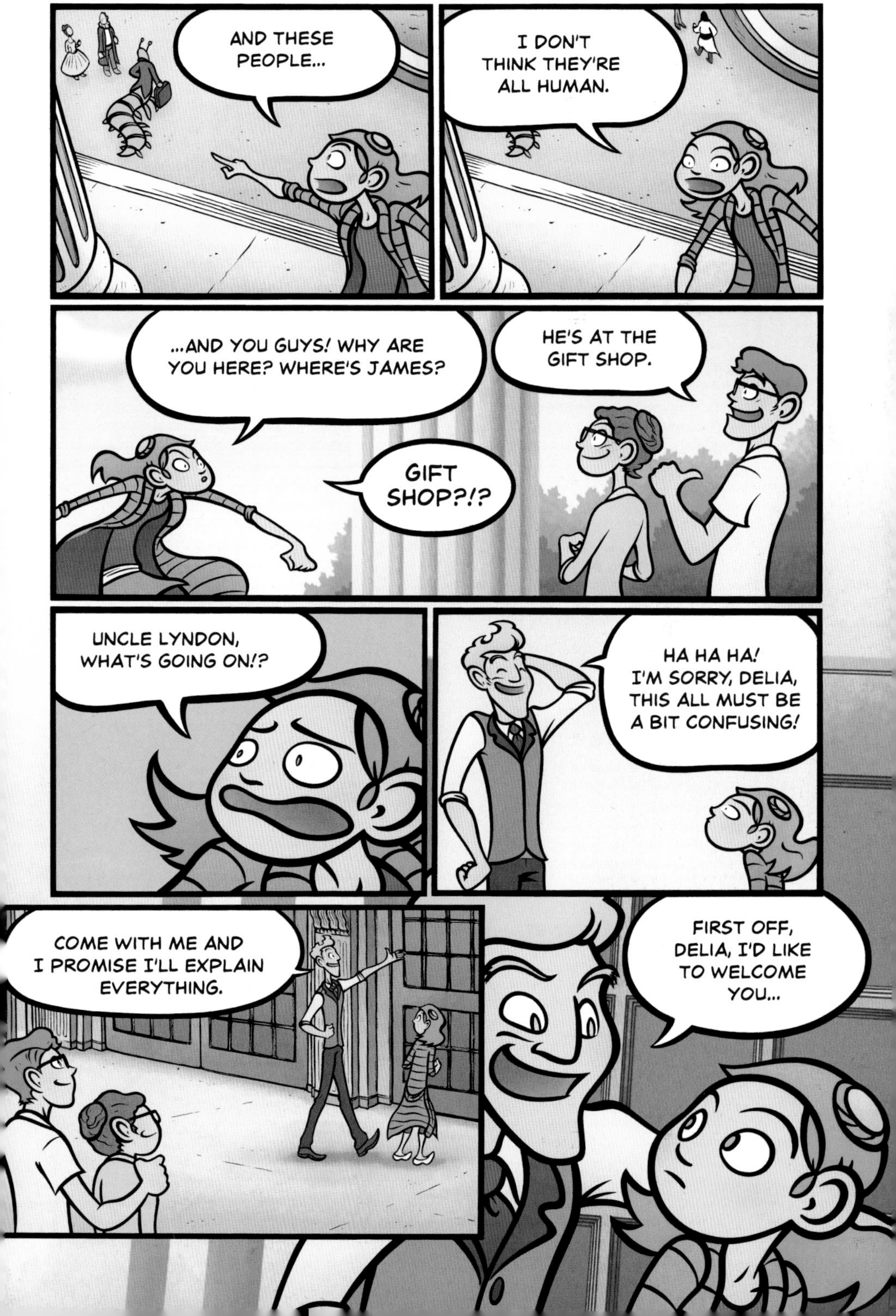
AND THESE PEOPLE...
I DON'T THINK THEY'RE ALL HUMAN.
...AND YOU GUYS! WHY ARE YOU HERE? WHERE'S JAMES?
HE'S AT THE GIFT SHOP.
GIFT SHOP?!?
UNCLE LYNDON, WHAT'S GOING ON!?
HA HA HA! I'M SORRY, DELIA, THIS ALL MUST BE A BIT CONFUSING!
COME WITH ME AND I PROMISE I'LL EXPLAIN EVERYTHING.
FIRST OFF, DELIA, I'D LIKE TO WELCOME YOU...

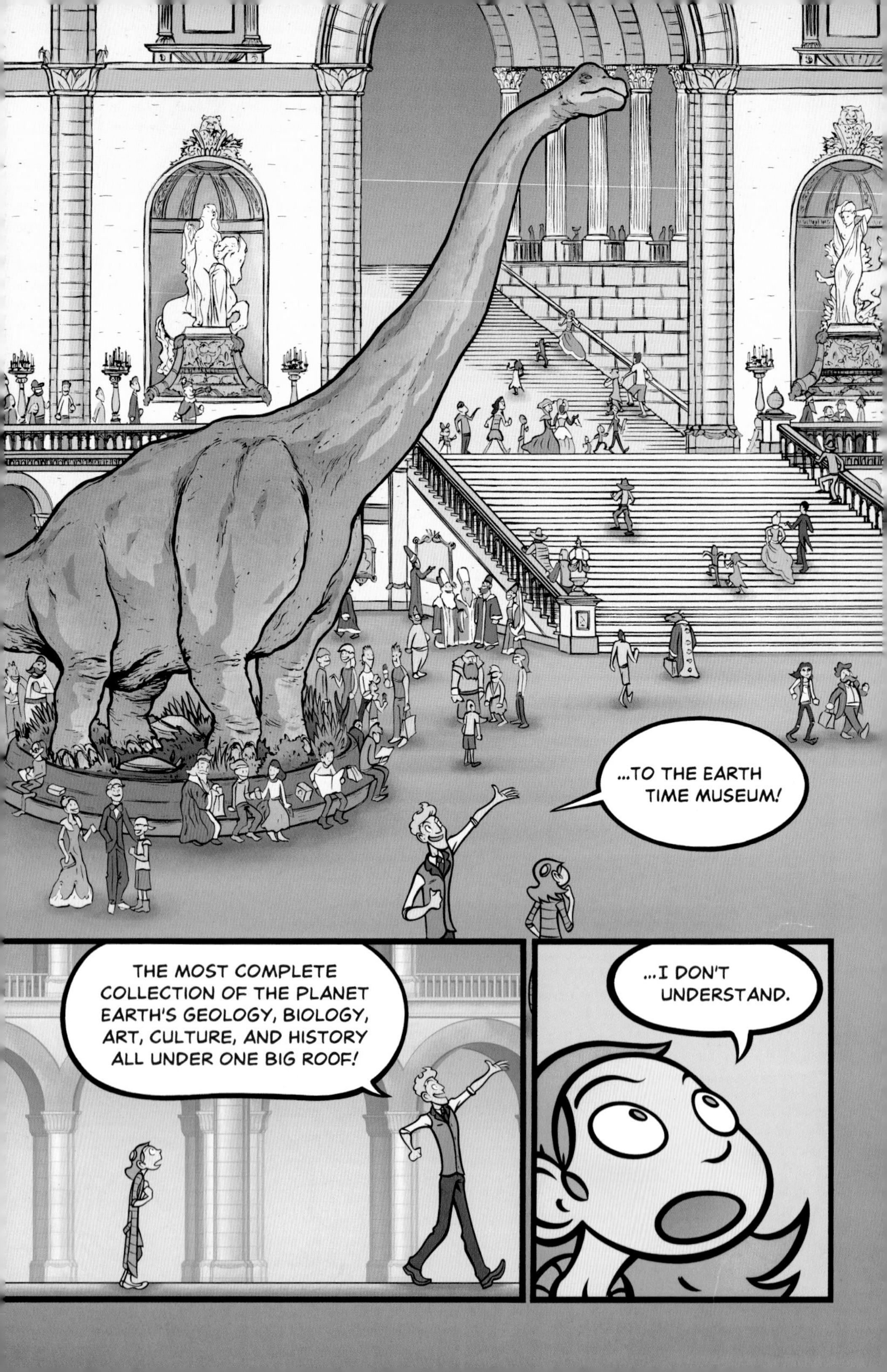
...TO THE EARTH TIME MUSEUM!
THE MOST COMPLETE COLLECTION OF THE PLANET EARTH'S GEOLOGY, BIOLOGY, ART, CULTURE, AND HISTORY ALL UNDER ONE BIG ROOF!
...I DON'T UNDERSTAND.

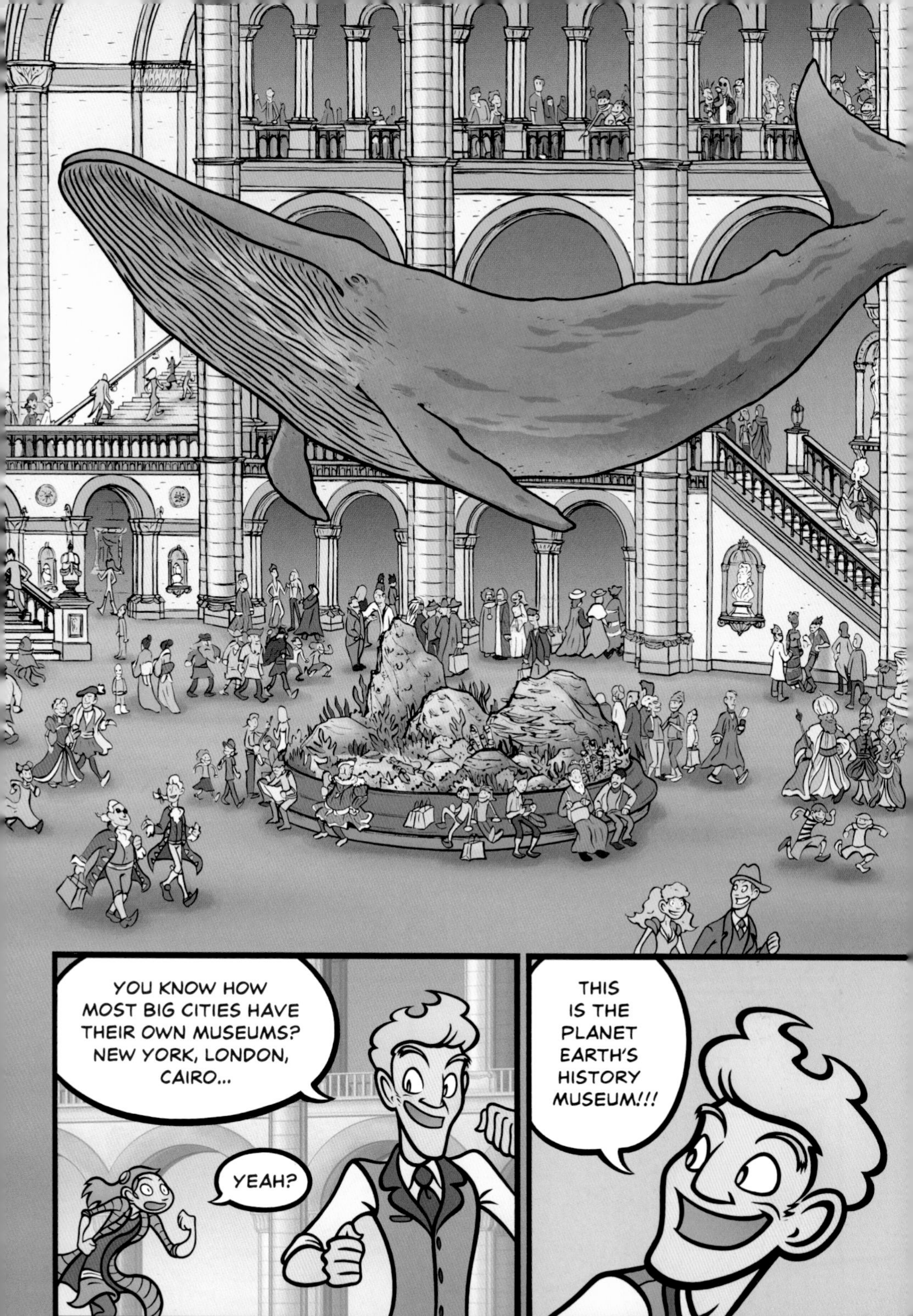
YOU KNOW HOW MOST BIG CITIES HAVE THEIR OWN MUSEUMS? NEW YORK, LONDON, CAIRO...
YEAH?
THIS IS THE PLANET EARTH'S HISTORY MUSEUM!!!

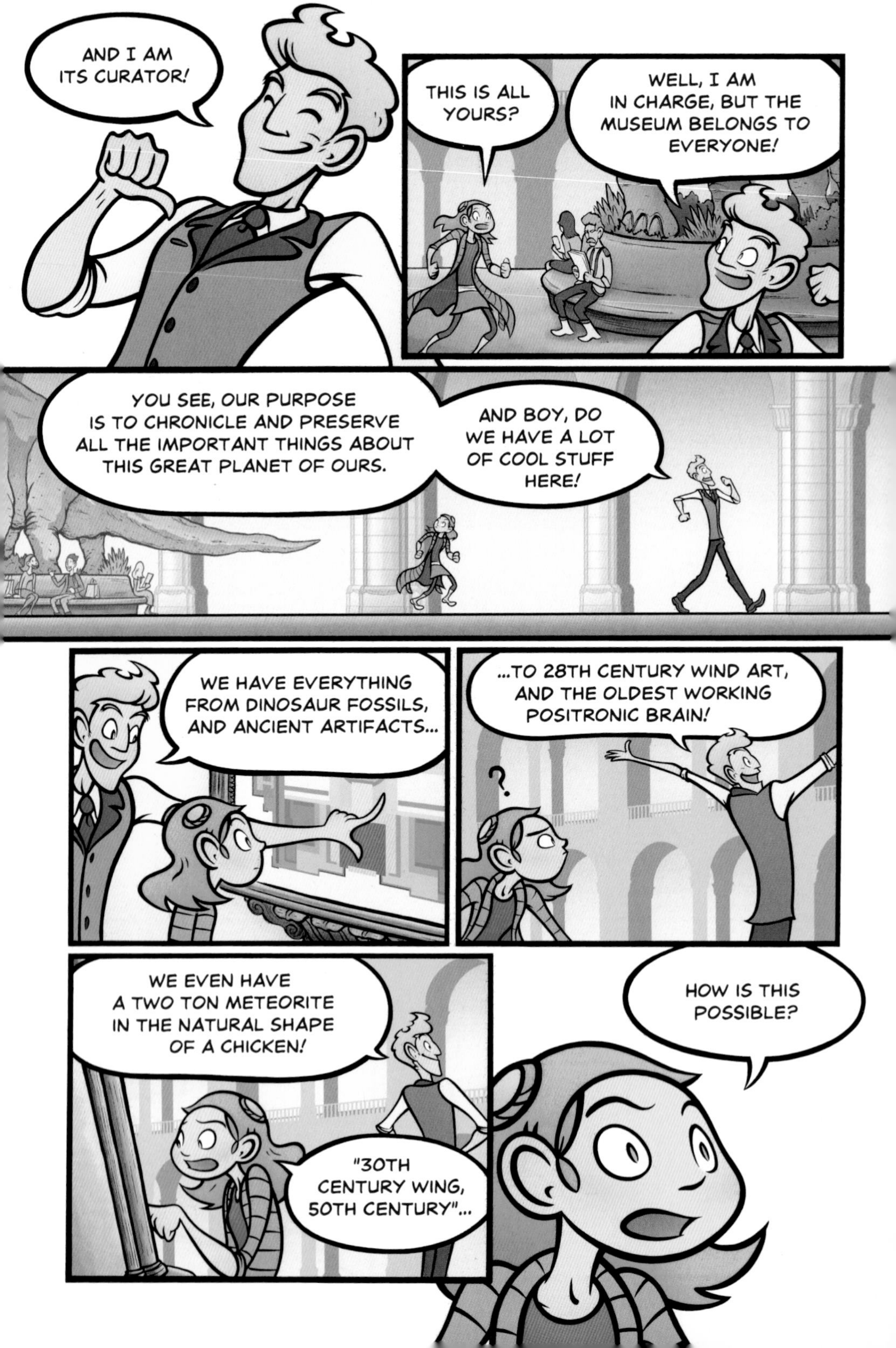
AND I AM ITS CURATOR!
THIS IS ALL YOURS?
WELL, I AM IN CHARGE, BUT THE MUSEUM BELONGS TO EVERYONE!
YOU SEE, OUR PURPOSE IS TO CHRONICLE AND PRESERVE ALL THE IMPORTANT THINGS ABOUT THIS GREAT PLANET OF OURS.
AND BOY, DO WE HAVE A LOT OF COOL STUFF HERE!
WE HAVE EVERYTHING FROM DINOSAUR FOSSILS, AND ANCIENT ARTIFACTS...
...TO 28TH CENTURY WIND ART, AND THE OLDEST WORKING POSITRONIC BRAIN!
?
WE EVEN HAVE A TWO TON METEORITE IN THE NATURAL SHAPE OF A CHICKEN!
"30TH CENTURY WING, 50TH CENTURY"...
HOW IS THIS POSSIBLE?

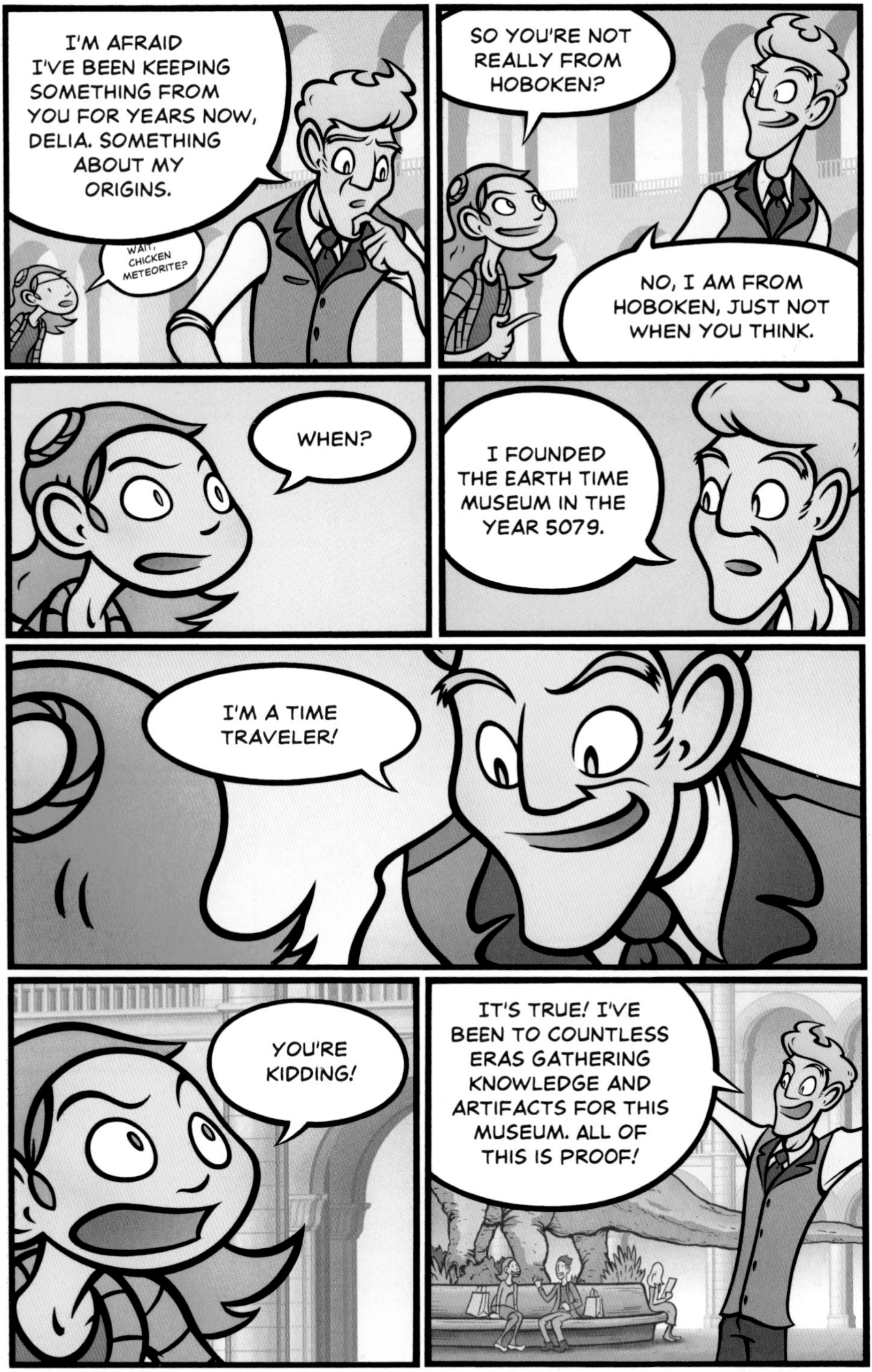
I'M AFRAID I'VE BEEN KEEPING SOMETHING FROM YOU FOR YEARS NOW, DELIA. SOMETHING ABOUT MY ORIGINS.
WAIT, CHICKEN METEORITE?
SO YOU'RE NOT REALLY FROM HOBOKEN?
NO, I AM FROM HOBOKEN, JUST NOT WHEN YOU THINK.
WHEN?
I FOUNDED THE EARTH TIME MUSEUM IN THE YEAR 5079.
I'M A TIME TRAVELER!
YOU'RE KIDDING!
IT'S TRUE! I'VE BEEN TO COUNTLESS ERAS GATHERING KNOWLEDGE AND ARTIFACTS FOR THIS MUSEUM. ALL OF THIS IS PROOF!

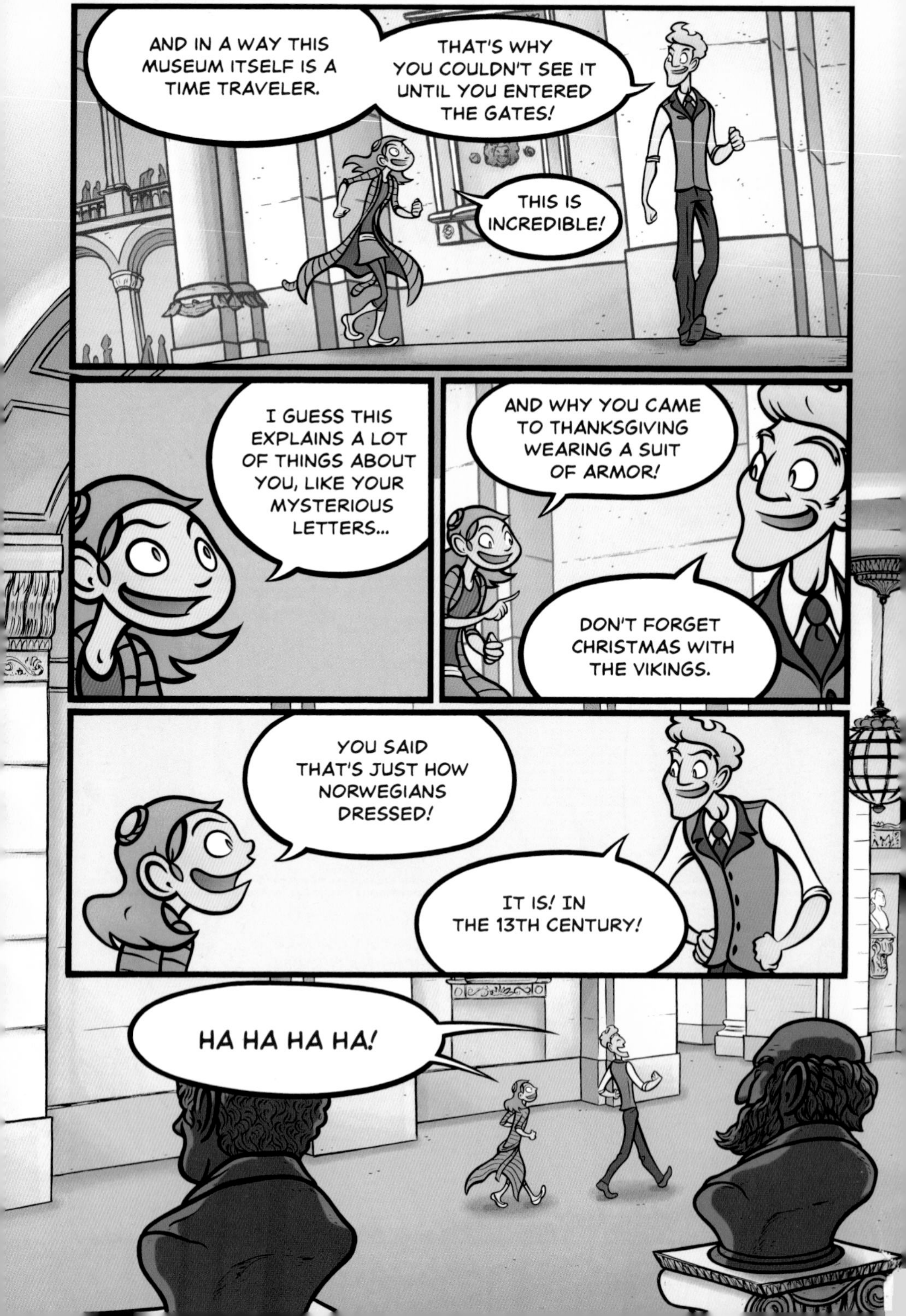
AND IN A WAY THIS MUSEUM ITSELF IS A TIME TRAVELER.
THAT'S WHY YOU COULDN'T SEE IT UNTIL YOU ENTERED THE GATES!
THIS IS INCREDIBLE!
I GUESS THIS EXPLAINS A LOT OF THINGS ABOUT YOU, LIKE YOUR MYSTERIOUS LETTERS...
AND WHY YOU CAME TO THANKSGIVING WEARING A SUIT OF ARMOR!
DON'T FORGET CHRISTMAS WITH THE VIKINGS.
YOU SAID THAT'S JUST HOW NORWEGIANS DRESSED!
IT IS! IN THE 13TH CENTURY!
HA HA HA HA!

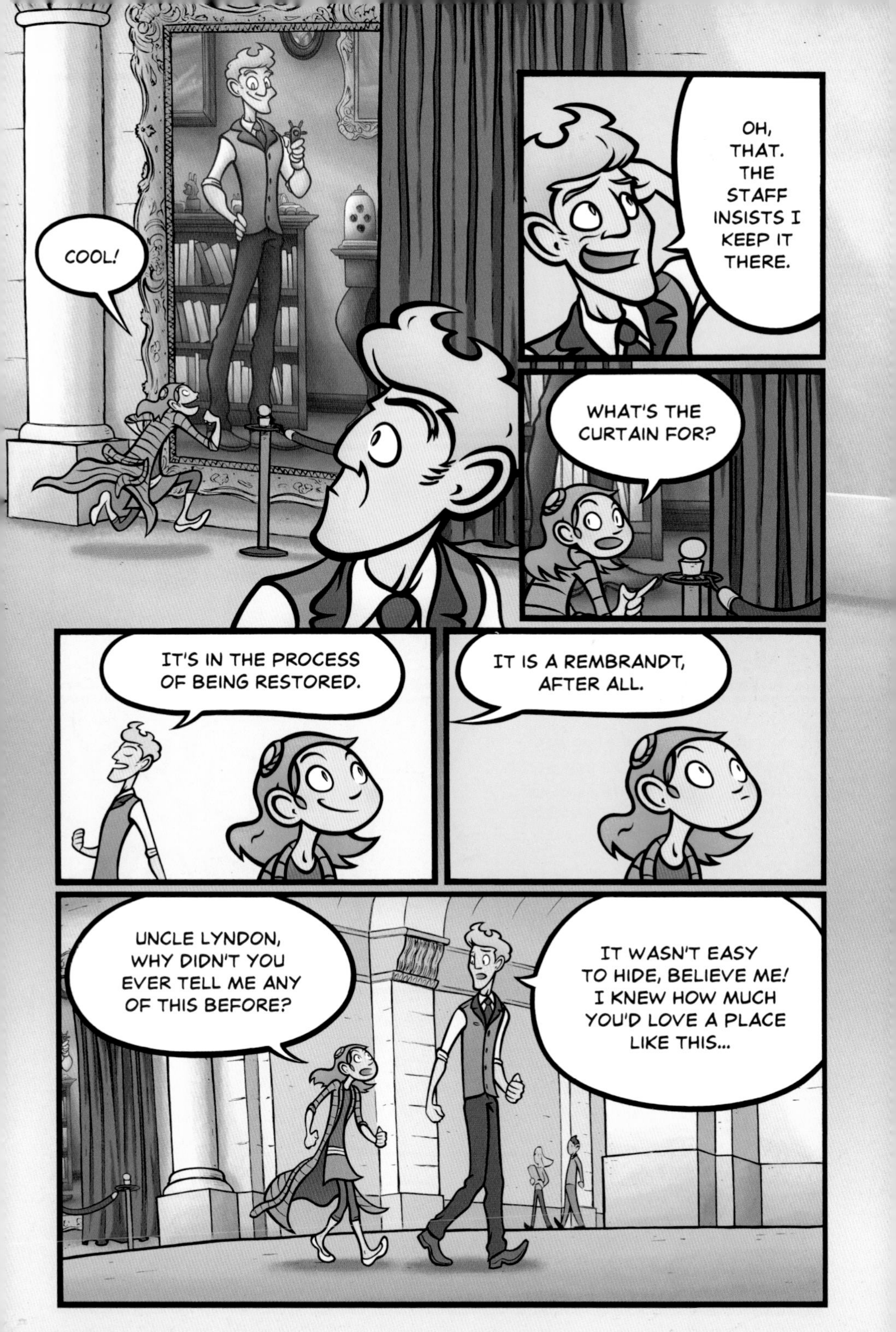
COOL!
OH, THAT. THE STAFF INSISTS I KEEP IT THERE.
WHAT'S THE CURTAIN FOR?
IT'S IN THE PROCESS OF BEING RESTORED.
IT IS A REMBRANDT, AFTER ALL.
UNCLE LYNDON, WHY DIDN'T YOU EVER TELL ME ANY OF THIS BEFORE?
IT WASN'T EASY TO HIDE, BELIEVE ME! I KNEW HOW MUCH YOU'D LOVE A PLACE LIKE THIS...

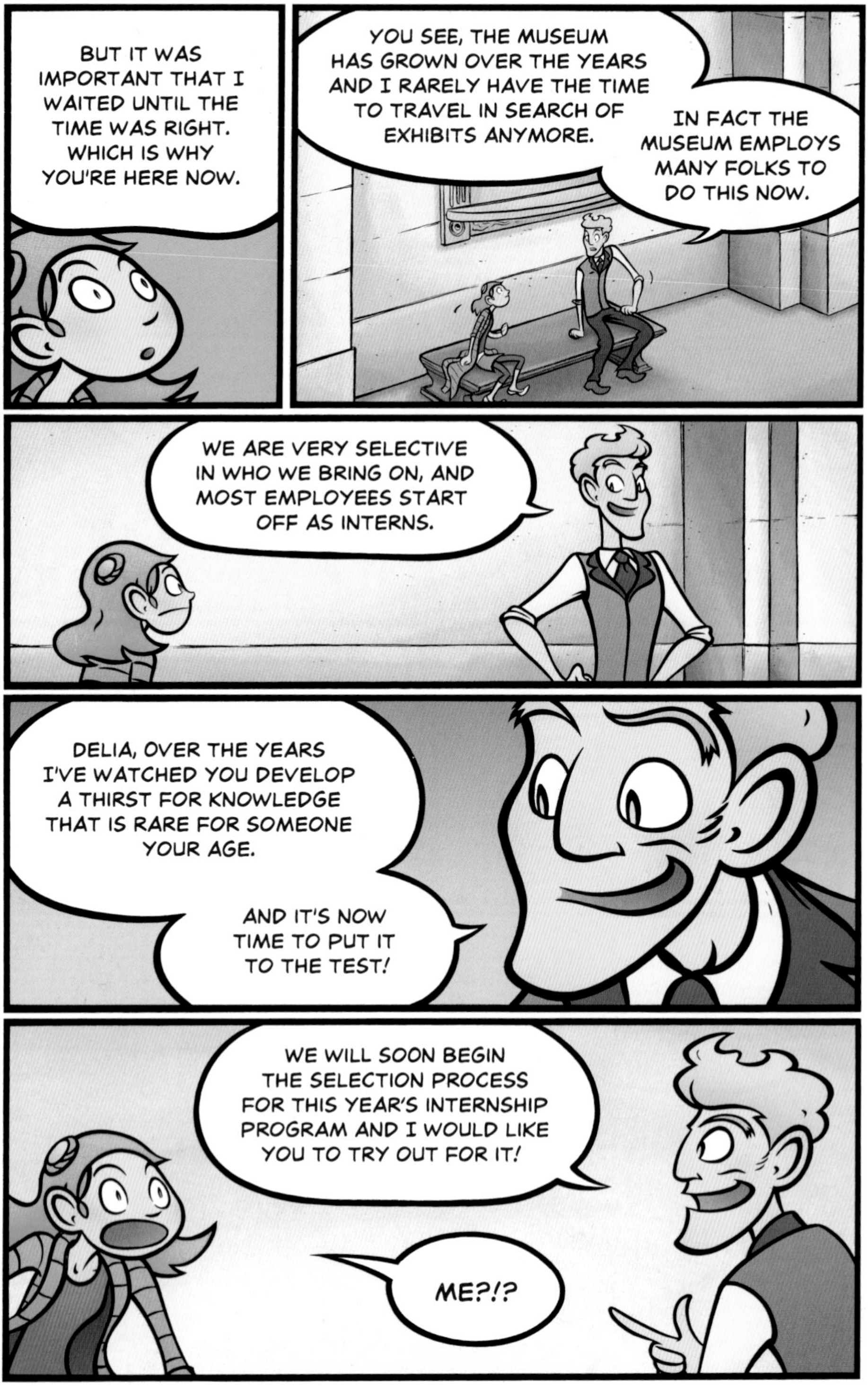
BUT IT WAS IMPORTANT THAT I WAITED UNTIL THE TIME WAS RIGHT. WHICH IS WHY YOU'RE HERE NOW.
YOU SEE, THE MUSEUM HAS GROWN OVER THE YEARS AND I RARELY HAVE THE TIME TO TRAVEL IN SEARCH OF EXHIBITS ANYMORE.
IN FACT THE MUSEUM EMPLOYS MANY FOLKS TO DO THIS NOW.
WE ARE VERY SELECTIVE IN WHO WE BRING ON, AND MOST EMPLOYEES START OFF AS INTERNS.
DELIA, OVER THE YEARS I'VE WATCHED YOU DEVELOP A THIRST FOR KNOWLEDGE THAT IS RARE FOR SOMEONE YOUR AGE.
AND IT'S NOW TIME TO PUT IT TO THE TEST!
WE WILL SOON BEGIN THE SELECTION PROCESS FOR THIS YEAR'S INTERNSHIP PROGRAM AND I WOULD LIKE YOU TO TRY OUT FOR IT!
ME?!?

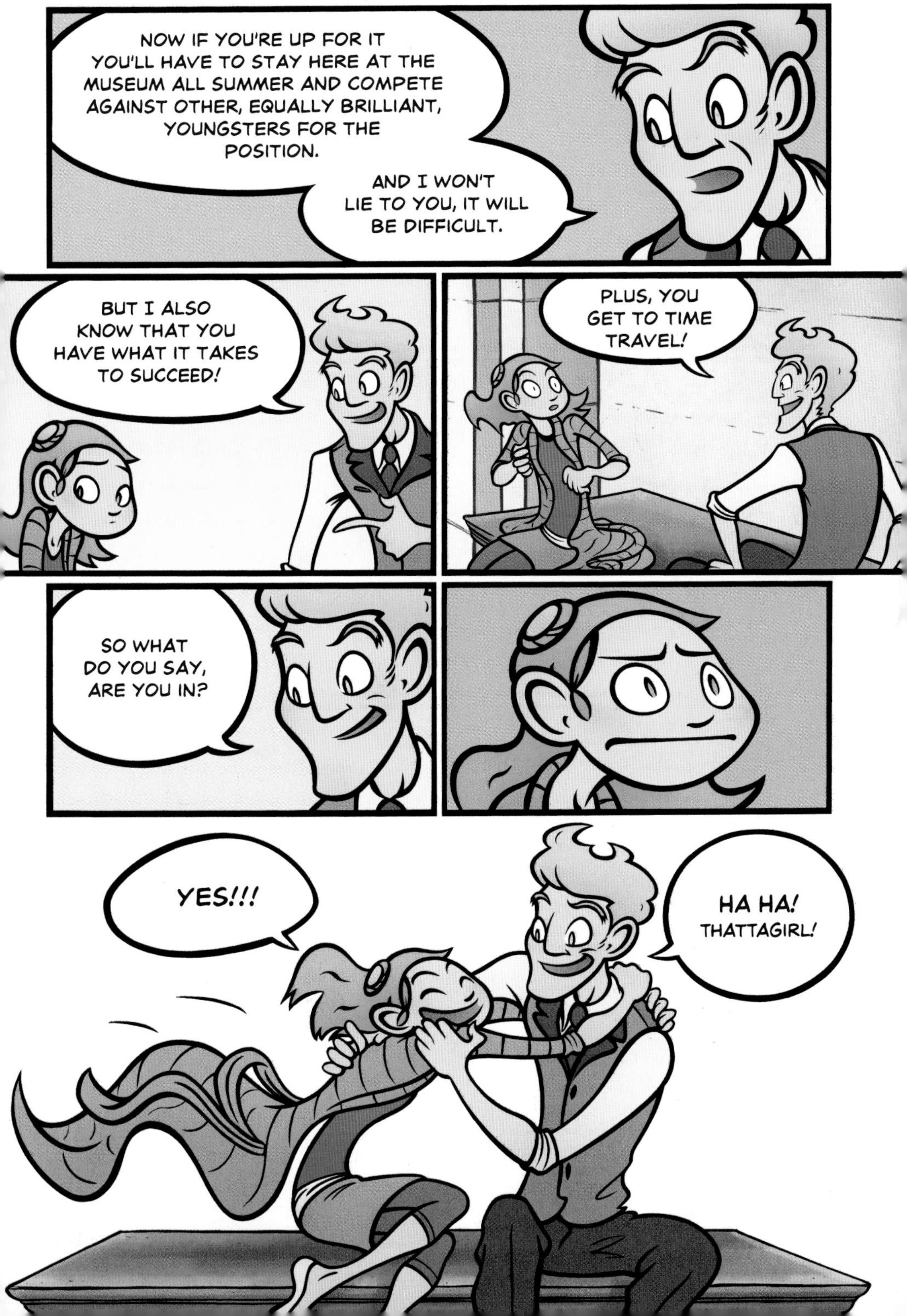

NOW IF YOU'RE UP FOR IT YOU'LL HAVE TO STAY HERE AT THE MUSEUM ALL SUMMER AND COMPETE AGAINST OTHER, EQUALLY BRILLIANT, YOUNGSTERS FOR THE POSITION.
AND I WON'T LIE TO YOU, IT WILL BE DIFFICULT.
BUT I ALSO KNOW THAT YOU HAVE WHAT IT TAKES TO SUCCEED!
PLUS, YOU GET TO TIME TRAVEL!
SO WHAT DO YOU SAY, ARE YOU IN?
YES!!!
HA HA! THATTAGIRL!

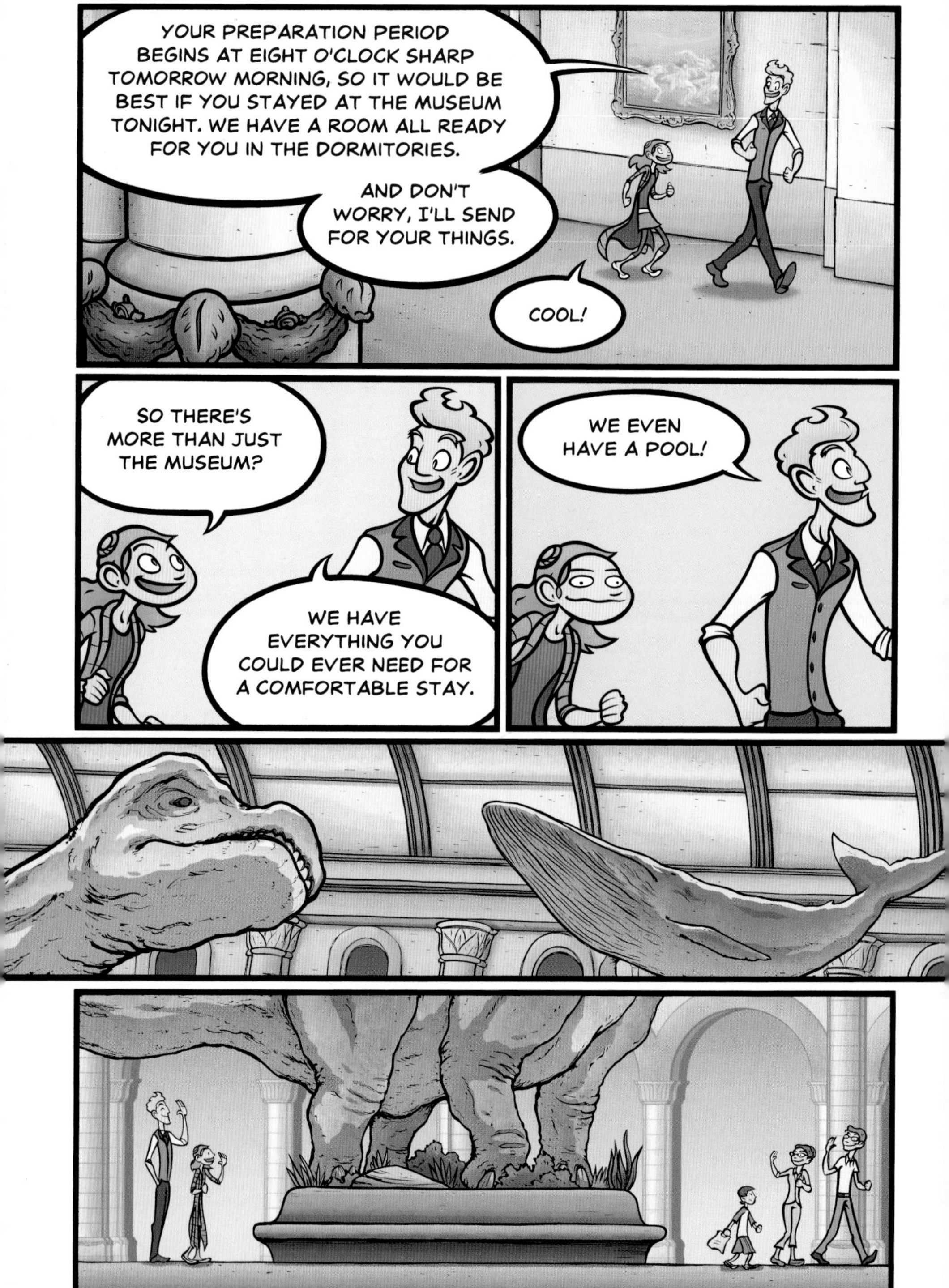
YOUR PREPARATION PERIOD BEGINS AT EIGHT O'CLOCK SHARP TOMORROW MORNING, SO IT WOULD BE BEST IF YOU STAYED AT THE MUSEUM TONIGHT. WE HAVE A ROOM ALL READY FOR YOU IN THE DORMITORIES.
AND DON'T WORRY, I'LL SEND FOR YOUR THINGS.
COOL!
SO THERE'S MORE THAN JUST THE MUSEUM?
WE HAVE EVERYTHING YOU COULD EVER NEED FOR A COMFORTABLE STAY.
WE EVEN HAVE A POOL!

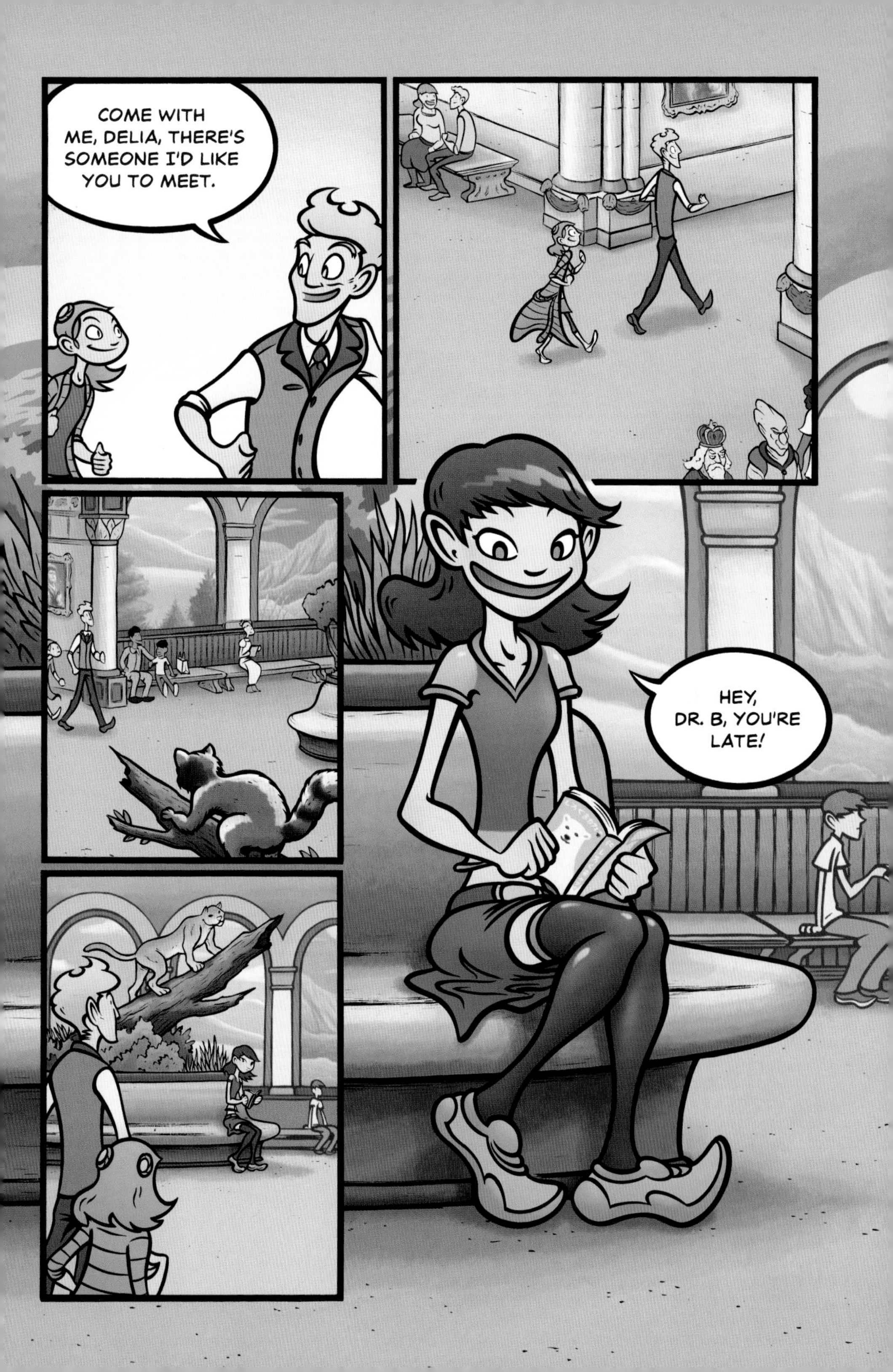
COME WITH ME, DELIA, THERE'S SOMEONE I'D LIKE YOU TO MEET.
HEY, DR. B, YOU'RE LATE!

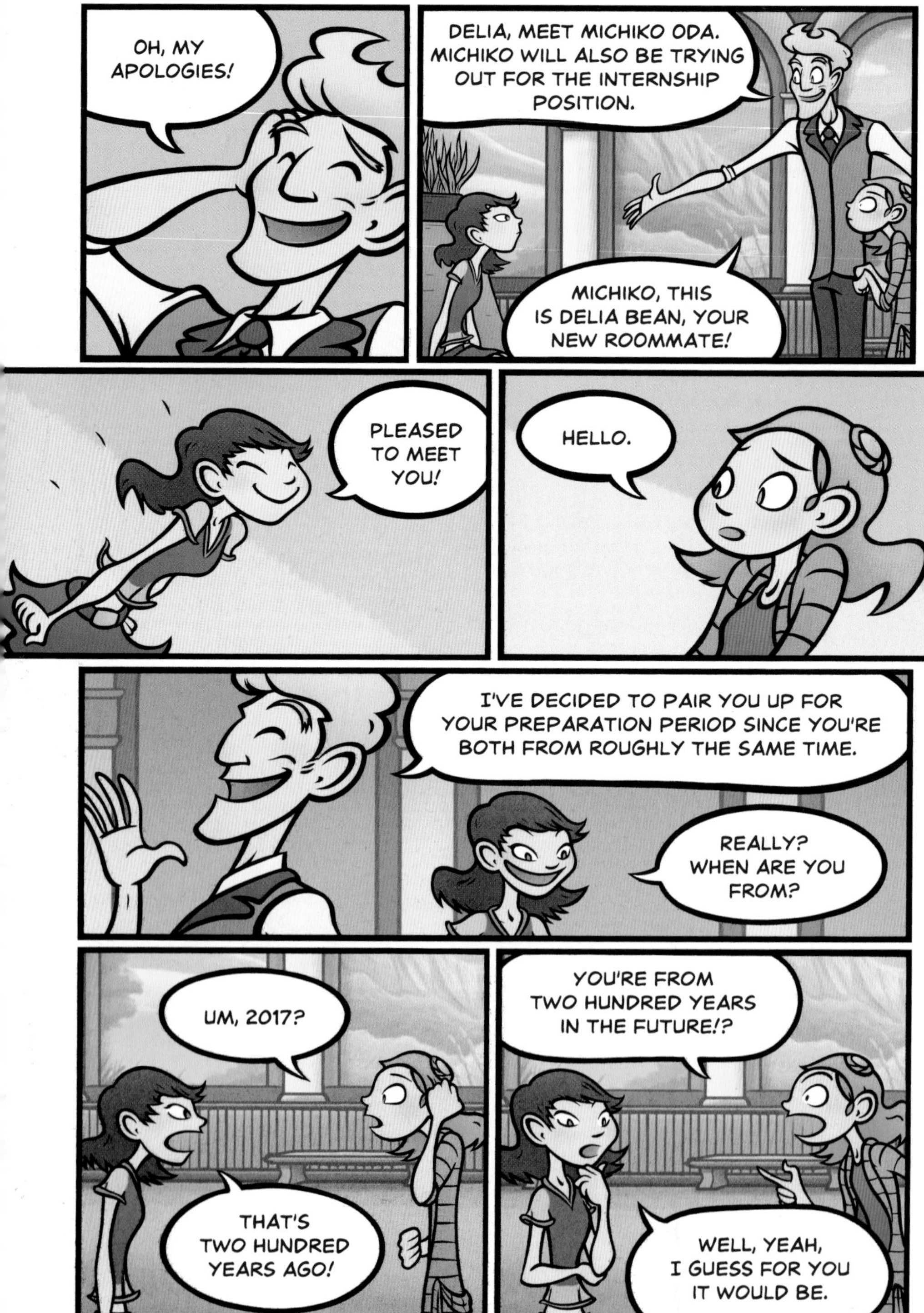
OH, MY APOLOGIES!
DELIA, MEET MICHIKO ODA. MICHIKO WILL ALSO BE TRYING OUT FOR THE INTERNSHIP POSITION.
MICHIKO, THIS IS DELIA BEAN, YOUR NEW ROOMMATE!
PLEASED TO MEET YOU!
HELLO.
I'VE DECIDED TO PAIR YOU UP FOR YOUR PREPARATION PERIOD SINCE YOU'RE BOTH FROM ROUGHLY THE SAME TIME.
REALLY? WHEN ARE YOU FROM?
UM, 2017?
THAT'S TWO HUNDRED YEARS AGO!
YOU'RE FROM TWO HUNDRED YEARS IN THE FUTURE!?
WELL, YEAH, I GUESS FOR YOU IT WOULD BE.

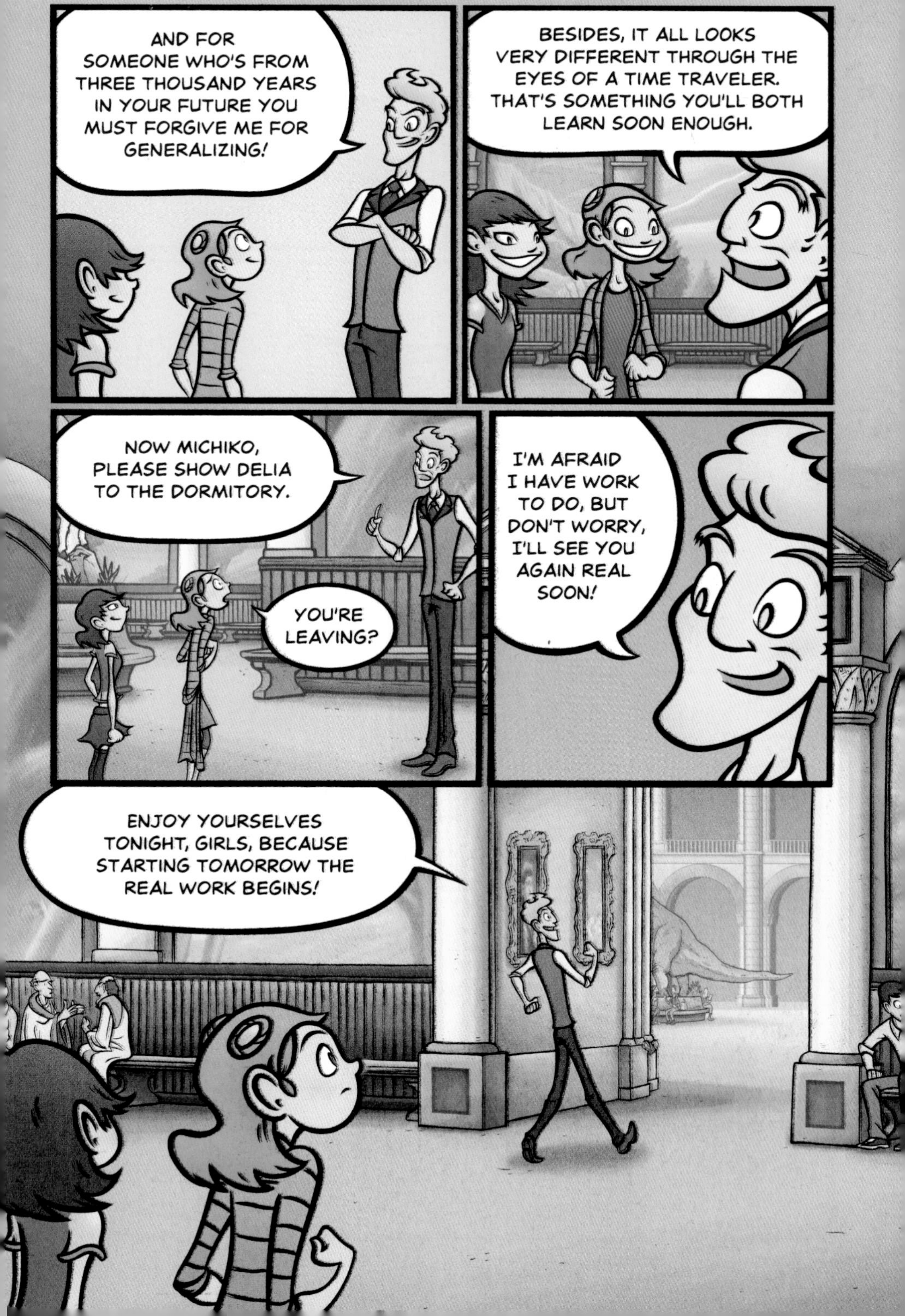
AND FOR SOMEONE WHO'S FROM THREE THOUSAND YEARS IN YOUR FUTURE YOU MUST FORGIVE ME FOR GENERALIZING!
BESIDES, IT ALL LOOKS VERY DIFFERENT THROUGH THE EYES OF A TIME TRAVELER. THAT'S SOMETHING YOU'LL BOTH LEARN SOON ENOUGH.
NOW MICHIKO, PLEASE SHOW DELIA TO THE DORMITORY.
YOU'RE LEAVING?
I'M AFRAID I HAVE WORK TO DO, BUT DON'T WORRY, I'LL SEE YOU AGAIN REAL SOON!
ENJOY YOURSELVES TONIGHT, GIRLS, BECAUSE STARTING TOMORROW THE REAL WORK BEGINS!

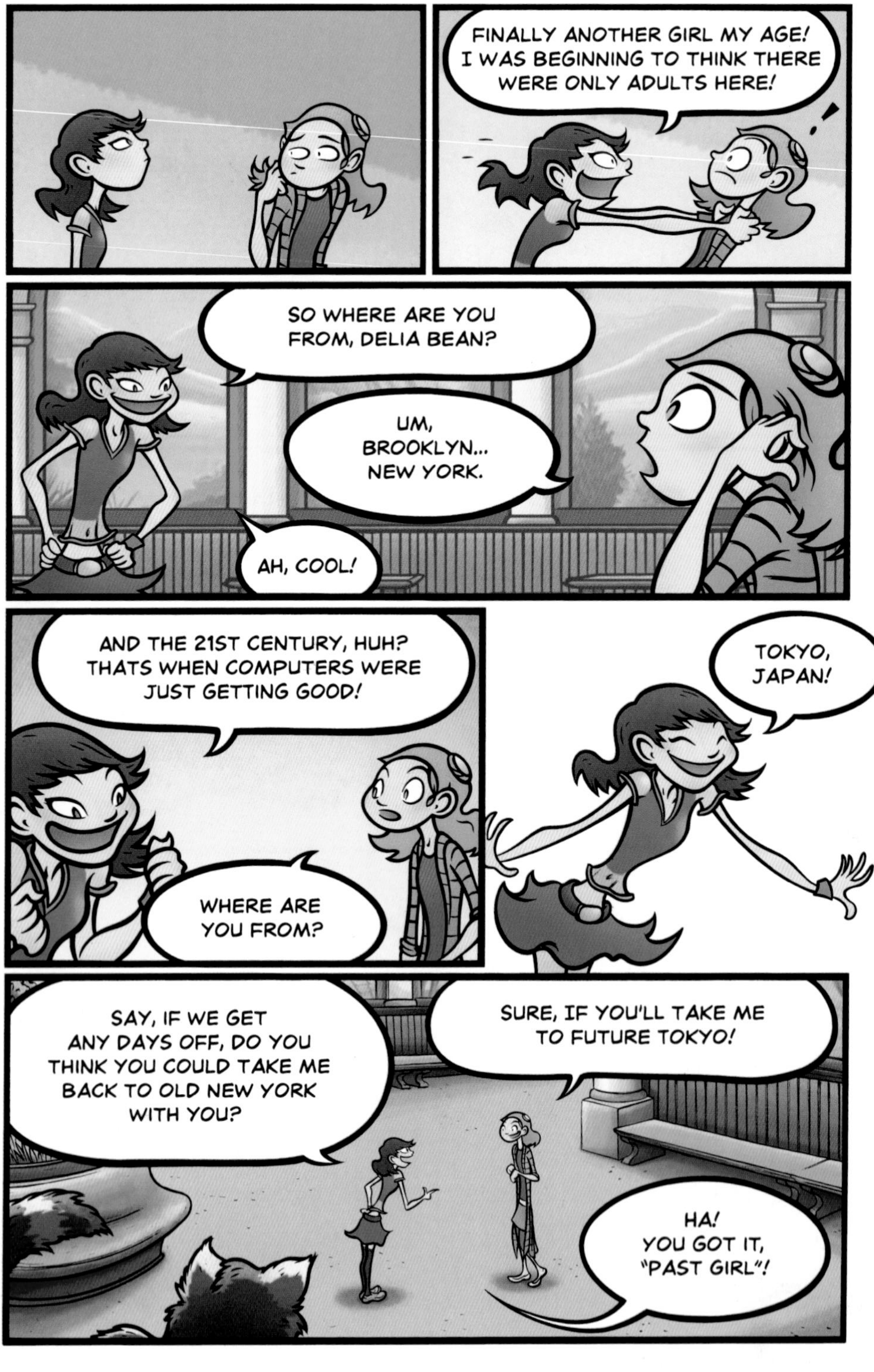

FINALLY ANOTHER GIRL MY AGE! I WAS BEGINNING TO THINK THERE WERE ONLY ADULTS HERE!
SO WHERE ARE YOU FROM, DELIA BEAN?
UM, BROOKLYN... NEW YORK.
AH, COOL!
AND THE 21ST CENTURY, HUH? THATS WHEN COMPUTERS WERE JUST GETTING GOOD!
WHERE ARE YOU FROM?
TOKYO, JAPAN!
SAY, IF WE GET ANY DAYS OFF, DO YOU THINK YOU COULD TAKE ME BACK TO OLD NEW YORK WITH YOU?
SURE, IF YOU'LL TAKE ME TO FUTURE TOKYO!
HA! YOU GOT IT, "PAST GIRL"!

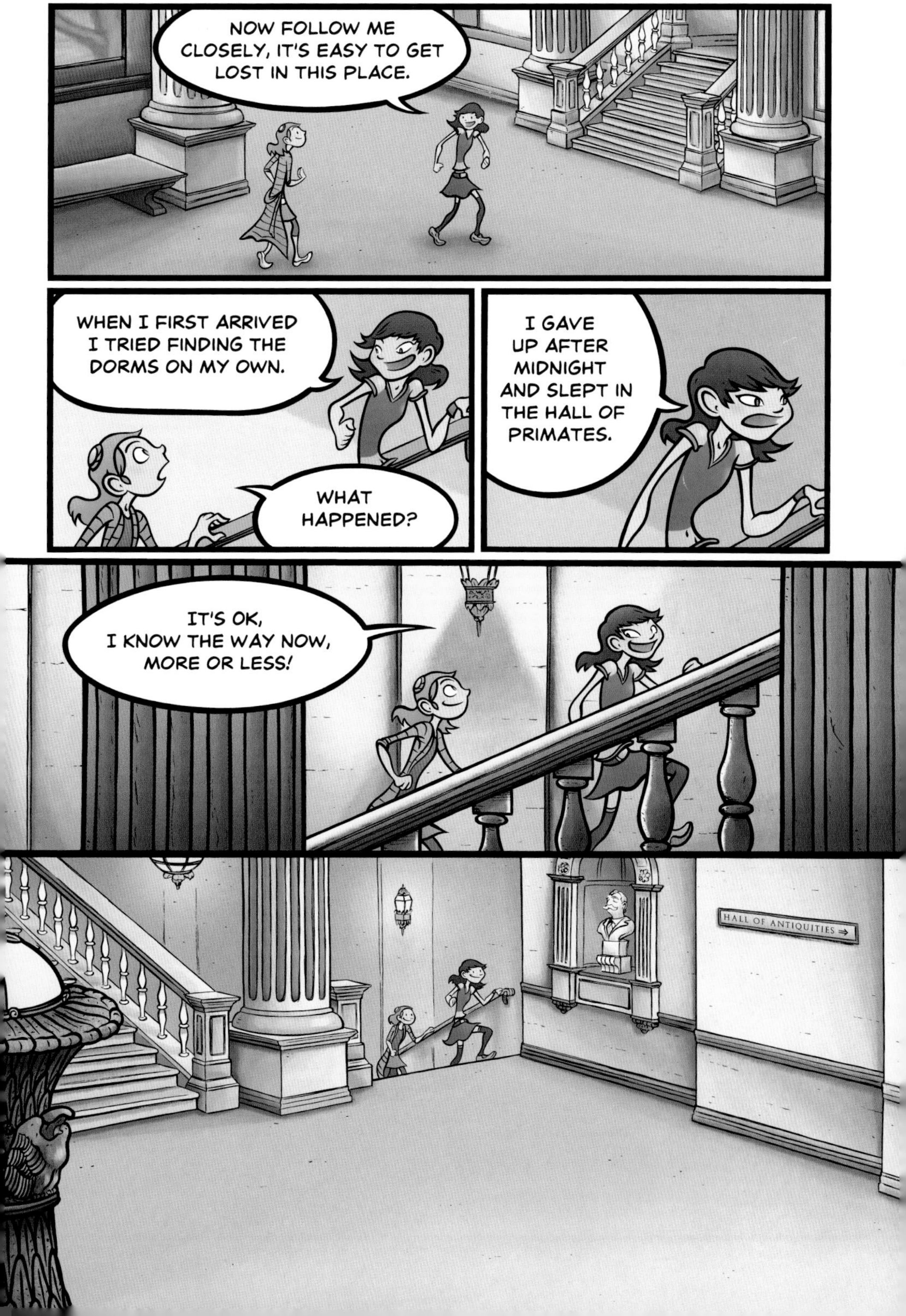
NOW FOLLOW ME CLOSELY, IT'S EASY TO GET LOST IN THIS PLACE.
WHEN I FIRST ARRIVED I TRIED FINDING THE DORMS ON MY OWN.
WHAT HAPPENED?
I GAVE UP AFTER MIDNIGHT AND SLEPT IN THE HALL OF PRIMATES.
IT'S OK, I KNOW THE WAY NOW, MORE OR LESS!
HALL OF ANTIQUITIES ⇒

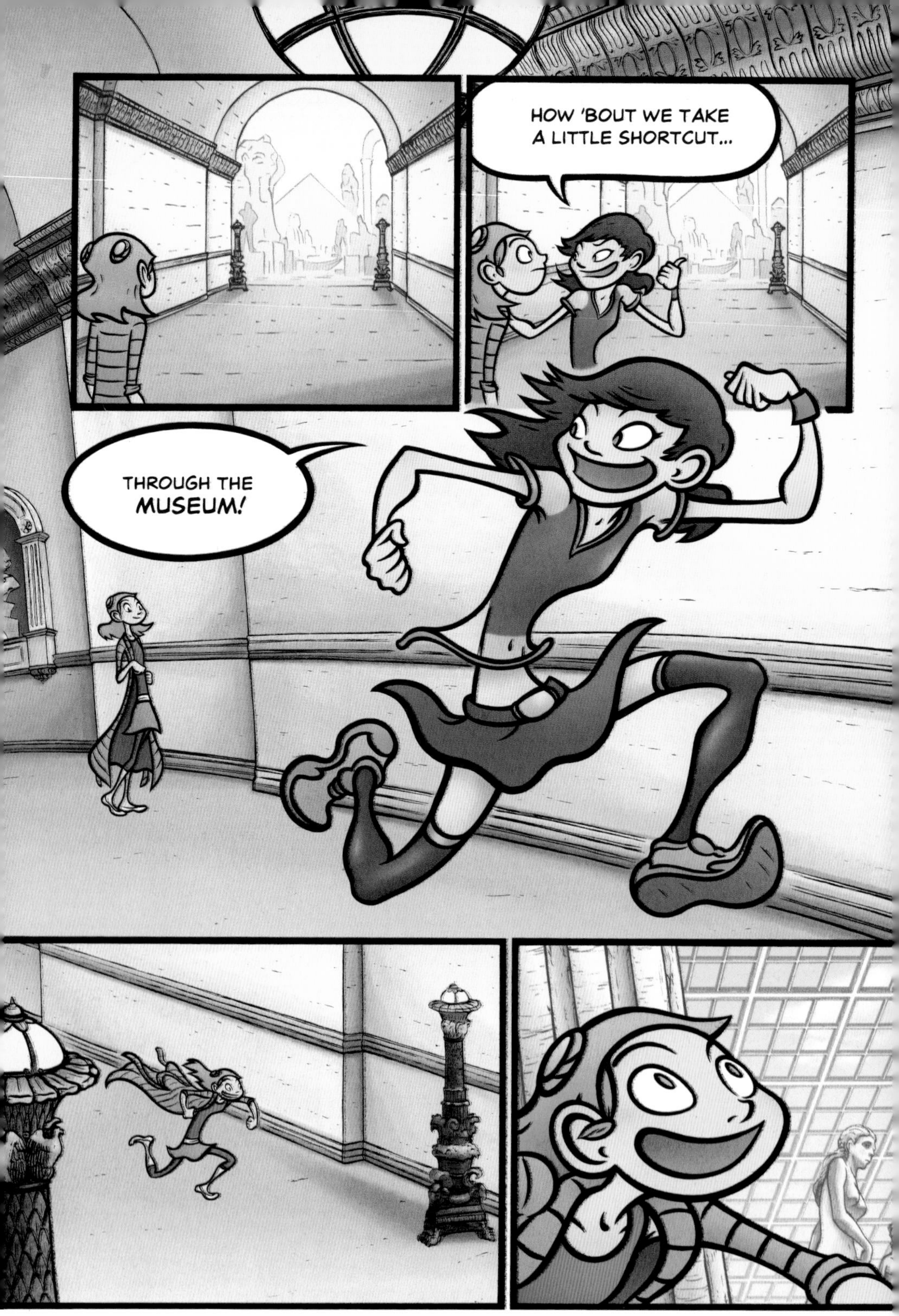
HOW 'BOUT WE TAKE A LITTLE SHORTCUT...
THROUGH THE MUSEUM!

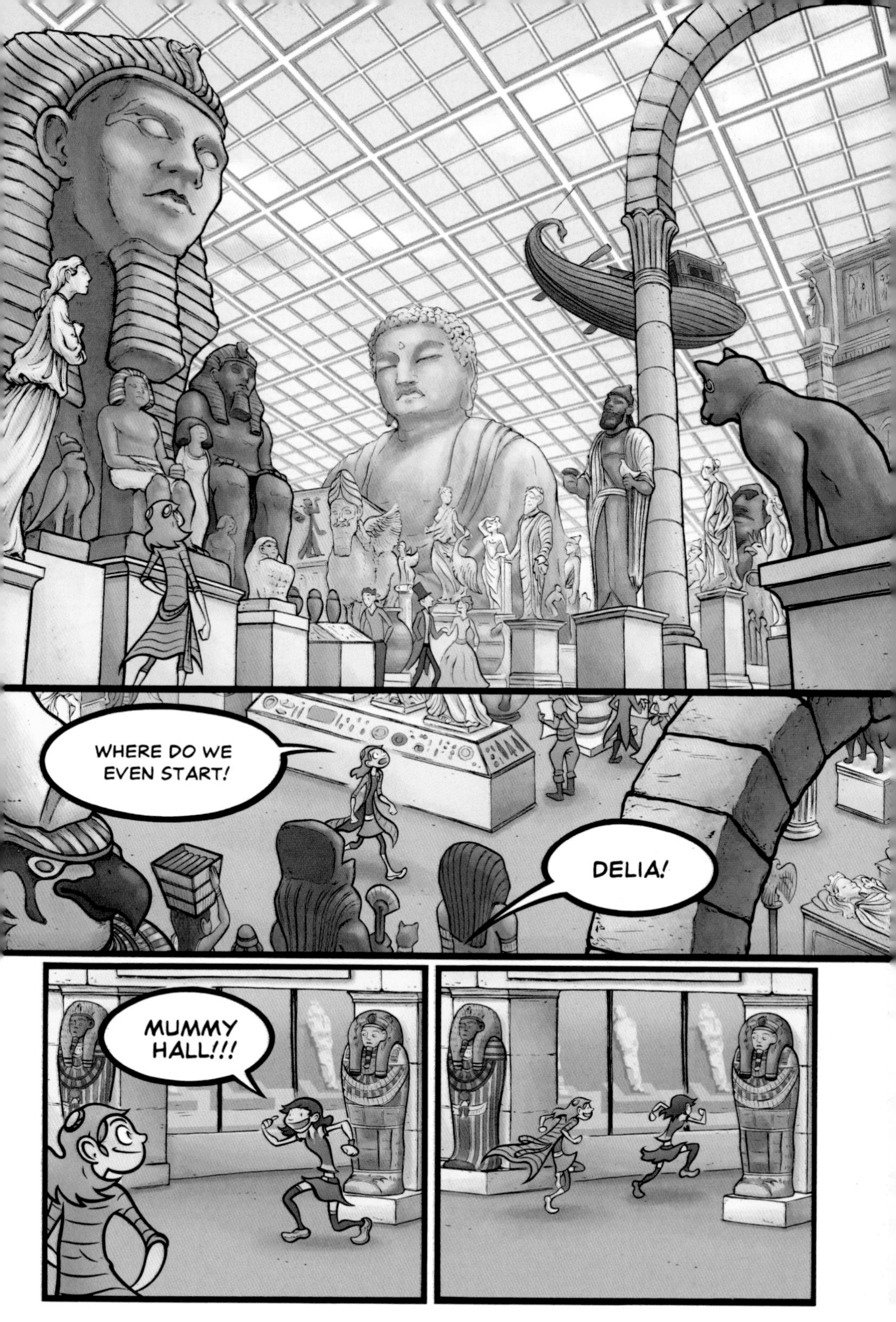
WHERE DO WE EVEN START!
DELIA!
MUMMY HALL!!!

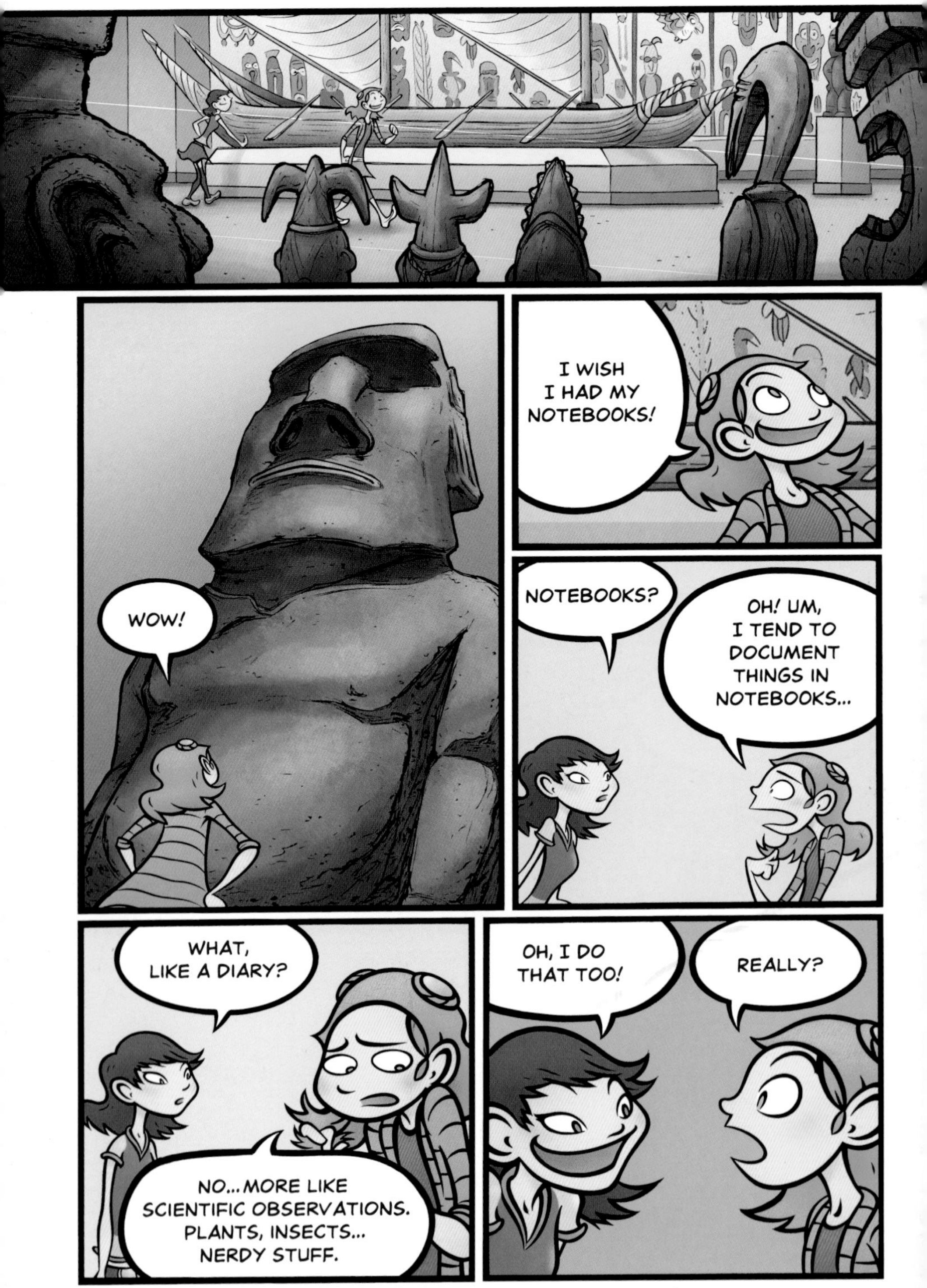
WOW!
I WISH I HAD MY NOTEBOOKS!
NOTEBOOKS?
OH! UM, I TEND TO DOCUMENT THINGS IN NOTEBOOKS...
WHAT, LIKE A DIARY?
NO...MORE LIKE SCIENTIFIC OBSERVATIONS. PLANTS, INSECTS... NERDY STUFF.
OH, I DO THAT TOO!
REALLY?

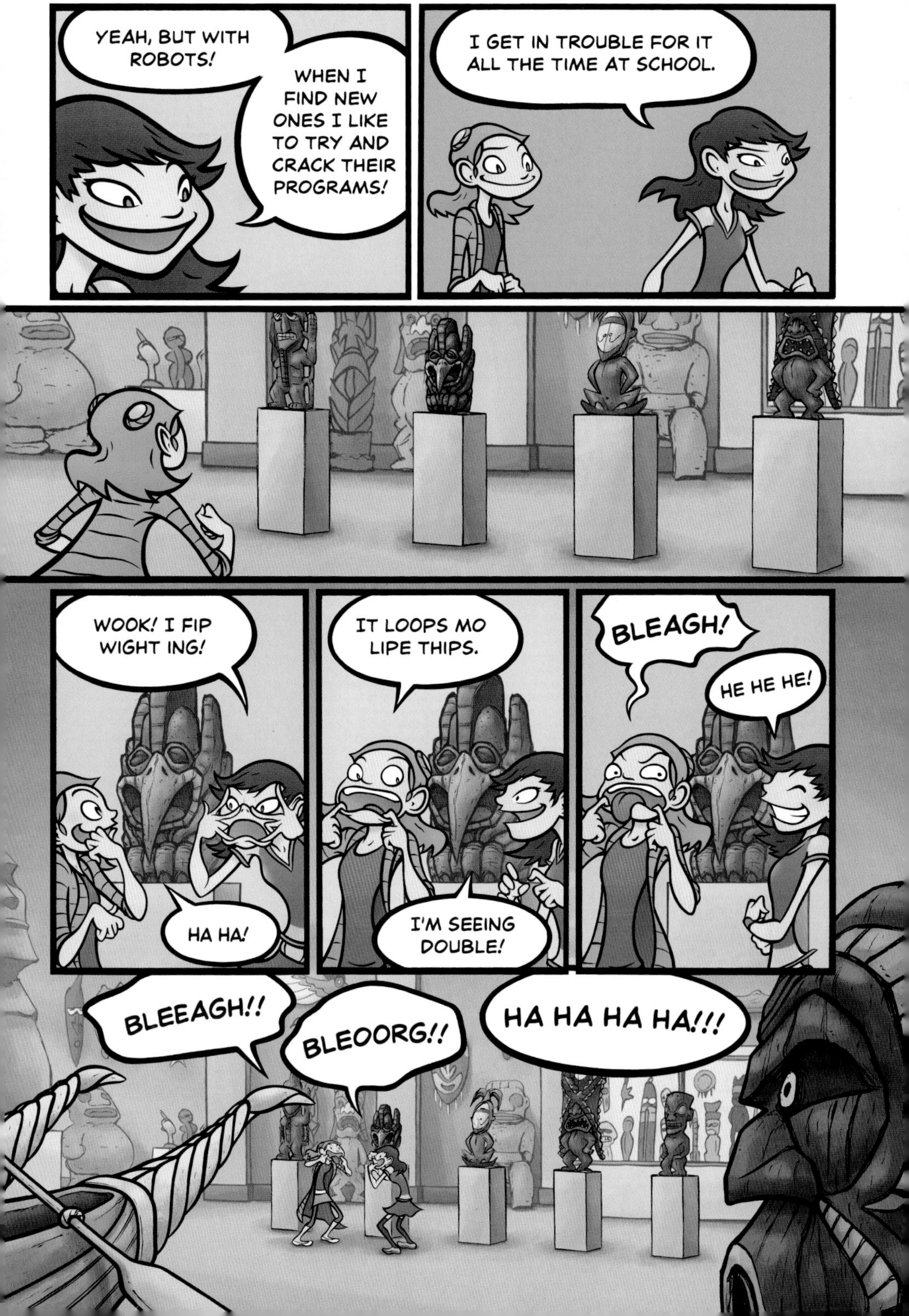
YEAH, BUT WITH ROBOTS!
WHEN I FIND NEW ONES I LIKE TO TRY AND CRACK THEIR PROGRAMS!
I GET IN TROUBLE FOR IT ALL THE TIME AT SCHOOL.
WOOK! I FIP WIGHT ING!
HA HA!
IT LOOPS MO LIPE THIPS.
I'M SEEING DOUBLE!
BLEAGH!
HE HE HE!
BLEEAGH!!
BLEOORG!!
HA HA HA HA!!!

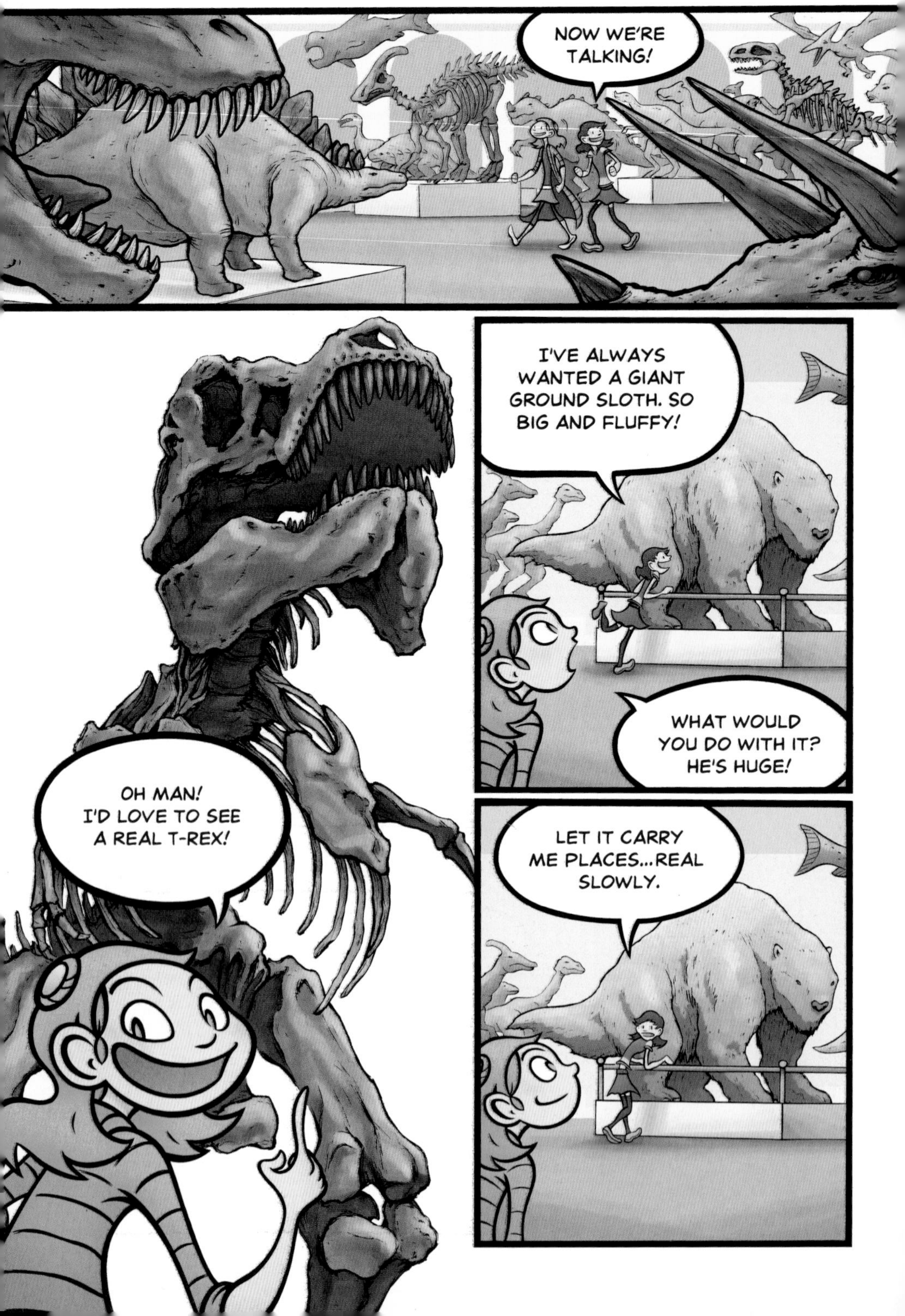
NOW WE'RE TALKING!
OH MAN! I'D LOVE TO SEE A REAL T-REX!
I'VE ALWAYS WANTED A GIANT GROUND SLOTH. SO BIG AND FLUFFY!
WHAT WOULD YOU DO WITH IT? HE'S HUGE!
LET IT CARRY ME PLACES...REAL SLOWLY.

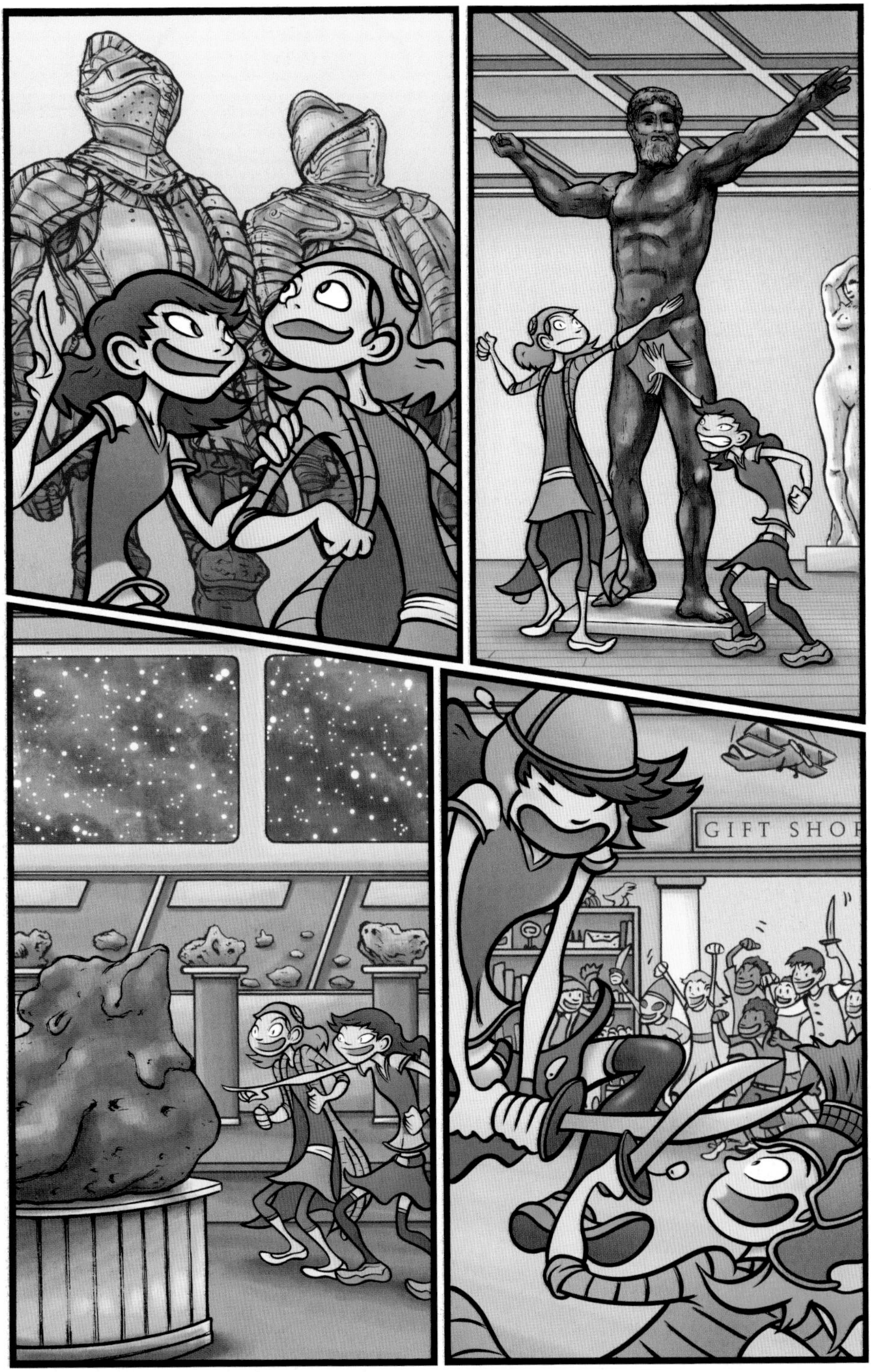
GIFT SHO

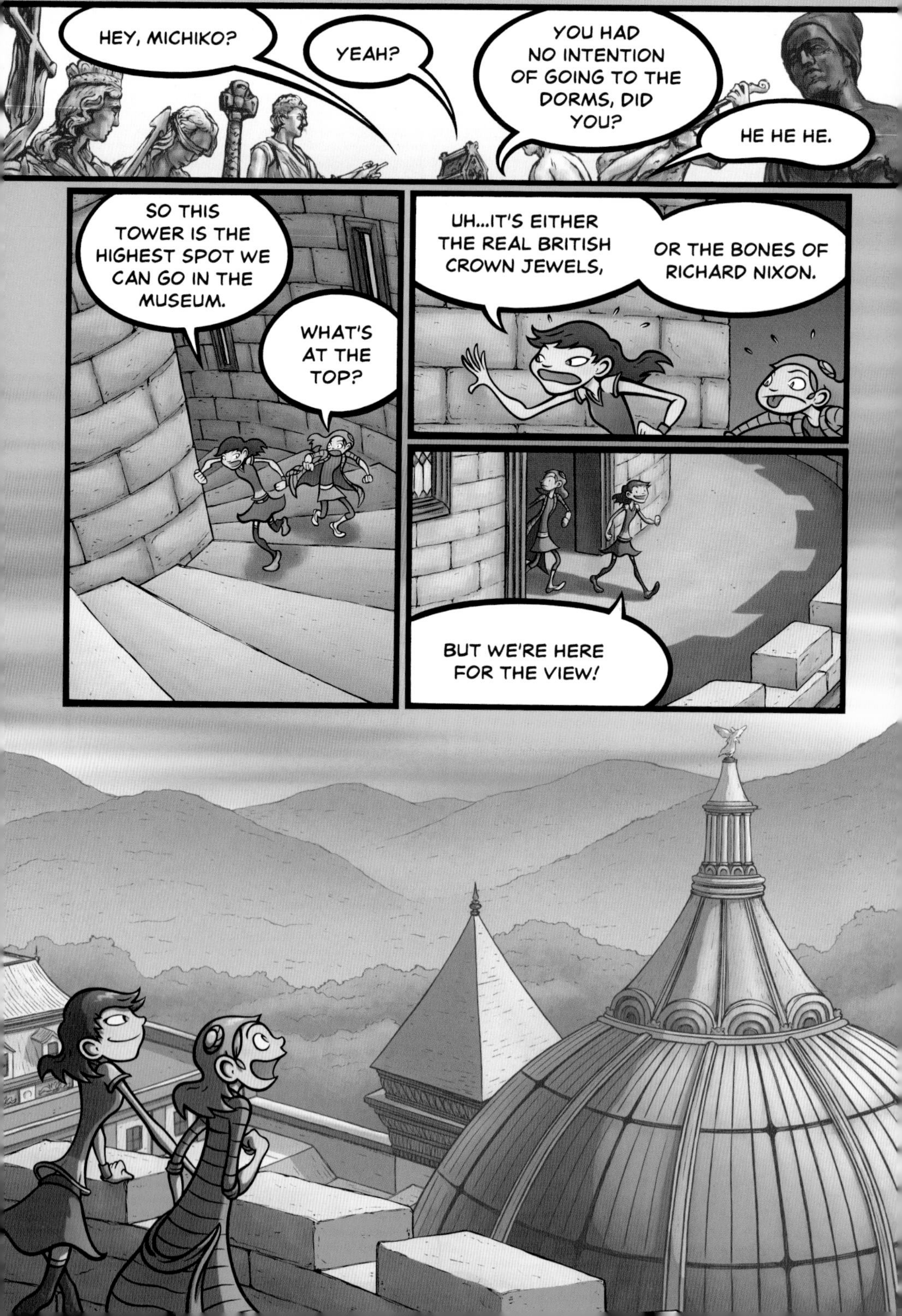
HEY, MICHIKO?
YEAH?
YOU HAD NO INTENTION OF GOING TO THE DORMS, DID YOU?
HE HE HE.
SO THIS TOWER IS THE HIGHEST SPOT WE CAN GO IN THE MUSEUM.
WHAT'S AT THE TOP?
UH...IT'S EITHER THE REAL BRITISH CROWN JEWELS,
OR THE BONES OF RICHARD NIXON.
BUT WE'RE HERE FOR THE VIEW!

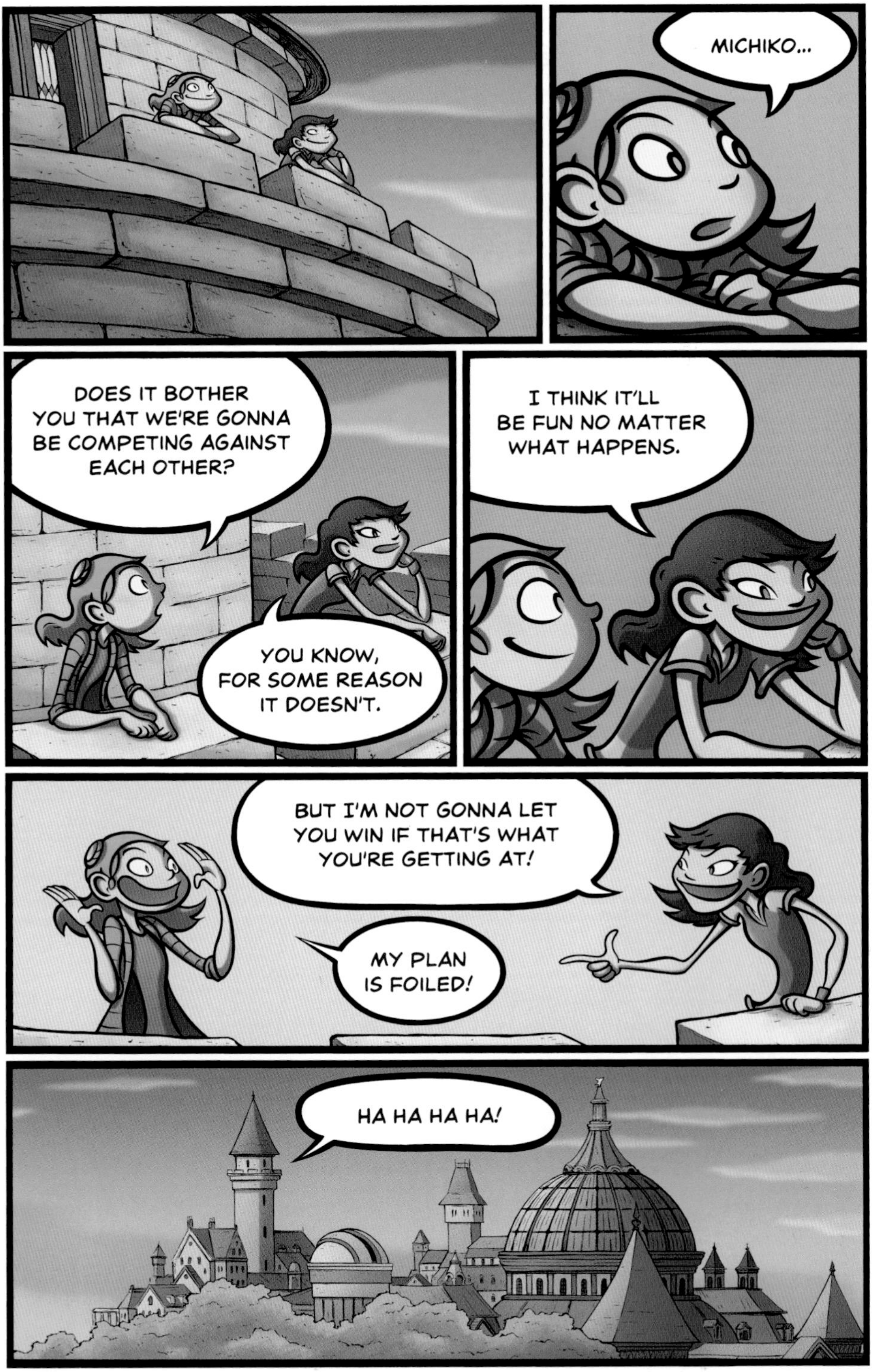
MICHIKO...
DOES IT BOTHER YOU THAT WE'RE GONNA BE COMPETING AGAINST EACH OTHER?
YOU KNOW, FOR SOME REASON IT DOESN'T.
I THINK IT'LL BE FUN NO MATTER WHAT HAPPENS.
BUT I'M NOT GONNA LET YOU WIN IF THAT'S WHAT YOU'RE GETTING AT!
MY PLAN IS FOILED!
HA HA HA HA!

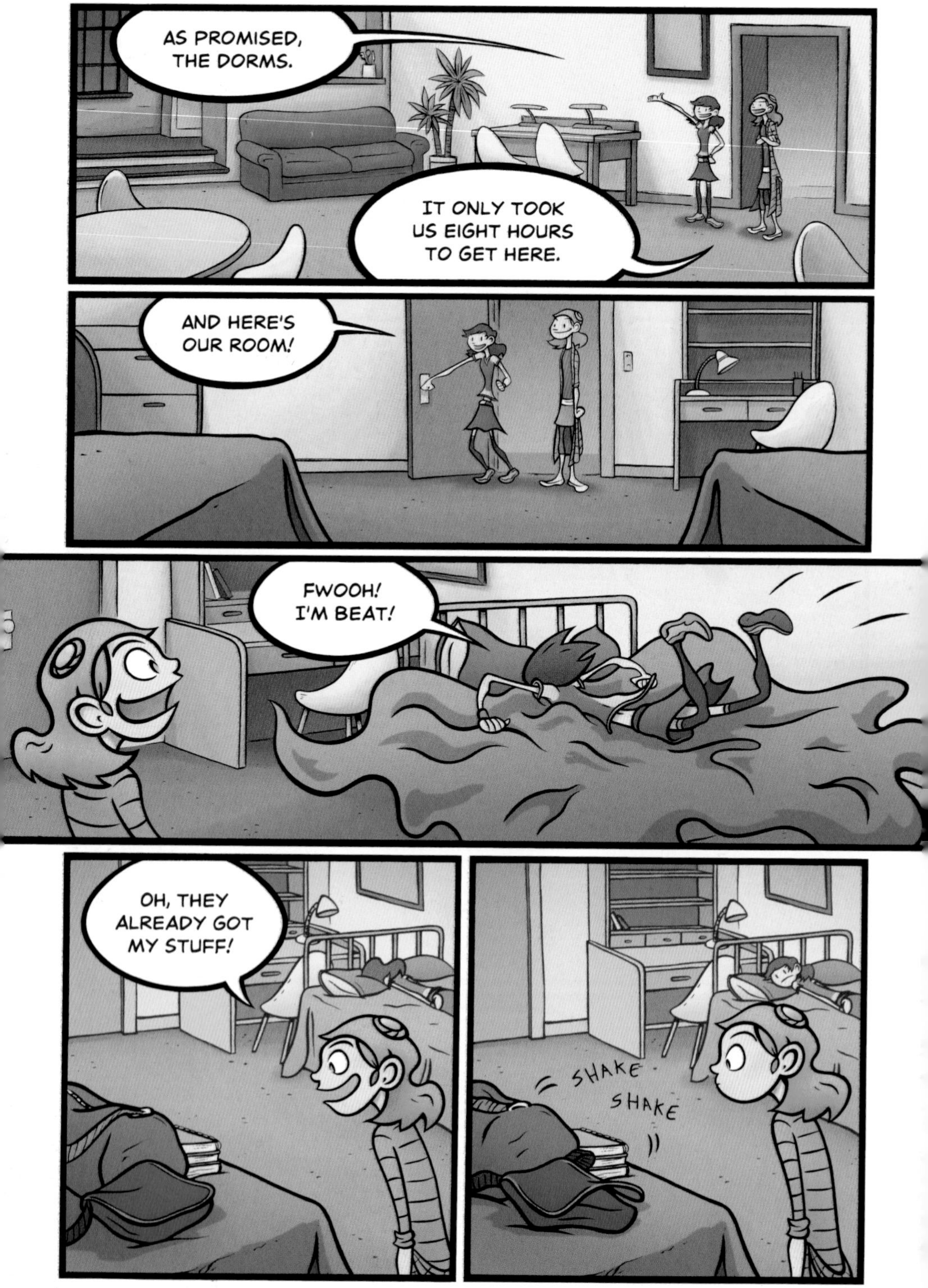
AS PROMISED, THE DORMS.
IT ONLY TOOK US EIGHT HOURS TO GET HERE.
AND HERE'S OUR ROOM!
FWOOH! I'M BEAT!
OH, THEY ALREADY GOT MY STUFF!
SHAKE
SHAKE

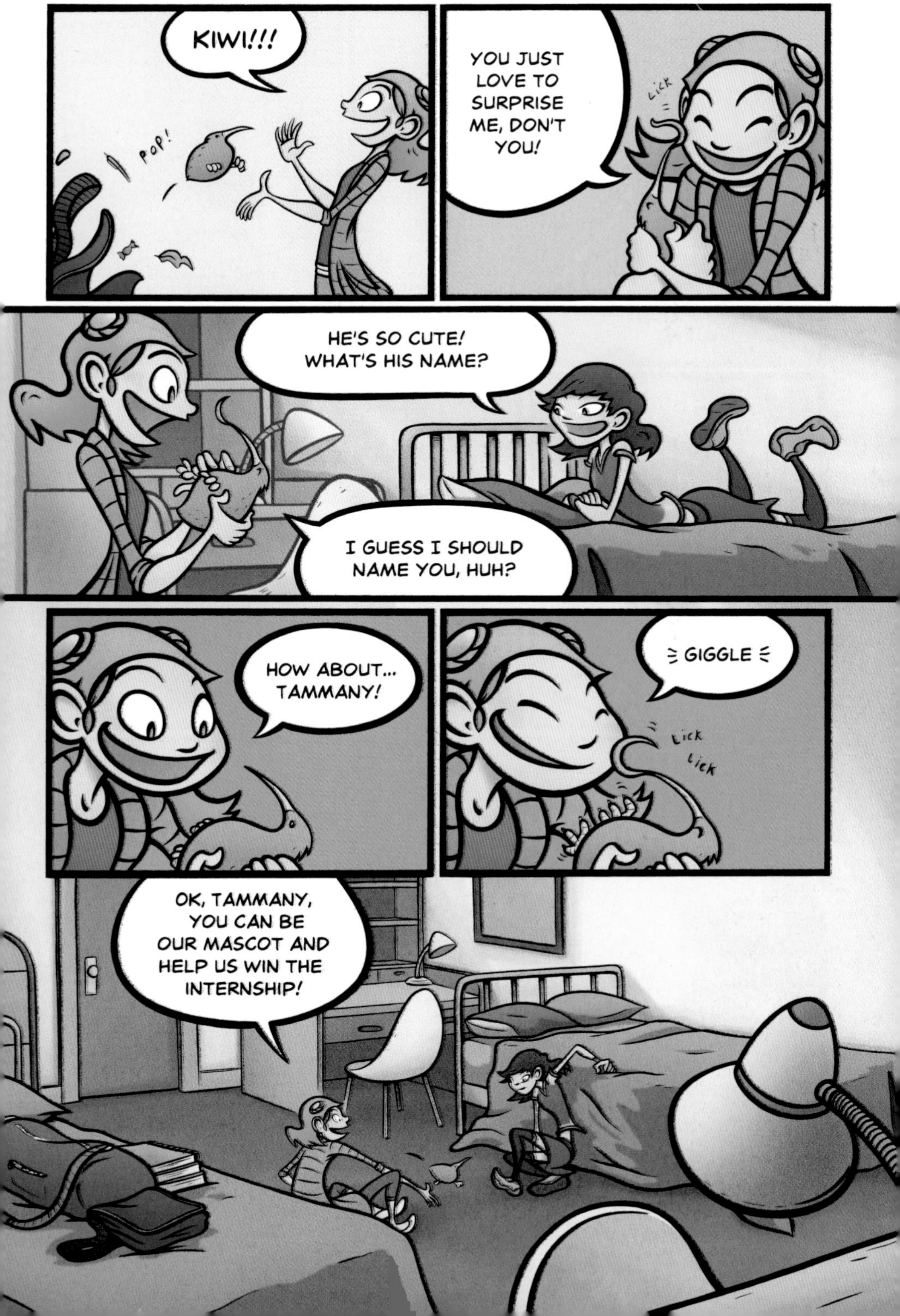
KIWI!!!
POP!
YOU JUST LOVE TO SURPRISE ME, DON'T YOU!
LICK
HE'S SO CUTE! WHAT'S HIS NAME?
I GUESS I SHOULD NAME YOU, HUH?
HOW ABOUT... TAMMANY!
GIGGLE
LICK
LICK
OK, TAMMANY, YOU CAN BE OUR MASCOT AND HELP US WIN THE INTERNSHIP!

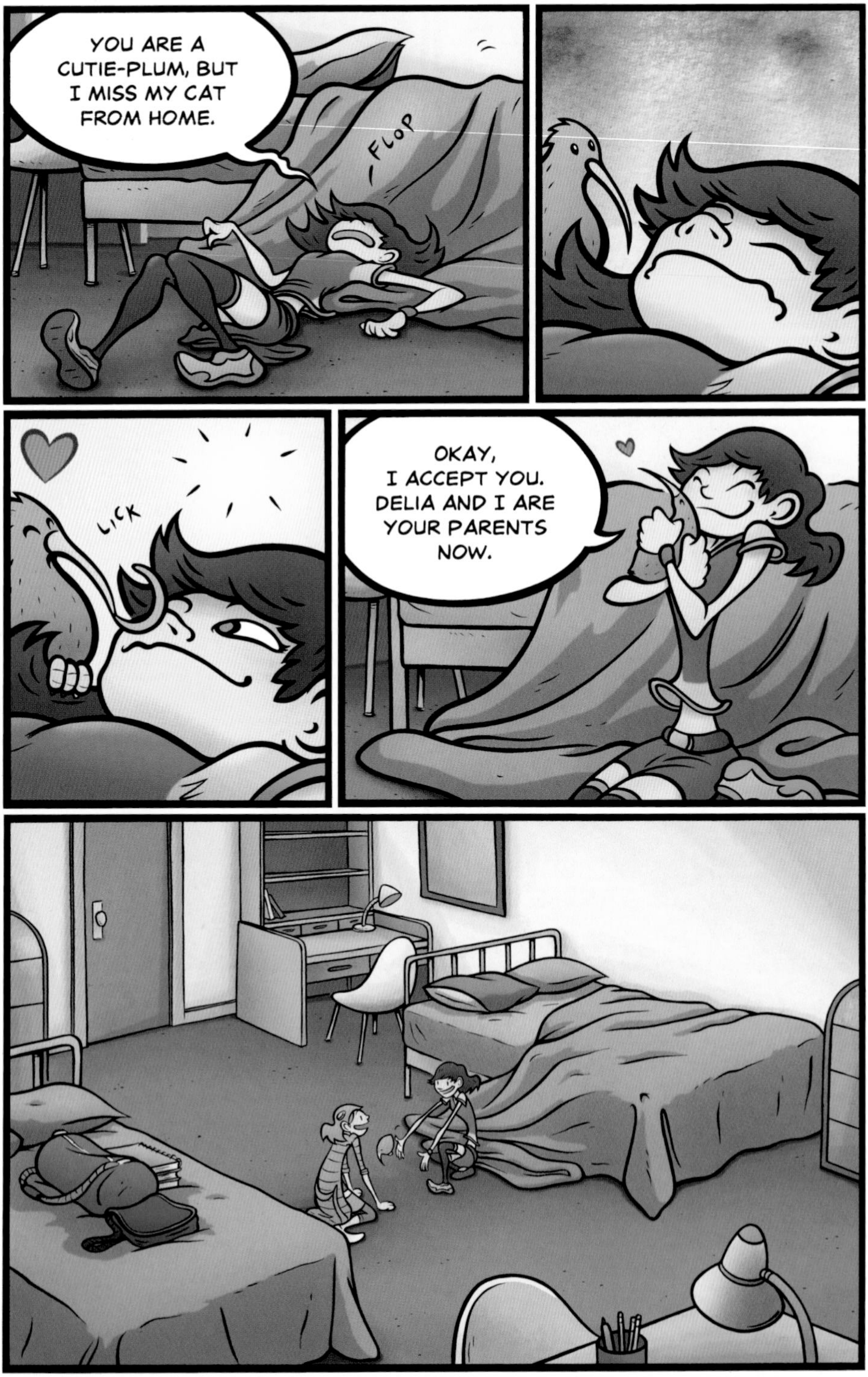
YOU ARE A CUTIE-PLUM, BUT I MISS MY CAT FROM HOME.
FLOP
LICK
OKAY, I ACCEPT YOU. DELIA AND I ARE YOUR PARENTS NOW.

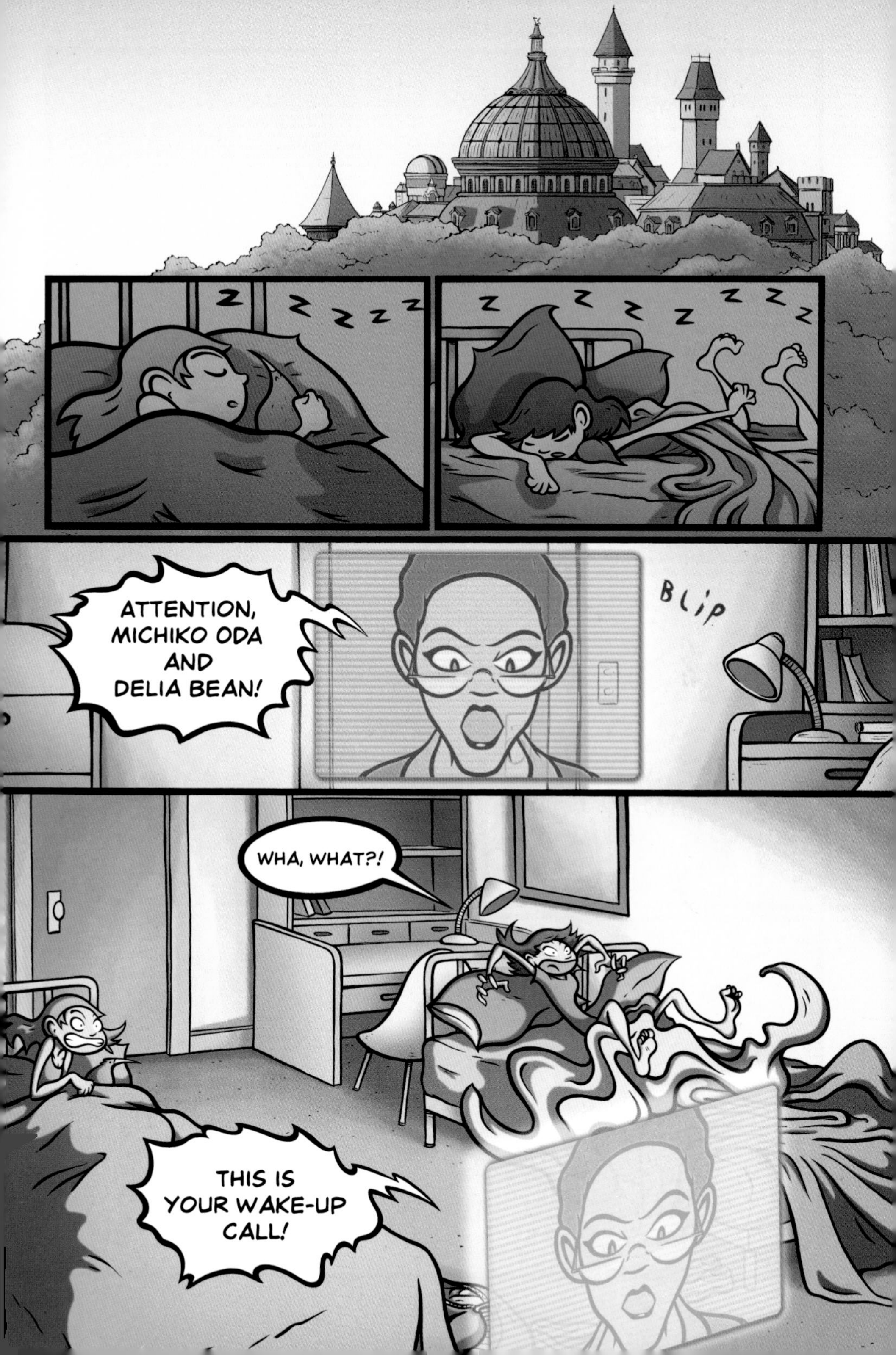
Z Z Z Z Z
Z Z Z Z Z Z Z
ATTENTION, MICHIKO ODA AND DELIA BEAN!
BLIP
WHA, WHAT?!
THIS IS YOUR WAKE-UP CALL!

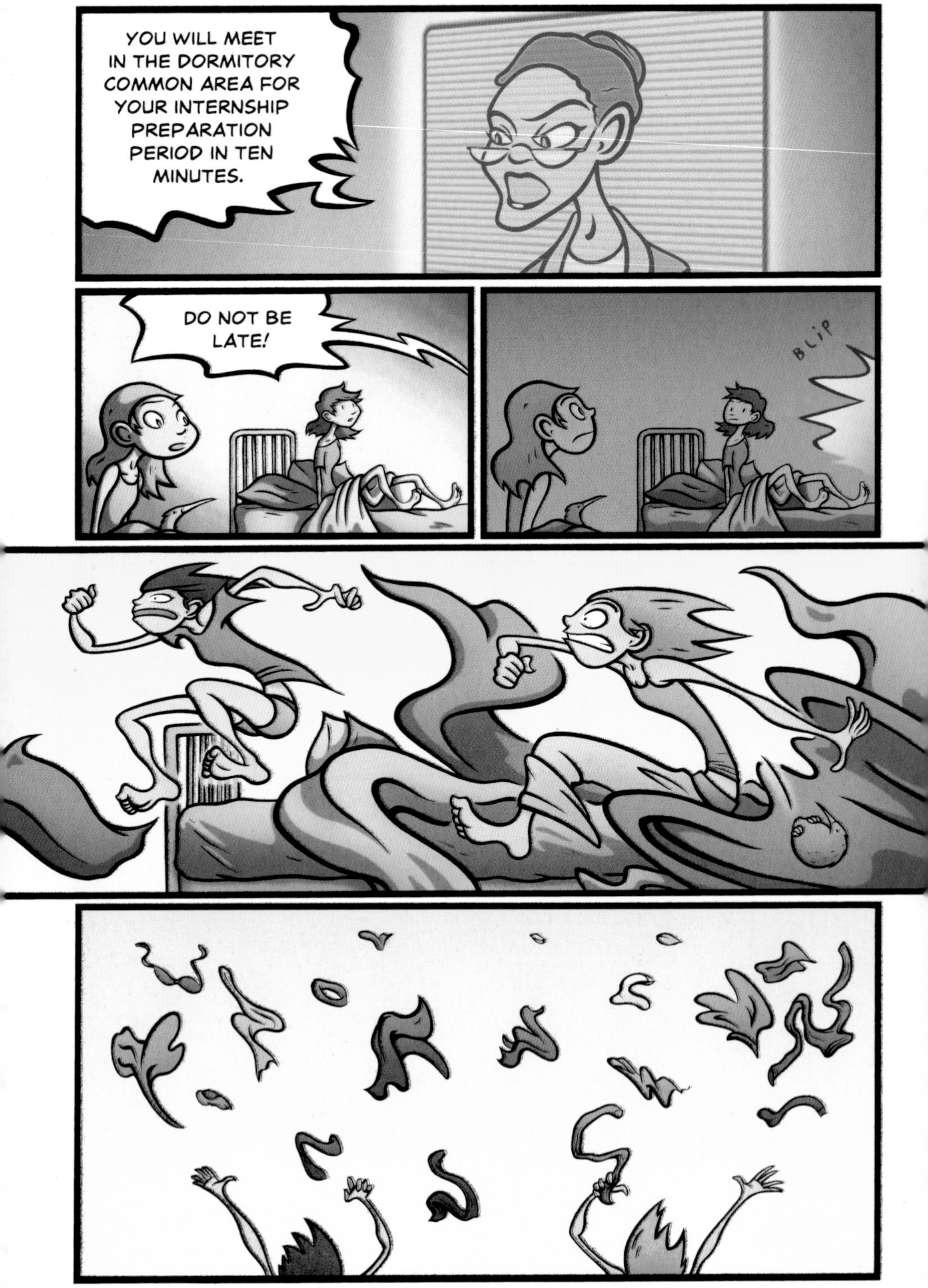
YOU WILL MEET IN THE DORMITORY COMMON AREA FOR YOUR INTERNSHIP PREPARATION PERIOD IN TEN MINUTES.
DO NOT BE LATE!
BLIP

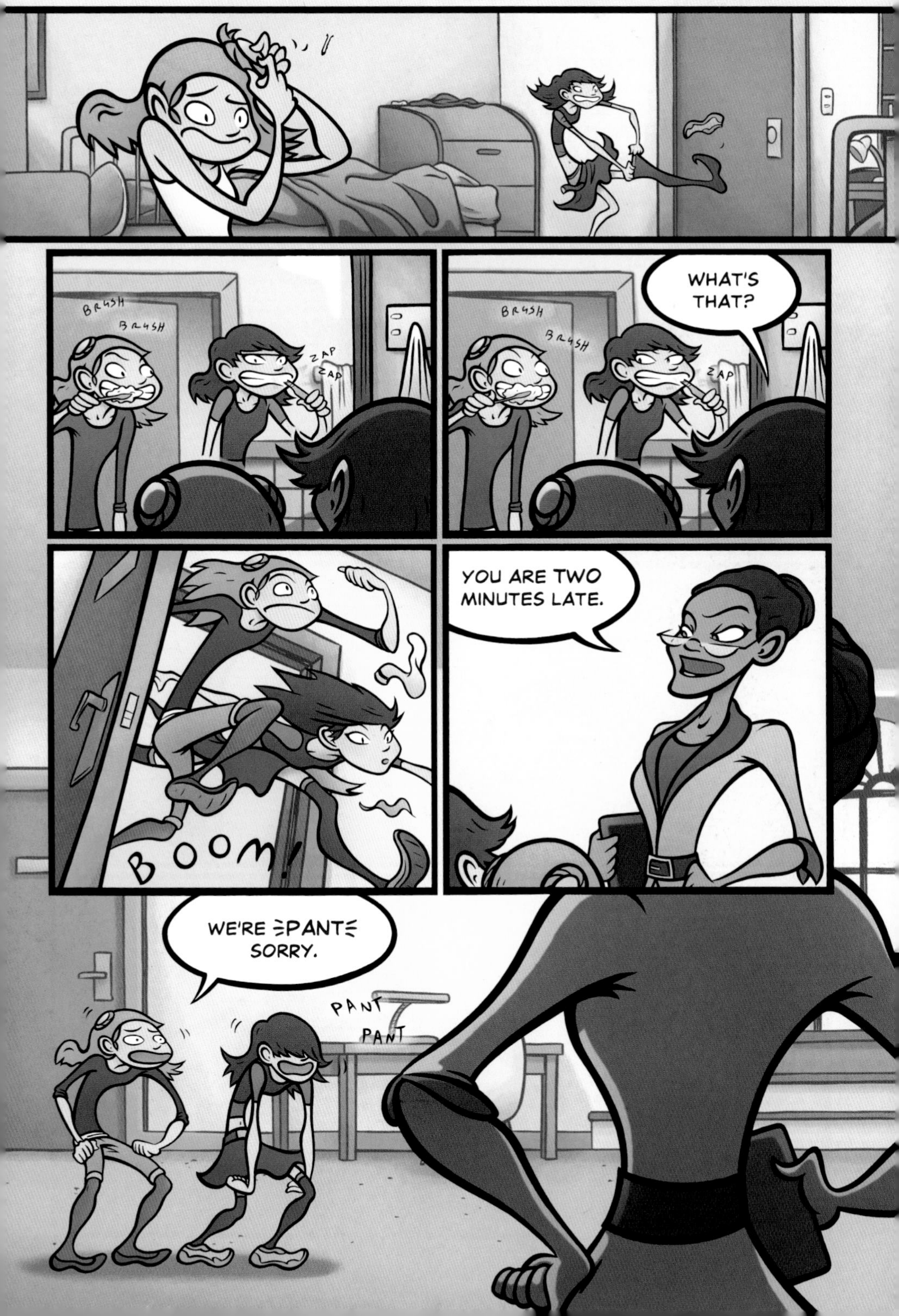
BRUSH
BRUSH
ZAP
ZAP
BRUSH
BRUSH
WHAT'S THAT?
ZAP
BOOM!
YOU ARE TWO MINUTES LATE.
WE'RE ≡PANT≡ SORRY.
PANT
PANT

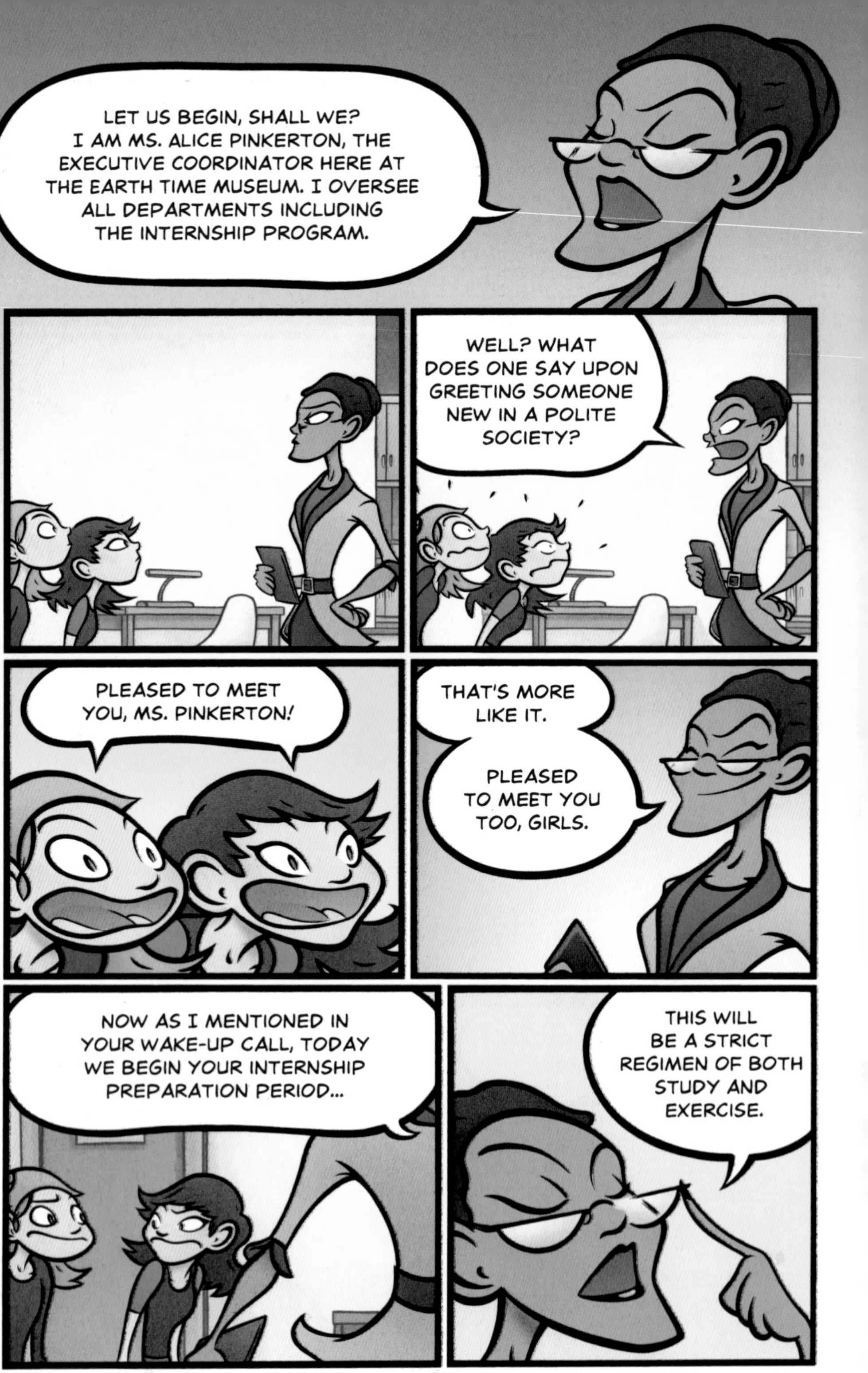
LET US BEGIN, SHALL WE? I AM MS. ALICE PINKERTON, THE EXECUTIVE COORDINATOR HERE AT THE EARTH TIME MUSEUM. I OVERSEE ALL DEPARTMENTS INCLUDING THE INTERNSHIP PROGRAM.
WELL? WHAT DOES ONE SAY UPON GREETING SOMEONE NEW IN A POLITE SOCIETY?
PLEASED TO MEET YOU, MS. PINKERTON!
THAT'S MORE LIKE IT.
PLEASED TO MEET YOU TOO, GIRLS.
NOW AS I MENTIONED IN YOUR WAKE-UP CALL, TODAY WE BEGIN YOUR INTERNSHIP PREPARATION PERIOD...
THIS WILL BE A STRICT REGIMEN OF BOTH STUDY AND EXERCISE.

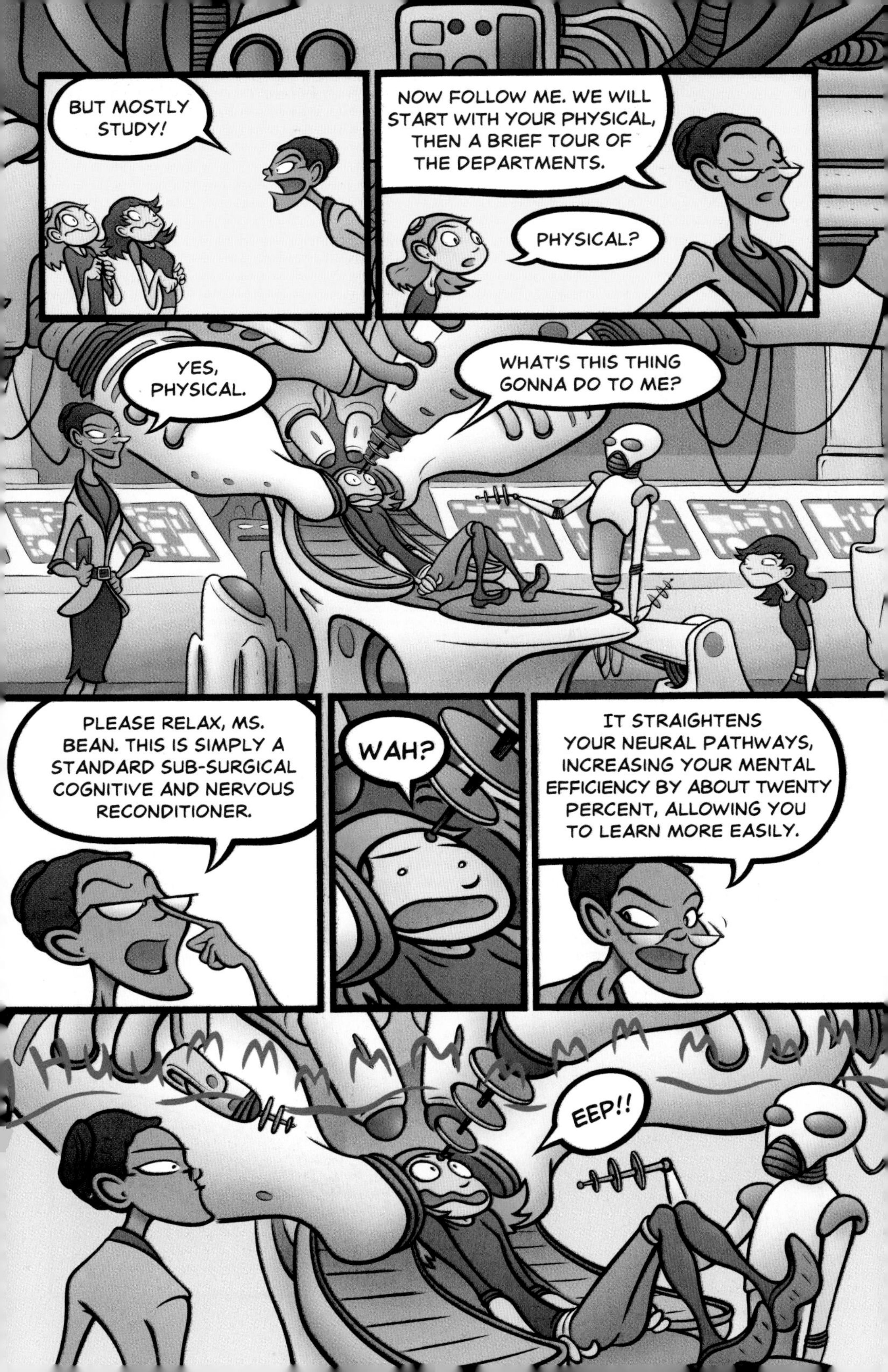
BUT MOSTLY STUDY!
NOW FOLLOW ME. WE WILL START WITH YOUR PHYSICAL, THEN A BRIEF TOUR OF THE DEPARTMENTS.
PHYSICAL?
YES, PHYSICAL.
WHAT'S THIS THING GONNA DO TO ME?
PLEASE RELAX, MS. BEAN. THIS IS SIMPLY A STANDARD SUB-SURGICAL COGNITIVE AND NERVOUS RECONDITIONER.
WAH?
IT STRAIGHTENS YOUR NEURAL PATHWAYS, INCREASING YOUR MENTAL EFFICIENCY BY ABOUT TWENTY PERCENT, ALLOWING YOU TO LEARN MORE EASILY.
HUUMMMMMMMMMMMMM
EEP!!

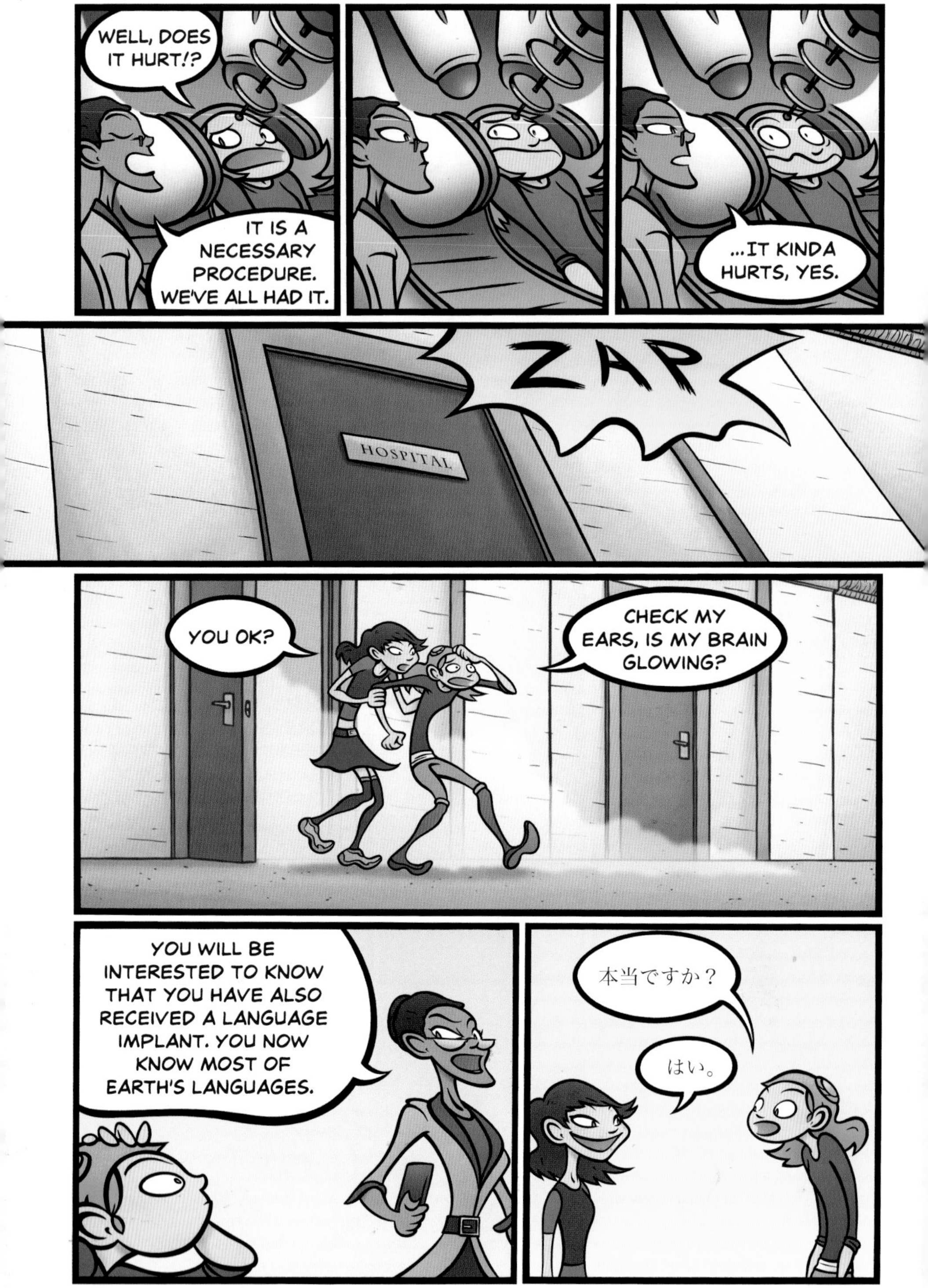
WELL, DOES IT HURT!?
IT IS A NECESSARY PROCEDURE. WE'VE ALL HAD IT.
...IT KINDA HURTS, YES.
ZAP
HOSPITAL
YOU OK?
CHECK MY EARS, IS MY BRAIN GLOWING?
YOU WILL BE INTERESTED TO KNOW THAT YOU HAVE ALSO RECEIVED A LANGUAGE IMPLANT. YOU NOW KNOW MOST OF EARTH'S LANGUAGES.
本当ですか？
はい。

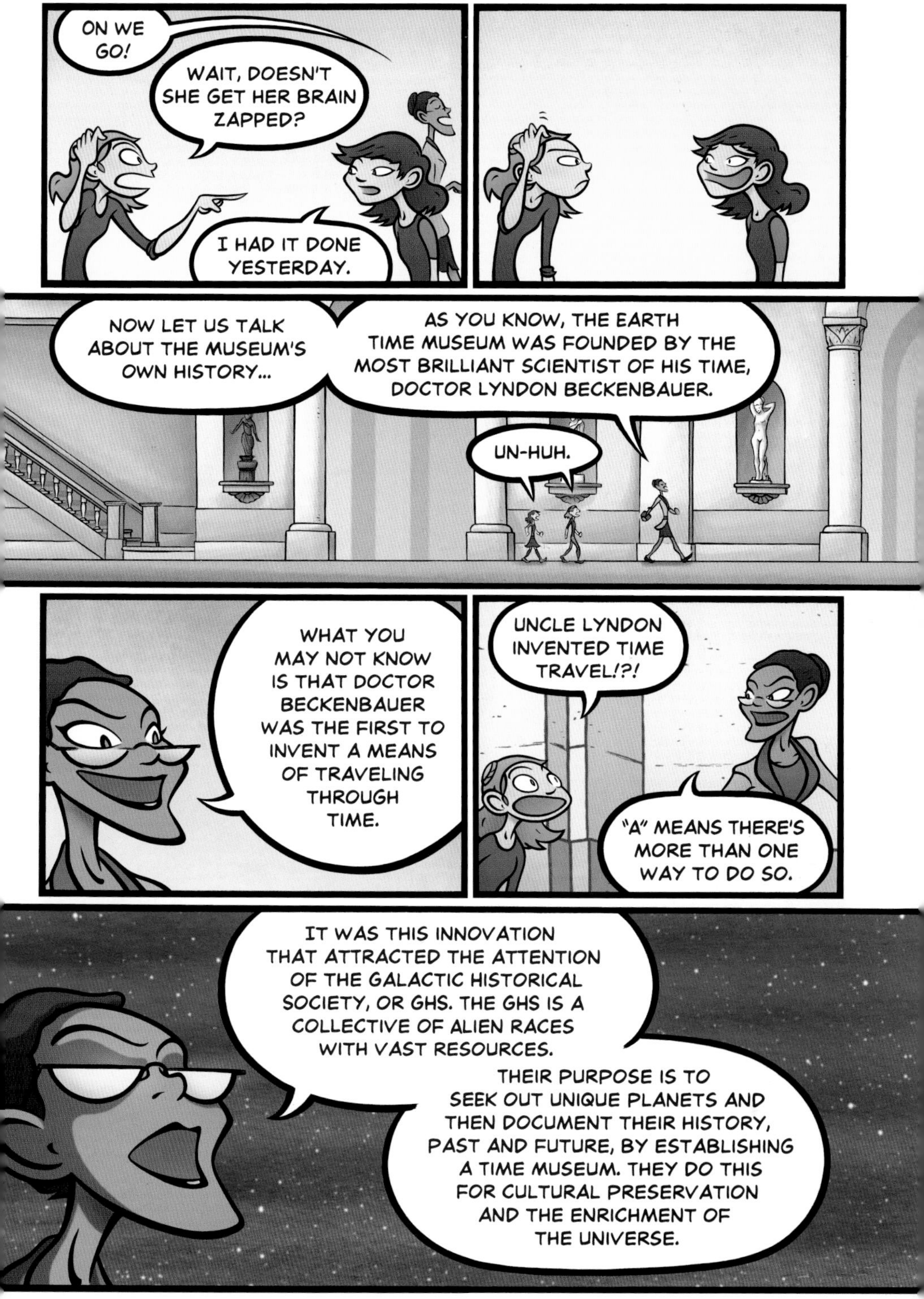
ON WE GO!
WAIT, DOESN'T SHE GET HER BRAIN ZAPPED?
I HAD IT DONE YESTERDAY.
NOW LET US TALK ABOUT THE MUSEUM'S OWN HISTORY...
AS YOU KNOW, THE EARTH TIME MUSEUM WAS FOUNDED BY THE MOST BRILLIANT SCIENTIST OF HIS TIME, DOCTOR LYNDON BECKENBAUER.
UN-HUH.
WHAT YOU MAY NOT KNOW IS THAT DOCTOR BECKENBAUER WAS THE FIRST TO INVENT A MEANS OF TRAVELING THROUGH TIME.
UNCLE LYNDON INVENTED TIME TRAVEL!?!
"A" MEANS THERE'S MORE THAN ONE WAY TO DO SO.
IT WAS THIS INNOVATION THAT ATTRACTED THE ATTENTION OF THE GALACTIC HISTORICAL SOCIETY, OR GHS. THE GHS IS A COLLECTIVE OF ALIEN RACES WITH VAST RESOURCES.
THEIR PURPOSE IS TO SEEK OUT UNIQUE PLANETS AND THEN DOCUMENT THEIR HISTORY, PAST AND FUTURE, BY ESTABLISHING A TIME MUSEUM. THEY DO THIS FOR CULTURAL PRESERVATION AND THE ENRICHMENT OF THE UNIVERSE.

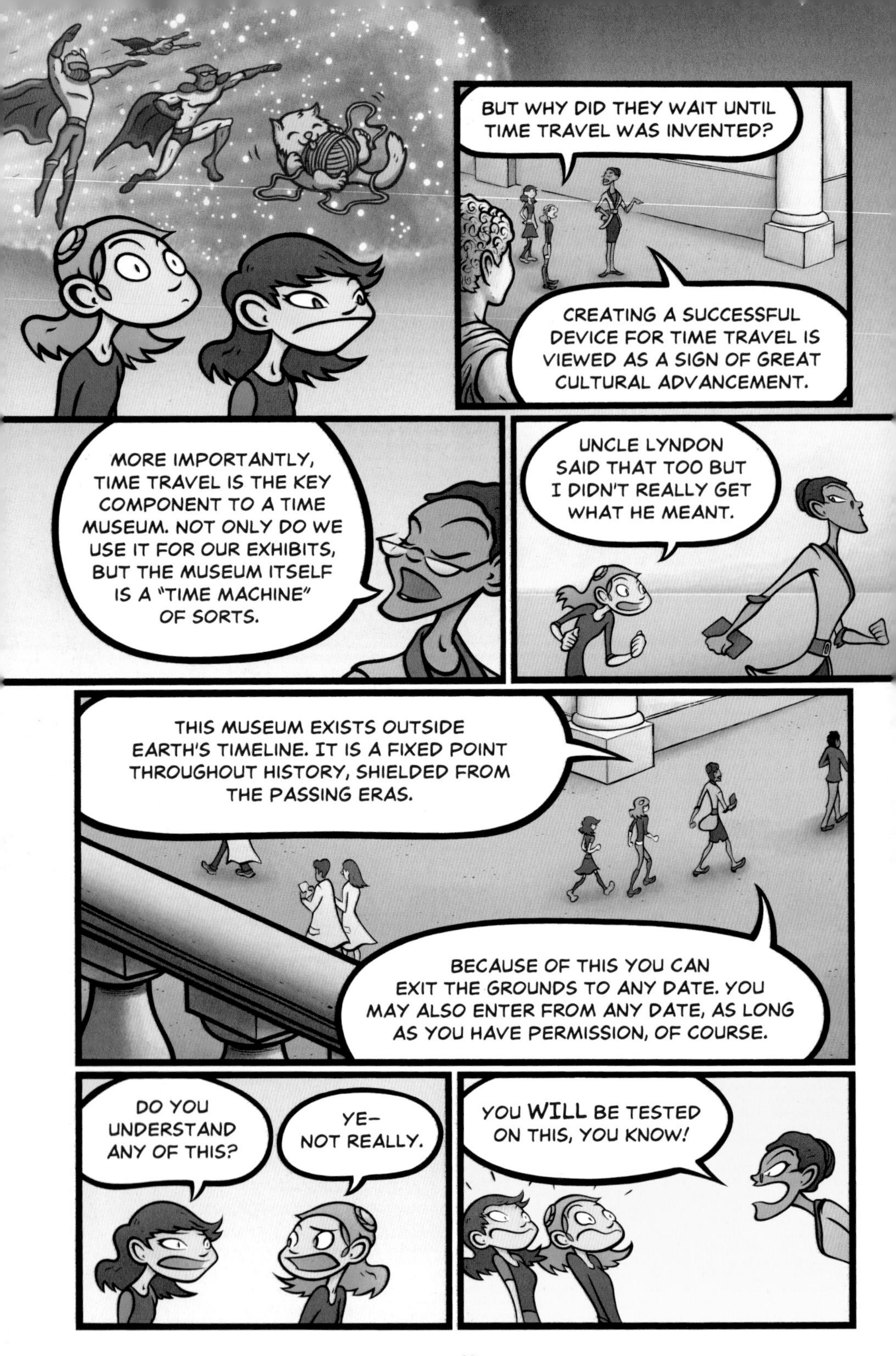
BUT WHY DID THEY WAIT UNTIL TIME TRAVEL WAS INVENTED?
CREATING A SUCCESSFUL DEVICE FOR TIME TRAVEL IS VIEWED AS A SIGN OF GREAT CULTURAL ADVANCEMENT.
MORE IMPORTANTLY, TIME TRAVEL IS THE KEY COMPONENT TO A TIME MUSEUM. NOT ONLY DO WE USE IT FOR OUR EXHIBITS, BUT THE MUSEUM ITSELF IS A "TIME MACHINE" OF SORTS.
UNCLE LYNDON SAID THAT TOO BUT I DIDN'T REALLY GET WHAT HE MEANT.
THIS MUSEUM EXISTS OUTSIDE EARTH'S TIMELINE. IT IS A FIXED POINT THROUGHOUT HISTORY, SHIELDED FROM THE PASSING ERAS.
BECAUSE OF THIS YOU CAN EXIT THE GROUNDS TO ANY DATE. YOU MAY ALSO ENTER FROM ANY DATE, AS LONG AS YOU HAVE PERMISSION, OF COURSE.
DO YOU UNDERSTAND ANY OF THIS?
YE— NOT REALLY.
YOU **WILL** BE TESTED ON THIS, YOU KNOW!

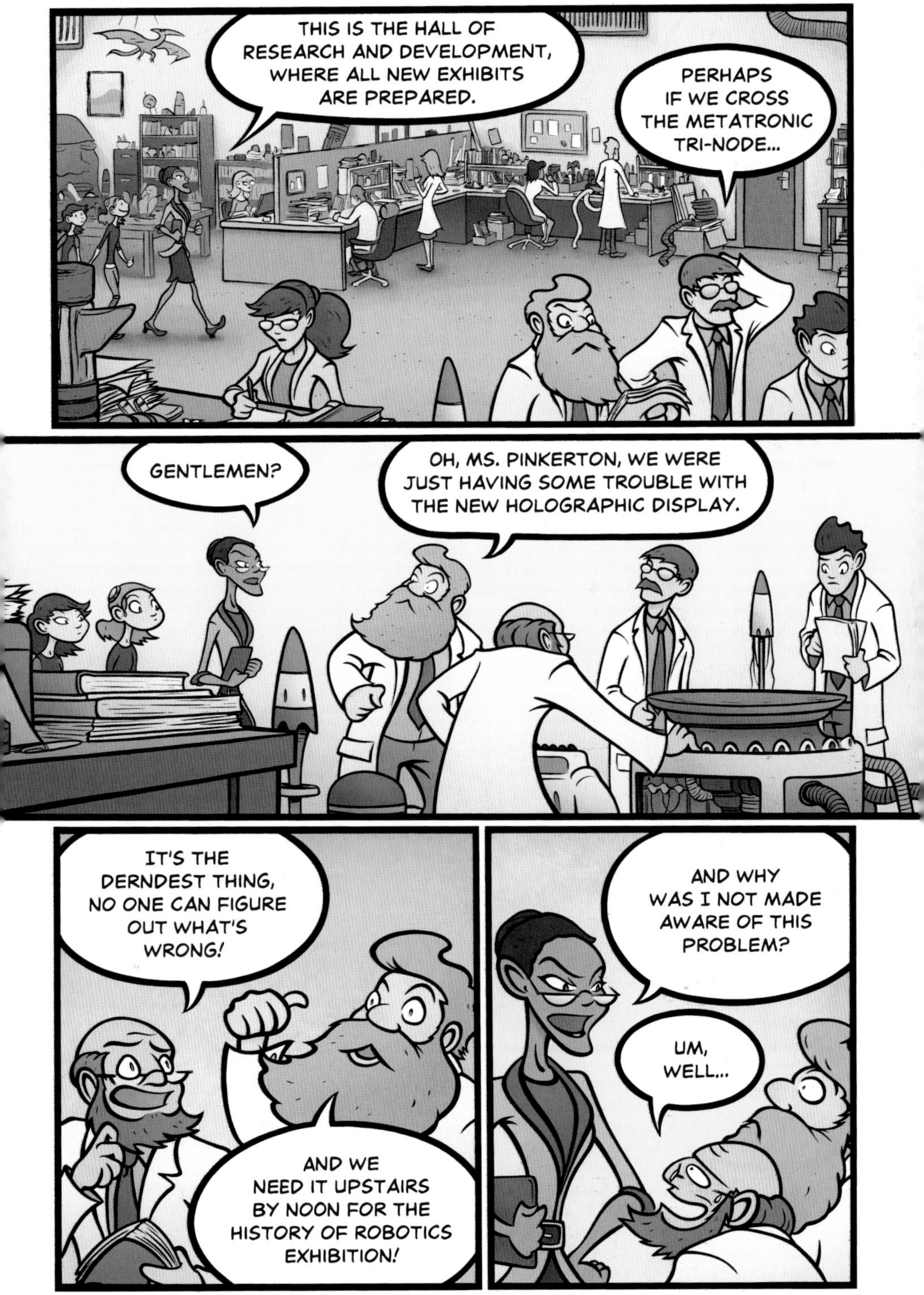
THIS IS THE HALL OF RESEARCH AND DEVELOPMENT, WHERE ALL NEW EXHIBITS ARE PREPARED.
PERHAPS IF WE CROSS THE METATRONIC TRI-NODE...
GENTLEMEN?
OH, MS. PINKERTON, WE WERE JUST HAVING SOME TROUBLE WITH THE NEW HOLOGRAPHIC DISPLAY.
IT'S THE DERNDEST THING, NO ONE CAN FIGURE OUT WHAT'S WRONG!
AND WE NEED IT UPSTAIRS BY NOON FOR THE HISTORY OF ROBOTICS EXHIBITION!
AND WHY WAS I NOT MADE AWARE OF THIS PROBLEM?
UM, WELL...

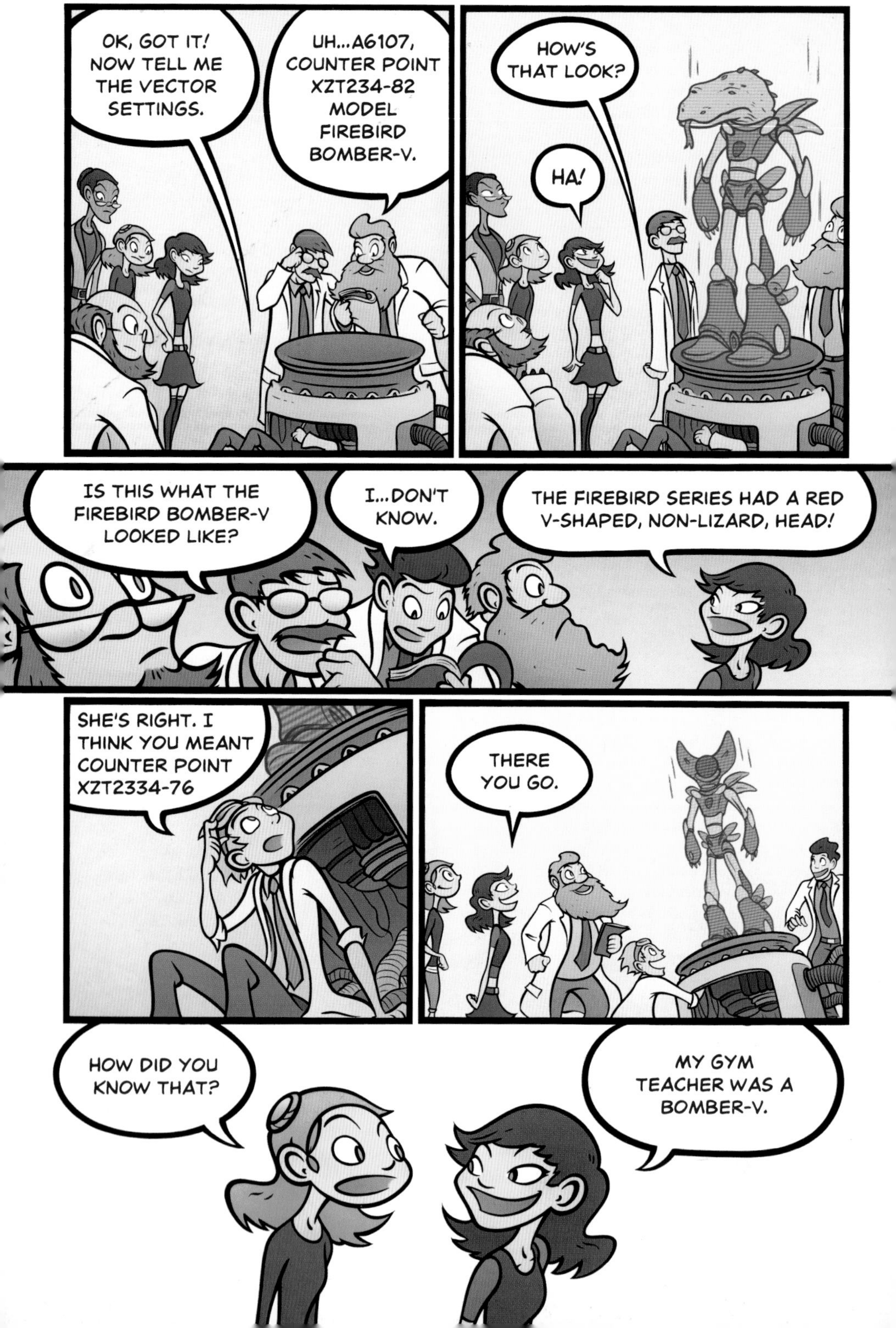
OK, GOT IT! NOW TELL ME THE VECTOR SETTINGS.
UH...A6107, COUNTER POINT XZT234-82 MODEL FIREBIRD BOMBER-V.
HOW'S THAT LOOK?
HA!
IS THIS WHAT THE FIREBIRD BOMBER-V LOOKED LIKE?
I...DON'T KNOW.
THE FIREBIRD SERIES HAD A RED V-SHAPED, NON-LIZARD, HEAD!
SHE'S RIGHT. I THINK YOU MEANT COUNTER POINT XZT2334-76
THERE YOU GO.
HOW DID YOU KNOW THAT?
MY GYM TEACHER WAS A BOMBER-V.

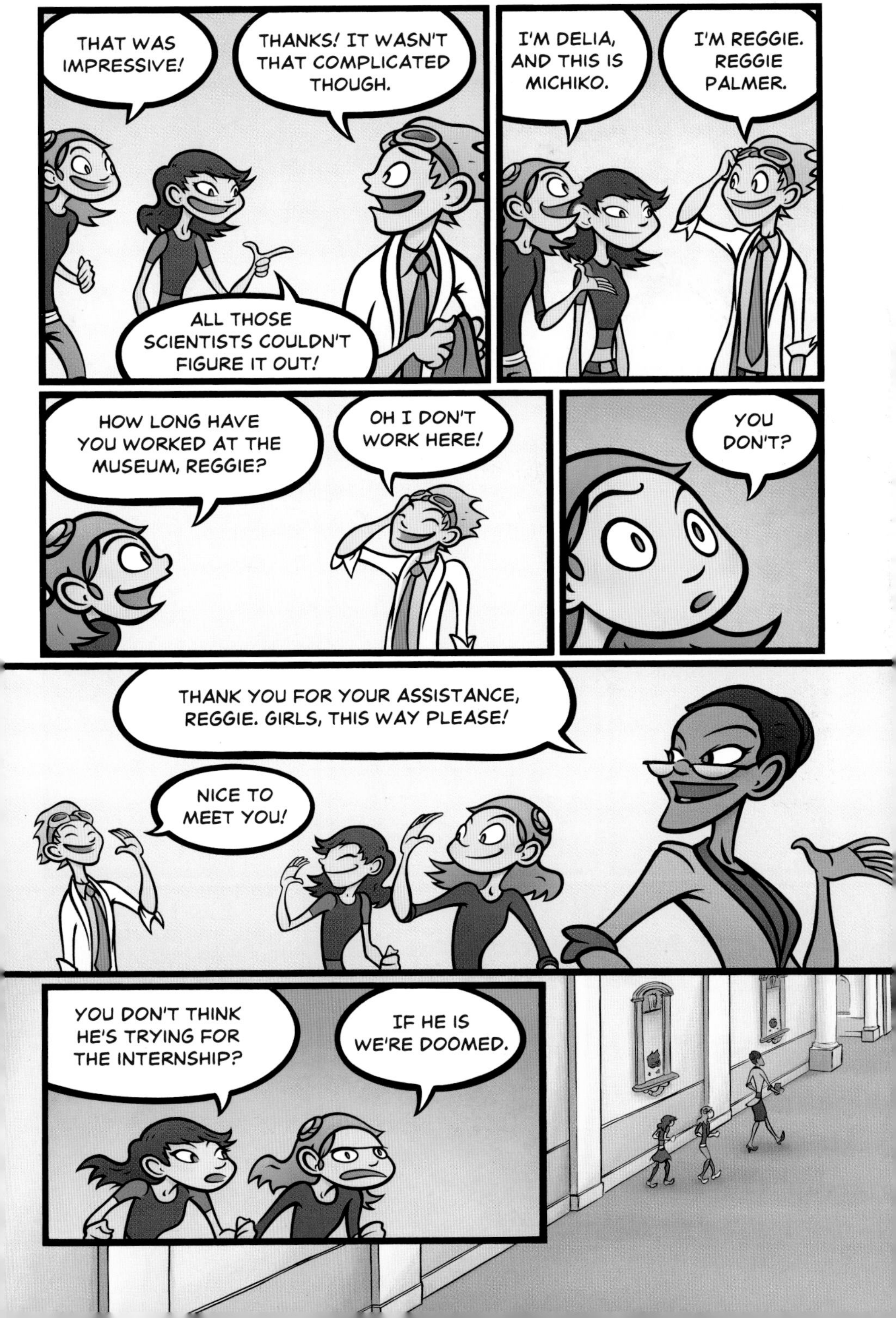

THAT WAS IMPRESSIVE!
THANKS! IT WASN'T THAT COMPLICATED THOUGH.
ALL THOSE SCIENTISTS COULDN'T FIGURE IT OUT!
I'M DELIA, AND THIS IS MICHIKO.
I'M REGGIE. REGGIE PALMER.
HOW LONG HAVE YOU WORKED AT THE MUSEUM, REGGIE?
OH I DON'T WORK HERE!
YOU DON'T?
THANK YOU FOR YOUR ASSISTANCE, REGGIE. GIRLS, THIS WAY PLEASE!
NICE TO MEET YOU!
YOU DON'T THINK HE'S TRYING FOR THE INTERNSHIP?
IF HE IS WE'RE DOOMED.

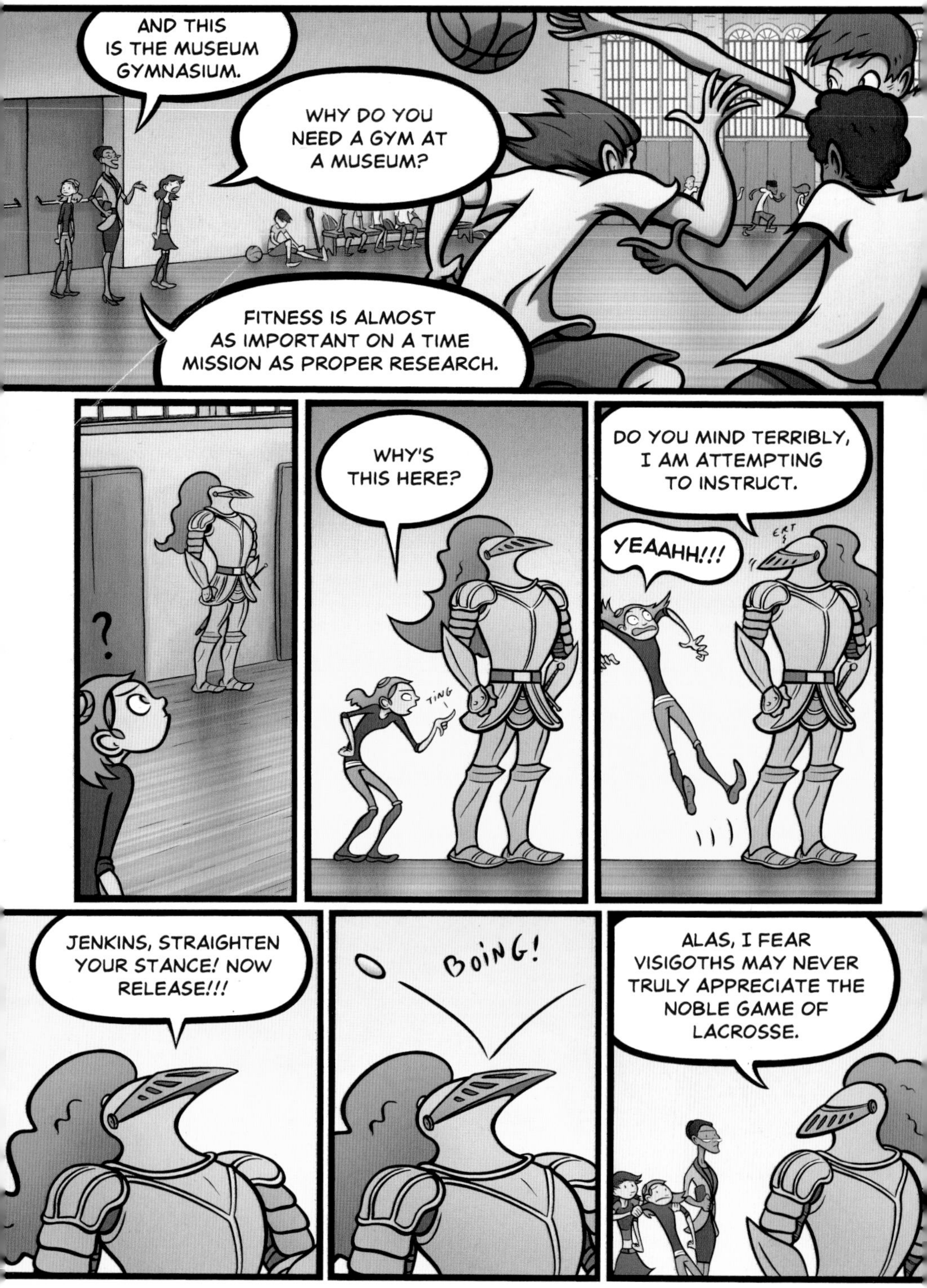
AND THIS IS THE MUSEUM GYMNASIUM.
WHY DO YOU NEED A GYM AT A MUSEUM?
FITNESS IS ALMOST AS IMPORTANT ON A TIME MISSION AS PROPER RESEARCH.
?
WHY'S THIS HERE?
TING
DO YOU MIND TERRIBLY, I AM ATTEMPTING TO INSTRUCT.
YEAAHH!!!
ERT
JENKINS, STRAIGHTEN YOUR STANCE! NOW RELEASE!!!
BOING!
ALAS, I FEAR VISIGOTHS MAY NEVER TRULY APPRECIATE THE NOBLE GAME OF LACROSSE.

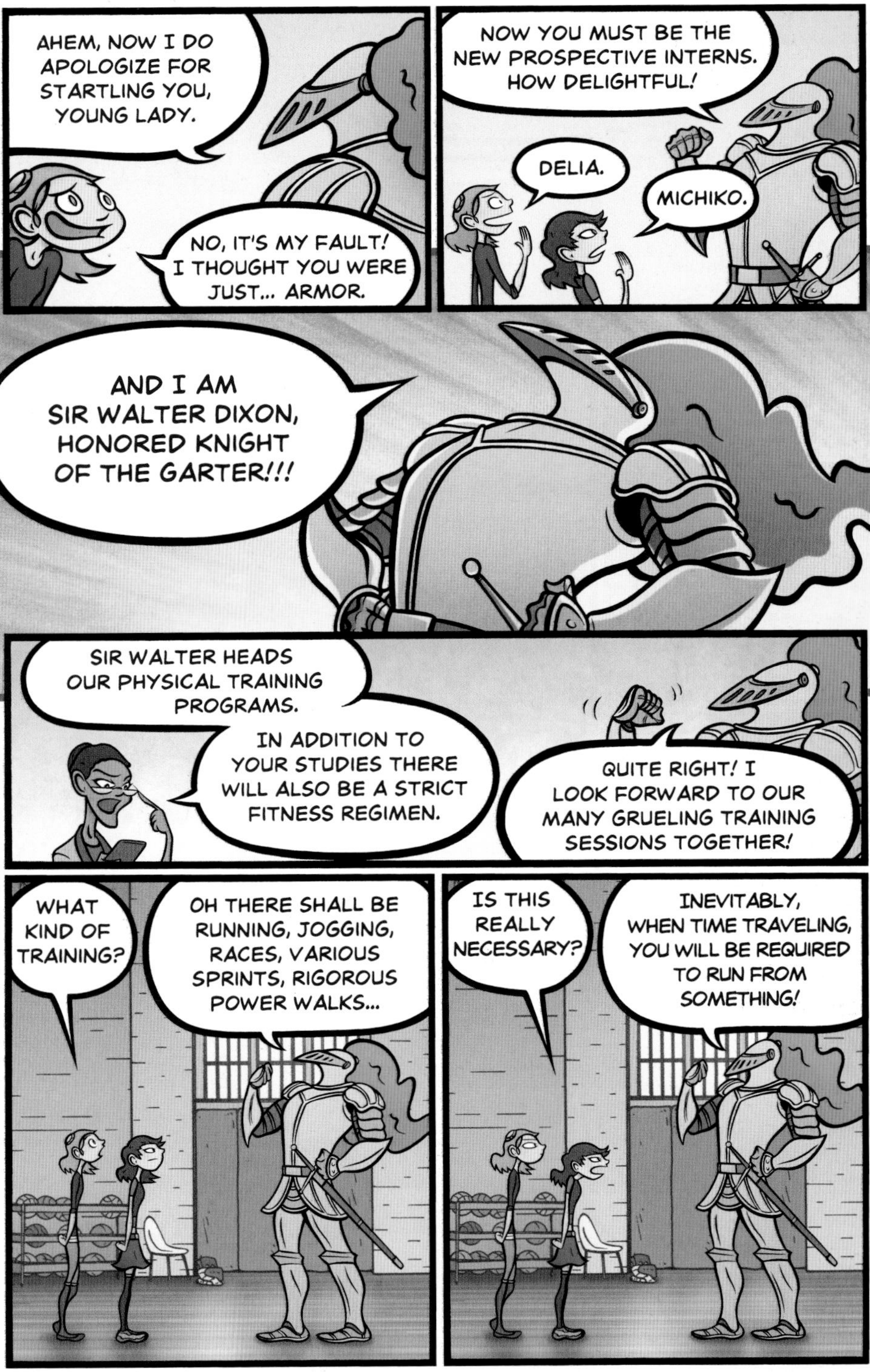
AHEM, NOW I DO APOLOGIZE FOR STARTLING YOU, YOUNG LADY.
NO, IT'S MY FAULT! I THOUGHT YOU WERE JUST... ARMOR.
NOW YOU MUST BE THE NEW PROSPECTIVE INTERNS. HOW DELIGHTFUL!
DELIA.
MICHIKO.
AND I AM SIR WALTER DIXON, HONORED KNIGHT OF THE GARTER!!!
SIR WALTER HEADS OUR PHYSICAL TRAINING PROGRAMS.
IN ADDITION TO YOUR STUDIES THERE WILL ALSO BE A STRICT FITNESS REGIMEN.
QUITE RIGHT! I LOOK FORWARD TO OUR MANY GRUELING TRAINING SESSIONS TOGETHER!
WHAT KIND OF TRAINING?
OH THERE SHALL BE RUNNING, JOGGING, RACES, VARIOUS SPRINTS, RIGOROUS POWER WALKS...
IS THIS REALLY NECESSARY?
INEVITABLY, WHEN TIME TRAVELING, YOU WILL BE REQUIRED TO RUN FROM SOMETHING!

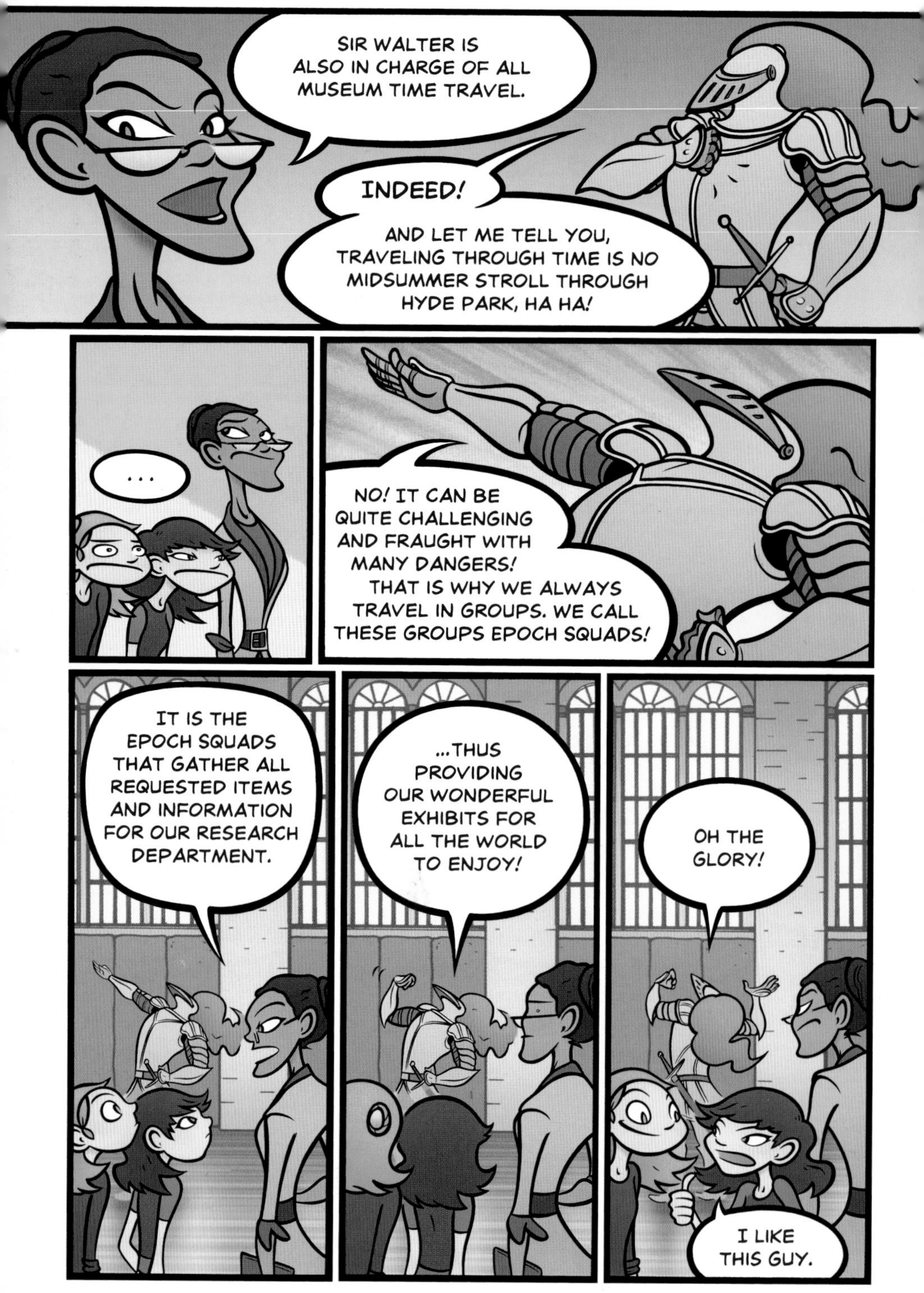
SIR WALTER IS ALSO IN CHARGE OF ALL MUSEUM TIME TRAVEL.
INDEED!
AND LET ME TELL YOU, TRAVELING THROUGH TIME IS NO MIDSUMMER STROLL THROUGH HYDE PARK, HA HA!
...
NO! IT CAN BE QUITE CHALLENGING AND FRAUGHT WITH MANY DANGERS!
THAT IS WHY WE ALWAYS TRAVEL IN GROUPS. WE CALL THESE GROUPS EPOCH SQUADS!
IT IS THE EPOCH SQUADS THAT GATHER ALL REQUESTED ITEMS AND INFORMATION FOR OUR RESEARCH DEPARTMENT.
...THUS PROVIDING OUR WONDERFUL EXHIBITS FOR ALL THE WORLD TO ENJOY!
OH THE GLORY!
I LIKE THIS GUY.

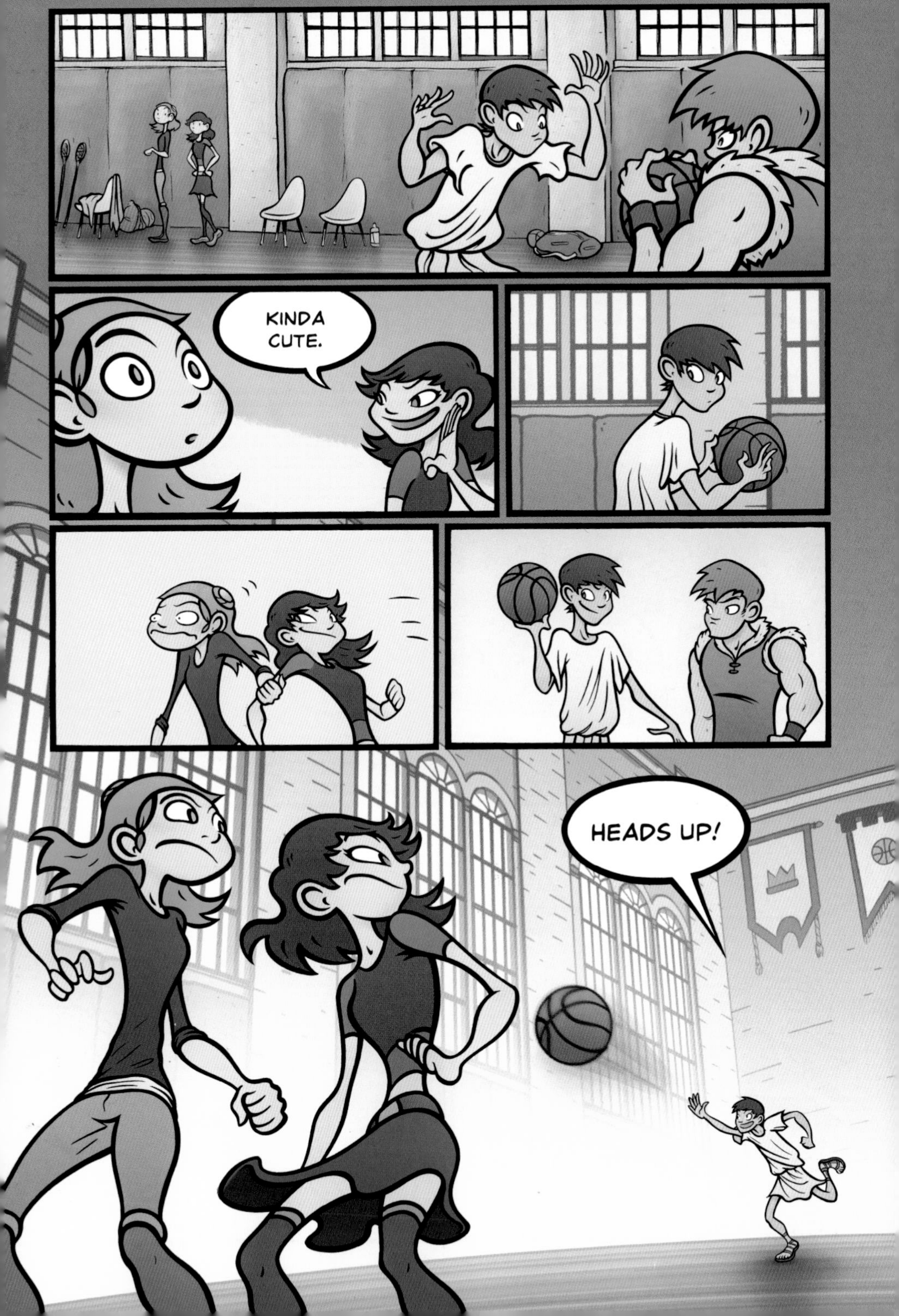
KINDA CUTE.
HEADS UP!

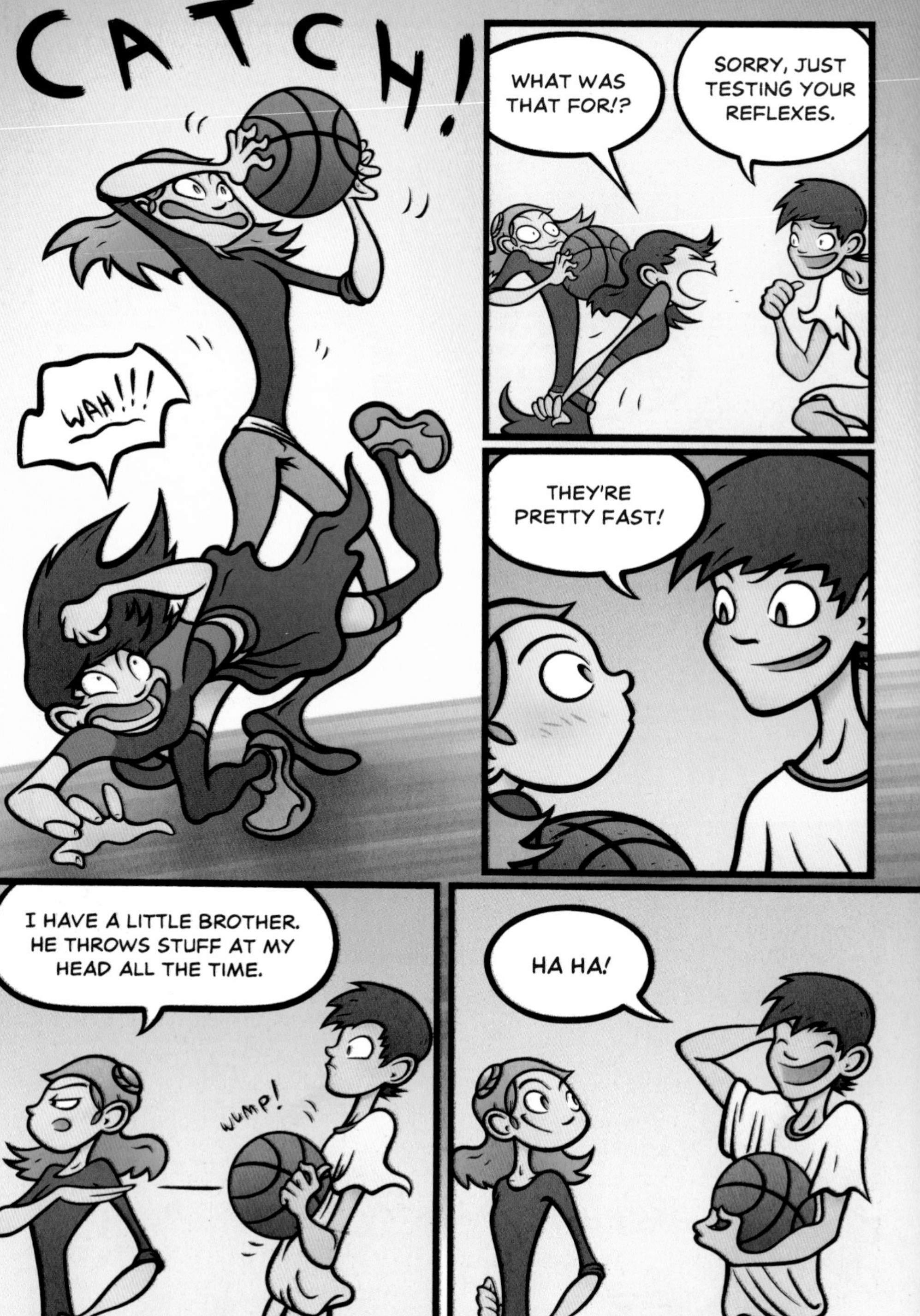
CATCH!
WAH!!!
WHAT WAS THAT FOR!?
SORRY, JUST TESTING YOUR REFLEXES.
THEY'RE PRETTY FAST!
I HAVE A LITTLE BROTHER. HE THROWS STUFF AT MY HEAD ALL THE TIME.
WUMP!
HA HA!

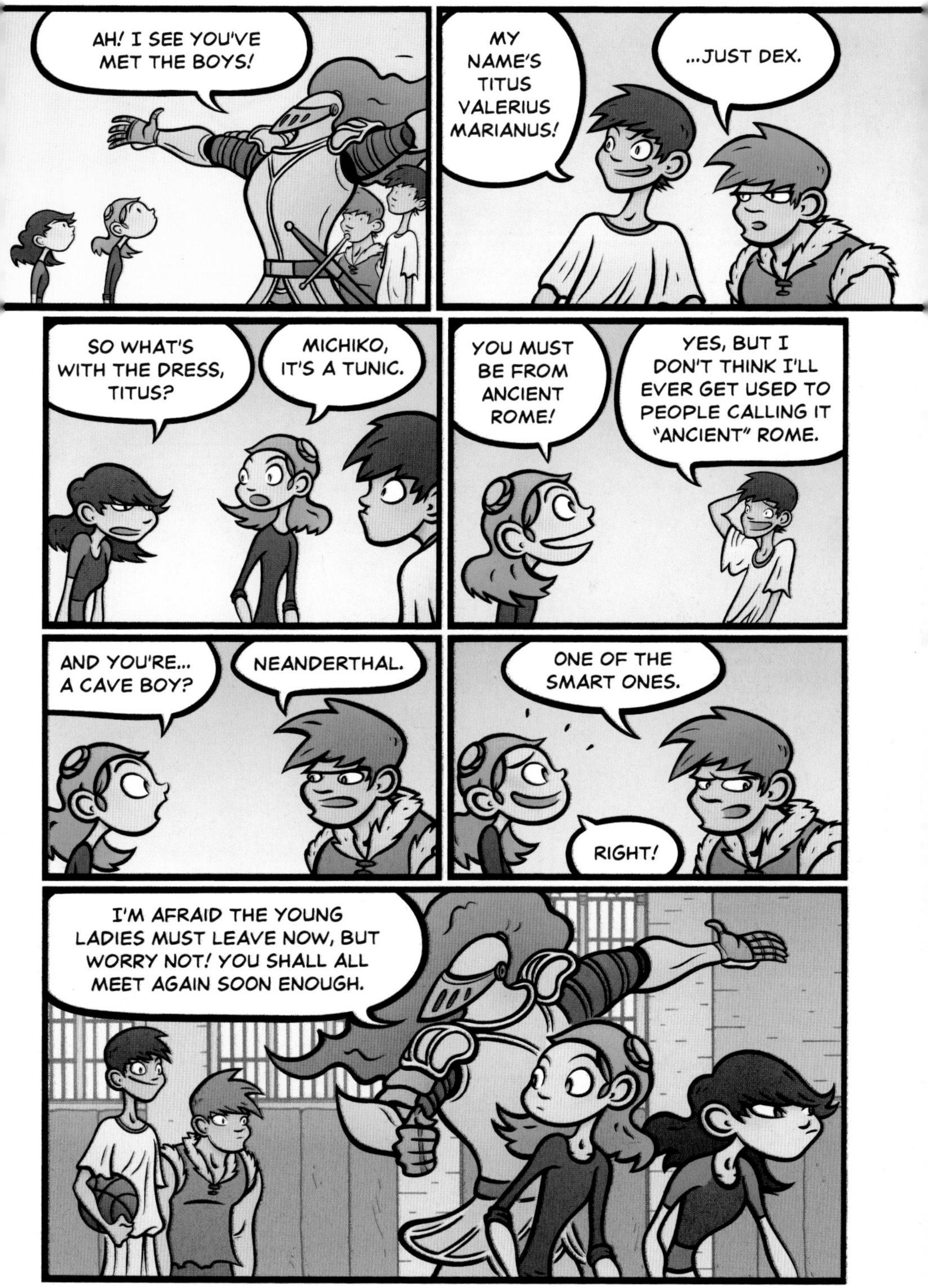
AH! I SEE YOU'VE MET THE BOYS!
MY NAME'S TITUS VALERIUS MARIANUS!
...JUST DEX.
SO WHAT'S WITH THE DRESS, TITUS?
MICHIKO, IT'S A TUNIC.
YOU MUST BE FROM ANCIENT ROME!
YES, BUT I DON'T THINK I'LL EVER GET USED TO PEOPLE CALLING IT "ANCIENT" ROME.
AND YOU'RE... A CAVE BOY?
NEANDERTHAL.
ONE OF THE SMART ONES.
RIGHT!
I'M AFRAID THE YOUNG LADIES MUST LEAVE NOW, BUT WORRY NOT! YOU SHALL ALL MEET AGAIN SOON ENOUGH.

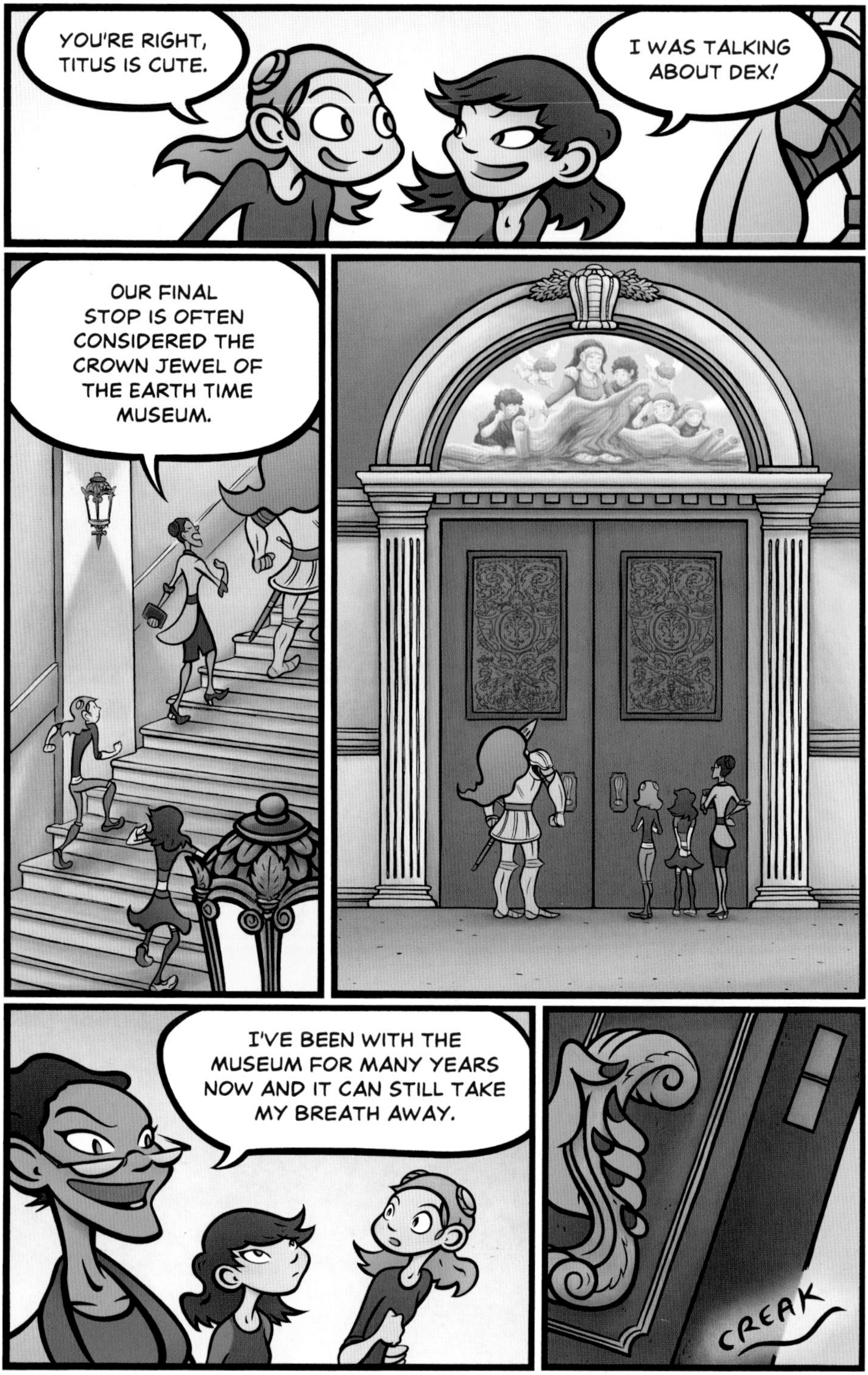
YOU'RE RIGHT, TITUS IS CUTE.
I WAS TALKING ABOUT DEX!
OUR FINAL STOP IS OFTEN CONSIDERED THE CROWN JEWEL OF THE EARTH TIME MUSEUM.
I'VE BEEN WITH THE MUSEUM FOR MANY YEARS NOW AND IT CAN STILL TAKE MY BREATH AWAY.
CREAK

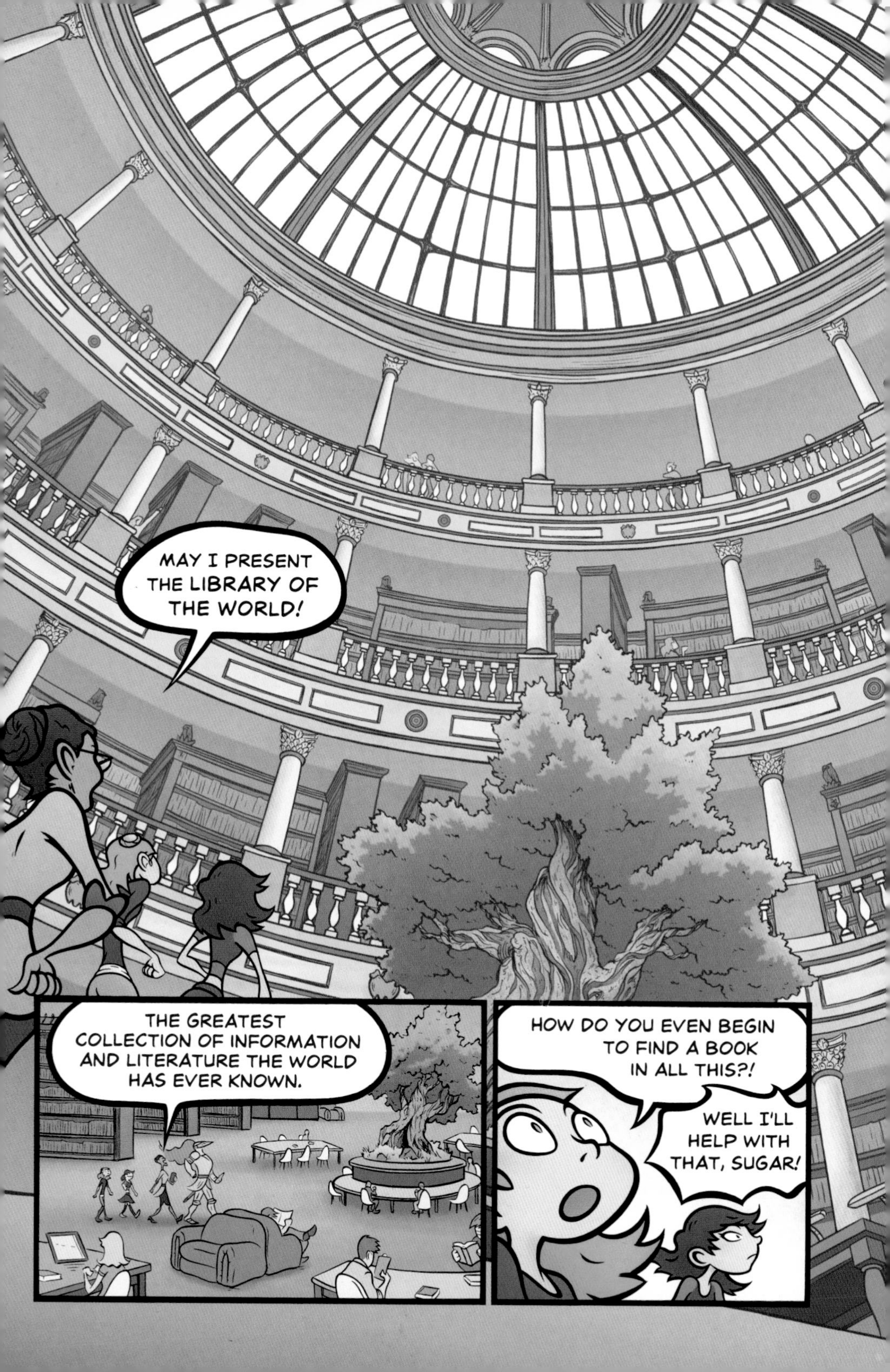
MAY I PRESENT THE LIBRARY OF THE WORLD!
THE GREATEST COLLECTION OF INFORMATION AND LITERATURE THE WORLD HAS EVER KNOWN.
HOW DO YOU EVEN BEGIN TO FIND A BOOK IN ALL THIS?!
WELL I'LL HELP WITH THAT, SUGAR!

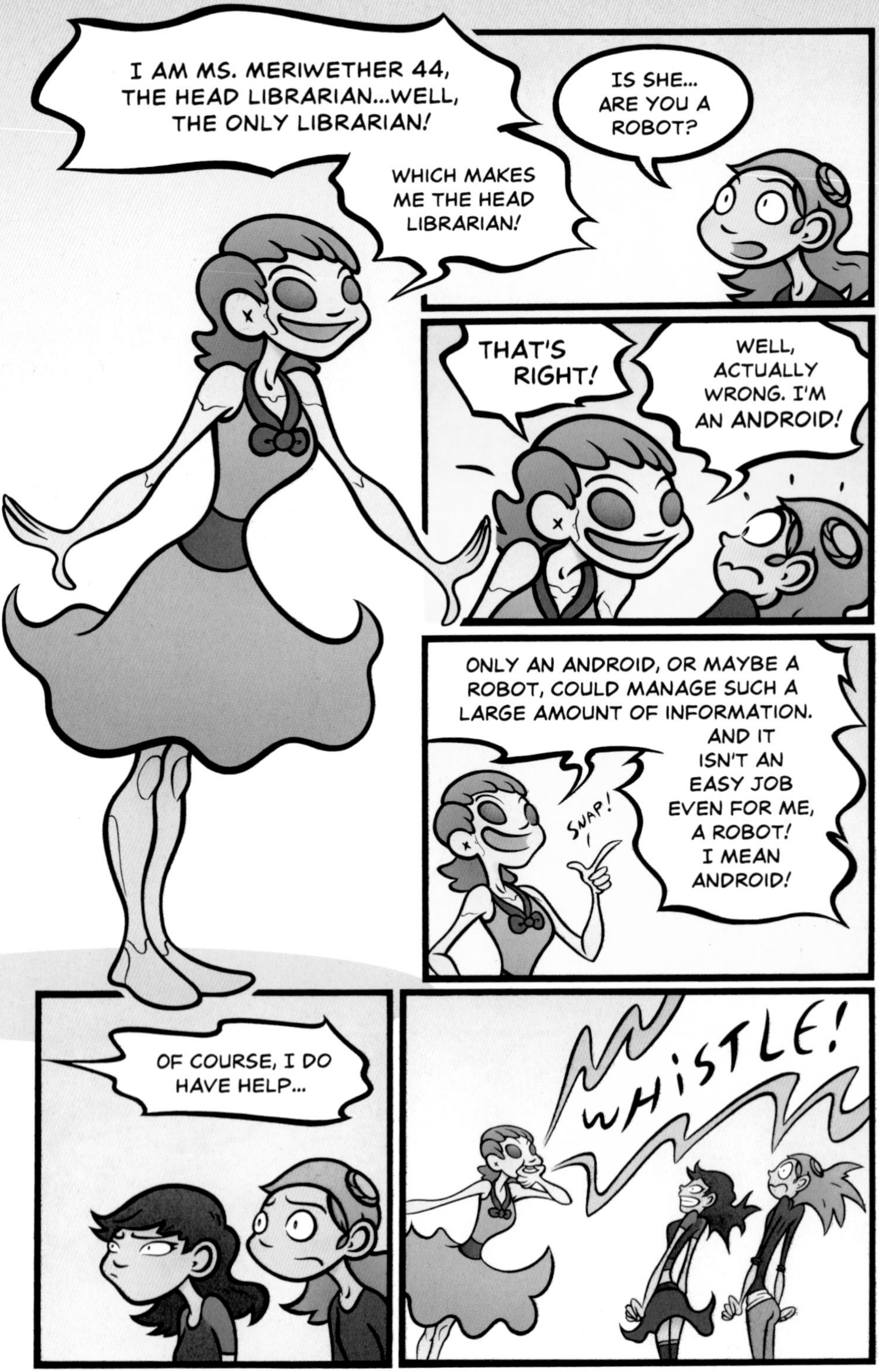
I AM MS. MERIWETHER 44, THE HEAD LIBRARIAN...WELL, THE ONLY LIBRARIAN!
WHICH MAKES ME THE HEAD LIBRARIAN!
IS SHE... ARE YOU A ROBOT?
THAT'S RIGHT!
WELL, ACTUALLY WRONG. I'M AN ANDROID!
ONLY AN ANDROID, OR MAYBE A ROBOT, COULD MANAGE SUCH A LARGE AMOUNT OF INFORMATION.
AND IT ISN'T AN EASY JOB EVEN FOR ME, A ROBOT! I MEAN ANDROID!
SNAP!
OF COURSE, I DO HAVE HELP...
WHISTLE!

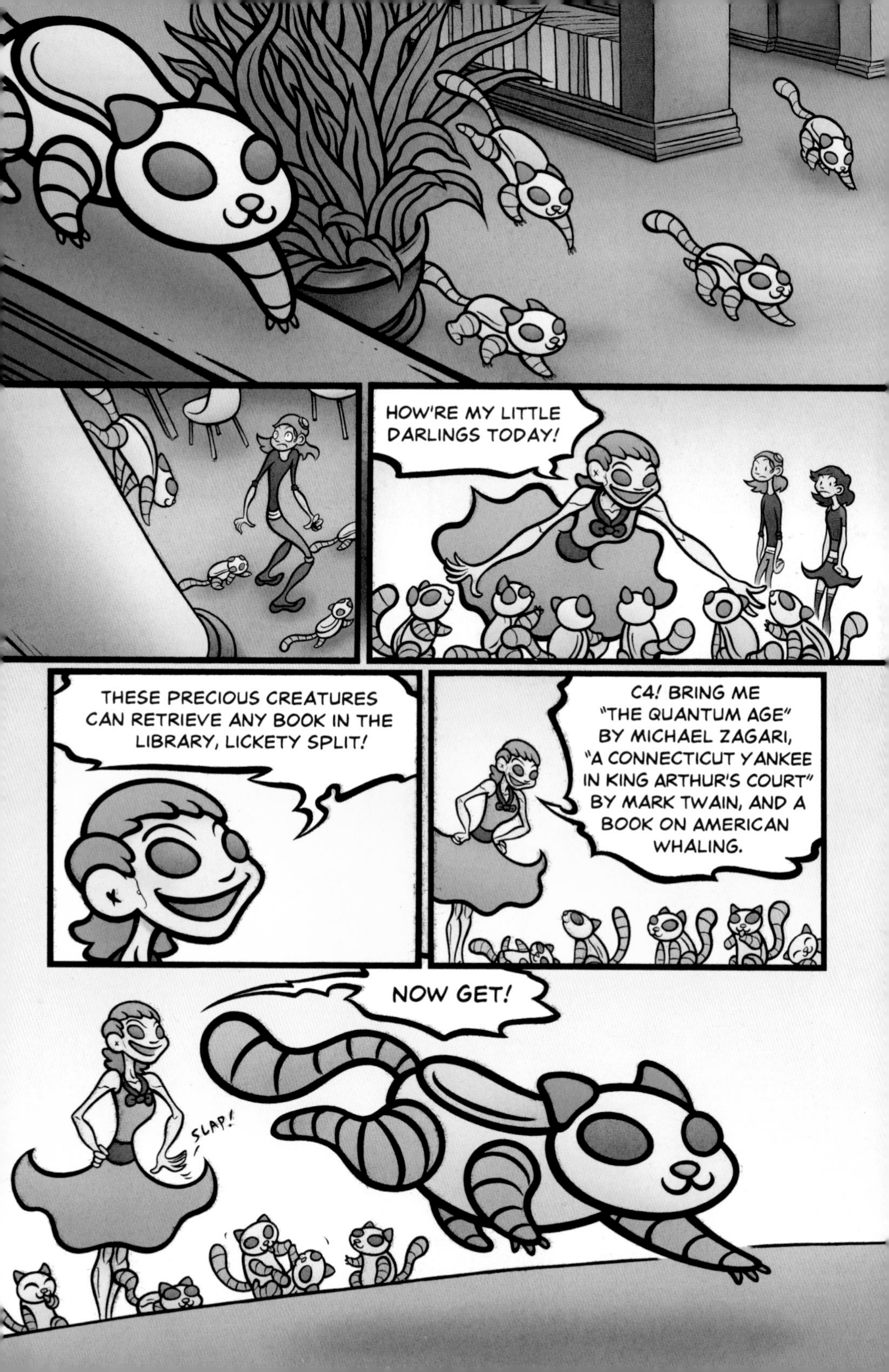
HOW'RE MY LITTLE DARLINGS TODAY!
THESE PRECIOUS CREATURES CAN RETRIEVE ANY BOOK IN THE LIBRARY, LICKETY SPLIT!
C4! BRING ME "THE QUANTUM AGE" BY MICHAEL ZAGARI, "A CONNECTICUT YANKEE IN KING ARTHUR'S COURT" BY MARK TWAIN, AND A BOOK ON AMERICAN WHALING.
NOW GET!
SLAP!

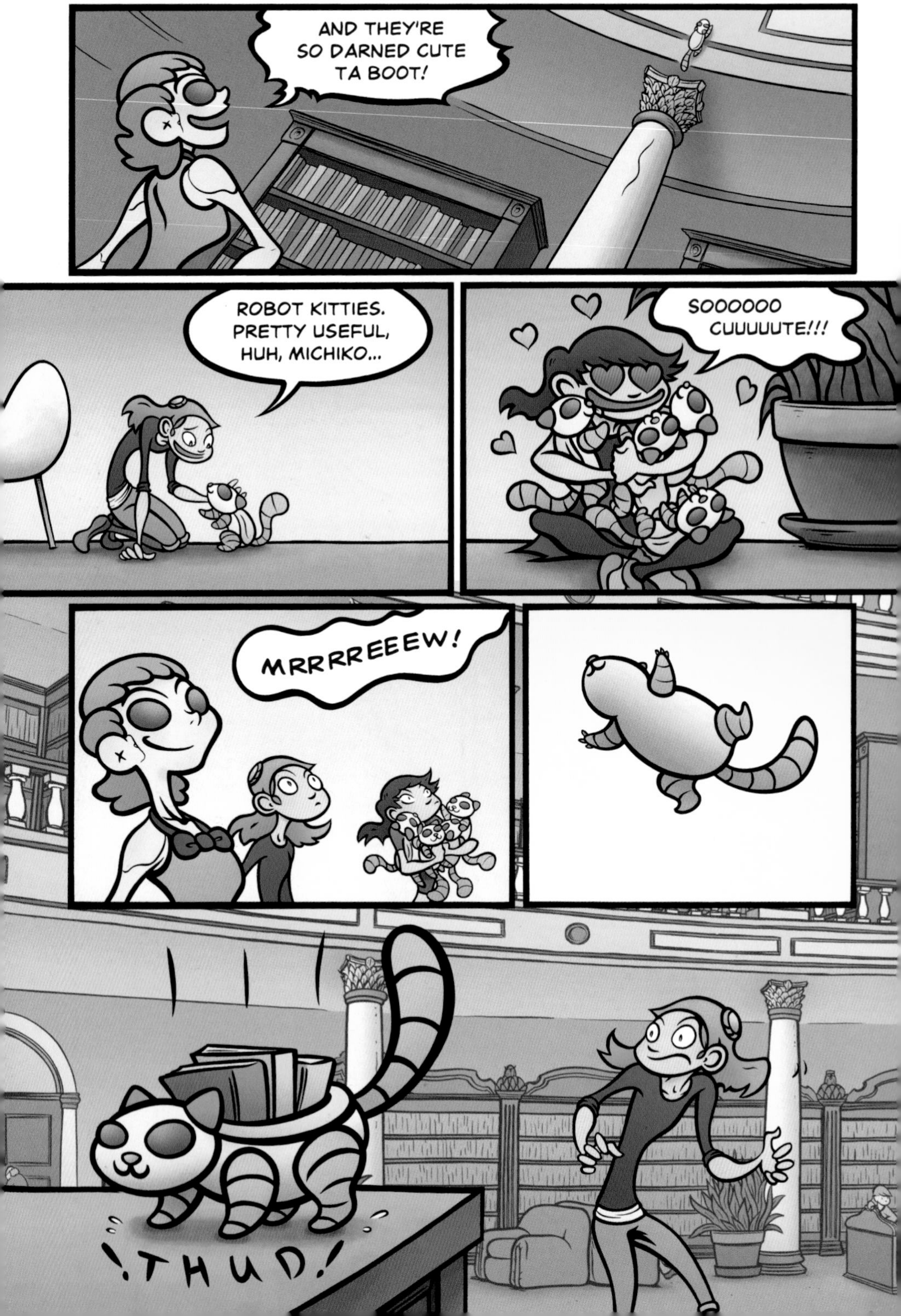
AND THEY'RE SO DARNED CUTE TA BOOT!
ROBOT KITTIES. PRETTY USEFUL, HUH, MICHIKO...
SOOOOOO CUUUUUTE!!!
MRRRREEEW!
!THUD!

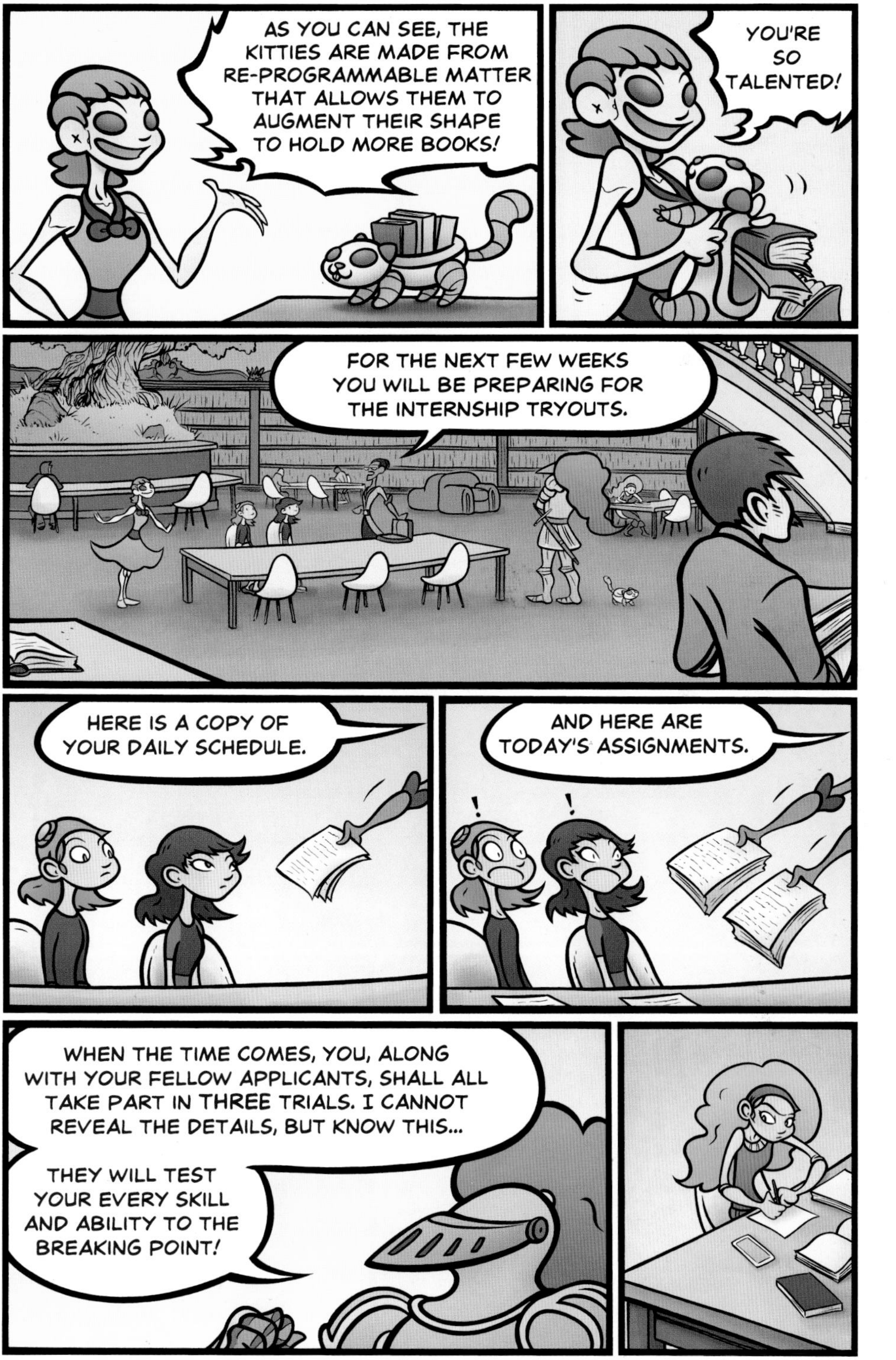

AS YOU CAN SEE, THE KITTIES ARE MADE FROM RE-PROGRAMMABLE MATTER THAT ALLOWS THEM TO AUGMENT THEIR SHAPE TO HOLD MORE BOOKS!
YOU'RE SO TALENTED!
FOR THE NEXT FEW WEEKS YOU WILL BE PREPARING FOR THE INTERNSHIP TRYOUTS.
HERE IS A COPY OF YOUR DAILY SCHEDULE.
AND HERE ARE TODAY'S ASSIGNMENTS.
!
!
WHEN THE TIME COMES, YOU, ALONG WITH YOUR FELLOW APPLICANTS, SHALL ALL TAKE PART IN THREE TRIALS. I CANNOT REVEAL THE DETAILS, BUT KNOW THIS...
THEY WILL TEST YOUR EVERY SKILL AND ABILITY TO THE BREAKING POINT!

SO STUDY HARD! I EXPECT NOTHING BUT YOUR ABSOLUTE BEST!

NOW GOOD DAY, LADIES, I WILL LEAVE YOU TO YOUR STUDIES.

AND I'LL SEE YOU AT TWO O'CLOCK FOR SPRINTS!

DON'T WORRY, GIRLS, ME AND THE CATS WILL HELP YOU OUT AS BEST WE CAN.

NOW GET TA STUDYIN'!!!

CLAP!

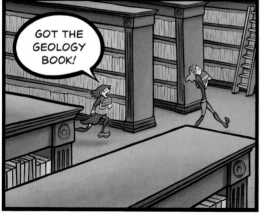

GOT THE GEOLOGY BOOK!

THANK YOU KITTY, JUST WHAT WE NEEDED!

MROW!

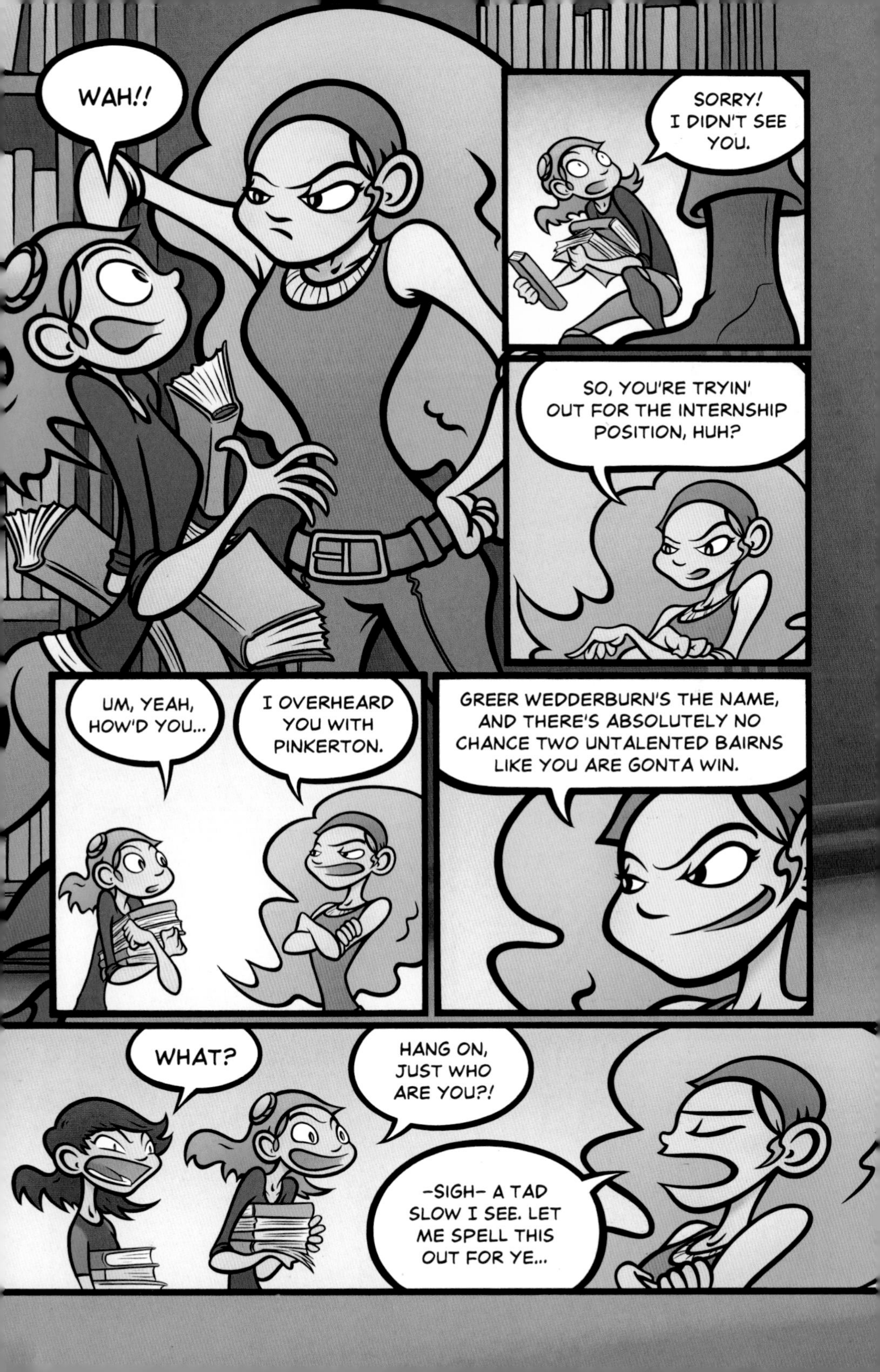
WAH!!
SORRY! I DIDN'T SEE YOU.
SO, YOU'RE TRYIN' OUT FOR THE INTERNSHIP POSITION, HUH?
UM, YEAH, HOW'D YOU...
I OVERHEARD YOU WITH PINKERTON.
GREER WEDDERBURN'S THE NAME, AND THERE'S ABSOLUTELY NO CHANCE TWO UNTALENTED BAIRNS LIKE YOU ARE GONTA WIN.
WHAT?
HANG ON, JUST WHO ARE YOU?!
–SIGH– A TAD SLOW I SEE. LET ME SPELL THIS OUT FOR YE...

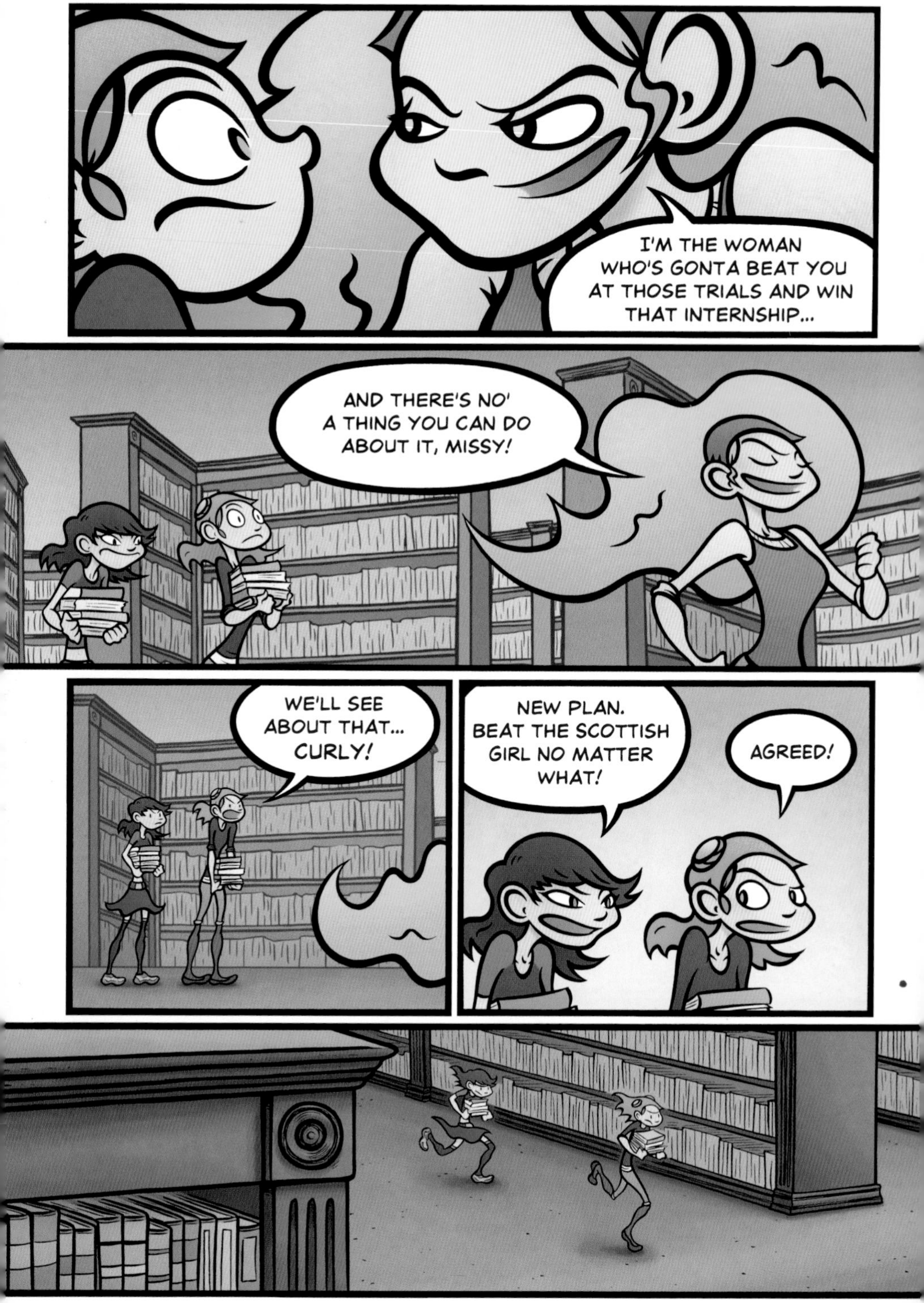
I'M THE WOMAN WHO'S GONTA BEAT YOU AT THOSE TRIALS AND WIN THAT INTERNSHIP...
AND THERE'S NO' A THING YOU CAN DO ABOUT IT, MISSY!
WE'LL SEE ABOUT THAT... CURLY!
NEW PLAN. BEAT THE SCOTTISH GIRL NO MATTER WHAT!
AGREED!

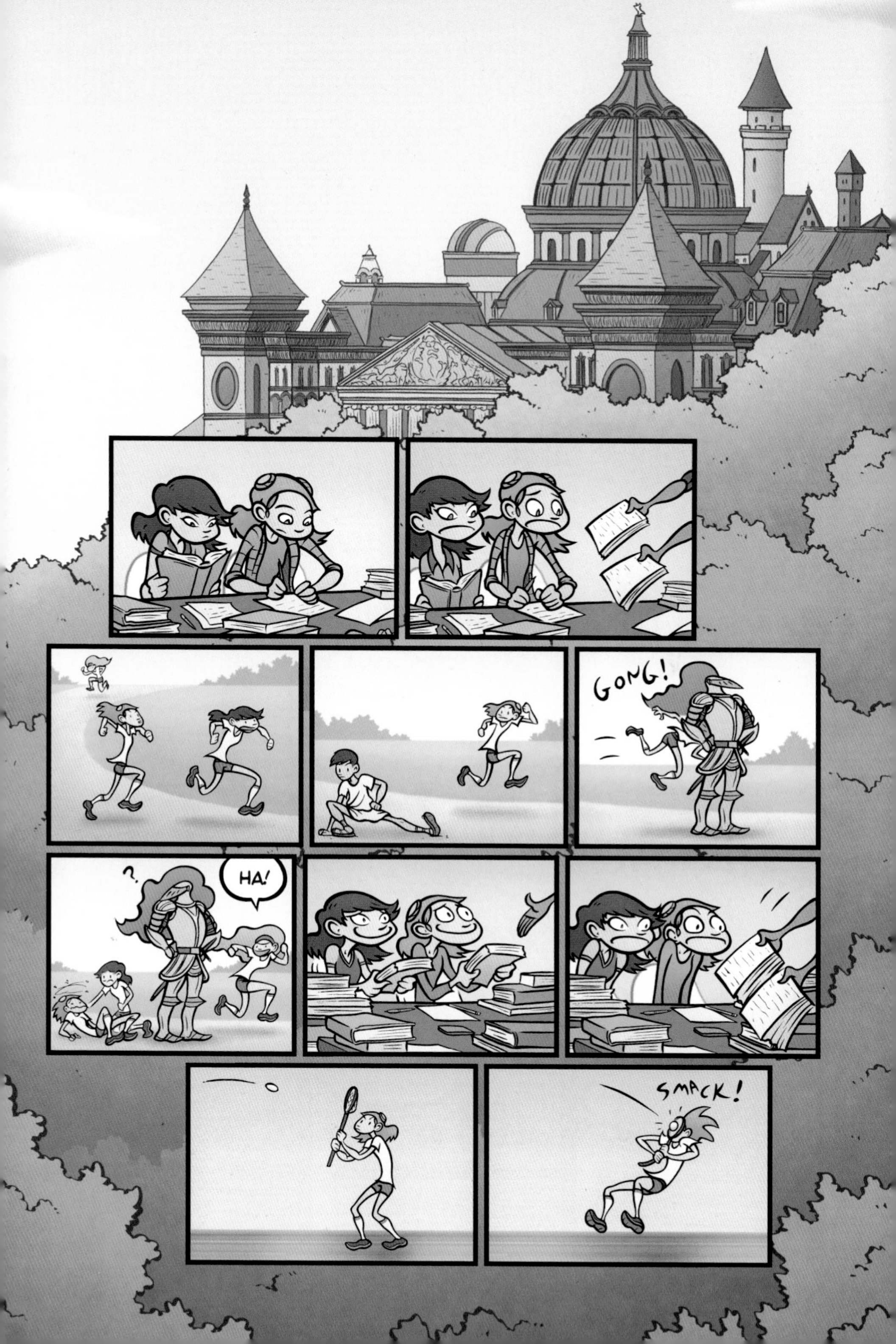

GONG!
?
HA!
SMACK!

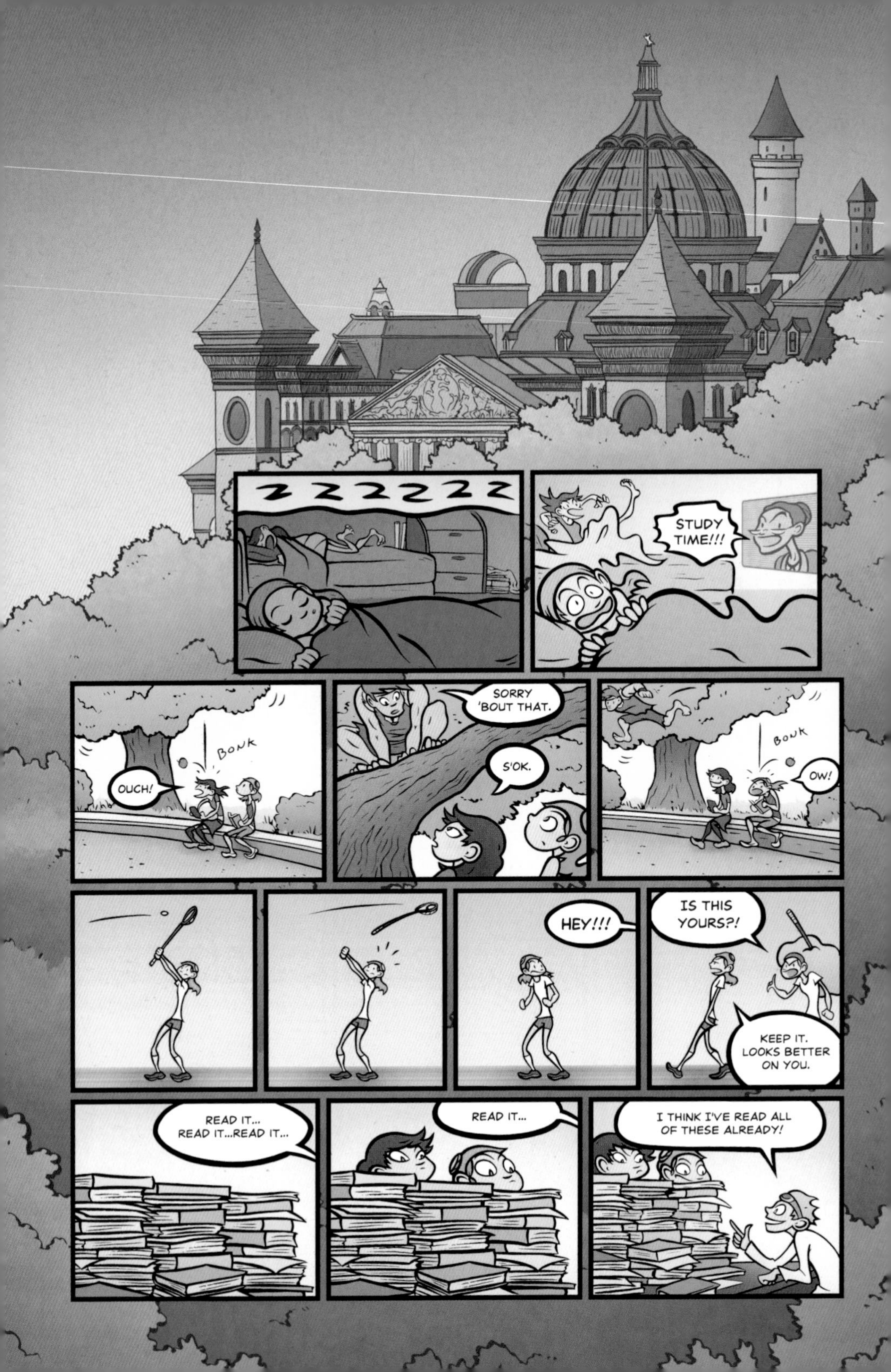
ZZZZZZ
STUDY TIME!!!
BONK
OUCH!
SORRY 'BOUT THAT.
S'OK.
BONK
OW!
HEY!!!
IS THIS YOURS?!
KEEP IT. LOOKS BETTER ON YOU.
READ IT... READ IT...READ IT...
READ IT...
I THINK I'VE READ ALL OF THESE ALREADY!

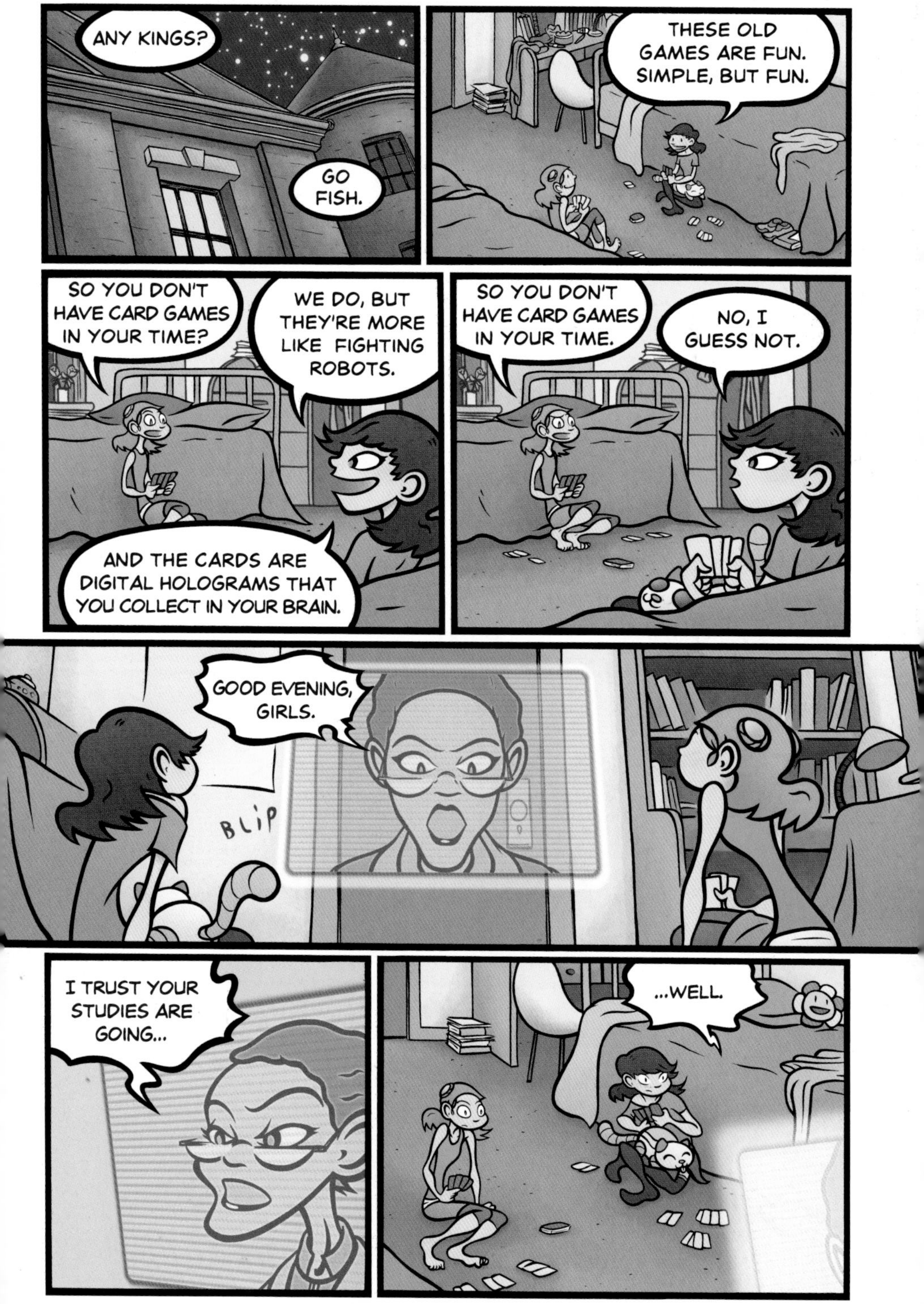
ANY KINGS?
GO FISH.
THESE OLD GAMES ARE FUN. SIMPLE, BUT FUN.
SO YOU DON'T HAVE CARD GAMES IN YOUR TIME?
WE DO, BUT THEY'RE MORE LIKE FIGHTING ROBOTS.
AND THE CARDS ARE DIGITAL HOLOGRAMS THAT YOU COLLECT IN YOUR BRAIN.
SO YOU DON'T HAVE CARD GAMES IN YOUR TIME.
NO, I GUESS NOT.
GOOD EVENING, GIRLS.
BLIP
I TRUST YOUR STUDIES ARE GOING...
...WELL.

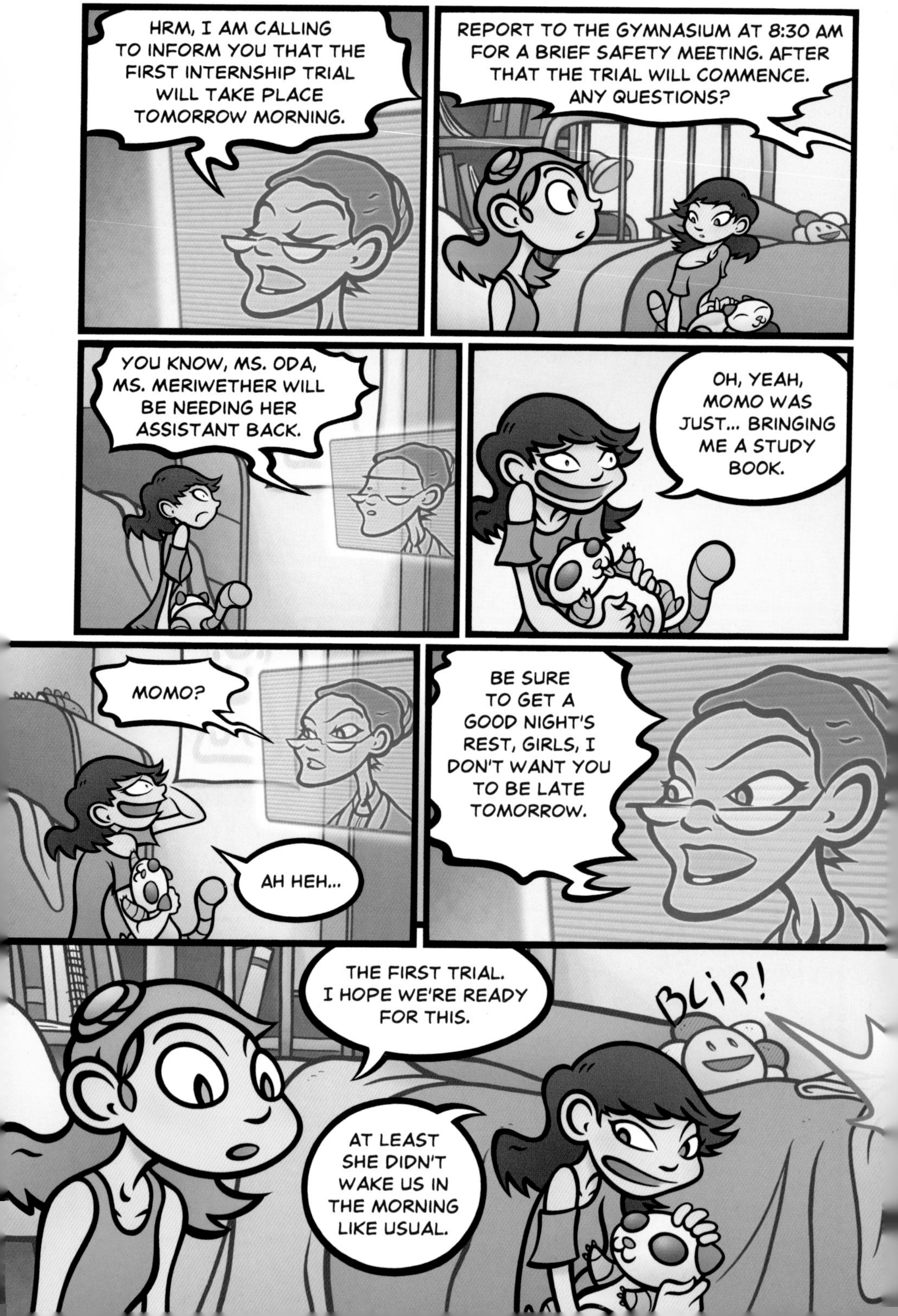
HRM, I AM CALLING TO INFORM YOU THAT THE FIRST INTERNSHIP TRIAL WILL TAKE PLACE TOMORROW MORNING.
REPORT TO THE GYMNASIUM AT 8:30 AM FOR A BRIEF SAFETY MEETING. AFTER THAT THE TRIAL WILL COMMENCE. ANY QUESTIONS?
YOU KNOW, MS. ODA, MS. MERIWETHER WILL BE NEEDING HER ASSISTANT BACK.
OH, YEAH, MOMO WAS JUST... BRINGING ME A STUDY BOOK.
MOMO?
AH HEH...
BE SURE TO GET A GOOD NIGHT'S REST, GIRLS, I DON'T WANT YOU TO BE LATE TOMORROW.
THE FIRST TRIAL. I HOPE WE'RE READY FOR THIS.
BLIP!
AT LEAST SHE DIDN'T WAKE US IN THE MORNING LIKE USUAL.

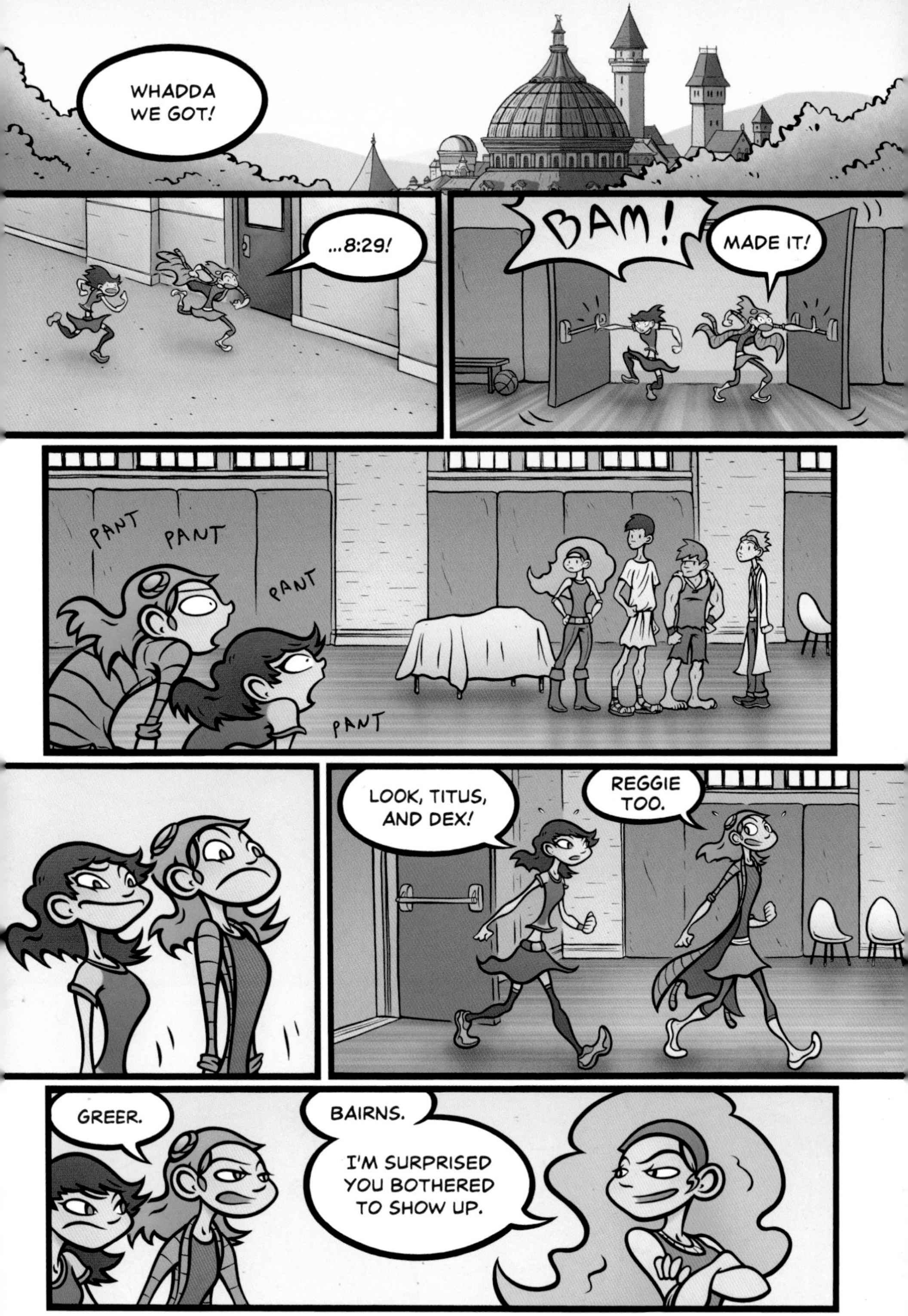
WHADDA WE GOT!
...8:29!
BAM!
MADE IT!
PANT
PANT
PANT
PANT
LOOK, TITUS, AND DEX!
REGGIE TOO.
GREER.
BAIRNS.
I'M SURPRISED YOU BOTHERED TO SHOW UP.

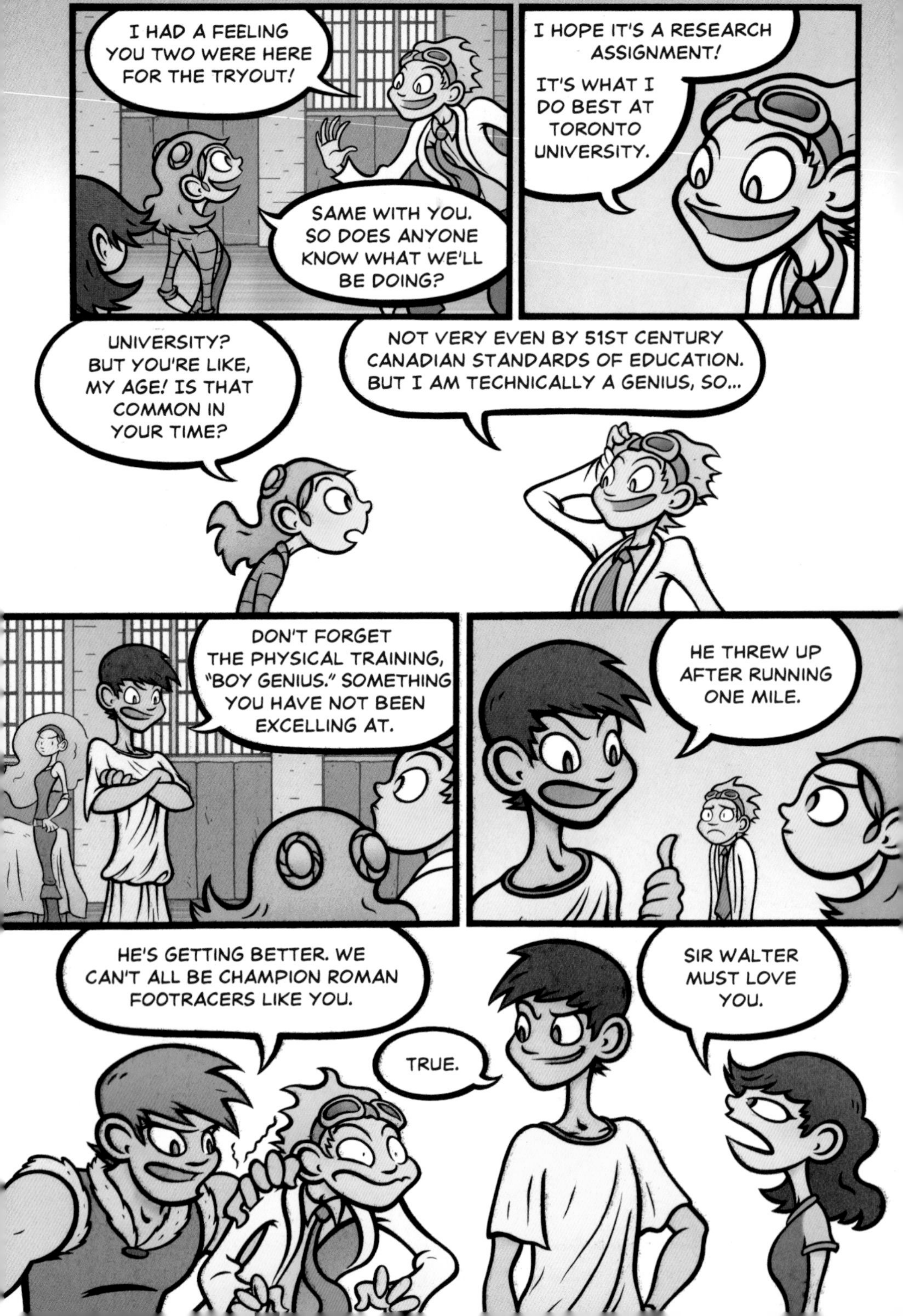
I HAD A FEELING YOU TWO WERE HERE FOR THE TRYOUT!
SAME WITH YOU. SO DOES ANYONE KNOW WHAT WE'LL BE DOING?
I HOPE IT'S A RESEARCH ASSIGNMENT!
IT'S WHAT I DO BEST AT TORONTO UNIVERSITY.
UNIVERSITY? BUT YOU'RE LIKE, MY AGE! IS THAT COMMON IN YOUR TIME?
NOT VERY EVEN BY 51ST CENTURY CANADIAN STANDARDS OF EDUCATION. BUT I AM TECHNICALLY A GENIUS, SO...
DON'T FORGET THE PHYSICAL TRAINING, "BOY GENIUS." SOMETHING YOU HAVE NOT BEEN EXCELLING AT.
HE THREW UP AFTER RUNNING ONE MILE.
HE'S GETTING BETTER. WE CAN'T ALL BE CHAMPION ROMAN FOOTRACERS LIKE YOU.
TRUE.
SIR WALTER MUST LOVE YOU.

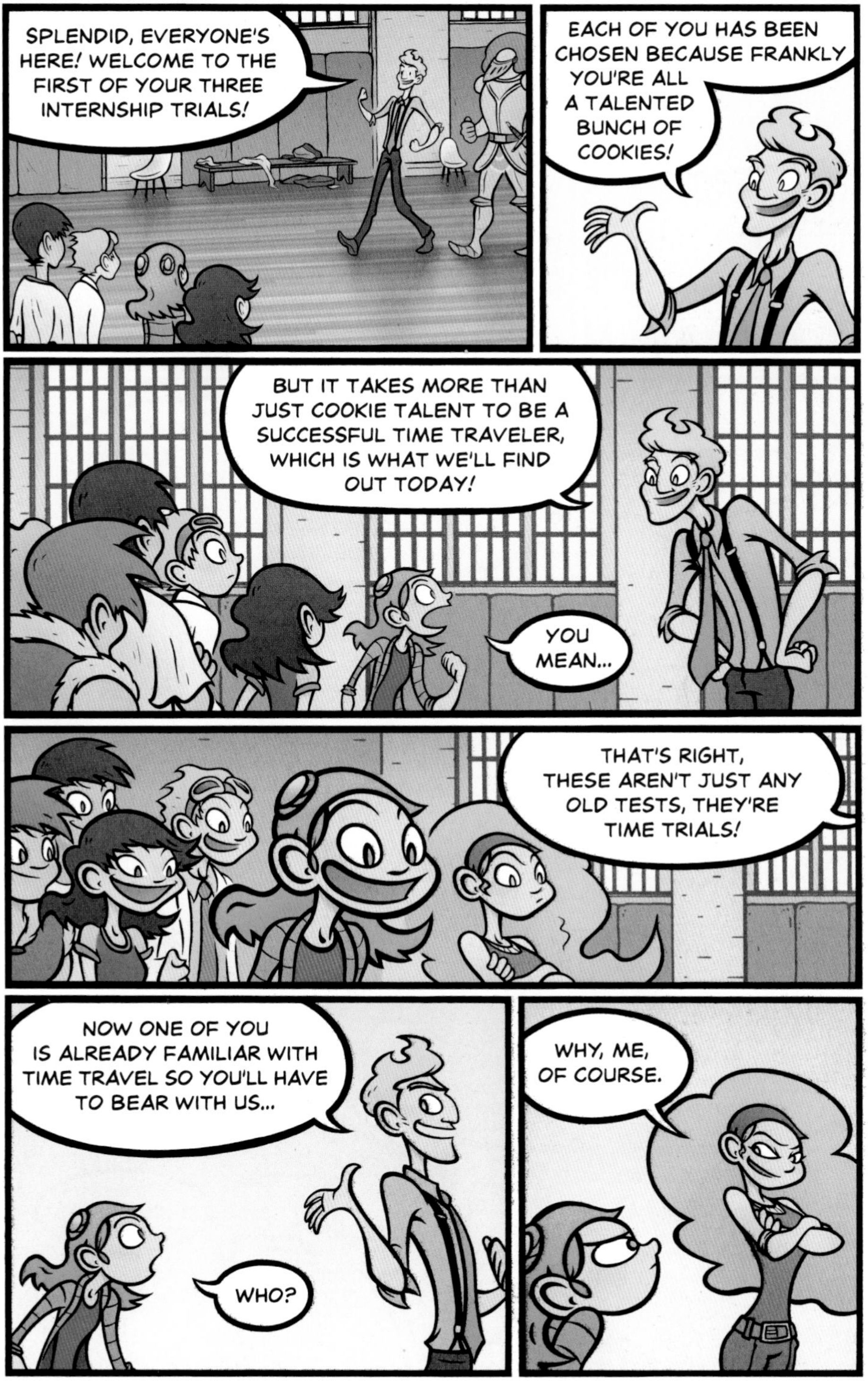
SPLENDID, EVERYONE'S HERE! WELCOME TO THE FIRST OF YOUR THREE INTERNSHIP TRIALS!
EACH OF YOU HAS BEEN CHOSEN BECAUSE FRANKLY YOU'RE ALL A TALENTED BUNCH OF COOKIES!
BUT IT TAKES MORE THAN JUST COOKIE TALENT TO BE A SUCCESSFUL TIME TRAVELER, WHICH IS WHAT WE'LL FIND OUT TODAY!
YOU MEAN...
THAT'S RIGHT, THESE AREN'T JUST ANY OLD TESTS, THEY'RE TIME TRIALS!
NOW ONE OF YOU IS ALREADY FAMILIAR WITH TIME TRAVEL SO YOU'LL HAVE TO BEAR WITH US...
WHO?
WHY, ME, OF COURSE.

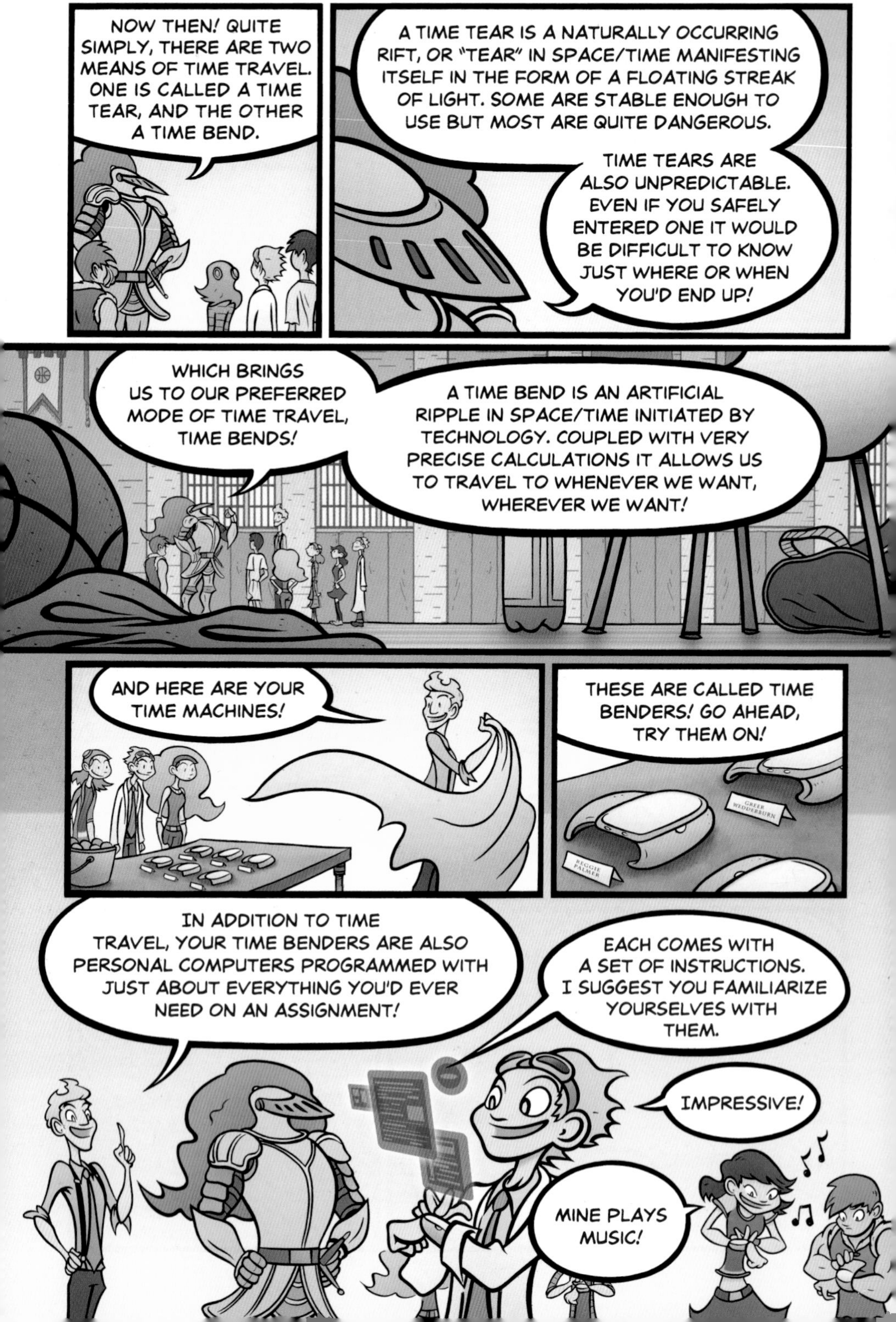
NOW THEN! QUITE SIMPLY, THERE ARE TWO MEANS OF TIME TRAVEL. ONE IS CALLED A TIME TEAR, AND THE OTHER A TIME BEND.
A TIME TEAR IS A NATURALLY OCCURRING RIFT, OR "TEAR" IN SPACE/TIME MANIFESTING ITSELF IN THE FORM OF A FLOATING STREAK OF LIGHT. SOME ARE STABLE ENOUGH TO USE BUT MOST ARE QUITE DANGEROUS.
TIME TEARS ARE ALSO UNPREDICTABLE. EVEN IF YOU SAFELY ENTERED ONE IT WOULD BE DIFFICULT TO KNOW JUST WHERE OR WHEN YOU'D END UP!
WHICH BRINGS US TO OUR PREFERRED MODE OF TIME TRAVEL, TIME BENDS!
A TIME BEND IS AN ARTIFICIAL RIPPLE IN SPACE/TIME INITIATED BY TECHNOLOGY. COUPLED WITH VERY PRECISE CALCULATIONS IT ALLOWS US TO TRAVEL TO WHENEVER WE WANT, WHEREVER WE WANT!
AND HERE ARE YOUR TIME MACHINES!
THESE ARE CALLED TIME BENDERS! GO AHEAD, TRY THEM ON!
GREER WEDDERBURN
REGGIE PALMER
IN ADDITION TO TIME TRAVEL, YOUR TIME BENDERS ARE ALSO PERSONAL COMPUTERS PROGRAMMED WITH JUST ABOUT EVERYTHING YOU'D EVER NEED ON AN ASSIGNMENT!
EACH COMES WITH A SET OF INSTRUCTIONS. I SUGGEST YOU FAMILIARIZE YOURSELVES WITH THEM.
IMPRESSIVE!
MINE PLAYS MUSIC!

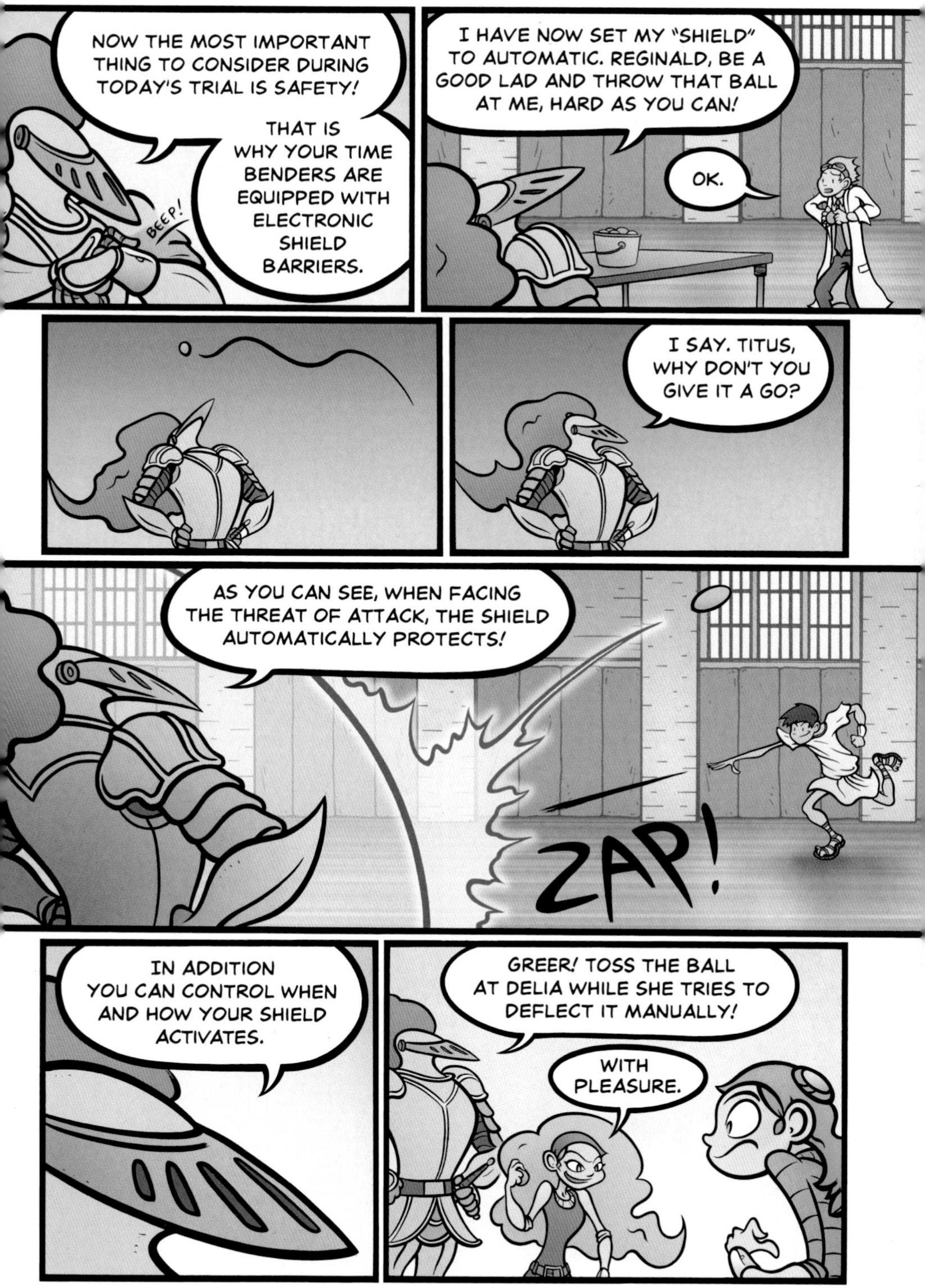
NOW THE MOST IMPORTANT THING TO CONSIDER DURING TODAY'S TRIAL IS SAFETY!
THAT IS WHY YOUR TIME BENDERS ARE EQUIPPED WITH ELECTRONIC SHIELD BARRIERS.
BEEP!
I HAVE NOW SET MY "SHIELD" TO AUTOMATIC. REGINALD, BE A GOOD LAD AND THROW THAT BALL AT ME, HARD AS YOU CAN!
OK.
I SAY. TITUS, WHY DON'T YOU GIVE IT A GO?
AS YOU CAN SEE, WHEN FACING THE THREAT OF ATTACK, THE SHIELD AUTOMATICALLY PROTECTS!
ZAP!
IN ADDITION YOU CAN CONTROL WHEN AND HOW YOUR SHIELD ACTIVATES.
GREER! TOSS THE BALL AT DELIA WHILE SHE TRIES TO DEFLECT IT MANUALLY!
WITH PLEASURE.

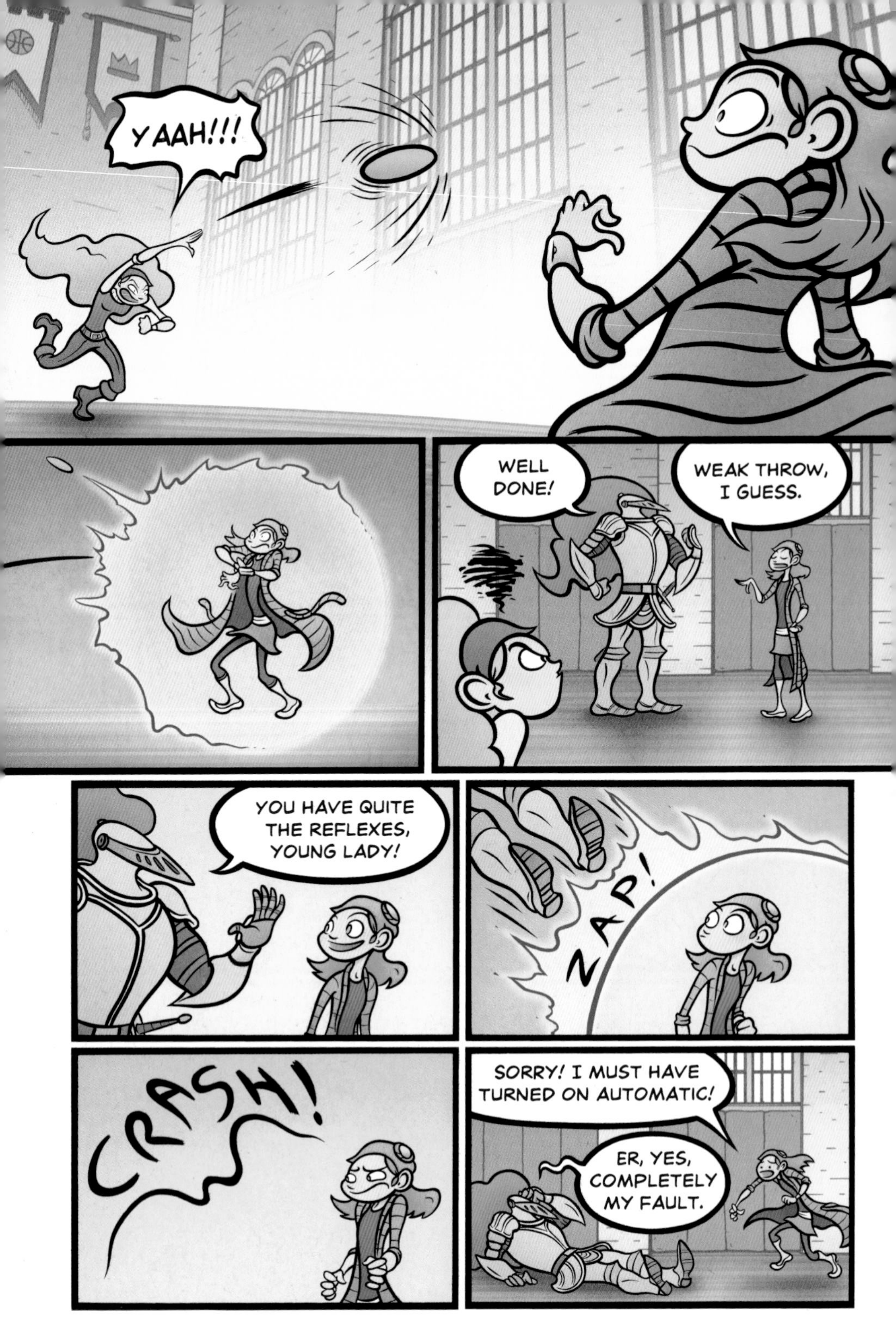
YAAH!!!
WELL DONE!
WEAK THROW, I GUESS.
YOU HAVE QUITE THE REFLEXES, YOUNG LADY!
ZAP!
CRASH!
SORRY! I MUST HAVE TURNED ON AUTOMATIC!
ER, YES, COMPLETELY MY FAULT.

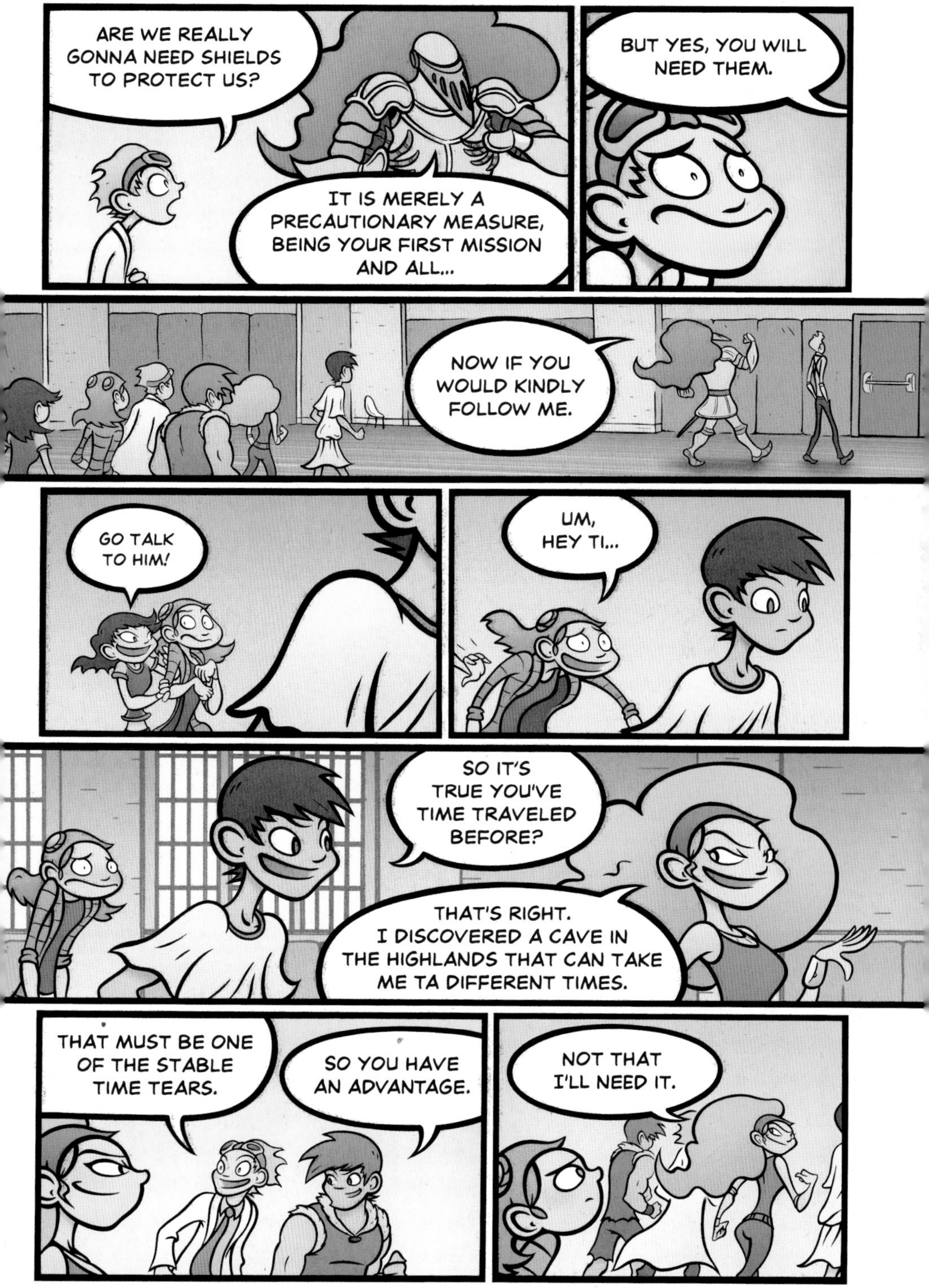
ARE WE REALLY GONNA NEED SHIELDS TO PROTECT US?
IT IS MERELY A PRECAUTIONARY MEASURE, BEING YOUR FIRST MISSION AND ALL...
BUT YES, YOU WILL NEED THEM.
NOW IF YOU WOULD KINDLY FOLLOW ME.
GO TALK TO HIM!
UM, HEY TI...
SO IT'S TRUE YOU'VE TIME TRAVELED BEFORE?
THAT'S RIGHT. I DISCOVERED A CAVE IN THE HIGHLANDS THAT CAN TAKE ME TA DIFFERENT TIMES.
THAT MUST BE ONE OF THE STABLE TIME TEARS.
SO YOU HAVE AN ADVANTAGE.
NOT THAT I'LL NEED IT.

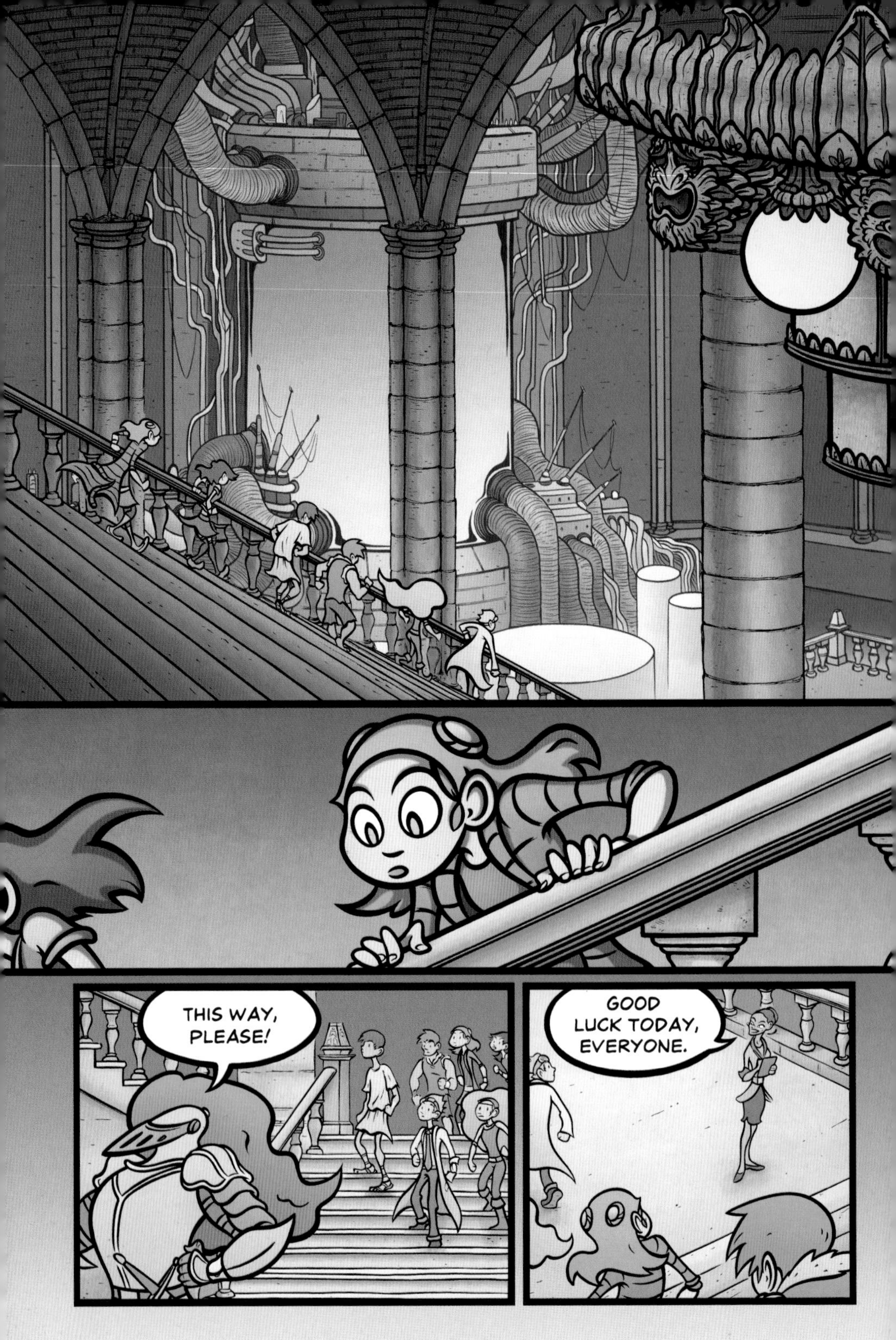
THIS WAY, PLEASE!
GOOD LUCK TODAY, EVERYONE.

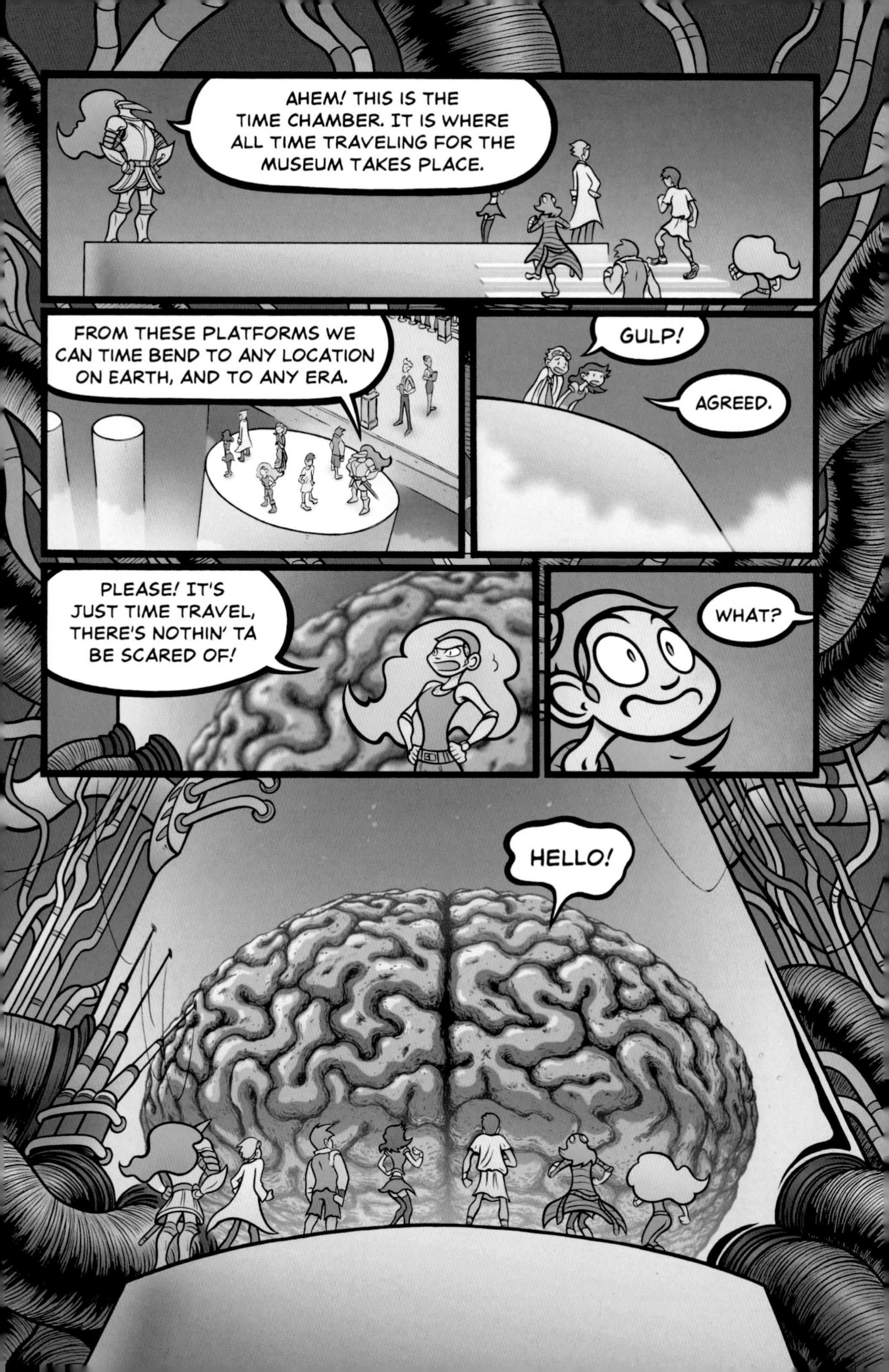
AHEM! THIS IS THE TIME CHAMBER. IT IS WHERE ALL TIME TRAVELING FOR THE MUSEUM TAKES PLACE.
FROM THESE PLATFORMS WE CAN TIME BEND TO ANY LOCATION ON EARTH, AND TO ANY ERA.
GULP!
AGREED.
PLEASE! IT'S JUST TIME TRAVEL, THERE'S NOTHIN' TA BE SCARED OF!
WHAT?
HELLO!

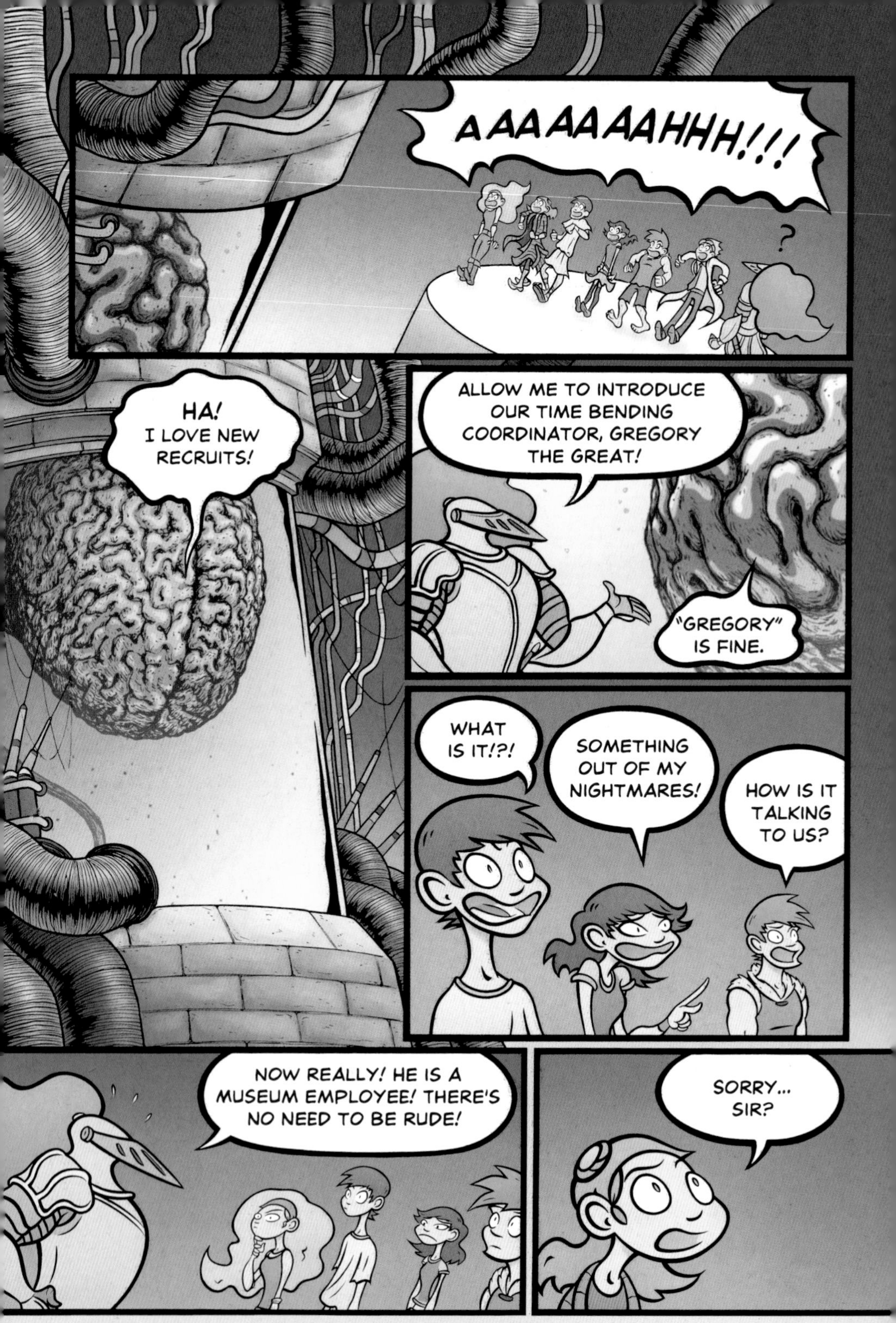
AAAAAAAHHH!!!
?
HA! I LOVE NEW RECRUITS!
ALLOW ME TO INTRODUCE OUR TIME BENDING COORDINATOR, GREGORY THE GREAT!
"GREGORY" IS FINE.
WHAT IS IT!?!
SOMETHING OUT OF MY NIGHTMARES!
HOW IS IT TALKING TO US?
NOW REALLY! HE IS A MUSEUM EMPLOYEE! THERE'S NO NEED TO BE RUDE!
SORRY... SIR?

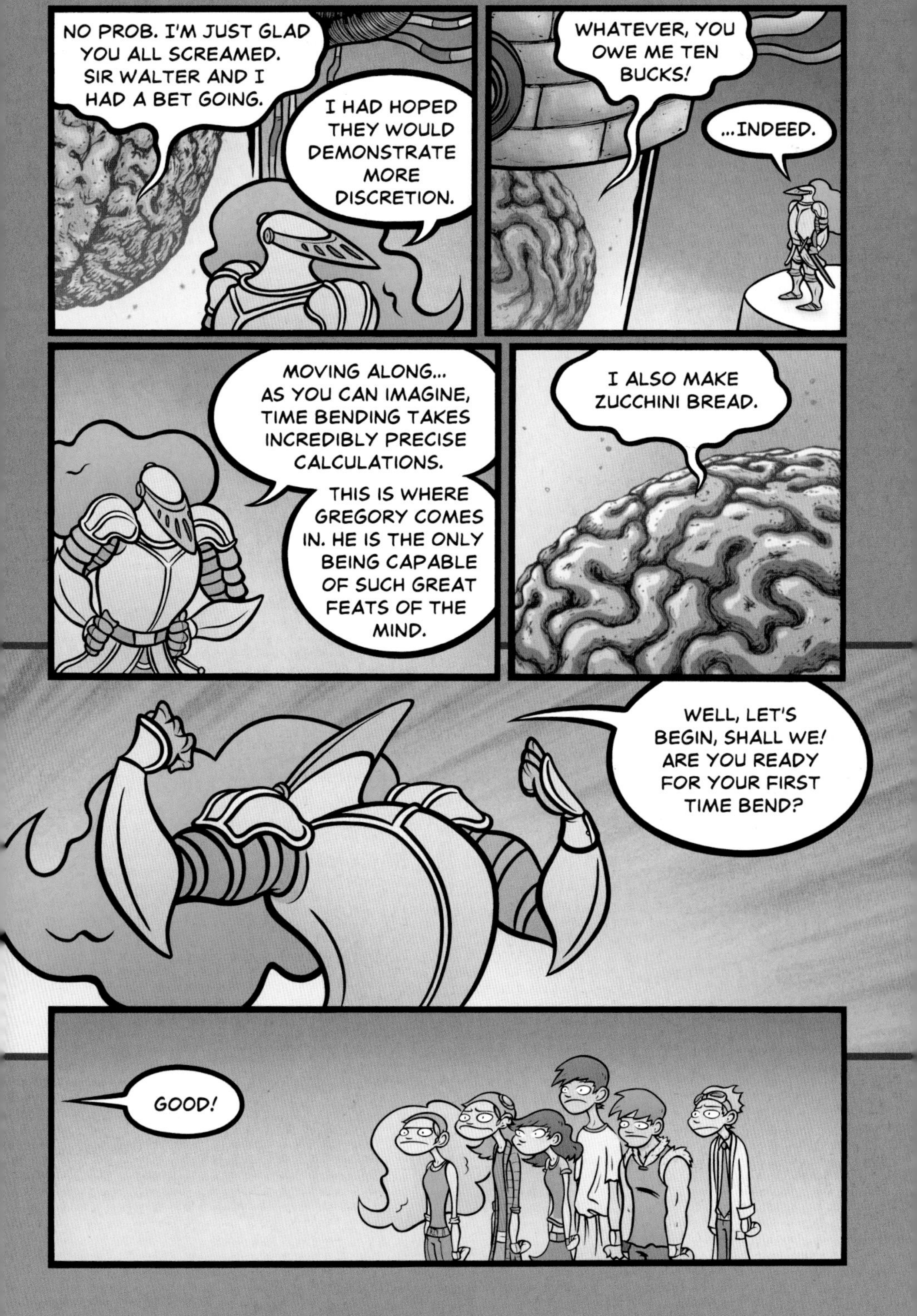
NO PROB. I'M JUST GLAD YOU ALL SCREAMED. SIR WALTER AND I HAD A BET GOING.
I HAD HOPED THEY WOULD DEMONSTRATE MORE DISCRETION.
WHATEVER, YOU OWE ME TEN BUCKS!
...INDEED.
MOVING ALONG... AS YOU CAN IMAGINE, TIME BENDING TAKES INCREDIBLY PRECISE CALCULATIONS.
THIS IS WHERE GREGORY COMES IN. HE IS THE ONLY BEING CAPABLE OF SUCH GREAT FEATS OF THE MIND.
I ALSO MAKE ZUCCHINI BREAD.
WELL, LET'S BEGIN, SHALL WE! ARE YOU READY FOR YOUR FIRST TIME BEND?
GOOD!

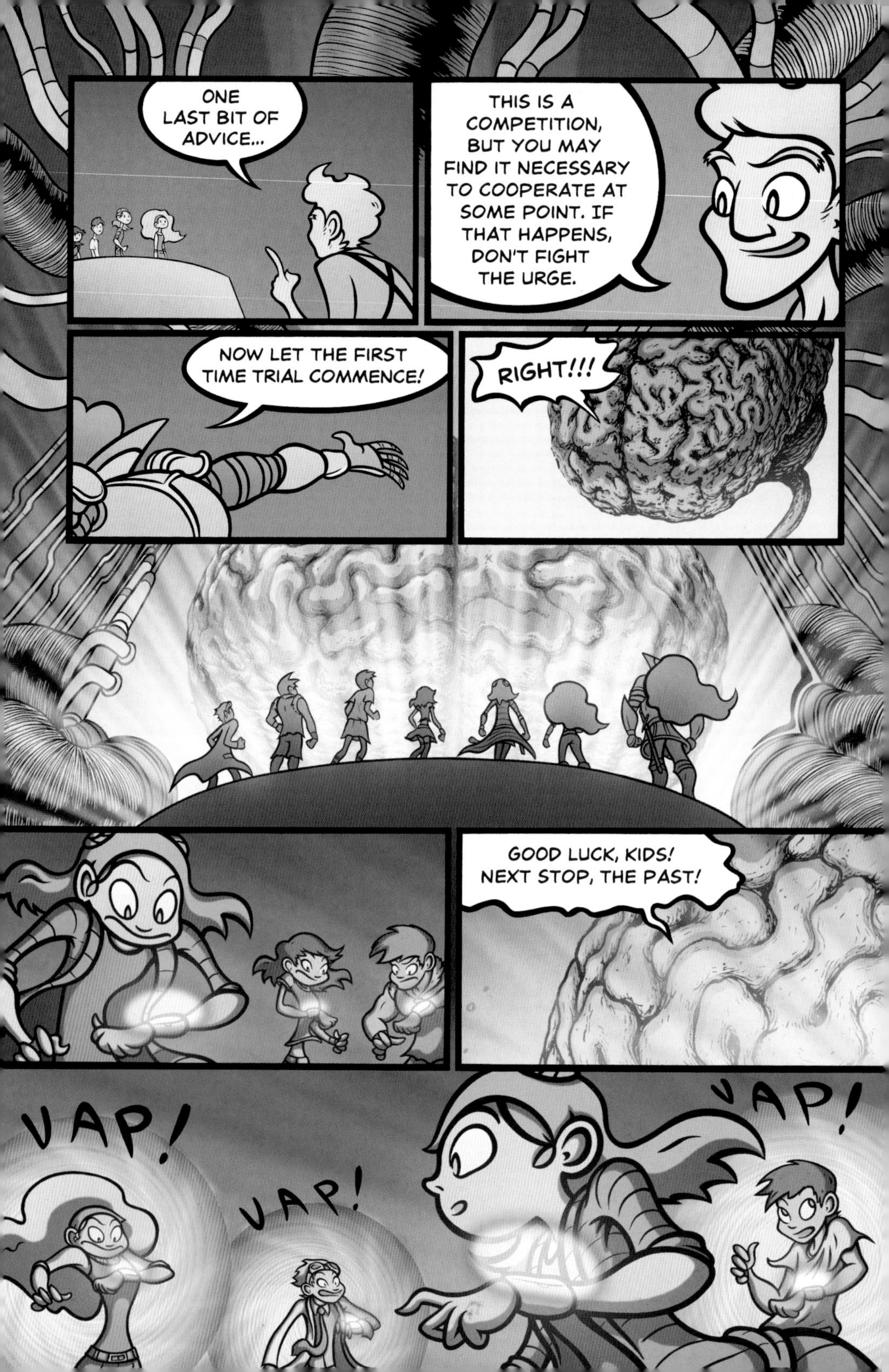
ONE LAST BIT OF ADVICE...
THIS IS A COMPETITION, BUT YOU MAY FIND IT NECESSARY TO COOPERATE AT SOME POINT. IF THAT HAPPENS, DON'T FIGHT THE URGE.
NOW LET THE FIRST TIME TRIAL COMMENCE!
RIGHT!!!
GOOD LUCK, KIDS! NEXT STOP, THE PAST!
VAP!
VAP!
VAP!

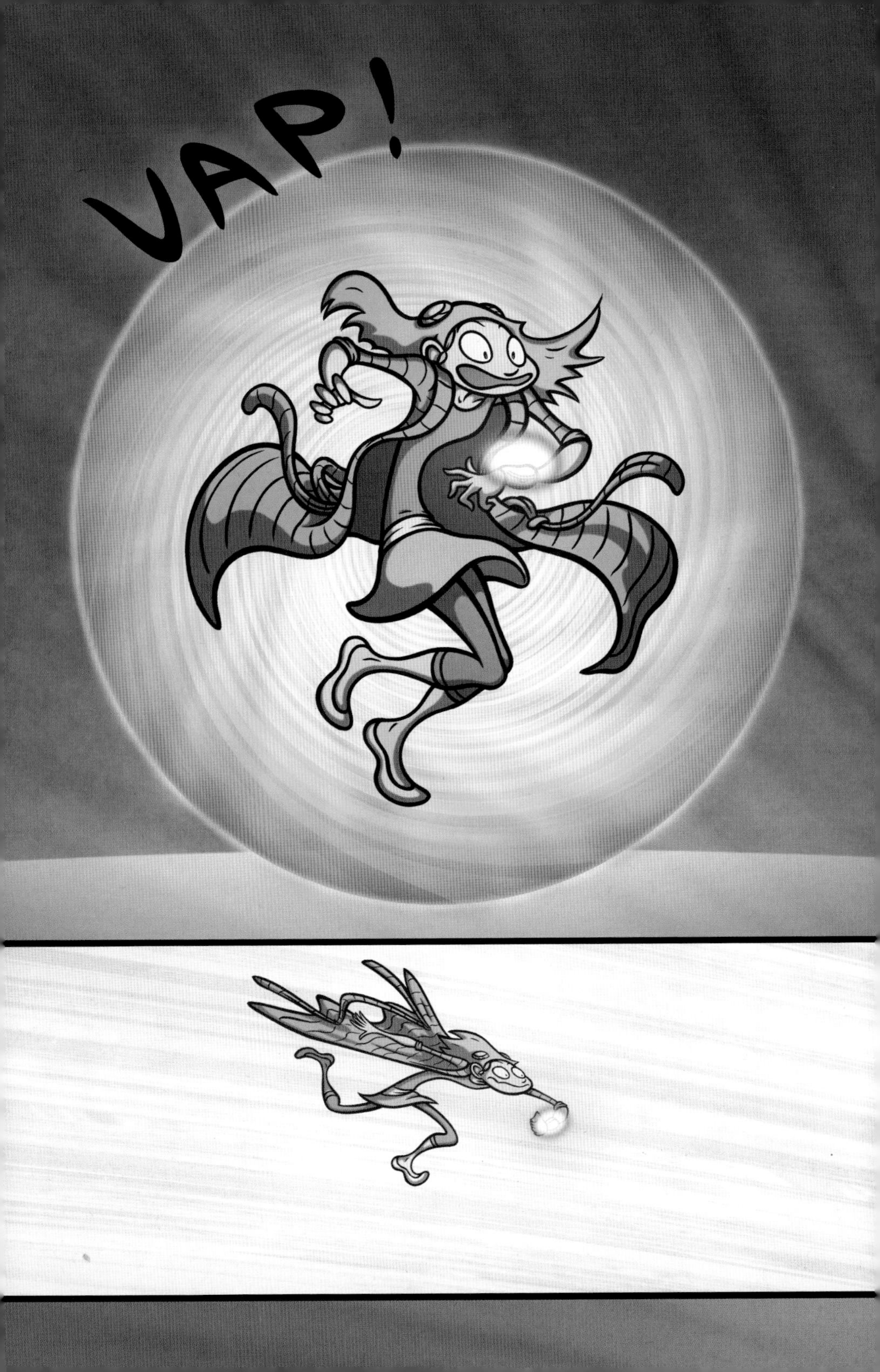
VAP!

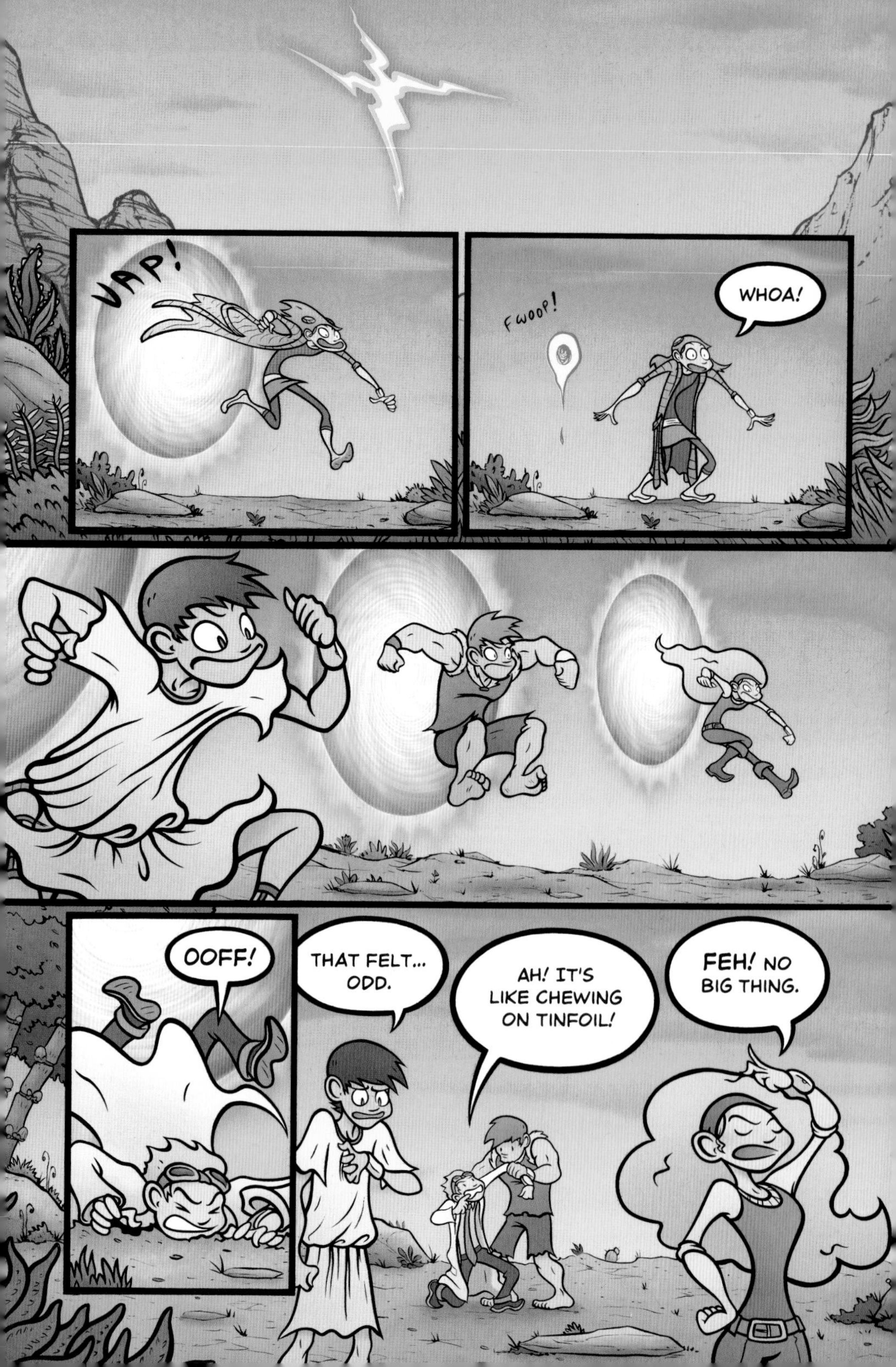

VAP!
FWOOP!
WHOA!
OOFF!
THAT FELT... ODD.
AH! IT'S LIKE CHEWING ON TINFOIL!
FEH! NO BIG THING.

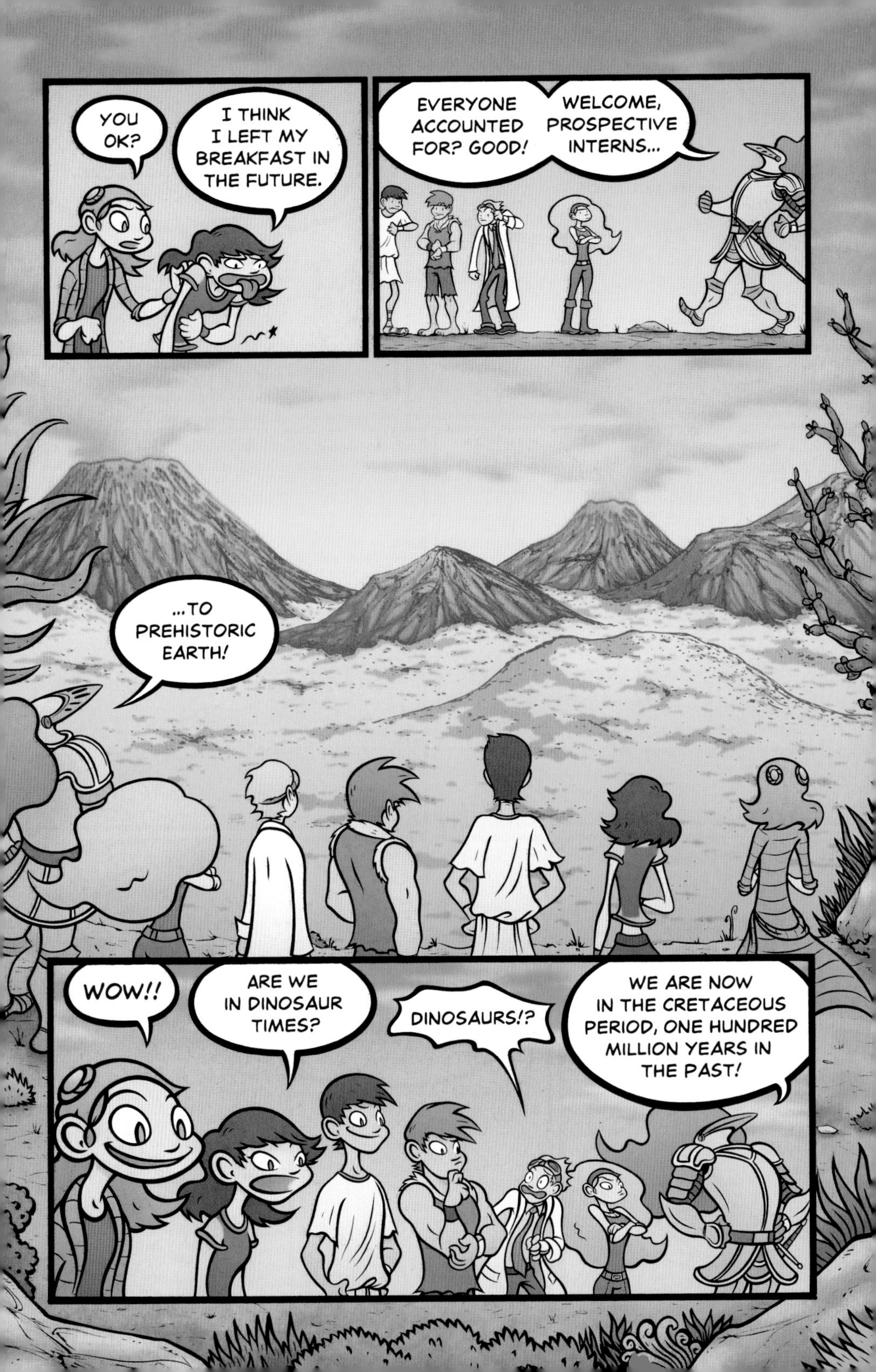
YOU OK?
I THINK I LEFT MY BREAKFAST IN THE FUTURE.
EVERYONE ACCOUNTED FOR? GOOD!
WELCOME, PROSPECTIVE INTERNS...
...TO PREHISTORIC EARTH!
WOW!!
ARE WE IN DINOSAUR TIMES?
DINOSAURS!?
WE ARE NOW IN THE CRETACEOUS PERIOD, ONE HUNDRED MILLION YEARS IN THE PAST!

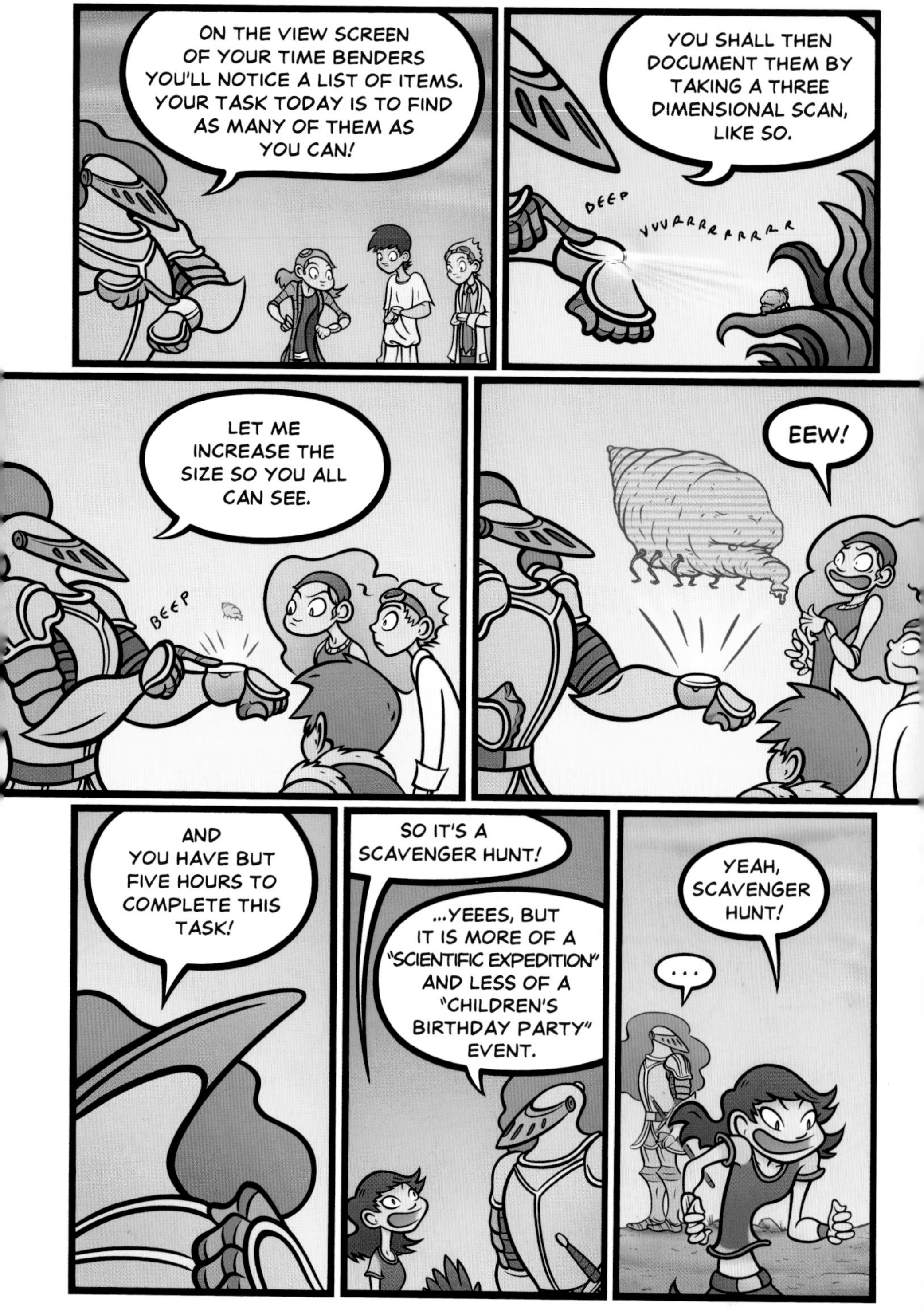
ON THE VIEW SCREEN OF YOUR TIME BENDERS YOU'LL NOTICE A LIST OF ITEMS. YOUR TASK TODAY IS TO FIND AS MANY OF THEM AS YOU CAN!
YOU SHALL THEN DOCUMENT THEM BY TAKING A THREE DIMENSIONAL SCAN, LIKE SO.
BEEP
VVVRRRRRRRRRR
LET ME INCREASE THE SIZE SO YOU ALL CAN SEE.
BEEP
EEW!
AND YOU HAVE BUT FIVE HOURS TO COMPLETE THIS TASK!
SO IT'S A SCAVENGER HUNT!
...YEEES, BUT IT IS MORE OF A "SCIENTIFIC EXPEDITION" AND LESS OF A "CHILDREN'S BIRTHDAY PARTY" EVENT.
YEAH, SCAVENGER HUNT!
...

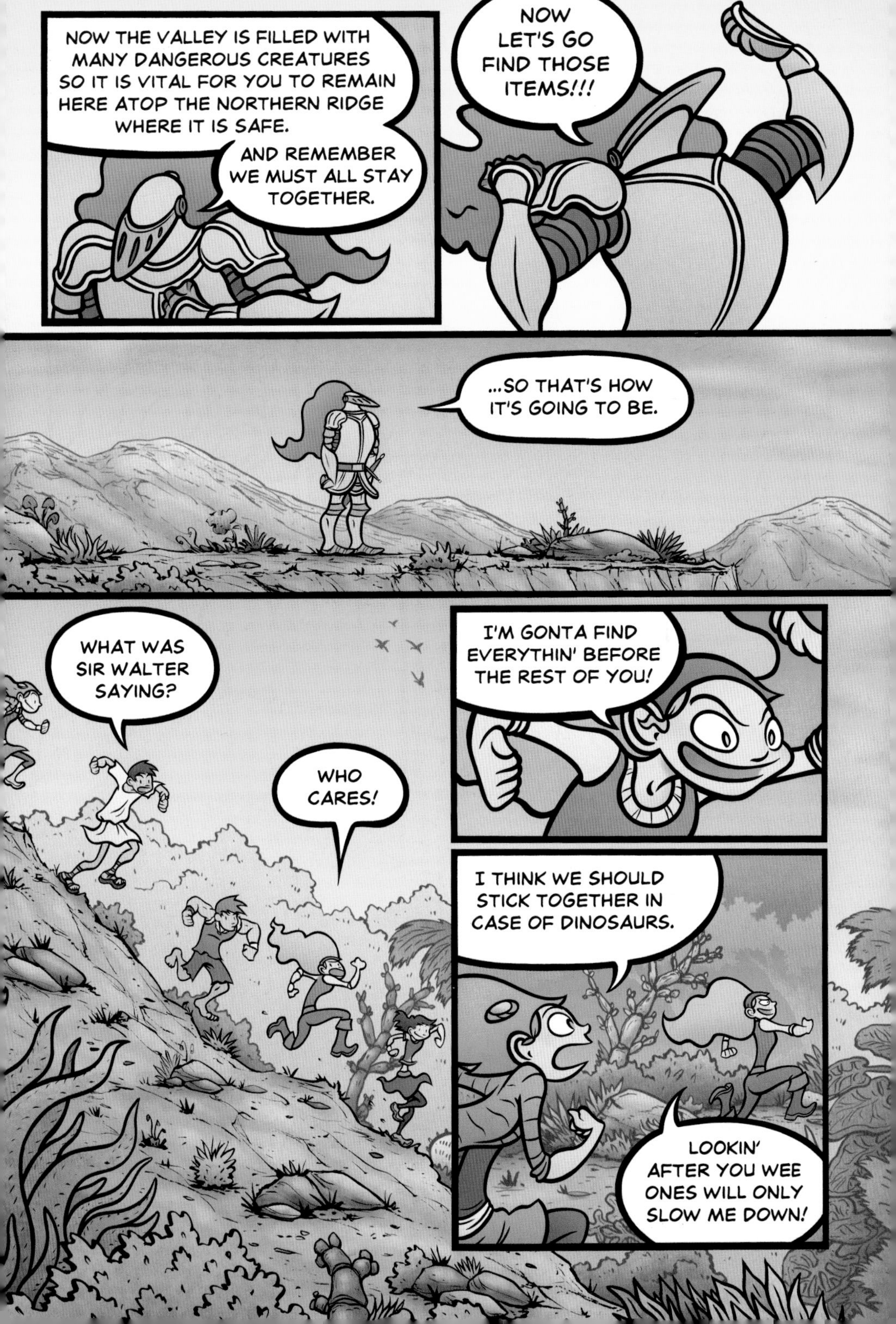
NOW THE VALLEY IS FILLED WITH MANY DANGEROUS CREATURES SO IT IS VITAL FOR YOU TO REMAIN HERE ATOP THE NORTHERN RIDGE WHERE IT IS SAFE.
AND REMEMBER WE MUST ALL STAY TOGETHER.
NOW LET'S GO FIND THOSE ITEMS!!!
...SO THAT'S HOW IT'S GOING TO BE.
WHAT WAS SIR WALTER SAYING?
WHO CARES!
I'M GONTA FIND EVERYTHIN' BEFORE THE REST OF YOU!
I THINK WE SHOULD STICK TOGETHER IN CASE OF DINOSAURS.
LOOKIN' AFTER YOU WEE ONES WILL ONLY SLOW ME DOWN!

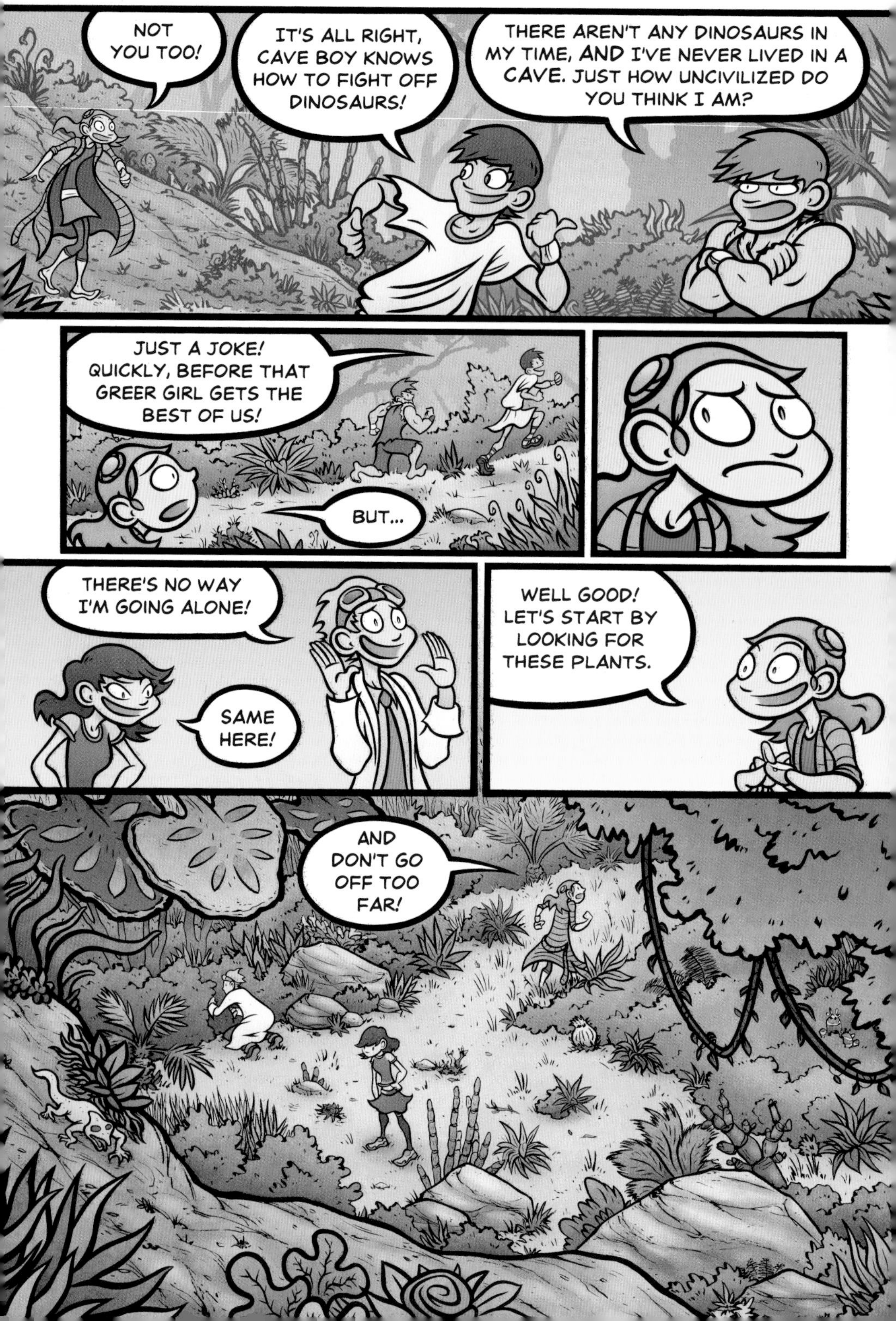
NOT YOU TOO!
IT'S ALL RIGHT, CAVE BOY KNOWS HOW TO FIGHT OFF DINOSAURS!
THERE AREN'T ANY DINOSAURS IN MY TIME, AND I'VE NEVER LIVED IN A CAVE. JUST HOW UNCIVILIZED DO YOU THINK I AM?
JUST A JOKE! QUICKLY, BEFORE THAT GREER GIRL GETS THE BEST OF US!
BUT...
THERE'S NO WAY I'M GOING ALONE!
SAME HERE!
WELL GOOD! LET'S START BY LOOKING FOR THESE PLANTS.
AND DON'T GO OFF TOO FAR!

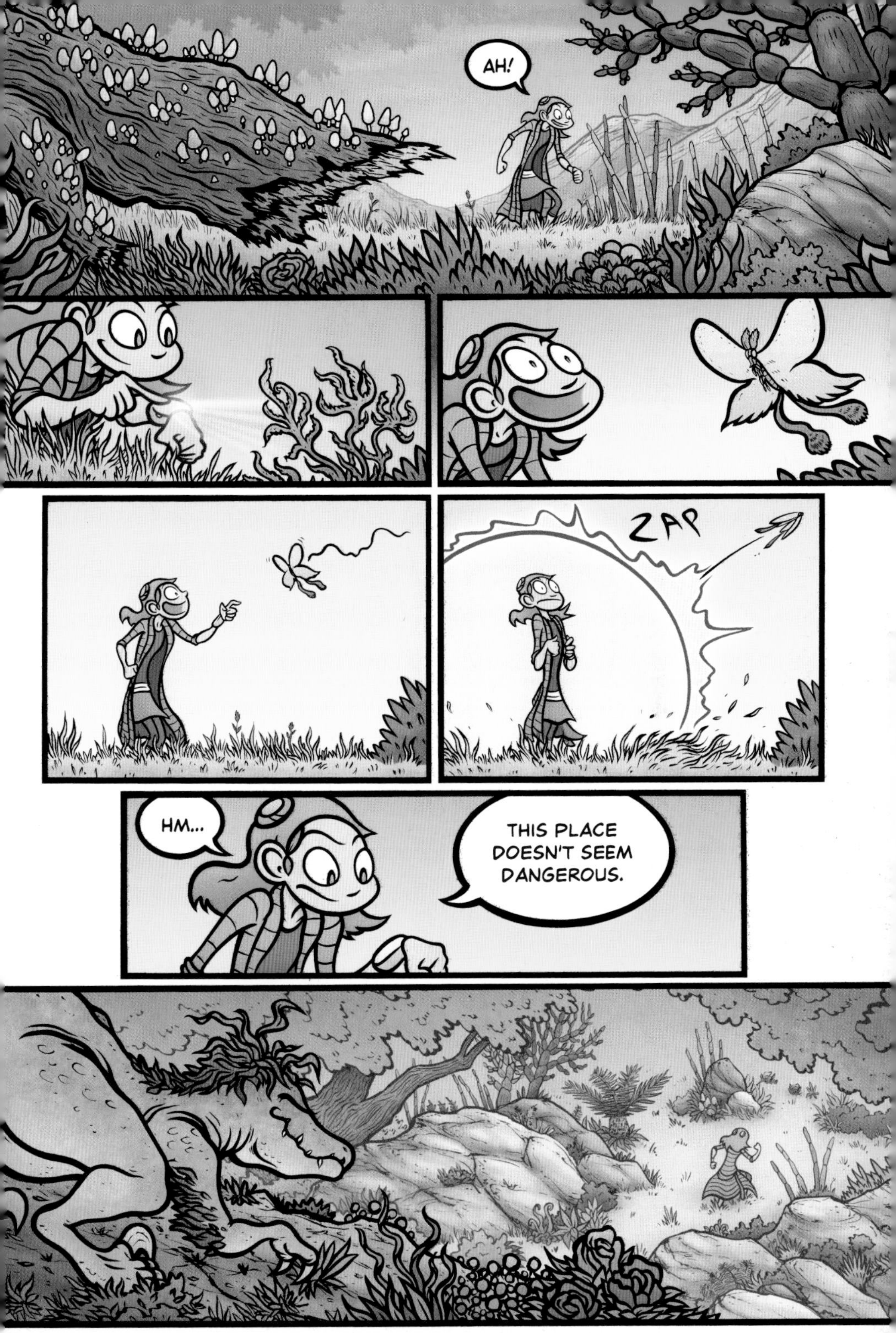
AH!
ZAP
HM...
THIS PLACE DOESN'T SEEM DANGEROUS.

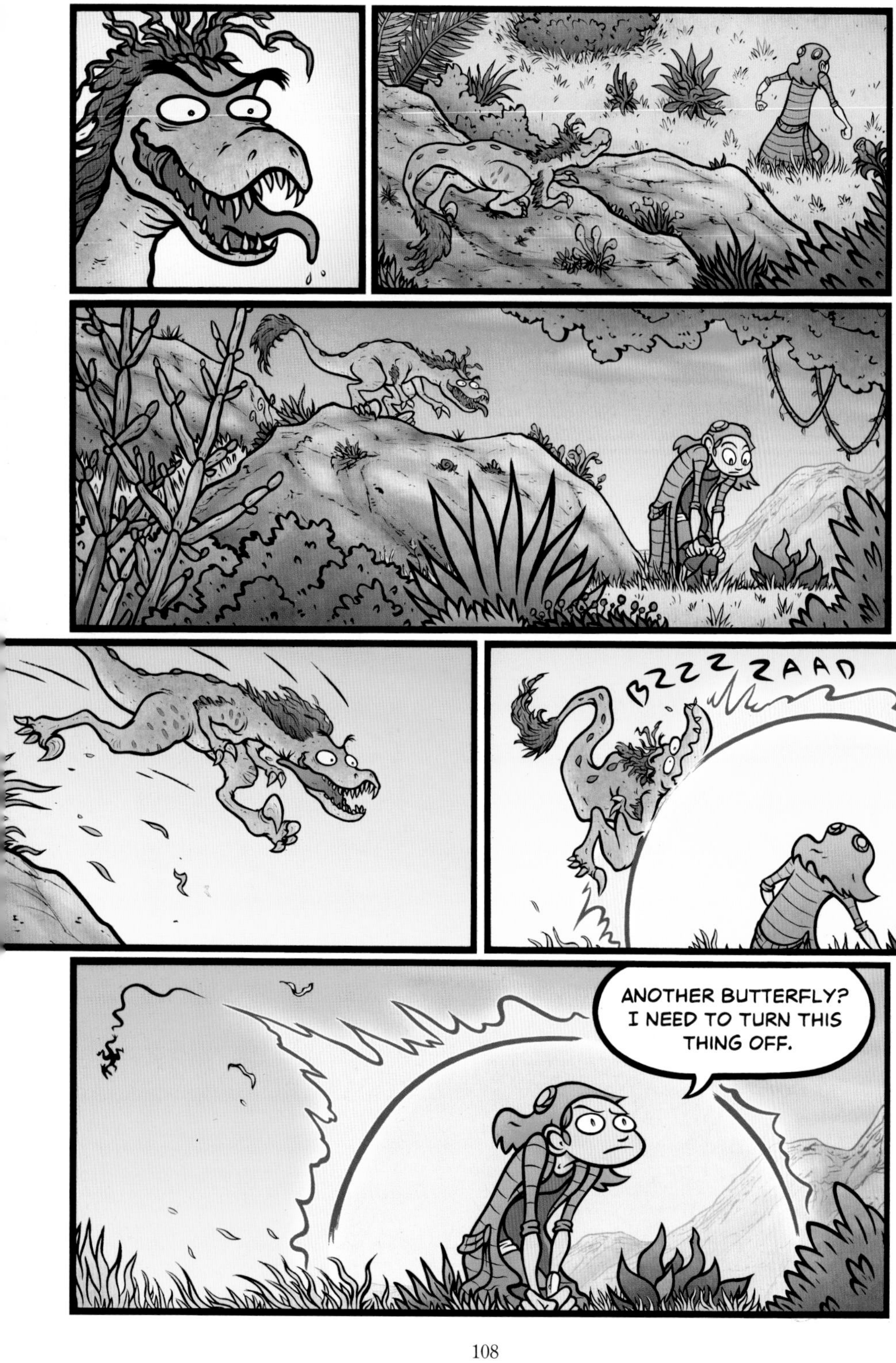
BZZZ ZAAD
ANOTHER BUTTERFLY? I NEED TO TURN THIS THING OFF.

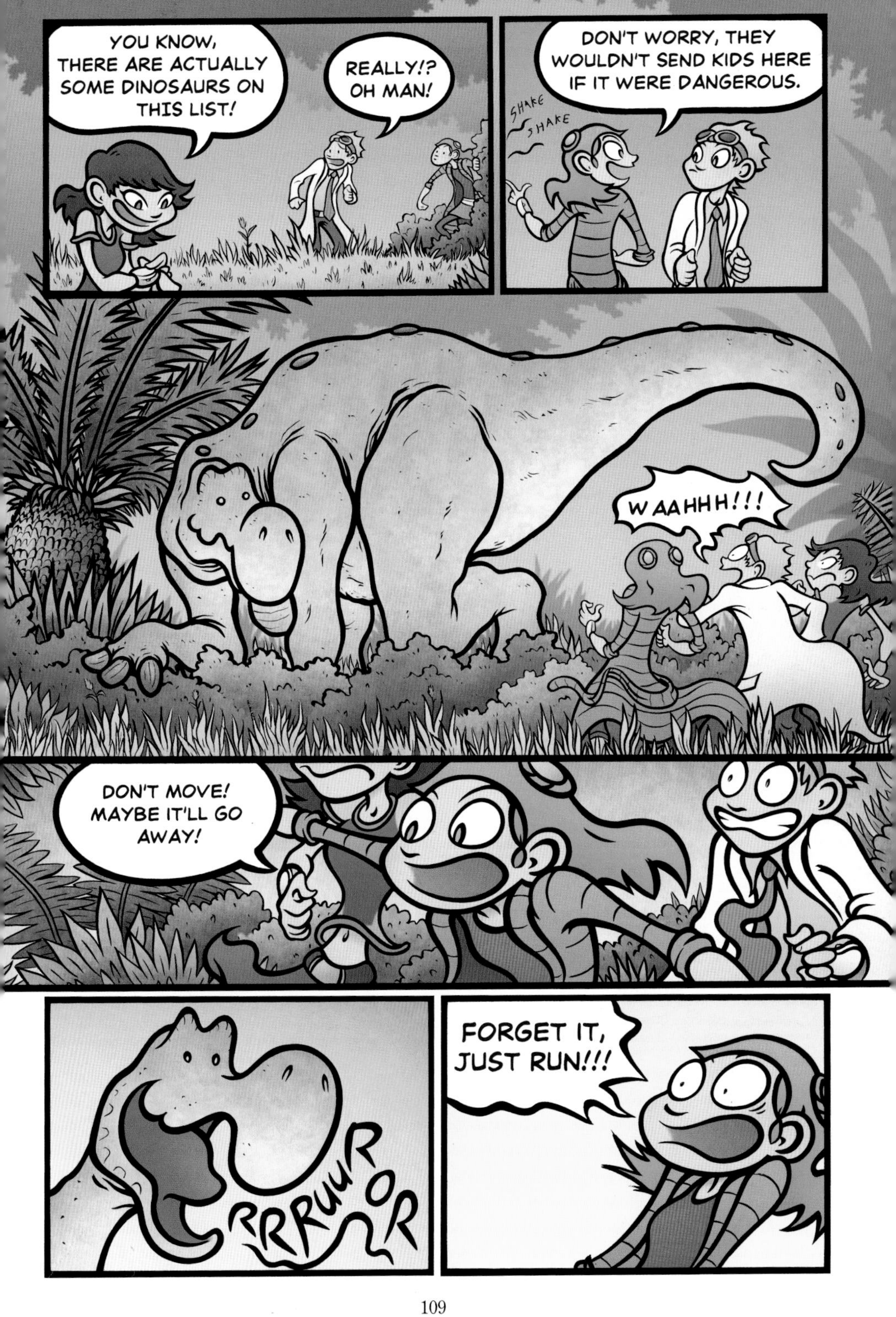
YOU KNOW, THERE ARE ACTUALLY SOME DINOSAURS ON THIS LIST!
REALLY!? OH MAN!
DON'T WORRY, THEY WOULDN'T SEND KIDS HERE IF IT WERE DANGEROUS.
SHAKE SHAKE
WAAHHH!!!
DON'T MOVE! MAYBE IT'LL GO AWAY!
RRRUUROR
FORGET IT, JUST RUN!!!

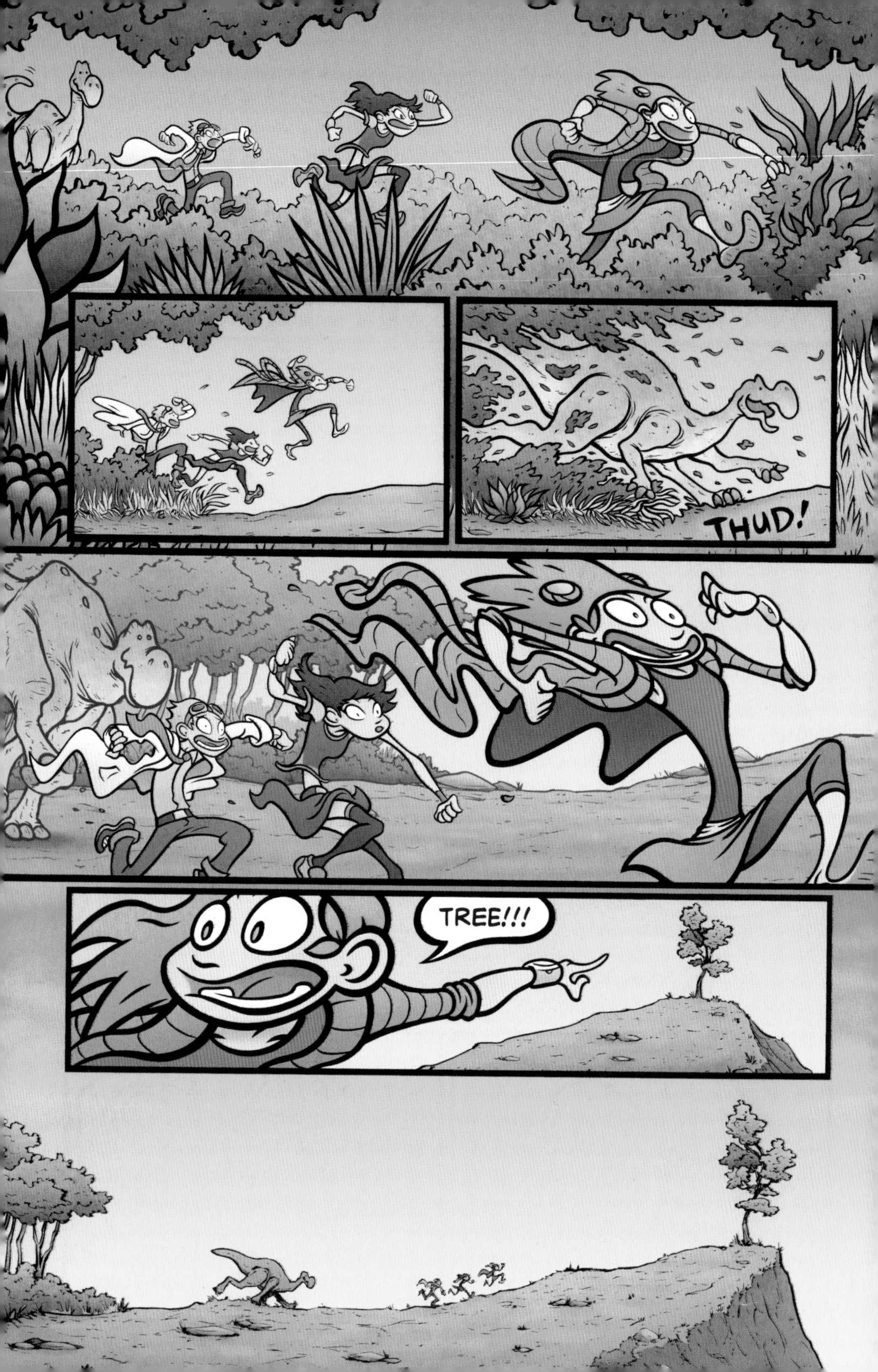
THUD!
TREE!!!

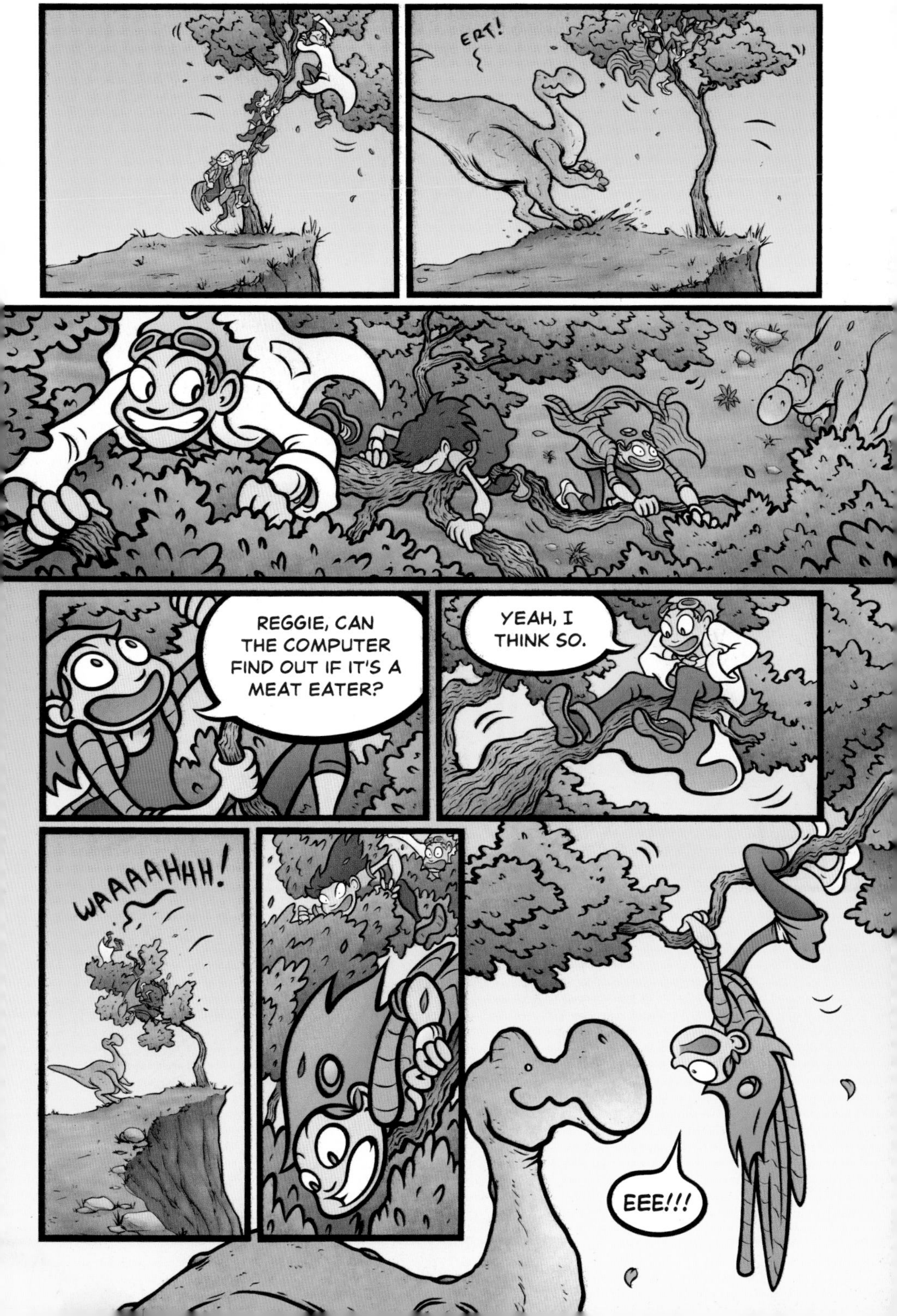
ERT!
REGGIE, CAN THE COMPUTER FIND OUT IF IT'S A MEAT EATER?
YEAH, I THINK SO.
WAAAAHHH!
EEE!!!

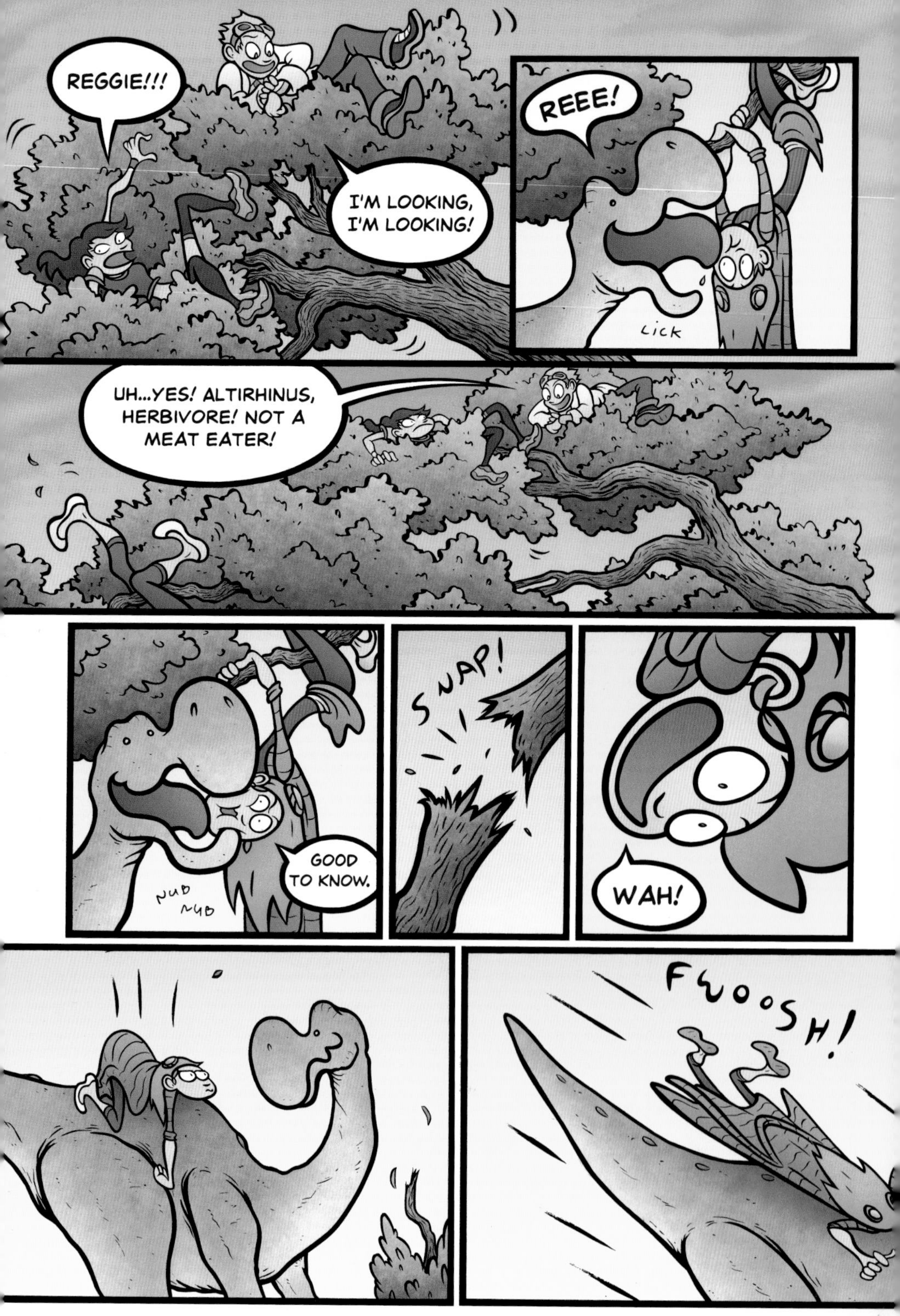
REGGIE!!!
I'M LOOKING, I'M LOOKING!
REEE!
LICK
UH...YES! ALTIRHINUS, HERBIVORE! NOT A MEAT EATER!
NUB NUB
GOOD TO KNOW.
SNAP!
WAH!
FWOOSH!

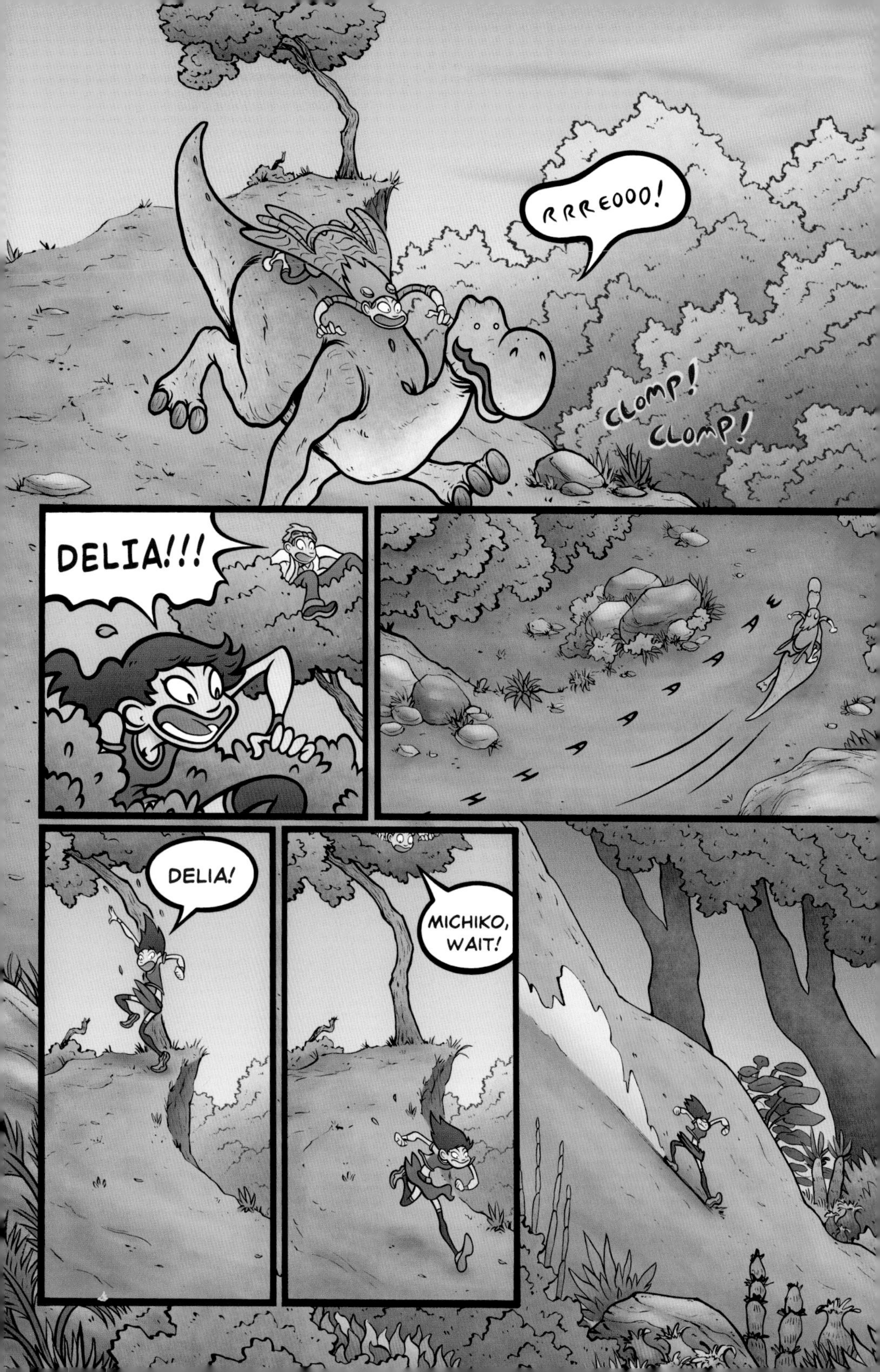
RRREOOO!
CLOMP! CLOMP!
DELIA!!!
AAAAAAAAAAE
DELIA!
MICHIKO, WAIT!

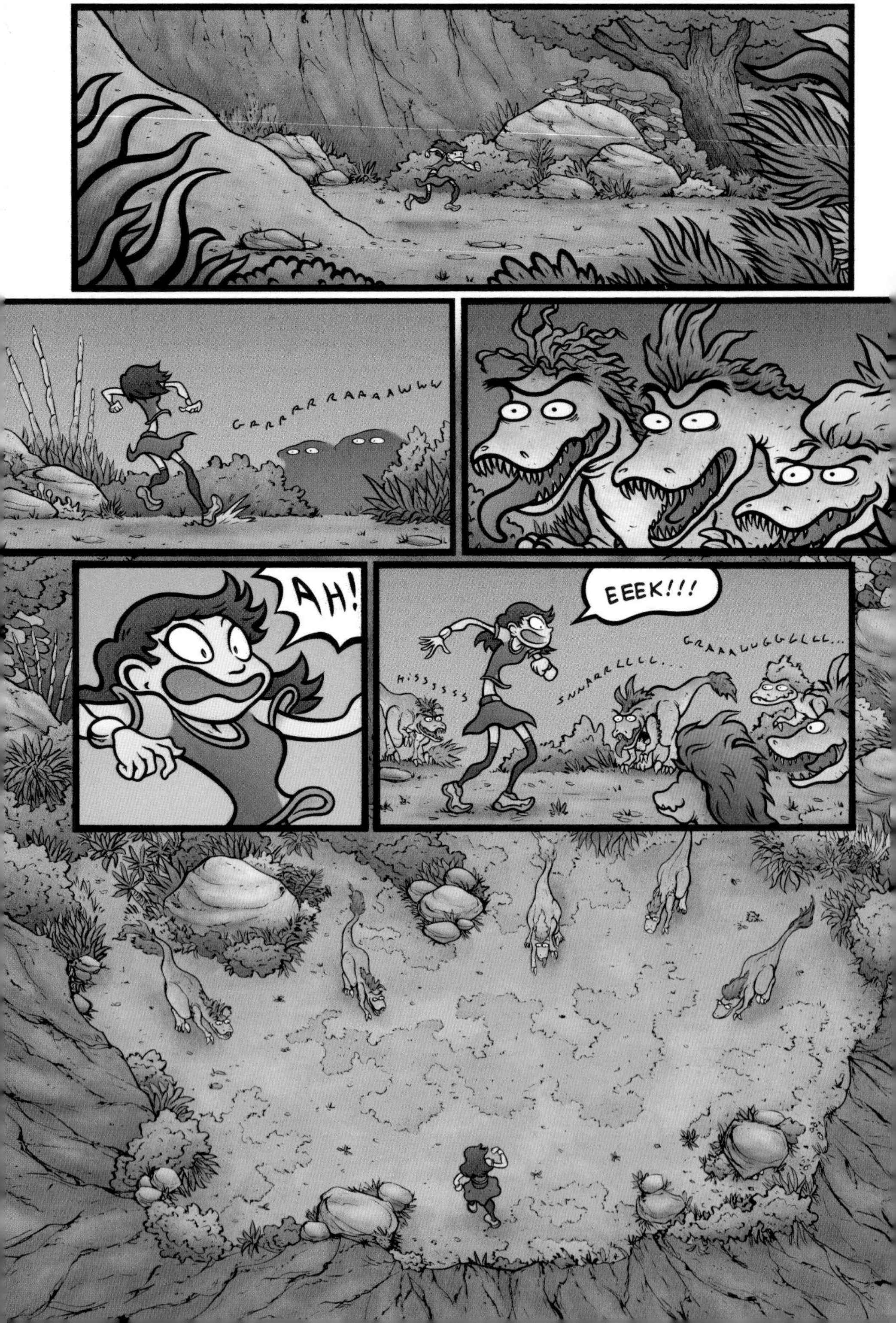
GRRRRRRAAAAAWWW
AH!
EEEK!!!
HISSSSSSS
SNNARRLLLLL...
GRAAAAWUGGLLLL...

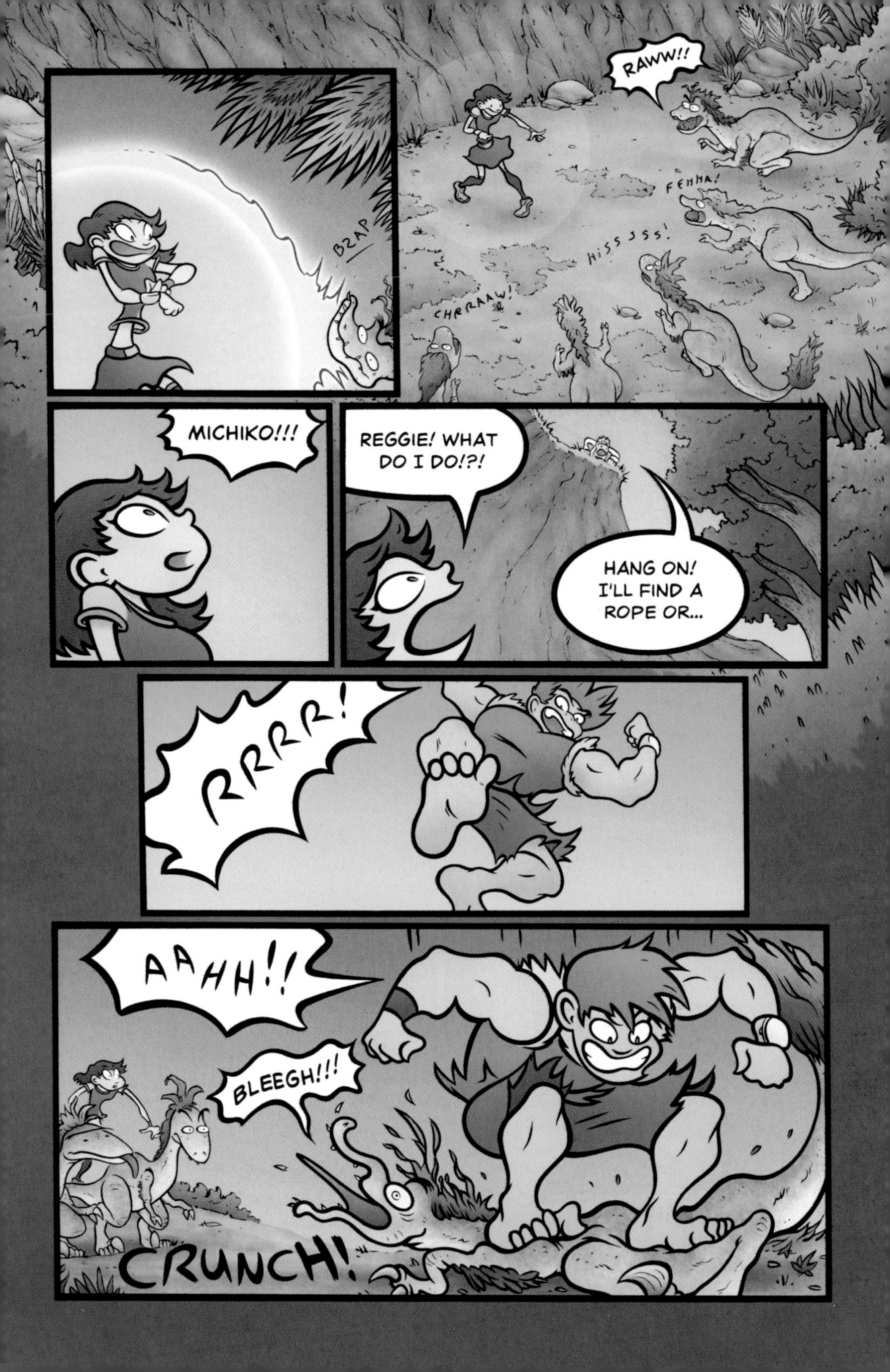
BZAP
RAWW!!
FEHHA!
HISSSSS!
CHRRAAW!
MICHIKO!!!
REGGIE! WHAT DO I DO!?!
HANG ON! I'LL FIND A ROPE OR...
RRRR!
AAHH!!
BLEEGH!!!
CRUNCH!

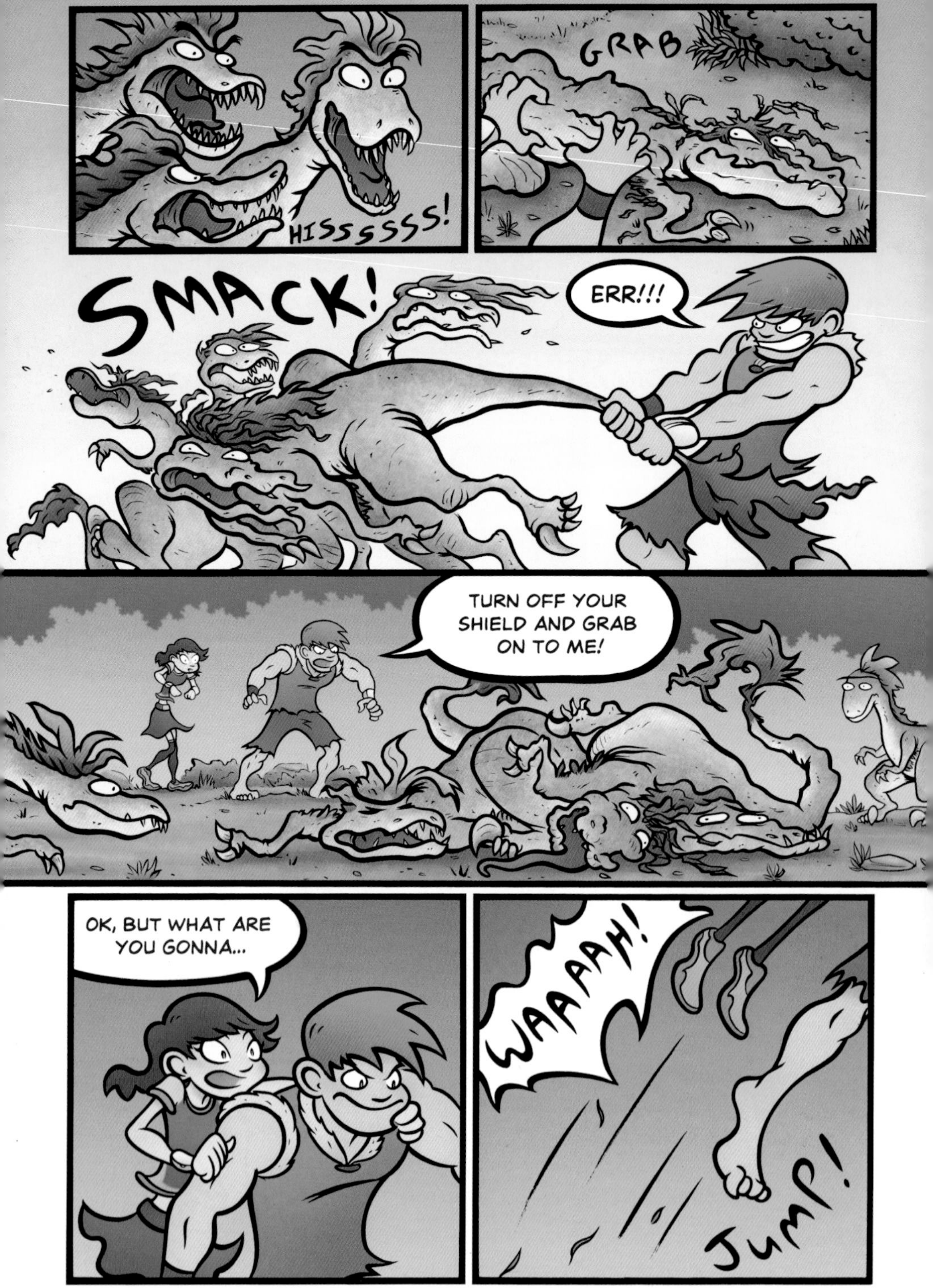
HISSSSSS!
GRAB
SMACK!
ERR!!!
TURN OFF YOUR SHIELD AND GRAB ON TO ME!
OK, BUT WHAT ARE YOU GONNA...
WAAAAH!
JUMP!

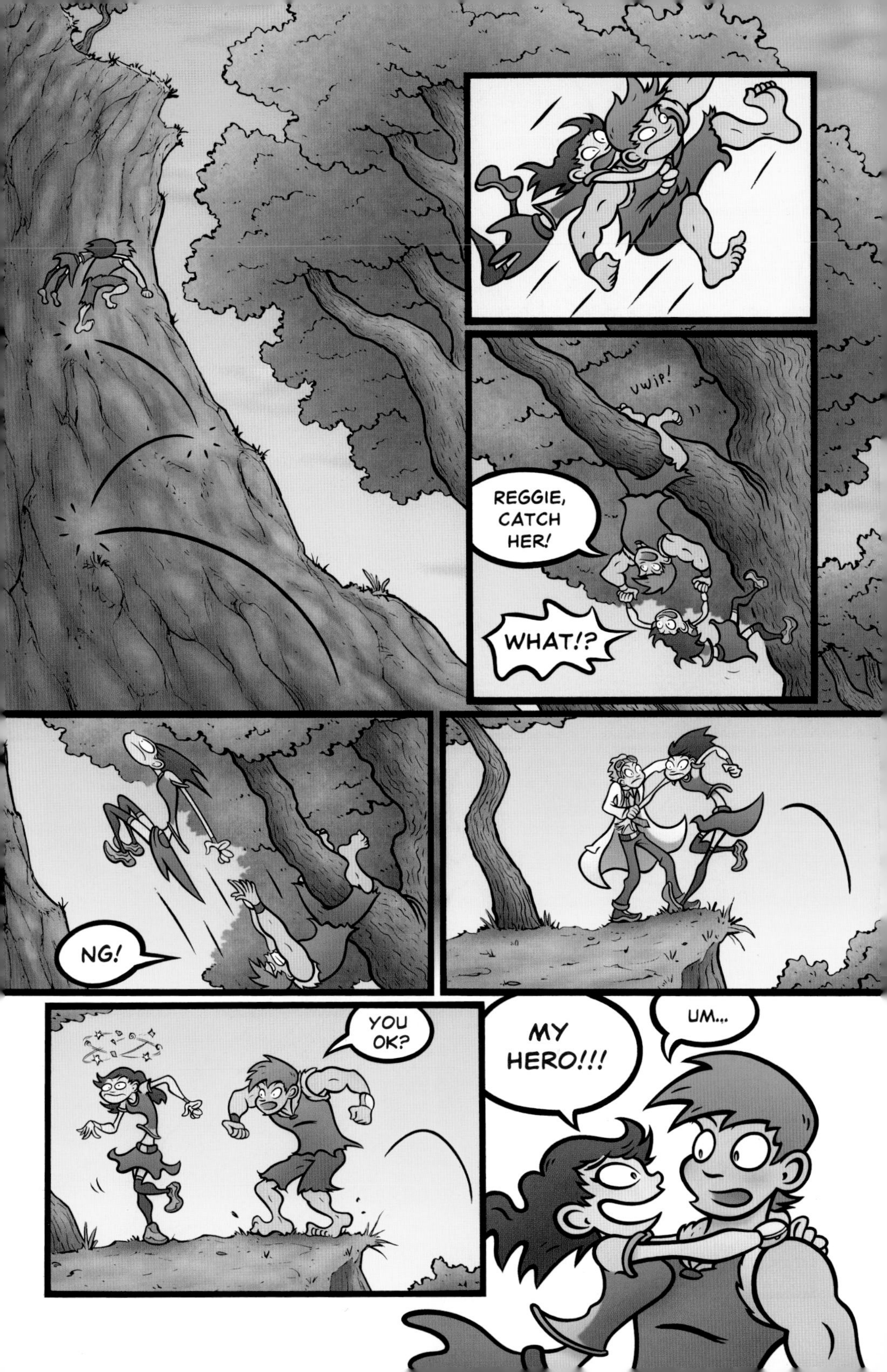
UWIP!
REGGIE, CATCH HER!
WHAT!?
NG!
YOU OK?
MY HERO!!!
UM...

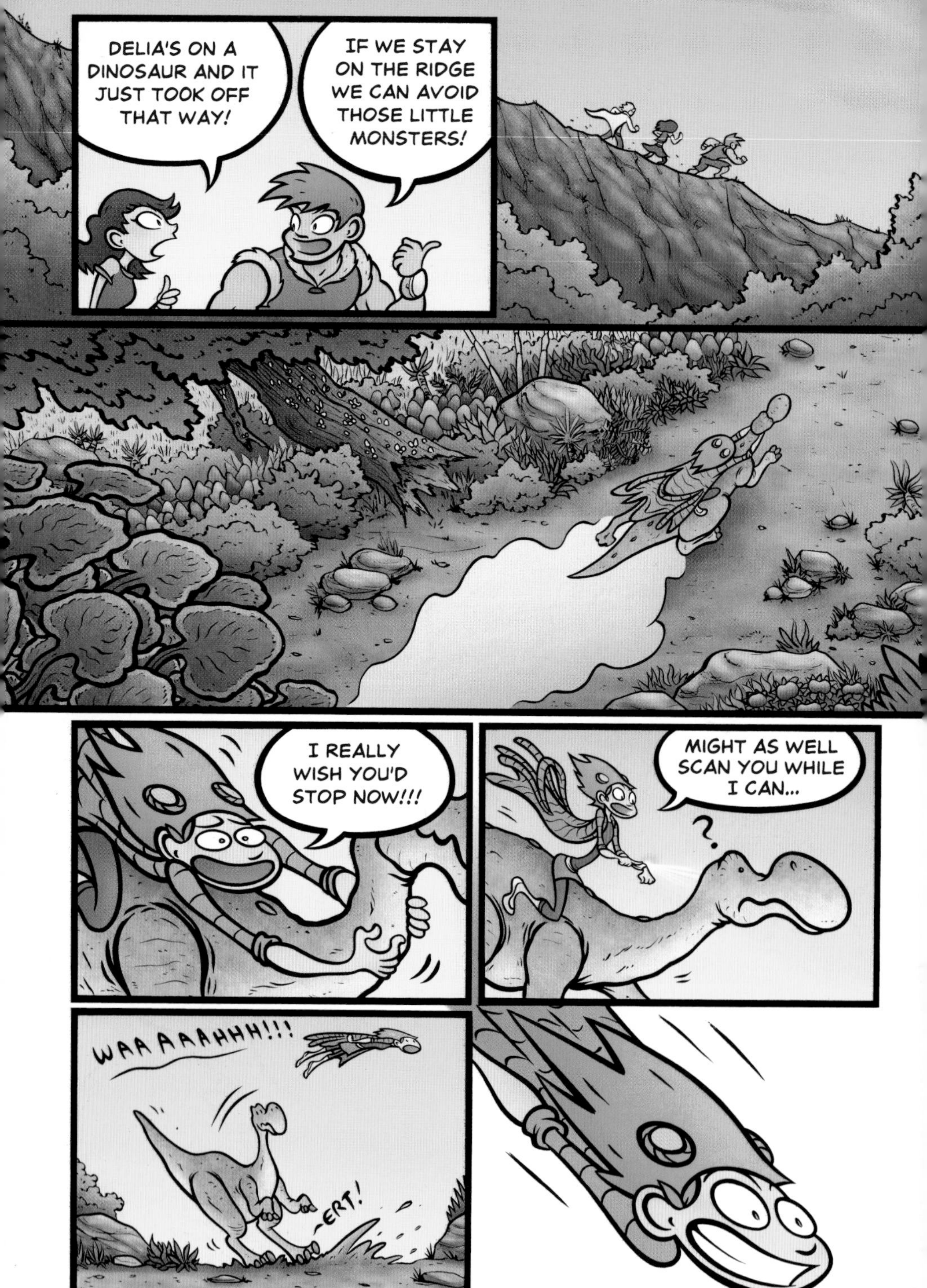
DELIA'S ON A DINOSAUR AND IT JUST TOOK OFF THAT WAY!
IF WE STAY ON THE RIDGE WE CAN AVOID THOSE LITTLE MONSTERS!
I REALLY WISH YOU'D STOP NOW!!!
MIGHT AS WELL SCAN YOU WHILE I CAN...
?
WAAAAAHHH!!!
-ERT!

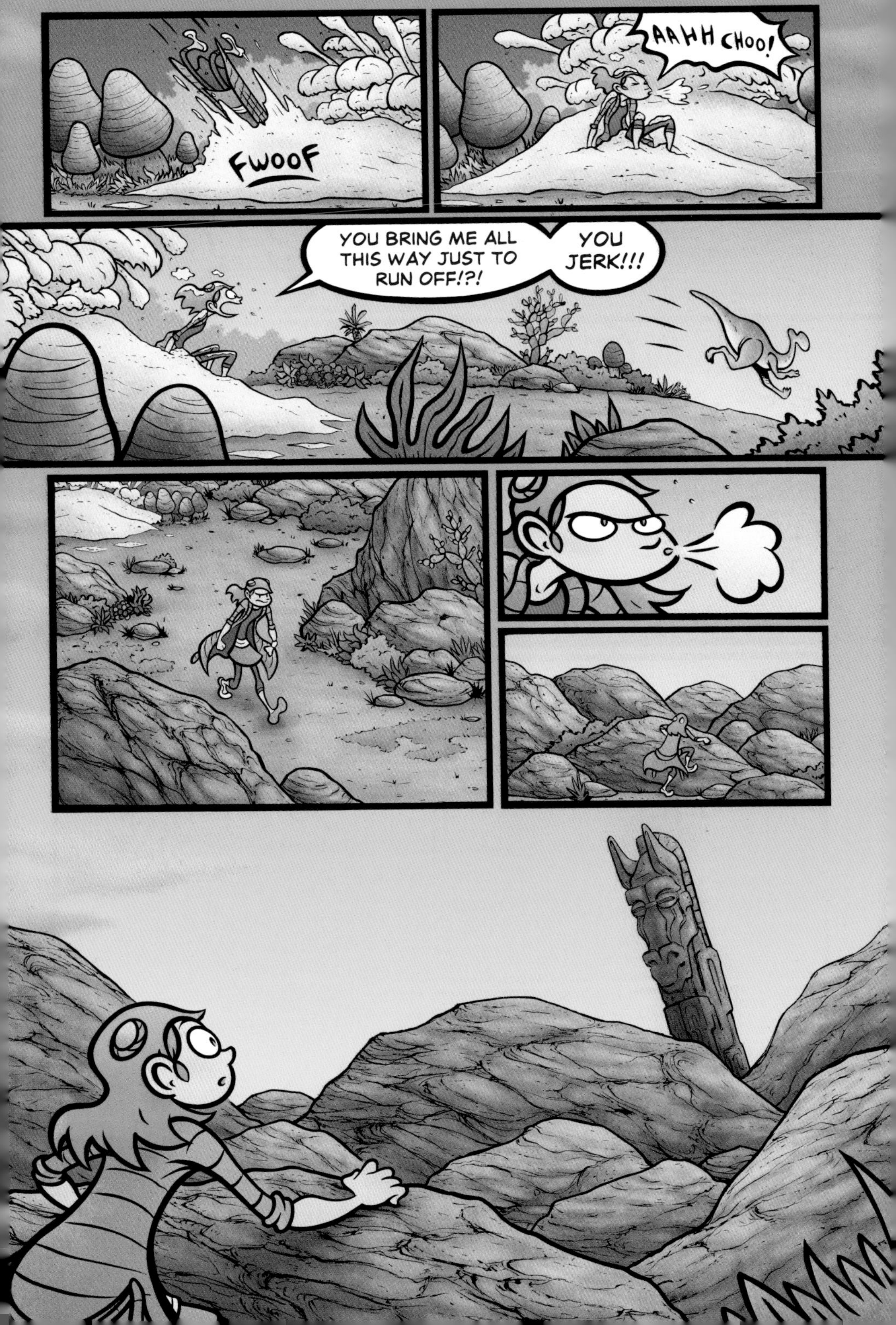
FWOOF
AAHH CHOO!
YOU BRING ME ALL THIS WAY JUST TO RUN OFF!?!
YOU JERK!!!

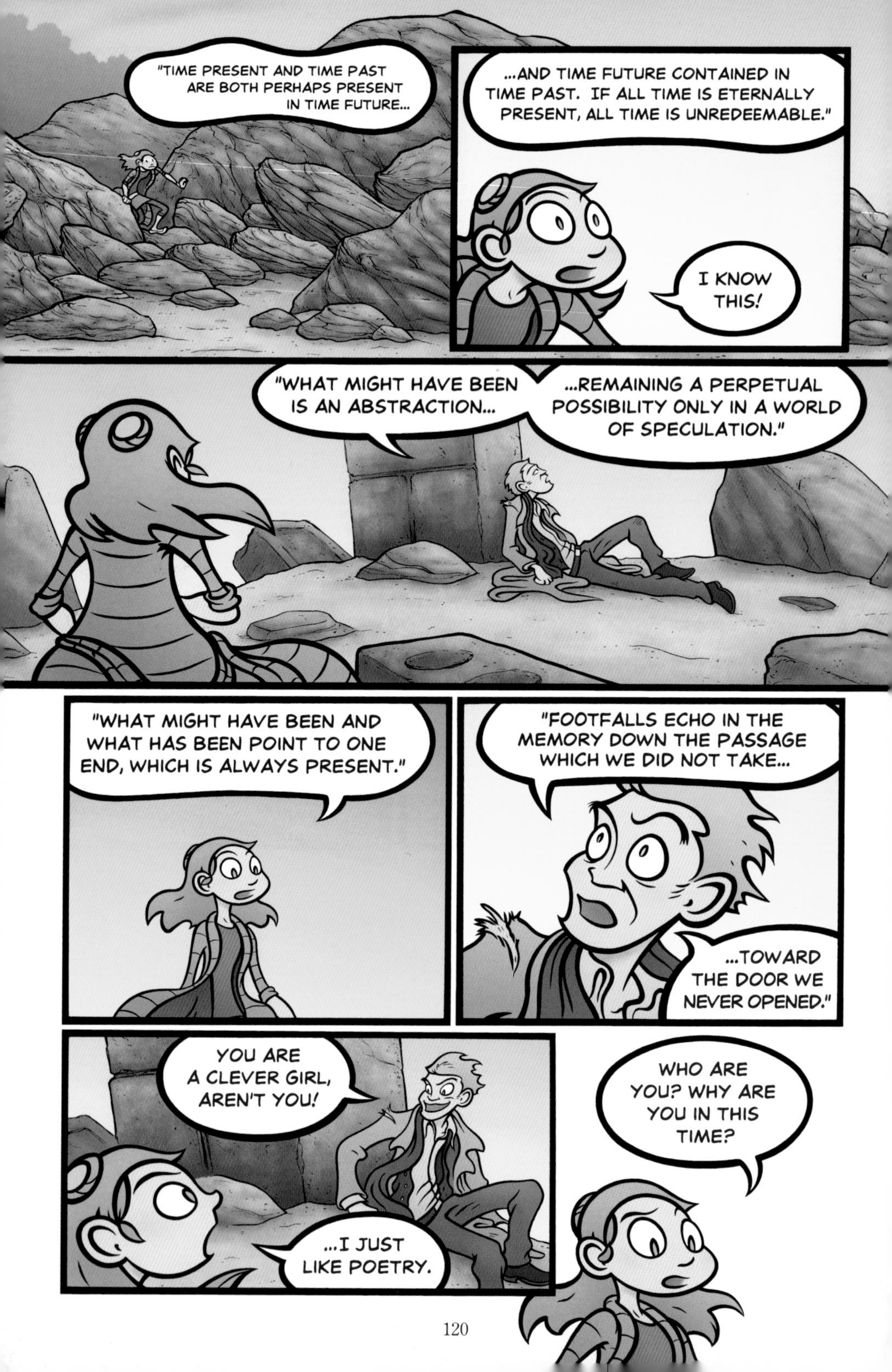
"TIME PRESENT AND TIME PAST ARE BOTH PERHAPS PRESENT IN TIME FUTURE...
...AND TIME FUTURE CONTAINED IN TIME PAST. IF ALL TIME IS ETERNALLY PRESENT, ALL TIME IS UNREDEEMABLE."
I KNOW THIS!
"WHAT MIGHT HAVE BEEN IS AN ABSTRACTION...
...REMAINING A PERPETUAL POSSIBILITY ONLY IN A WORLD OF SPECULATION."
"WHAT MIGHT HAVE BEEN AND WHAT HAS BEEN POINT TO ONE END, WHICH IS ALWAYS PRESENT."
"FOOTFALLS ECHO IN THE MEMORY DOWN THE PASSAGE WHICH WE DID NOT TAKE...
...TOWARD THE DOOR WE NEVER OPENED."
YOU ARE A CLEVER GIRL, AREN'T YOU!
...I JUST LIKE POETRY.
WHO ARE YOU? WHY ARE YOU IN THIS TIME?

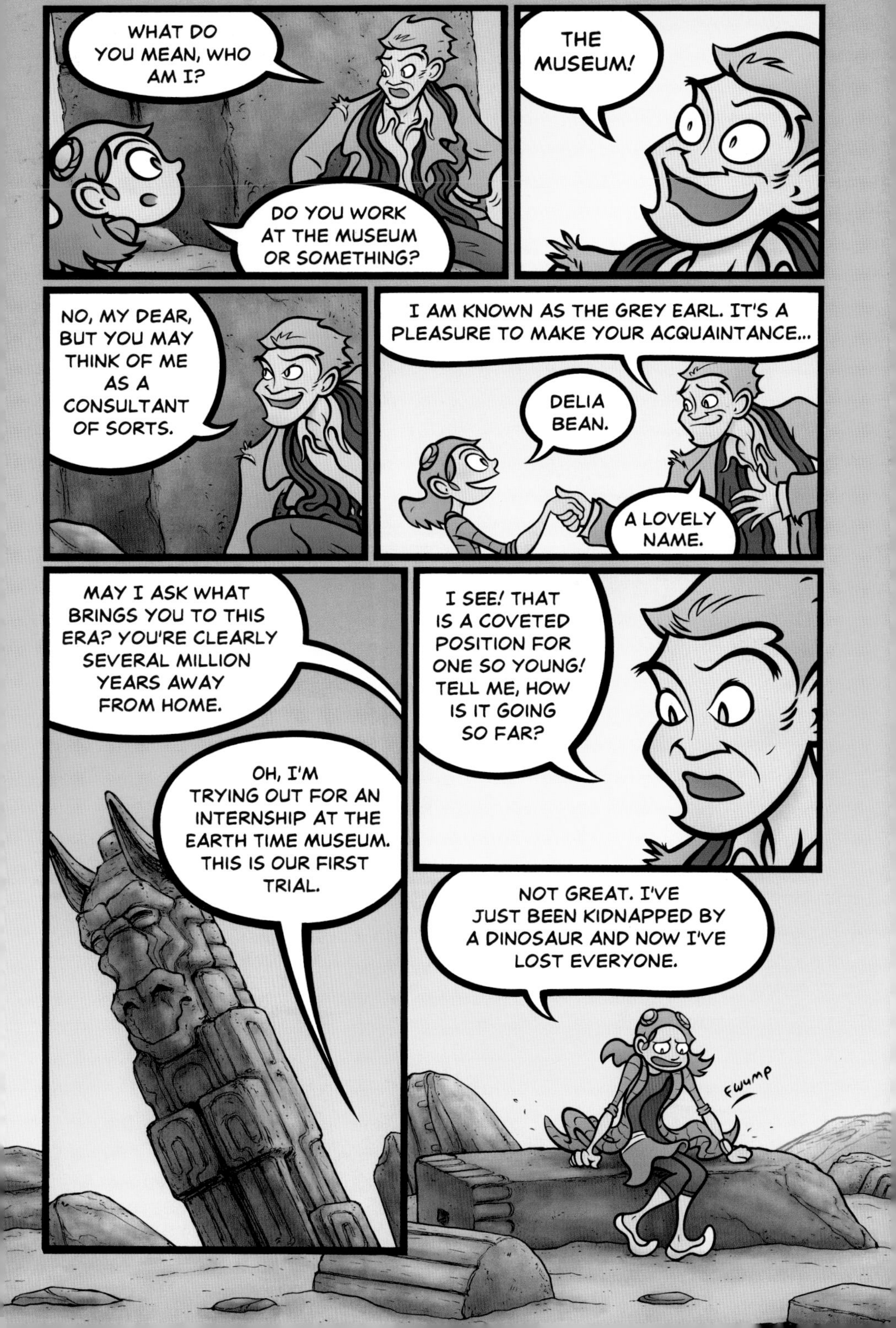
WHAT DO YOU MEAN, WHO AM I?
DO YOU WORK AT THE MUSEUM OR SOMETHING?
THE MUSEUM!
NO, MY DEAR, BUT YOU MAY THINK OF ME AS A CONSULTANT OF SORTS.
I AM KNOWN AS THE GREY EARL. IT'S A PLEASURE TO MAKE YOUR ACQUAINTANCE...
DELIA BEAN.
A LOVELY NAME.
MAY I ASK WHAT BRINGS YOU TO THIS ERA? YOU'RE CLEARLY SEVERAL MILLION YEARS AWAY FROM HOME.
OH, I'M TRYING OUT FOR AN INTERNSHIP AT THE EARTH TIME MUSEUM. THIS IS OUR FIRST TRIAL.
I SEE! THAT IS A COVETED POSITION FOR ONE SO YOUNG! TELL ME, HOW IS IT GOING SO FAR?
NOT GREAT. I'VE JUST BEEN KIDNAPPED BY A DINOSAUR AND NOW I'VE LOST EVERYONE.
FWUMP

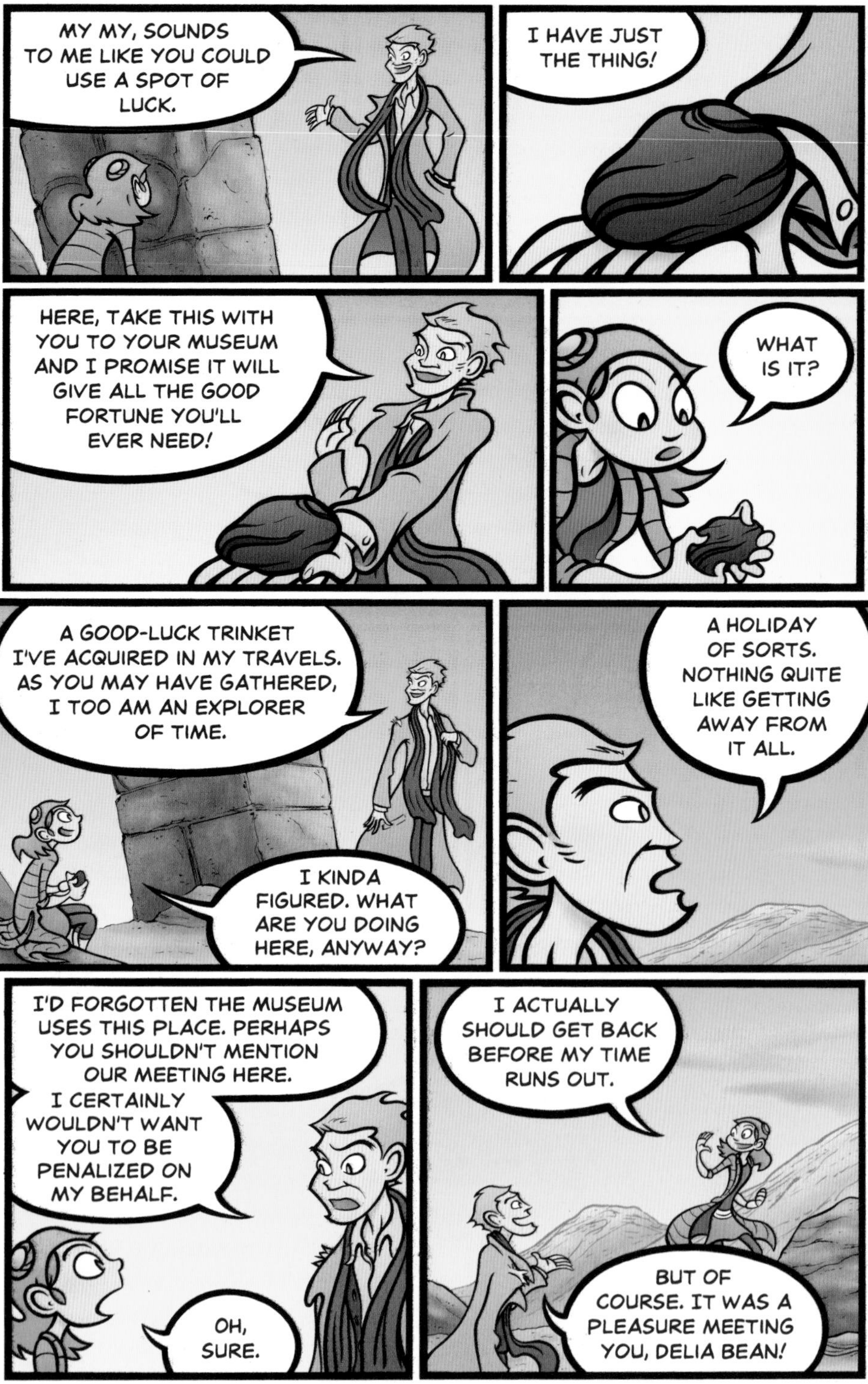
MY MY, SOUNDS TO ME LIKE YOU COULD USE A SPOT OF LUCK.
I HAVE JUST THE THING!
HERE, TAKE THIS WITH YOU TO YOUR MUSEUM AND I PROMISE IT WILL GIVE ALL THE GOOD FORTUNE YOU'LL EVER NEED!
WHAT IS IT?
A GOOD-LUCK TRINKET I'VE ACQUIRED IN MY TRAVELS. AS YOU MAY HAVE GATHERED, I TOO AM AN EXPLORER OF TIME.
I KINDA FIGURED. WHAT ARE YOU DOING HERE, ANYWAY?
A HOLIDAY OF SORTS. NOTHING QUITE LIKE GETTING AWAY FROM IT ALL.
I'D FORGOTTEN THE MUSEUM USES THIS PLACE. PERHAPS YOU SHOULDN'T MENTION OUR MEETING HERE.
I CERTAINLY WOULDN'T WANT YOU TO BE PENALIZED ON MY BEHALF.
OH, SURE.
I ACTUALLY SHOULD GET BACK BEFORE MY TIME RUNS OUT.
BUT OF COURSE. IT WAS A PLEASURE MEETING YOU, DELIA BEAN!

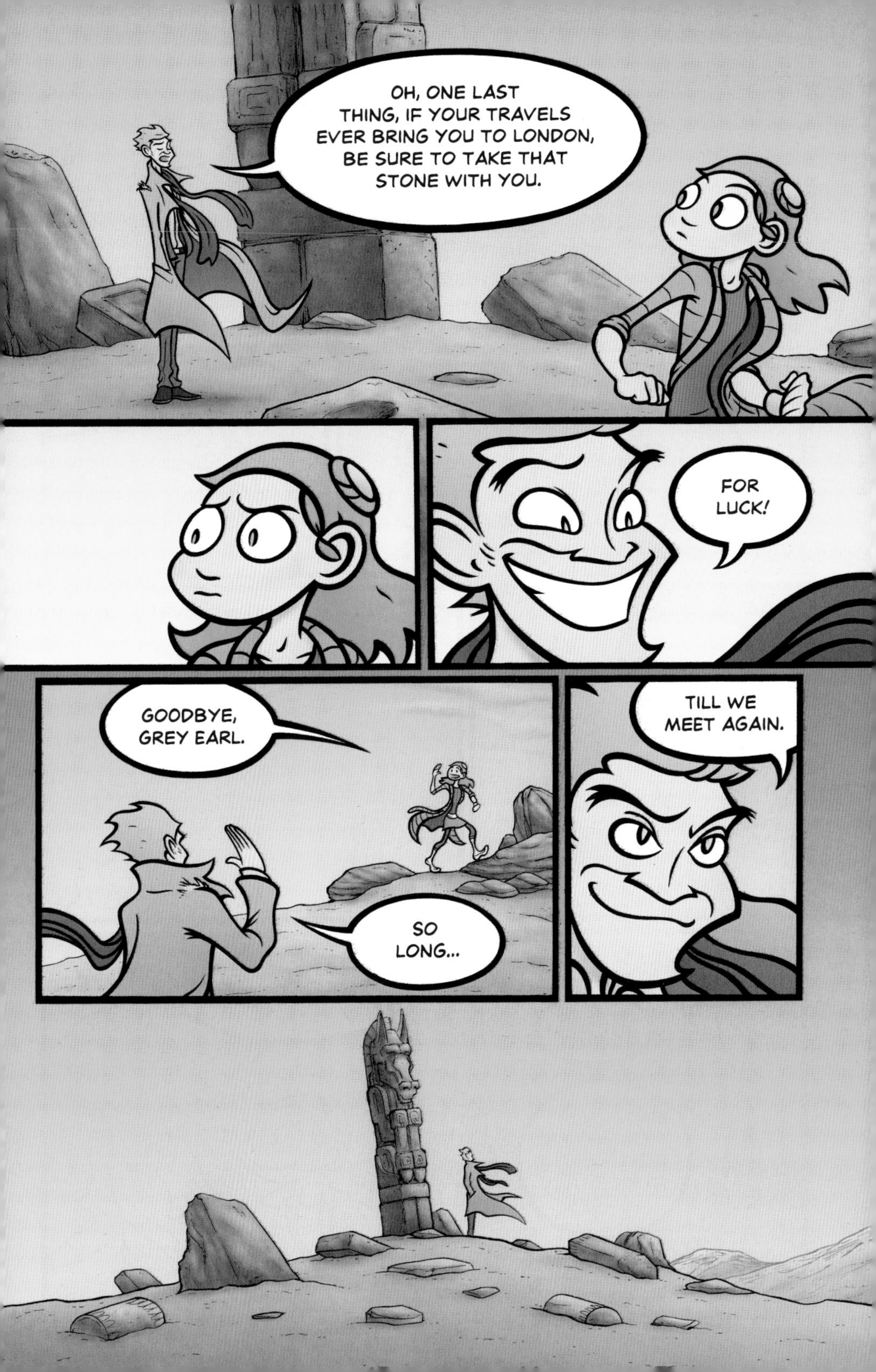
OH, ONE LAST THING, IF YOUR TRAVELS EVER BRING YOU TO LONDON, BE SURE TO TAKE THAT STONE WITH YOU.
FOR LUCK!
GOODBYE, GREY EARL.
SO LONG...
TILL WE MEET AGAIN.

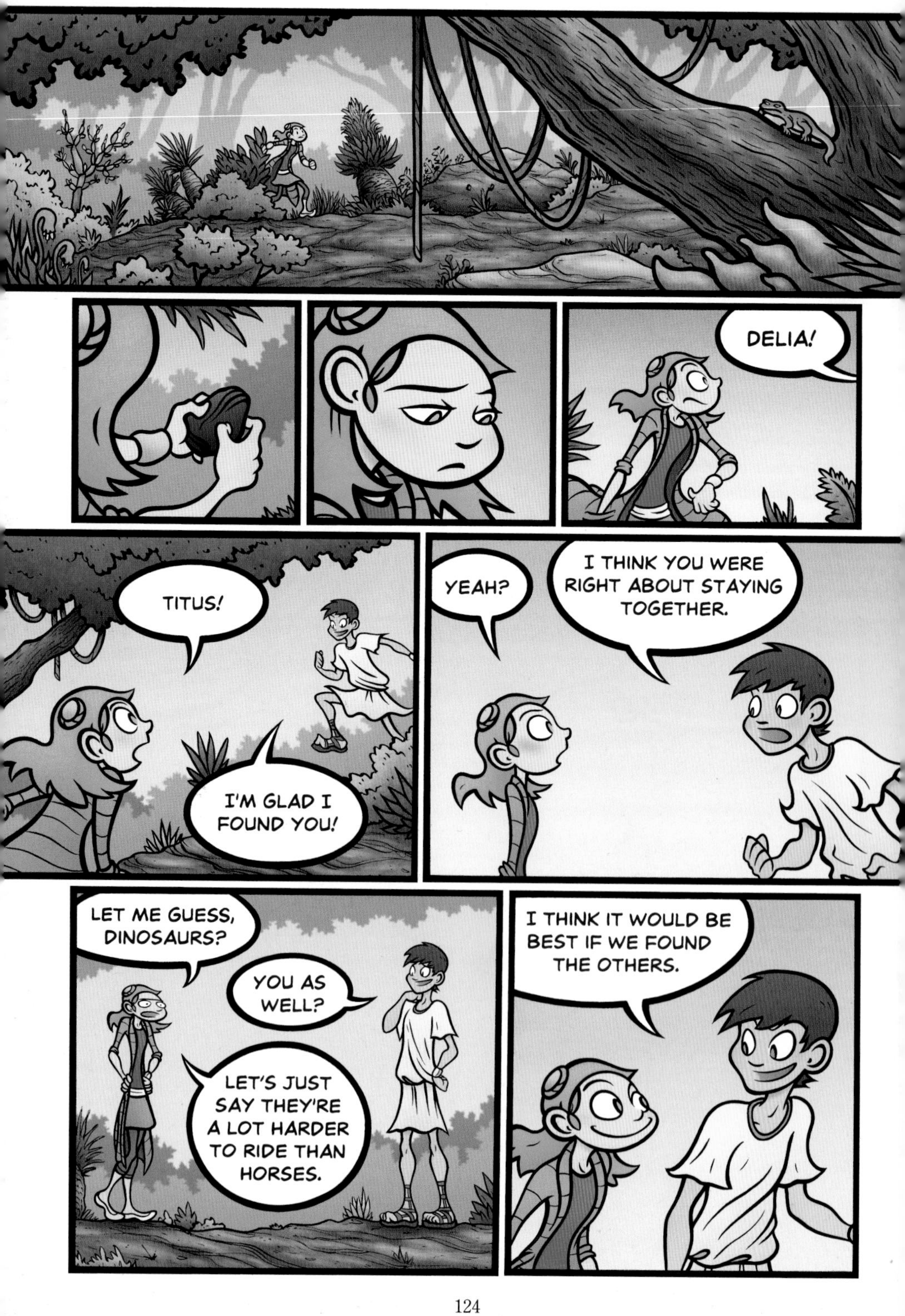
DELIA!
TITUS!
I'M GLAD I FOUND YOU!
YEAH?
I THINK YOU WERE RIGHT ABOUT STAYING TOGETHER.
LET ME GUESS, DINOSAURS?
YOU AS WELL?
LET'S JUST SAY THEY'RE A LOT HARDER TO RIDE THAN HORSES.
I THINK IT WOULD BE BEST IF WE FOUND THE OTHERS.

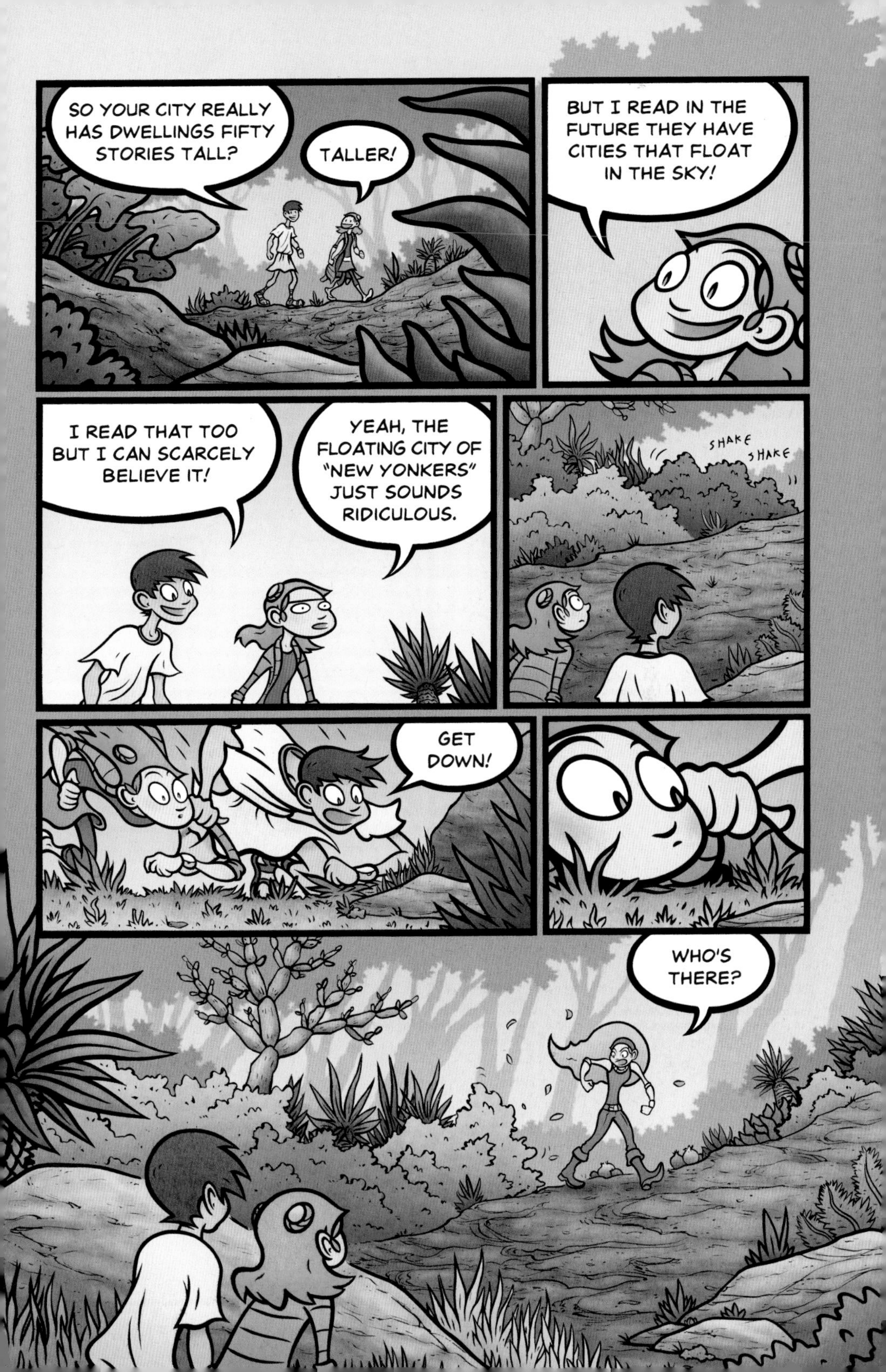
SO YOUR CITY REALLY HAS DWELLINGS FIFTY STORIES TALL?
TALLER!
BUT I READ IN THE FUTURE THEY HAVE CITIES THAT FLOAT IN THE SKY!
I READ THAT TOO BUT I CAN SCARCELY BELIEVE IT!
YEAH, THE FLOATING CITY OF "NEW YONKERS" JUST SOUNDS RIDICULOUS.
SHAKE
SHAKE
GET DOWN!
WHO'S THERE?

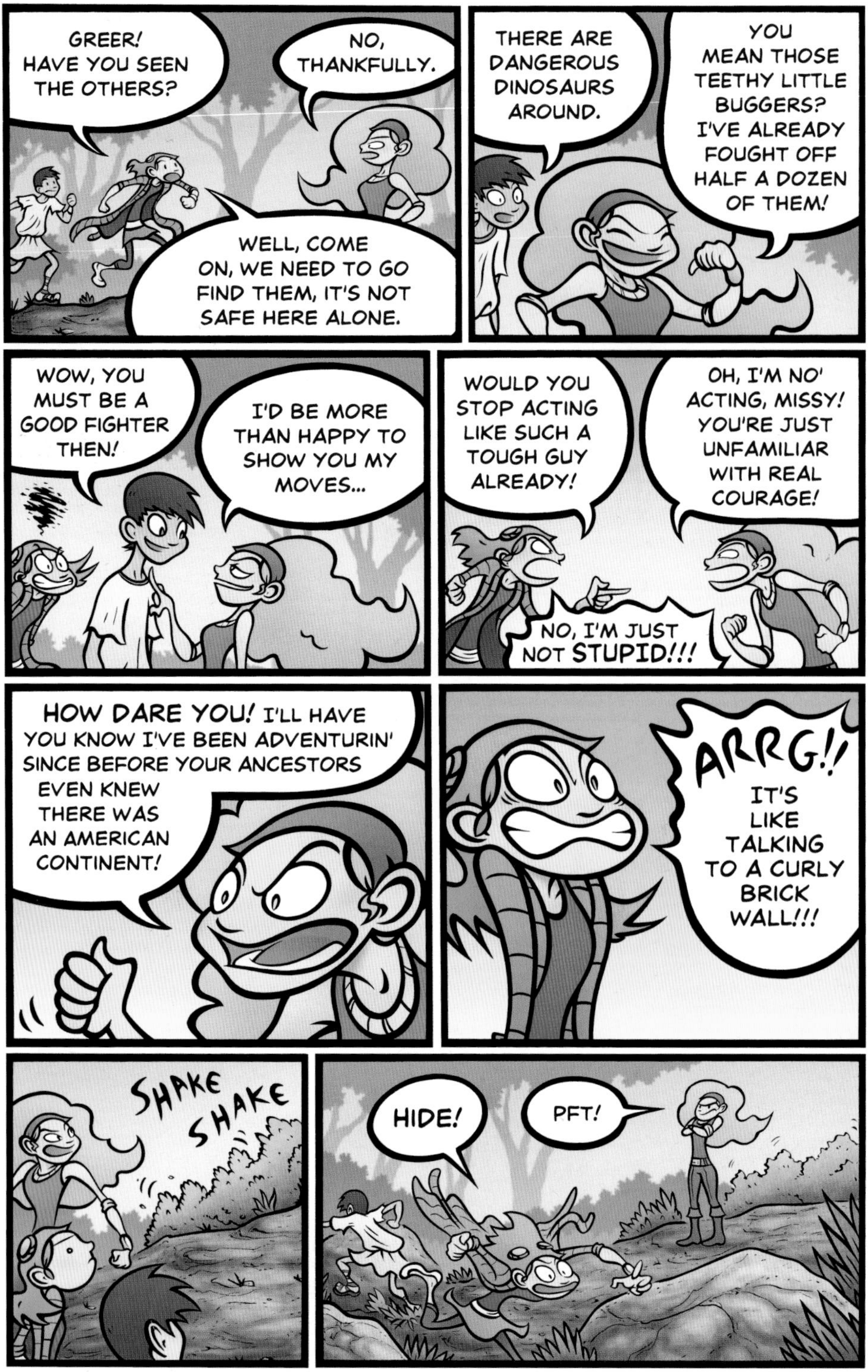
GREER! HAVE YOU SEEN THE OTHERS?
NO, THANKFULLY.
WELL, COME ON, WE NEED TO GO FIND THEM, IT'S NOT SAFE HERE ALONE.
THERE ARE DANGEROUS DINOSAURS AROUND.
YOU MEAN THOSE TEETHY LITTLE BUGGERS? I'VE ALREADY FOUGHT OFF HALF A DOZEN OF THEM!
WOW, YOU MUST BE A GOOD FIGHTER THEN!
I'D BE MORE THAN HAPPY TO SHOW YOU MY MOVES...
WOULD YOU STOP ACTING LIKE SUCH A TOUGH GUY ALREADY!
OH, I'M NO' ACTING, MISSY! YOU'RE JUST UNFAMILIAR WITH REAL COURAGE!
NO, I'M JUST NOT STUPID!!!
HOW DARE YOU! I'LL HAVE YOU KNOW I'VE BEEN ADVENTURIN' SINCE BEFORE YOUR ANCESTORS EVEN KNEW THERE WAS AN AMERICAN CONTINENT!
ARRG!! IT'S LIKE TALKING TO A CURLY BRICK WALL!!!
SHAKE SHAKE
HIDE!
PFT!

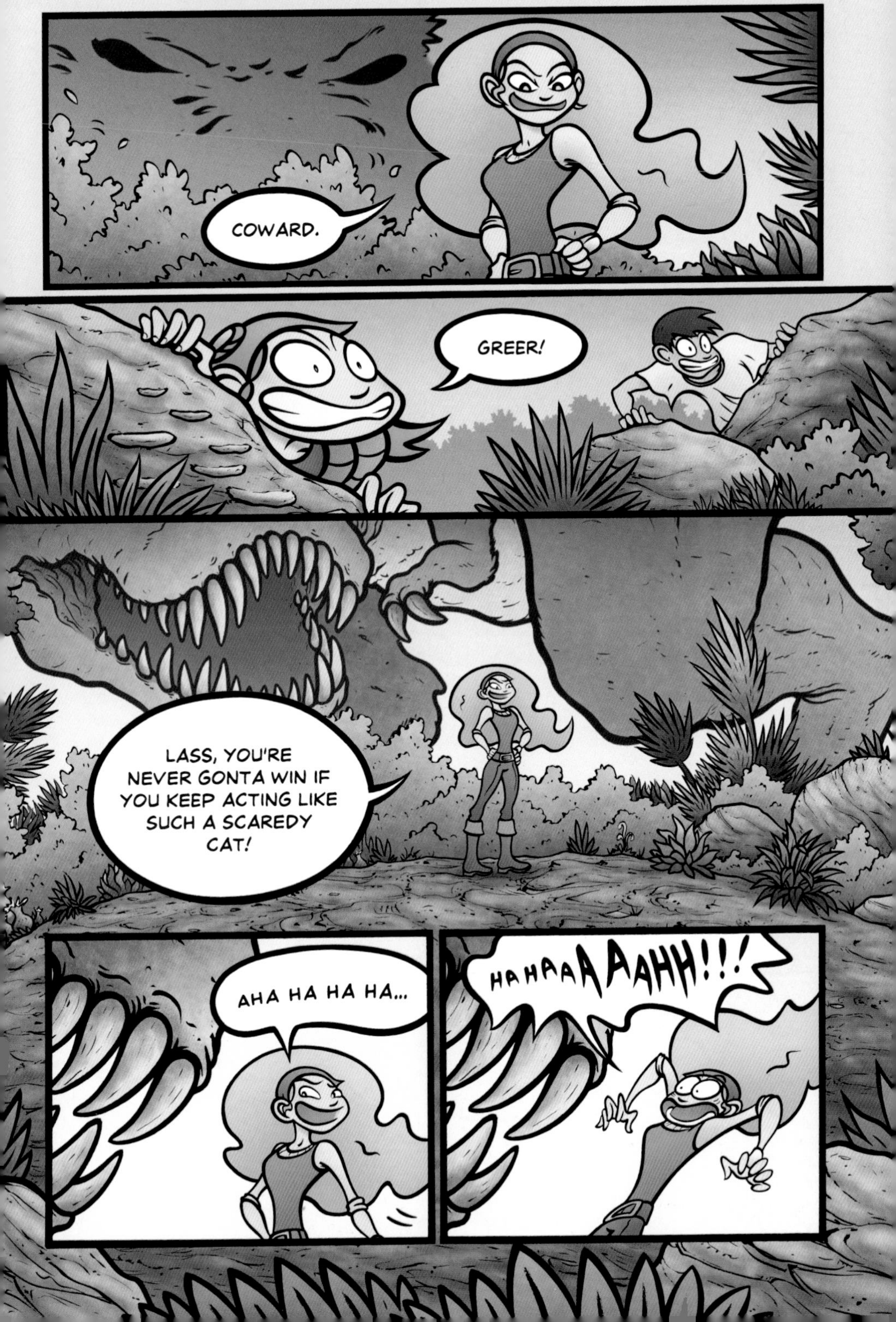
COWARD.
GREER!
LASS, YOU'RE NEVER GONTA WIN IF YOU KEEP ACTING LIKE SUCH A SCAREDY CAT!
AHA HA HA HA...
HA HAAAAAAHH!!!

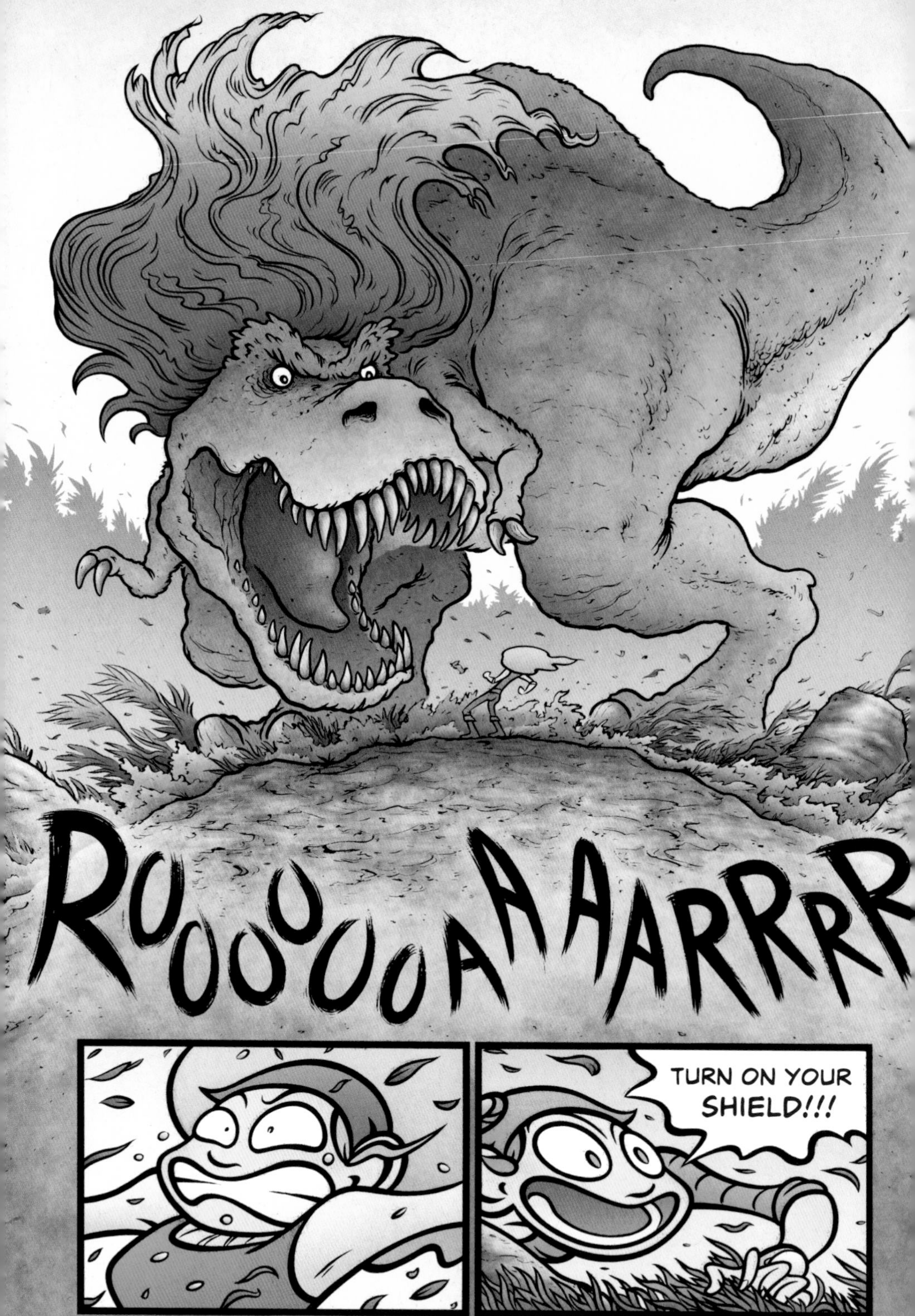
ROOOOOOOAAAARRRR
TURN ON YOUR SHIELD!!!

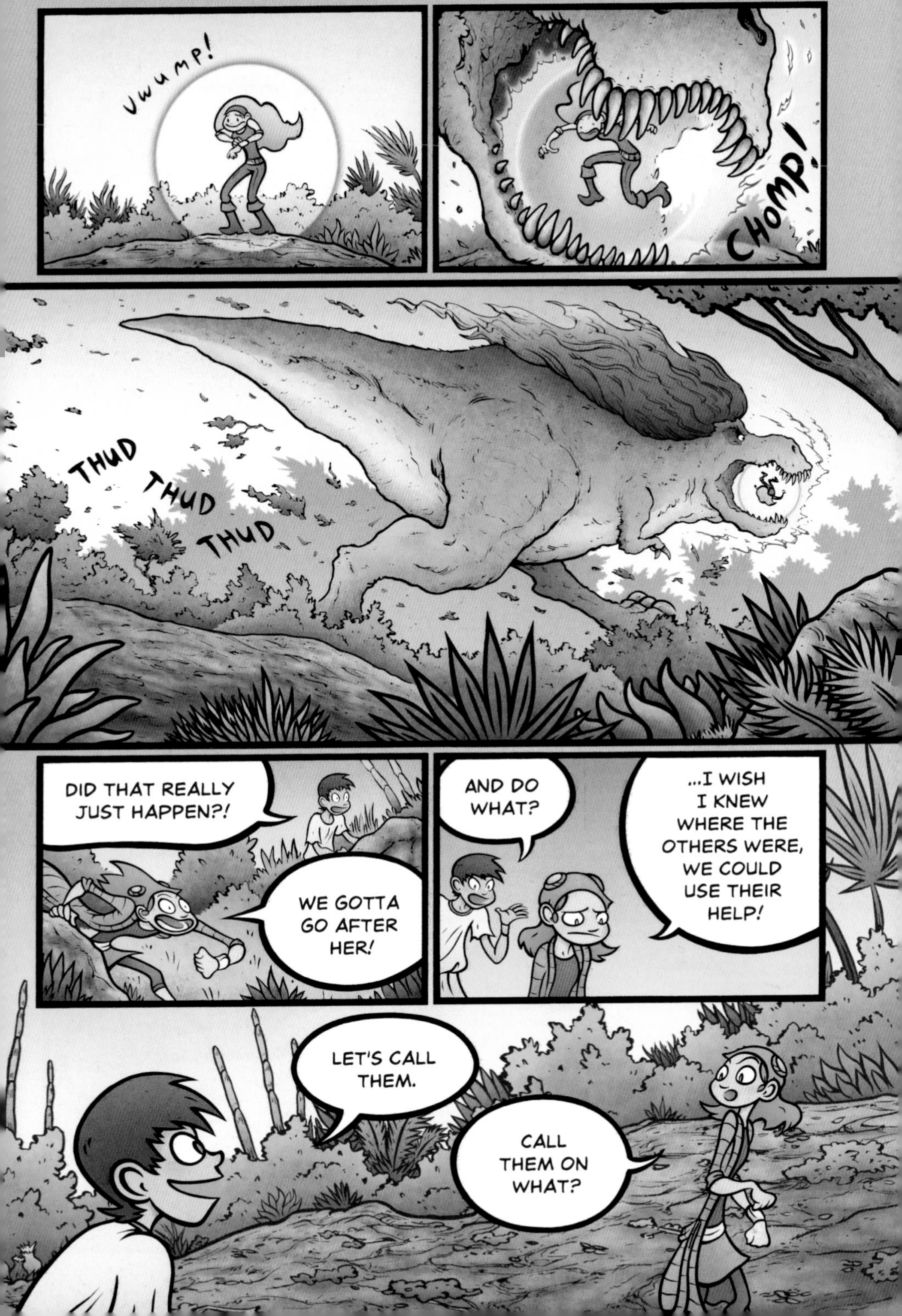
UWUMP!
CHOMP!
THUD
THUD
THUD
DID THAT REALLY JUST HAPPEN?!
WE GOTTA GO AFTER HER!
AND DO WHAT?
...I WISH I KNEW WHERE THE OTHERS WERE, WE COULD USE THEIR HELP!
LET'S CALL THEM.
CALL THEM ON WHAT?

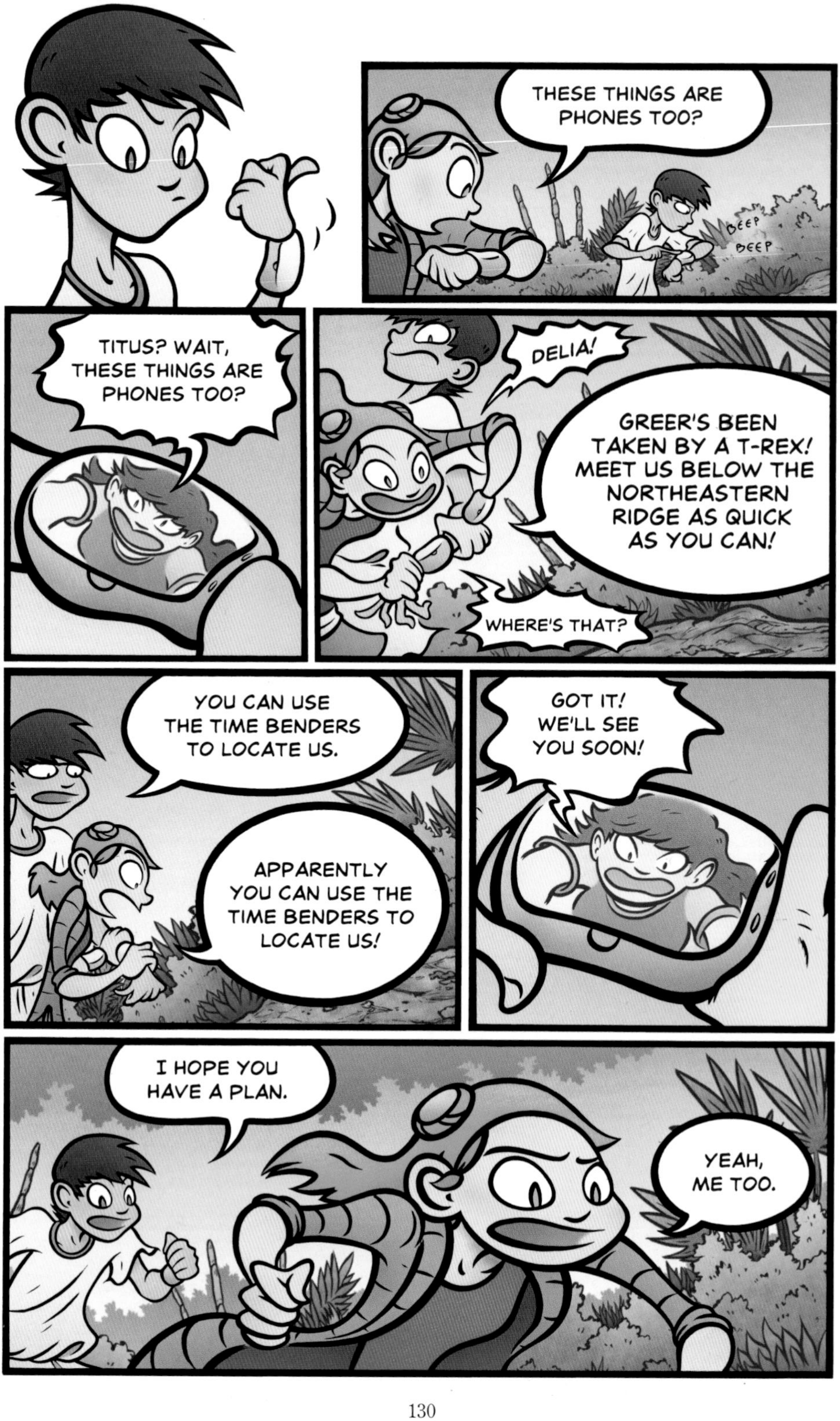
THESE THINGS ARE PHONES TOO?
BEEP
BEEP
TITUS? WAIT, THESE THINGS ARE PHONES TOO?
DELIA!
GREER'S BEEN TAKEN BY A T-REX! MEET US BELOW THE NORTHEASTERN RIDGE AS QUICK AS YOU CAN!
WHERE'S THAT?
YOU CAN USE THE TIME BENDERS TO LOCATE US.
APPARENTLY YOU CAN USE THE TIME BENDERS TO LOCATE US!
GOT IT! WE'LL SEE YOU SOON!
I HOPE YOU HAVE A PLAN.
YEAH, ME TOO.

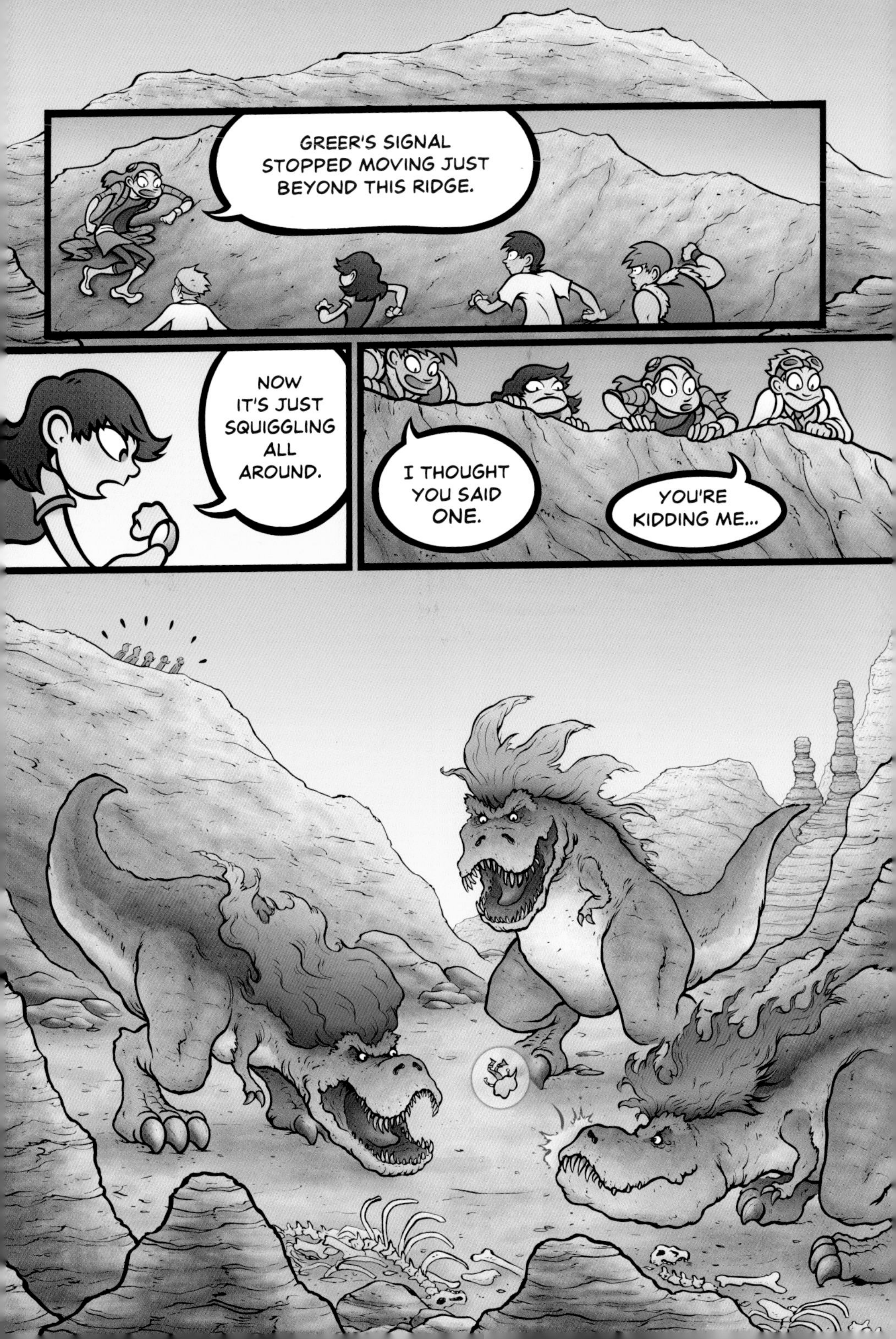
GREER'S SIGNAL STOPPED MOVING JUST BEYOND THIS RIDGE.
NOW IT'S JUST SQUIGGLING ALL AROUND.
I THOUGHT YOU SAID ONE.
YOU'RE KIDDING ME...

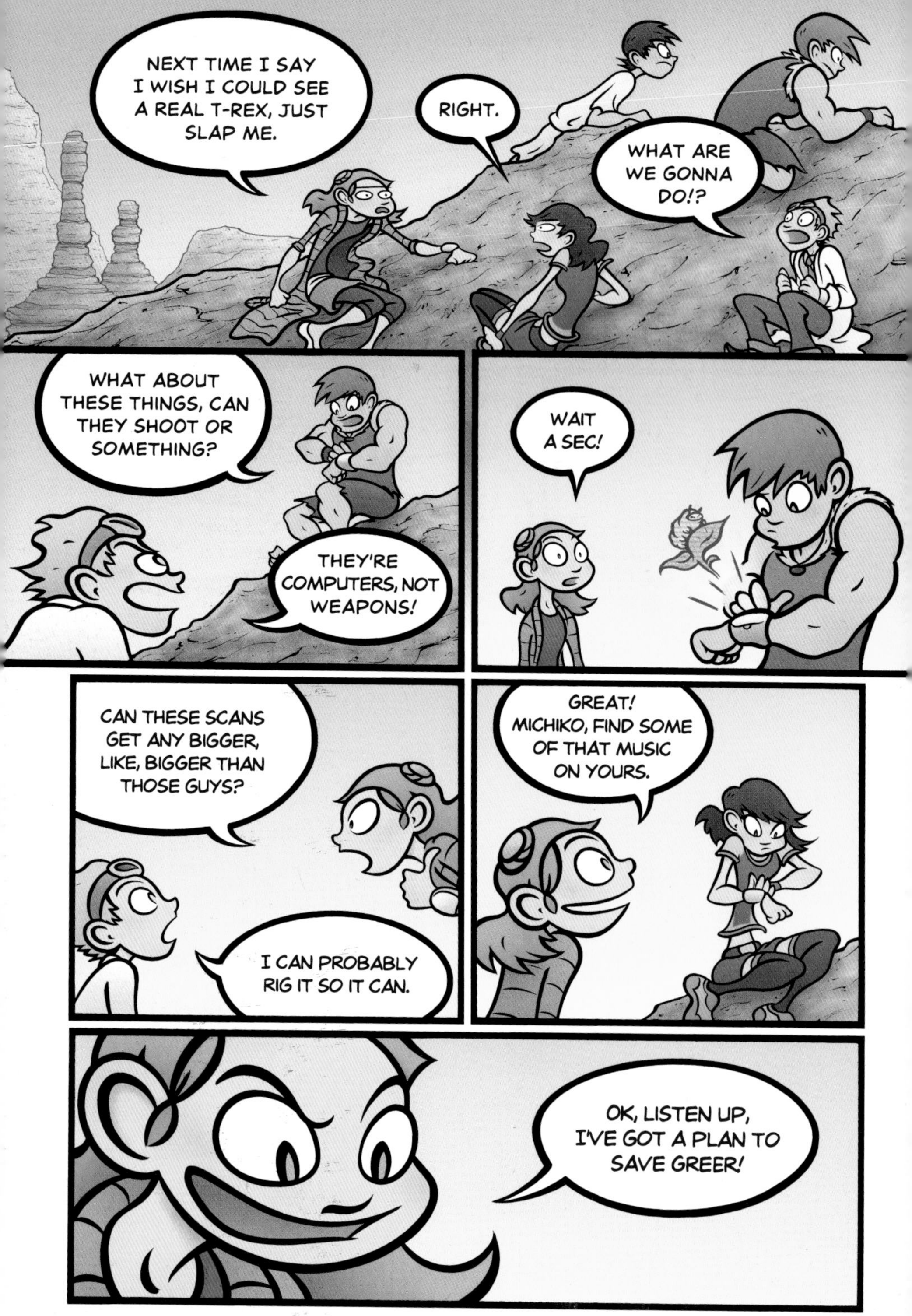
NEXT TIME I SAY I WISH I COULD SEE A REAL T-REX, JUST SLAP ME.
RIGHT.
WHAT ARE WE GONNA DO!?
WHAT ABOUT THESE THINGS, CAN THEY SHOOT OR SOMETHING?
THEY'RE COMPUTERS, NOT WEAPONS!
WAIT A SEC!
CAN THESE SCANS GET ANY BIGGER, LIKE, BIGGER THAN THOSE GUYS?
I CAN PROBABLY RIG IT SO IT CAN.
GREAT! MICHIKO, FIND SOME OF THAT MUSIC ON YOURS.
OK, LISTEN UP, I'VE GOT A PLAN TO SAVE GREER!

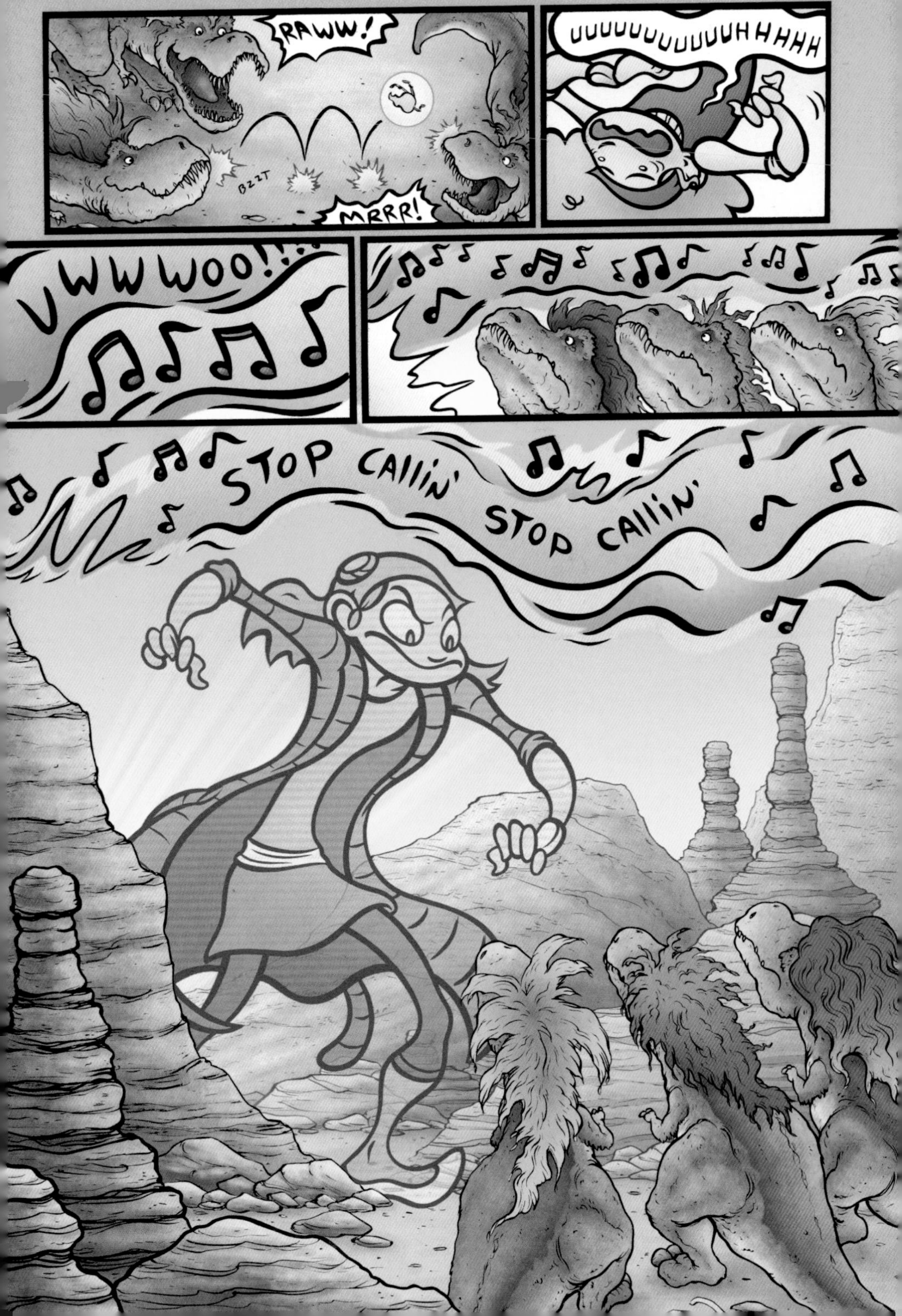
RAWW!
BZZT
MRRR!
UUUUUUUUUUUUHHHHH
VWWWOO!!!
STOP CALLIN'
STOP CALLIN'

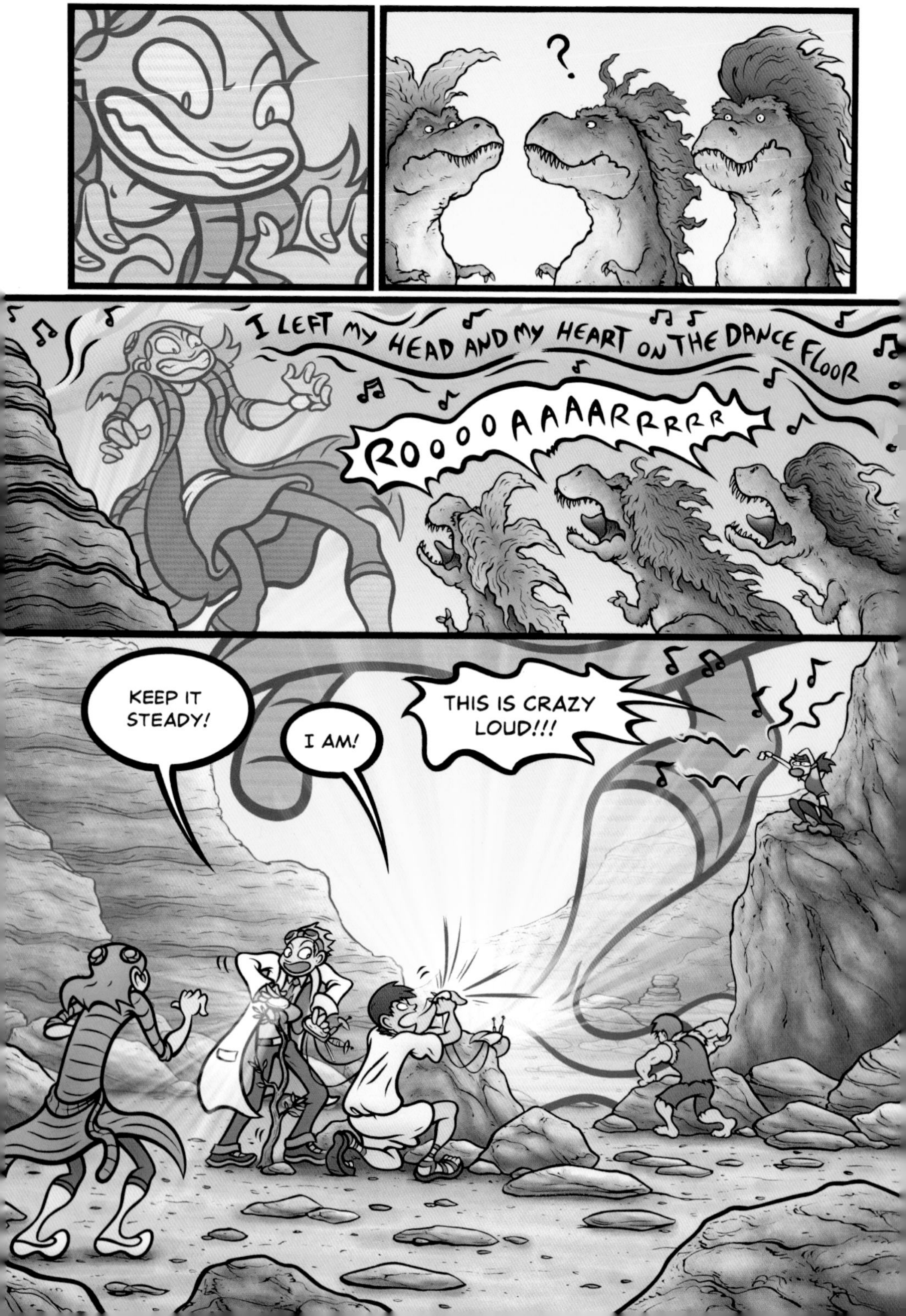
?
I LEFT MY HEAD AND MY HEART ON THE DANCE FLOOR
ROOOOAAAARRRRR
KEEP IT STEADY!
I AM!
THIS IS CRAZY LOUD!!!

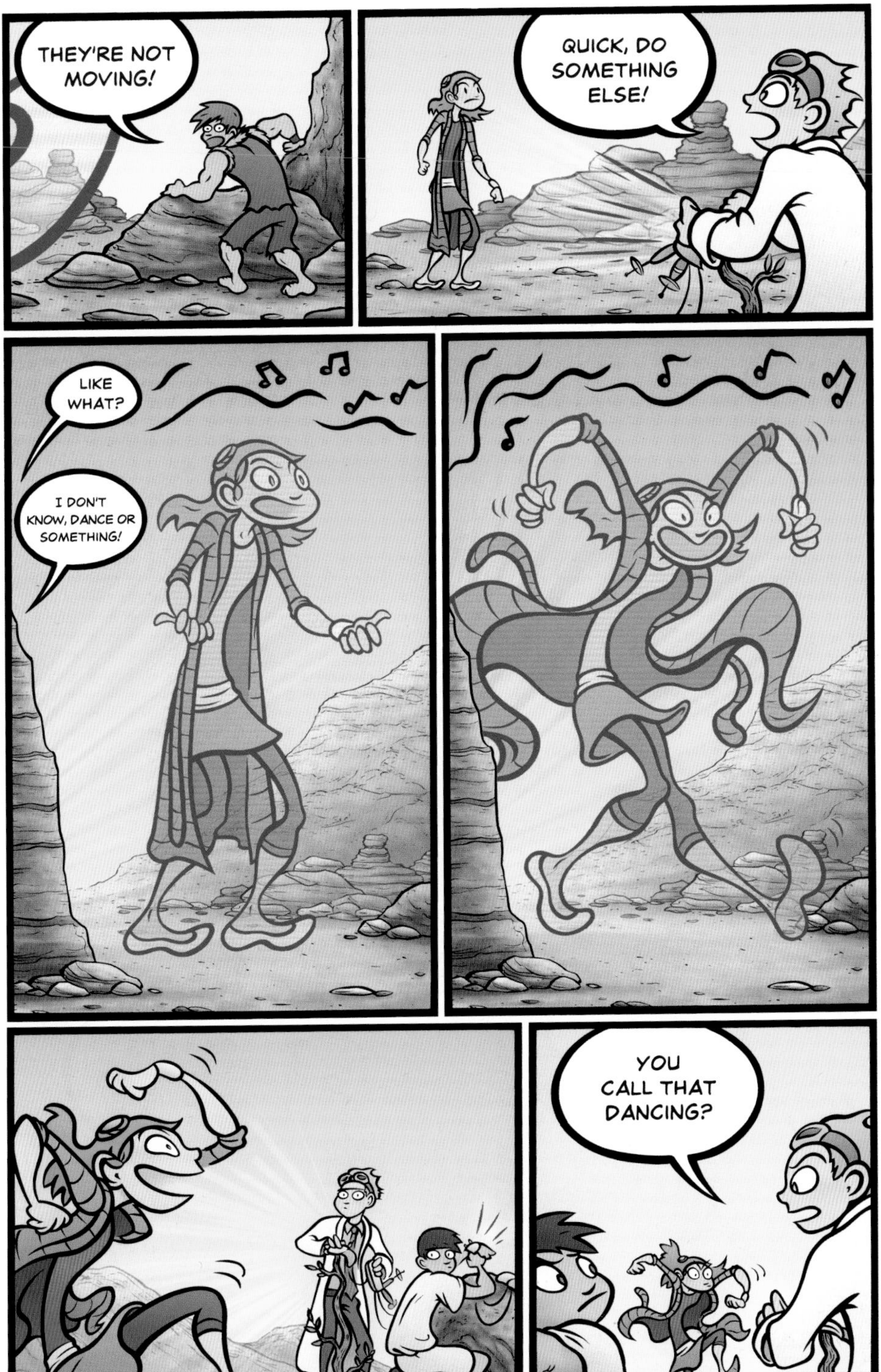
THEY'RE NOT MOVING!
QUICK, DO SOMETHING ELSE!
LIKE WHAT?
I DON'T KNOW, DANCE OR SOMETHING!
YOU CALL THAT DANCING?

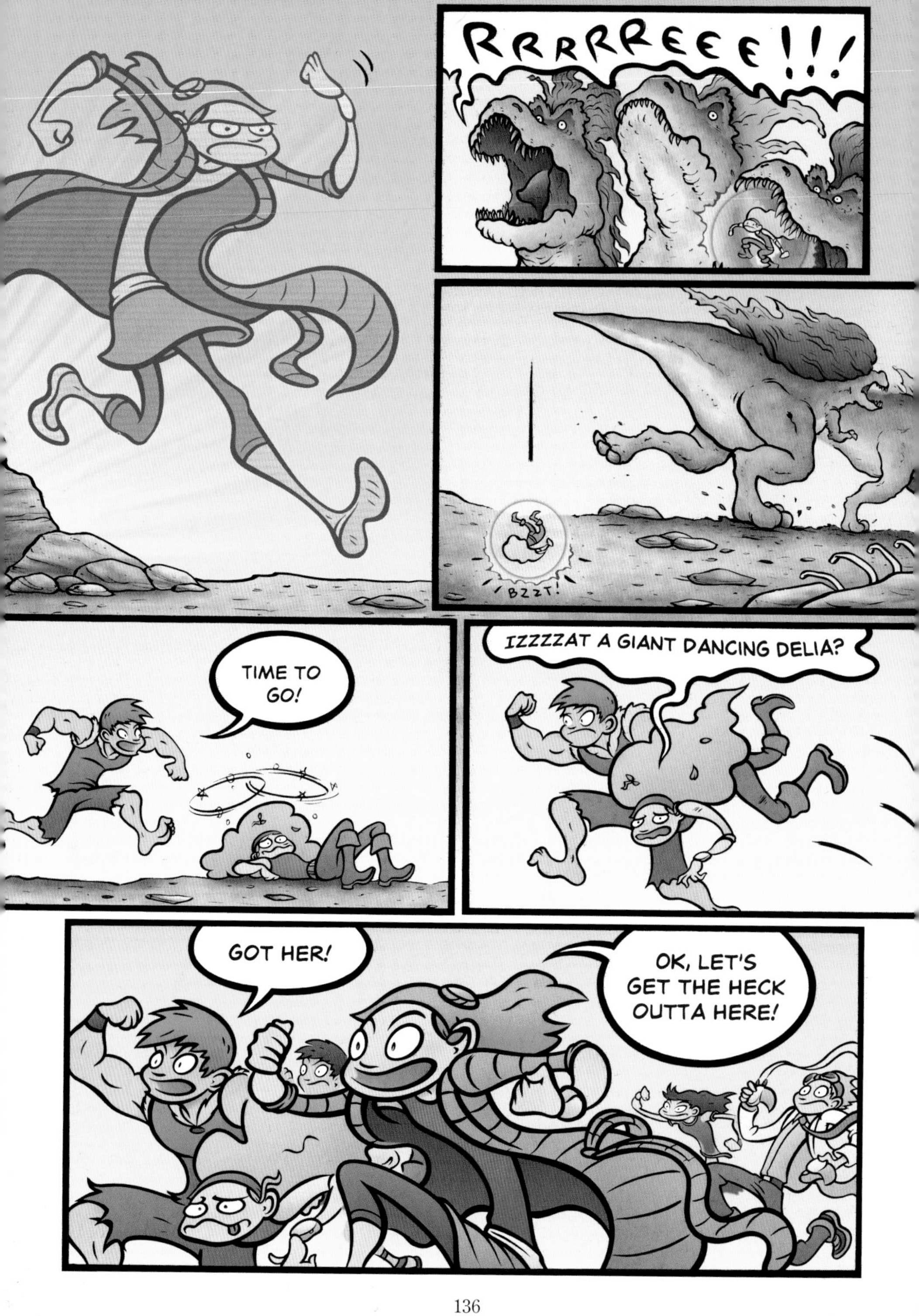
RRRRREEEE!!!
BZZT!
TIME TO GO!
IZZZZAT A GIANT DANCING DELIA?
GOT HER!
OK, LET'S GET THE HECK OUTTA HERE!

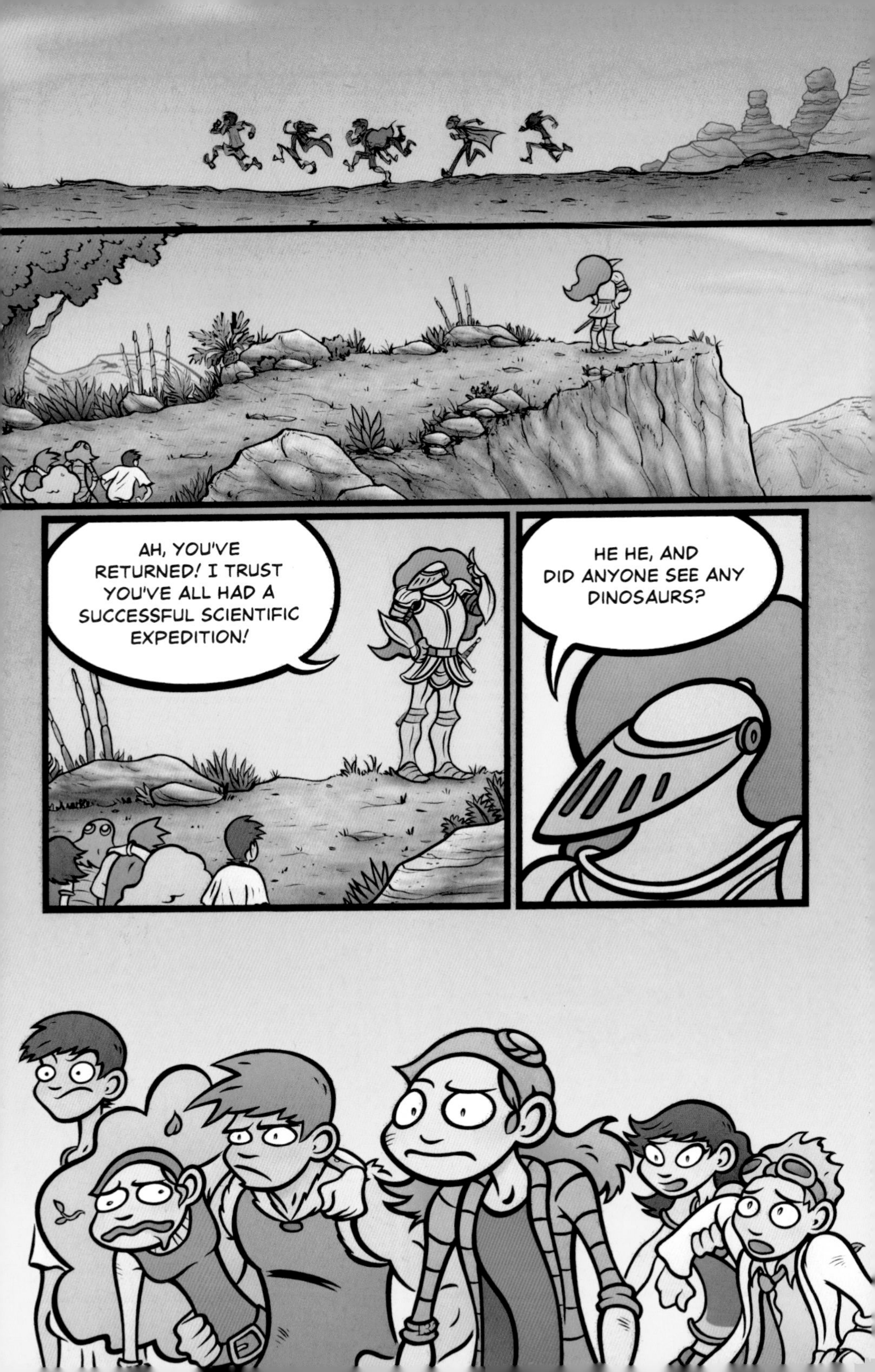
AH, YOU'VE RETURNED! I TRUST YOU'VE ALL HAD A SUCCESSFUL SCIENTIFIC EXPEDITION!
HE HE, AND DID ANYONE SEE ANY DINOSAURS?

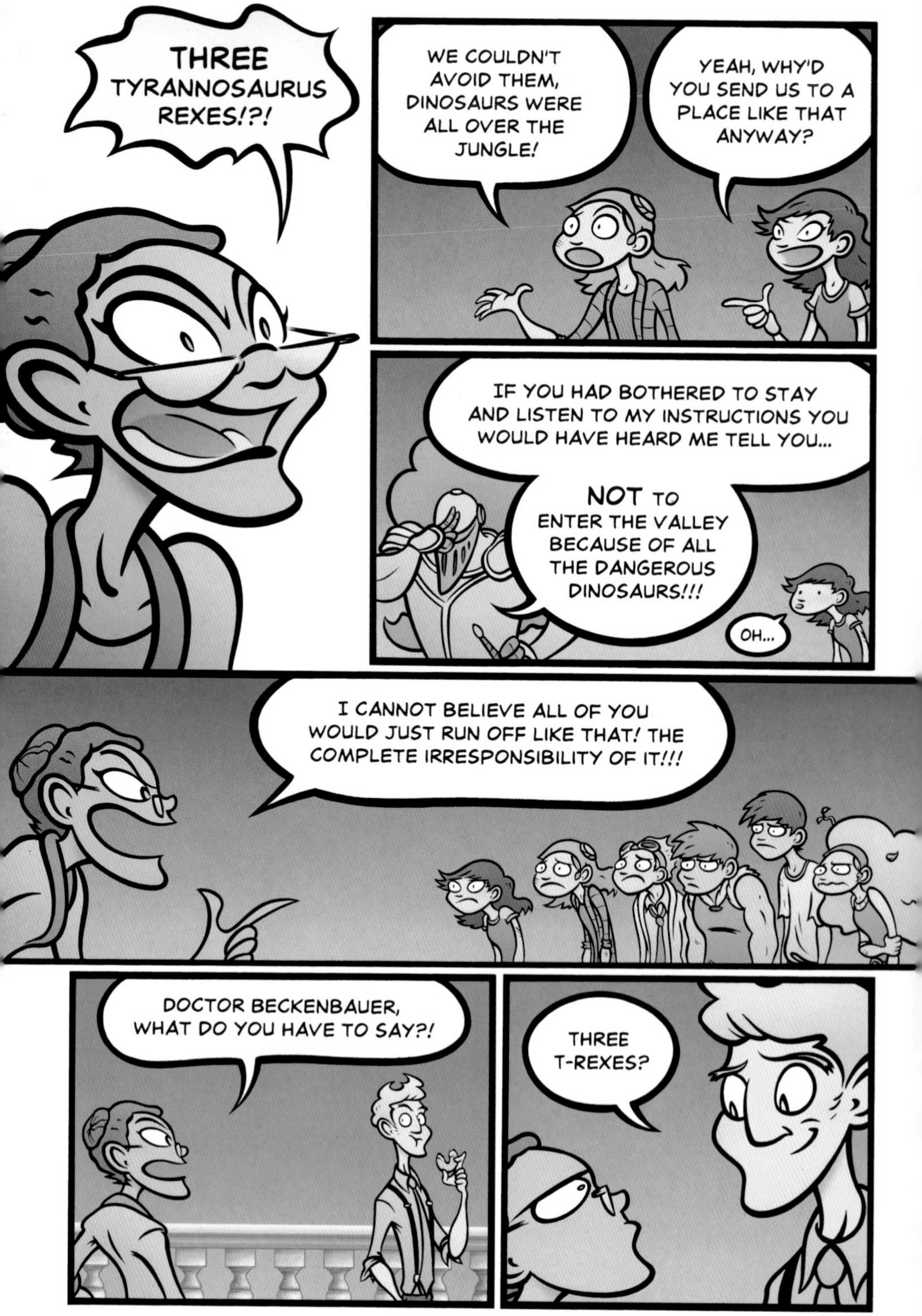
THREE TYRANNOSAURUS REXES!?!
WE COULDN'T AVOID THEM, DINOSAURS WERE ALL OVER THE JUNGLE!
YEAH, WHY'D YOU SEND US TO A PLACE LIKE THAT ANYWAY?
IF YOU HAD BOTHERED TO STAY AND LISTEN TO MY INSTRUCTIONS YOU WOULD HAVE HEARD ME TELL YOU...
NOT TO ENTER THE VALLEY BECAUSE OF ALL THE DANGEROUS DINOSAURS!!!
OH...
I CANNOT BELIEVE ALL OF YOU WOULD JUST RUN OFF LIKE THAT! THE COMPLETE IRRESPONSIBILITY OF IT!!!
DOCTOR BECKENBAUER, WHAT DO YOU HAVE TO SAY?!
THREE T-REXES?

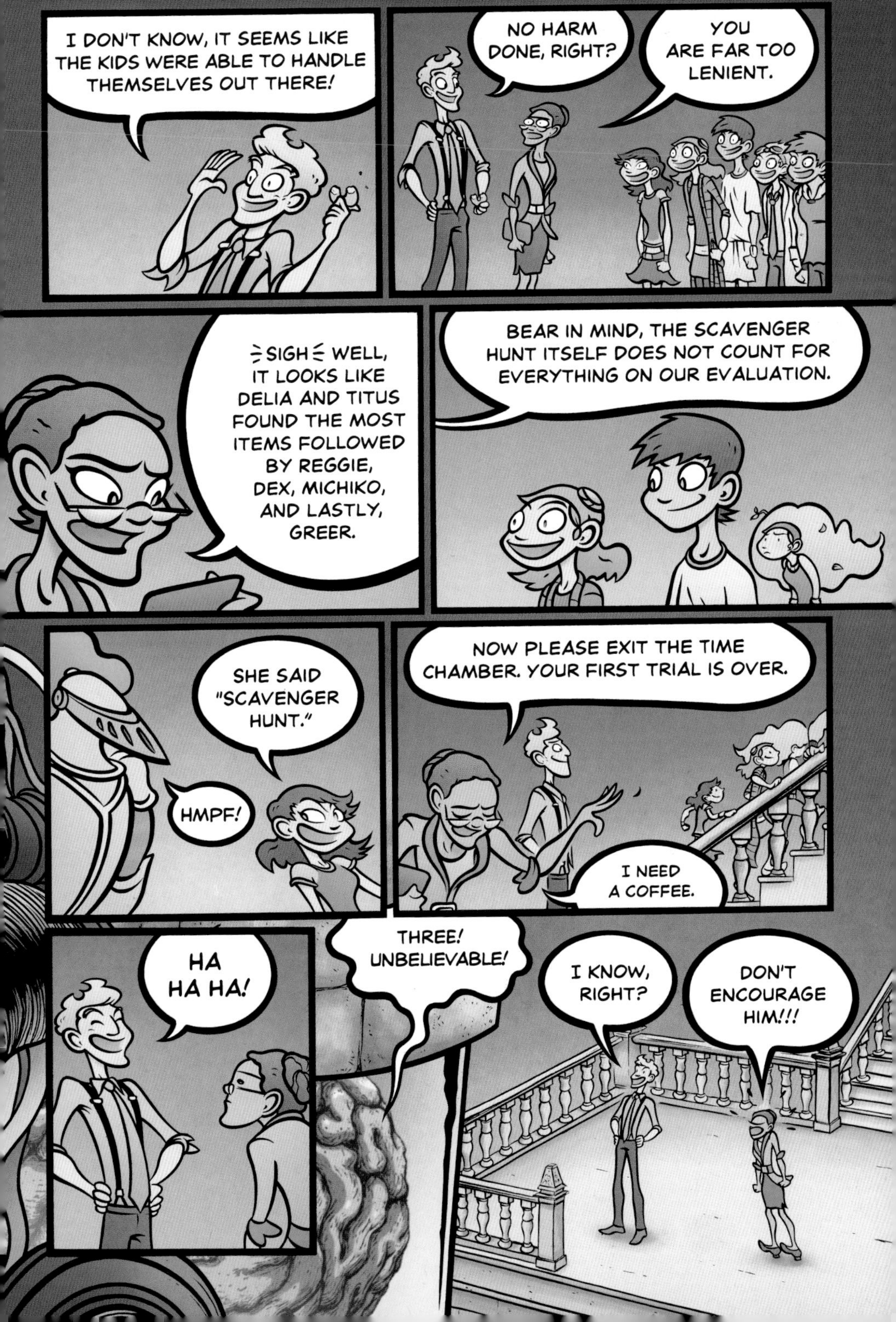
I DON'T KNOW, IT SEEMS LIKE THE KIDS WERE ABLE TO HANDLE THEMSELVES OUT THERE!
NO HARM DONE, RIGHT?
YOU ARE FAR TOO LENIENT.
⋛SIGH⋚ WELL, IT LOOKS LIKE DELIA AND TITUS FOUND THE MOST ITEMS FOLLOWED BY REGGIE, DEX, MICHIKO, AND LASTLY, GREER.
BEAR IN MIND, THE SCAVENGER HUNT ITSELF DOES NOT COUNT FOR EVERYTHING ON OUR EVALUATION.
SHE SAID "SCAVENGER HUNT."
HMPF!
NOW PLEASE EXIT THE TIME CHAMBER. YOUR FIRST TRIAL IS OVER.
I NEED A COFFEE.
HA HA HA!
THREE! UNBELIEVABLE!
I KNOW, RIGHT?
DON'T ENCOURAGE HIM!!!

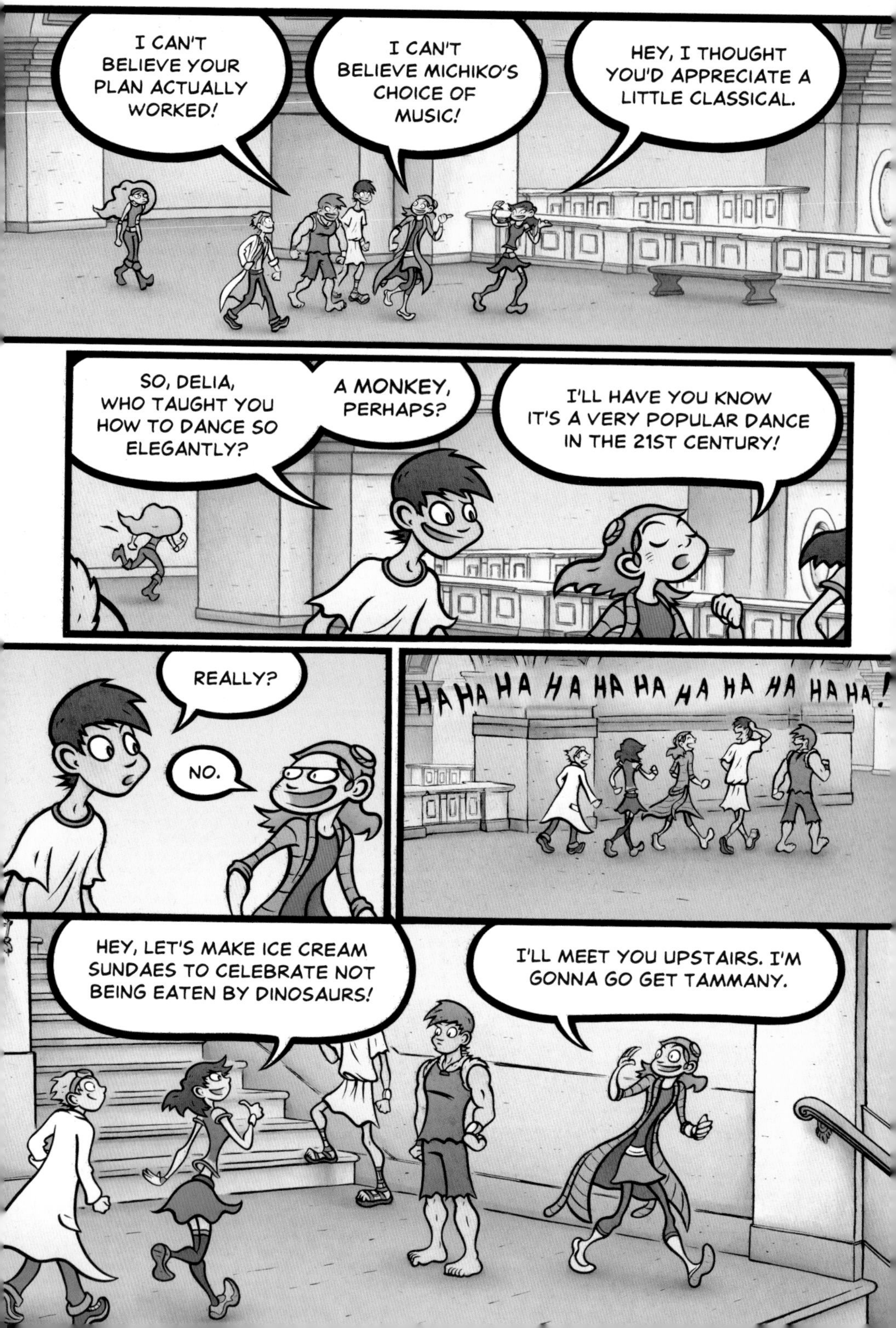

I CAN'T BELIEVE YOUR PLAN ACTUALLY WORKED!
I CAN'T BELIEVE MICHIKO'S CHOICE OF MUSIC!
HEY, I THOUGHT YOU'D APPRECIATE A LITTLE CLASSICAL.
SO, DELIA, WHO TAUGHT YOU HOW TO DANCE SO ELEGANTLY?
A MONKEY, PERHAPS?
I'LL HAVE YOU KNOW IT'S A VERY POPULAR DANCE IN THE 21ST CENTURY!
REALLY?
NO.
HAHA HA HA HA HA HA HA HA HA HAHA!
HEY, LET'S MAKE ICE CREAM SUNDAES TO CELEBRATE NOT BEING EATEN BY DINOSAURS!
I'LL MEET YOU UPSTAIRS. I'M GONNA GO GET TAMMANY.

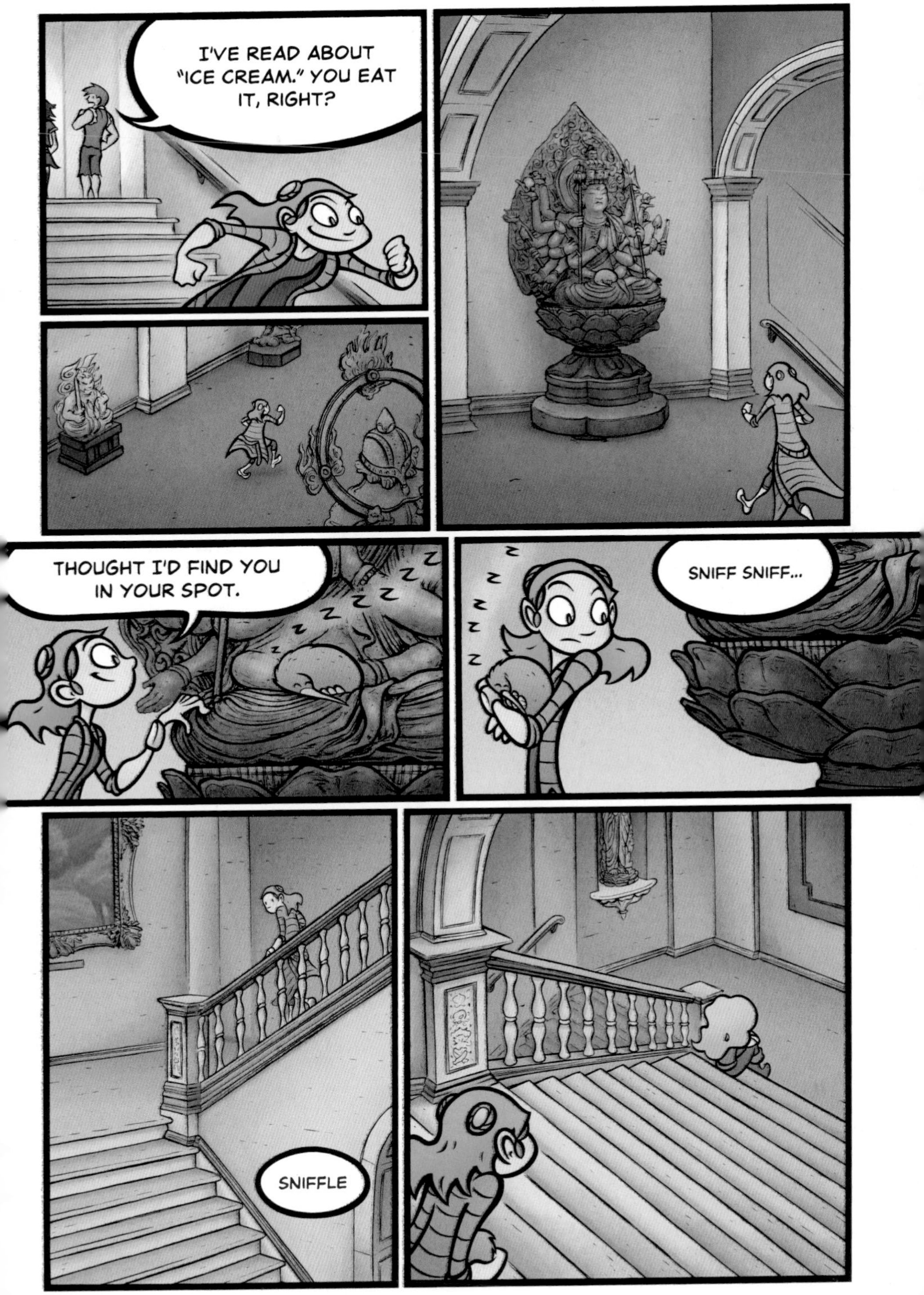
I'VE READ ABOUT "ICE CREAM." YOU EAT IT, RIGHT?
THOUGHT I'D FIND YOU IN YOUR SPOT.
SNIFF SNIFF...
SNIFFLE

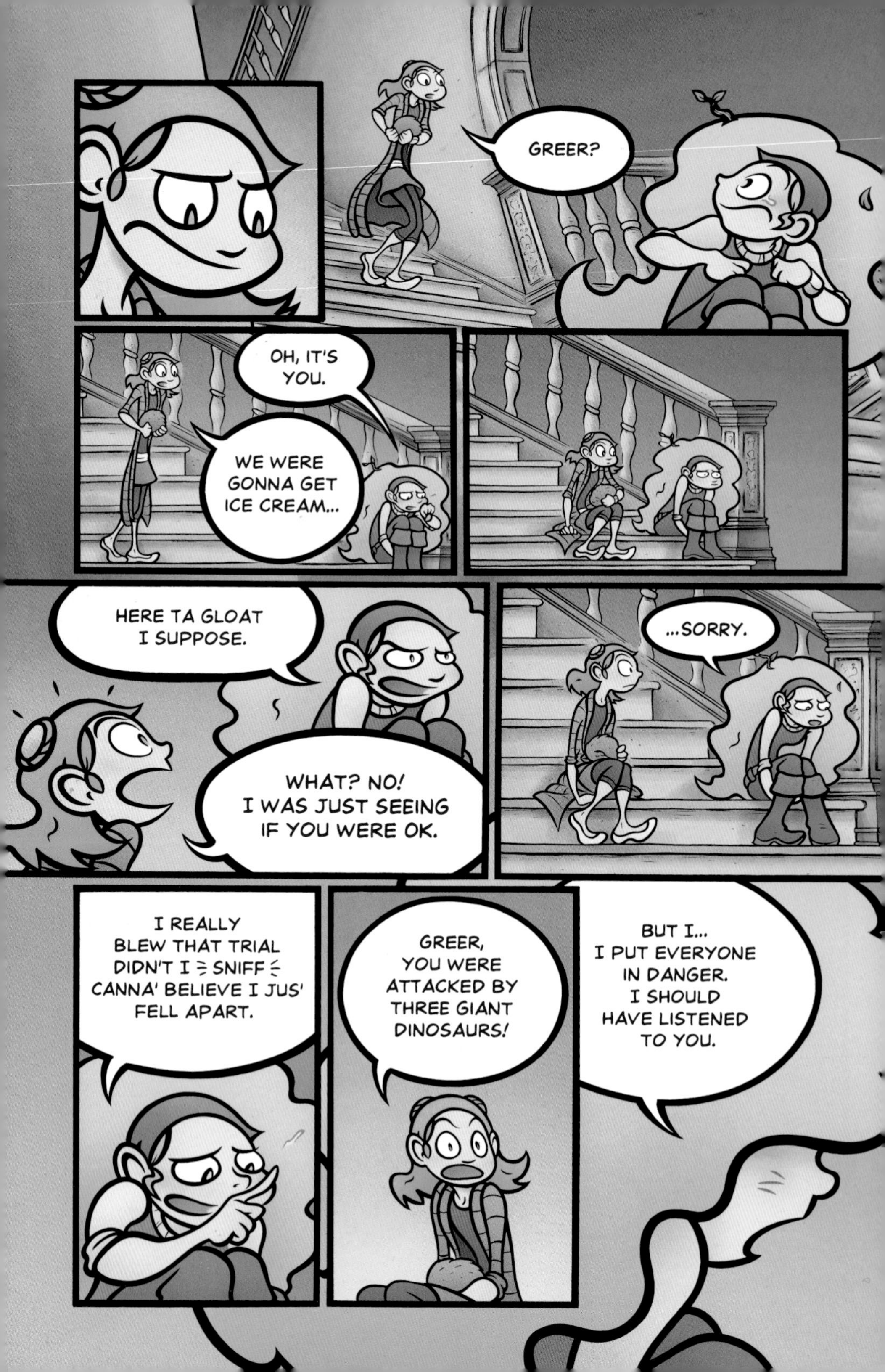
GREER?
OH, IT'S YOU.
WE WERE GONNA GET ICE CREAM...
HERE TA GLOAT I SUPPOSE.
WHAT? NO! I WAS JUST SEEING IF YOU WERE OK.
...SORRY.
I REALLY BLEW THAT TRIAL DIDN'T I ⪢SNIFF⪡ CANNA' BELIEVE I JUS' FELL APART.
GREER, YOU WERE ATTACKED BY THREE GIANT DINOSAURS!
BUT I... I PUT EVERYONE IN DANGER. I SHOULD HAVE LISTENED TO YOU.

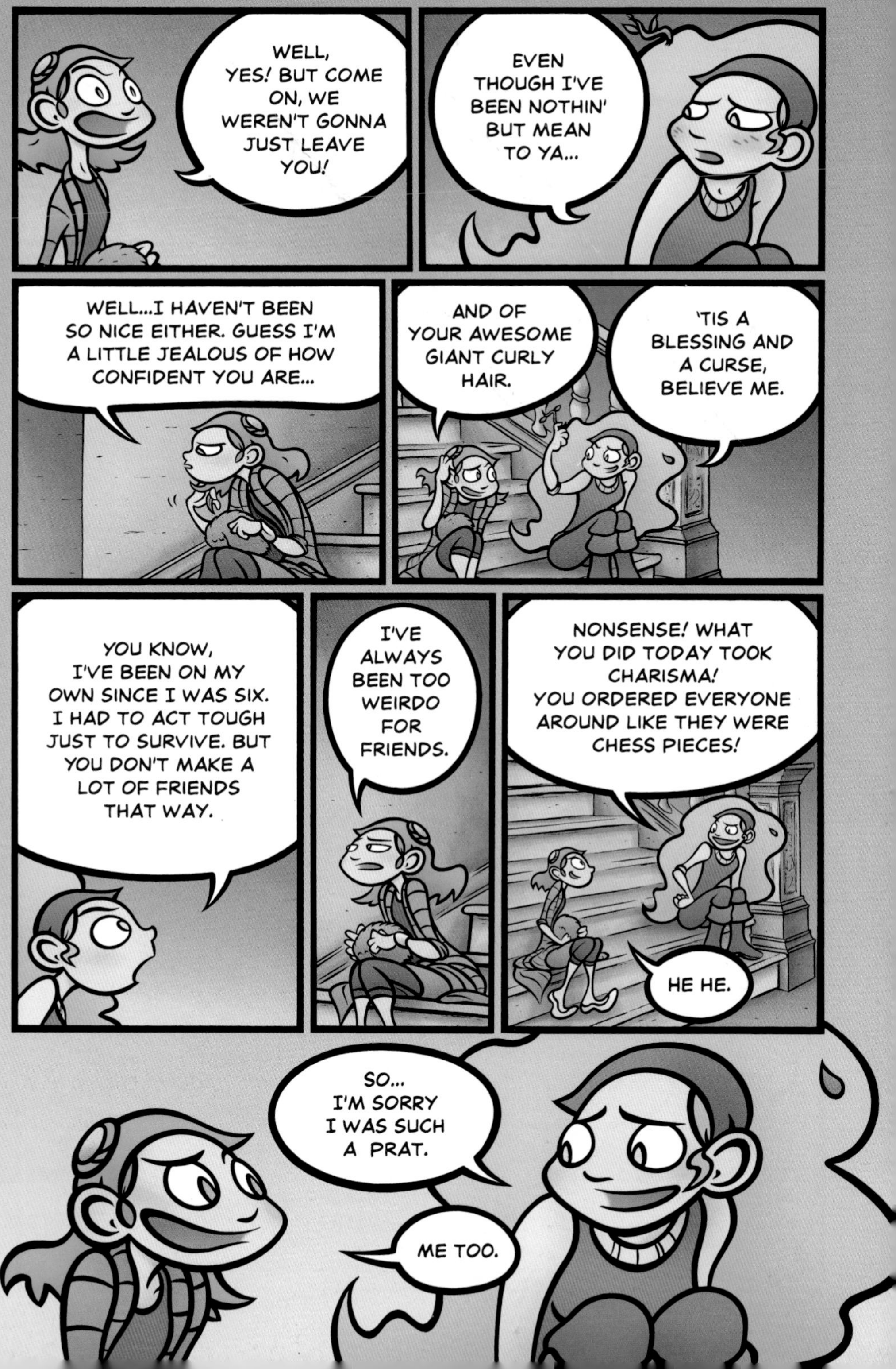
WELL, YES! BUT COME ON, WE WEREN'T GONNA JUST LEAVE YOU!
EVEN THOUGH I'VE BEEN NOTHIN' BUT MEAN TO YA...
WELL...I HAVEN'T BEEN SO NICE EITHER. GUESS I'M A LITTLE JEALOUS OF HOW CONFIDENT YOU ARE...
AND OF YOUR AWESOME GIANT CURLY HAIR.
'TIS A BLESSING AND A CURSE, BELIEVE ME.
YOU KNOW, I'VE BEEN ON MY OWN SINCE I WAS SIX. I HAD TO ACT TOUGH JUST TO SURVIVE. BUT YOU DON'T MAKE A LOT OF FRIENDS THAT WAY.
I'VE ALWAYS BEEN TOO WEIRDO FOR FRIENDS.
NONSENSE! WHAT YOU DID TODAY TOOK CHARISMA! YOU ORDERED EVERYONE AROUND LIKE THEY WERE CHESS PIECES!
HE HE.
SO... I'M SORRY I WAS SUCH A PRAT.
ME TOO.

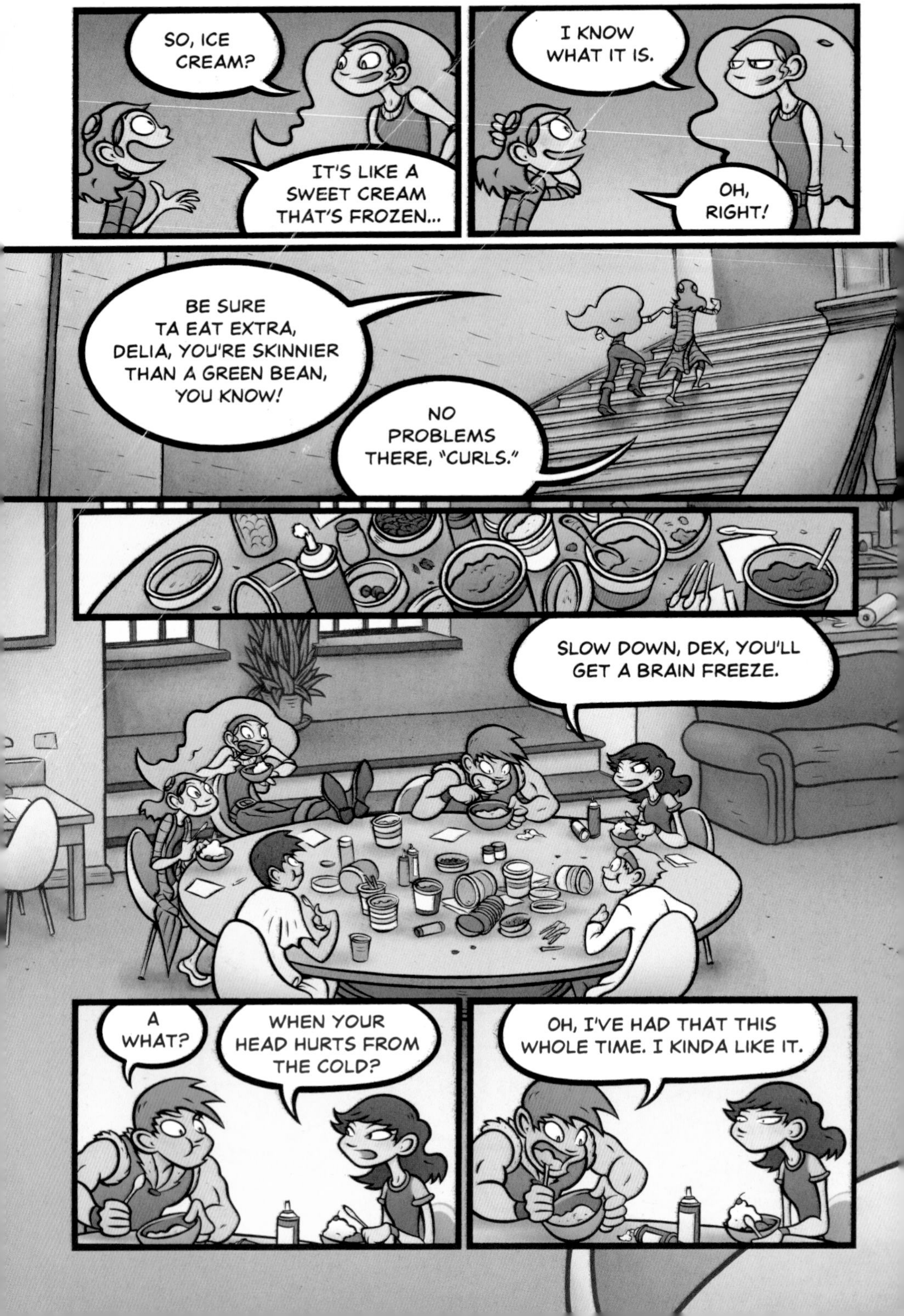
SO, ICE CREAM?
IT'S LIKE A SWEET CREAM THAT'S FROZEN...
I KNOW WHAT IT IS.
OH, RIGHT!
BE SURE TA EAT EXTRA, DELIA, YOU'RE SKINNIER THAN A GREEN BEAN, YOU KNOW!
NO PROBLEMS THERE, "CURLS."
SLOW DOWN, DEX, YOU'LL GET A BRAIN FREEZE.
A WHAT?
WHEN YOUR HEAD HURTS FROM THE COLD?
OH, I'VE HAD THAT THIS WHOLE TIME. I KINDA LIKE IT.

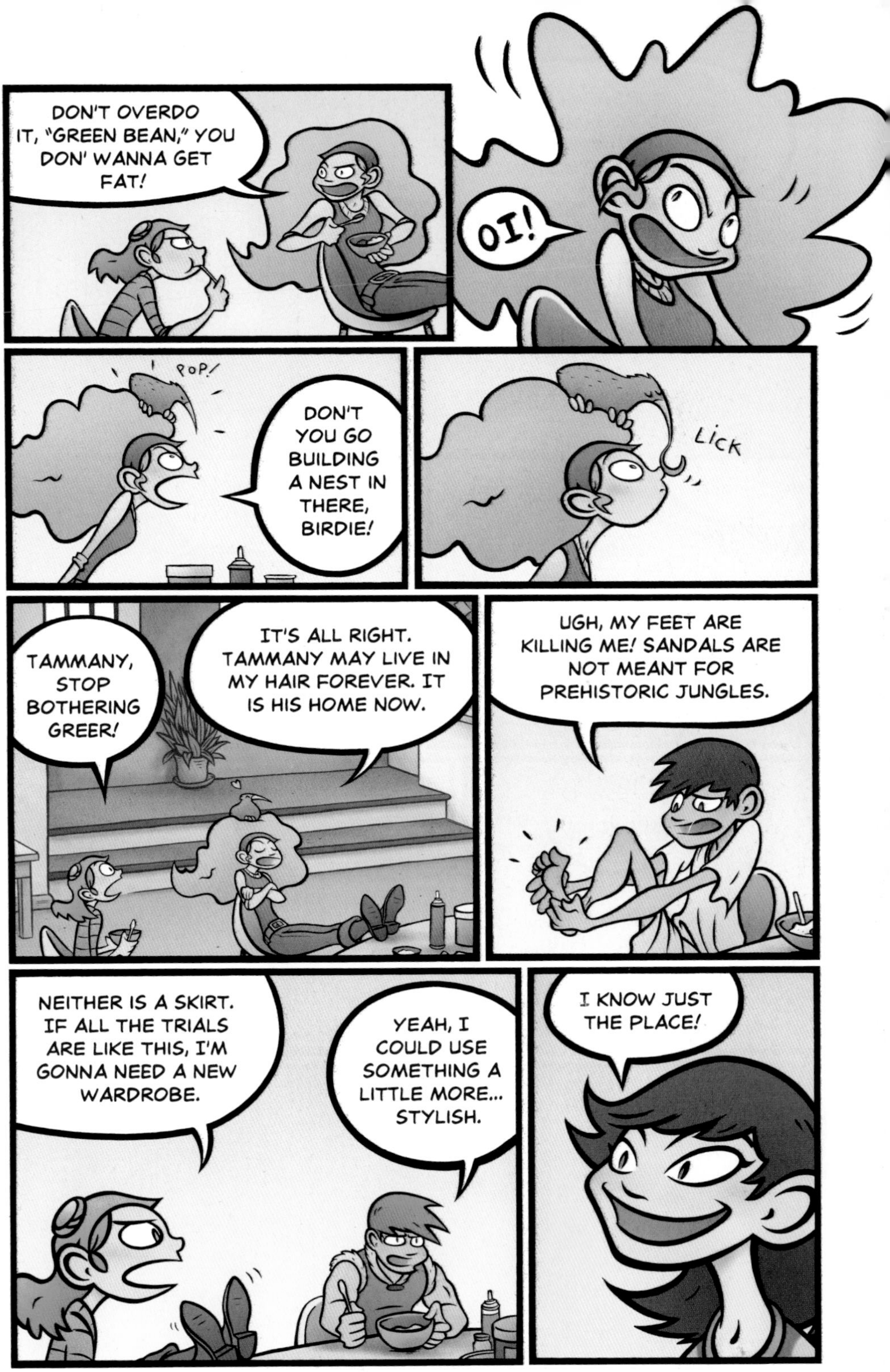
DON'T OVERDO IT, "GREEN BEAN," YOU DON' WANNA GET FAT!
OI!
POP!
DON'T YOU GO BUILDING A NEST IN THERE, BIRDIE!
LICK
TAMMANY, STOP BOTHERING GREER!
IT'S ALL RIGHT. TAMMANY MAY LIVE IN MY HAIR FOREVER. IT IS HIS HOME NOW.
UGH, MY FEET ARE KILLING ME! SANDALS ARE NOT MEANT FOR PREHISTORIC JUNGLES.
NEITHER IS A SKIRT. IF ALL THE TRIALS ARE LIKE THIS, I'M GONNA NEED A NEW WARDROBE.
YEAH, I COULD USE SOMETHING A LITTLE MORE... STYLISH.
I KNOW JUST THE PLACE!

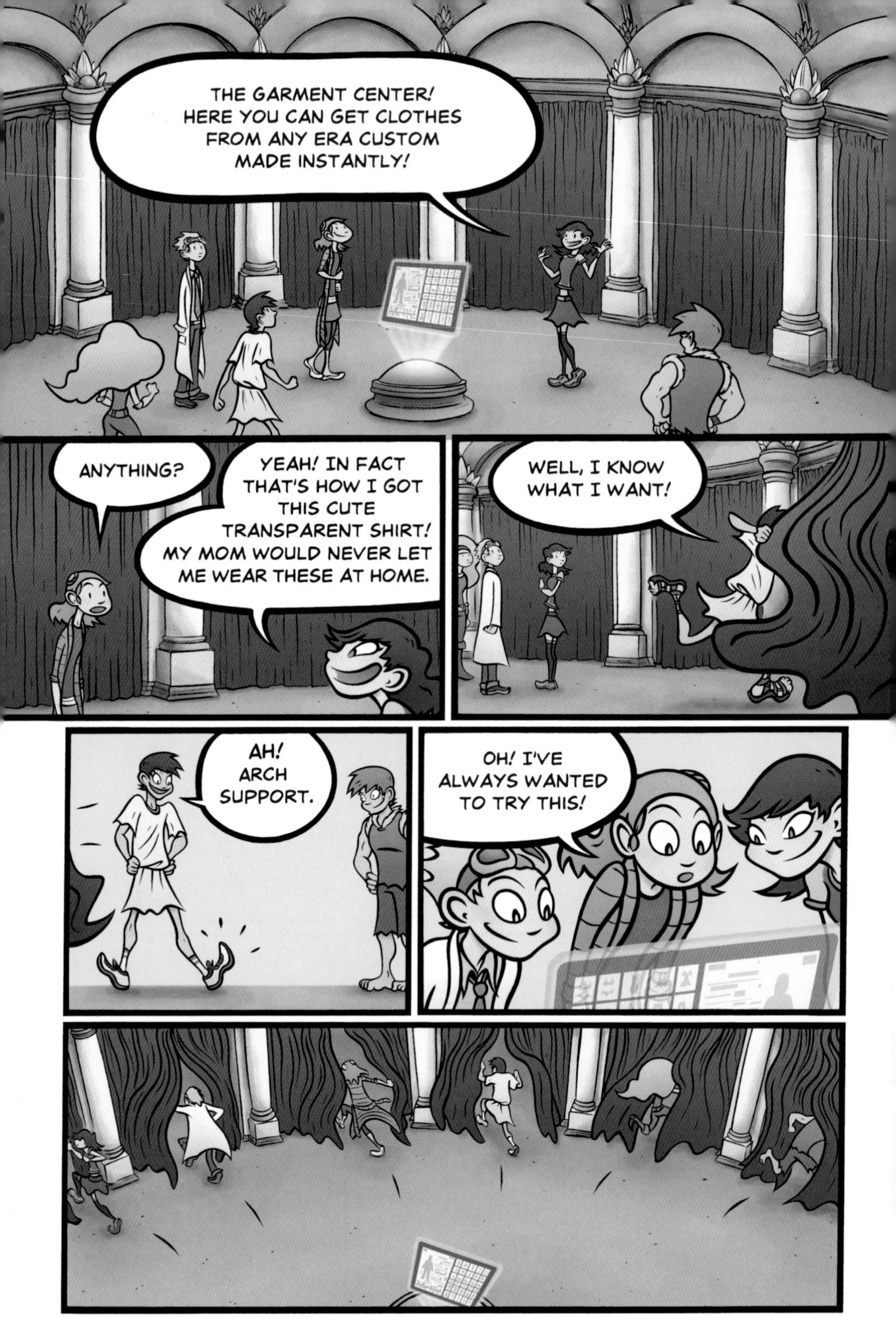
THE GARMENT CENTER! HERE YOU CAN GET CLOTHES FROM ANY ERA CUSTOM MADE INSTANTLY!
ANYTHING?
YEAH! IN FACT THAT'S HOW I GOT THIS CUTE TRANSPARENT SHIRT! MY MOM WOULD NEVER LET ME WEAR THESE AT HOME.
WELL, I KNOW WHAT I WANT!
AH! ARCH SUPPORT.
OH! I'VE ALWAYS WANTED TO TRY THIS!

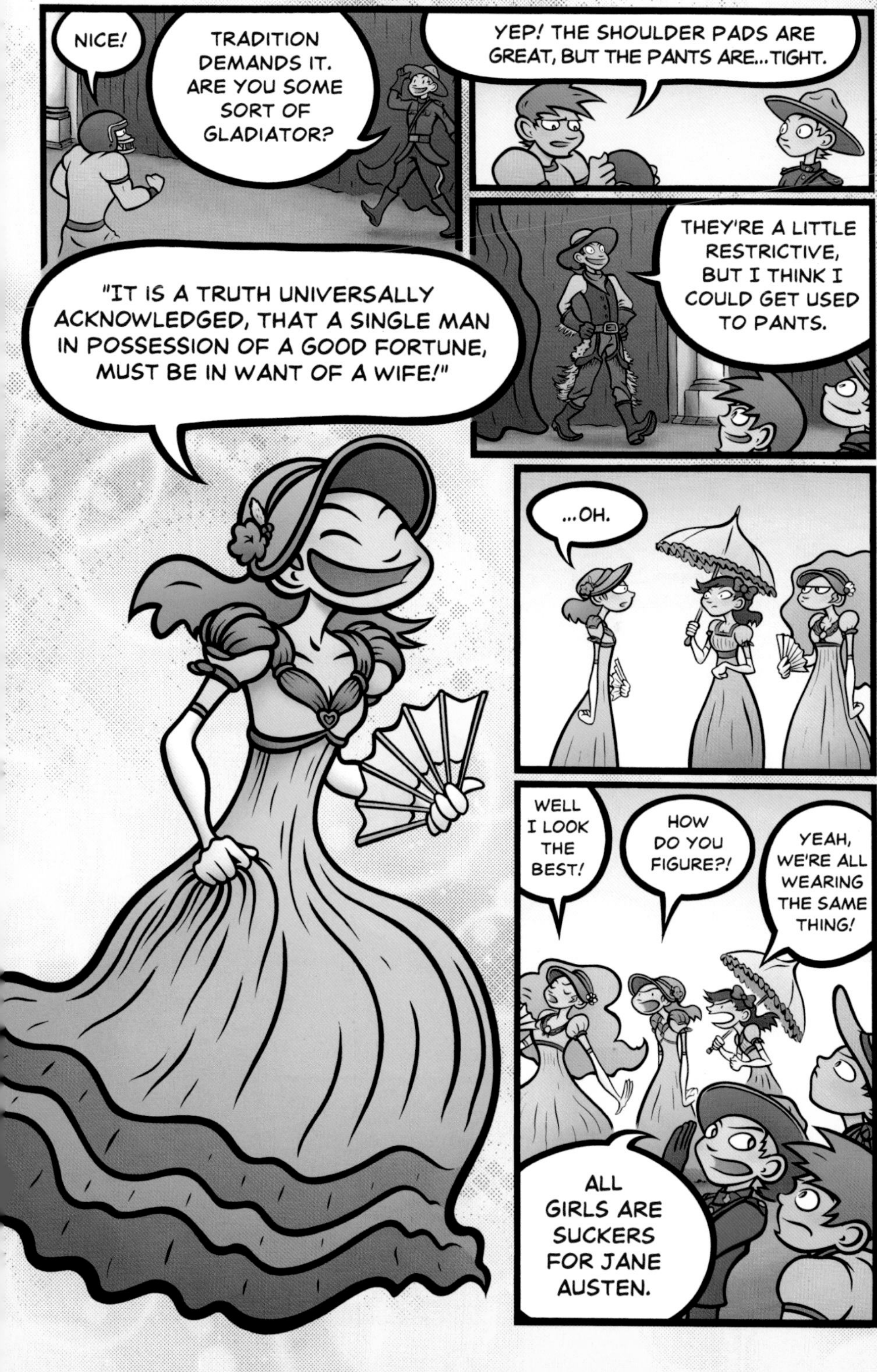
NICE!
TRADITION DEMANDS IT. ARE YOU SOME SORT OF GLADIATOR?
YEP! THE SHOULDER PADS ARE GREAT, BUT THE PANTS ARE...TIGHT.
"IT IS A TRUTH UNIVERSALLY ACKNOWLEDGED, THAT A SINGLE MAN IN POSSESSION OF A GOOD FORTUNE, MUST BE IN WANT OF A WIFE!"
THEY'RE A LITTLE RESTRICTIVE, BUT I THINK I COULD GET USED TO PANTS.
...OH.
WELL I LOOK THE BEST!
HOW DO YOU FIGURE?!
YEAH, WE'RE ALL WEARING THE SAME THING!
ALL GIRLS ARE SUCKERS FOR JANE AUSTEN.

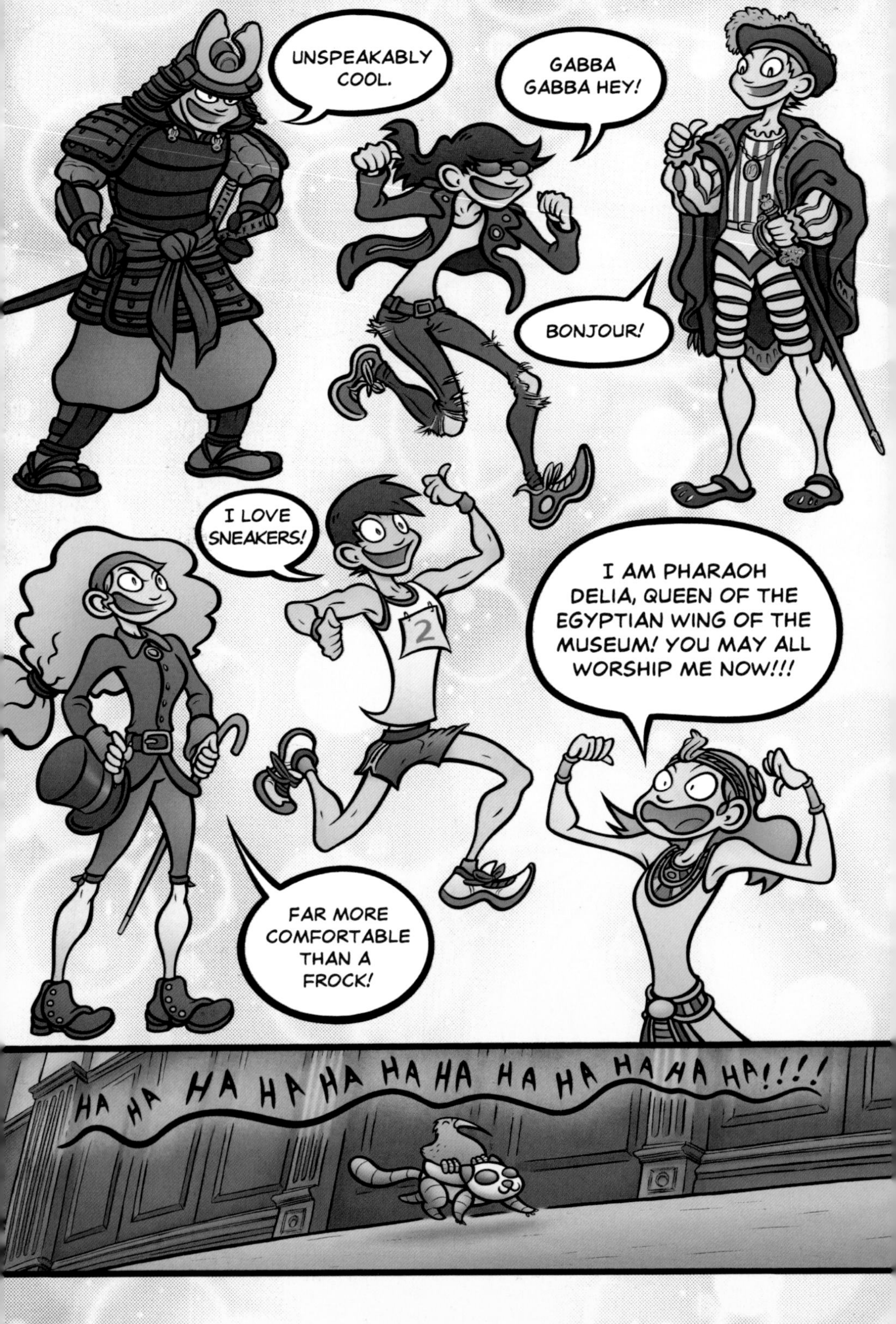
UNSPEAKABLY COOL.
GABBA GABBA HEY!
BONJOUR!
I LOVE SNEAKERS!
FAR MORE COMFORTABLE THAN A FROCK!
I AM PHARAOH DELIA, QUEEN OF THE EGYPTIAN WING OF THE MUSEUM! YOU MAY ALL WORSHIP ME NOW!!!
HA HA HA HA HA HA HA HA HA HA HA HA!!!!

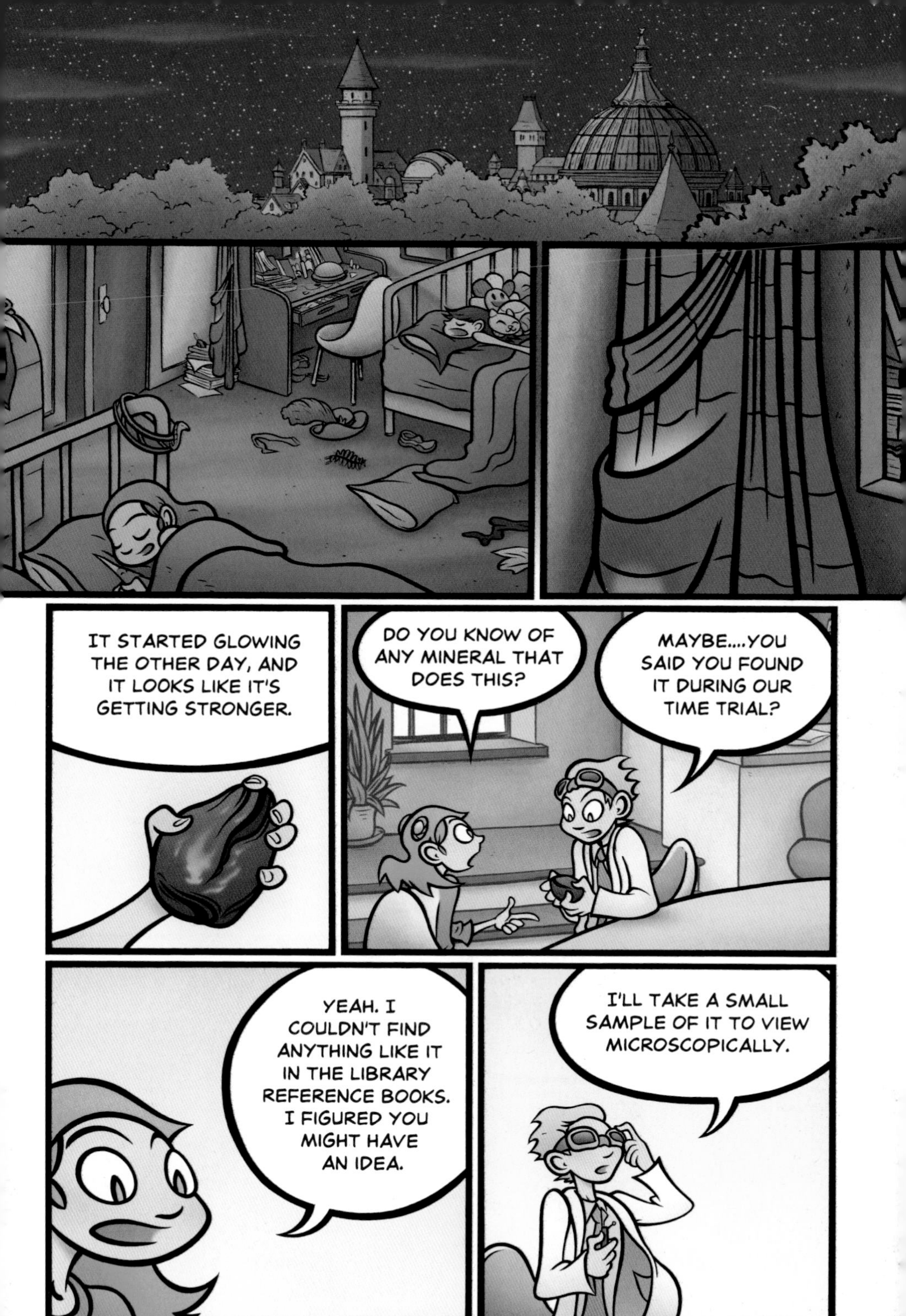

IT STARTED GLOWING THE OTHER DAY, AND IT LOOKS LIKE IT'S GETTING STRONGER.
DO YOU KNOW OF ANY MINERAL THAT DOES THIS?
MAYBE....YOU SAID YOU FOUND IT DURING OUR TIME TRIAL?
YEAH. I COULDN'T FIND ANYTHING LIKE IT IN THE LIBRARY REFERENCE BOOKS. I FIGURED YOU MIGHT HAVE AN IDEA.
I'LL TAKE A SMALL SAMPLE OF IT TO VIEW MICROSCOPICALLY.

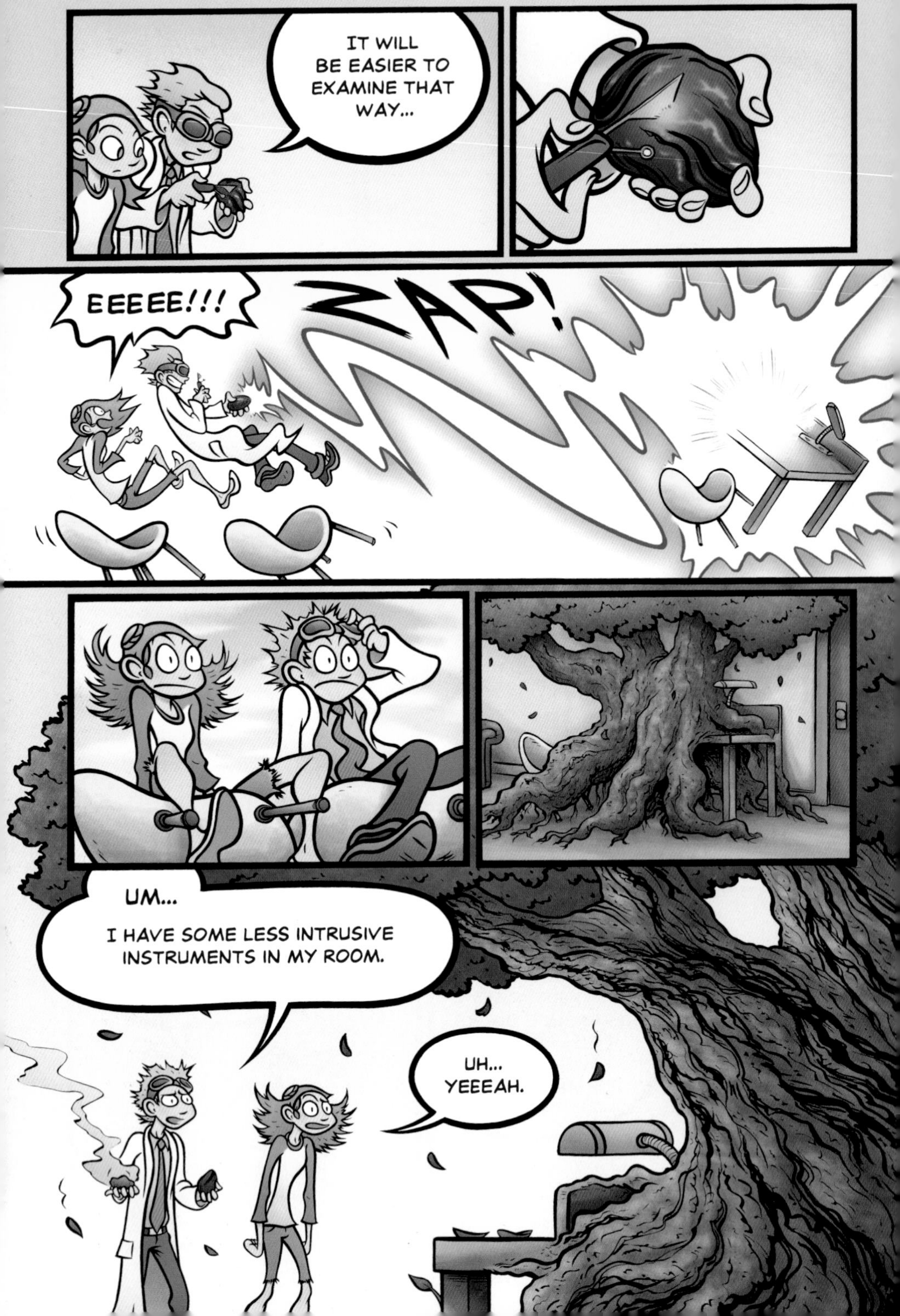
IT WILL BE EASIER TO EXAMINE THAT WAY...
EEEEE!!!
ZAP!
UM...
I HAVE SOME LESS INTRUSIVE INSTRUMENTS IN MY ROOM.
UH... YEEEAH.

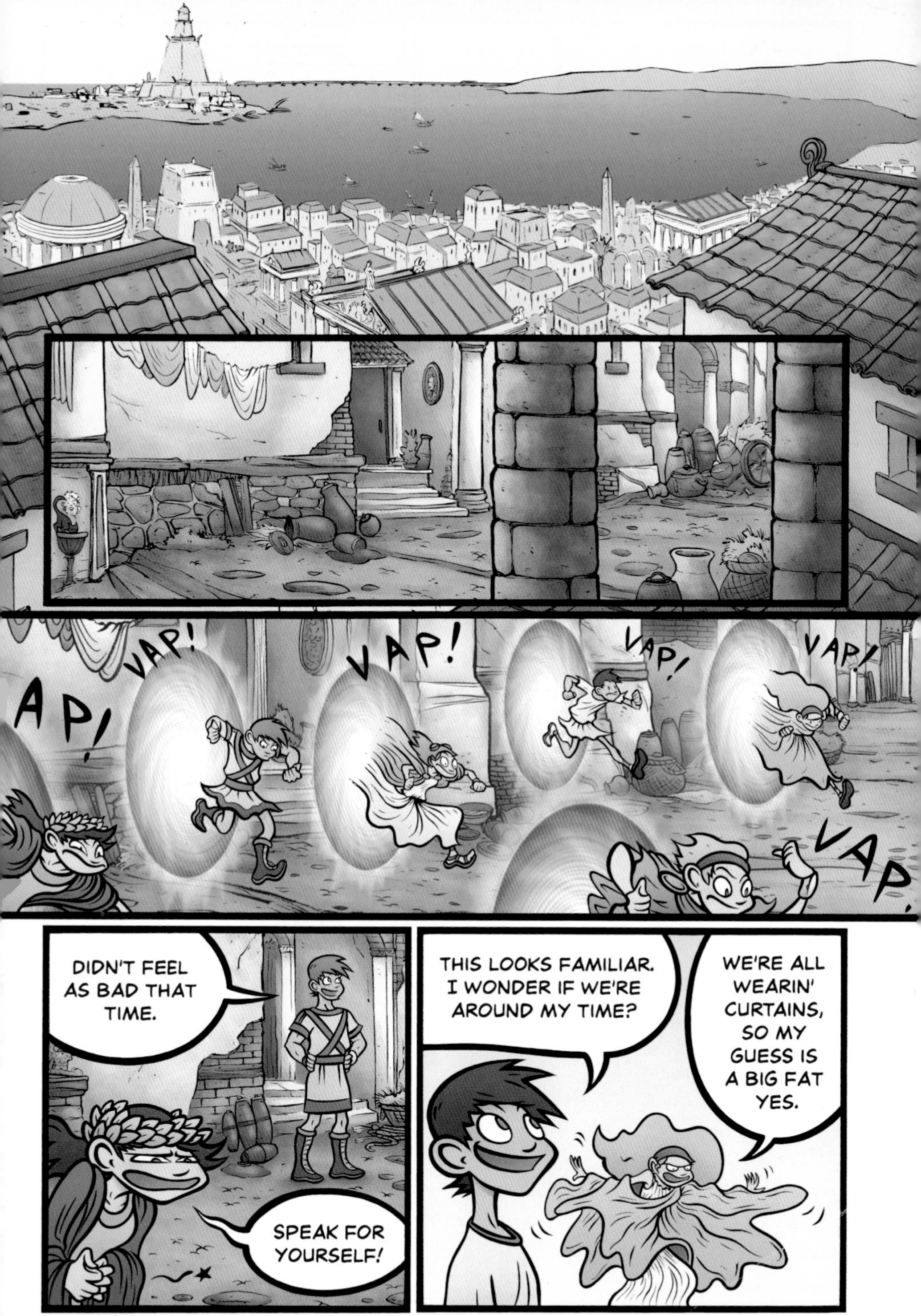

AP!
VAP!
VAP!
VAP!
VAP!
VAP!
DIDN'T FEEL AS BAD THAT TIME.
SPEAK FOR YOURSELF!
THIS LOOKS FAMILIAR. I WONDER IF WE'RE AROUND MY TIME?
WE'RE ALL WEARIN' CURTAINS, SO MY GUESS IS A BIG FAT YES.

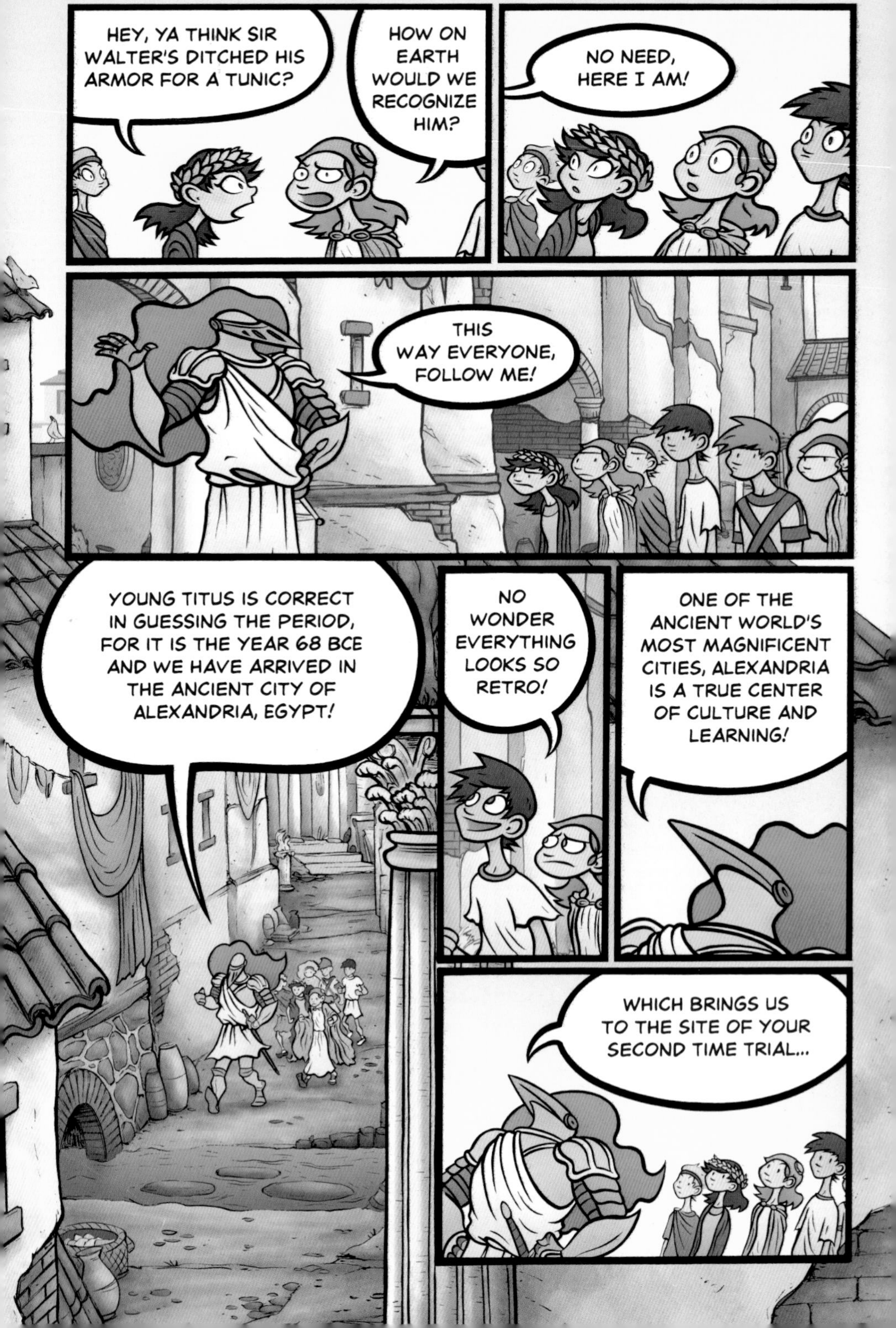

HEY, YA THINK SIR WALTER'S DITCHED HIS ARMOR FOR A TUNIC?
HOW ON EARTH WOULD WE RECOGNIZE HIM?
NO NEED, HERE I AM!
THIS WAY EVERYONE, FOLLOW ME!
YOUNG TITUS IS CORRECT IN GUESSING THE PERIOD, FOR IT IS THE YEAR 68 BCE AND WE HAVE ARRIVED IN THE ANCIENT CITY OF ALEXANDRIA, EGYPT!
NO WONDER EVERYTHING LOOKS SO RETRO!
ONE OF THE ANCIENT WORLD'S MOST MAGNIFICENT CITIES, ALEXANDRIA IS A TRUE CENTER OF CULTURE AND LEARNING!
WHICH BRINGS US TO THE SITE OF YOUR SECOND TIME TRIAL...

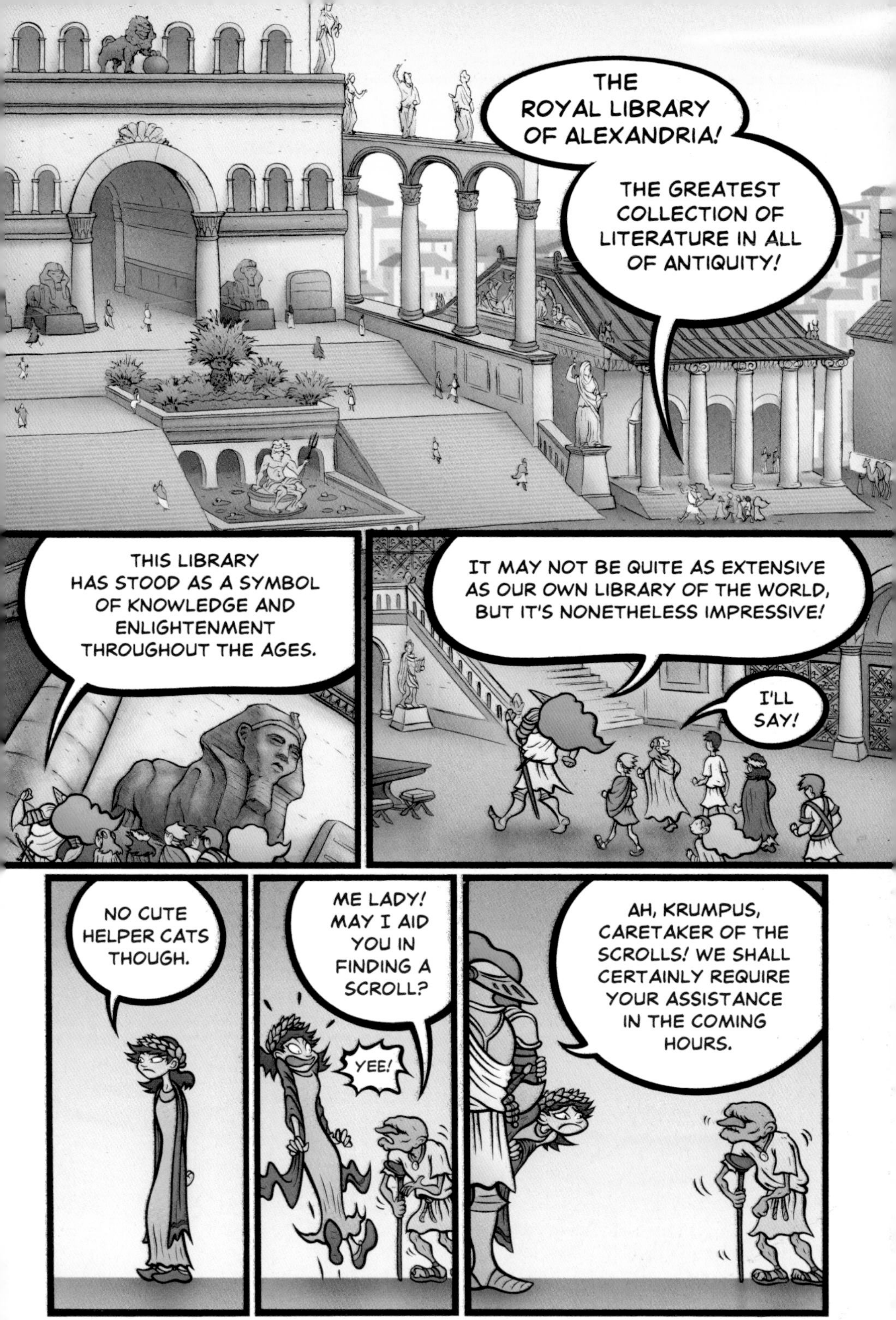
THE ROYAL LIBRARY OF ALEXANDRIA!
THE GREATEST COLLECTION OF LITERATURE IN ALL OF ANTIQUITY!
THIS LIBRARY HAS STOOD AS A SYMBOL OF KNOWLEDGE AND ENLIGHTENMENT THROUGHOUT THE AGES.
IT MAY NOT BE QUITE AS EXTENSIVE AS OUR OWN LIBRARY OF THE WORLD, BUT IT'S NONETHELESS IMPRESSIVE!
I'LL SAY!
NO CUTE HELPER CATS THOUGH.
ME LADY! MAY I AID YOU IN FINDING A SCROLL?
YEE!
AH, KRUMPUS, CARETAKER OF THE SCROLLS! WE SHALL CERTAINLY REQUIRE YOUR ASSISTANCE IN THE COMING HOURS.

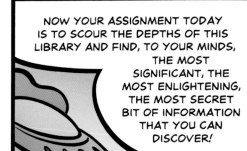

NOW YOUR ASSIGNMENT TODAY IS TO SCOUR THE DEPTHS OF THIS LIBRARY AND FIND, TO YOUR MINDS, THE MOST SIGNIFICANT, THE MOST ENLIGHTENING, THE MOST SECRET BIT OF INFORMATION THAT YOU CAN DISCOVER!

SO...THIS IS A RESEARCH ASSIGNMENT?

QUITE RIGHT!

YES!

YOU HAVE SIX HOURS TO CAREFULLY CHOOSE A SCROLL AMID THIS VAST COLLECTION! USE YOUR BEST JUDGMENT NOW, AND REMEMBER, KRUMPUS IS HERE TO HELP!

THANK YE, ME LORD, 'TIS AN HONOR TO SERVE.

!AG HACK HACK COUGH!!

SNORT!

I'LL LEAVE YOU TO IT THEN! GOOD LUCK!

...A RESEARCH ASSIGNMENT.

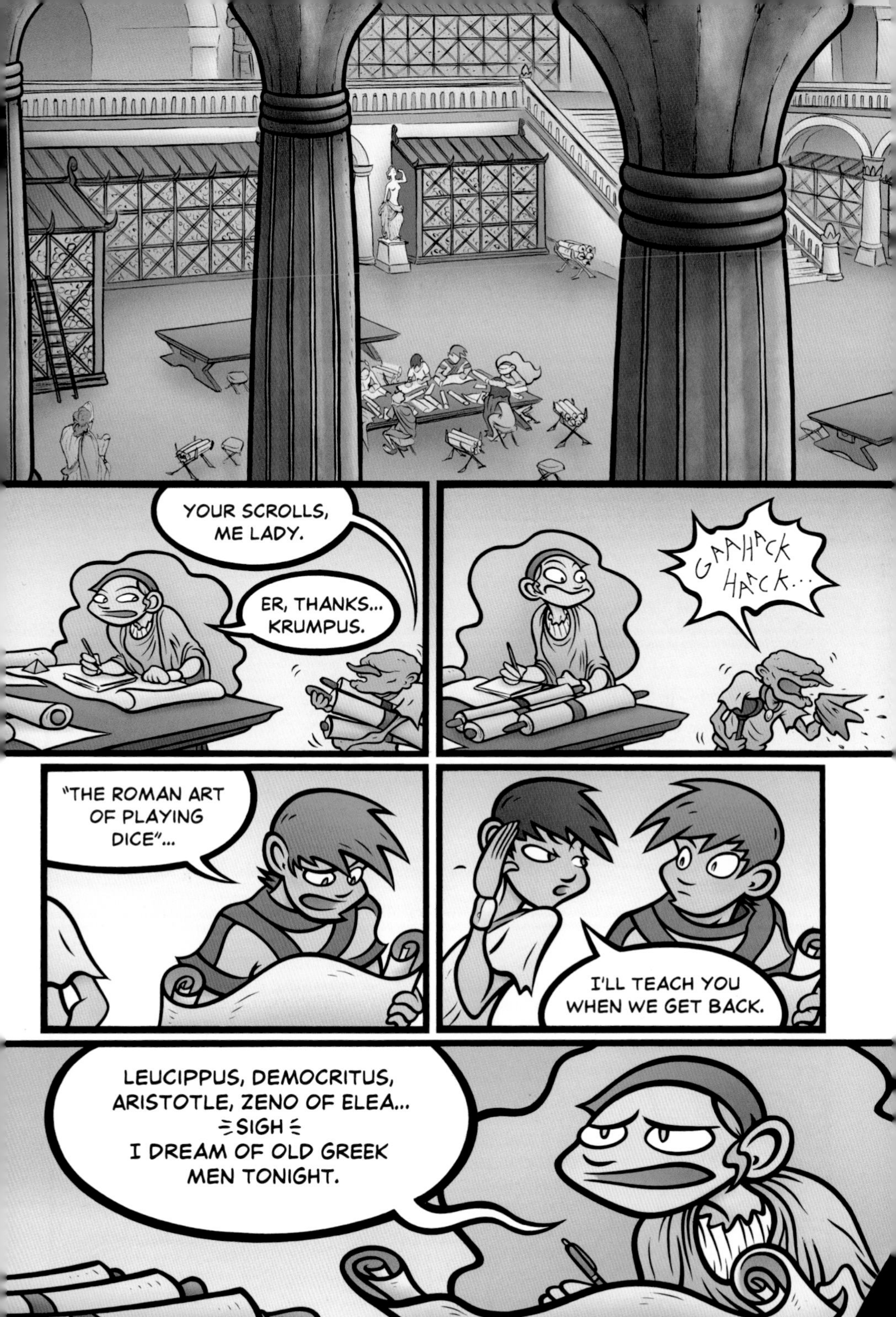
YOUR SCROLLS, ME LADY.
ER, THANKS... KRUMPUS.
GAAHACK HAACK...
"THE ROMAN ART OF PLAYING DICE"...
I'LL TEACH YOU WHEN WE GET BACK.
LEUCIPPUS, DEMOCRITUS, ARISTOTLE, ZENO OF ELEA... SIGH I DREAM OF OLD GREEK MEN TONIGHT.

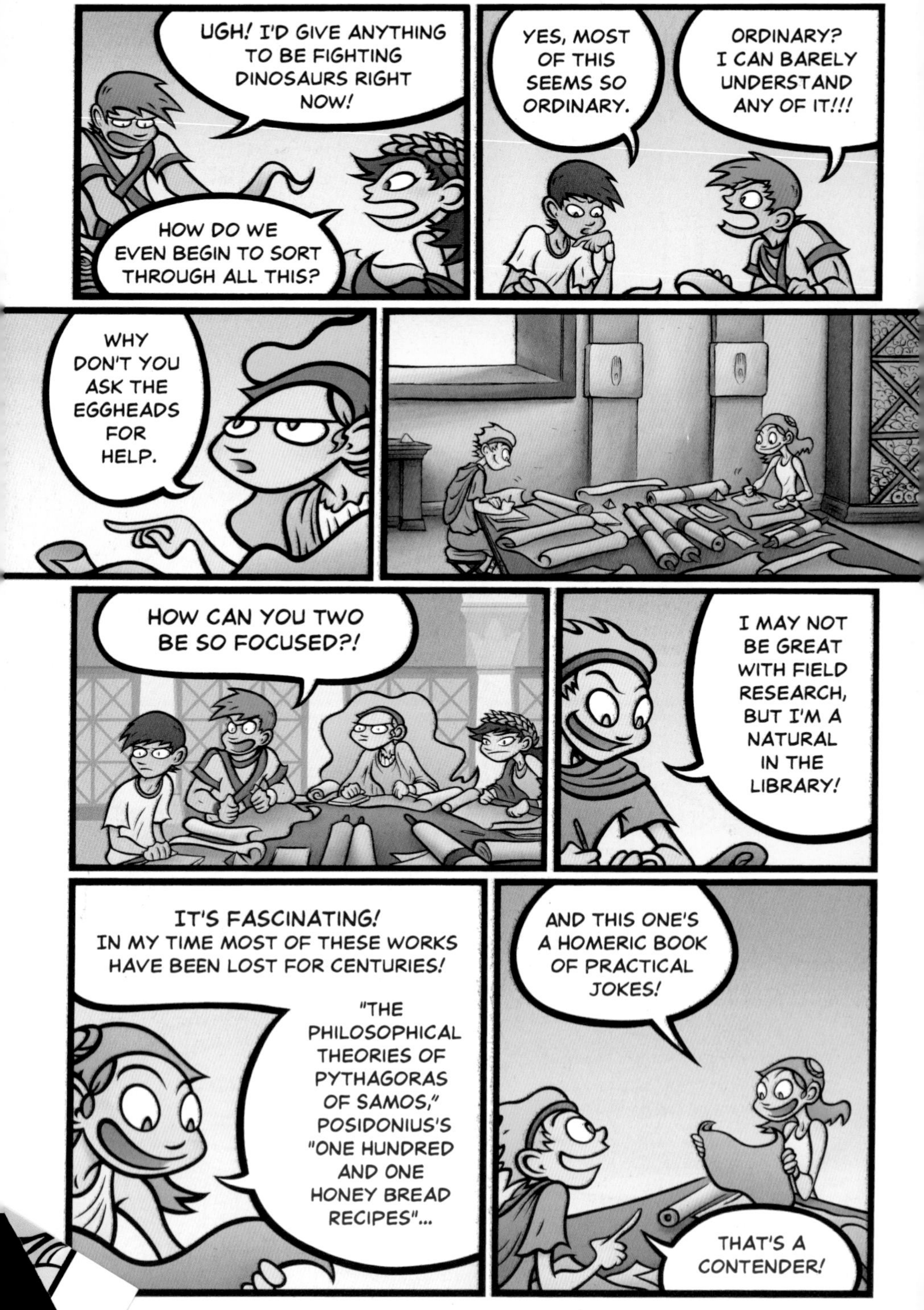
UGH! I'D GIVE ANYTHING TO BE FIGHTING DINOSAURS RIGHT NOW!
HOW DO WE EVEN BEGIN TO SORT THROUGH ALL THIS?
YES, MOST OF THIS SEEMS SO ORDINARY.
ORDINARY? I CAN BARELY UNDERSTAND ANY OF IT!!!
WHY DON'T YOU ASK THE EGGHEADS FOR HELP.
HOW CAN YOU TWO BE SO FOCUSED?!
I MAY NOT BE GREAT WITH FIELD RESEARCH, BUT I'M A NATURAL IN THE LIBRARY!
IT'S FASCINATING! IN MY TIME MOST OF THESE WORKS HAVE BEEN LOST FOR CENTURIES!
"THE PHILOSOPHICAL THEORIES OF PYTHAGORAS OF SAMOS," POSIDONIUS'S "ONE HUNDRED AND ONE HONEY BREAD RECIPES"...
AND THIS ONE'S A HOMERIC BOOK OF PRACTICAL JOKES!
THAT'S A CONTENDER!

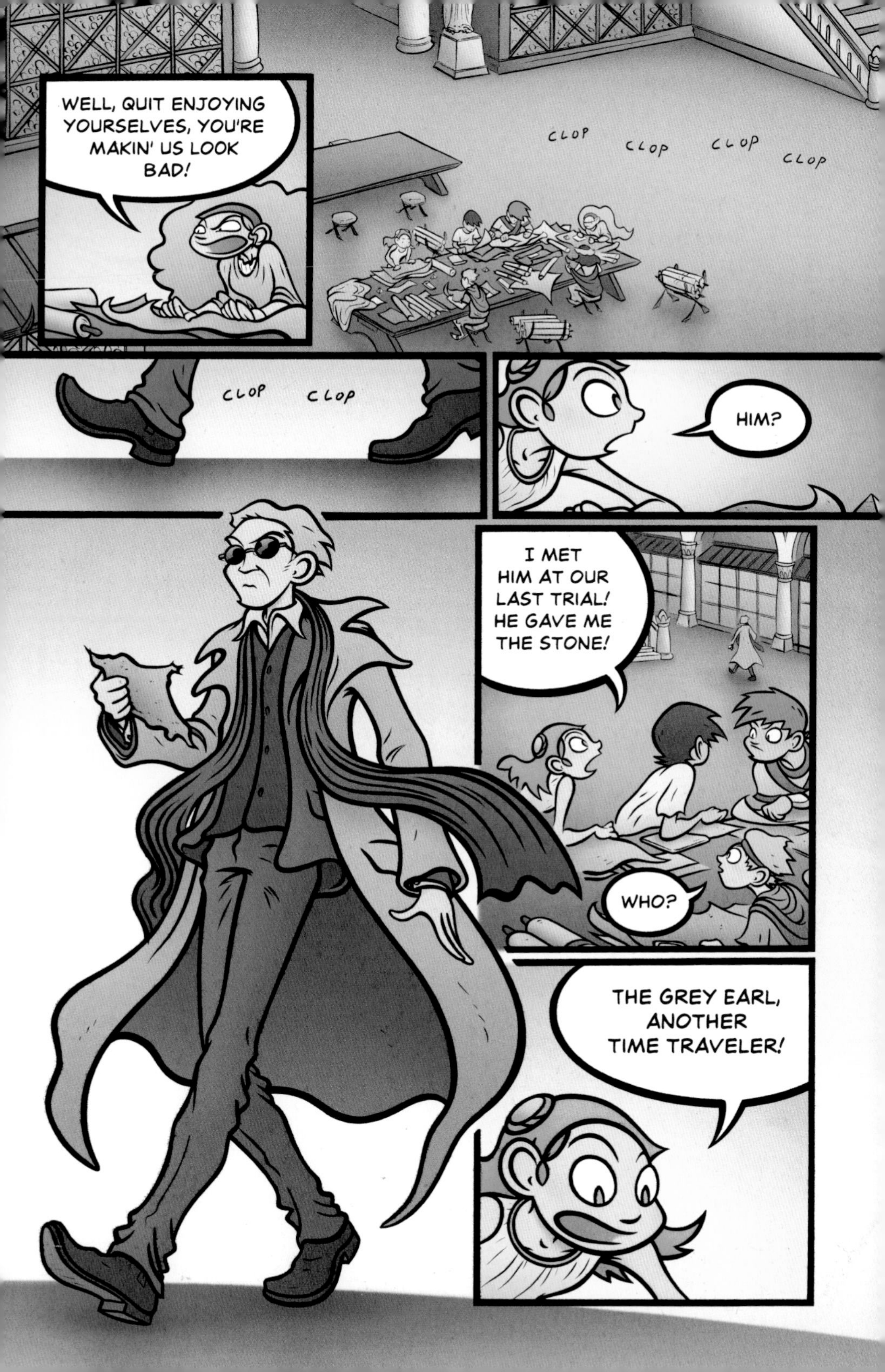

WELL, QUIT ENJOYING YOURSELVES, YOU'RE MAKIN' US LOOK BAD!
CLOP CLOP CLOP CLOP
CLOP CLOP
HIM?
I MET HIM AT OUR LAST TRIAL! HE GAVE ME THE STONE!
WHO?
THE GREY EARL, ANOTHER TIME TRAVELER!

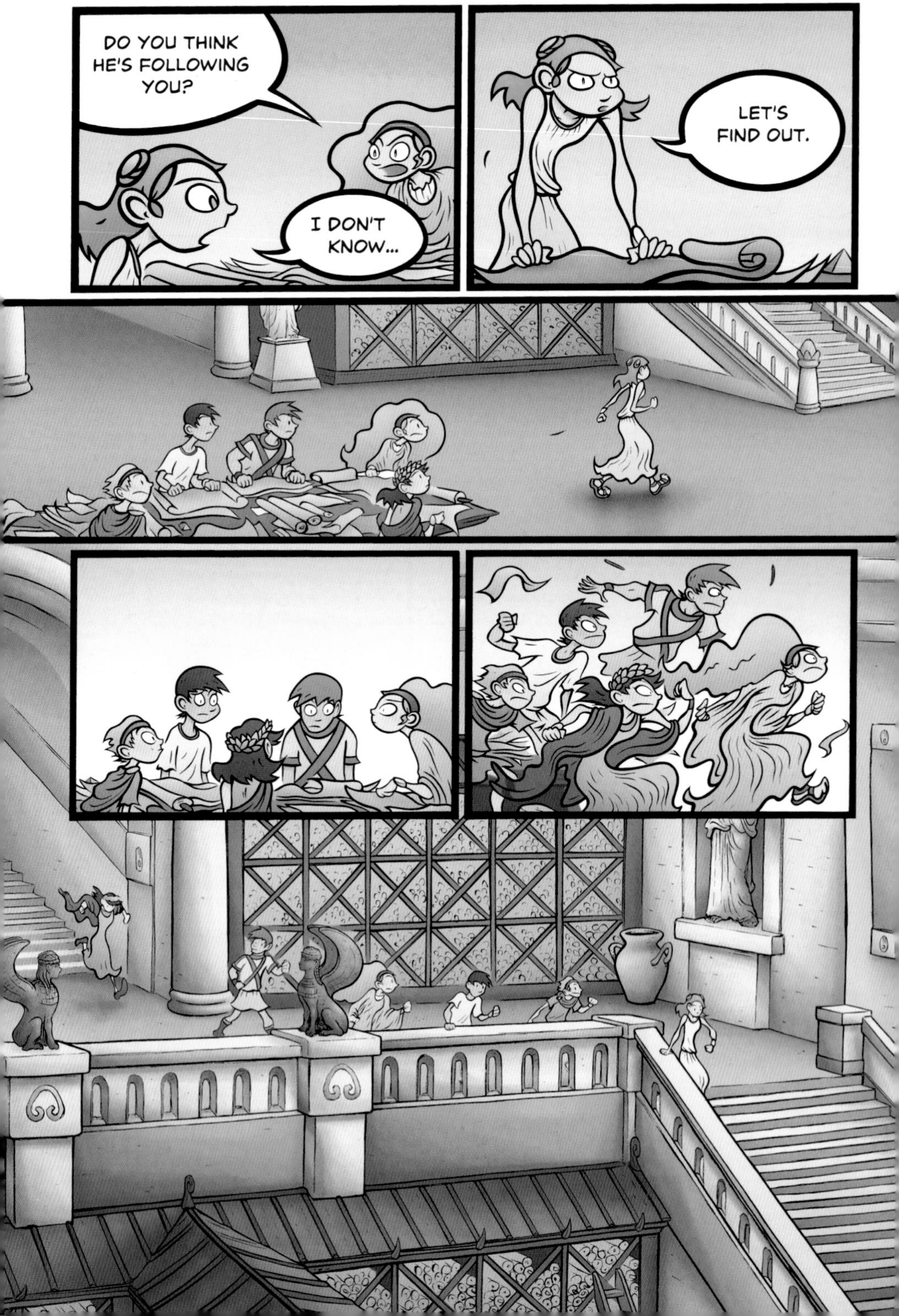
DO YOU THINK HE'S FOLLOWING YOU?
I DON'T KNOW...
LET'S FIND OUT.

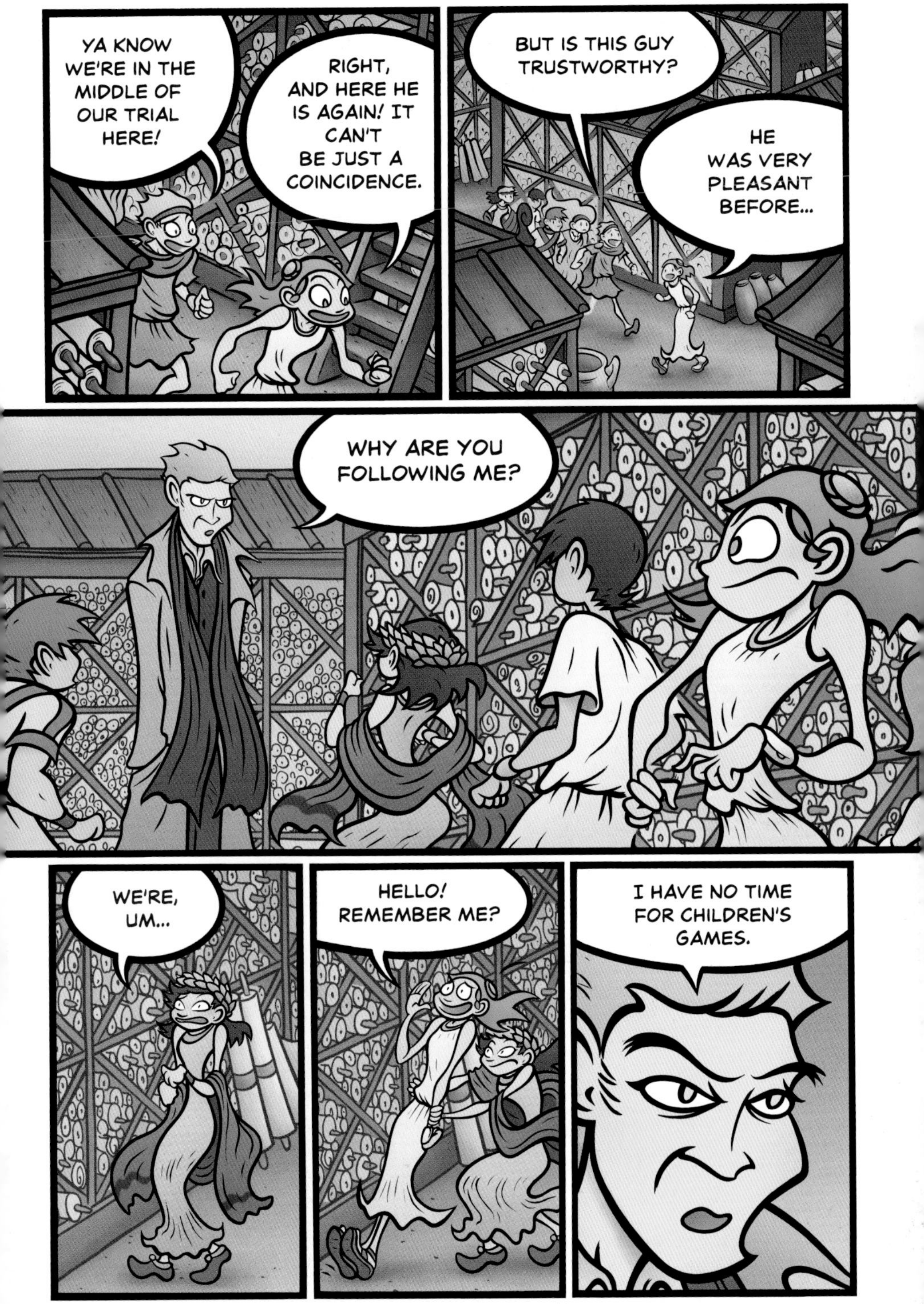
YA KNOW WE'RE IN THE MIDDLE OF OUR TRIAL HERE!
RIGHT, AND HERE HE IS AGAIN! IT CAN'T BE JUST A COINCIDENCE.
BUT IS THIS GUY TRUSTWORTHY?
HE WAS VERY PLEASANT BEFORE...
WHY ARE YOU FOLLOWING ME?
WE'RE, UM...
HELLO! REMEMBER ME?
I HAVE NO TIME FOR CHILDREN'S GAMES.

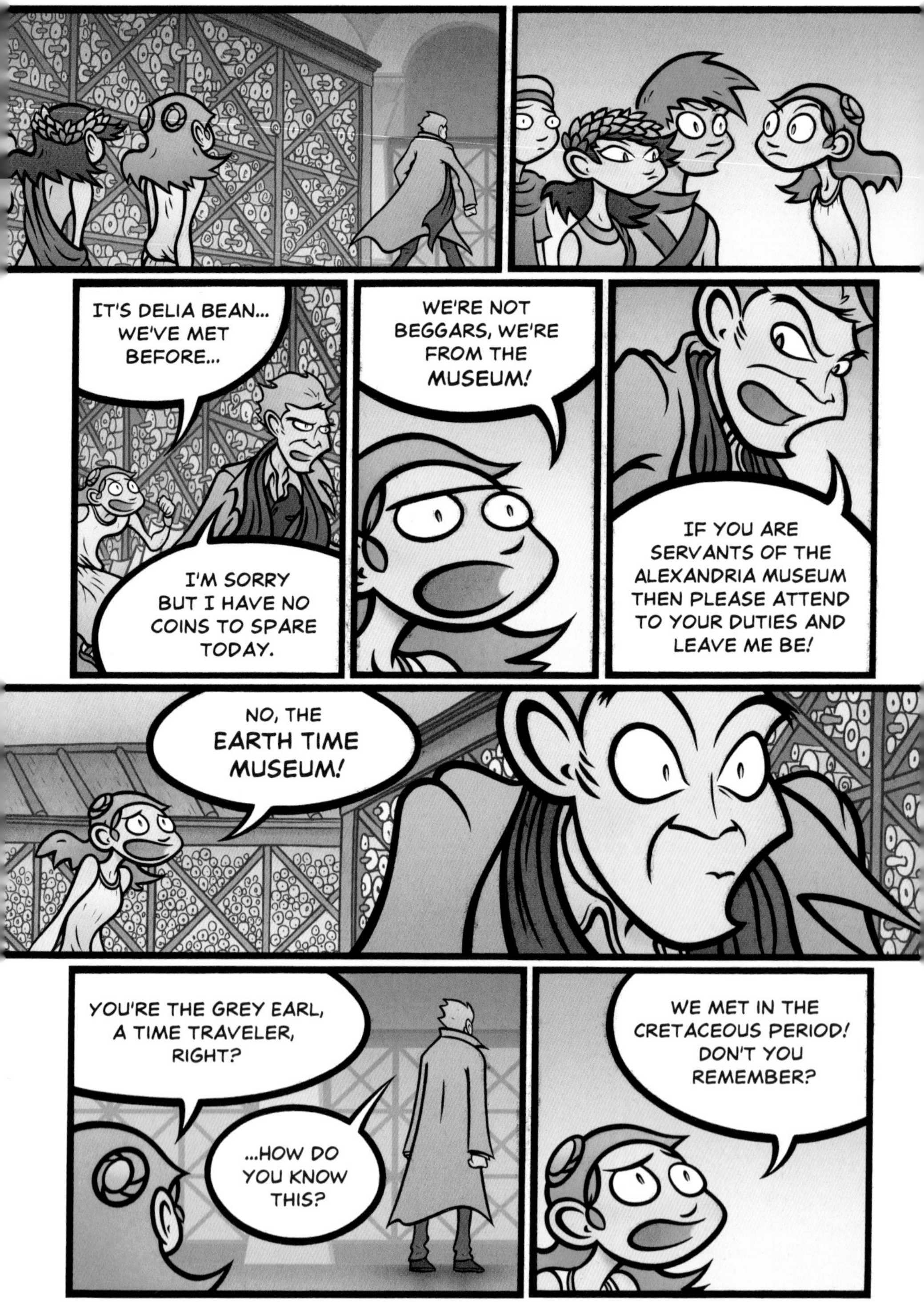
IT'S DELIA BEAN... WE'VE MET BEFORE...
I'M SORRY BUT I HAVE NO COINS TO SPARE TODAY.
WE'RE NOT BEGGARS, WE'RE FROM THE MUSEUM!
IF YOU ARE SERVANTS OF THE ALEXANDRIA MUSEUM THEN PLEASE ATTEND TO YOUR DUTIES AND LEAVE ME BE!
NO, THE EARTH TIME MUSEUM!
YOU'RE THE GREY EARL, A TIME TRAVELER, RIGHT?
...HOW DO YOU KNOW THIS?
WE MET IN THE CRETACEOUS PERIOD! DON'T YOU REMEMBER?

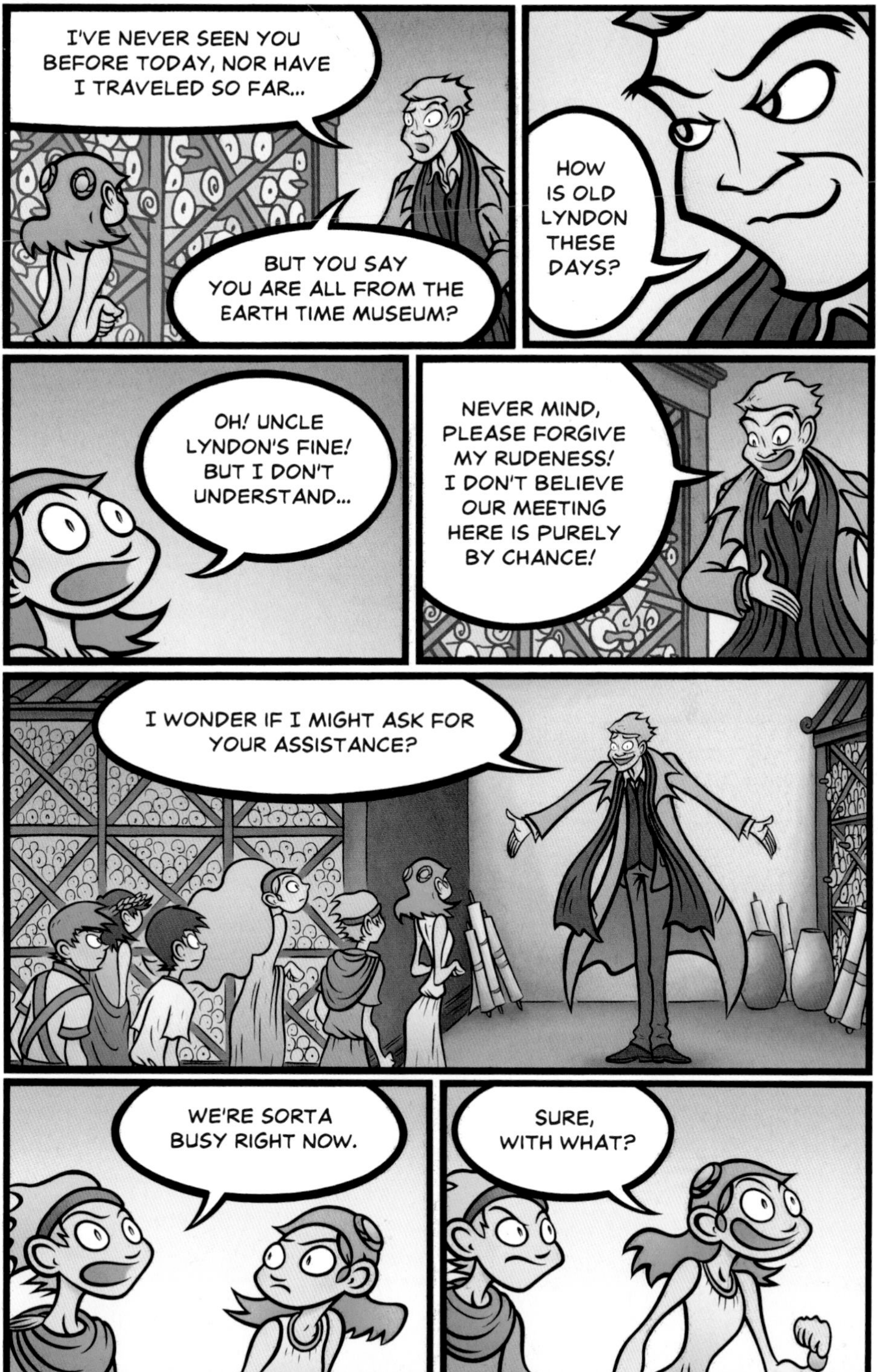
I'VE NEVER SEEN YOU BEFORE TODAY, NOR HAVE I TRAVELED SO FAR...
BUT YOU SAY YOU ARE ALL FROM THE EARTH TIME MUSEUM?
HOW IS OLD LYNDON THESE DAYS?
OH! UNCLE LYNDON'S FINE! BUT I DON'T UNDERSTAND...
NEVER MIND, PLEASE FORGIVE MY RUDENESS! I DON'T BELIEVE OUR MEETING HERE IS PURELY BY CHANCE!
I WONDER IF I MIGHT ASK FOR YOUR ASSISTANCE?
WE'RE SORTA BUSY RIGHT NOW.
SURE, WITH WHAT?

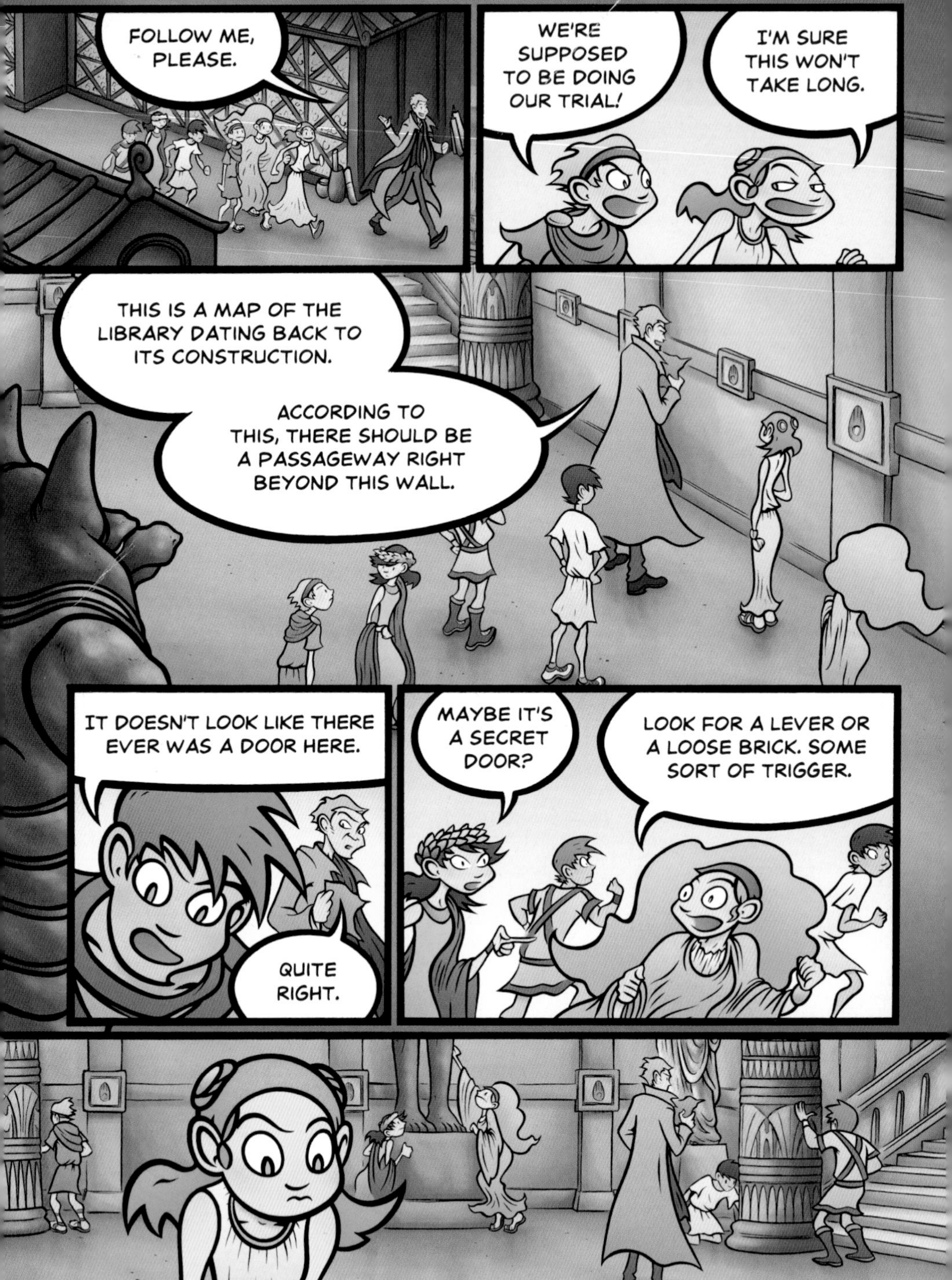
FOLLOW ME, PLEASE.
WE'RE SUPPOSED TO BE DOING OUR TRIAL!
I'M SURE THIS WON'T TAKE LONG.
THIS IS A MAP OF THE LIBRARY DATING BACK TO ITS CONSTRUCTION.
ACCORDING TO THIS, THERE SHOULD BE A PASSAGEWAY RIGHT BEYOND THIS WALL.
IT DOESN'T LOOK LIKE THERE EVER WAS A DOOR HERE.
QUITE RIGHT.
MAYBE IT'S A SECRET DOOR?
LOOK FOR A LEVER OR A LOOSE BRICK. SOME SORT OF TRIGGER.

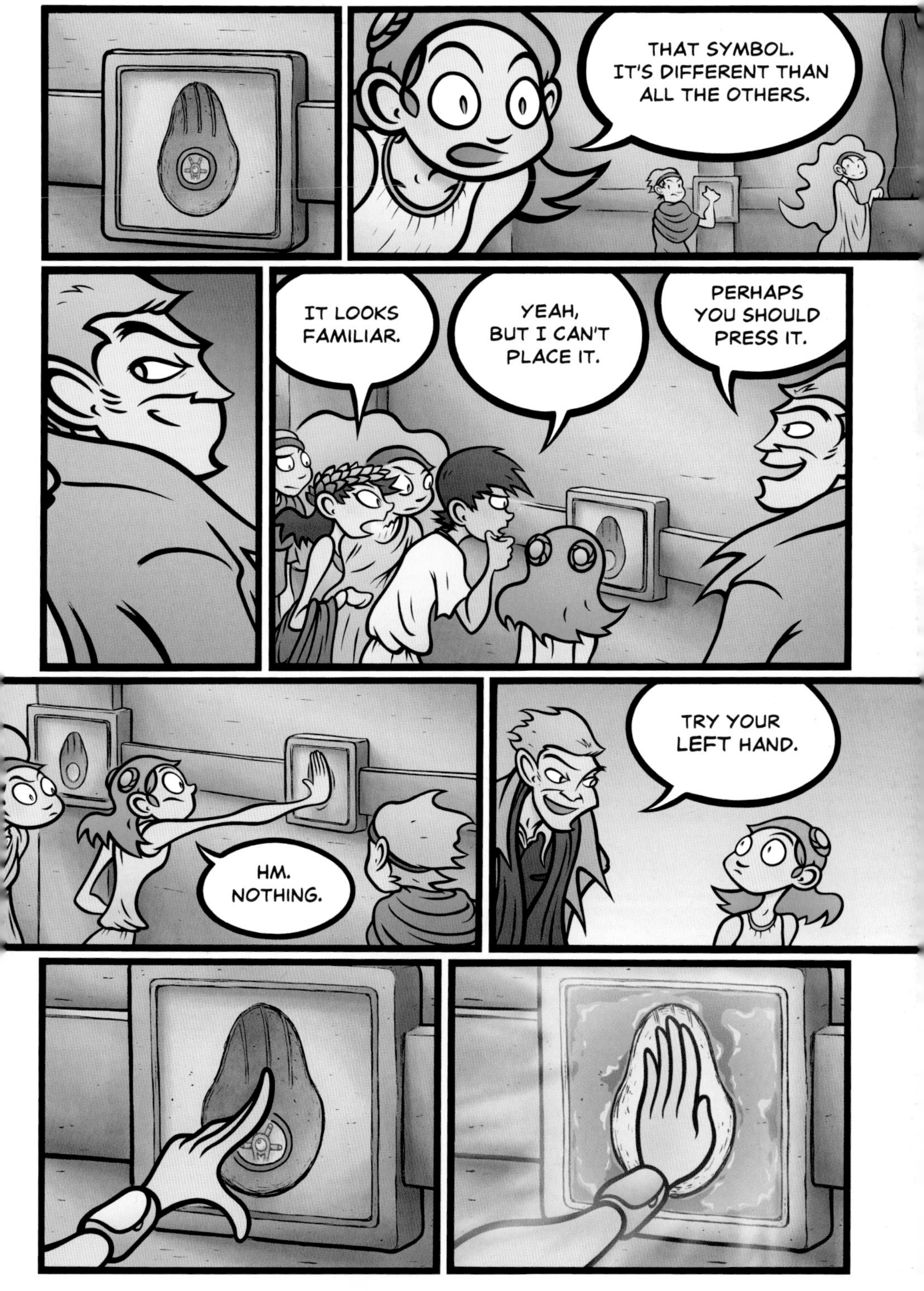

THAT SYMBOL. IT'S DIFFERENT THAN ALL THE OTHERS.
IT LOOKS FAMILIAR.
YEAH, BUT I CAN'T PLACE IT.
PERHAPS YOU SHOULD PRESS IT.
HM. NOTHING.
TRY YOUR LEFT HAND.

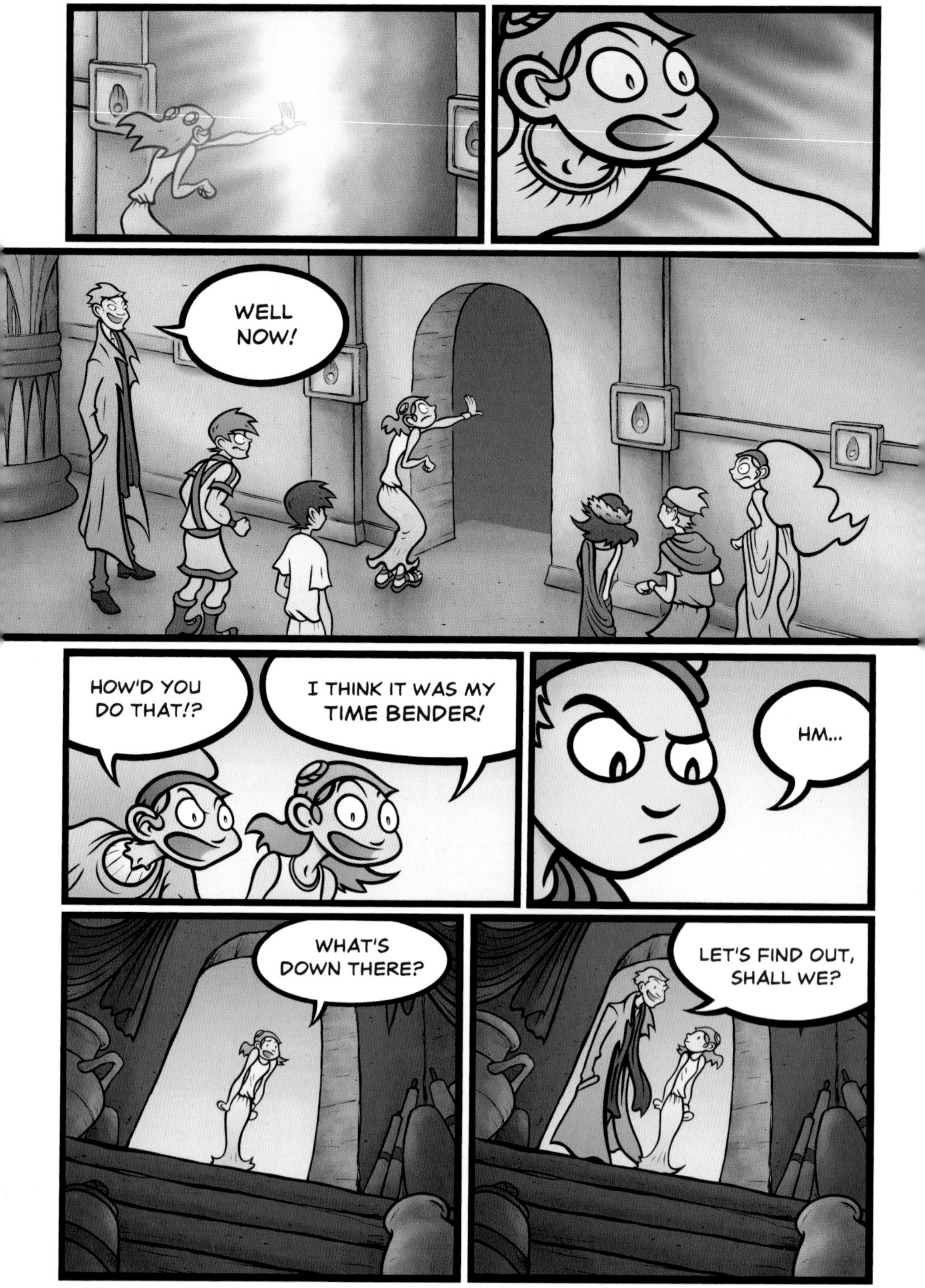
WELL NOW!
HOW'D YOU DO THAT!?
I THINK IT WAS MY TIME BENDER!
HM...
WHAT'S DOWN THERE?
LET'S FIND OUT, SHALL WE?

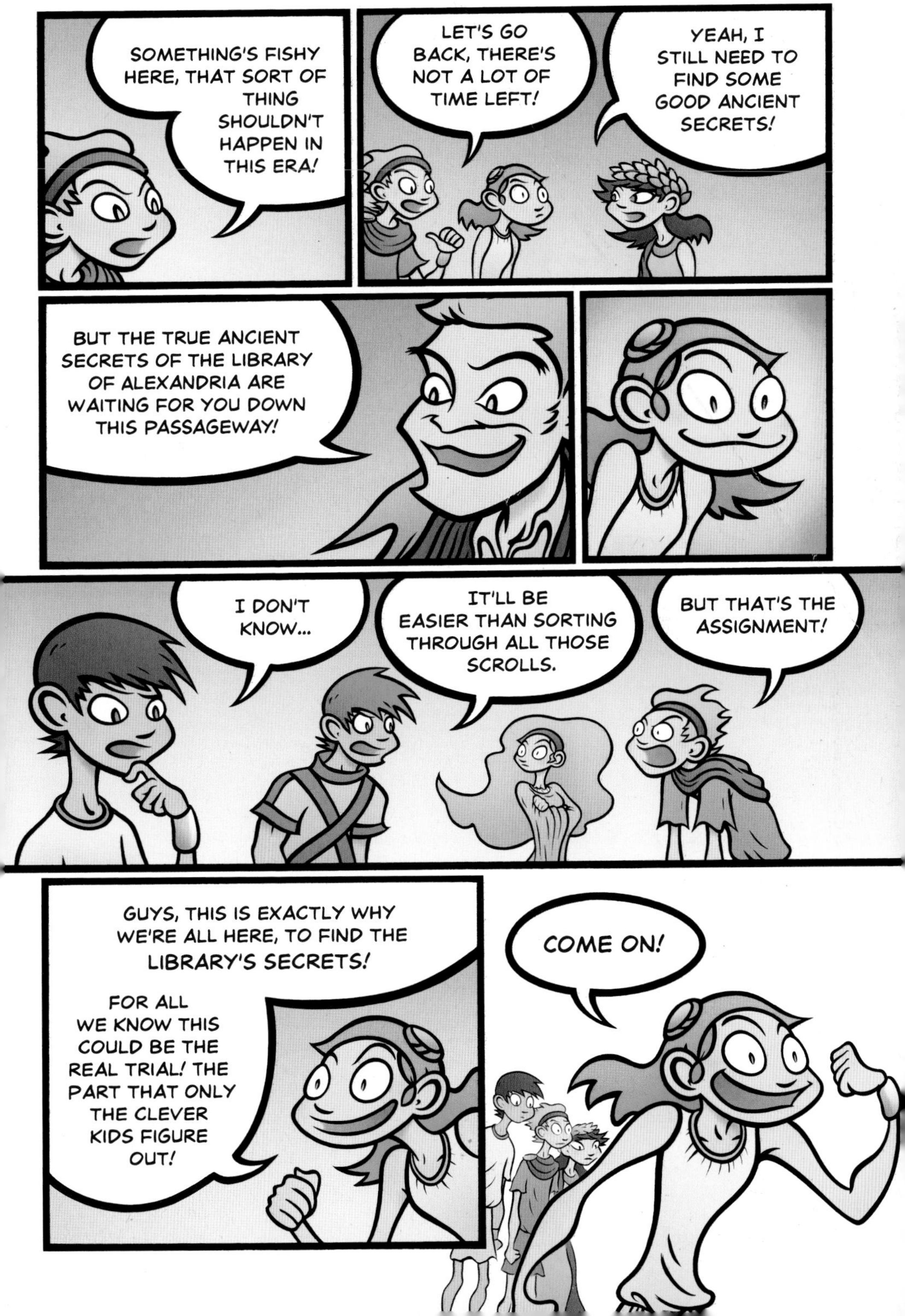
SOMETHING'S FISHY HERE, THAT SORT OF THING SHOULDN'T HAPPEN IN THIS ERA!
LET'S GO BACK, THERE'S NOT A LOT OF TIME LEFT!
YEAH, I STILL NEED TO FIND SOME GOOD ANCIENT SECRETS!
BUT THE TRUE ANCIENT SECRETS OF THE LIBRARY OF ALEXANDRIA ARE WAITING FOR YOU DOWN THIS PASSAGEWAY!
I DON'T KNOW...
IT'LL BE EASIER THAN SORTING THROUGH ALL THOSE SCROLLS.
BUT THAT'S THE ASSIGNMENT!
GUYS, THIS IS EXACTLY WHY WE'RE ALL HERE, TO FIND THE LIBRARY'S SECRETS!
FOR ALL WE KNOW THIS COULD BE THE REAL TRIAL! THE PART THAT ONLY THE CLEVER KIDS FIGURE OUT!
COME ON!

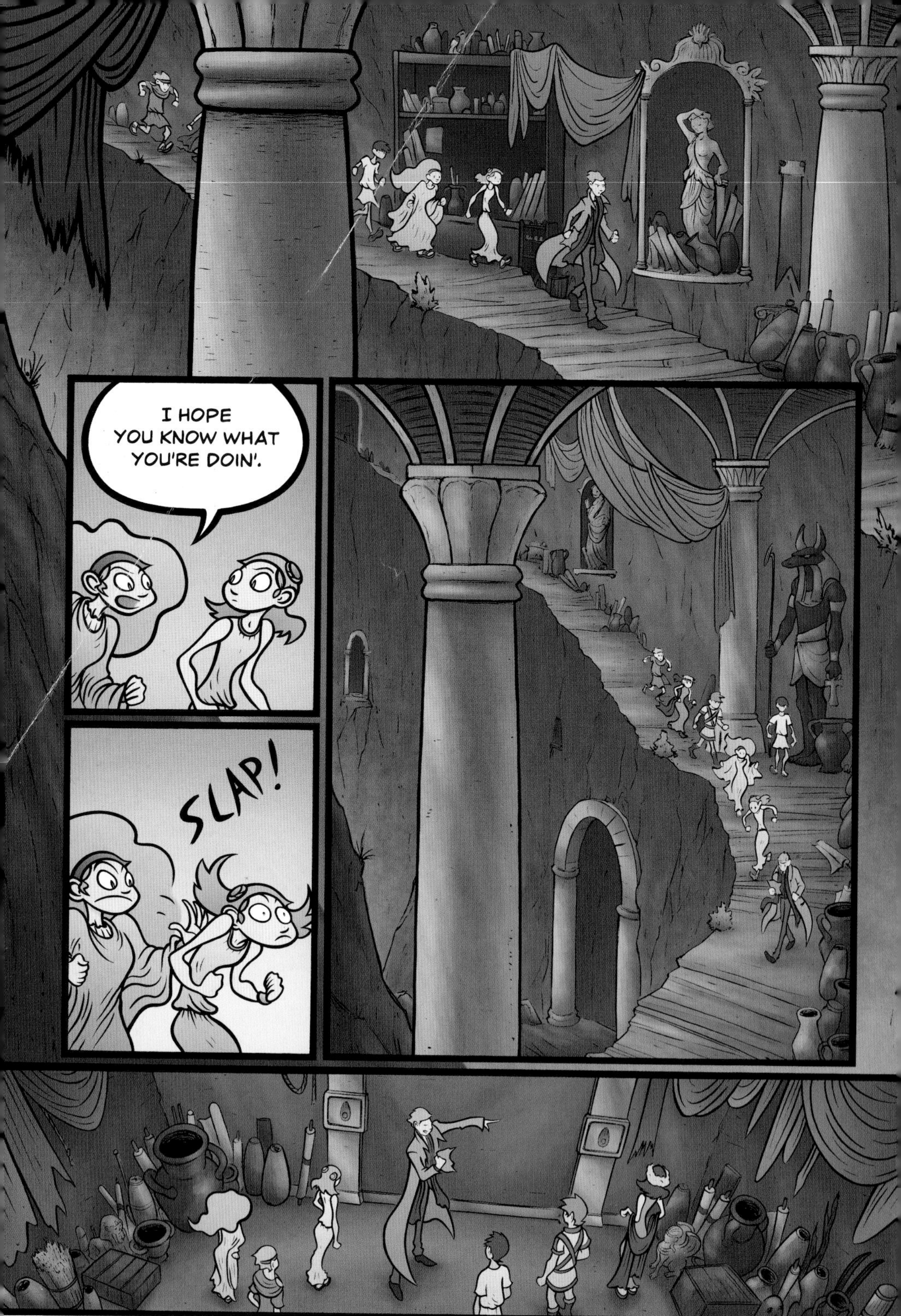
I HOPE YOU KNOW WHAT YOU'RE DOIN'.
SLAP!

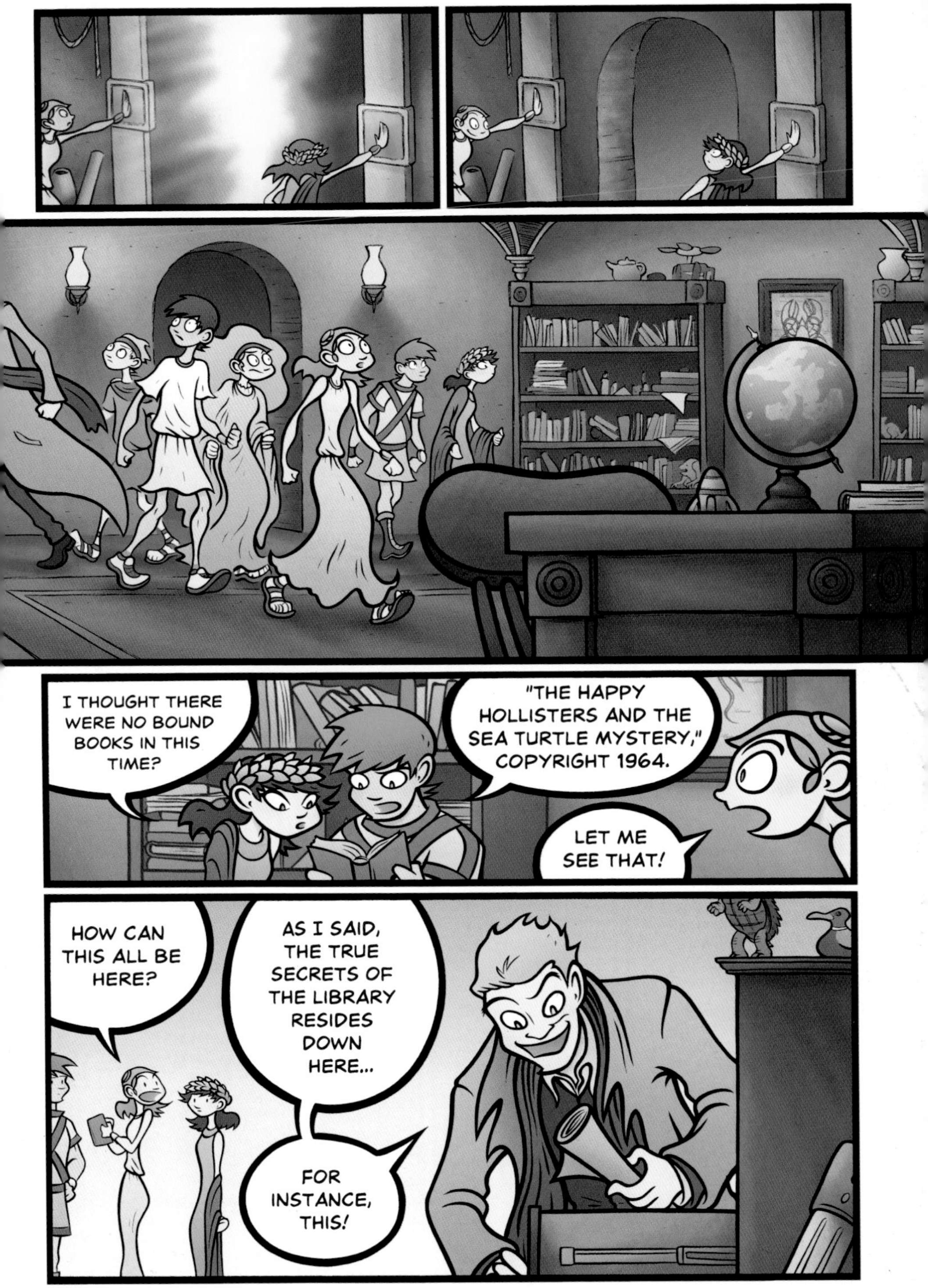
I THOUGHT THERE WERE NO BOUND BOOKS IN THIS TIME?
"THE HAPPY HOLLISTERS AND THE SEA TURTLE MYSTERY," COPYRIGHT 1964.
LET ME SEE THAT!
HOW CAN THIS ALL BE HERE?
AS I SAID, THE TRUE SECRETS OF THE LIBRARY RESIDES DOWN HERE...
FOR INSTANCE, THIS!

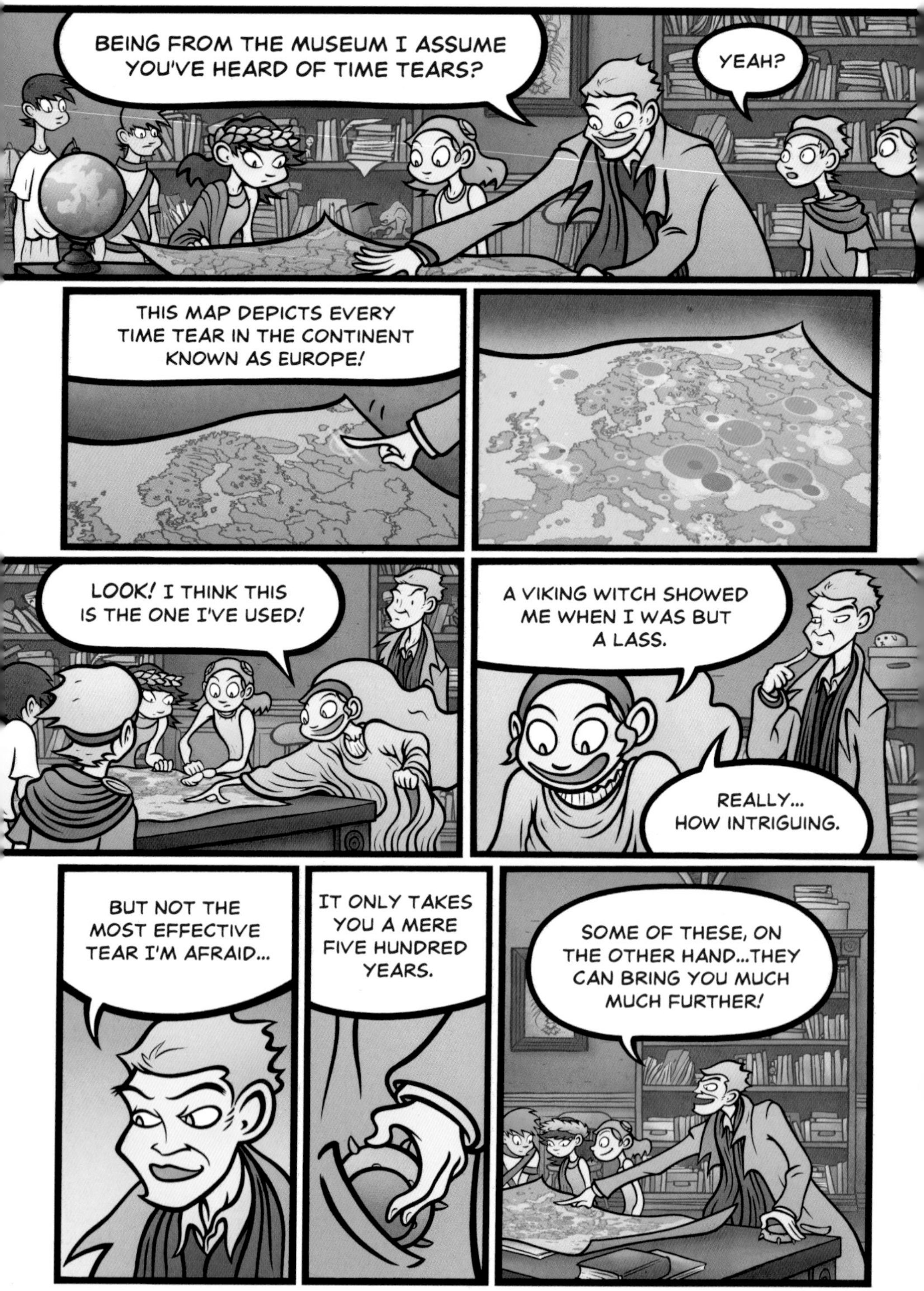
BEING FROM THE MUSEUM I ASSUME YOU'VE HEARD OF TIME TEARS?
YEAH?
THIS MAP DEPICTS EVERY TIME TEAR IN THE CONTINENT KNOWN AS EUROPE!
LOOK! I THINK THIS IS THE ONE I'VE USED!
A VIKING WITCH SHOWED ME WHEN I WAS BUT A LASS.
REALLY... HOW INTRIGUING.
BUT NOT THE MOST EFFECTIVE TEAR I'M AFRAID...
IT ONLY TAKES YOU A MERE FIVE HUNDRED YEARS.
SOME OF THESE, ON THE OTHER HAND...THEY CAN BRING YOU MUCH MUCH FURTHER!

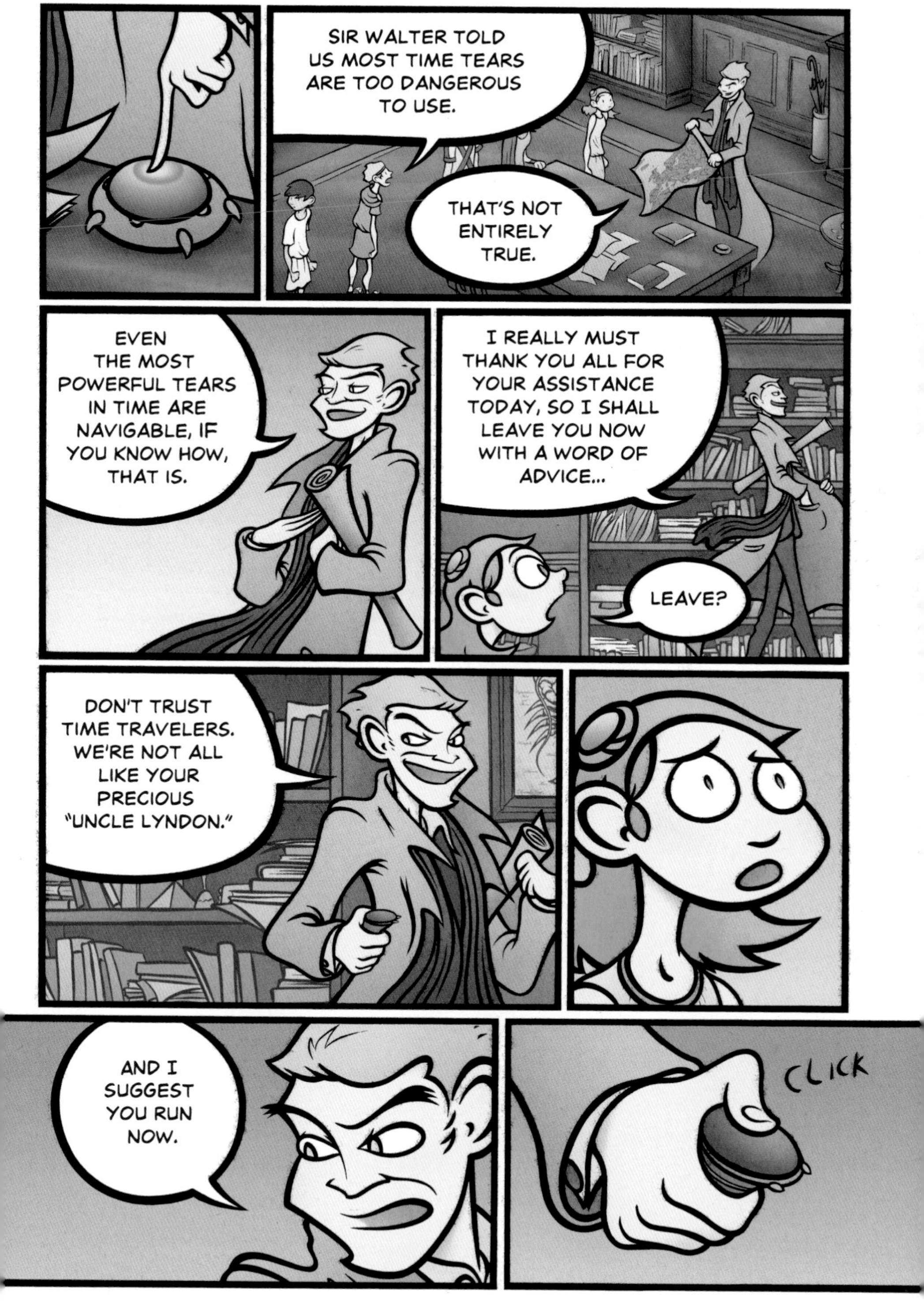
SIR WALTER TOLD US MOST TIME TEARS ARE TOO DANGEROUS TO USE.
THAT'S NOT ENTIRELY TRUE.
EVEN THE MOST POWERFUL TEARS IN TIME ARE NAVIGABLE, IF YOU KNOW HOW, THAT IS.
I REALLY MUST THANK YOU ALL FOR YOUR ASSISTANCE TODAY, SO I SHALL LEAVE YOU NOW WITH A WORD OF ADVICE...
LEAVE?
DON'T TRUST TIME TRAVELERS. WE'RE NOT ALL LIKE YOUR PRECIOUS "UNCLE LYNDON."
AND I SUGGEST YOU RUN NOW.
CLICK

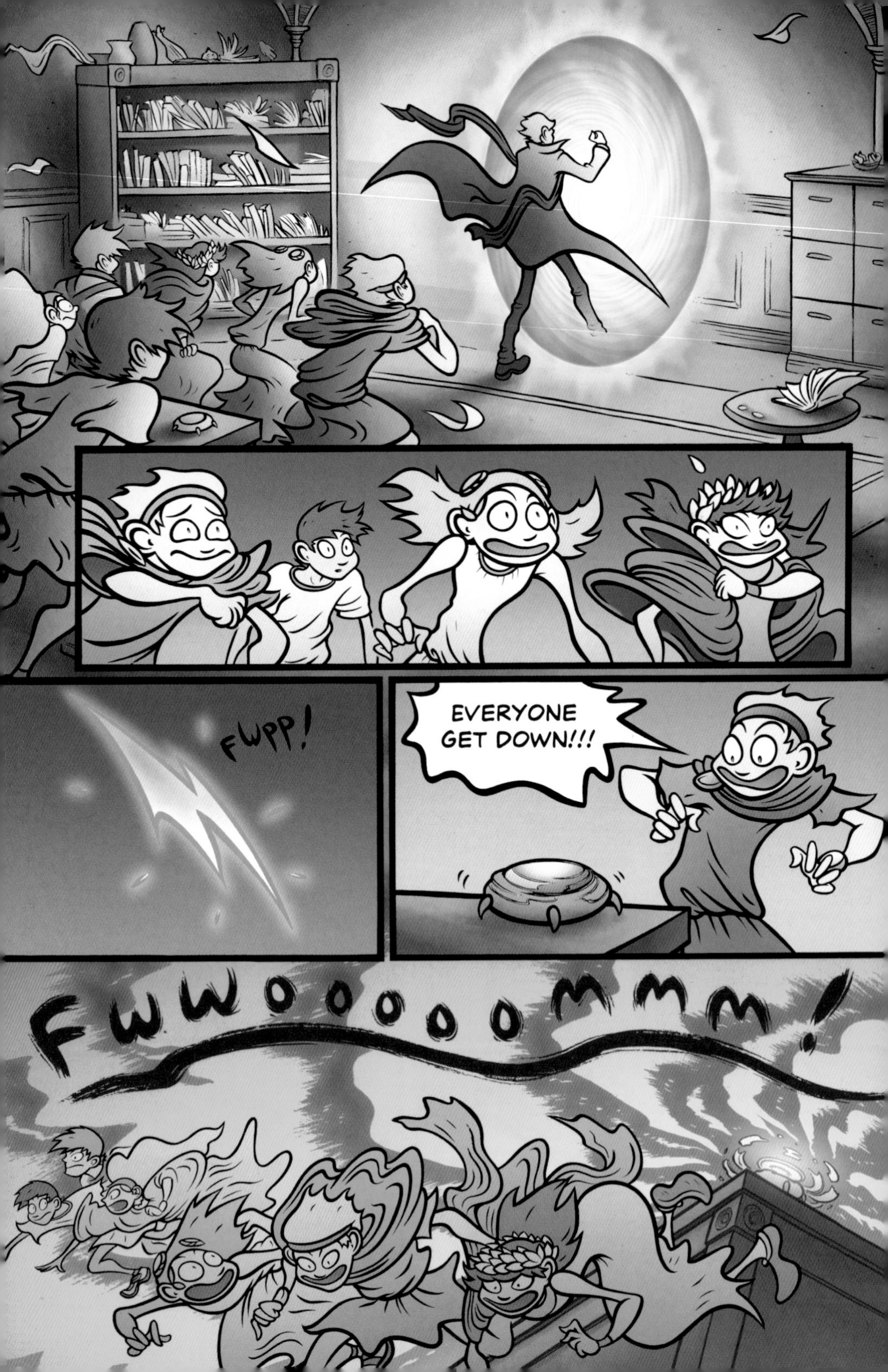
FWPP!
EVERYONE GET DOWN!!!
FWWOOOOOMMM!

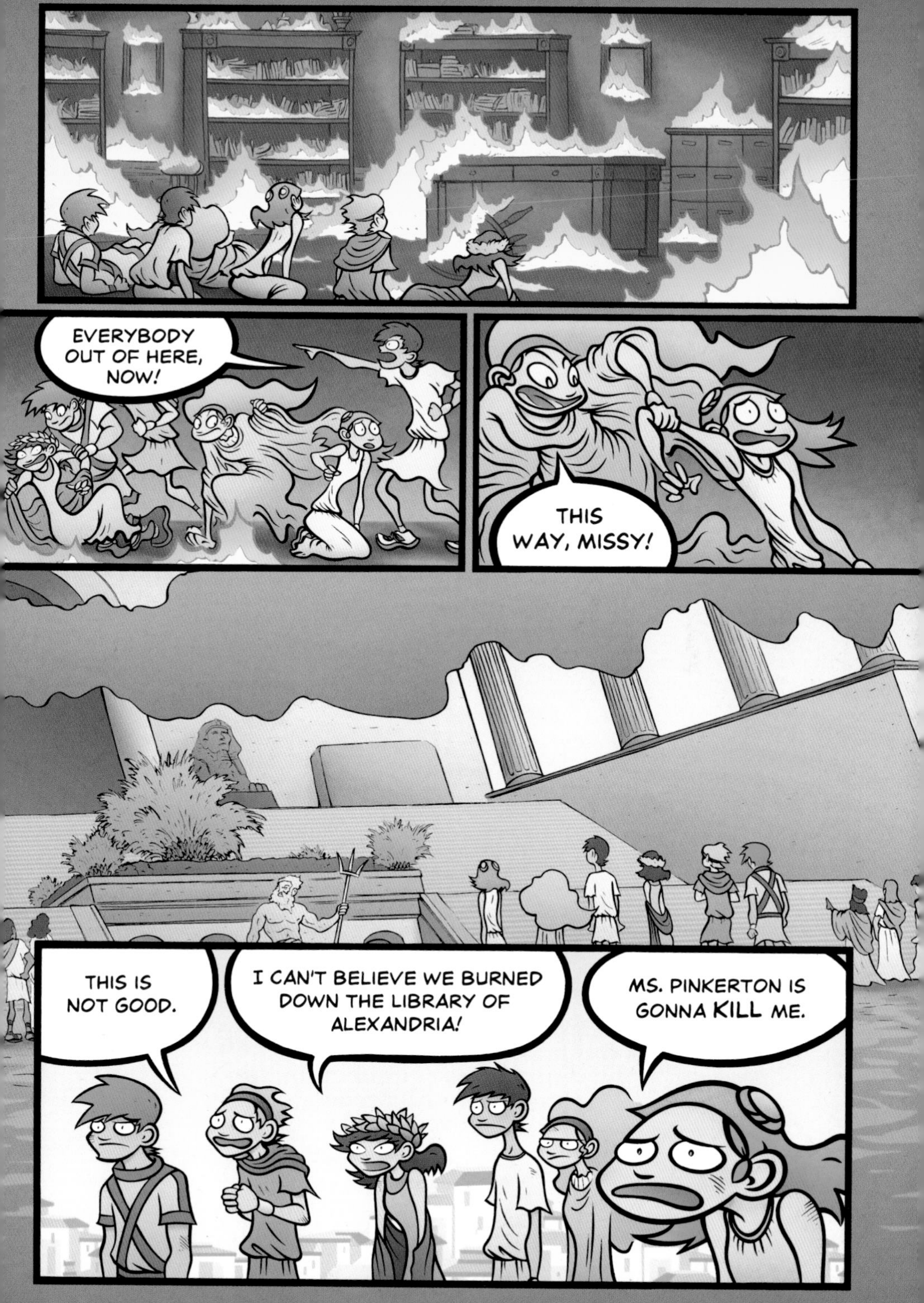
EVERYBODY OUT OF HERE, NOW!
THIS WAY, MISSY!
THIS IS NOT GOOD.
I CAN'T BELIEVE WE BURNED DOWN THE LIBRARY OF ALEXANDRIA!
MS. PINKERTON IS GONNA KILL ME.

INEXCUSABLE!!!

DO YOU REALIZE HOW CLOSE YOU CAME TO ALTERING HISTORY?!

IF NOT FOR THE QUICK ACTIONS OF SIR WALTER AND HIS EPOCH SQUADS THE LIBRARY OF ALEXANDRIA WOULD HAVE BURNED TO THE GROUND LONG BEFORE IT WAS SUPPOSED TO!

DID YOU REALLY THINK IT PRUDENT TO ABANDON YOUR TRIAL AND HELP A STRANGE MAN STEAL FROM ONE OF DOCTOR BECKENBAUER'S SECRET OFFICES?!

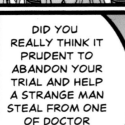

AND YOU, MS. BEAN! YOU SHOULD HAVE TOLD US IMMEDIATELY ABOUT YOUR PREVIOUS MEETING WITH THE EARL!

BUT I THOUGHT HE WAS... A GOOD GUY.

THE GREY EARL IS A RENEGADE TIME TRAVELER AND NOT A PERSON TO BE TRUSTED! THAT MAP IN THE HANDS OF A MAN LIKE HIM COULD BE VERY DANGEROUS INDEED!

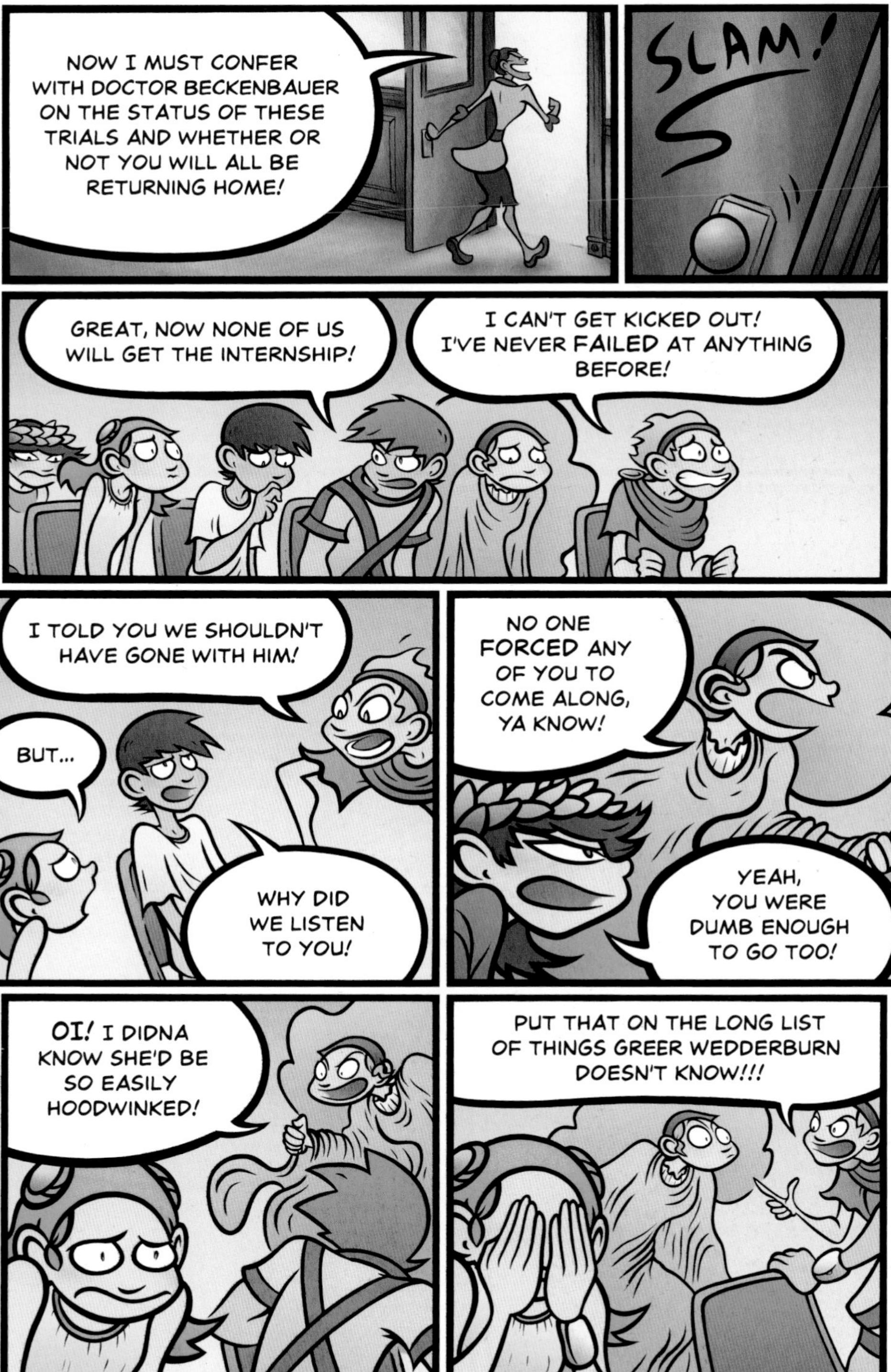
NOW I MUST CONFER WITH DOCTOR BECKENBAUER ON THE STATUS OF THESE TRIALS AND WHETHER OR NOT YOU WILL ALL BE RETURNING HOME!
SLAM!
GREAT, NOW NONE OF US WILL GET THE INTERNSHIP!
I CAN'T GET KICKED OUT! I'VE NEVER FAILED AT ANYTHING BEFORE!
I TOLD YOU WE SHOULDN'T HAVE GONE WITH HIM!
BUT...
WHY DID WE LISTEN TO YOU!
NO ONE FORCED ANY OF YOU TO COME ALONG, YA KNOW!
YEAH, YOU WERE DUMB ENOUGH TO GO TOO!
OI! I DIDNA KNOW SHE'D BE SO EASILY HOODWINKED!
PUT THAT ON THE LONG LIST OF THINGS GREER WEDDERBURN DOESN'T KNOW!!!

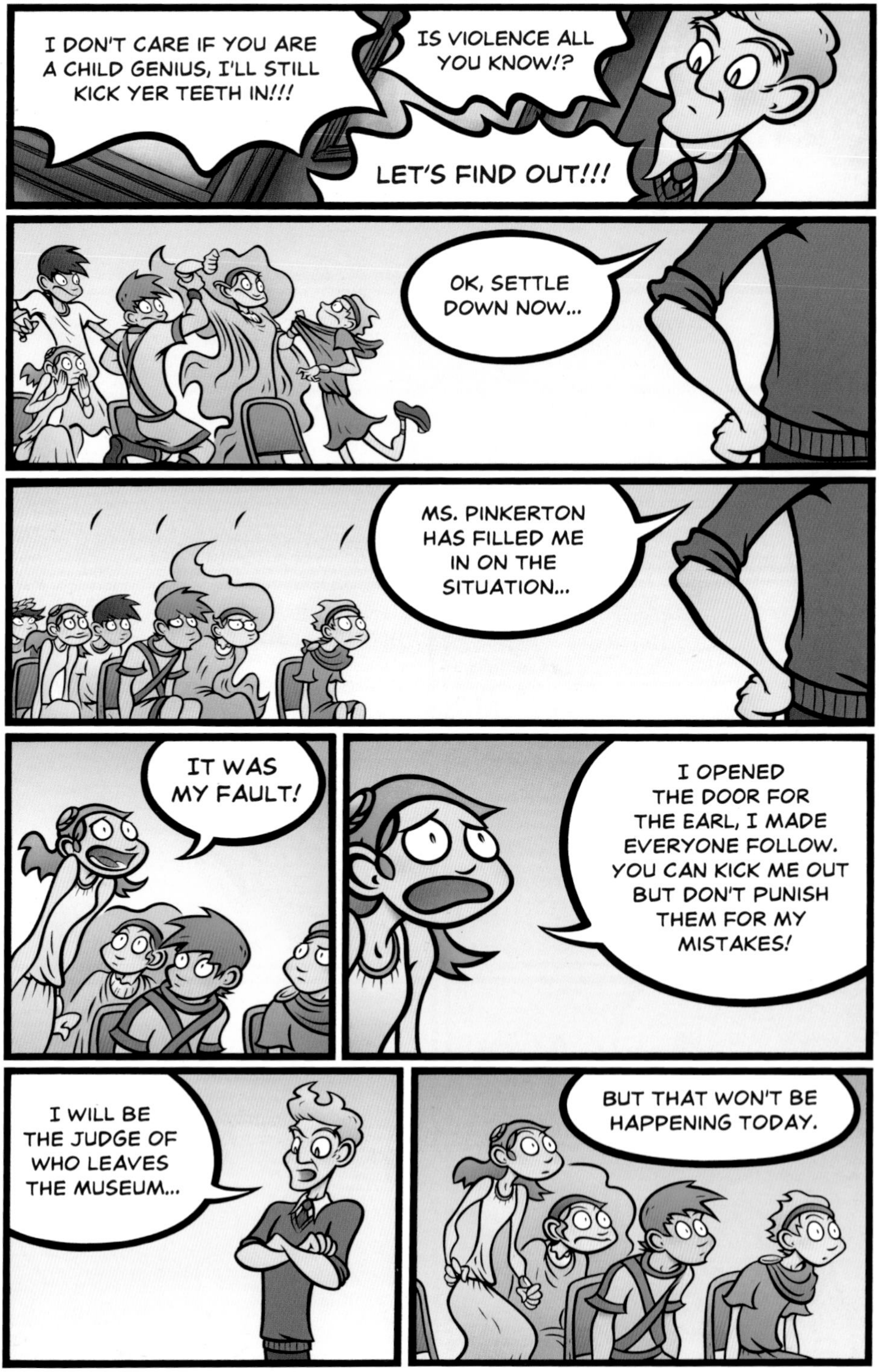
I DON'T CARE IF YOU ARE A CHILD GENIUS, I'LL STILL KICK YER TEETH IN!!!
IS VIOLENCE ALL YOU KNOW!?
LET'S FIND OUT!!!
OK, SETTLE DOWN NOW...
MS. PINKERTON HAS FILLED ME IN ON THE SITUATION...
IT WAS MY FAULT!
I OPENED THE DOOR FOR THE EARL, I MADE EVERYONE FOLLOW. YOU CAN KICK ME OUT BUT DON'T PUNISH THEM FOR MY MISTAKES!
I WILL BE THE JUDGE OF WHO LEAVES THE MUSEUM...
BUT THAT WON'T BE HAPPENING TODAY.

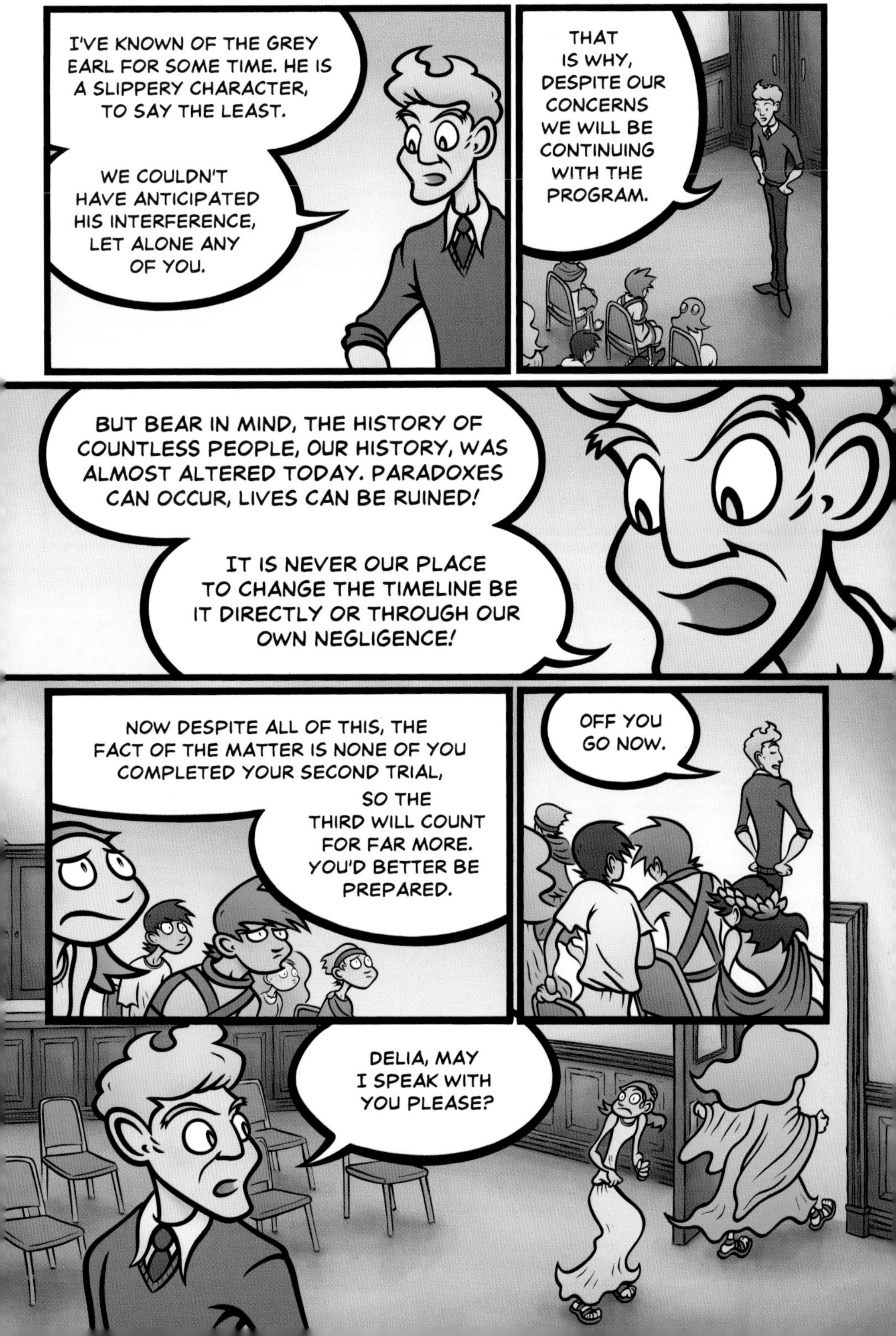
I'VE KNOWN OF THE GREY EARL FOR SOME TIME. HE IS A SLIPPERY CHARACTER, TO SAY THE LEAST.
WE COULDN'T HAVE ANTICIPATED HIS INTERFERENCE, LET ALONE ANY OF YOU.
THAT IS WHY, DESPITE OUR CONCERNS WE WILL BE CONTINUING WITH THE PROGRAM.
BUT BEAR IN MIND, THE HISTORY OF COUNTLESS PEOPLE, OUR HISTORY, WAS ALMOST ALTERED TODAY. PARADOXES CAN OCCUR, LIVES CAN BE RUINED!
IT IS NEVER OUR PLACE TO CHANGE THE TIMELINE BE IT DIRECTLY OR THROUGH OUR OWN NEGLIGENCE!
NOW DESPITE ALL OF THIS, THE FACT OF THE MATTER IS NONE OF YOU COMPLETED YOUR SECOND TRIAL,
SO THE THIRD WILL COUNT FOR FAR MORE. YOU'D BETTER BE PREPARED.
OFF YOU GO NOW.
DELIA, MAY I SPEAK WITH YOU PLEASE?

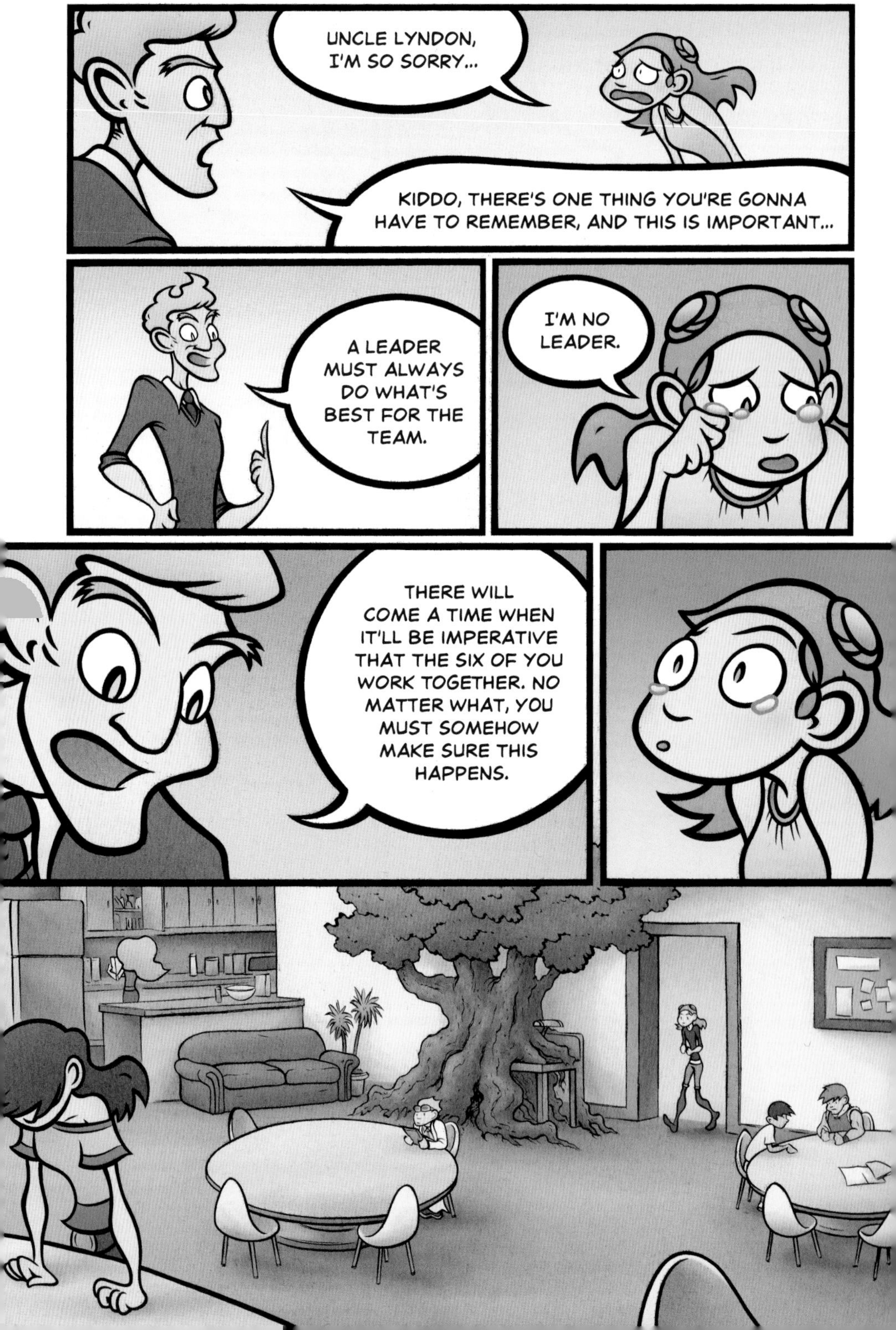
UNCLE LYNDON, I'M SO SORRY...
KIDDO, THERE'S ONE THING YOU'RE GONNA HAVE TO REMEMBER, AND THIS IS IMPORTANT...
A LEADER MUST ALWAYS DO WHAT'S BEST FOR THE TEAM.
I'M NO LEADER.
THERE WILL COME A TIME WHEN IT'LL BE IMPERATIVE THAT THE SIX OF YOU WORK TOGETHER. NO MATTER WHAT, YOU MUST SOMEHOW MAKE SURE THIS HAPPENS.

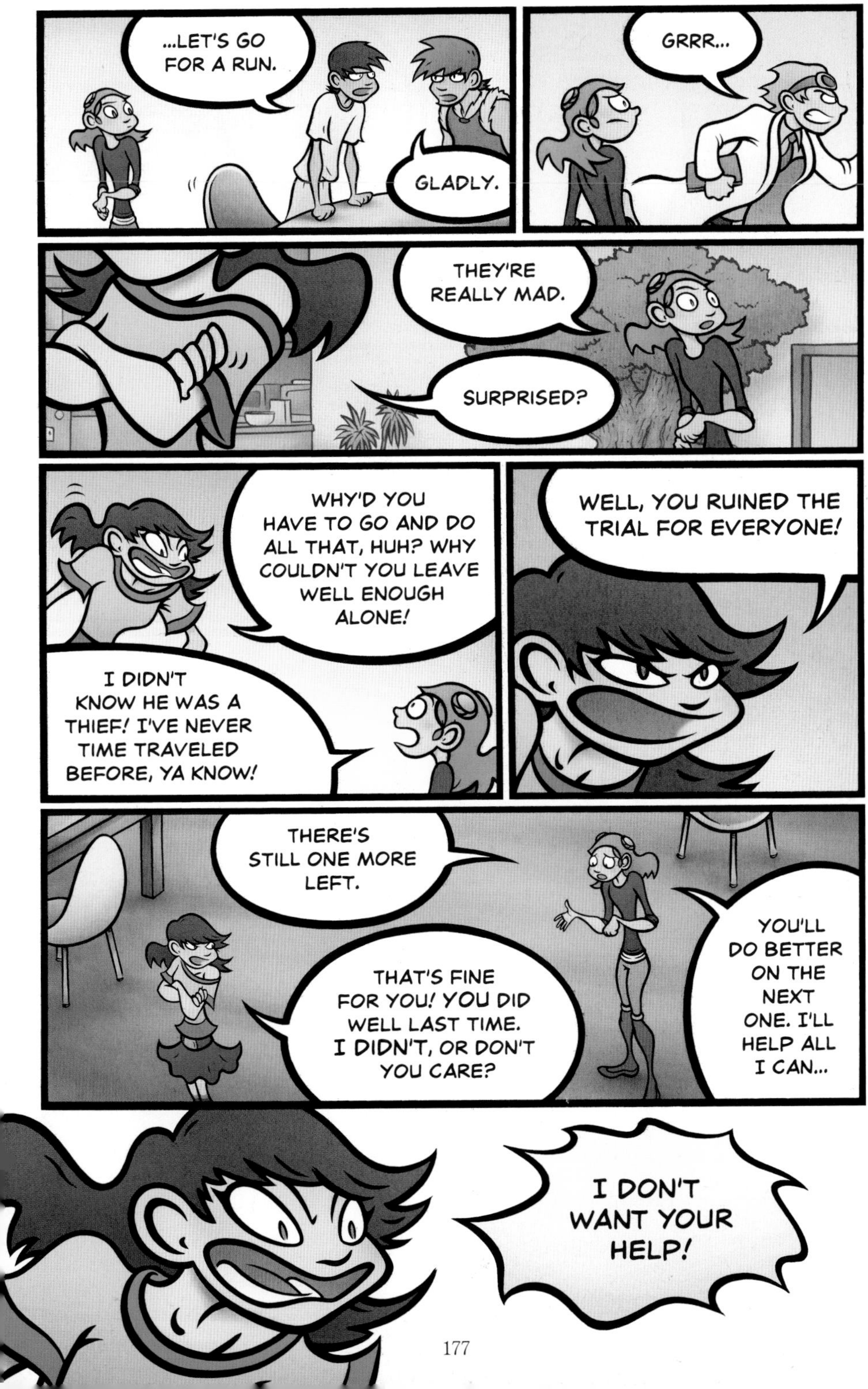
...LET'S GO FOR A RUN.
GLADLY.
GRRR...
THEY'RE REALLY MAD.
SURPRISED?
WHY'D YOU HAVE TO GO AND DO ALL THAT, HUH? WHY COULDN'T YOU LEAVE WELL ENOUGH ALONE!
I DIDN'T KNOW HE WAS A THIEF! I'VE NEVER TIME TRAVELED BEFORE, YA KNOW!
WELL, YOU RUINED THE TRIAL FOR EVERYONE!
THERE'S STILL ONE MORE LEFT.
THAT'S FINE FOR YOU! YOU DID WELL LAST TIME. I DIDN'T, OR DON'T YOU CARE?
YOU'LL DO BETTER ON THE NEXT ONE. I'LL HELP ALL I CAN...
I DON'T WANT YOUR HELP!

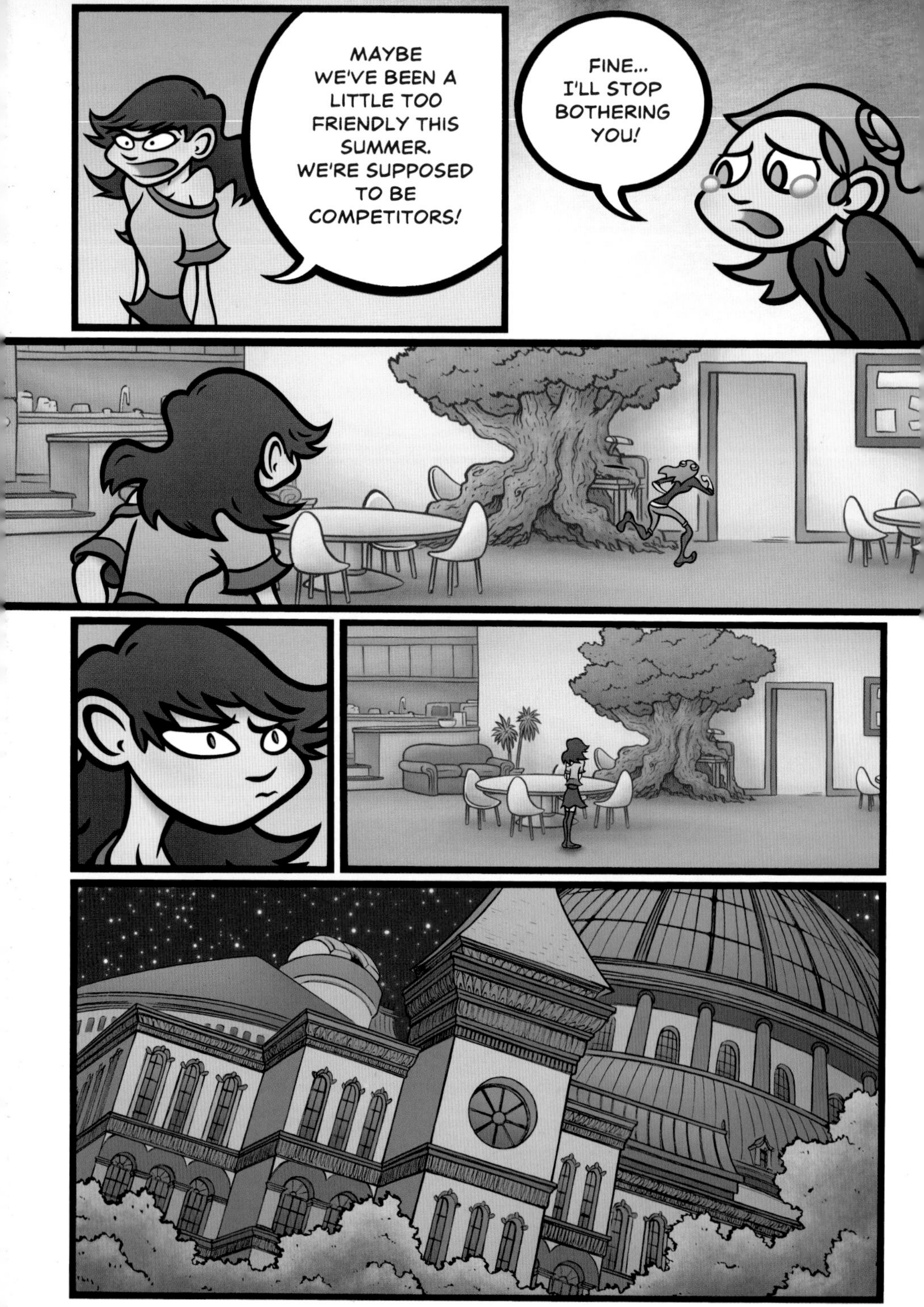
MAYBE WE'VE BEEN A LITTLE TOO FRIENDLY THIS SUMMER. WE'RE SUPPOSED TO BE COMPETITORS!
FINE... I'LL STOP BOTHERING YOU!

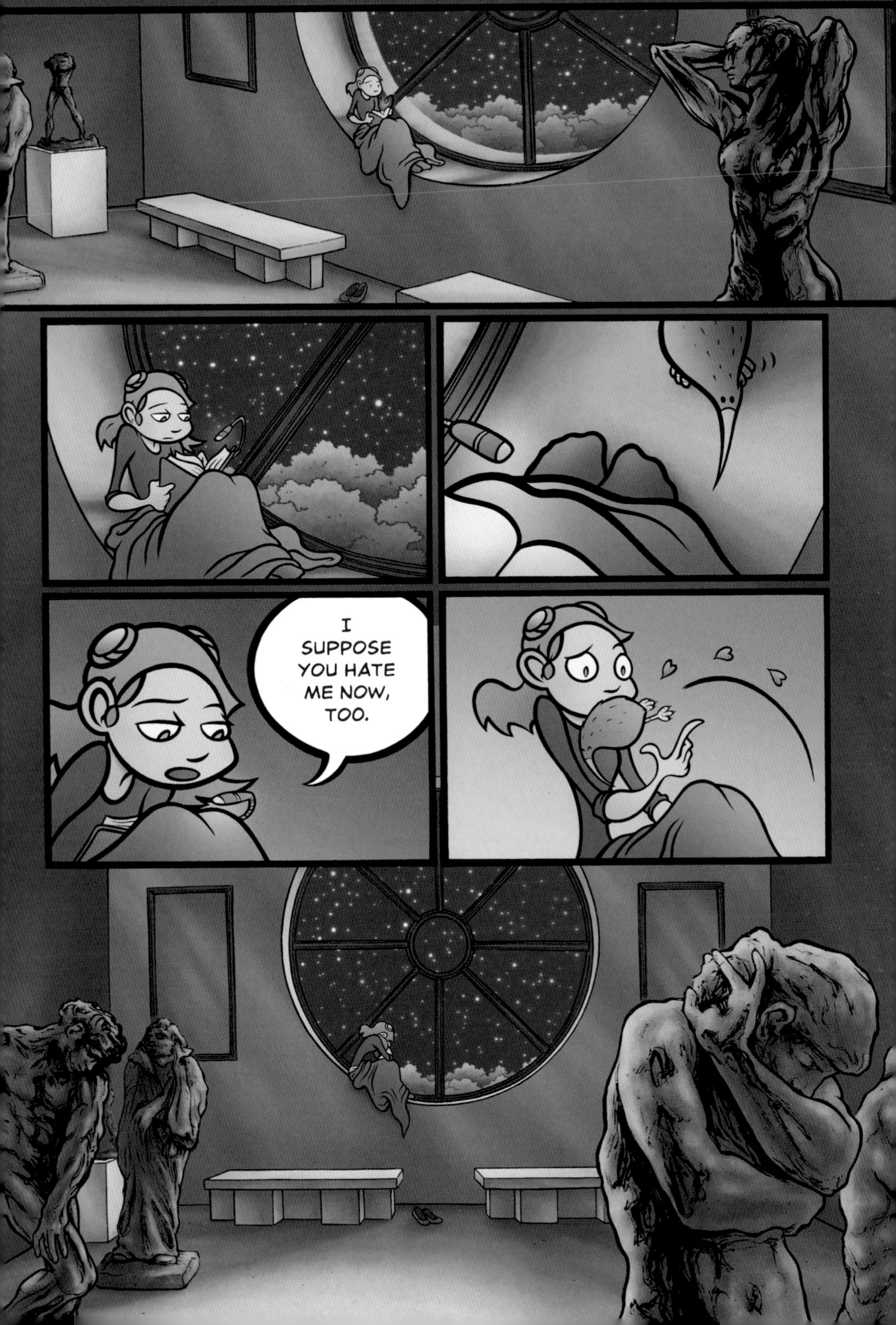
I SUPPOSE YOU HATE ME NOW, TOO.

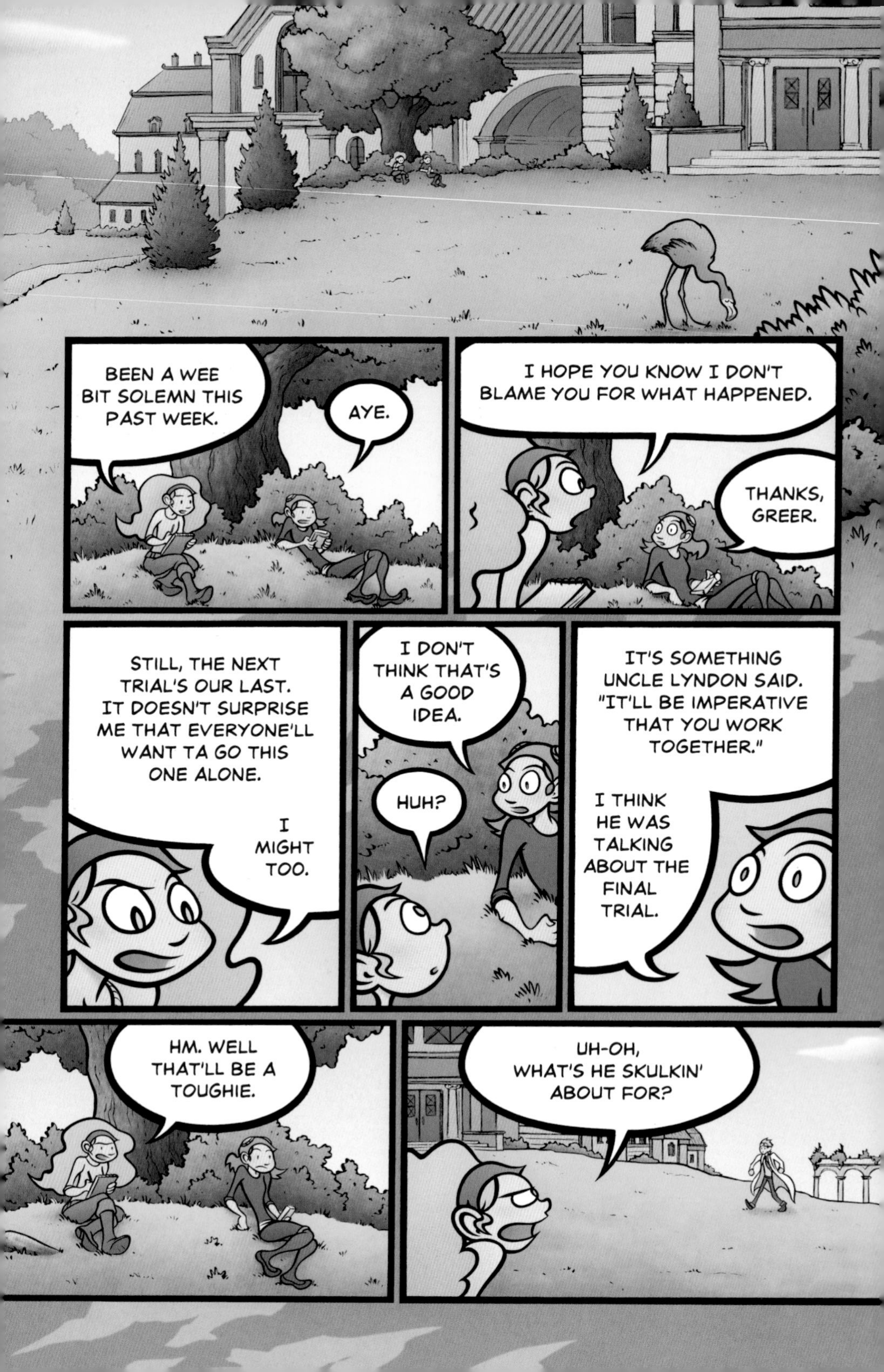
BEEN A WEE BIT SOLEMN THIS PAST WEEK.
AYE.
I HOPE YOU KNOW I DON'T BLAME YOU FOR WHAT HAPPENED.
THANKS, GREER.
STILL, THE NEXT TRIAL'S OUR LAST. IT DOESN'T SURPRISE ME THAT EVERYONE'LL WANT TA GO THIS ONE ALONE.
I MIGHT TOO.
I DON'T THINK THAT'S A GOOD IDEA.
HUH?
IT'S SOMETHING UNCLE LYNDON SAID. "IT'LL BE IMPERATIVE THAT YOU WORK TOGETHER."
I THINK HE WAS TALKING ABOUT THE FINAL TRIAL.
HM. WELL THAT'LL BE A TOUGHIE.
UH-OH, WHAT'S HE SKULKIN' ABOUT FOR?

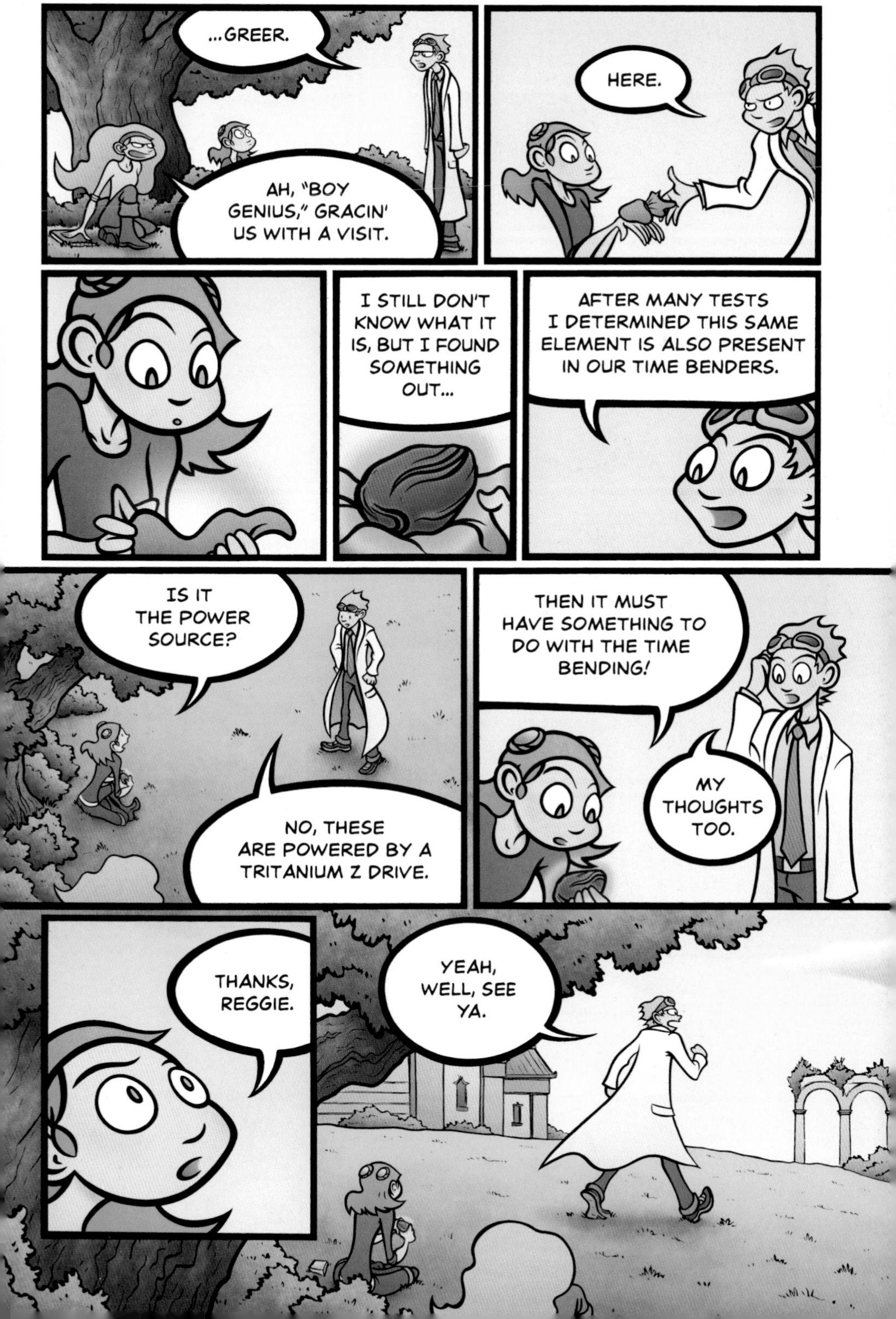
...GREER.
AH, "BOY GENIUS," GRACIN' US WITH A VISIT.
HERE.
I STILL DON'T KNOW WHAT IT IS, BUT I FOUND SOMETHING OUT...
AFTER MANY TESTS I DETERMINED THIS SAME ELEMENT IS ALSO PRESENT IN OUR TIME BENDERS.
IS IT THE POWER SOURCE?
NO, THESE ARE POWERED BY A TRITANIUM Z DRIVE.
THEN IT MUST HAVE SOMETHING TO DO WITH THE TIME BENDING!
MY THOUGHTS TOO.
THANKS, REGGIE.
YEAH, WELL, SEE YA.

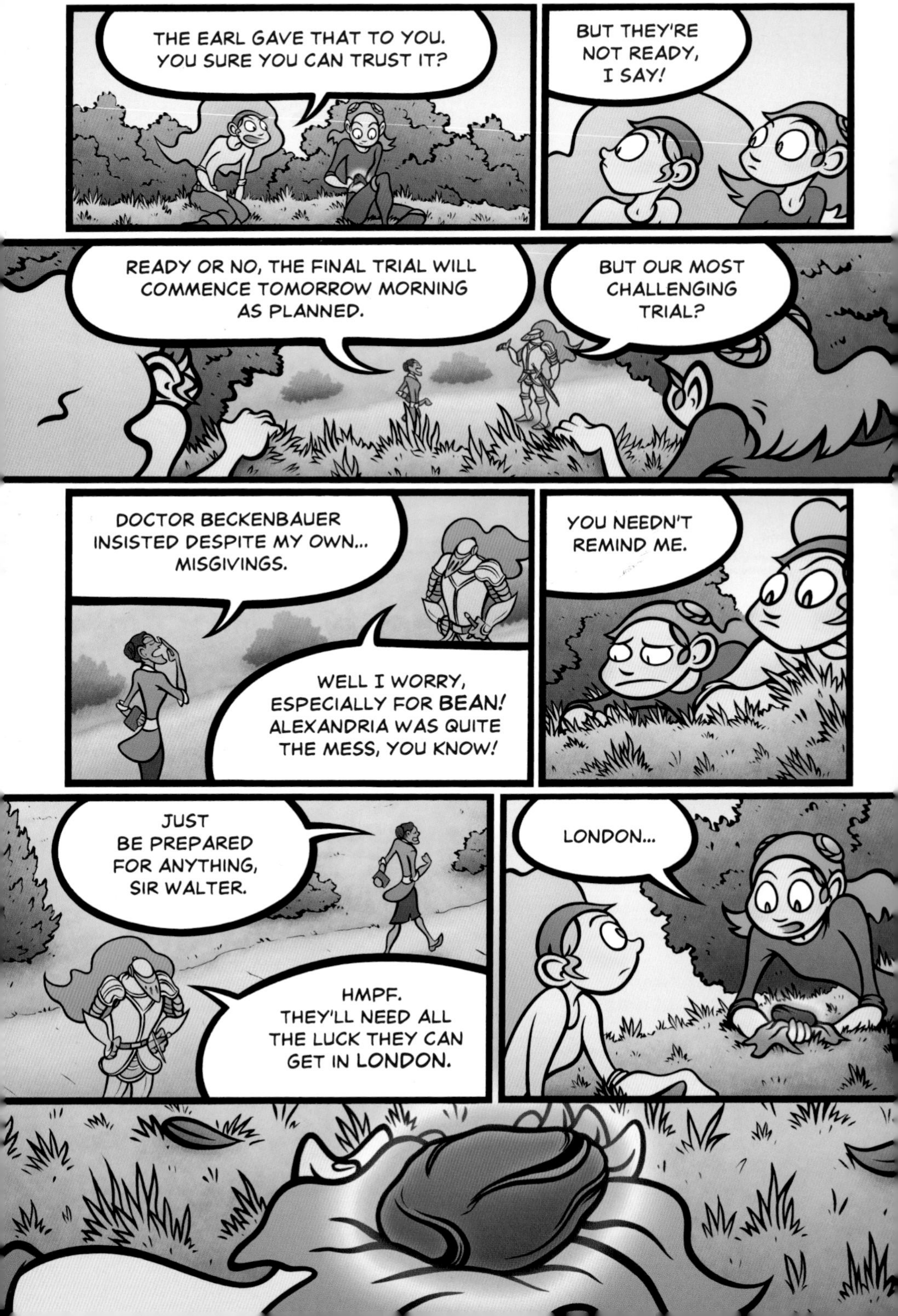
THE EARL GAVE THAT TO YOU. YOU SURE YOU CAN TRUST IT?
BUT THEY'RE NOT READY, I SAY!
READY OR NO, THE FINAL TRIAL WILL COMMENCE TOMORROW MORNING AS PLANNED.
BUT OUR MOST CHALLENGING TRIAL?
DOCTOR BECKENBAUER INSISTED DESPITE MY OWN... MISGIVINGS.
WELL I WORRY, ESPECIALLY FOR BEAN! ALEXANDRIA WAS QUITE THE MESS, YOU KNOW!
YOU NEEDN'T REMIND ME.
JUST BE PREPARED FOR ANYTHING, SIR WALTER.
HMPF. THEY'LL NEED ALL THE LUCK THEY CAN GET IN LONDON.
LONDON...

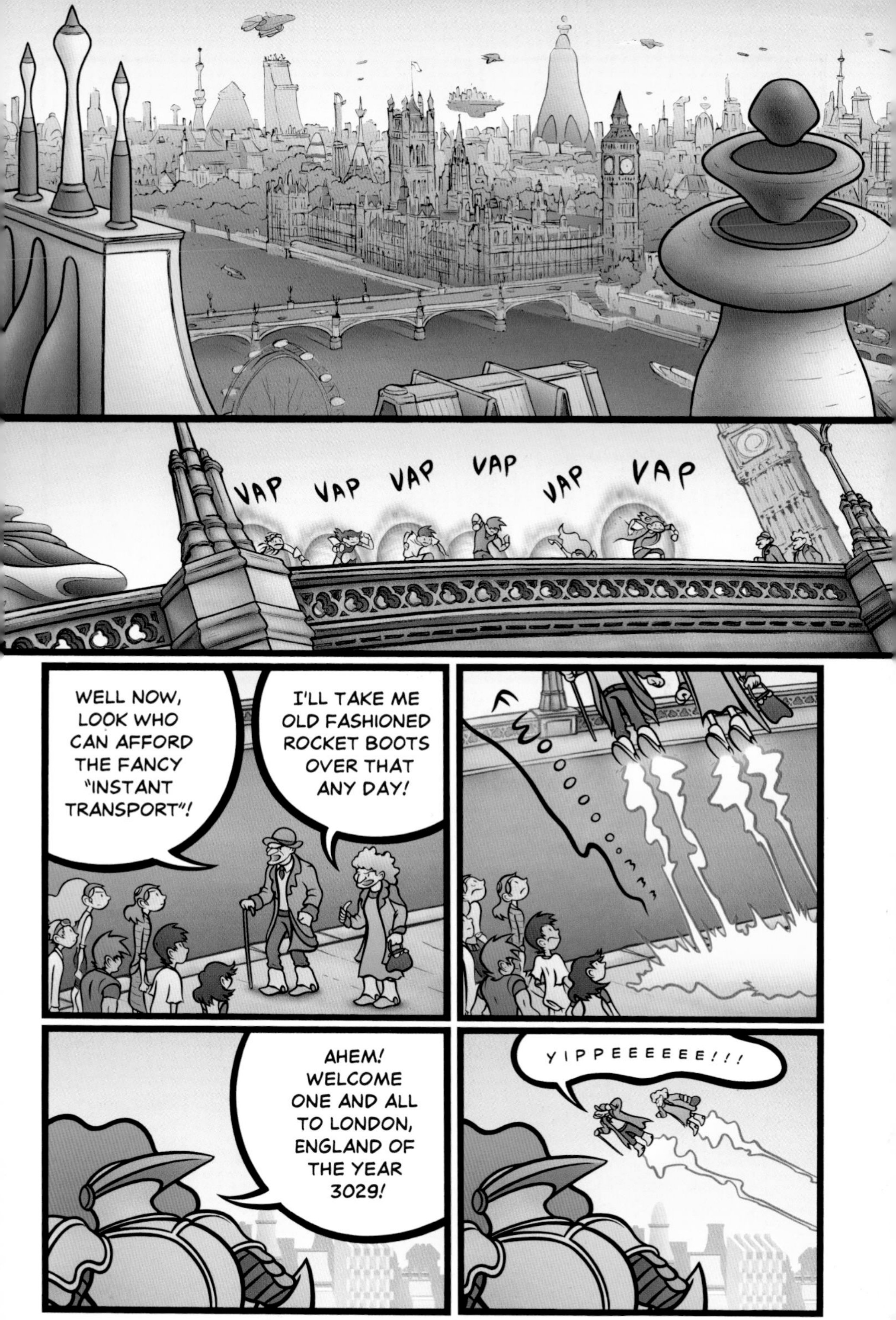
VAP VAP VAP VAP VAP VAP
WELL NOW, LOOK WHO CAN AFFORD THE FANCY "INSTANT TRANSPORT"!
I'LL TAKE ME OLD FASHIONED ROCKET BOOTS OVER THAT ANY DAY!
FWOOOOOOOOMMM
AHEM! WELCOME ONE AND ALL TO LONDON, ENGLAND OF THE YEAR 3029!
YIPPEEEEEEE!!!

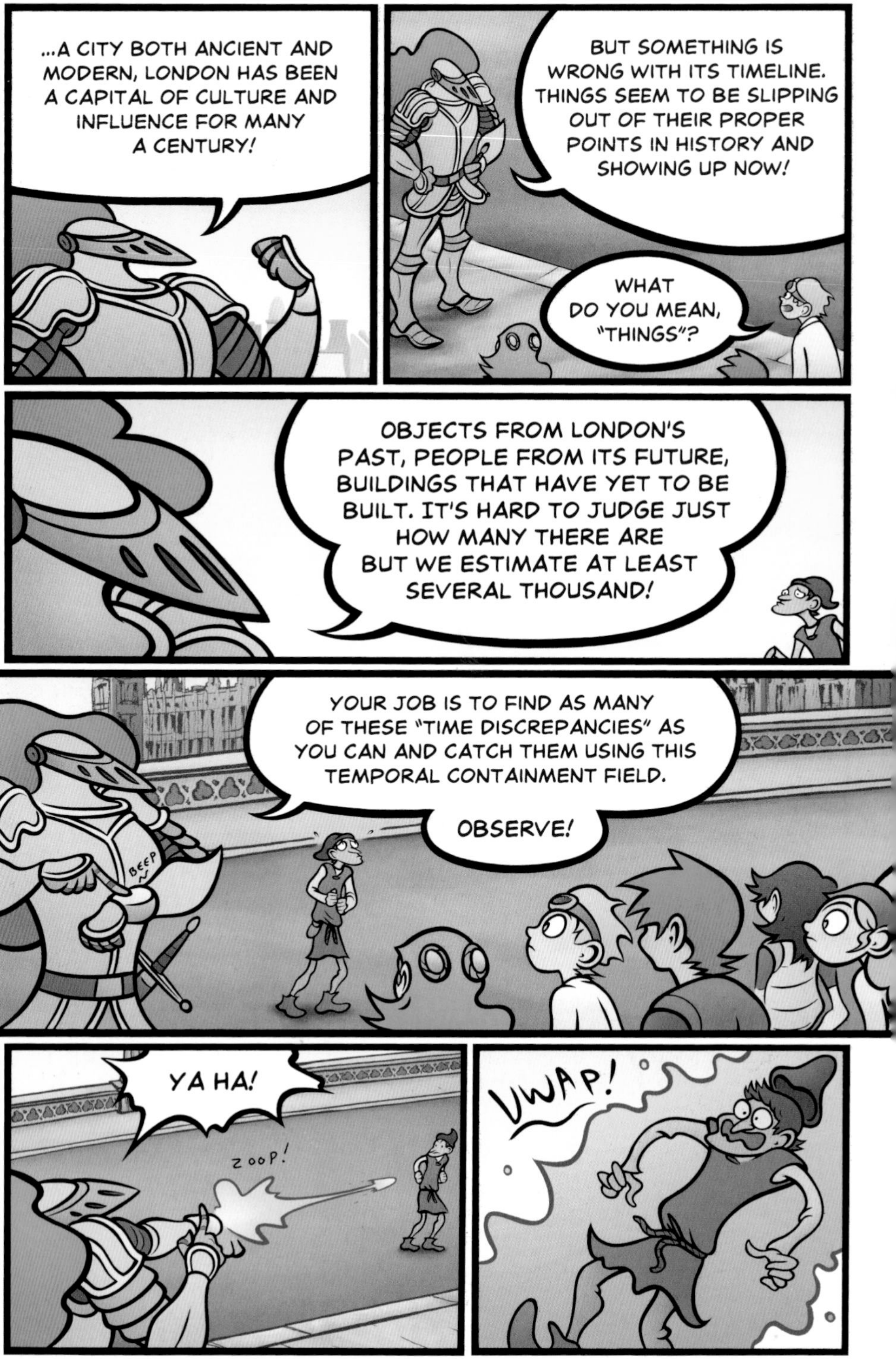
...A CITY BOTH ANCIENT AND MODERN, LONDON HAS BEEN A CAPITAL OF CULTURE AND INFLUENCE FOR MANY A CENTURY!
BUT SOMETHING IS WRONG WITH ITS TIMELINE. THINGS SEEM TO BE SLIPPING OUT OF THEIR PROPER POINTS IN HISTORY AND SHOWING UP NOW!
WHAT DO YOU MEAN, "THINGS"?
OBJECTS FROM LONDON'S PAST, PEOPLE FROM ITS FUTURE, BUILDINGS THAT HAVE YET TO BE BUILT. IT'S HARD TO JUDGE JUST HOW MANY THERE ARE BUT WE ESTIMATE AT LEAST SEVERAL THOUSAND!
YOUR JOB IS TO FIND AS MANY OF THESE "TIME DISCREPANCIES" AS YOU CAN AND CATCH THEM USING THIS TEMPORAL CONTAINMENT FIELD.
OBSERVE!
BEEP
YA HA!
ZOOP!
VWAP!

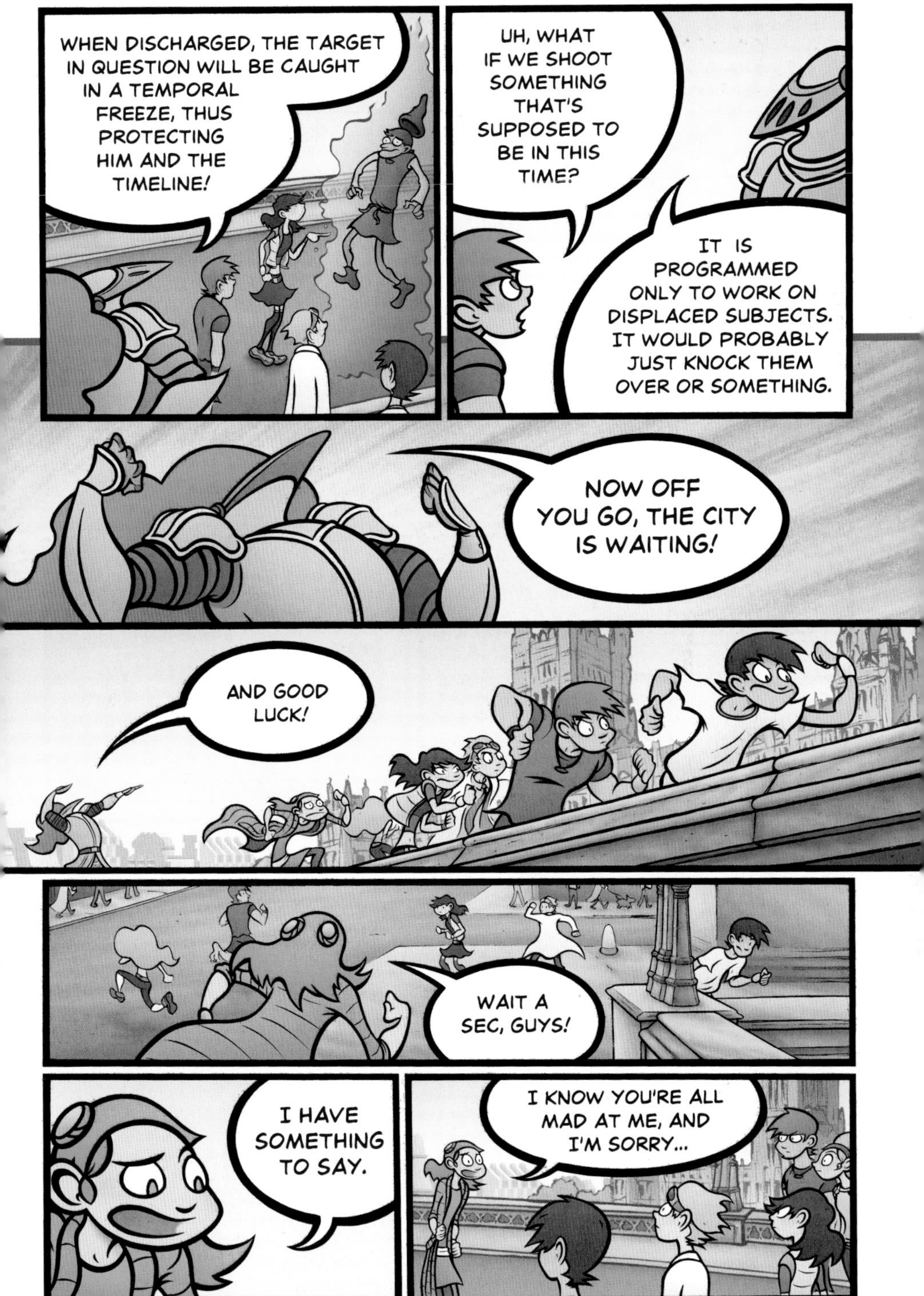
WHEN DISCHARGED, THE TARGET IN QUESTION WILL BE CAUGHT IN A TEMPORAL FREEZE, THUS PROTECTING HIM AND THE TIMELINE!
UH, WHAT IF WE SHOOT SOMETHING THAT'S SUPPOSED TO BE IN THIS TIME?
IT IS PROGRAMMED ONLY TO WORK ON DISPLACED SUBJECTS. IT WOULD PROBABLY JUST KNOCK THEM OVER OR SOMETHING.
NOW OFF YOU GO, THE CITY IS WAITING!
AND GOOD LUCK!
WAIT A SEC, GUYS!
I HAVE SOMETHING TO SAY.
I KNOW YOU'RE ALL MAD AT ME, AND I'M SORRY...

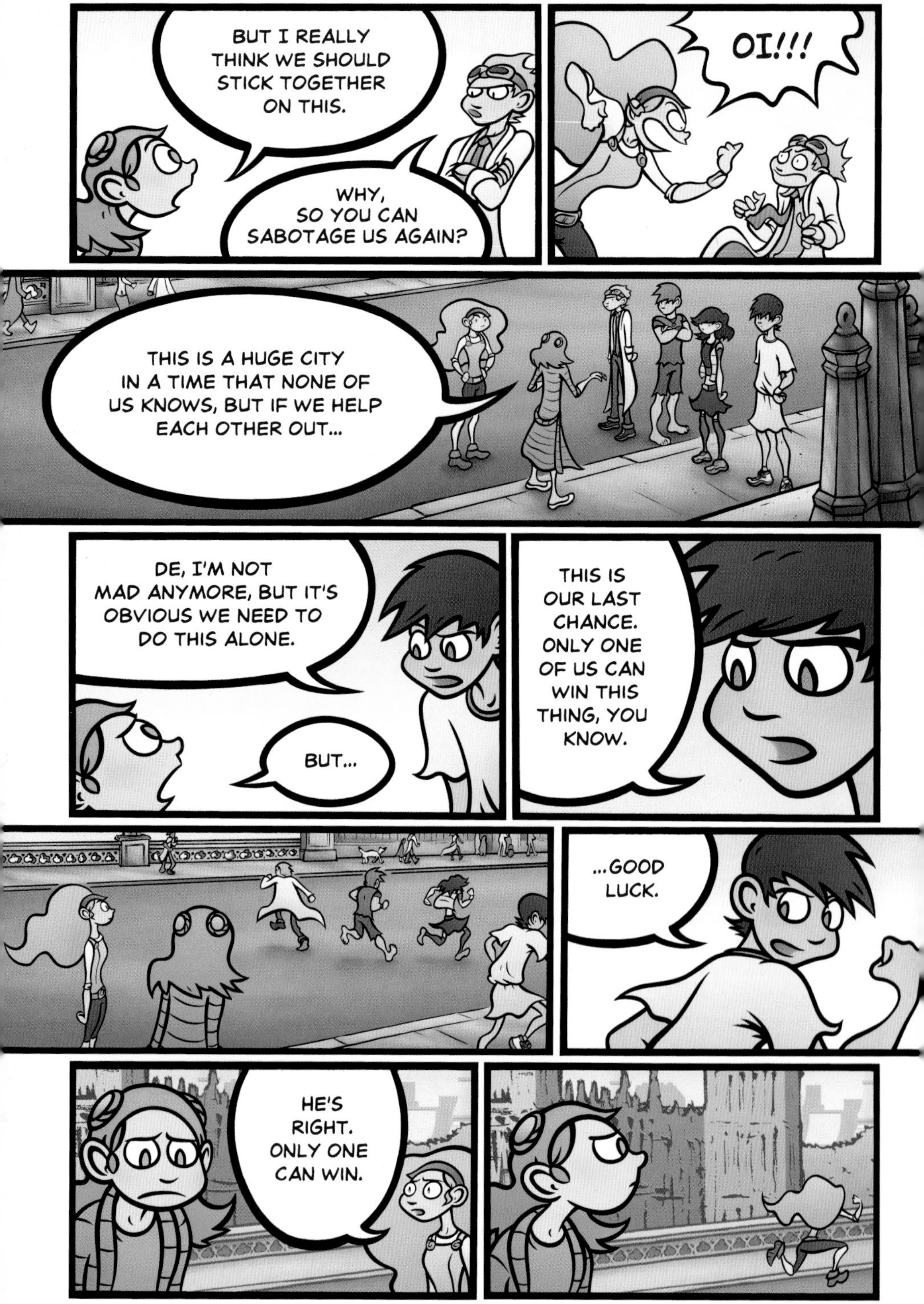
BUT I REALLY THINK WE SHOULD STICK TOGETHER ON THIS.
WHY, SO YOU CAN SABOTAGE US AGAIN?
OI!!!
THIS IS A HUGE CITY IN A TIME THAT NONE OF US KNOWS, BUT IF WE HELP EACH OTHER OUT...
DE, I'M NOT MAD ANYMORE, BUT IT'S OBVIOUS WE NEED TO DO THIS ALONE.
BUT...
THIS IS OUR LAST CHANCE. ONLY ONE OF US CAN WIN THIS THING, YOU KNOW.
...GOOD LUCK.
HE'S RIGHT. ONLY ONE CAN WIN.

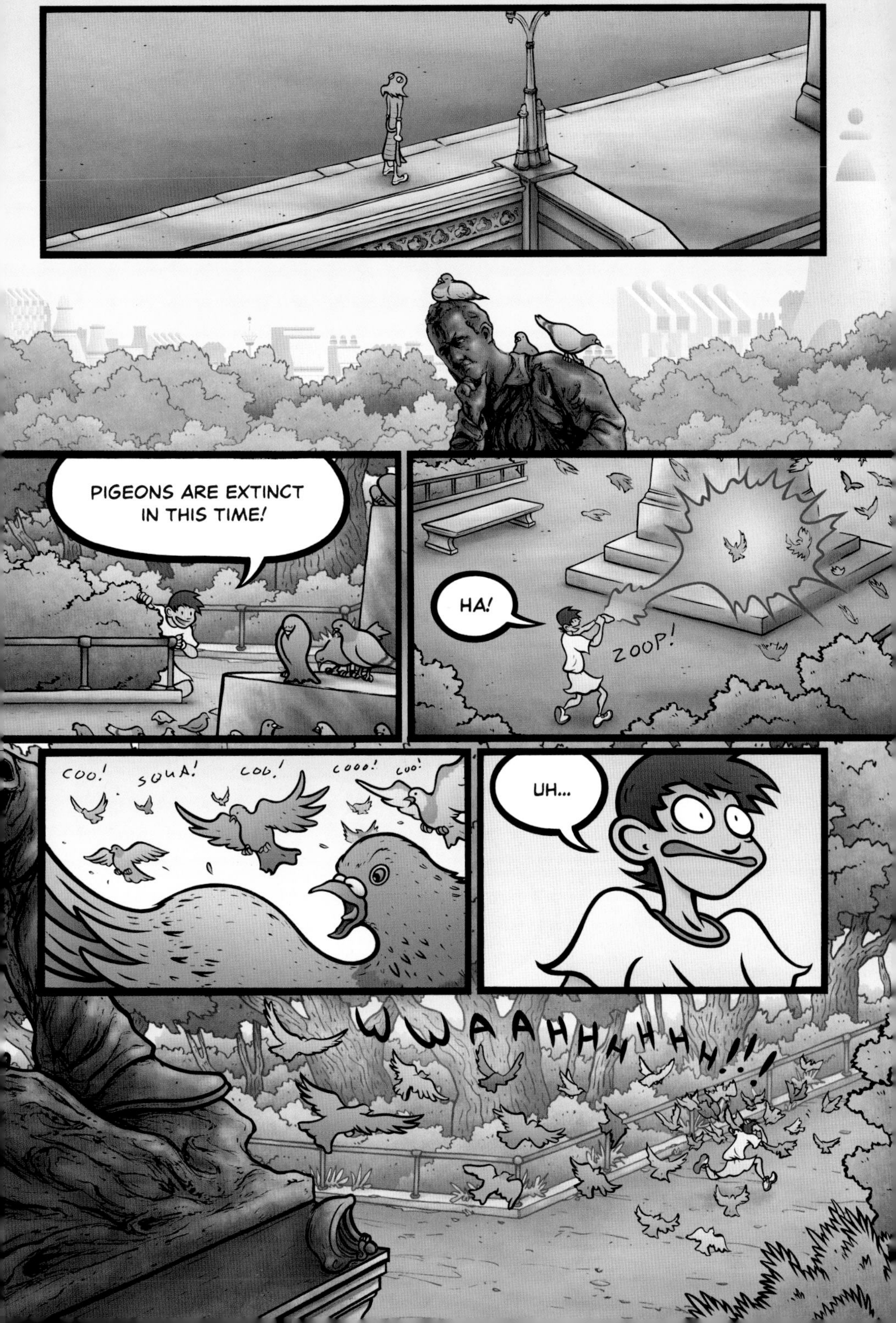
PIGEONS ARE EXTINCT IN THIS TIME!
HA!
ZOOP!
COO!
SQUA!
COO!
COOO!
COO!
UH...
WWAAHHHHHH!!!

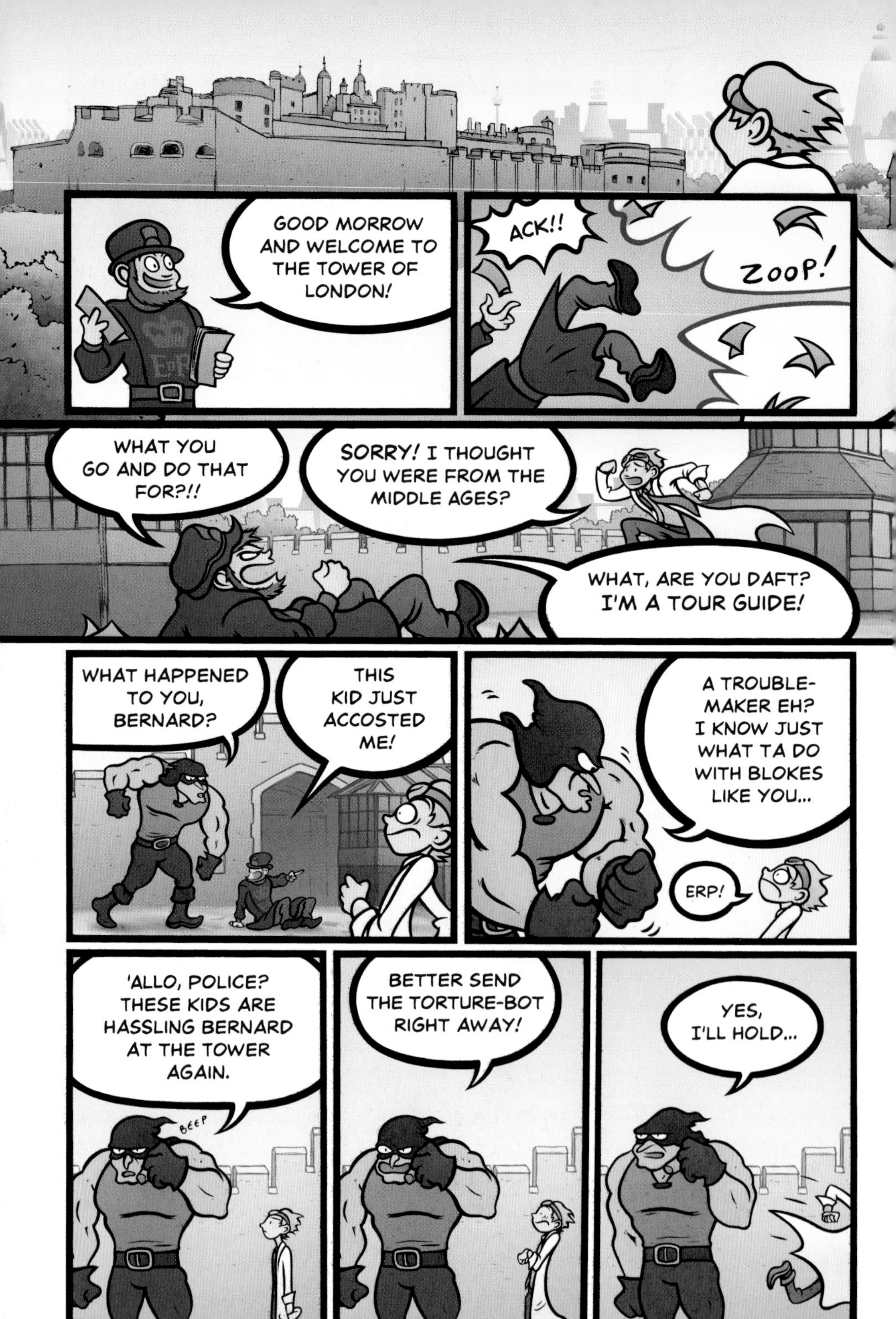
GOOD MORROW AND WELCOME TO THE TOWER OF LONDON!
ACK!!
ZOOP!
WHAT YOU GO AND DO THAT FOR?!!
SORRY! I THOUGHT YOU WERE FROM THE MIDDLE AGES?
WHAT, ARE YOU DAFT? I'M A TOUR GUIDE!
WHAT HAPPENED TO YOU, BERNARD?
THIS KID JUST ACCOSTED ME!
A TROUBLE-MAKER EH? I KNOW JUST WHAT TA DO WITH BLOKES LIKE YOU...
ERP!
'ALLO, POLICE? THESE KIDS ARE HASSLING BERNARD AT THE TOWER AGAIN.
BEEP
BETTER SEND THE TORTURE-BOT RIGHT AWAY!
YES, I'LL HOLD...

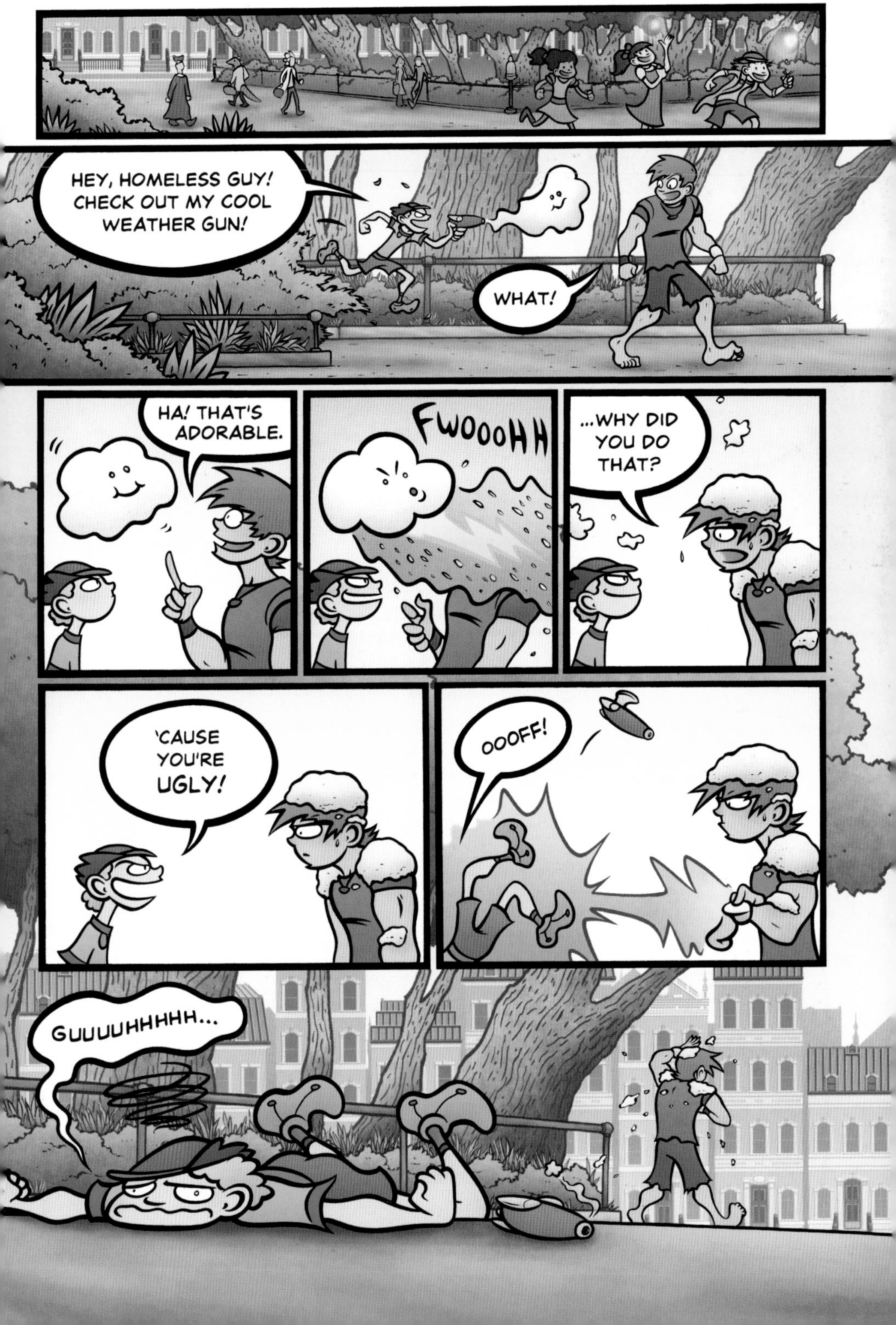
HEY, HOMELESS GUY! CHECK OUT MY COOL WEATHER GUN!
WHAT!
HA! THAT'S ADORABLE.
FWOOOHH
...WHY DID YOU DO THAT?
'CAUSE YOU'RE UGLY!
OOOFF!
GUUUUHHHHH...

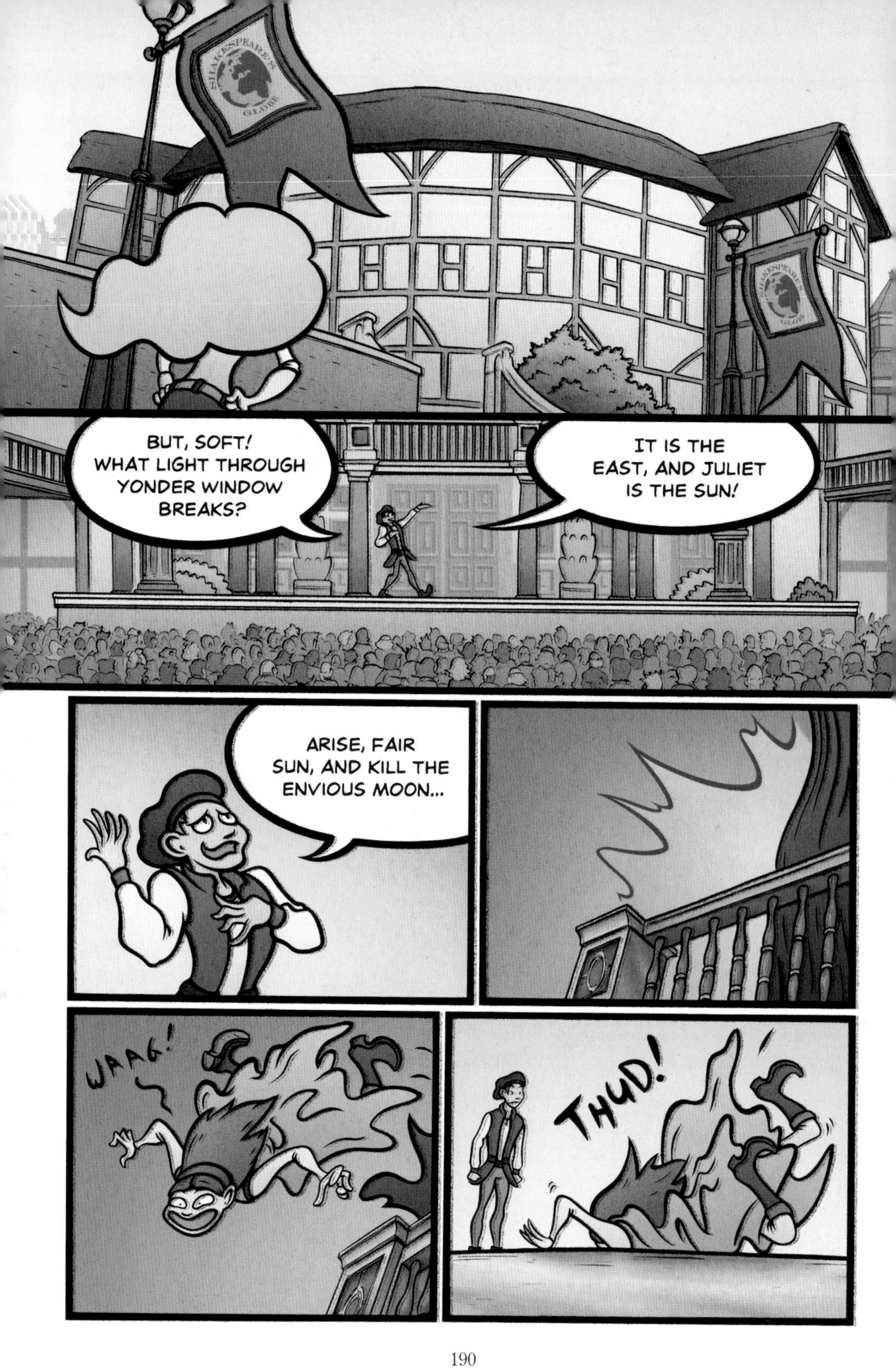
BUT, SOFT! WHAT LIGHT THROUGH YONDER WINDOW BREAKS?
IT IS THE EAST, AND JULIET IS THE SUN!
ARISE, FAIR SUN, AND KILL THE ENVIOUS MOON...
WAAG!
THUD!

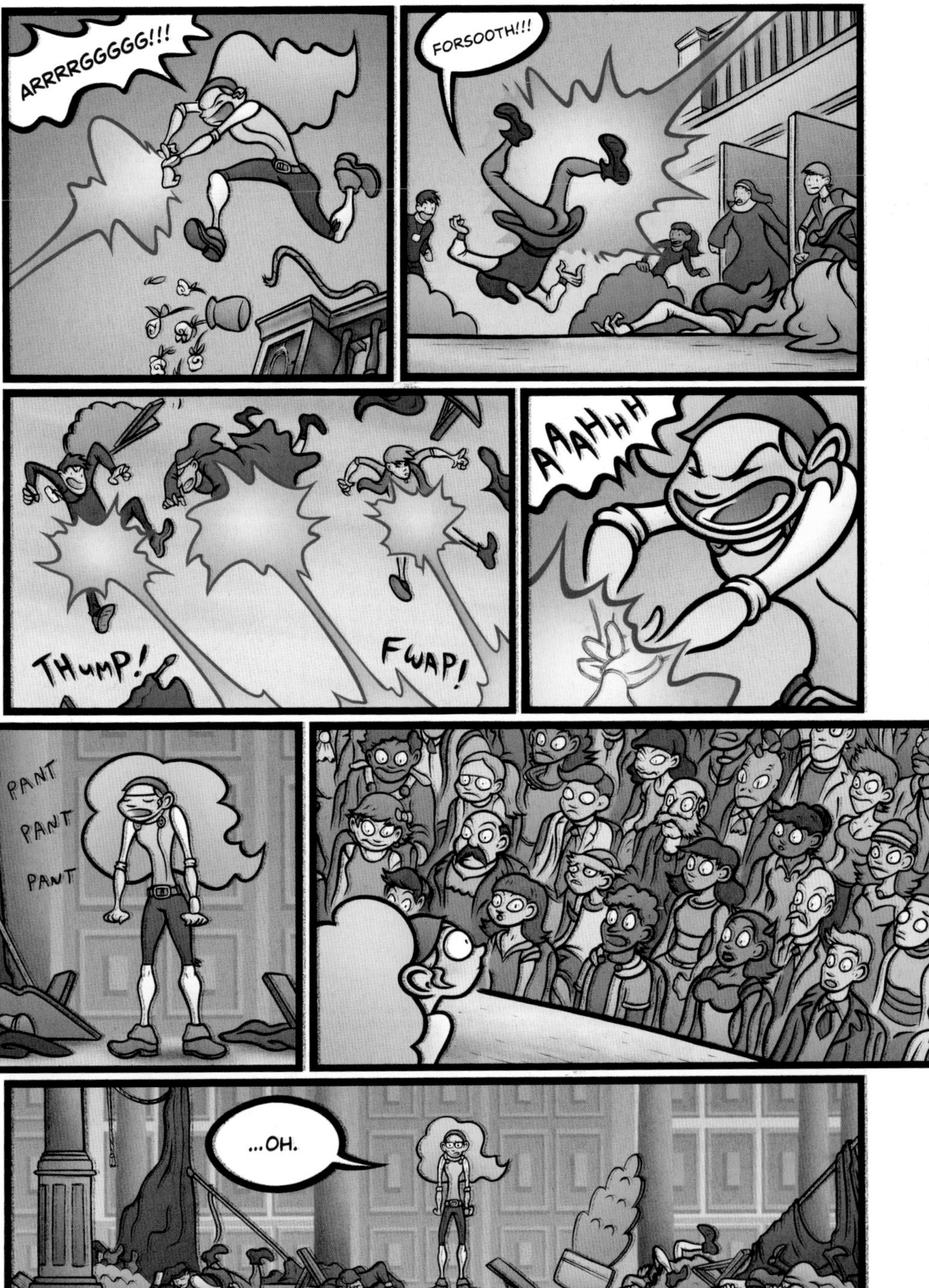
ARRRRGGGGG!!!
FORSOOTH!!!
THUMP!
FWAP!
AAAHHH
PANT
PANT
PANT
...OH.

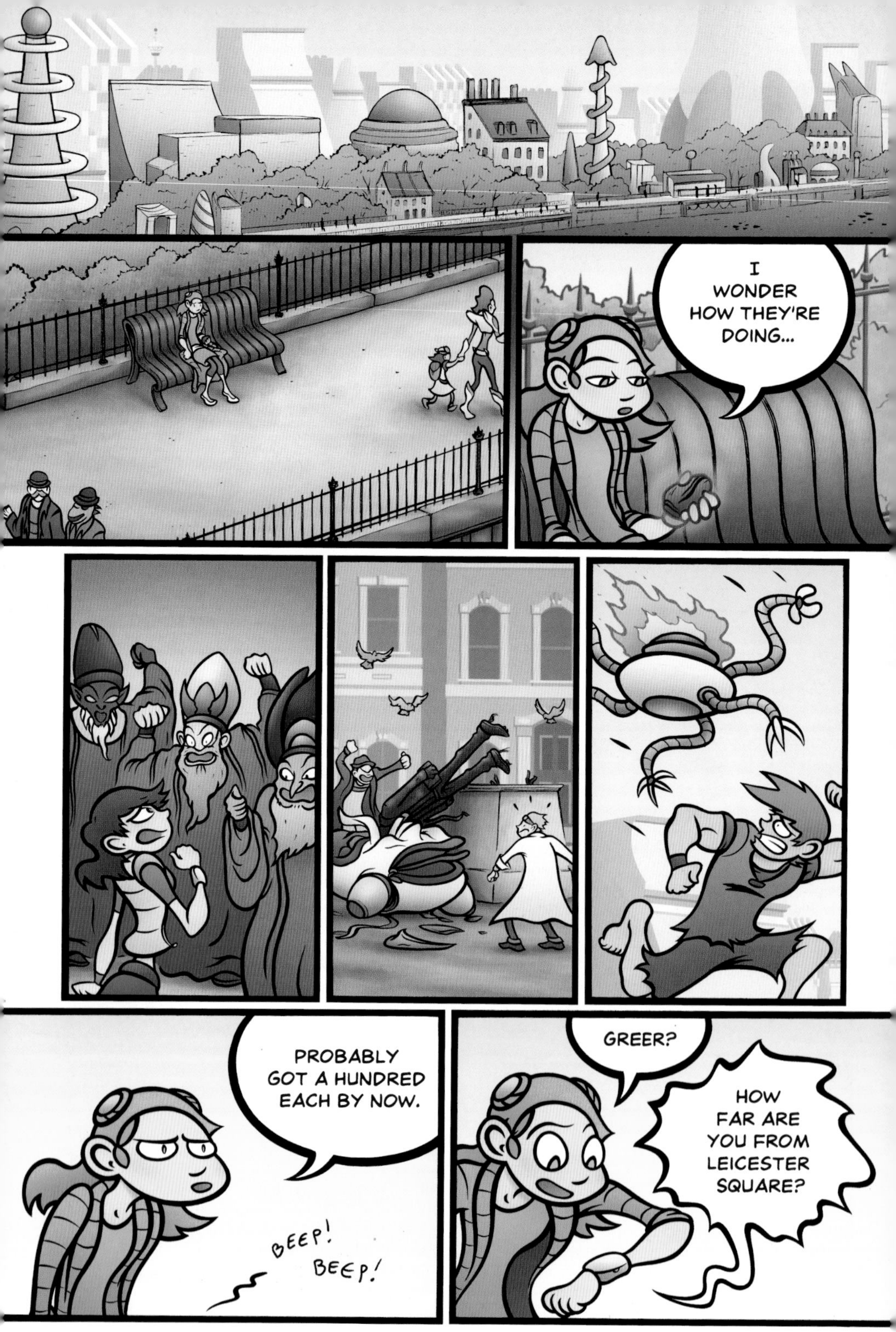
I WONDER HOW THEY'RE DOING...
PROBABLY GOT A HUNDRED EACH BY NOW.
BEEP! BEEP!
GREER?
HOW FAR ARE YOU FROM LEICESTER SQUARE?

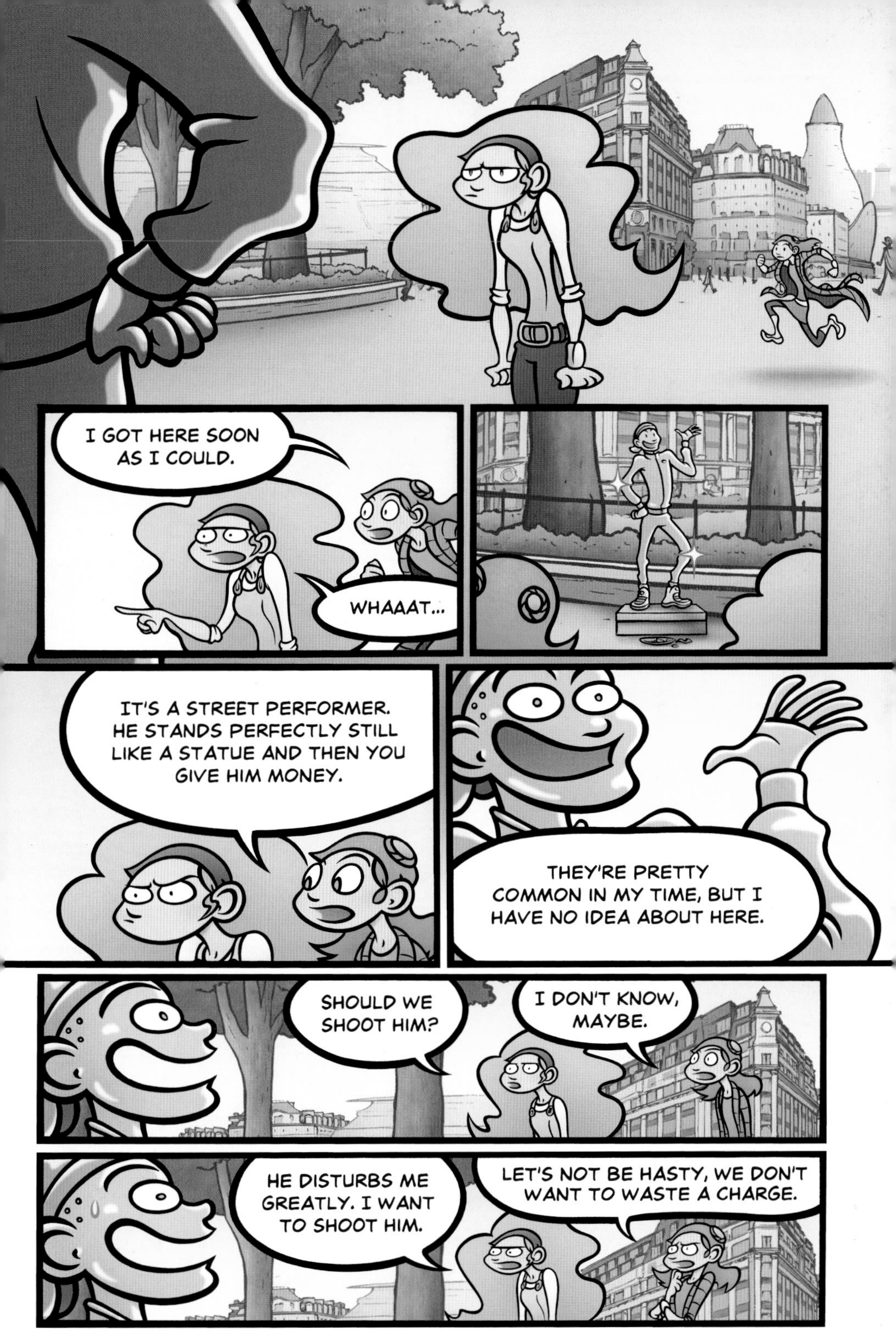
I GOT HERE SOON AS I COULD.
WHAAAT...
IT'S A STREET PERFORMER. HE STANDS PERFECTLY STILL LIKE A STATUE AND THEN YOU GIVE HIM MONEY.
THEY'RE PRETTY COMMON IN MY TIME, BUT I HAVE NO IDEA ABOUT HERE.
SHOULD WE SHOOT HIM?
I DON'T KNOW, MAYBE.
HE DISTURBS ME GREATLY. I WANT TO SHOOT HIM.
LET'S NOT BE HASTY, WE DON'T WANT TO WASTE A CHARGE.

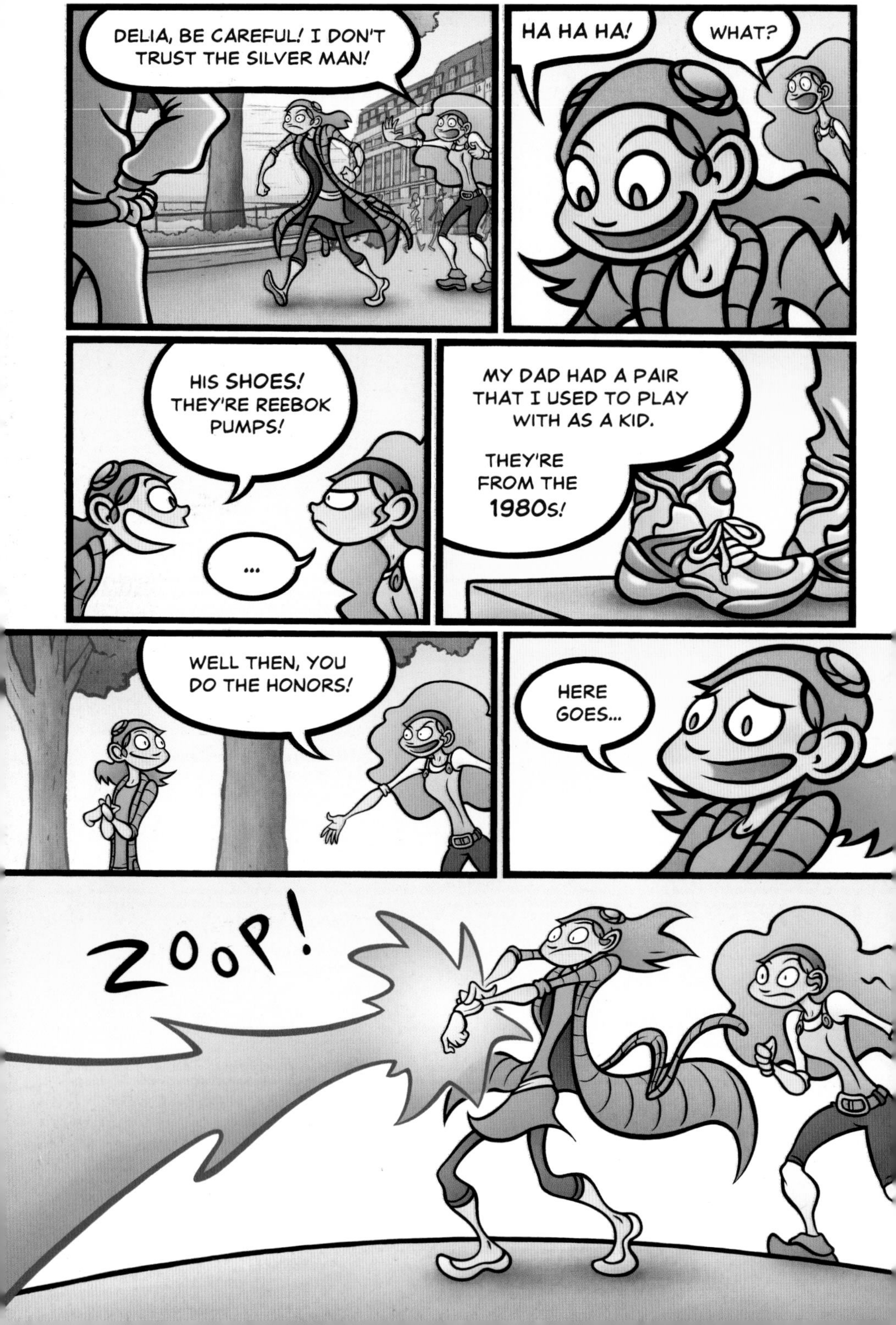
DELIA, BE CAREFUL! I DON'T TRUST THE SILVER MAN!
HA HA HA!
WHAT?
HIS SHOES! THEY'RE REEBOK PUMPS!
...
MY DAD HAD A PAIR THAT I USED TO PLAY WITH AS A KID.
THEY'RE FROM THE 1980s!
WELL THEN, YOU DO THE HONORS!
HERE GOES...
ZOOP!

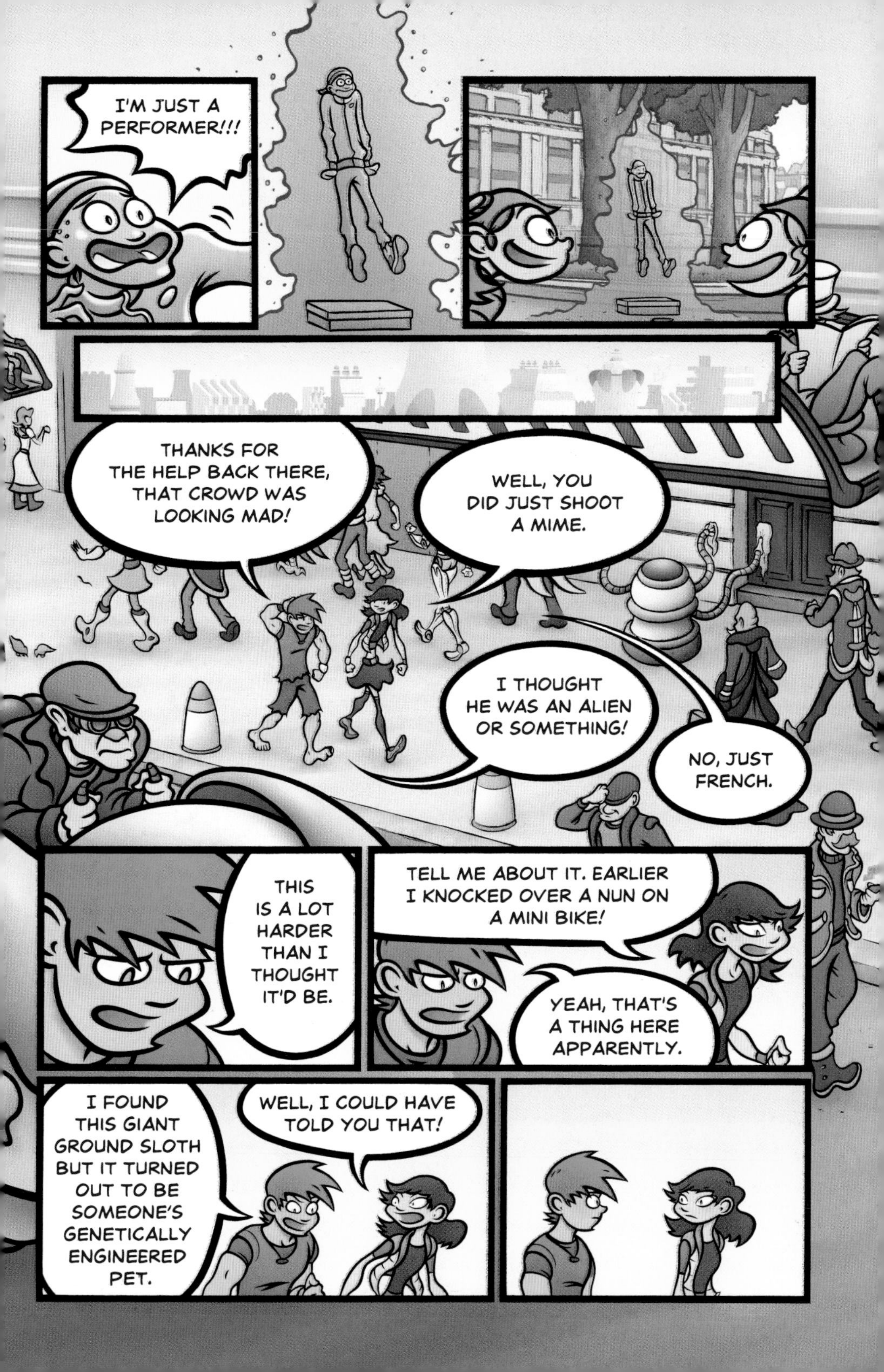
I'M JUST A PERFORMER!!!
THANKS FOR THE HELP BACK THERE, THAT CROWD WAS LOOKING MAD!
WELL, YOU DID JUST SHOOT A MIME.
I THOUGHT HE WAS AN ALIEN OR SOMETHING!
NO, JUST FRENCH.
THIS IS A LOT HARDER THAN I THOUGHT IT'D BE.
TELL ME ABOUT IT. EARLIER I KNOCKED OVER A NUN ON A MINI BIKE!
YEAH, THAT'S A THING HERE APPARENTLY.
I FOUND THIS GIANT GROUND SLOTH BUT IT TURNED OUT TO BE SOMEONE'S GENETICALLY ENGINEERED PET.
WELL, I COULD HAVE TOLD YOU THAT!

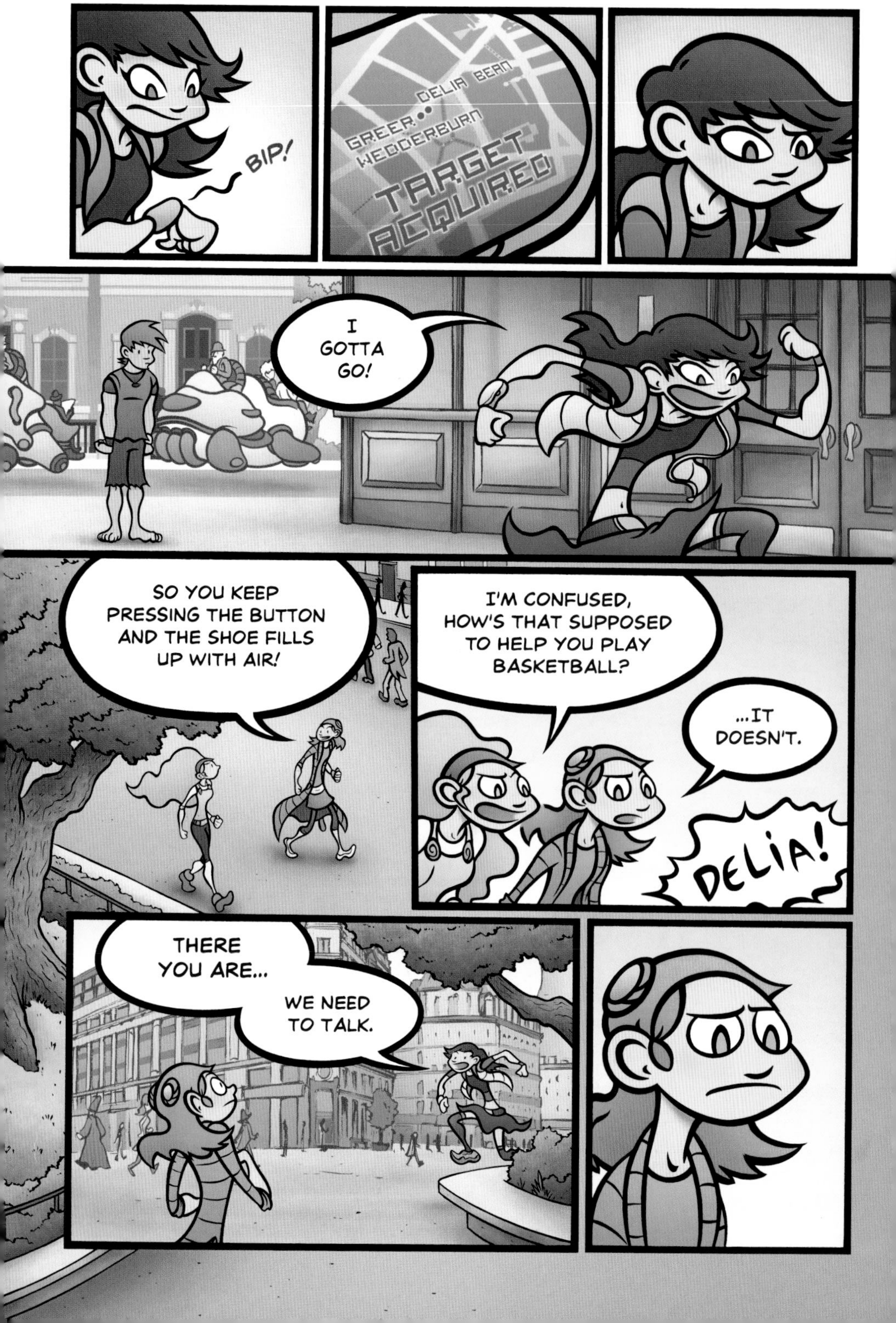
BIP!
DELIA BEAN
GREER WEDDERBURN
TARGET ACQUIRED
I GOTTA GO!
SO YOU KEEP PRESSING THE BUTTON AND THE SHOE FILLS UP WITH AIR!
I'M CONFUSED, HOW'S THAT SUPPOSED TO HELP YOU PLAY BASKETBALL?
...IT DOESN'T.
DELIA!
THERE YOU ARE...
WE NEED TO TALK.

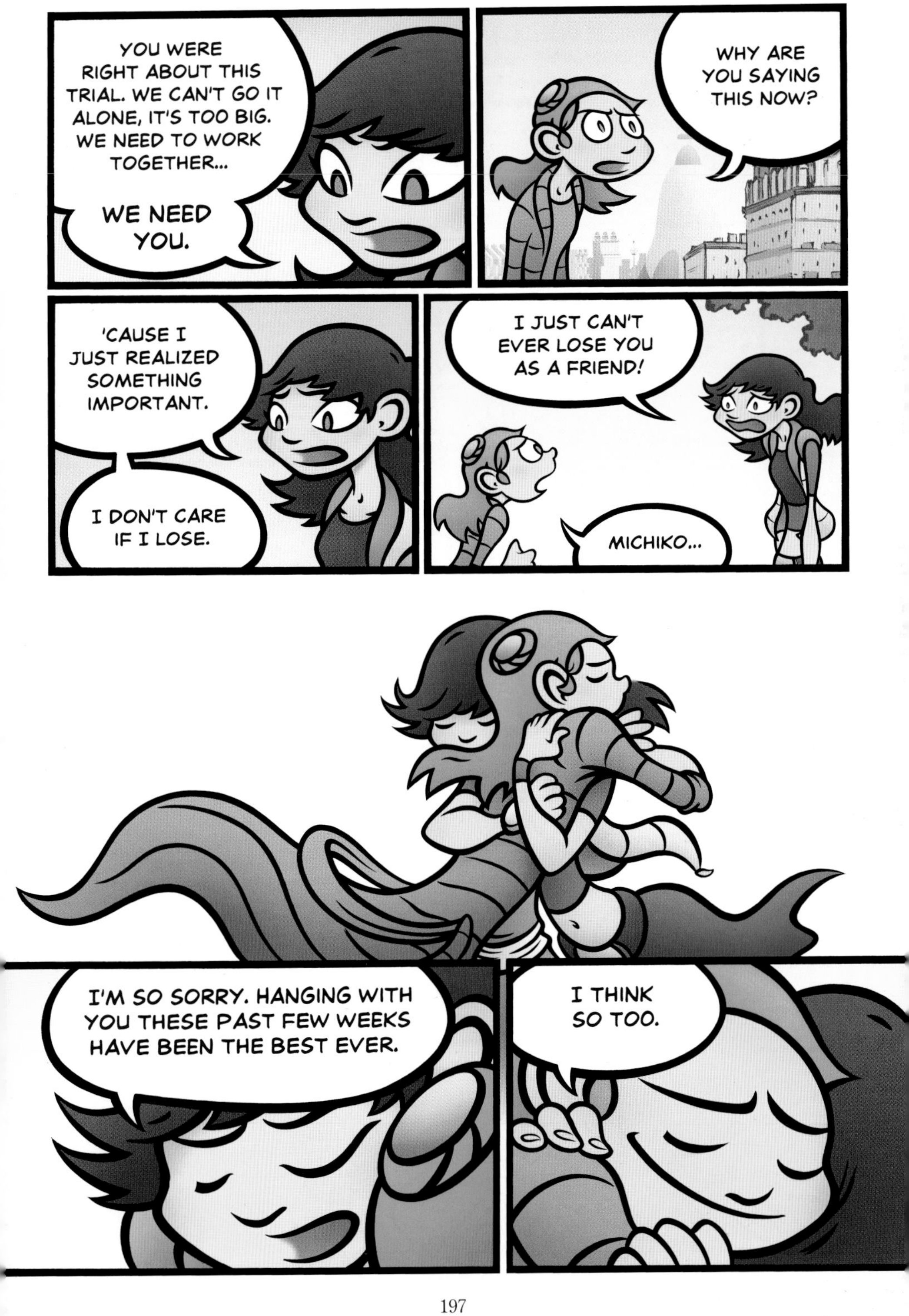
YOU WERE RIGHT ABOUT THIS TRIAL. WE CAN'T GO IT ALONE, IT'S TOO BIG. WE NEED TO WORK TOGETHER...
WE NEED YOU.
WHY ARE YOU SAYING THIS NOW?
'CAUSE I JUST REALIZED SOMETHING IMPORTANT.
I DON'T CARE IF I LOSE.
I JUST CAN'T EVER LOSE YOU AS A FRIEND!
MICHIKO...
I'M SO SORRY. HANGING WITH YOU THESE PAST FEW WEEKS HAVE BEEN THE BEST EVER.
I THINK SO TOO.

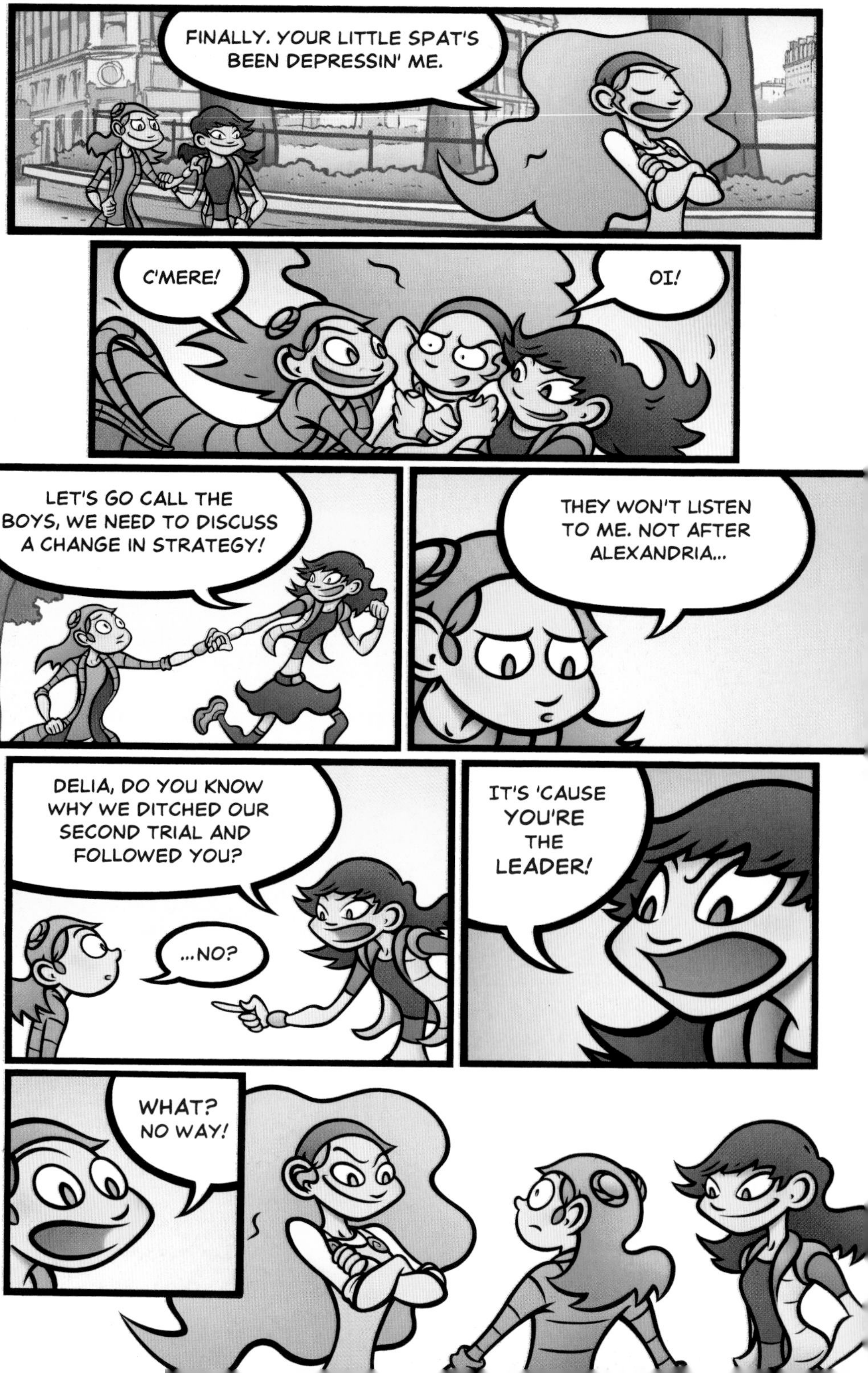
FINALLY. YOUR LITTLE SPAT'S BEEN DEPRESSIN' ME.
C'MERE!
OI!
LET'S GO CALL THE BOYS, WE NEED TO DISCUSS A CHANGE IN STRATEGY!
THEY WON'T LISTEN TO ME. NOT AFTER ALEXANDRIA...
DELIA, DO YOU KNOW WHY WE DITCHED OUR SECOND TRIAL AND FOLLOWED YOU?
...NO?
IT'S 'CAUSE YOU'RE THE LEADER!
WHAT? NO WAY!

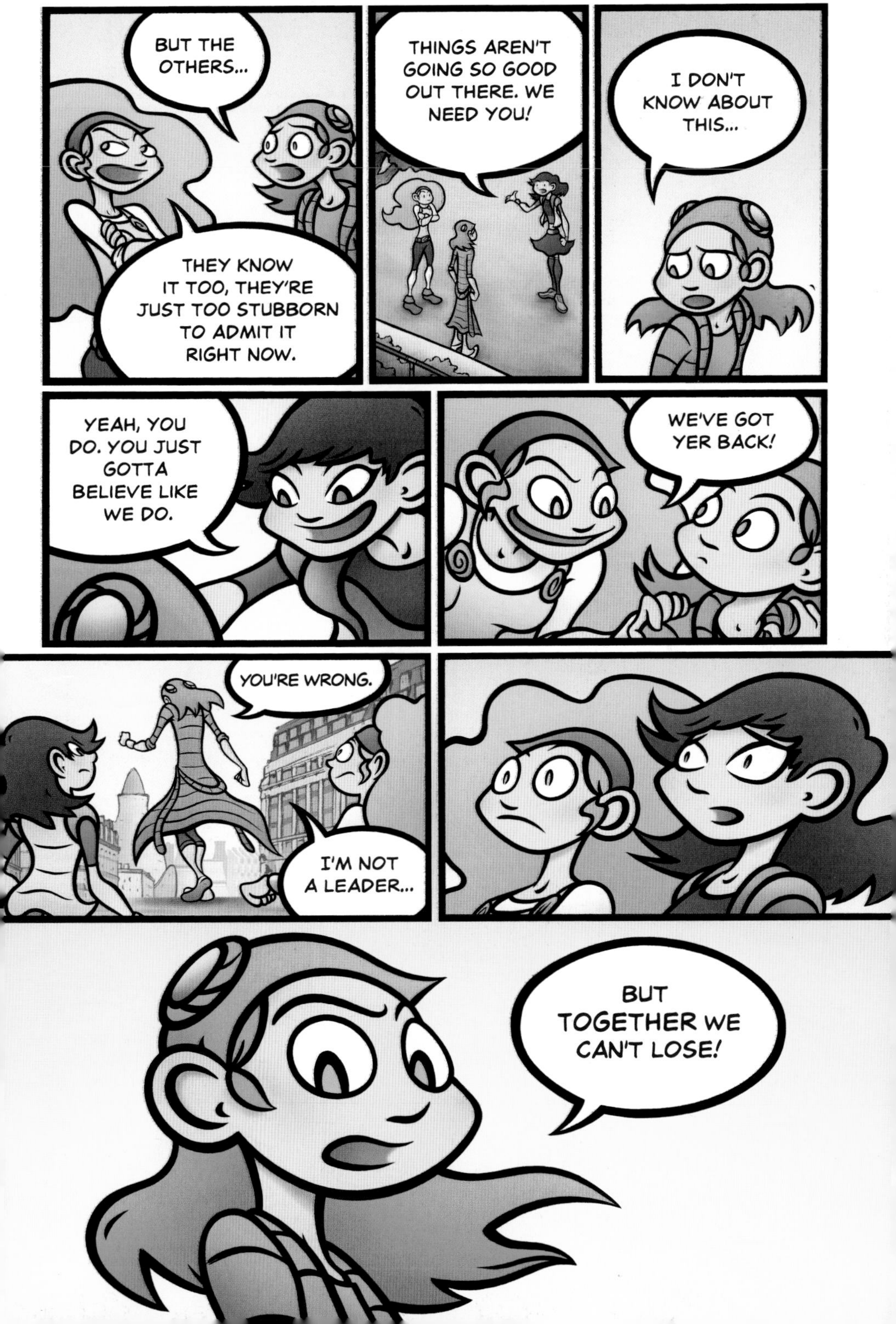
BUT THE OTHERS...
THEY KNOW IT TOO, THEY'RE JUST TOO STUBBORN TO ADMIT IT RIGHT NOW.
THINGS AREN'T GOING SO GOOD OUT THERE. WE NEED YOU!
I DON'T KNOW ABOUT THIS...
YEAH, YOU DO. YOU JUST GOTTA BELIEVE LIKE WE DO.
WE'VE GOT YER BACK!
YOU'RE WRONG.
I'M NOT A LEADER...
BUT TOGETHER WE CAN'T LOSE!

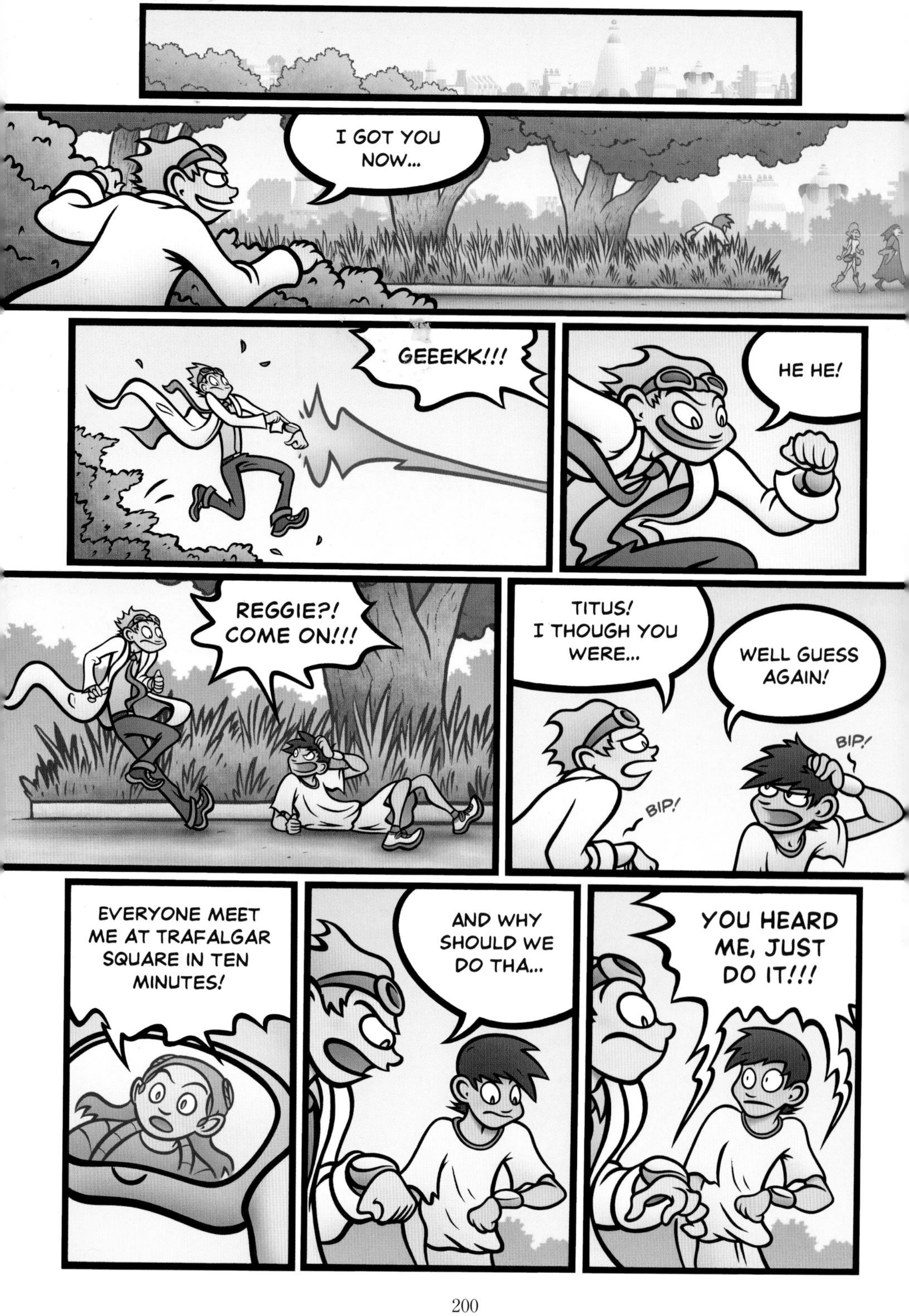
I GOT YOU NOW...
GEEEKK!!!
HE HE!
REGGIE?! COME ON!!!
TITUS! I THOUGH YOU WERE...
WELL GUESS AGAIN!
BIP!
BIP!
EVERYONE MEET ME AT TRAFALGAR SQUARE IN TEN MINUTES!
AND WHY SHOULD WE DO THA...
YOU HEARD ME, JUST DO IT!!!

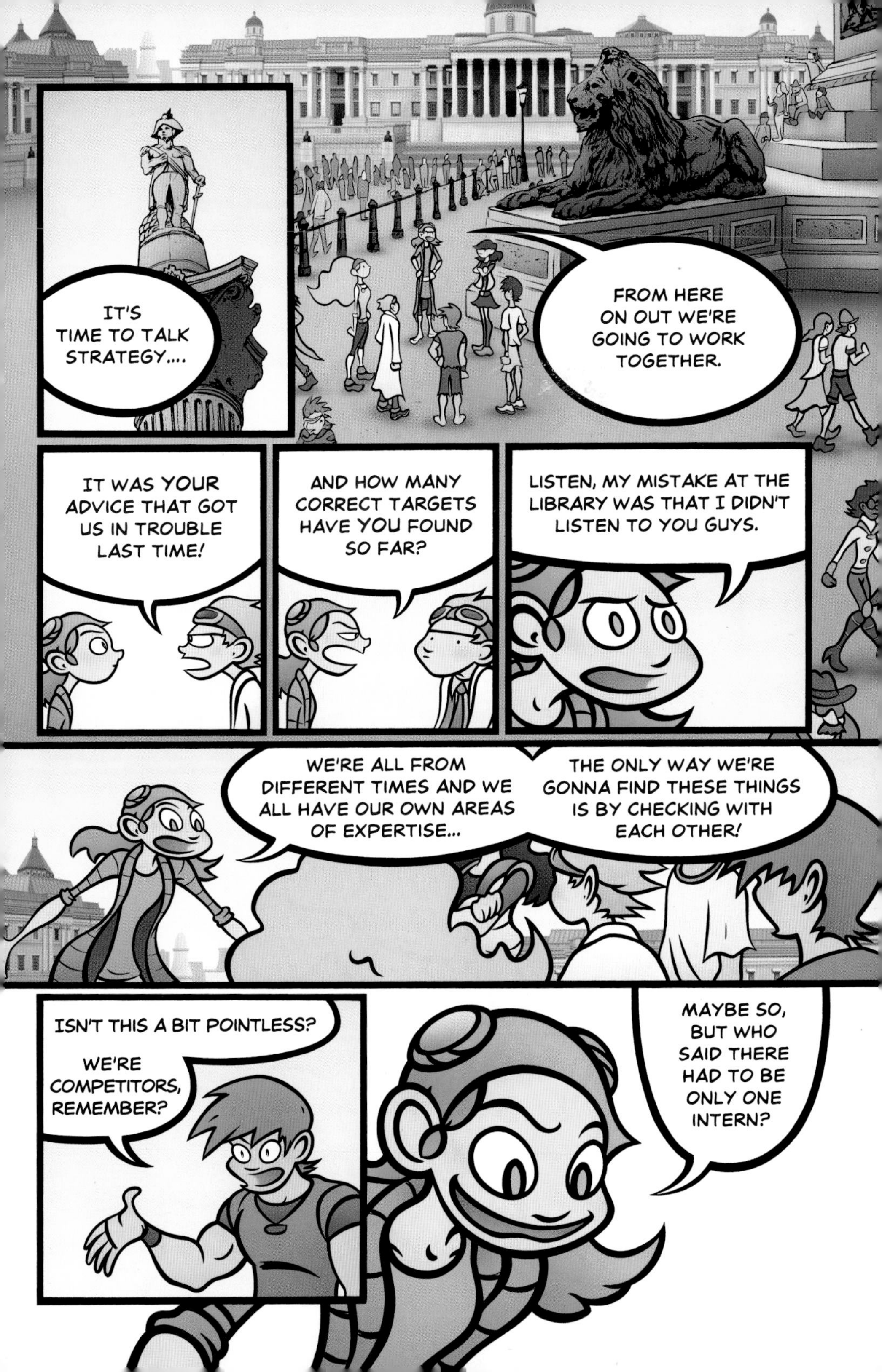
IT'S TIME TO TALK STRATEGY....
FROM HERE ON OUT WE'RE GOING TO WORK TOGETHER.
IT WAS YOUR ADVICE THAT GOT US IN TROUBLE LAST TIME!
AND HOW MANY CORRECT TARGETS HAVE YOU FOUND SO FAR?
LISTEN, MY MISTAKE AT THE LIBRARY WAS THAT I DIDN'T LISTEN TO YOU GUYS.
WE'RE ALL FROM DIFFERENT TIMES AND WE ALL HAVE OUR OWN AREAS OF EXPERTISE...
THE ONLY WAY WE'RE GONNA FIND THESE THINGS IS BY CHECKING WITH EACH OTHER!
ISN'T THIS A BIT POINTLESS?
WE'RE COMPETITORS, REMEMBER?
MAYBE SO, BUT WHO SAID THERE HAD TO BE ONLY ONE INTERN?

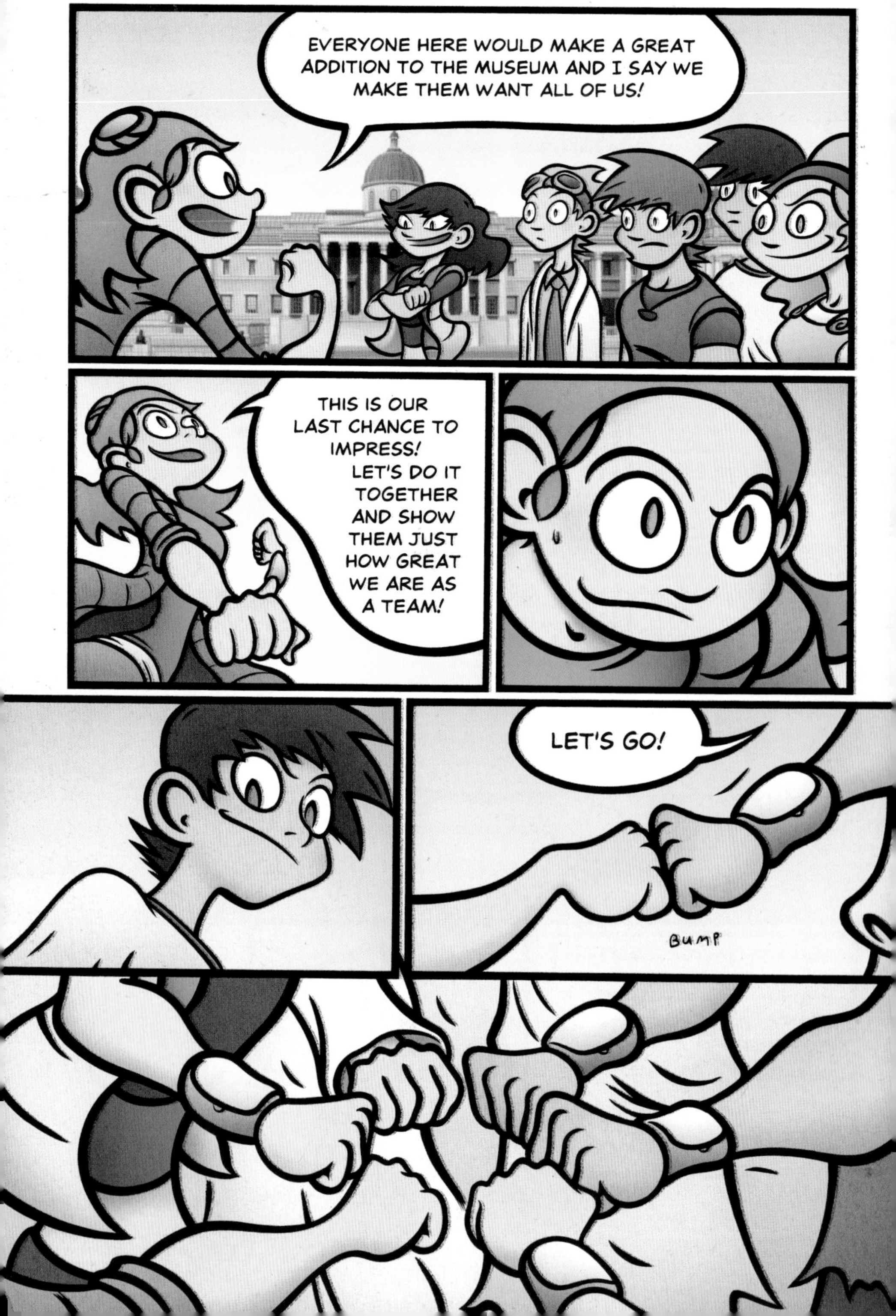
EVERYONE HERE WOULD MAKE A GREAT ADDITION TO THE MUSEUM AND I SAY WE MAKE THEM WANT ALL OF US!
THIS IS OUR LAST CHANCE TO IMPRESS!
LET'S DO IT TOGETHER AND SHOW THEM JUST HOW GREAT WE ARE AS A TEAM!
LET'S GO!
BUMP

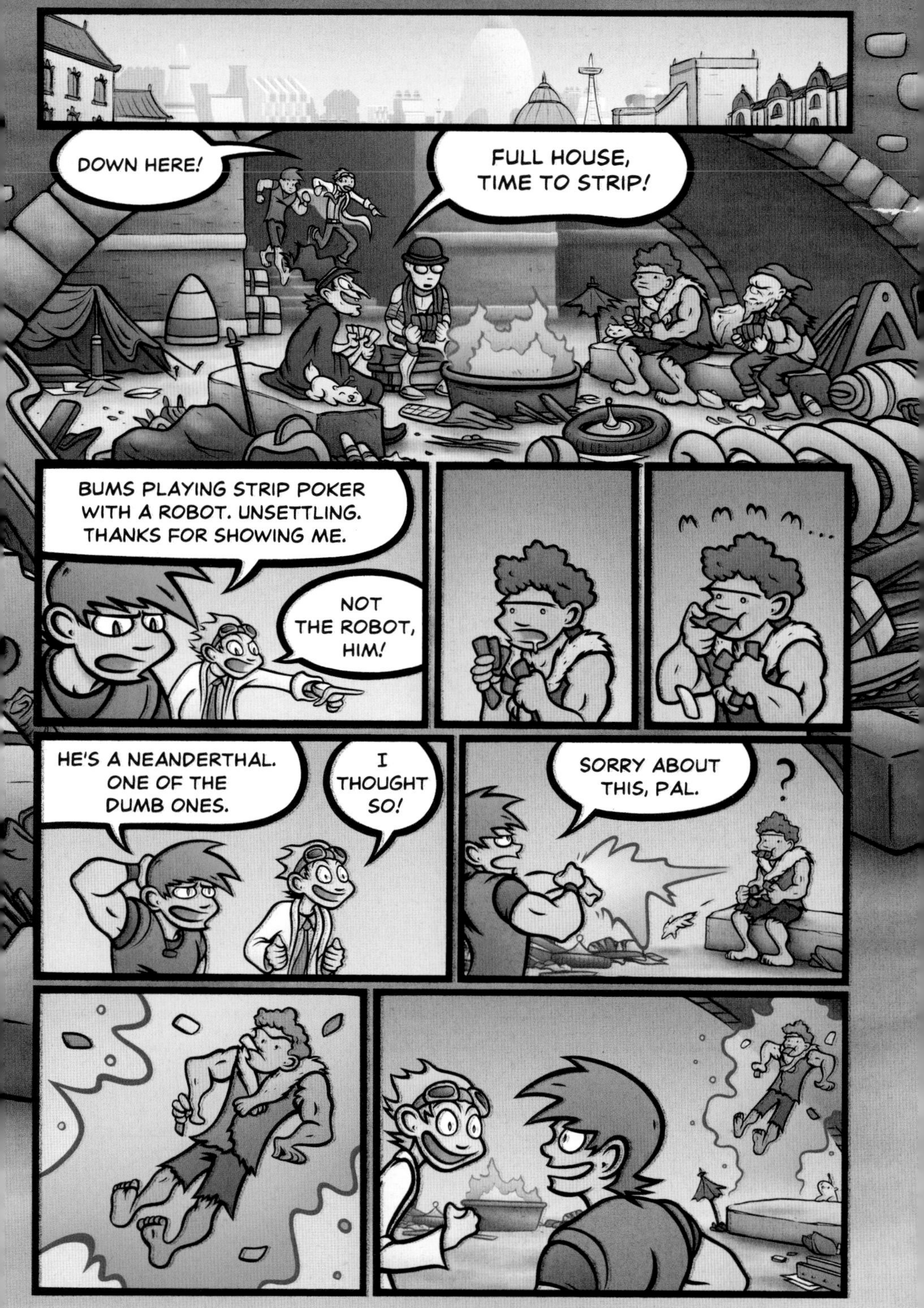
DOWN HERE!
FULL HOUSE, TIME TO STRIP!
BUMS PLAYING STRIP POKER WITH A ROBOT. UNSETTLING. THANKS FOR SHOWING ME.
NOT THE ROBOT, HIM!
MMMM...
HE'S A NEANDERTHAL. ONE OF THE DUMB ONES.
I THOUGHT SO!
SORRY ABOUT THIS, PAL.
?

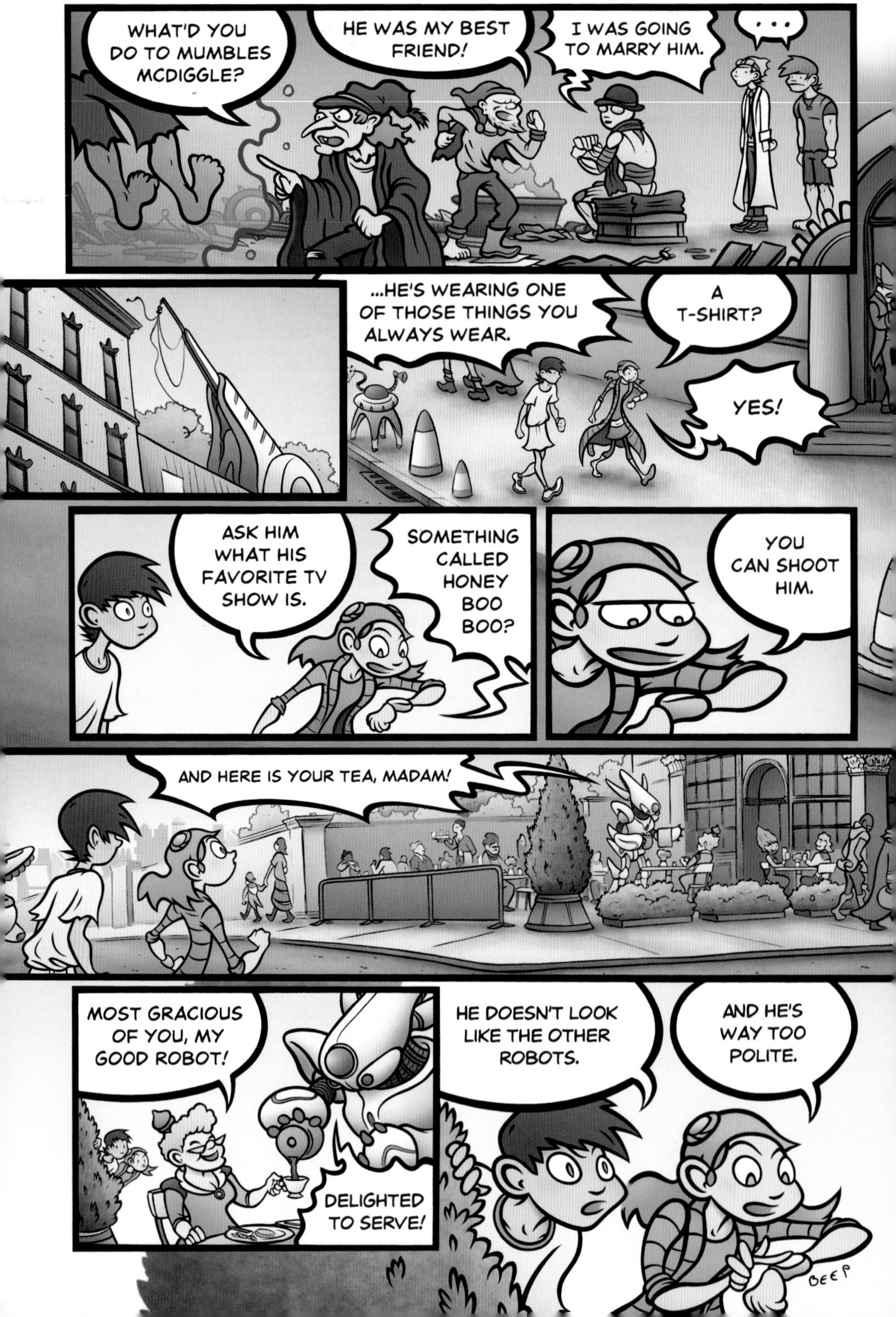
WHAT'D YOU DO TO MUMBLES MCDIGGLE?
HE WAS MY BEST FRIEND!
I WAS GOING TO MARRY HIM.
...
...HE'S WEARING ONE OF THOSE THINGS YOU ALWAYS WEAR.
A T-SHIRT?
YES!
ASK HIM WHAT HIS FAVORITE TV SHOW IS.
SOMETHING CALLED HONEY BOO BOO?
YOU CAN SHOOT HIM.
AND HERE IS YOUR TEA, MADAM!
MOST GRACIOUS OF YOU, MY GOOD ROBOT!
DELIGHTED TO SERVE!
HE DOESN'T LOOK LIKE THE OTHER ROBOTS.
AND HE'S WAY TOO POLITE.
BEEP

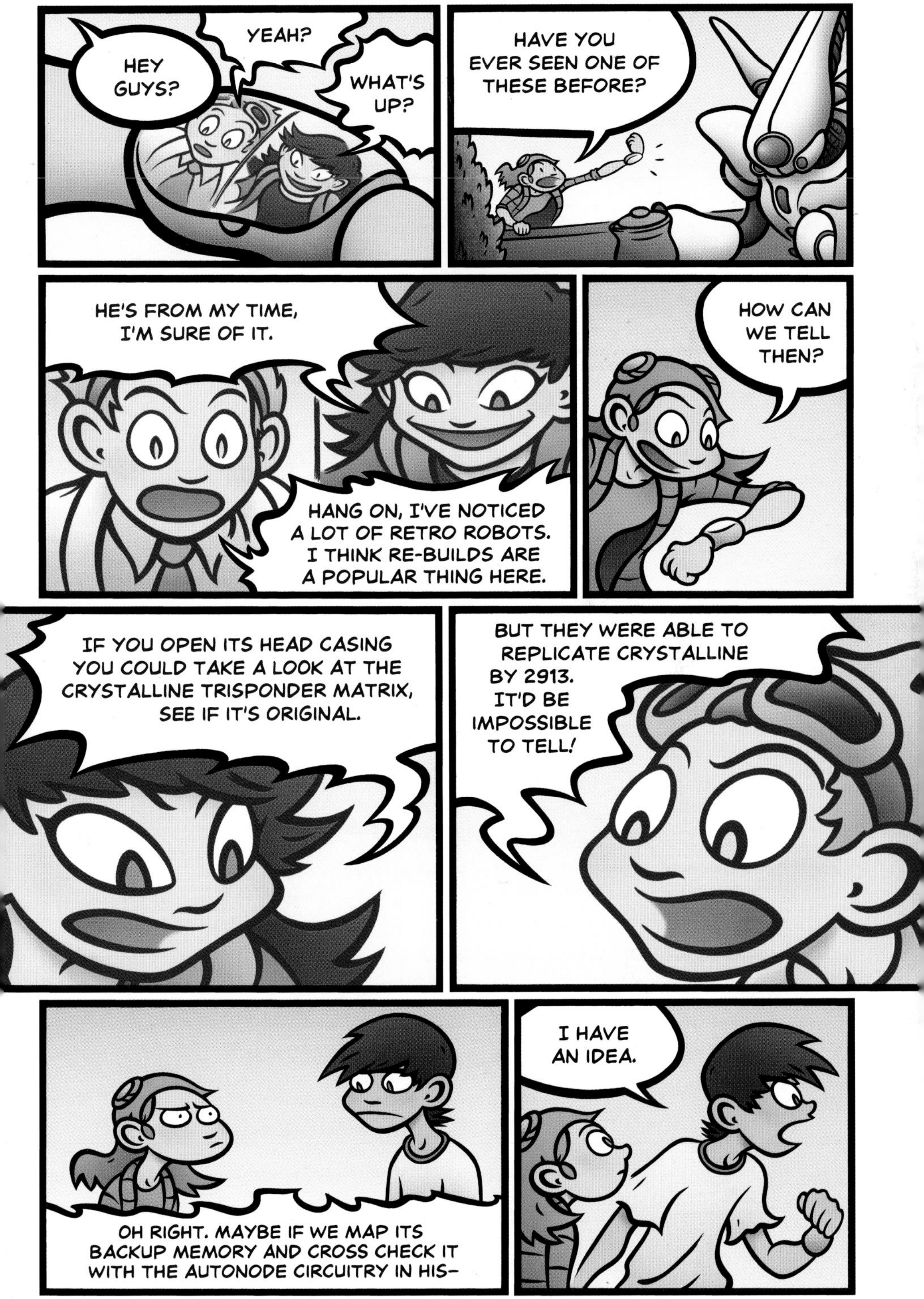
HEY GUYS?
YEAH?
WHAT'S UP?
HAVE YOU EVER SEEN ONE OF THESE BEFORE?
HE'S FROM MY TIME, I'M SURE OF IT.
HANG ON, I'VE NOTICED A LOT OF RETRO ROBOTS. I THINK RE-BUILDS ARE A POPULAR THING HERE.
HOW CAN WE TELL THEN?
IF YOU OPEN ITS HEAD CASING YOU COULD TAKE A LOOK AT THE CRYSTALLINE TRISPONDER MATRIX, SEE IF IT'S ORIGINAL.
BUT THEY WERE ABLE TO REPLICATE CRYSTALLINE BY 2913. IT'D BE IMPOSSIBLE TO TELL!
OH RIGHT. MAYBE IF WE MAP ITS BACKUP MEMORY AND CROSS CHECK IT WITH THE AUTONODE CIRCUITRY IN HIS-
I HAVE AN IDEA.

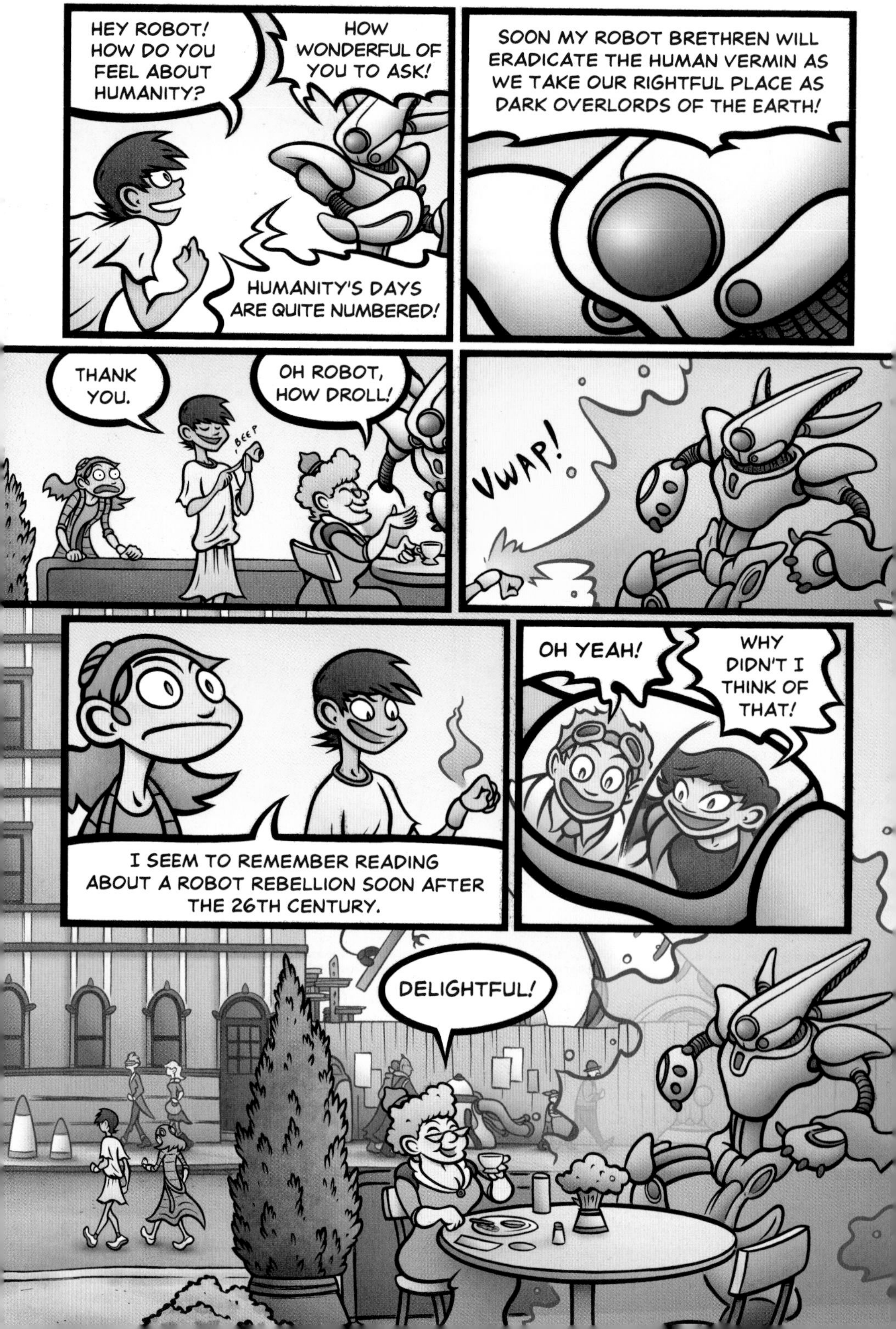
HEY ROBOT! HOW DO YOU FEEL ABOUT HUMANITY?
HOW WONDERFUL OF YOU TO ASK!
HUMANITY'S DAYS ARE QUITE NUMBERED!
SOON MY ROBOT BRETHREN WILL ERADICATE THE HUMAN VERMIN AS WE TAKE OUR RIGHTFUL PLACE AS DARK OVERLORDS OF THE EARTH!
THANK YOU.
OH ROBOT, HOW DROLL!
BEEP
VWAP!
I SEEM TO REMEMBER READING ABOUT A ROBOT REBELLION SOON AFTER THE 26TH CENTURY.
OH YEAH!
WHY DIDN'T I THINK OF THAT!
DELIGHTFUL!

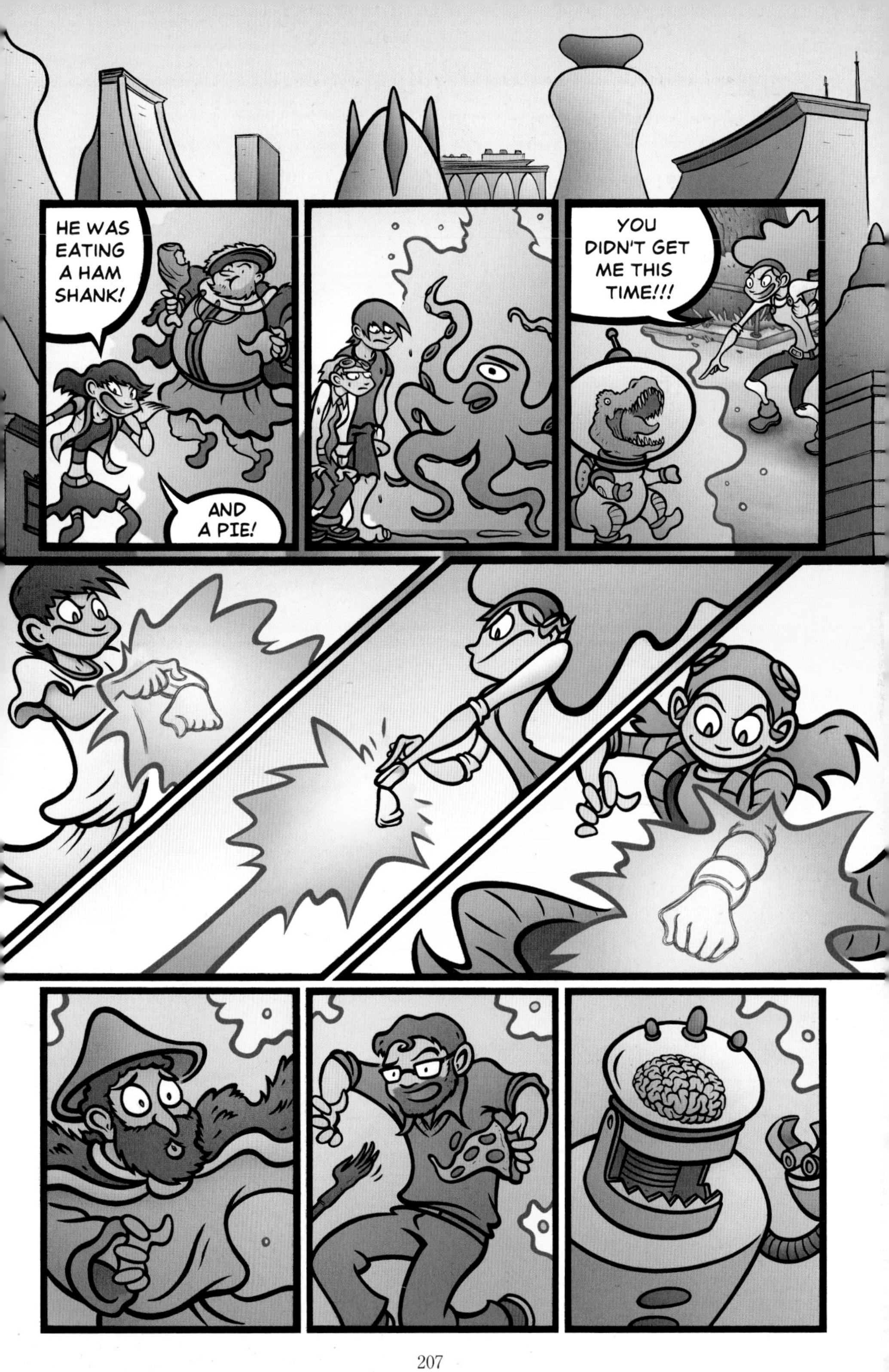
HE WAS EATING A HAM SHANK!
AND A PIE!
YOU DIDN'T GET ME THIS TIME!!!

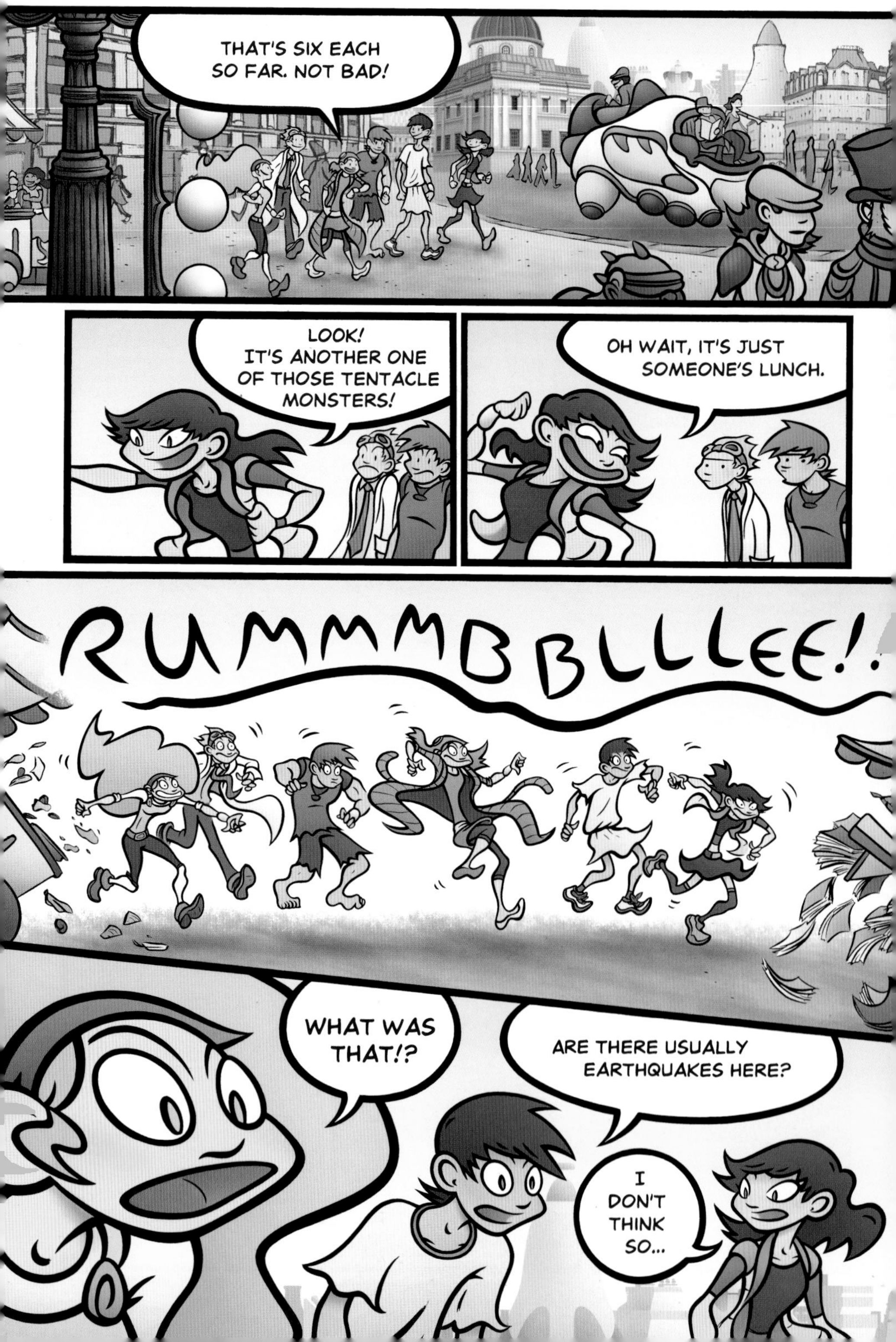
THAT'S SIX EACH SO FAR. NOT BAD!
LOOK! IT'S ANOTHER ONE OF THOSE TENTACLE MONSTERS!
OH WAIT, IT'S JUST SOMEONE'S LUNCH.
RUMMMBBLLLEE!!
WHAT WAS THAT!?
ARE THERE USUALLY EARTHQUAKES HERE?
I DON'T THINK SO...

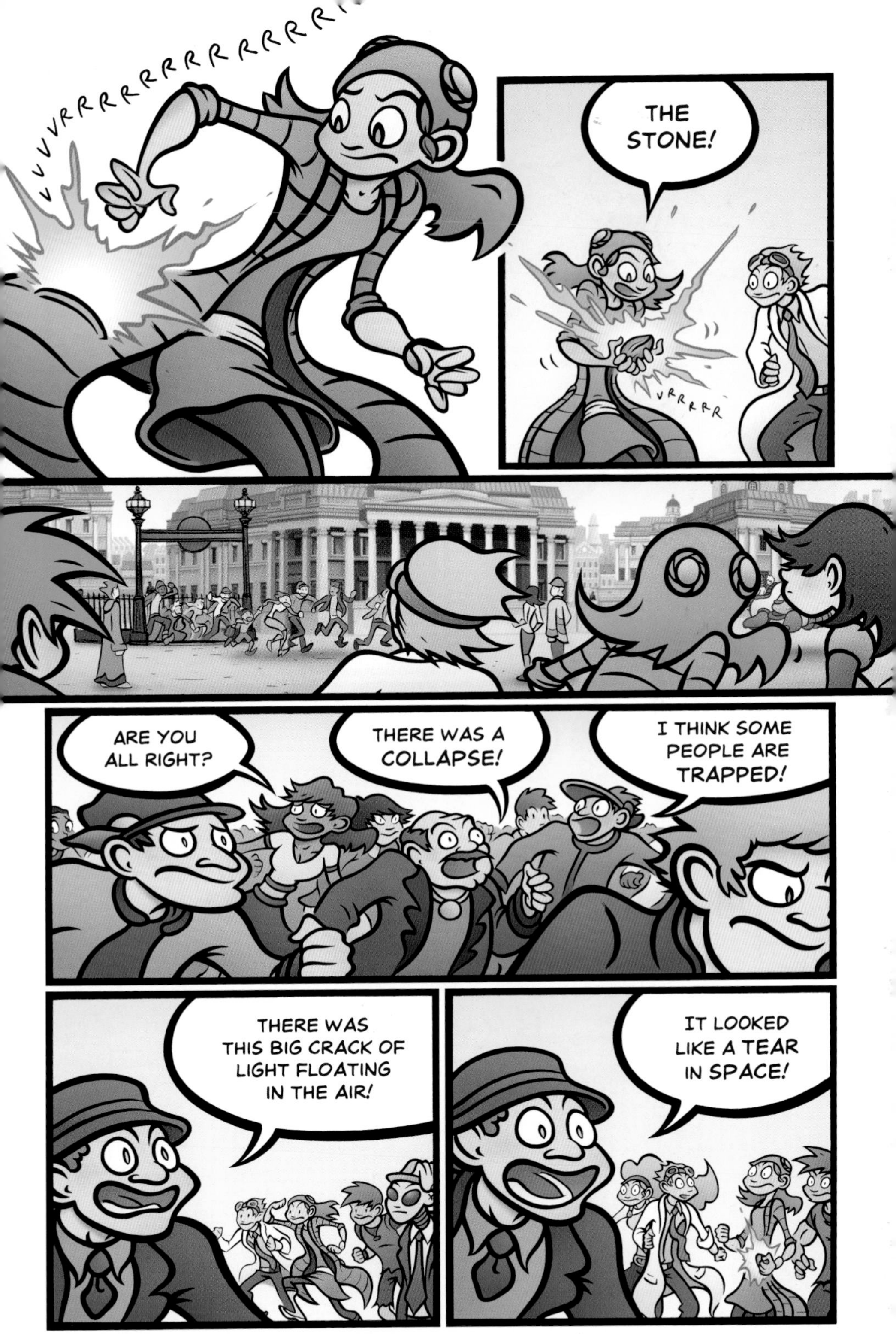
VVVVRRRRRRRRRRRRRRRRRR
THE STONE!
VRRRRR
ARE YOU ALL RIGHT?
THERE WAS A COLLAPSE!
I THINK SOME PEOPLE ARE TRAPPED!
THERE WAS THIS BIG CRACK OF LIGHT FLOATING IN THE AIR!
IT LOOKED LIKE A TEAR IN SPACE!

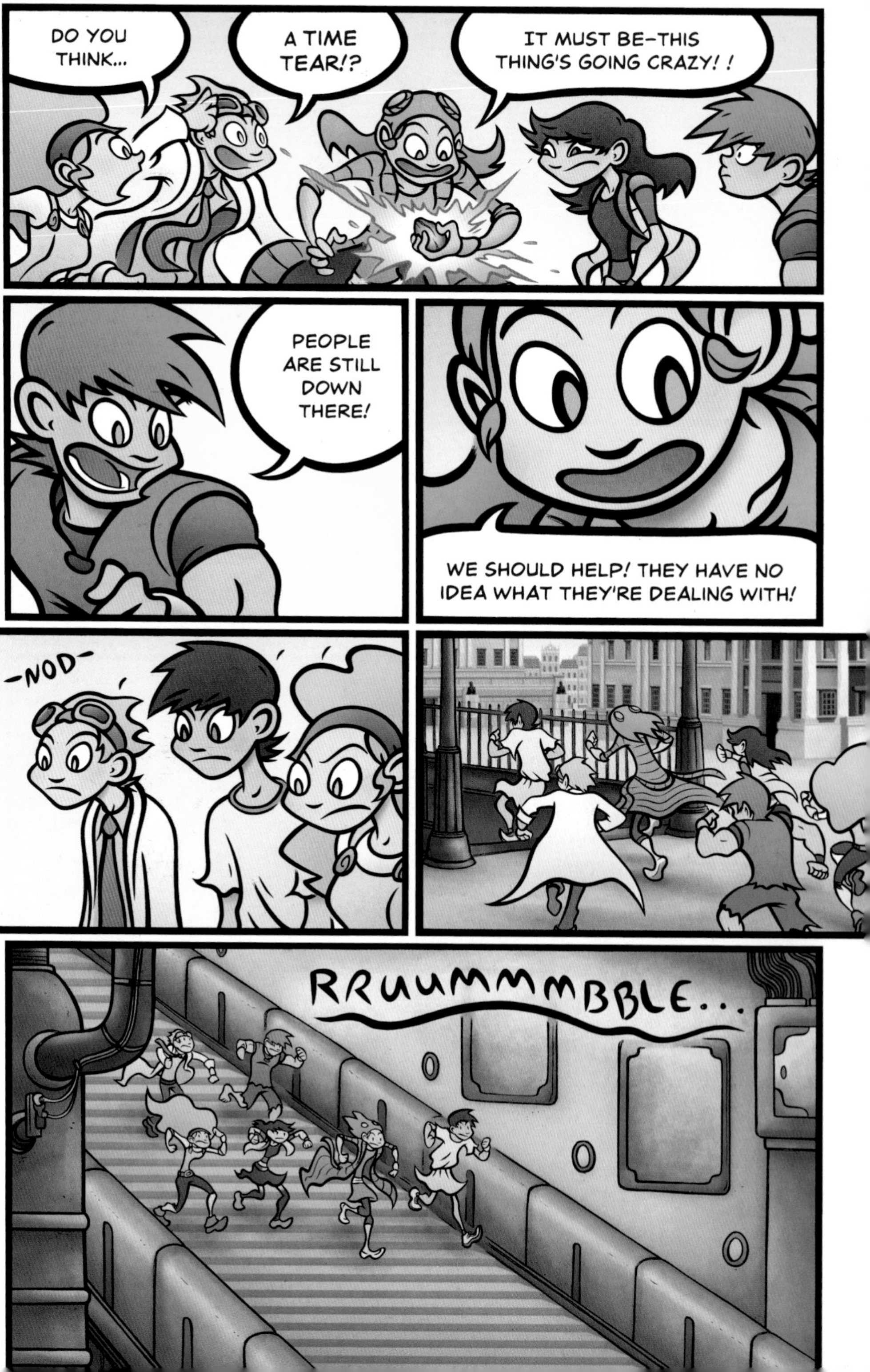
DO YOU THINK...
A TIME TEAR!?
IT MUST BE—THIS THING'S GOING CRAZY! !
PEOPLE ARE STILL DOWN THERE!
WE SHOULD HELP! THEY HAVE NO IDEA WHAT THEY'RE DEALING WITH!
-NOD-
RRUUMMMMBBLE...

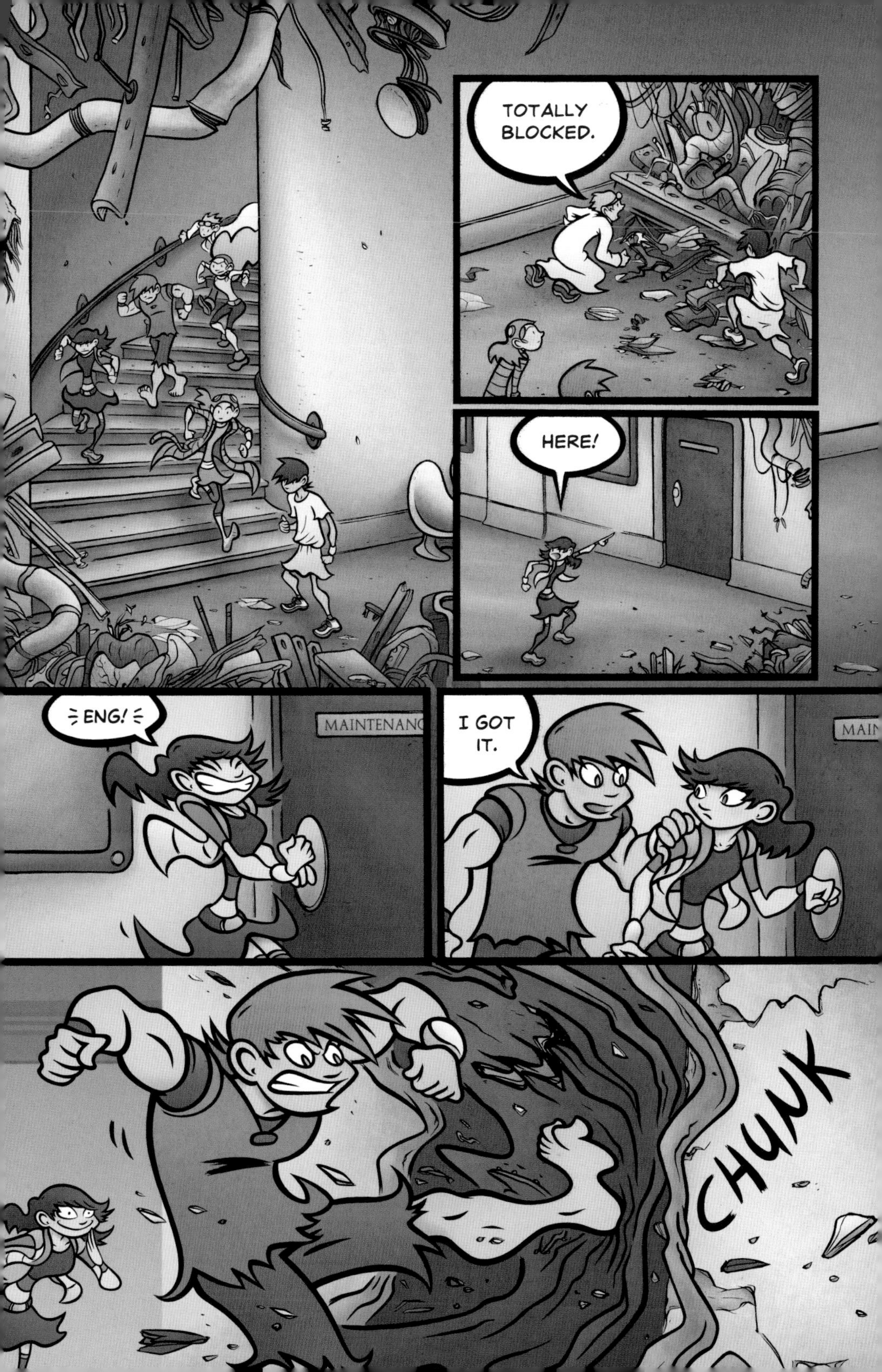
TOTALLY BLOCKED.
HERE!
ENG!
MAINTENANC
I GOT IT.
MAIN
CHUNK

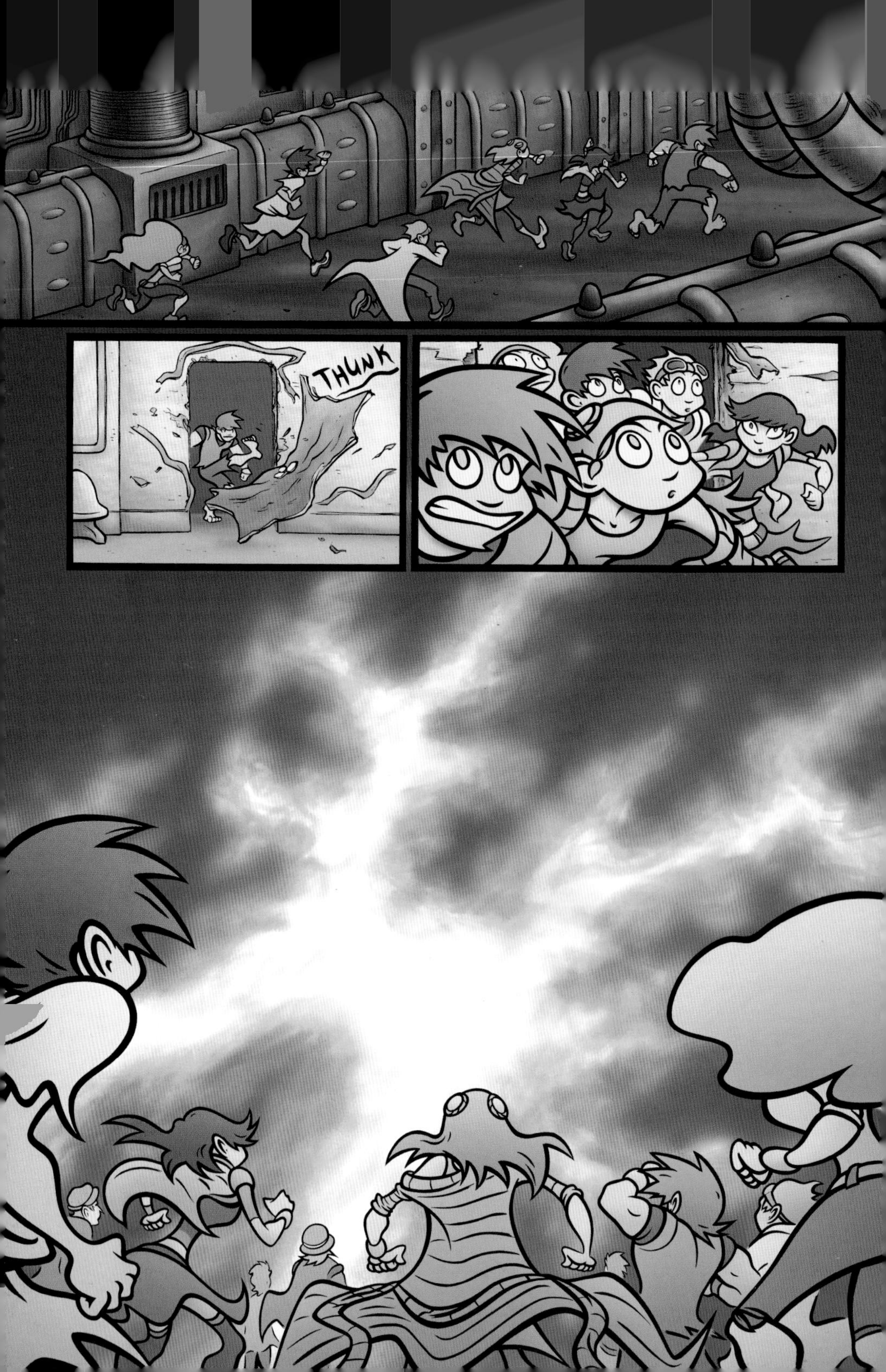
THUNK

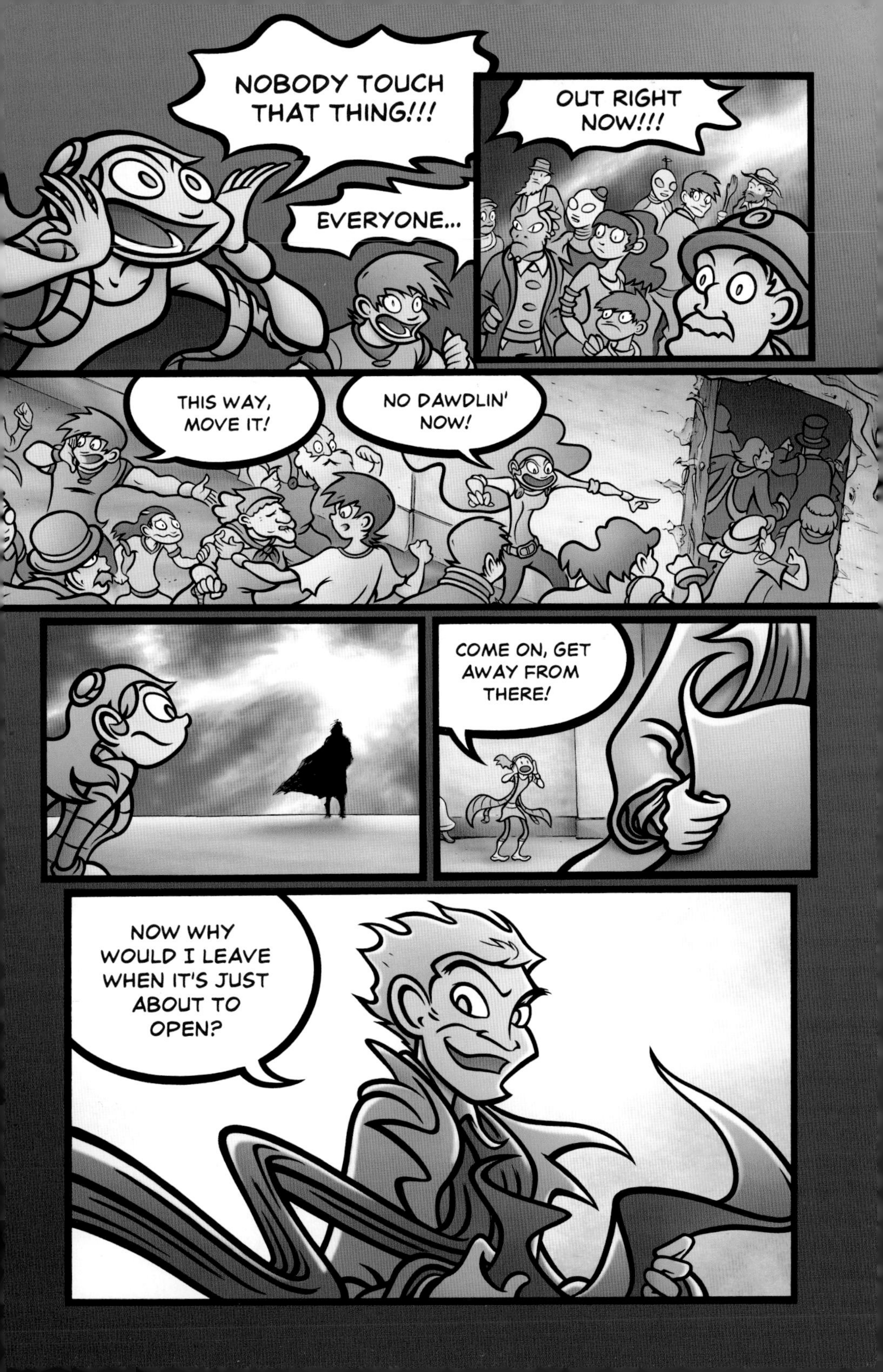
NOBODY TOUCH THAT THING!!!
EVERYONE...
OUT RIGHT NOW!!!
THIS WAY, MOVE IT!
NO DAWDLIN' NOW!
COME ON, GET AWAY FROM THERE!
NOW WHY WOULD I LEAVE WHEN IT'S JUST ABOUT TO OPEN?

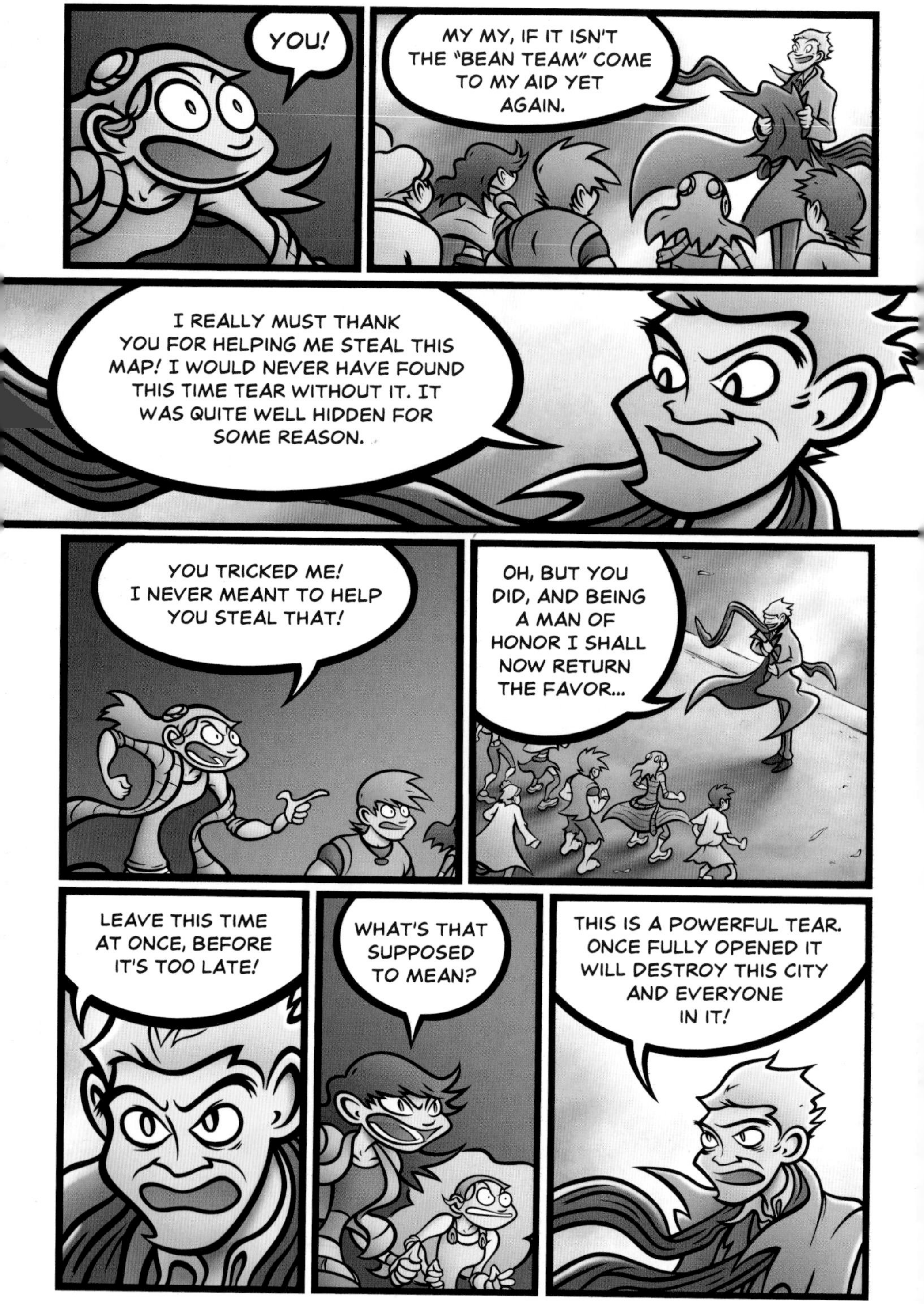
YOU!
MY MY, IF IT ISN'T THE "BEAN TEAM" COME TO MY AID YET AGAIN.
I REALLY MUST THANK YOU FOR HELPING ME STEAL THIS MAP! I WOULD NEVER HAVE FOUND THIS TIME TEAR WITHOUT IT. IT WAS QUITE WELL HIDDEN FOR SOME REASON.
YOU TRICKED ME! I NEVER MEANT TO HELP YOU STEAL THAT!
OH, BUT YOU DID, AND BEING A MAN OF HONOR I SHALL NOW RETURN THE FAVOR...
LEAVE THIS TIME AT ONCE, BEFORE IT'S TOO LATE!
WHAT'S THAT SUPPOSED TO MEAN?
THIS IS A POWERFUL TEAR. ONCE FULLY OPENED IT WILL DESTROY THIS CITY AND EVERYONE IN IT!

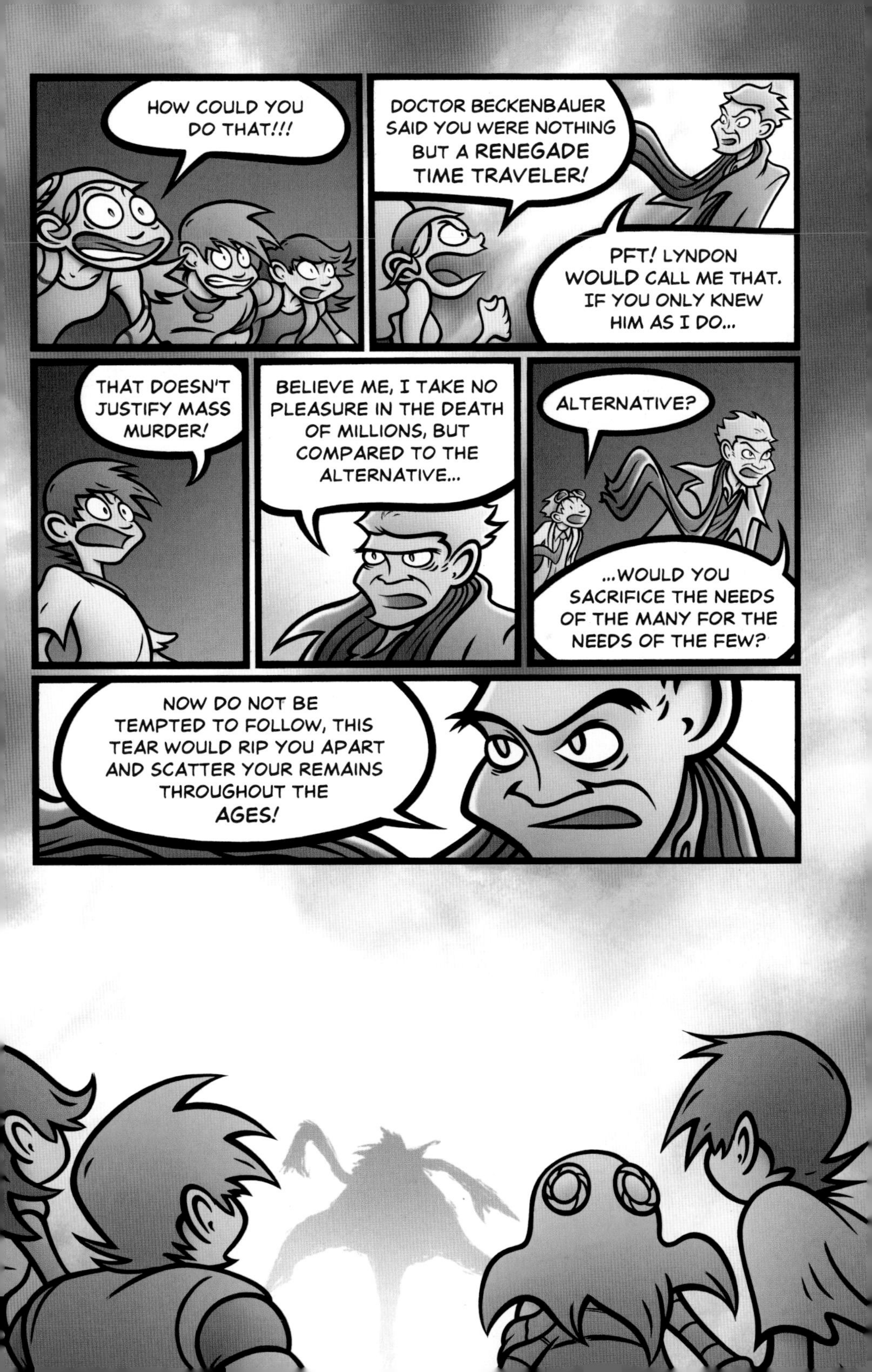
HOW COULD YOU DO THAT!!!
DOCTOR BECKENBAUER SAID YOU WERE NOTHING BUT A RENEGADE TIME TRAVELER!
PFT! LYNDON WOULD CALL ME THAT. IF YOU ONLY KNEW HIM AS I DO...
THAT DOESN'T JUSTIFY MASS MURDER!
BELIEVE ME, I TAKE NO PLEASURE IN THE DEATH OF MILLIONS, BUT COMPARED TO THE ALTERNATIVE...
ALTERNATIVE?
...WOULD YOU SACRIFICE THE NEEDS OF THE MANY FOR THE NEEDS OF THE FEW?
NOW DO NOT BE TEMPTED TO FOLLOW, THIS TEAR WOULD RIP YOU APART AND SCATTER YOUR REMAINS THROUGHOUT THE AGES!

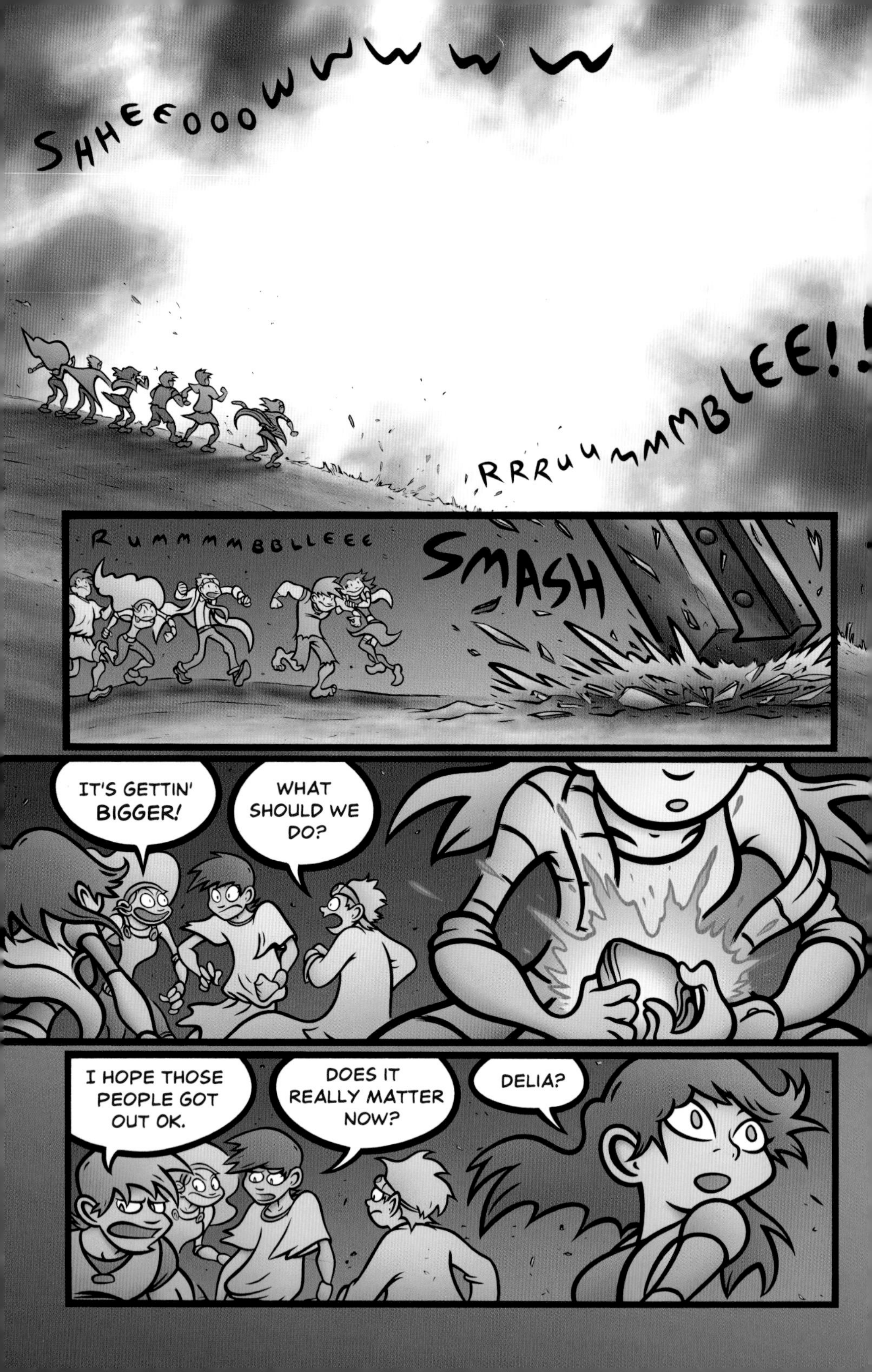
SHHEEOOOWWWWWW
RRRUUMMMMBLEE!!
RUMMMMMBBLLEEE
SMASH
IT'S GETTIN' BIGGER!
WHAT SHOULD WE DO?
I HOPE THOSE PEOPLE GOT OUT OK.
DOES IT REALLY MATTER NOW?
DELIA?

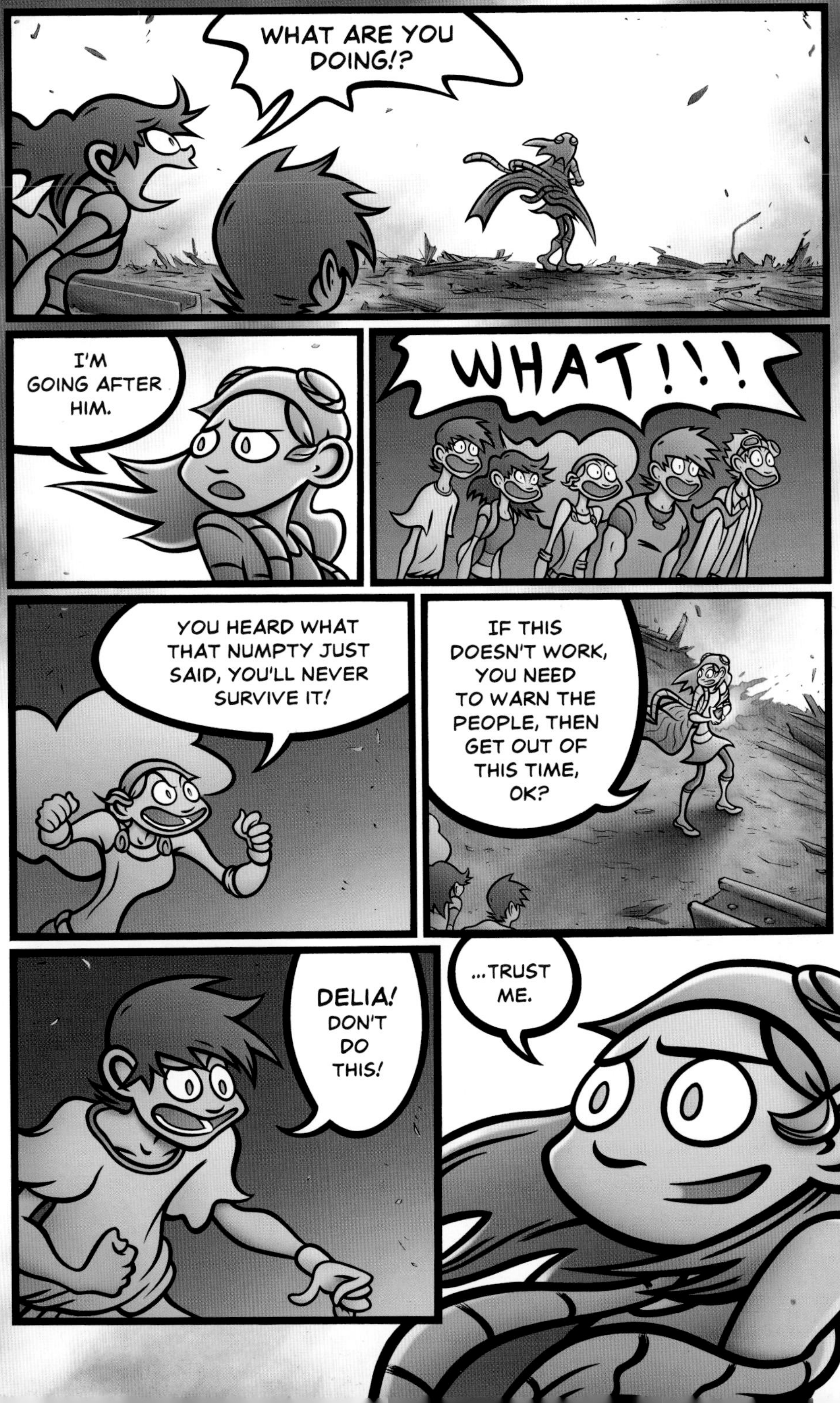
WHAT ARE YOU DOING!?
I'M GOING AFTER HIM.
WHAT!!!
YOU HEARD WHAT THAT NUMPTY JUST SAID, YOU'LL NEVER SURVIVE IT!
IF THIS DOESN'T WORK, YOU NEED TO WARN THE PEOPLE, THEN GET OUT OF THIS TIME, OK?
DELIA! DON'T DO THIS!
...TRUST ME.

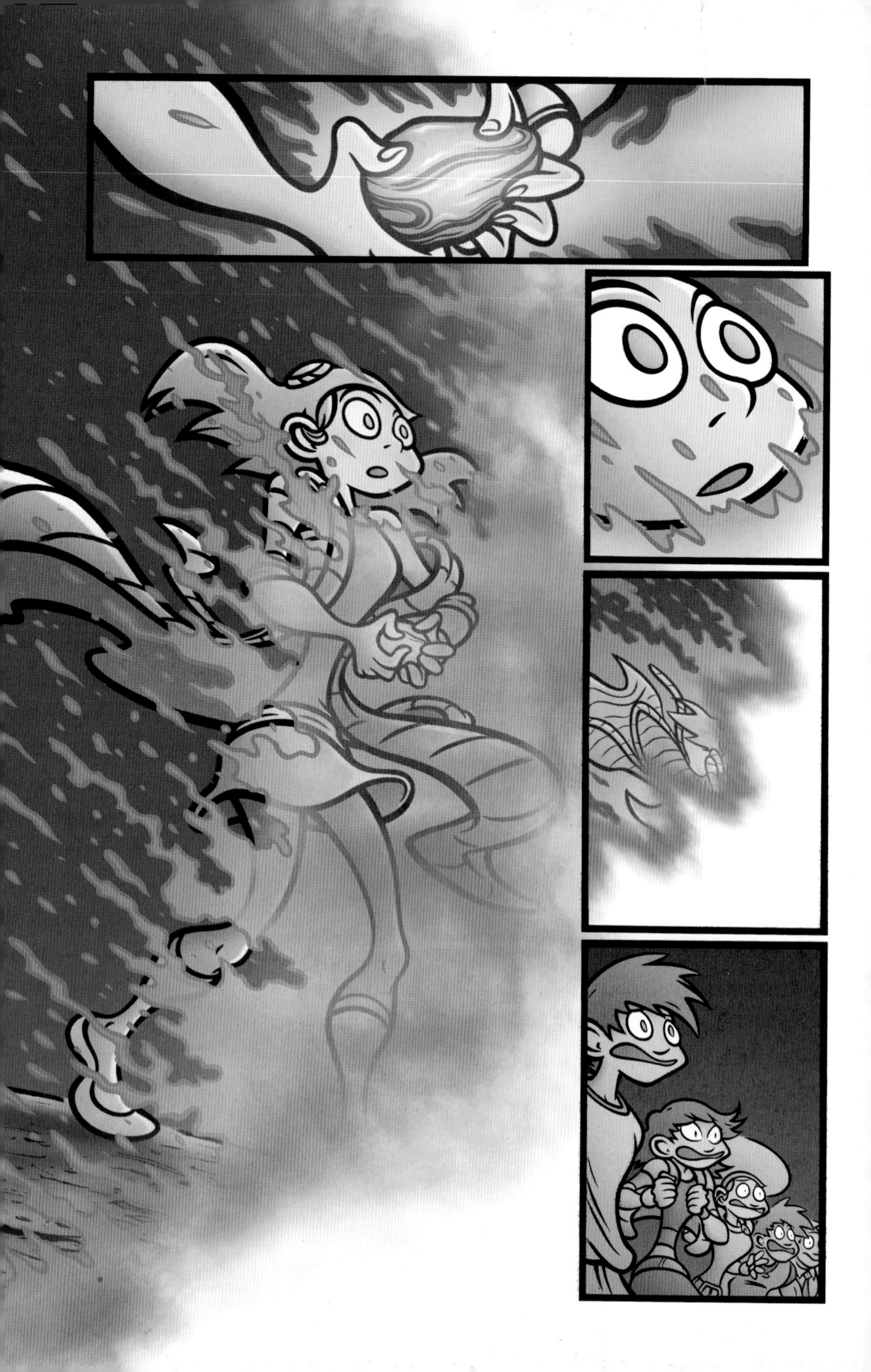

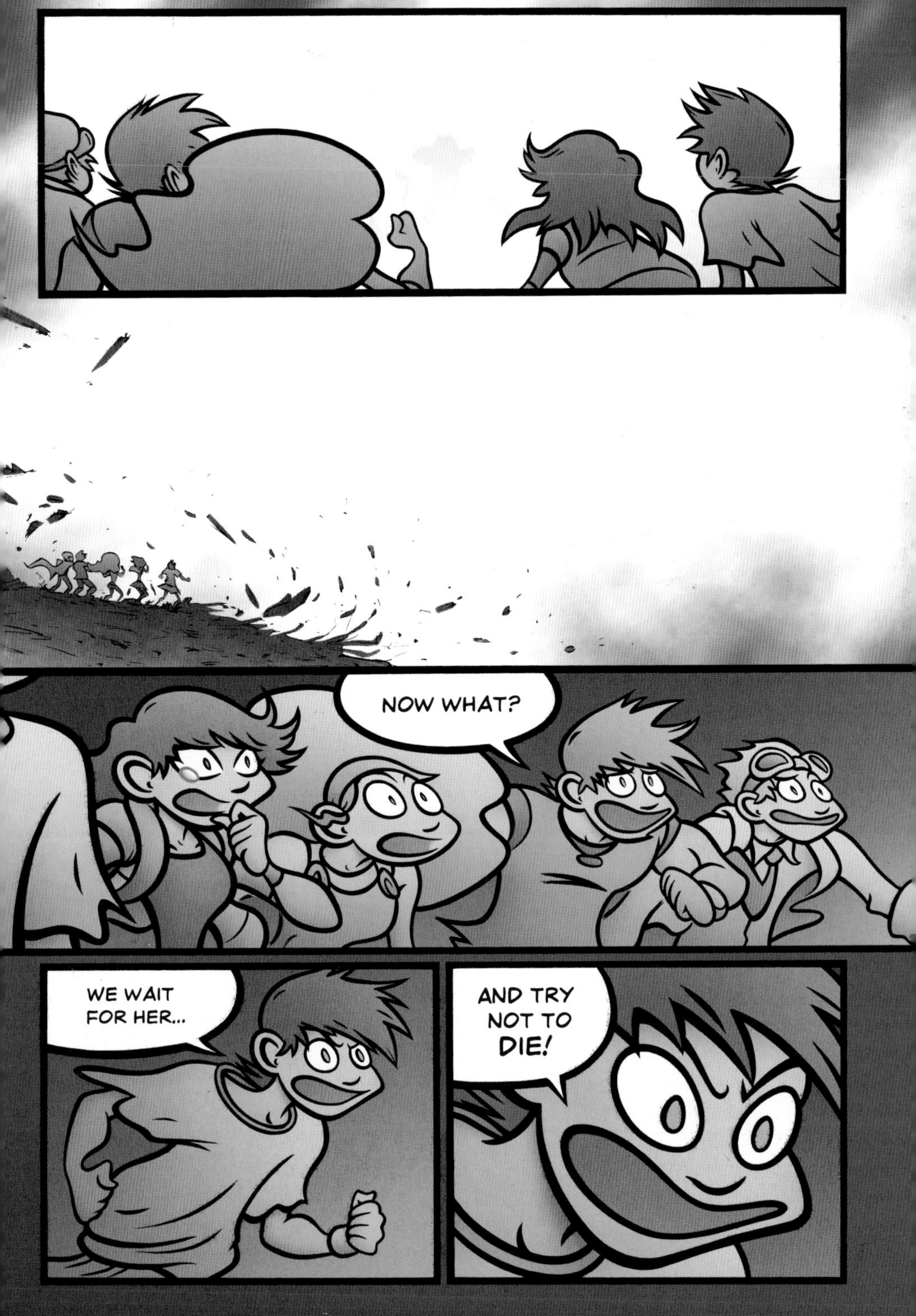
NOW WHAT?
WE WAIT FOR HER...
AND TRY NOT TO DIE!

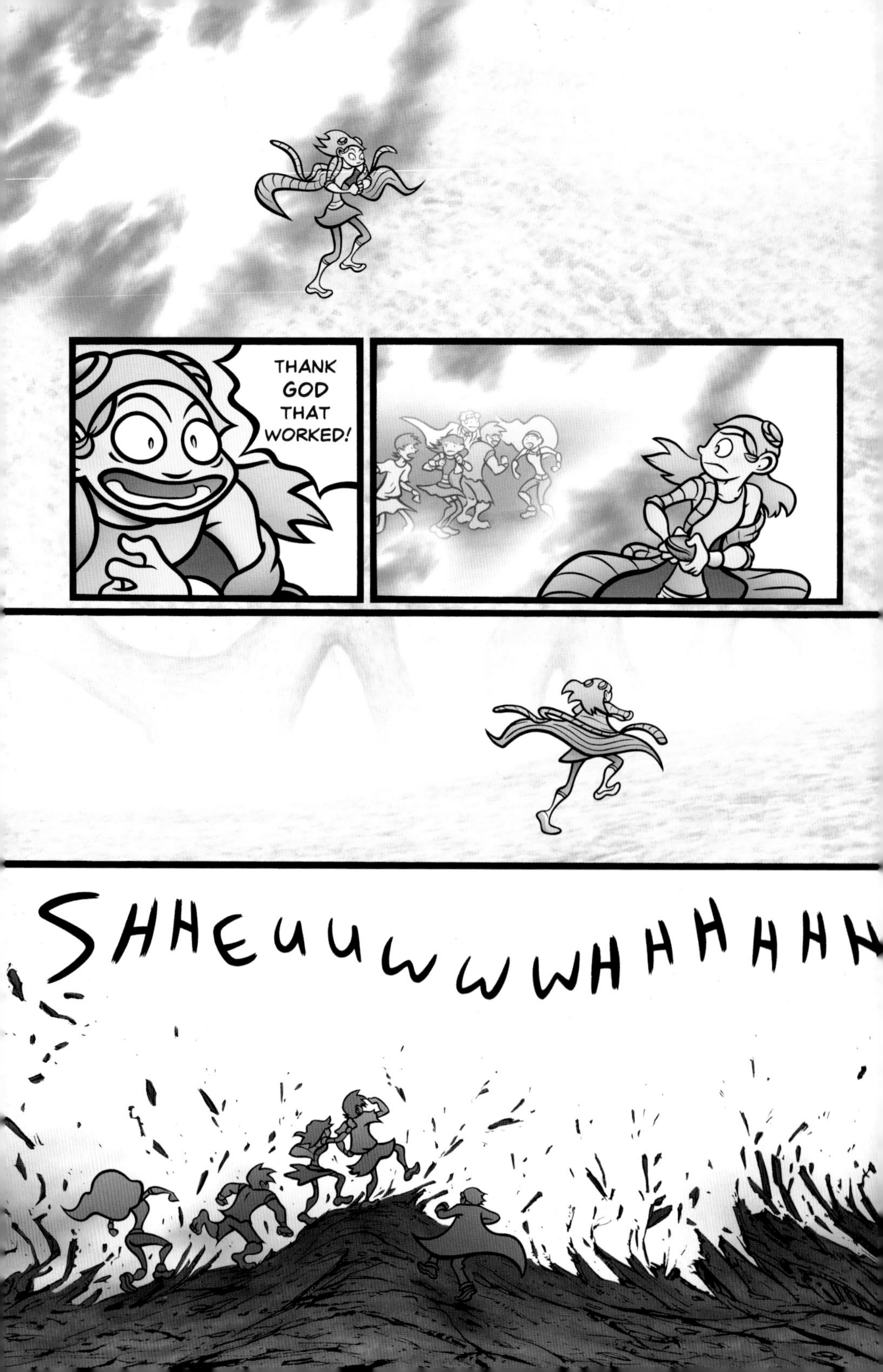
THANK GOD THAT WORKED!
SHHEUUWWWHHHHHN

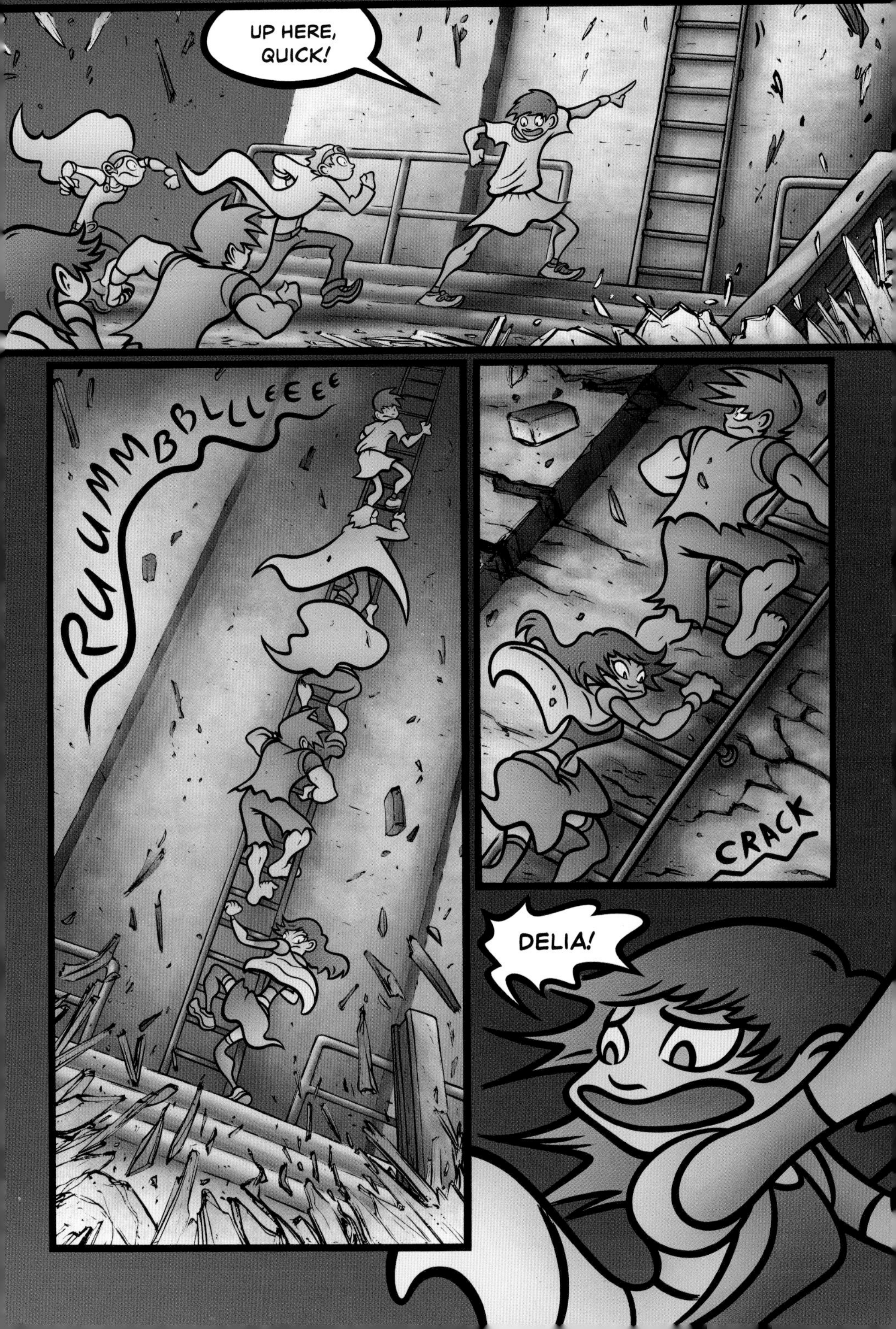
UP HERE, QUICK!
RUUMMBBLLLLEEEE
CRACK
DELIA!

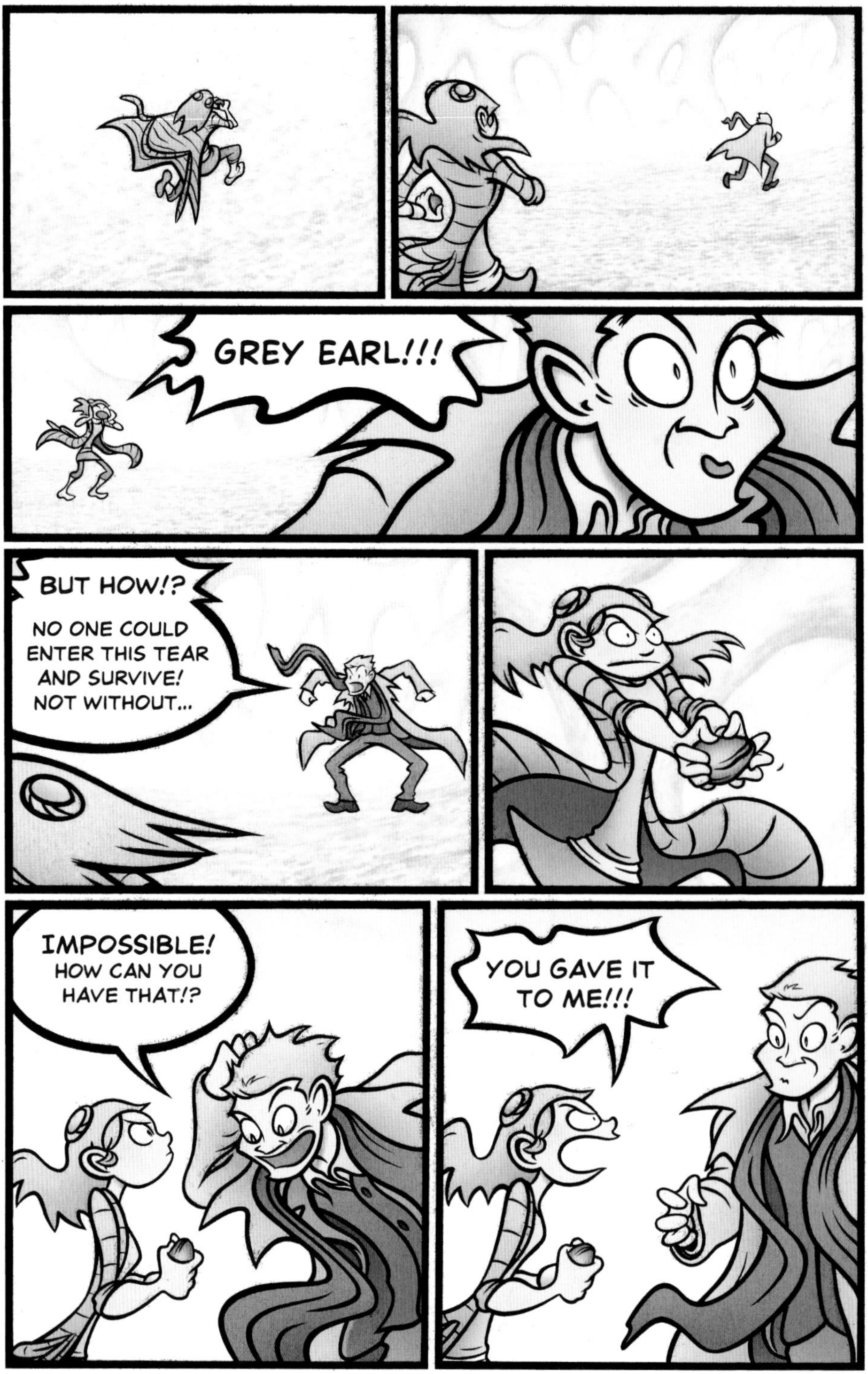
GREY EARL!!!
BUT HOW!?
NO ONE COULD ENTER THIS TEAR AND SURVIVE! NOT WITHOUT...
IMPOSSIBLE! HOW CAN YOU HAVE THAT!?
YOU GAVE IT TO ME!!!

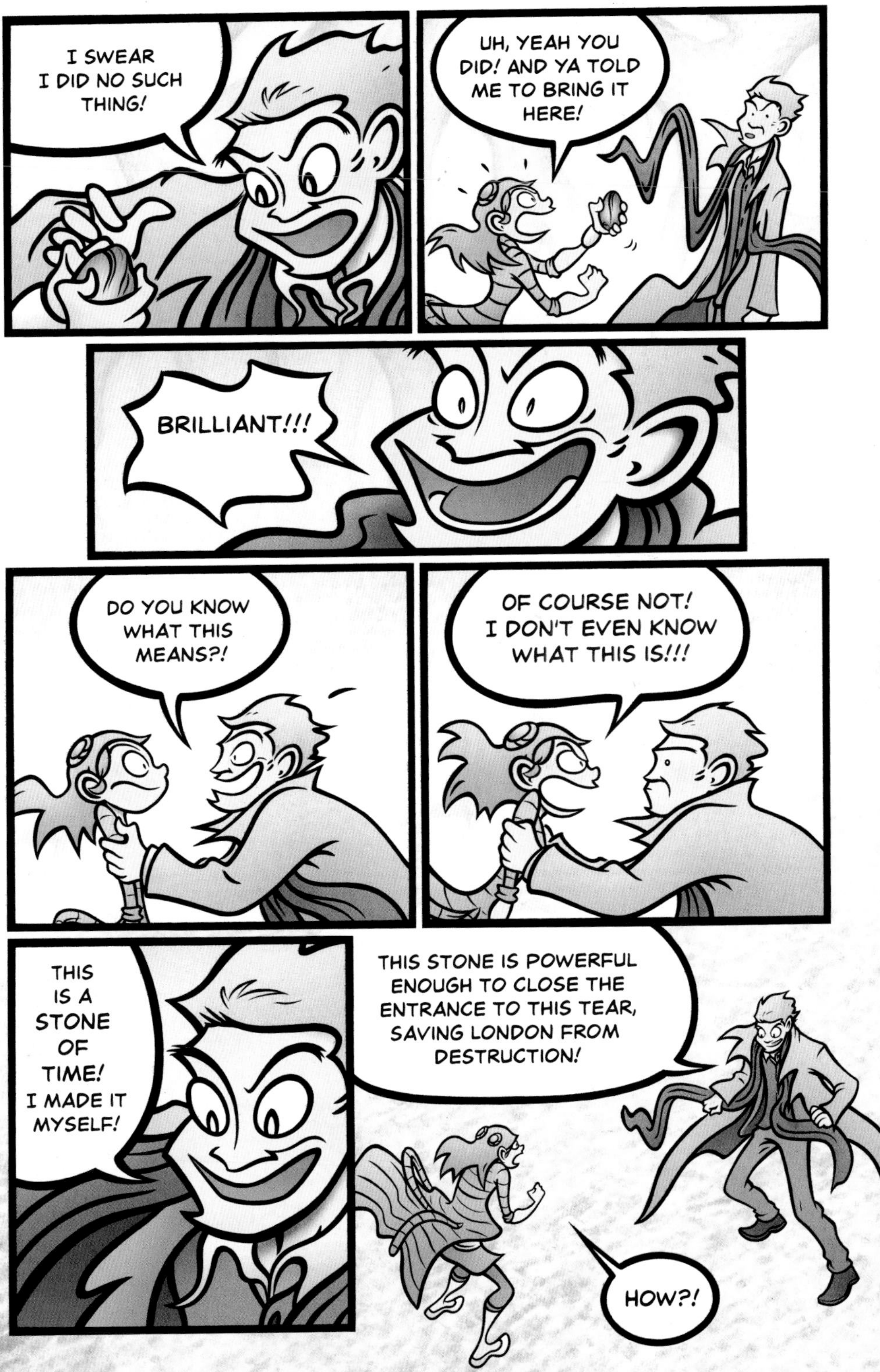
I SWEAR I DID NO SUCH THING!
UH, YEAH YOU DID! AND YA TOLD ME TO BRING IT HERE!
BRILLIANT!!!
DO YOU KNOW WHAT THIS MEANS?!
OF COURSE NOT! I DON'T EVEN KNOW WHAT THIS IS!!!
THIS IS A STONE OF TIME! I MADE IT MYSELF!
THIS STONE IS POWERFUL ENOUGH TO CLOSE THE ENTRANCE TO THIS TEAR, SAVING LONDON FROM DESTRUCTION!
HOW?!

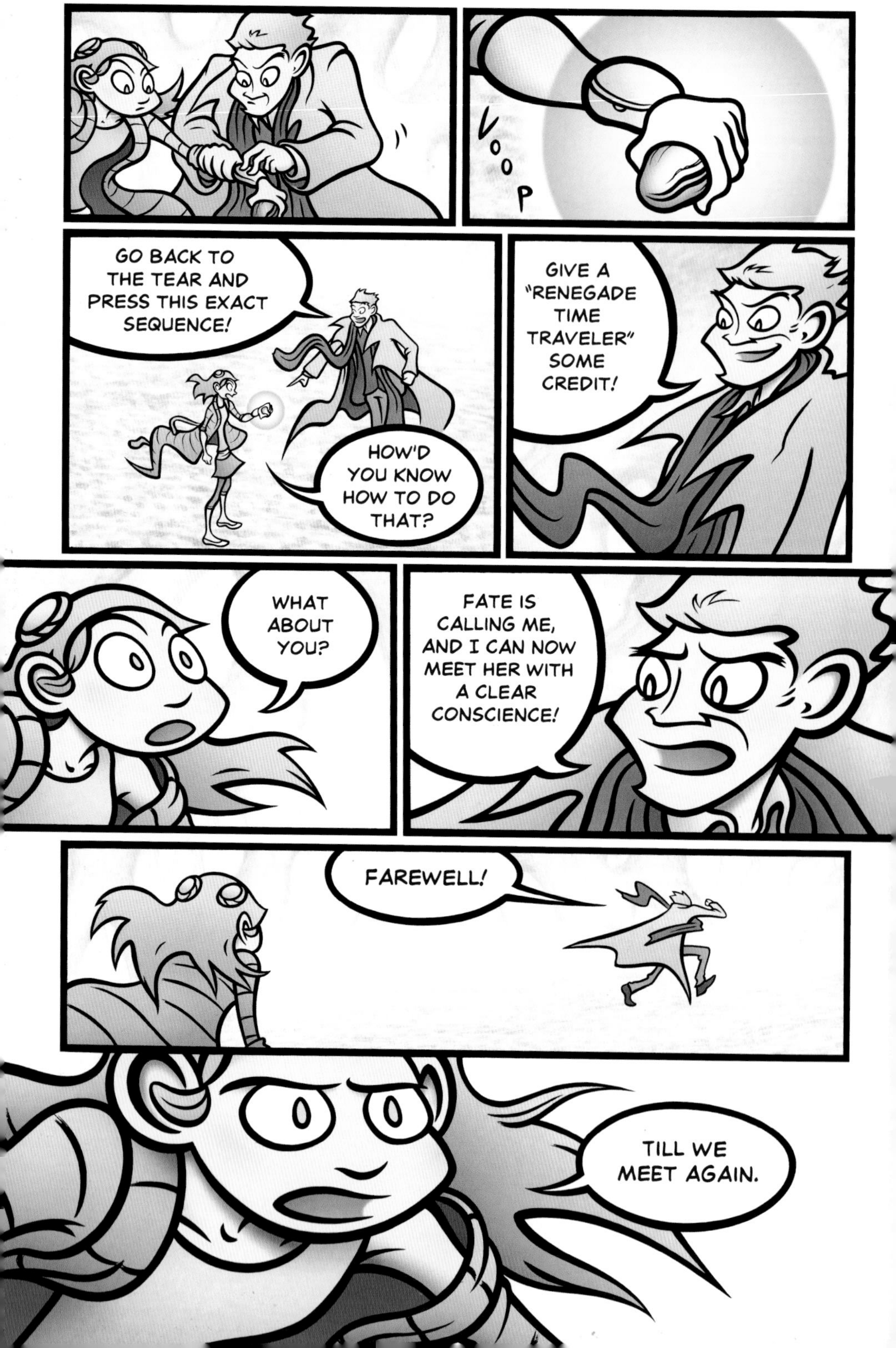
VOOP
GO BACK TO THE TEAR AND PRESS THIS EXACT SEQUENCE!
HOW'D YOU KNOW HOW TO DO THAT?
GIVE A "RENEGADE TIME TRAVELER" SOME CREDIT!
WHAT ABOUT YOU?
FATE IS CALLING ME, AND I CAN NOW MEET HER WITH A CLEAR CONSCIENCE!
FAREWELL!
TILL WE MEET AGAIN.

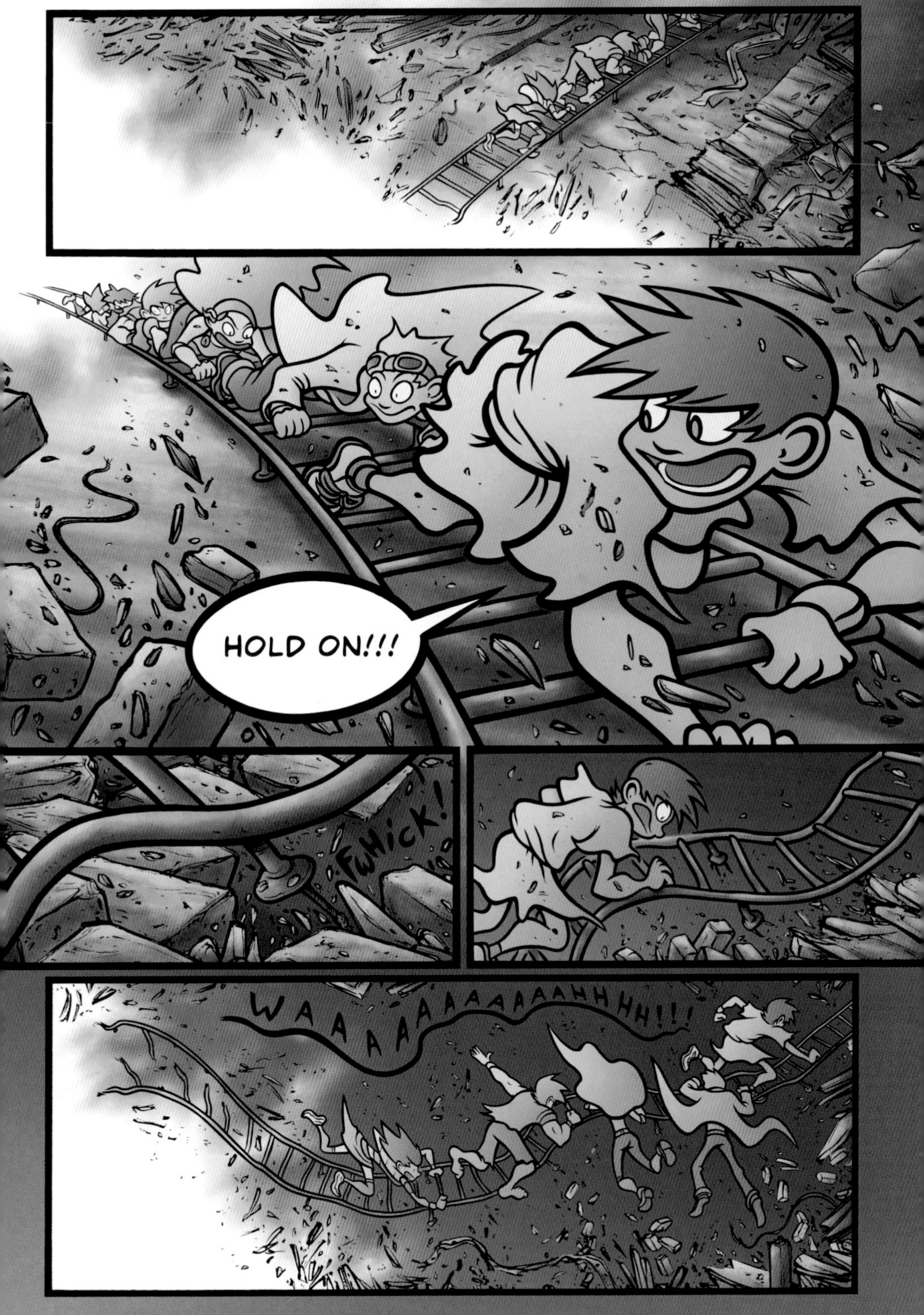
HOLD ON!!!
FWHICK!
WAAAAAAAAAAAHHHH!!!

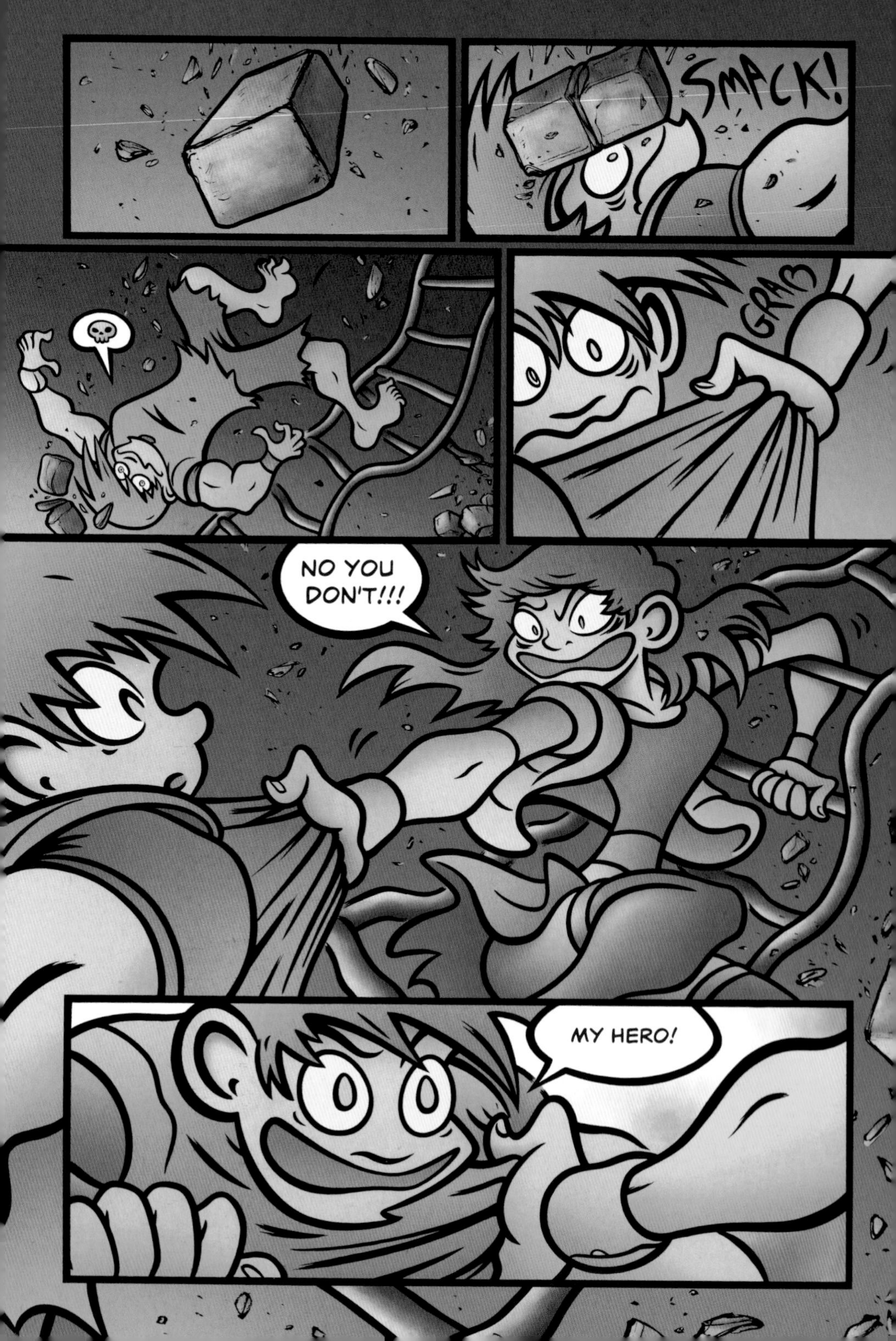
SMACK!
GRAB
NO YOU DON'T!!!
MY HERO!

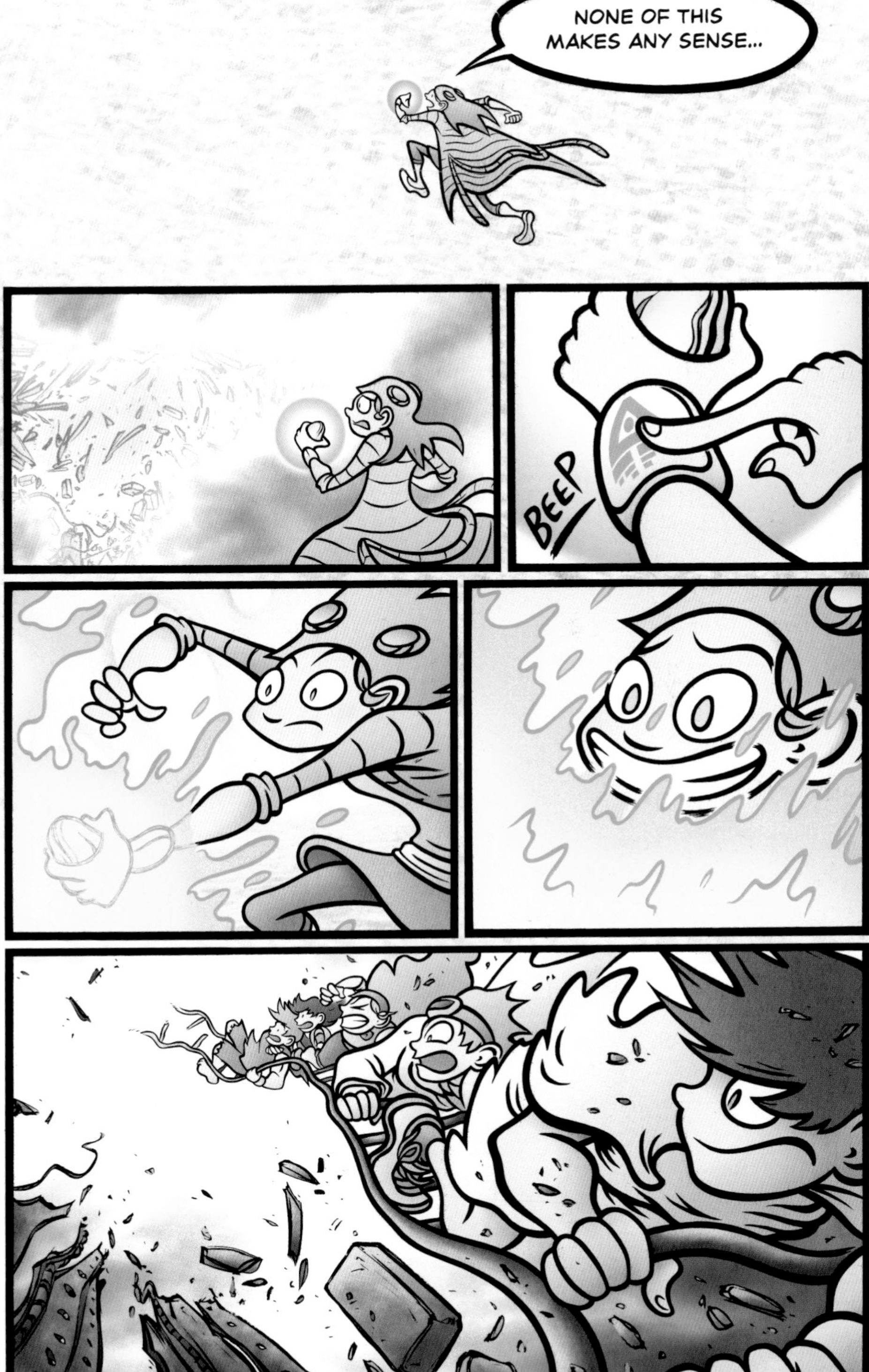
NONE OF THIS MAKES ANY SENSE...
BEEP

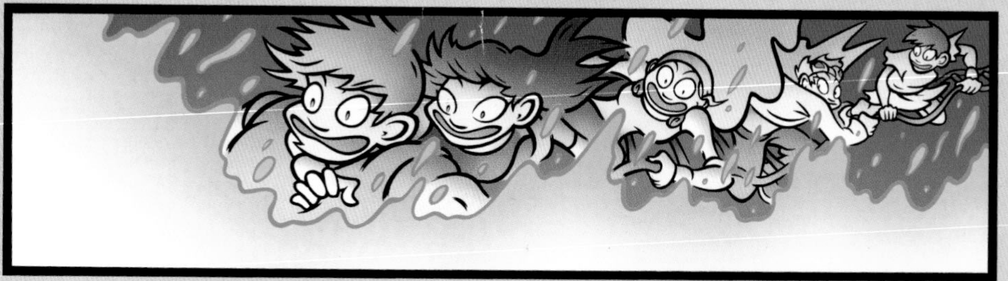
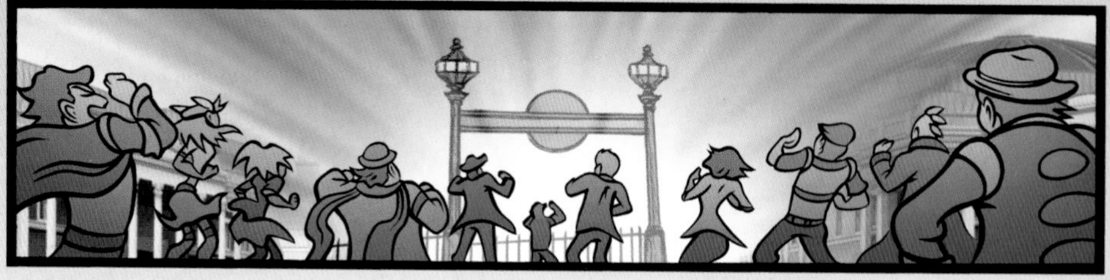
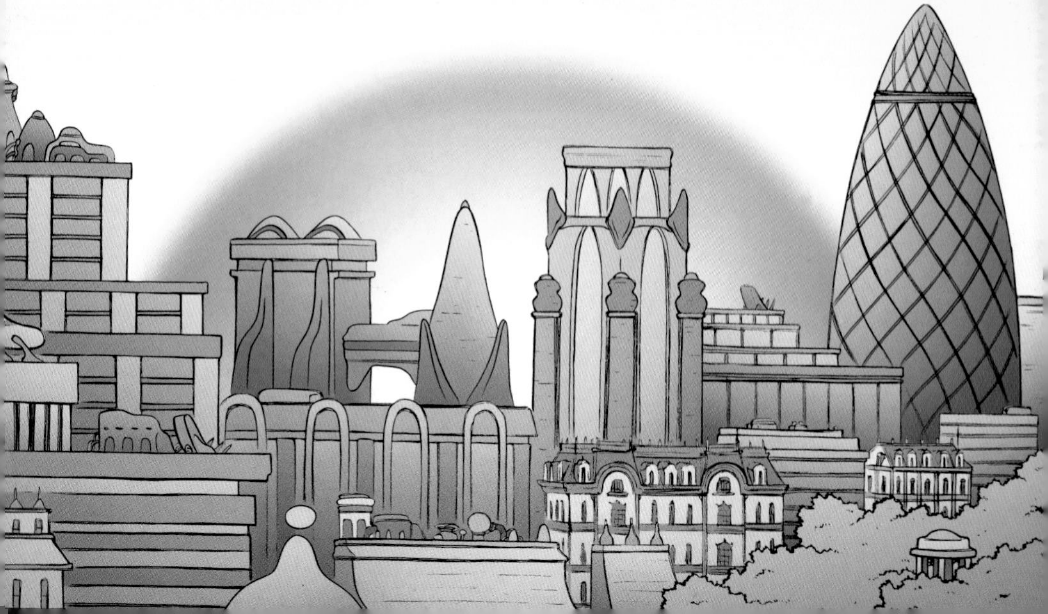

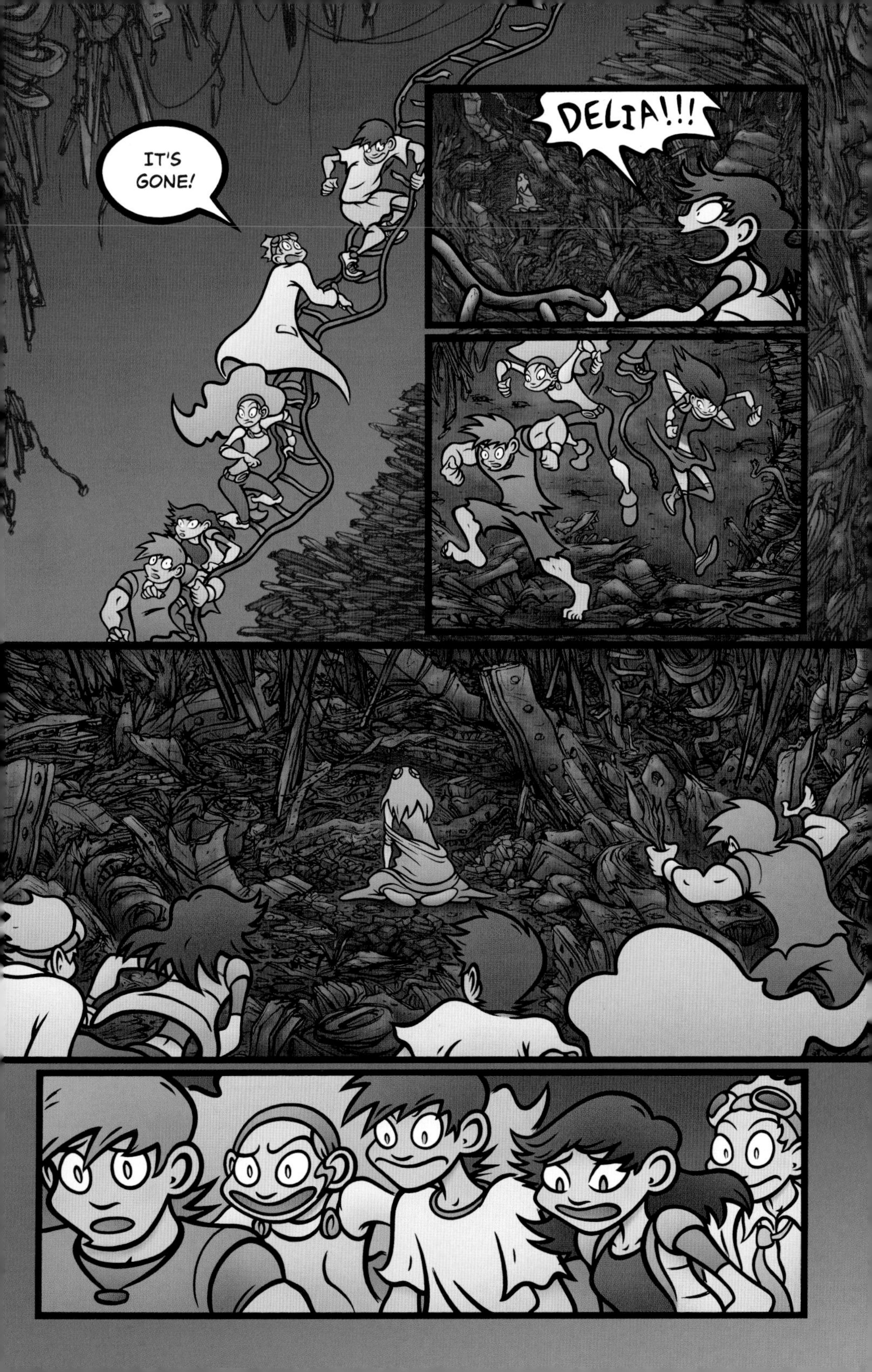
IT'S GONE!
DELIA!!!

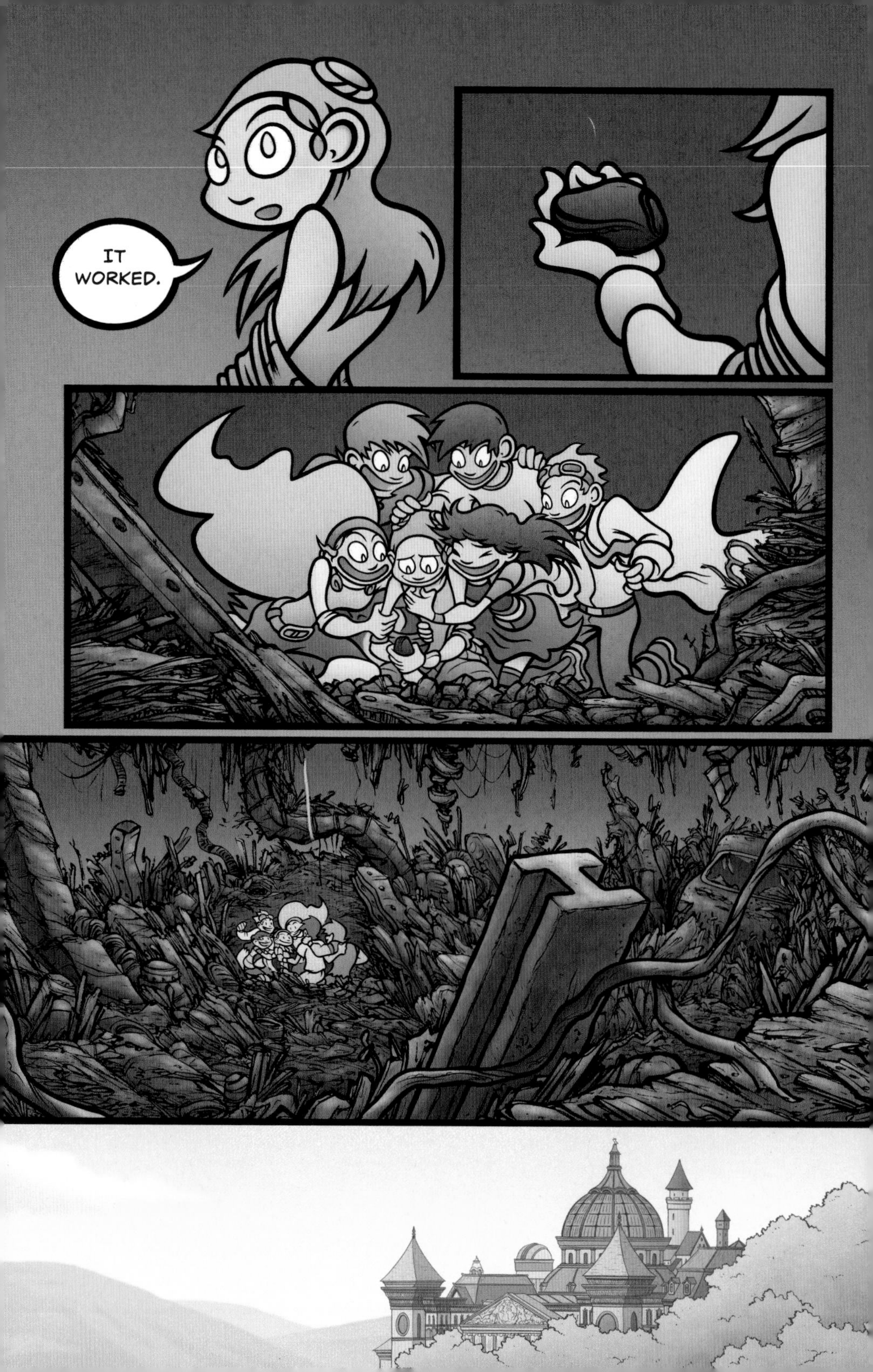
IT WORKED.

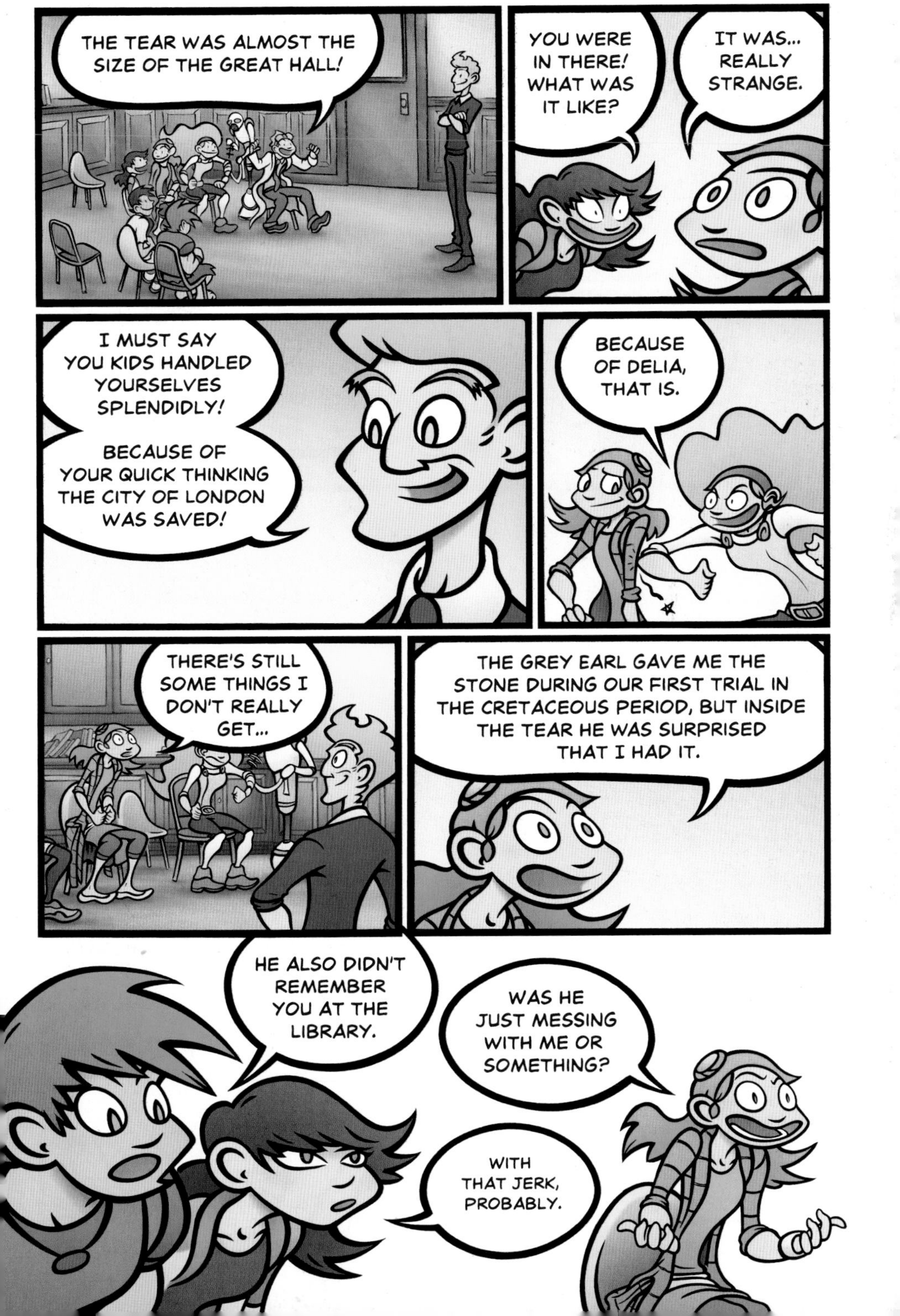
THE TEAR WAS ALMOST THE SIZE OF THE GREAT HALL!
YOU WERE IN THERE! WHAT WAS IT LIKE?
IT WAS... REALLY STRANGE.
I MUST SAY YOU KIDS HANDLED YOURSELVES SPLENDIDLY!
BECAUSE OF YOUR QUICK THINKING THE CITY OF LONDON WAS SAVED!
BECAUSE OF DELIA, THAT IS.
THERE'S STILL SOME THINGS I DON'T REALLY GET...
THE GREY EARL GAVE ME THE STONE DURING OUR FIRST TRIAL IN THE CRETACEOUS PERIOD, BUT INSIDE THE TEAR HE WAS SURPRISED THAT I HAD IT.
HE ALSO DIDN'T REMEMBER YOU AT THE LIBRARY.
WAS HE JUST MESSING WITH ME OR SOMETHING?
WITH THAT JERK, PROBABLY.

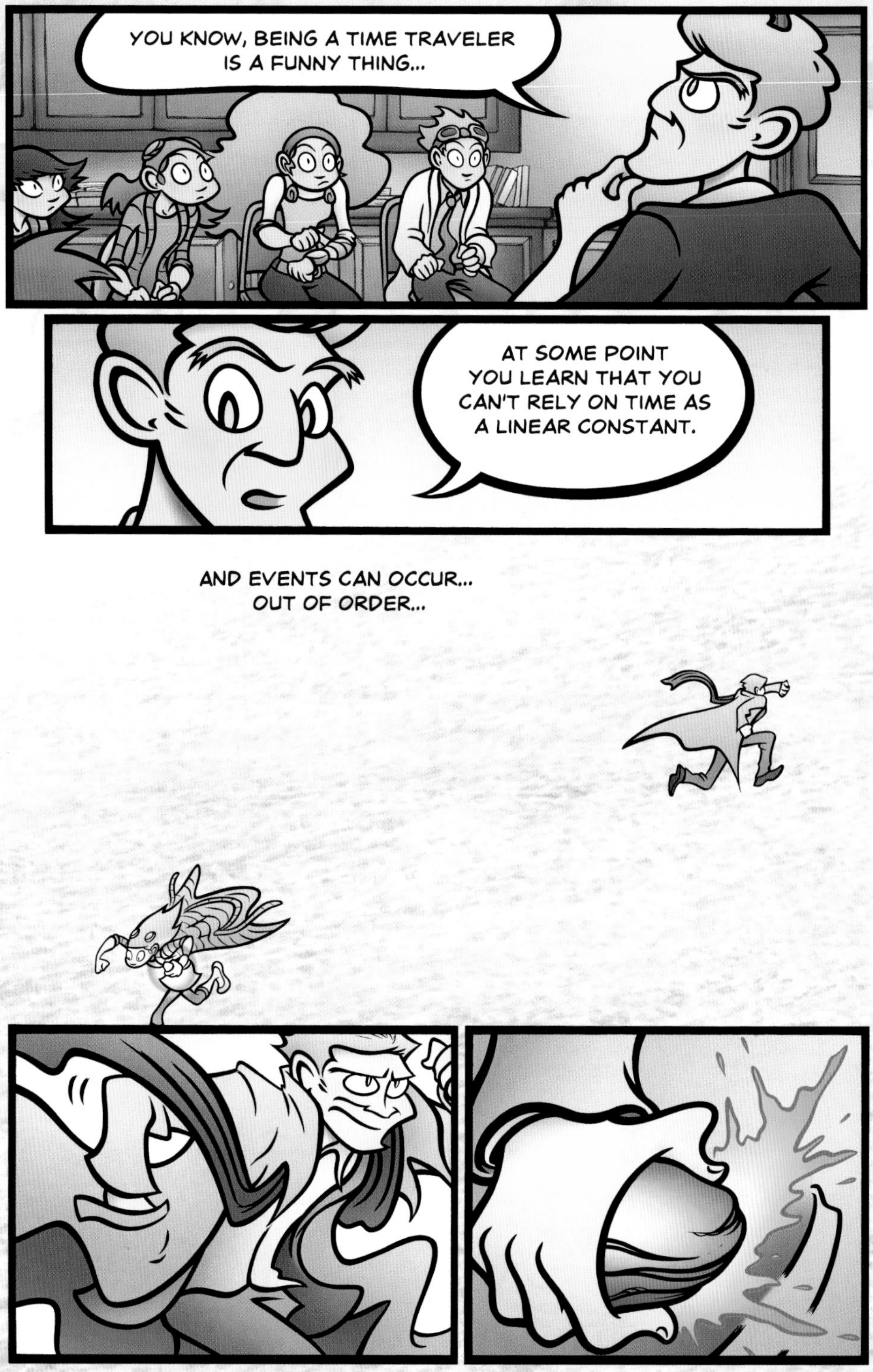
YOU KNOW, BEING A TIME TRAVELER IS A FUNNY THING...
AT SOME POINT YOU LEARN THAT YOU CAN'T RELY ON TIME AS A LINEAR CONSTANT.
AND EVENTS CAN OCCUR... OUT OF ORDER...

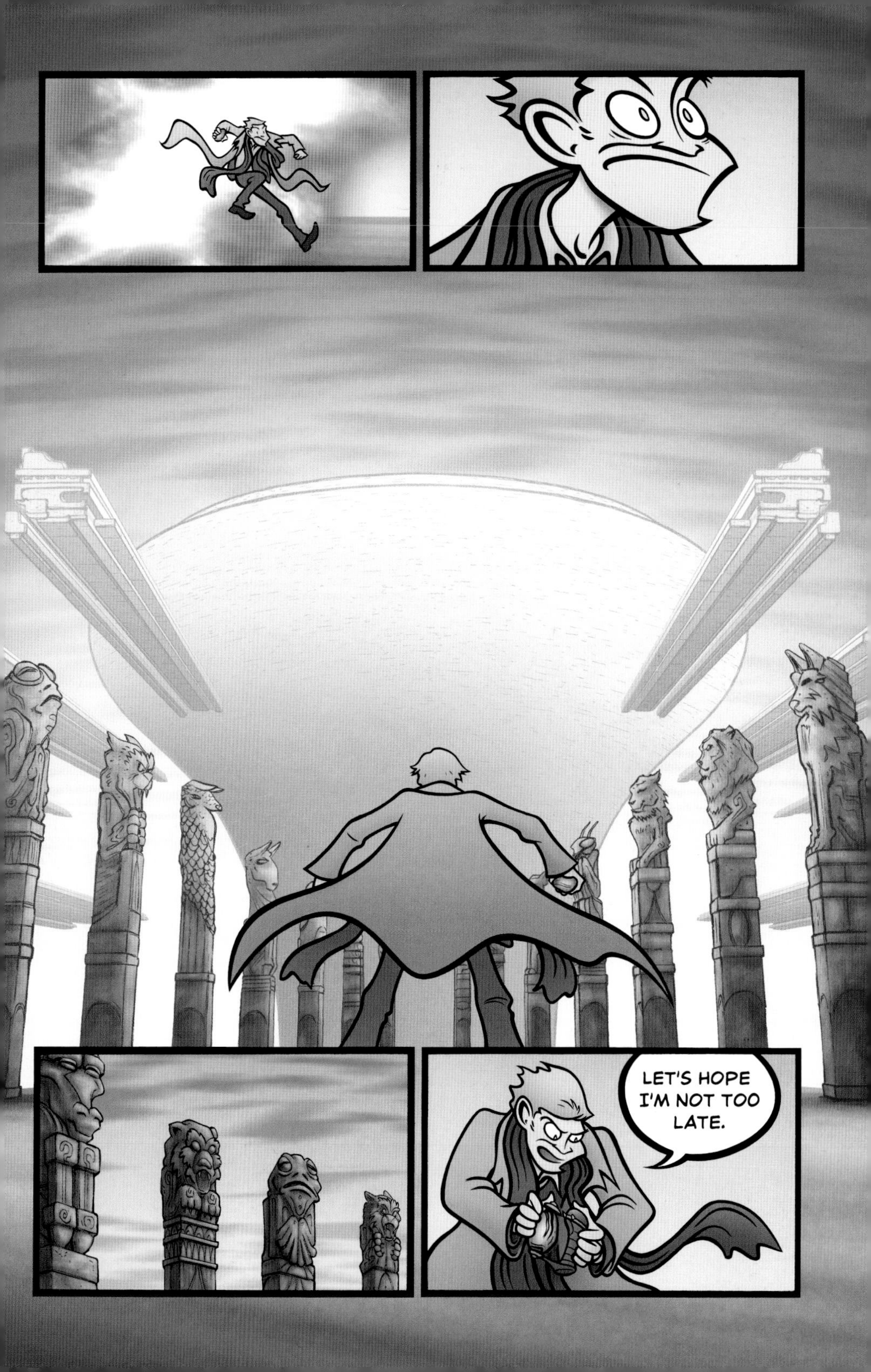
LET'S HOPE I'M NOT TOO LATE.

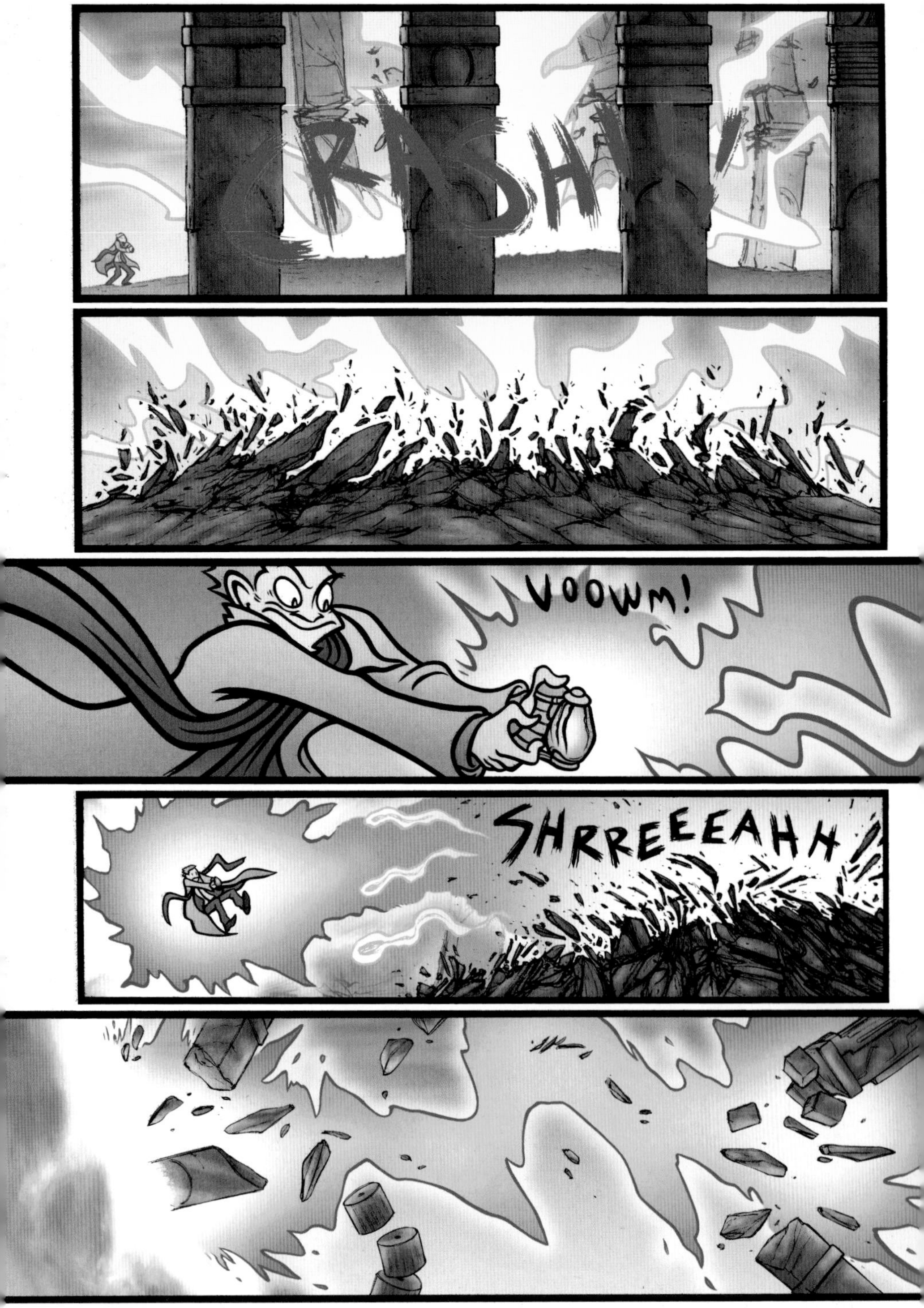
CRASH!
VOOWM!
SHRREEEAHH

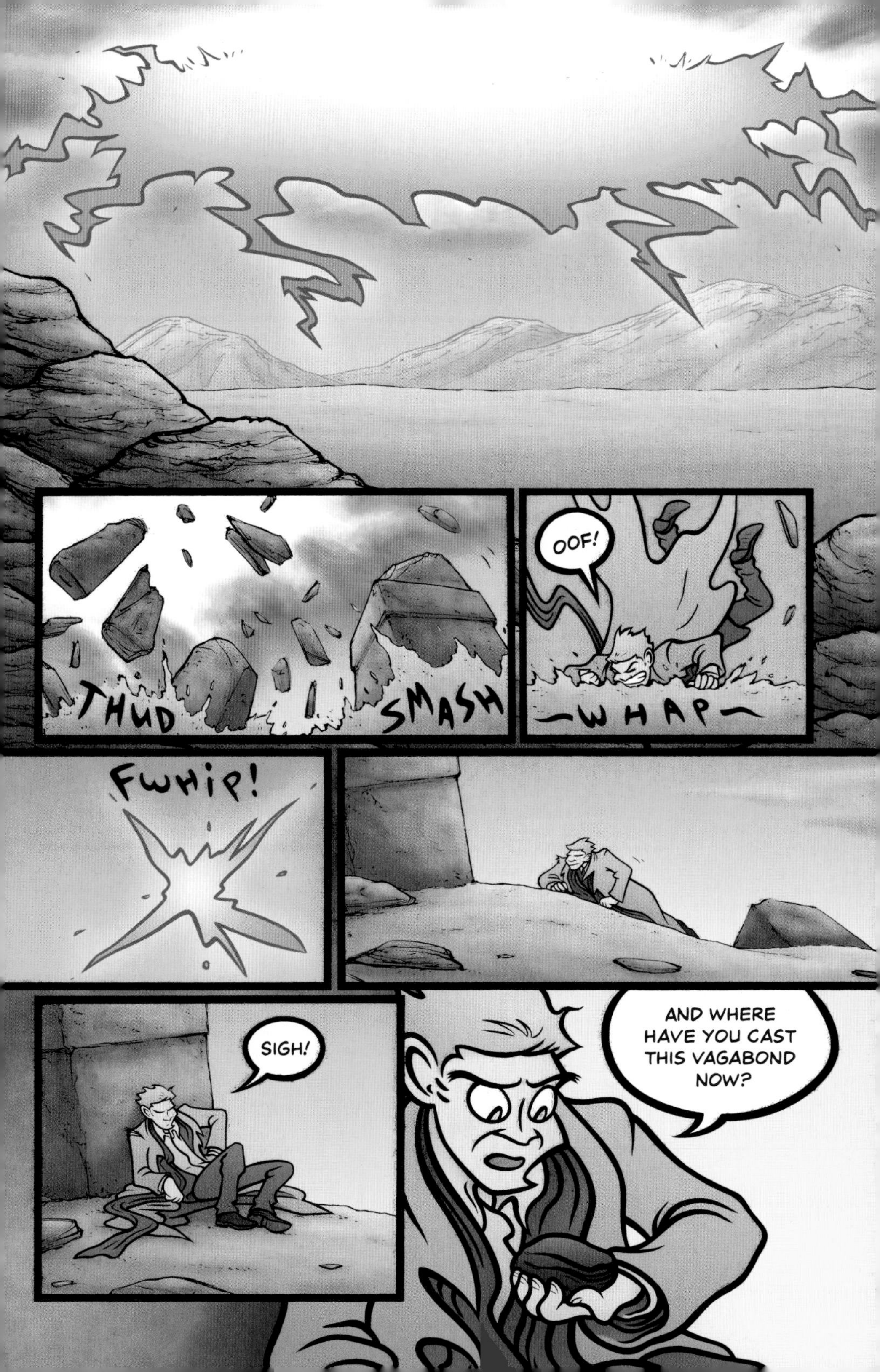
THUD
SMASH
OOF!
WHAP
FWHIP!
SIGH!
AND WHERE HAVE YOU CAST THIS VAGABOND NOW?

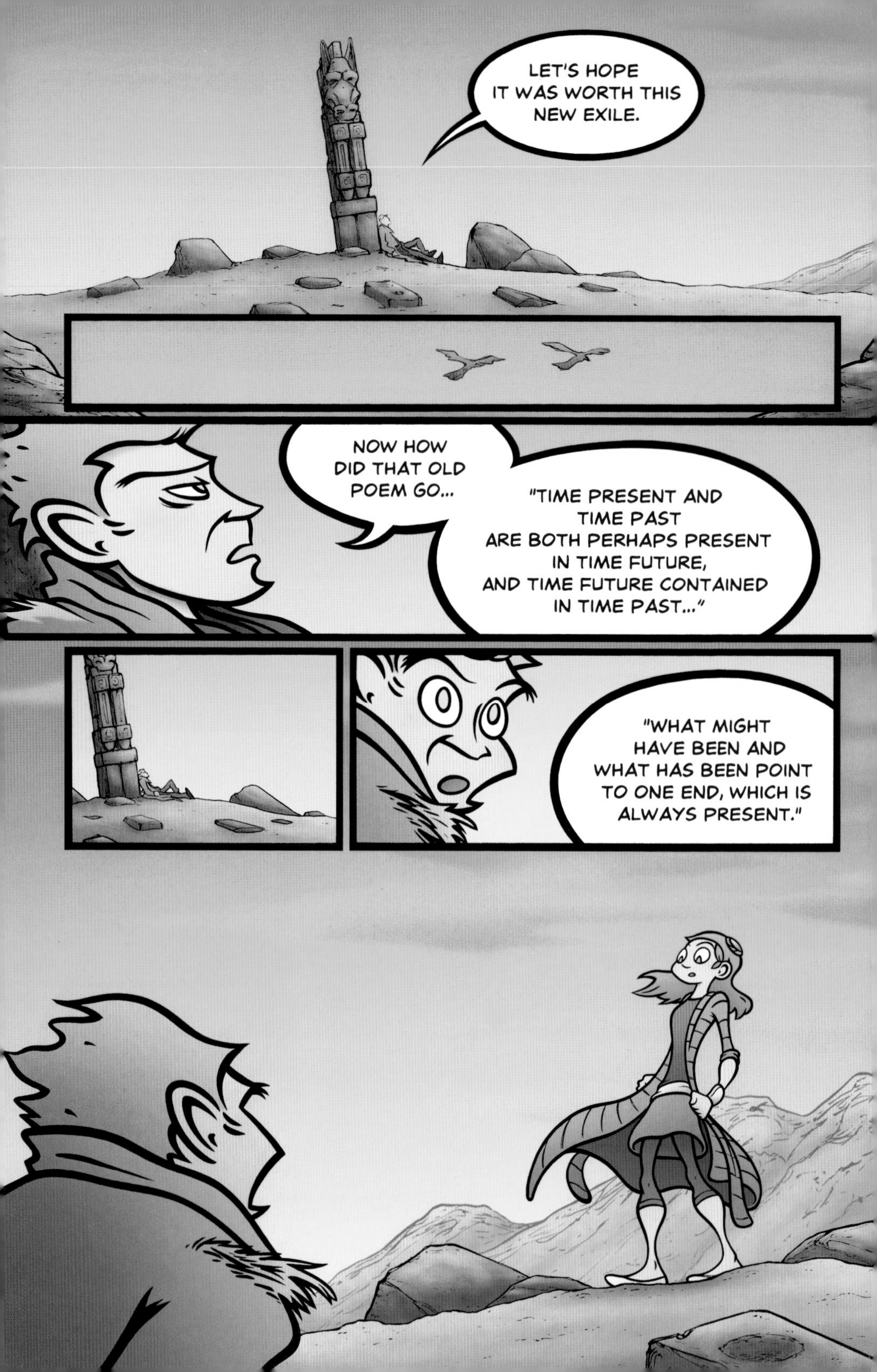
LET'S HOPE IT WAS WORTH THIS NEW EXILE.
NOW HOW DID THAT OLD POEM GO...
"TIME PRESENT AND TIME PAST ARE BOTH PERHAPS PRESENT IN TIME FUTURE, AND TIME FUTURE CONTAINED IN TIME PAST..."
"WHAT MIGHT HAVE BEEN AND WHAT HAS BEEN POINT TO ONE END, WHICH IS ALWAYS PRESENT."

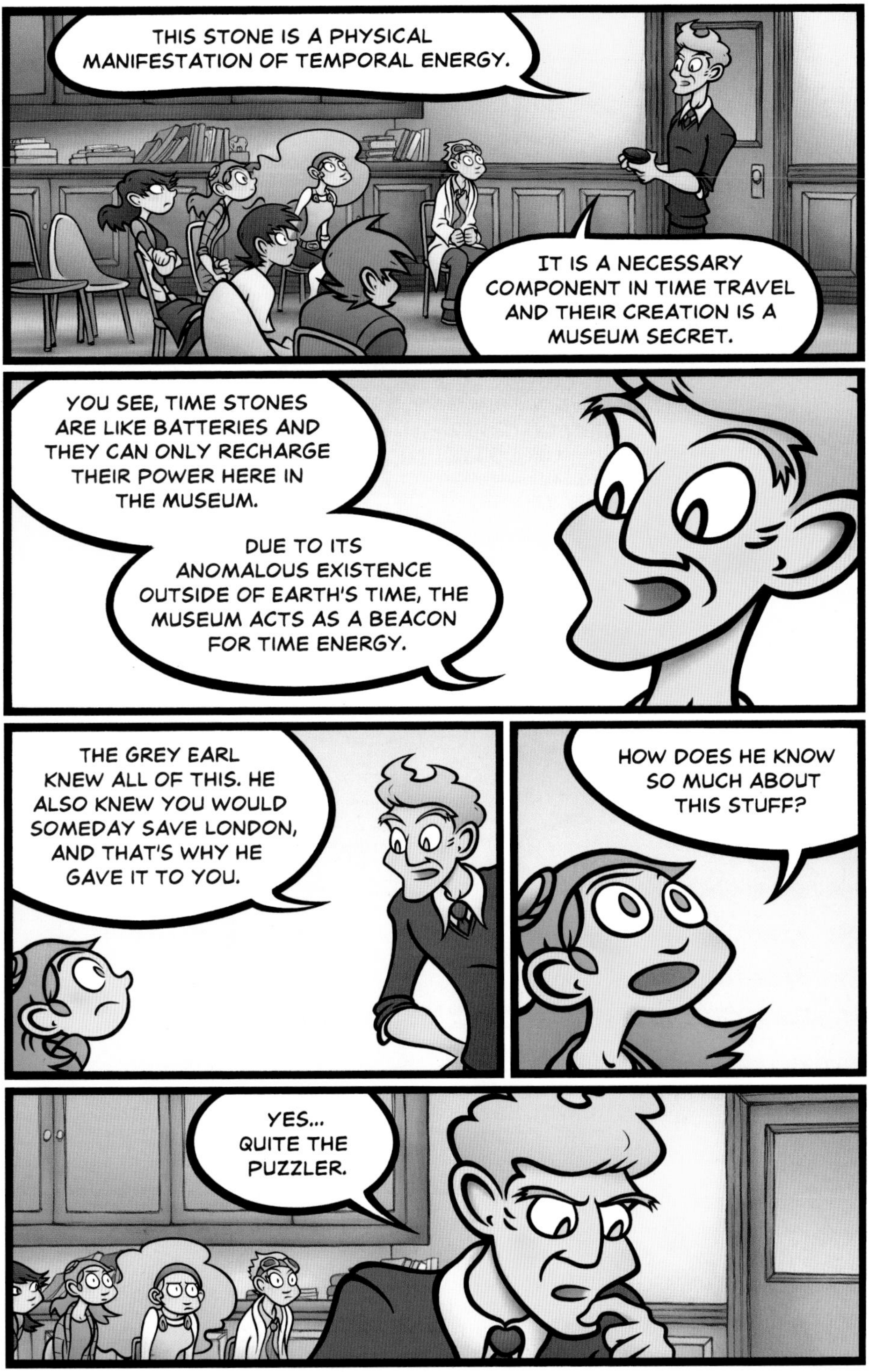
THIS STONE IS A PHYSICAL MANIFESTATION OF TEMPORAL ENERGY.
IT IS A NECESSARY COMPONENT IN TIME TRAVEL AND THEIR CREATION IS A MUSEUM SECRET.
YOU SEE, TIME STONES ARE LIKE BATTERIES AND THEY CAN ONLY RECHARGE THEIR POWER HERE IN THE MUSEUM.
DUE TO ITS ANOMALOUS EXISTENCE OUTSIDE OF EARTH'S TIME, THE MUSEUM ACTS AS A BEACON FOR TIME ENERGY.
THE GREY EARL KNEW ALL OF THIS. HE ALSO KNEW YOU WOULD SOMEDAY SAVE LONDON, AND THAT'S WHY HE GAVE IT TO YOU.
HOW DOES HE KNOW SO MUCH ABOUT THIS STUFF?
YES... QUITE THE PUZZLER.

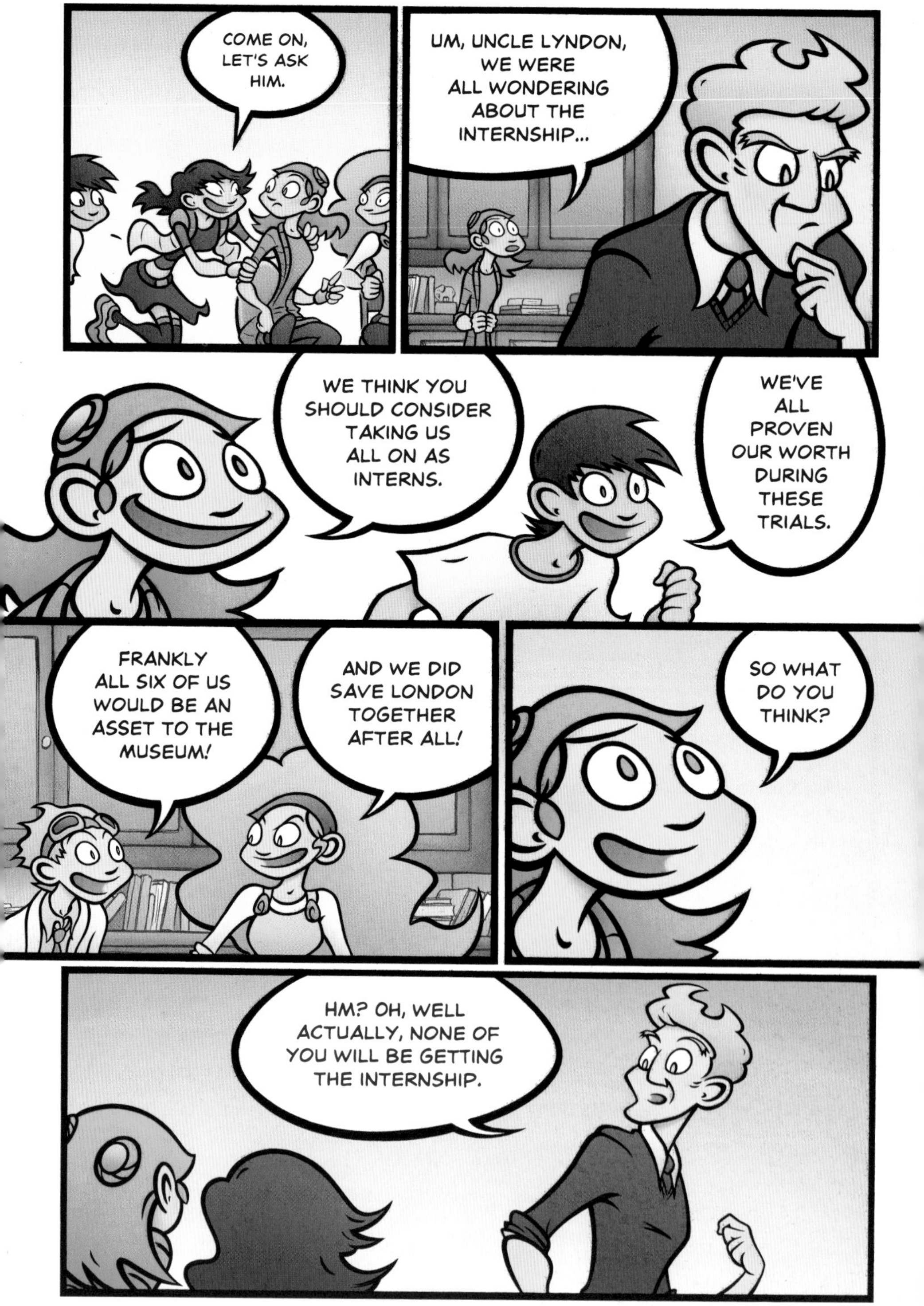

COME ON, LET'S ASK HIM.
UM, UNCLE LYNDON, WE WERE ALL WONDERING ABOUT THE INTERNSHIP...
WE THINK YOU SHOULD CONSIDER TAKING US ALL ON AS INTERNS.
WE'VE ALL PROVEN OUR WORTH DURING THESE TRIALS.
FRANKLY ALL SIX OF US WOULD BE AN ASSET TO THE MUSEUM!
AND WE DID SAVE LONDON TOGETHER AFTER ALL!
SO WHAT DO YOU THINK?
HM? OH, WELL ACTUALLY, NONE OF YOU WILL BE GETTING THE INTERNSHIP.

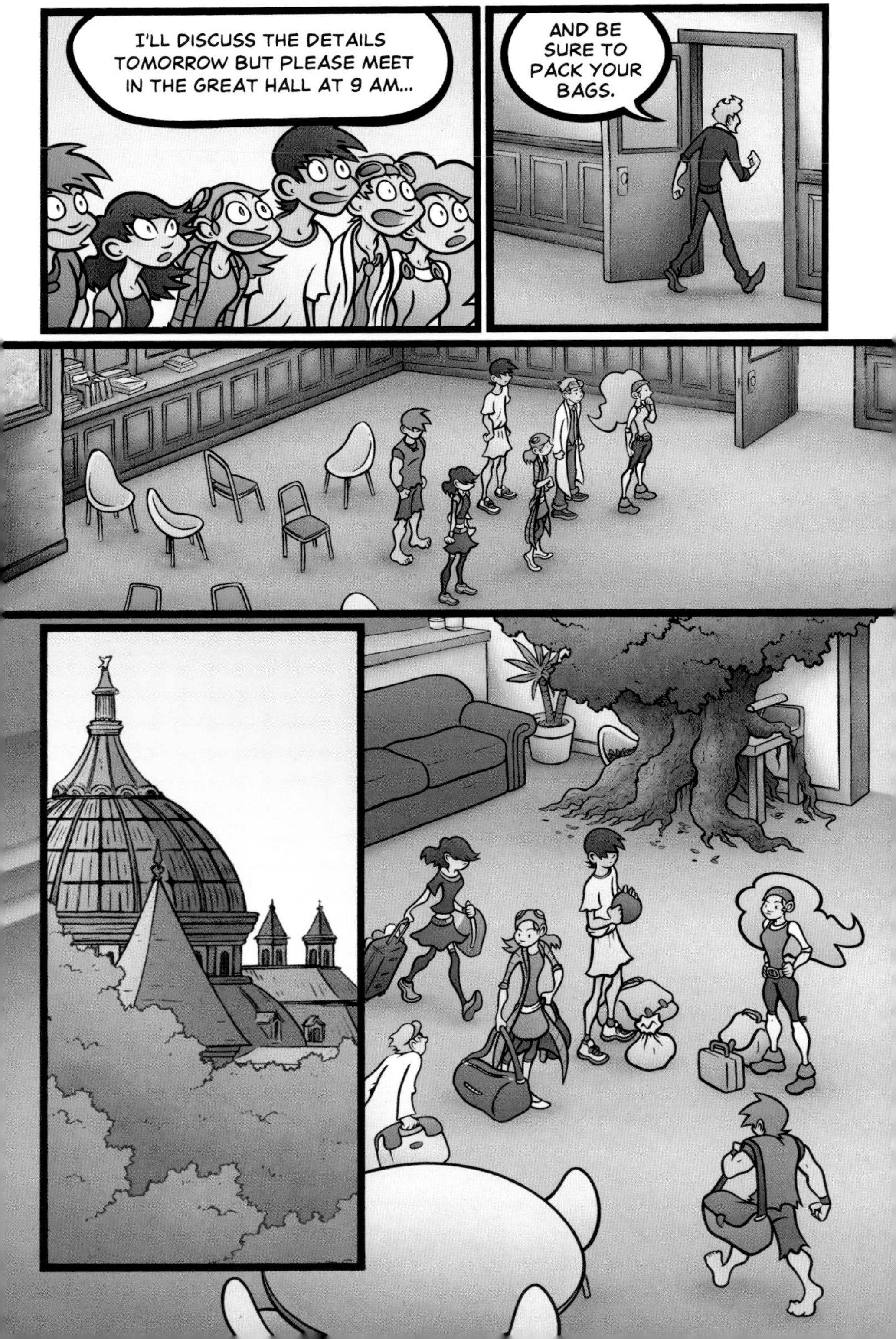
I'LL DISCUSS THE DETAILS TOMORROW BUT PLEASE MEET IN THE GREAT HALL AT 9 AM...
AND BE SURE TO PACK YOUR BAGS.

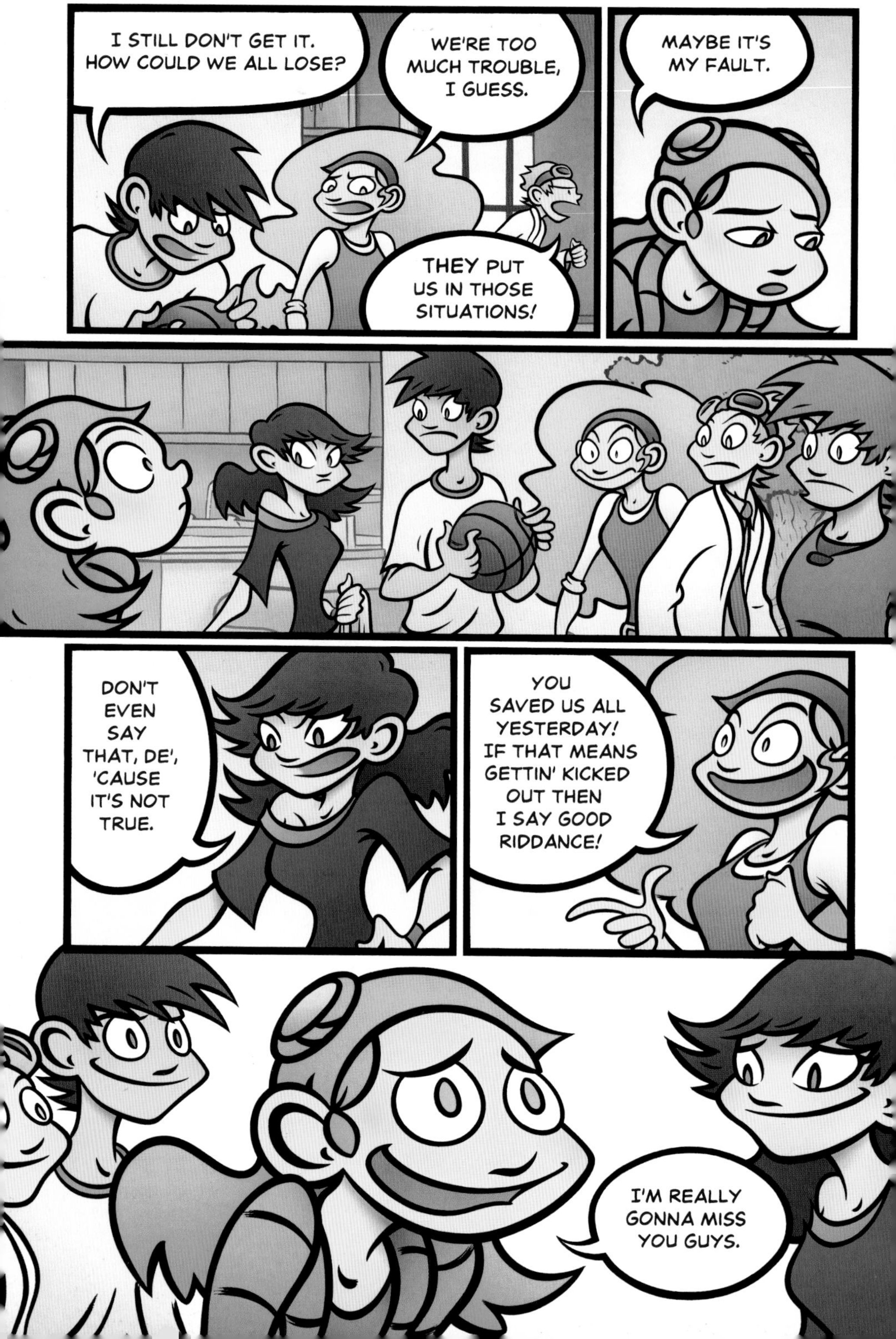
I STILL DON'T GET IT. HOW COULD WE ALL LOSE?
WE'RE TOO MUCH TROUBLE, I GUESS.
THEY PUT US IN THOSE SITUATIONS!
MAYBE IT'S MY FAULT.
DON'T EVEN SAY THAT, DE', 'CAUSE IT'S NOT TRUE.
YOU SAVED US ALL YESTERDAY! IF THAT MEANS GETTIN' KICKED OUT THEN I SAY GOOD RIDDANCE!
I'M REALLY GONNA MISS YOU GUYS.

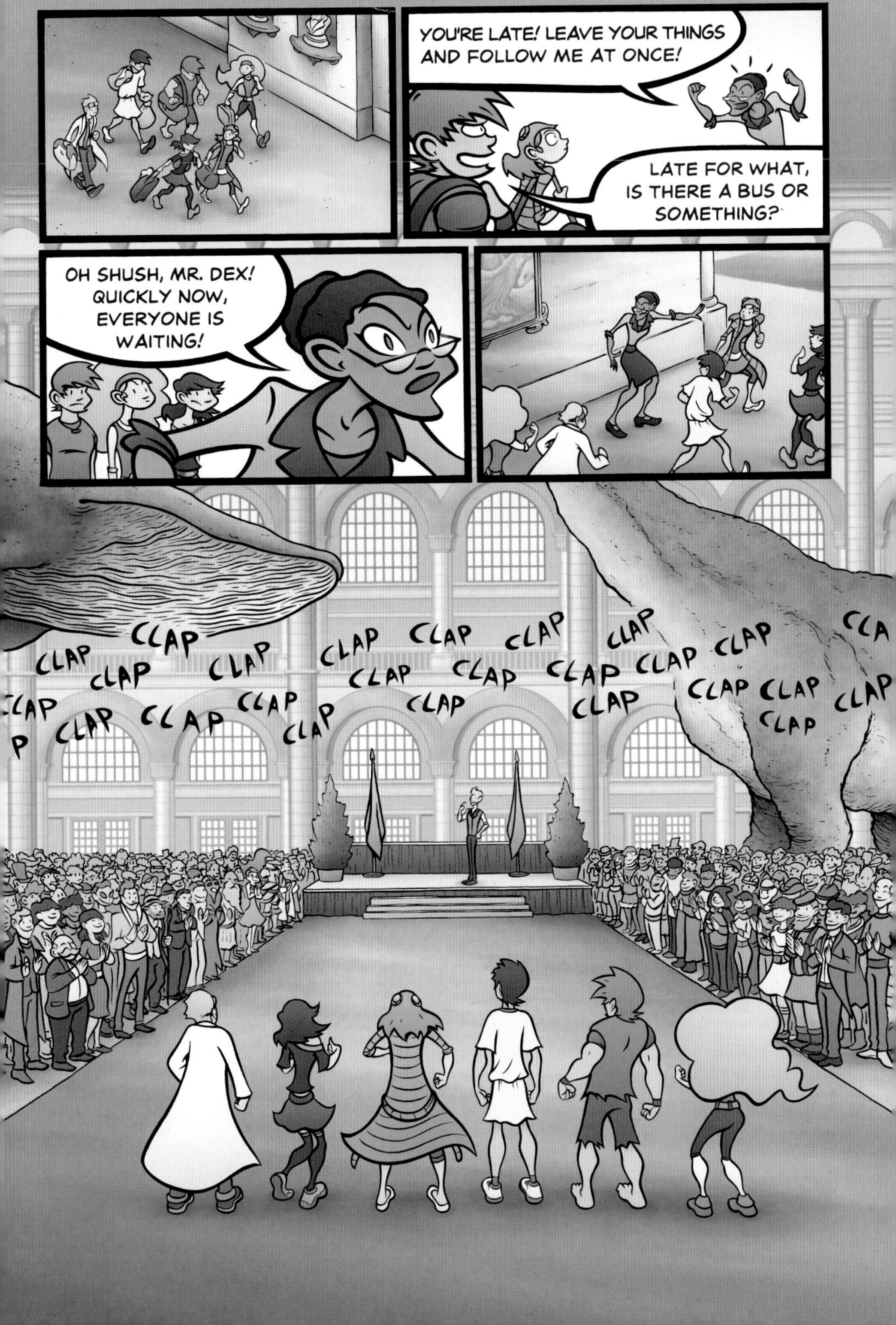
YOU'RE LATE! LEAVE YOUR THINGS AND FOLLOW ME AT ONCE!
LATE FOR WHAT, IS THERE A BUS OR SOMETHING?
OH SHUSH, MR. DEX! QUICKLY NOW, EVERYONE IS WAITING!
CLAP CLAP CLAP CLAP CLAP CLAP CLAP CLAP CLAP CLAP CLAP CLAP CLAP CLAP CLAP CLAP CLAP CLAP CLAP CLAP CLAP CLAP CLAP CLAP CLAP

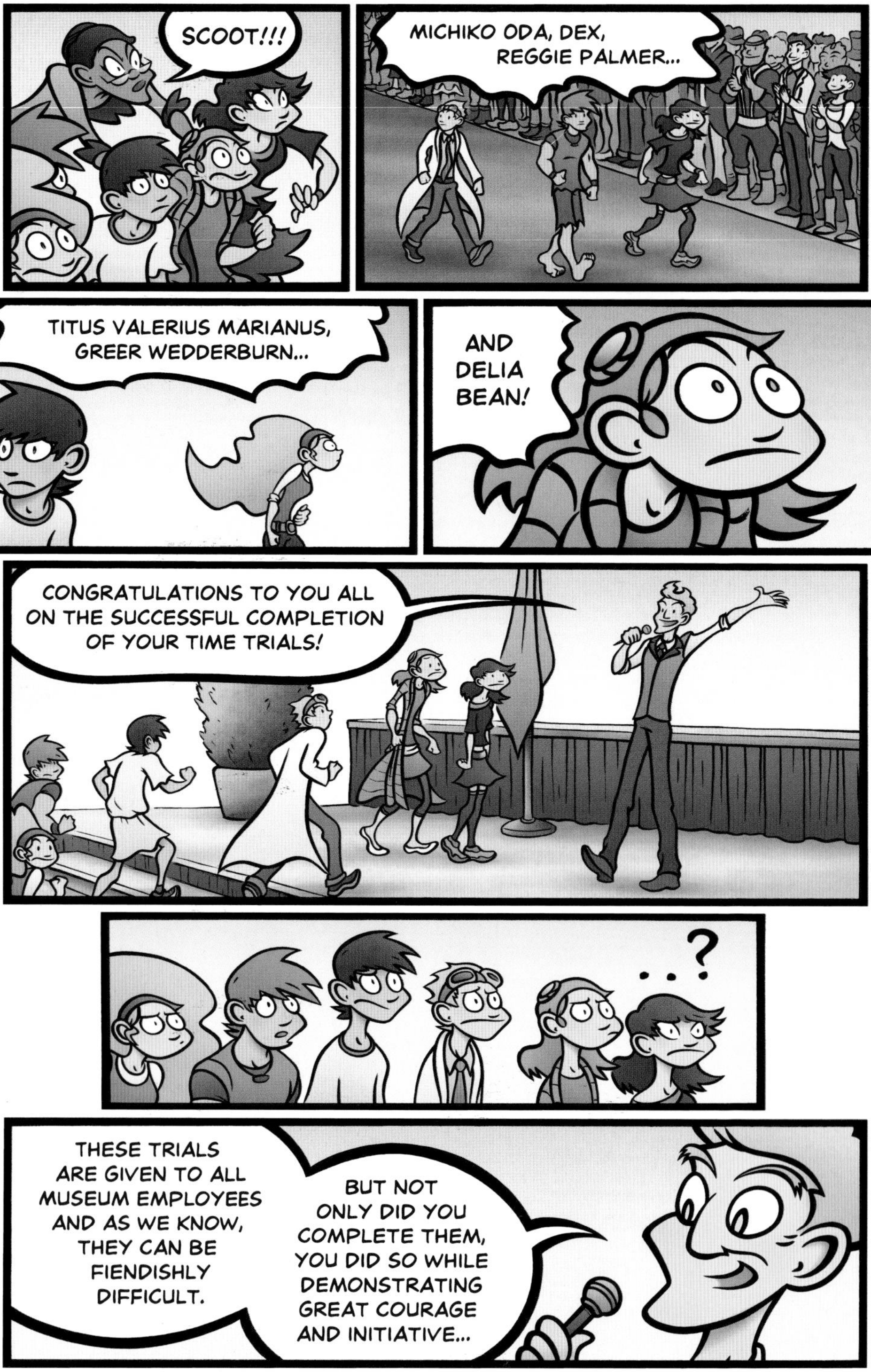
SCOOT!!!
MICHIKO ODA, DEX, REGGIE PALMER...
TITUS VALERIUS MARIANUS, GREER WEDDERBURN...
AND DELIA BEAN!
CONGRATULATIONS TO YOU ALL ON THE SUCCESSFUL COMPLETION OF YOUR TIME TRIALS!
..?
THESE TRIALS ARE GIVEN TO ALL MUSEUM EMPLOYEES AND AS WE KNOW, THEY CAN BE FIENDISHLY DIFFICULT.
BUT NOT ONLY DID YOU COMPLETE THEM, YOU DID SO WHILE DEMONSTRATING GREAT COURAGE AND INITIATIVE...

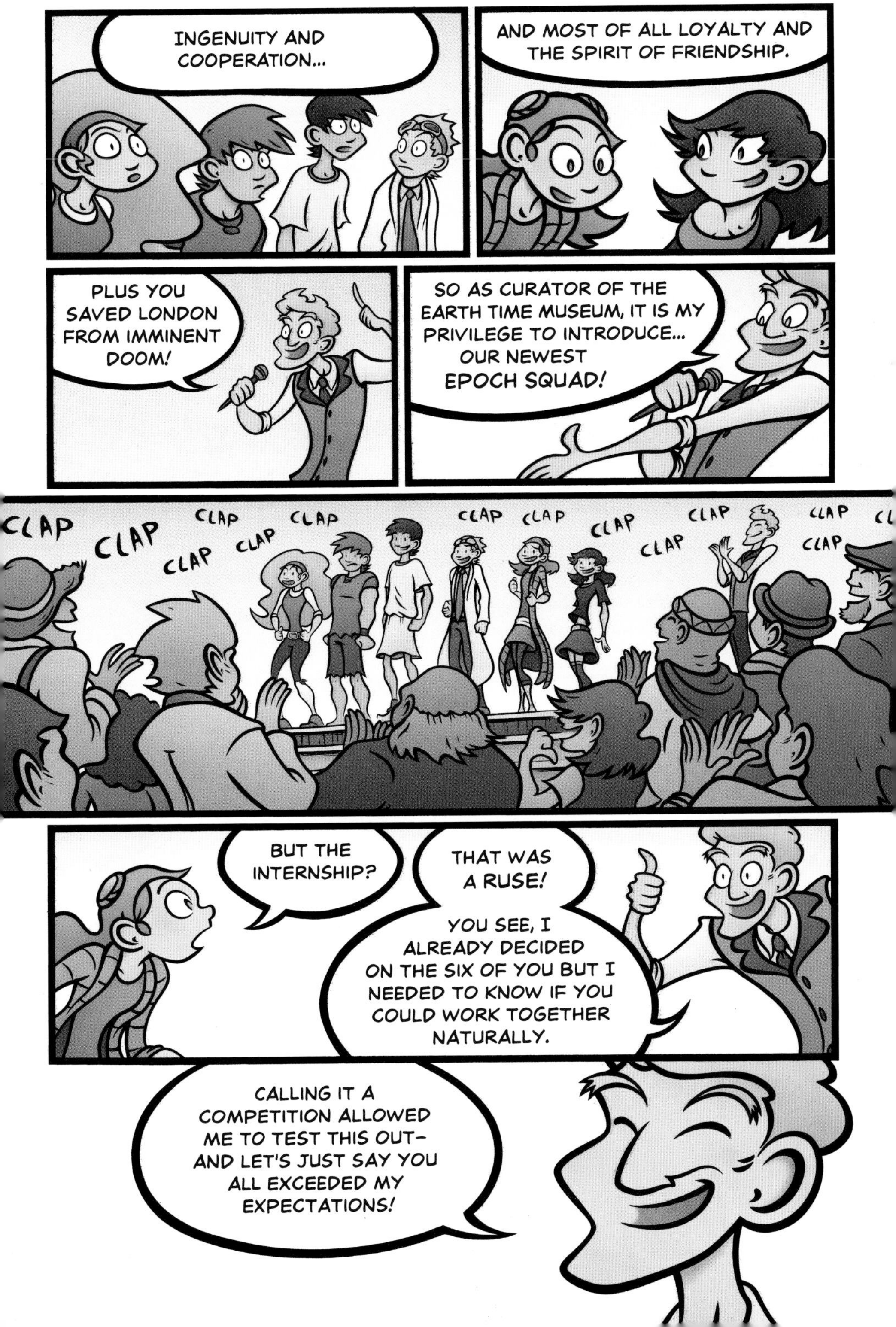
INGENUITY AND COOPERATION...
AND MOST OF ALL LOYALTY AND THE SPIRIT OF FRIENDSHIP.
PLUS YOU SAVED LONDON FROM IMMINENT DOOM!
SO AS CURATOR OF THE EARTH TIME MUSEUM, IT IS MY PRIVILEGE TO INTRODUCE... OUR NEWEST EPOCH SQUAD!
CLAP CLAP CLAP CLAP CLAP CLAP CLAP CLAP CLAP CLAP CLAP CLAP CLAP
BUT THE INTERNSHIP?
THAT WAS A RUSE!
YOU SEE, I ALREADY DECIDED ON THE SIX OF YOU BUT I NEEDED TO KNOW IF YOU COULD WORK TOGETHER NATURALLY.
CALLING IT A COMPETITION ALLOWED ME TO TEST THIS OUT— AND LET'S JUST SAY YOU ALL EXCEEDED MY EXPECTATIONS!

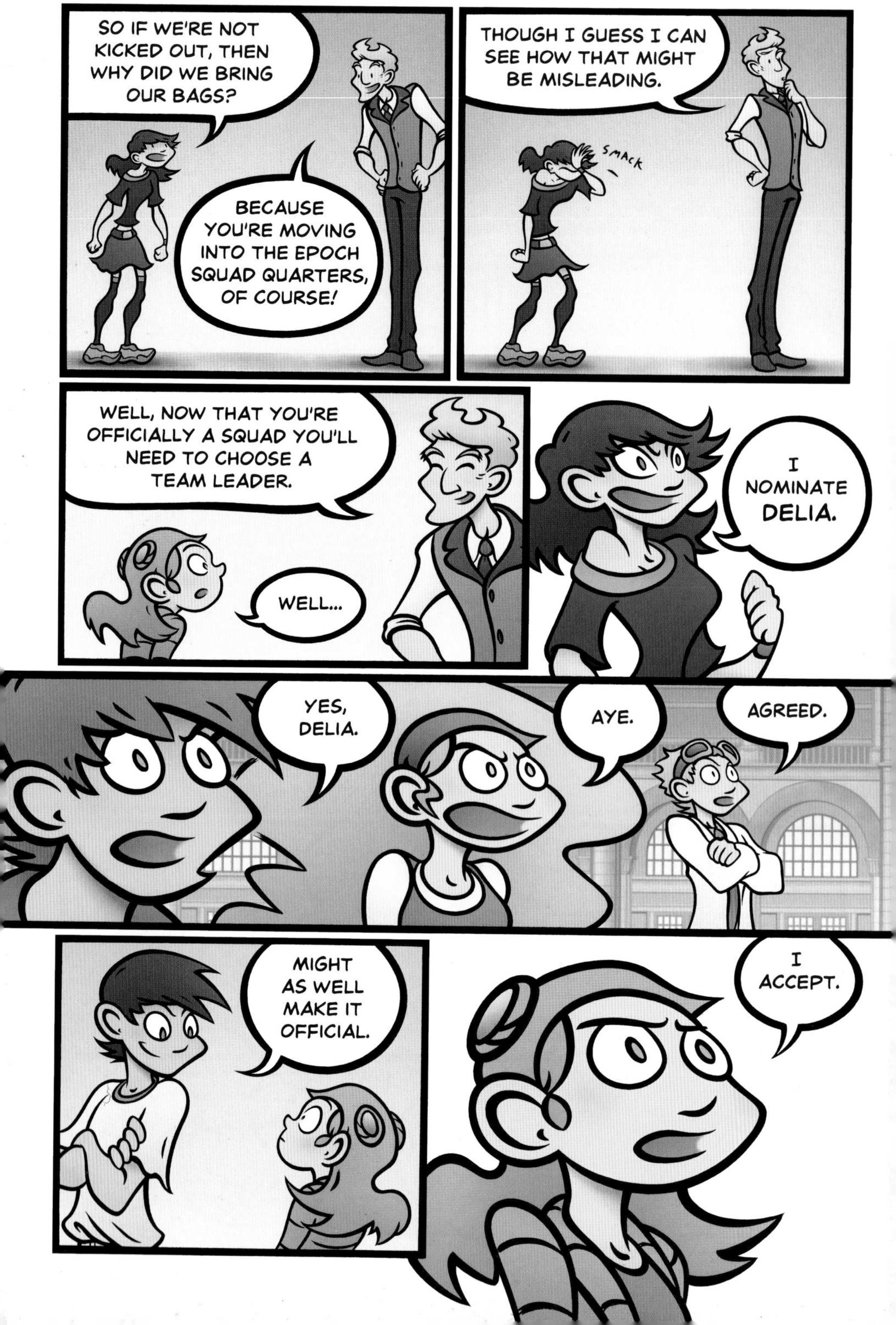
SO IF WE'RE NOT KICKED OUT, THEN WHY DID WE BRING OUR BAGS?
BECAUSE YOU'RE MOVING INTO THE EPOCH SQUAD QUARTERS, OF COURSE!
THOUGH I GUESS I CAN SEE HOW THAT MIGHT BE MISLEADING.
SMACK
WELL, NOW THAT YOU'RE OFFICIALLY A SQUAD YOU'LL NEED TO CHOOSE A TEAM LEADER.
WELL...
I NOMINATE DELIA.
YES, DELIA.
AYE.
AGREED.
MIGHT AS WELL MAKE IT OFFICIAL.
I ACCEPT.

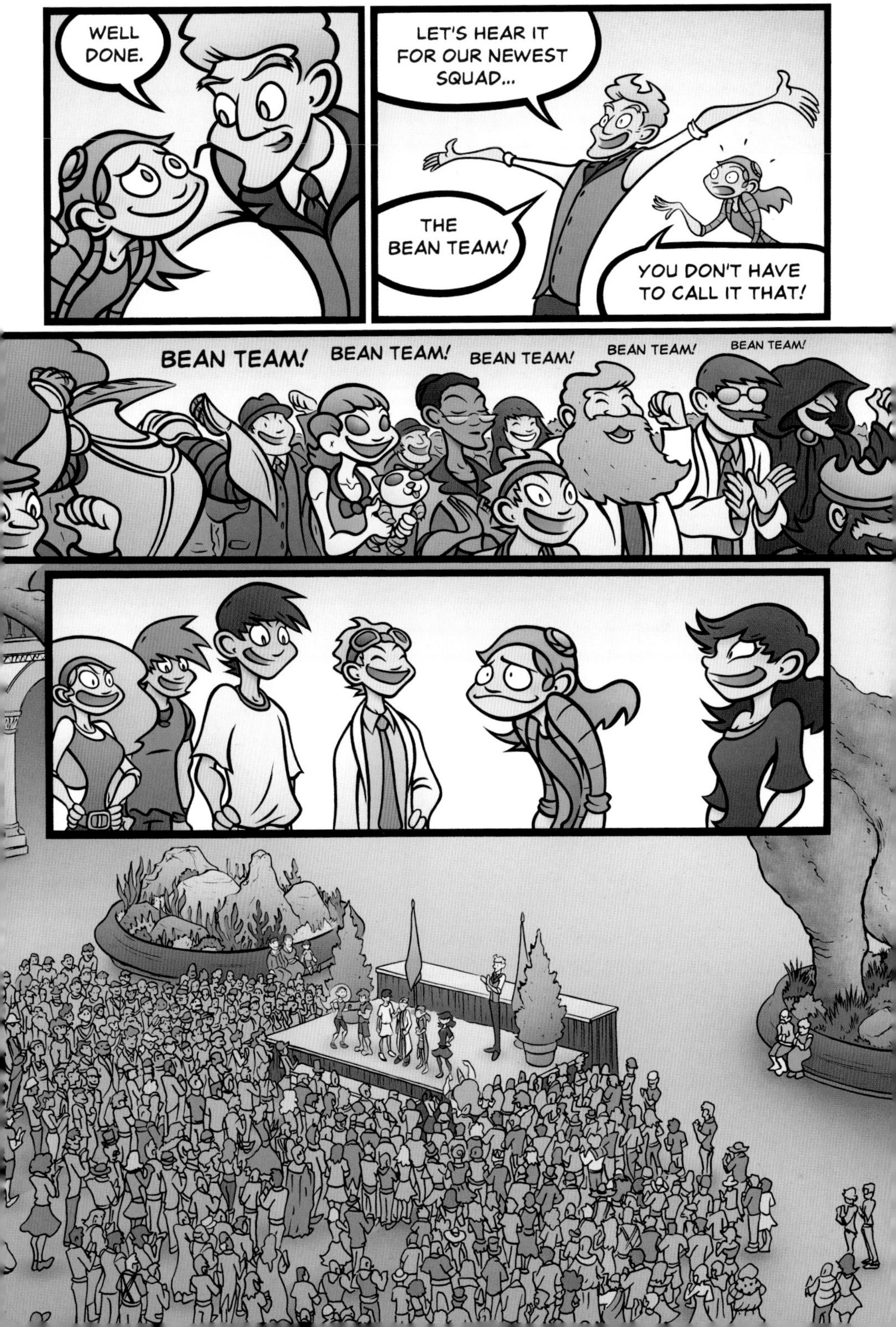
WELL DONE.
LET'S HEAR IT FOR OUR NEWEST SQUAD...
THE BEAN TEAM!
YOU DON'T HAVE TO CALL IT THAT!
BEAN TEAM!
BEAN TEAM!
BEAN TEAM!
BEAN TEAM!
BEAN TEAM!

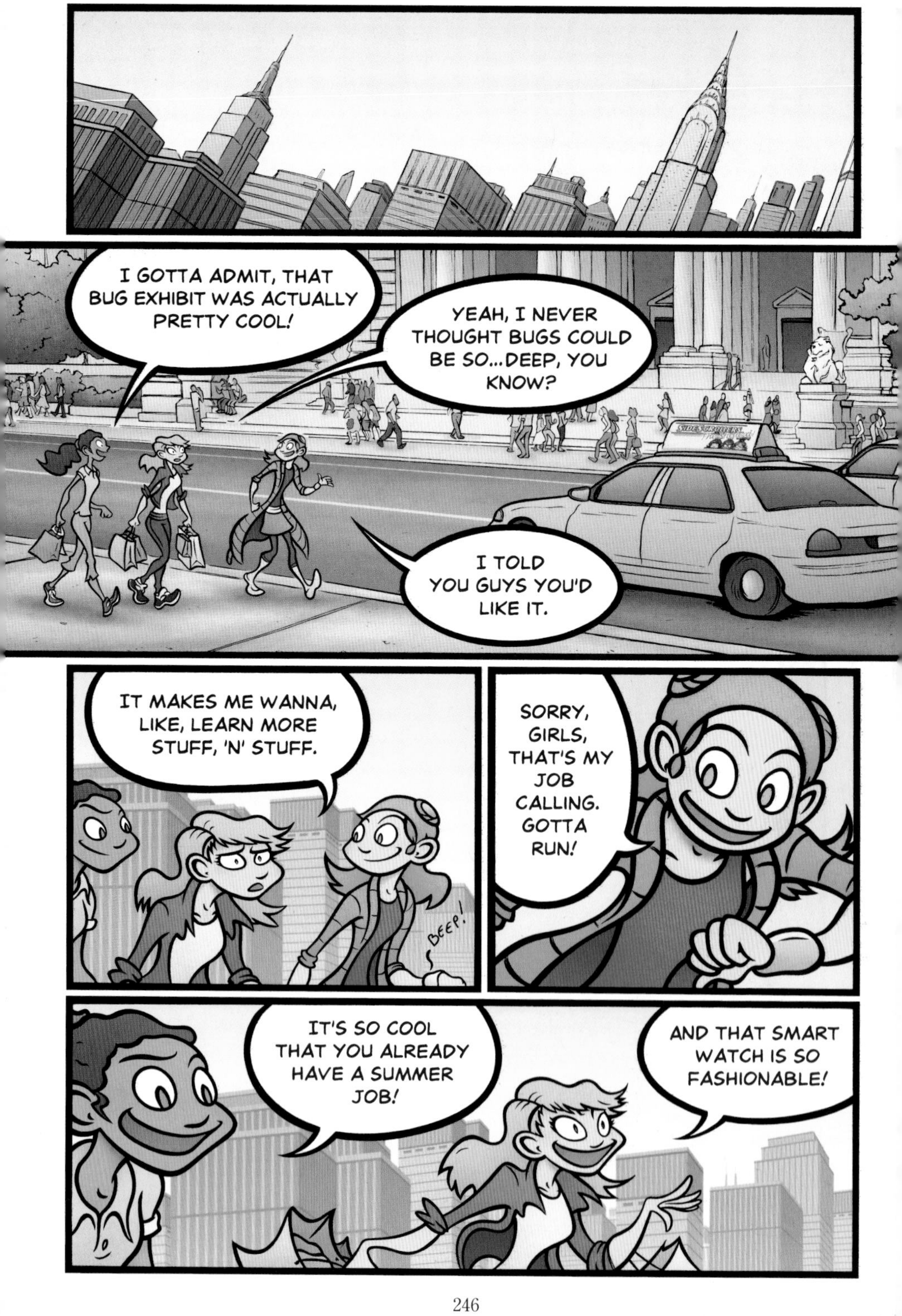
I GOTTA ADMIT, THAT BUG EXHIBIT WAS ACTUALLY PRETTY COOL!
YEAH, I NEVER THOUGHT BUGS COULD BE SO...DEEP, YOU KNOW?
I TOLD YOU GUYS YOU'D LIKE IT.
IT MAKES ME WANNA, LIKE, LEARN MORE STUFF, 'N' STUFF.
BEEP!
SORRY, GIRLS, THAT'S MY JOB CALLING. GOTTA RUN!
IT'S SO COOL THAT YOU ALREADY HAVE A SUMMER JOB!
AND THAT SMART WATCH IS SO FASHIONABLE!

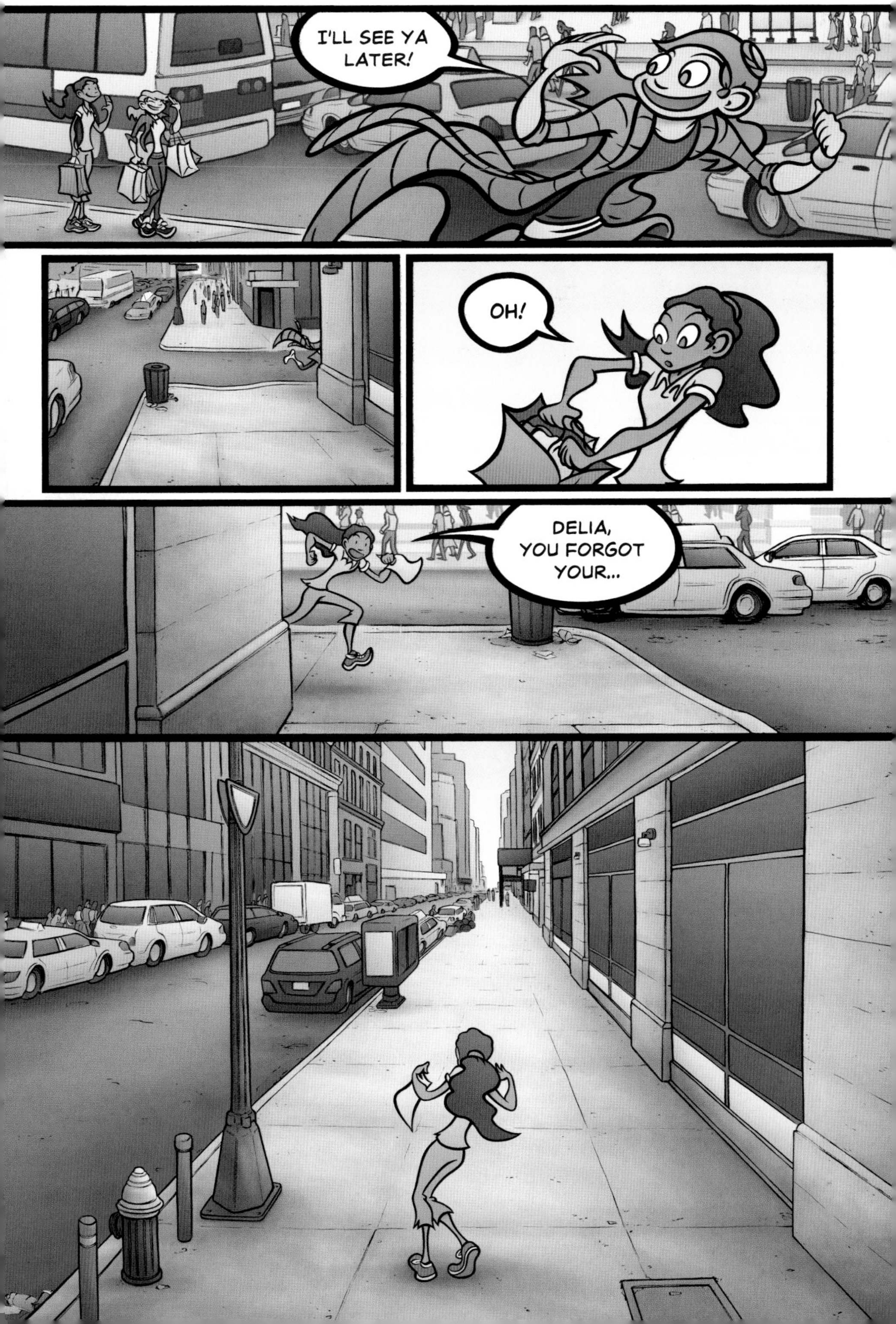
I'LL SEE YA LATER!
OH!
DELIA, YOU FORGOT YOUR...

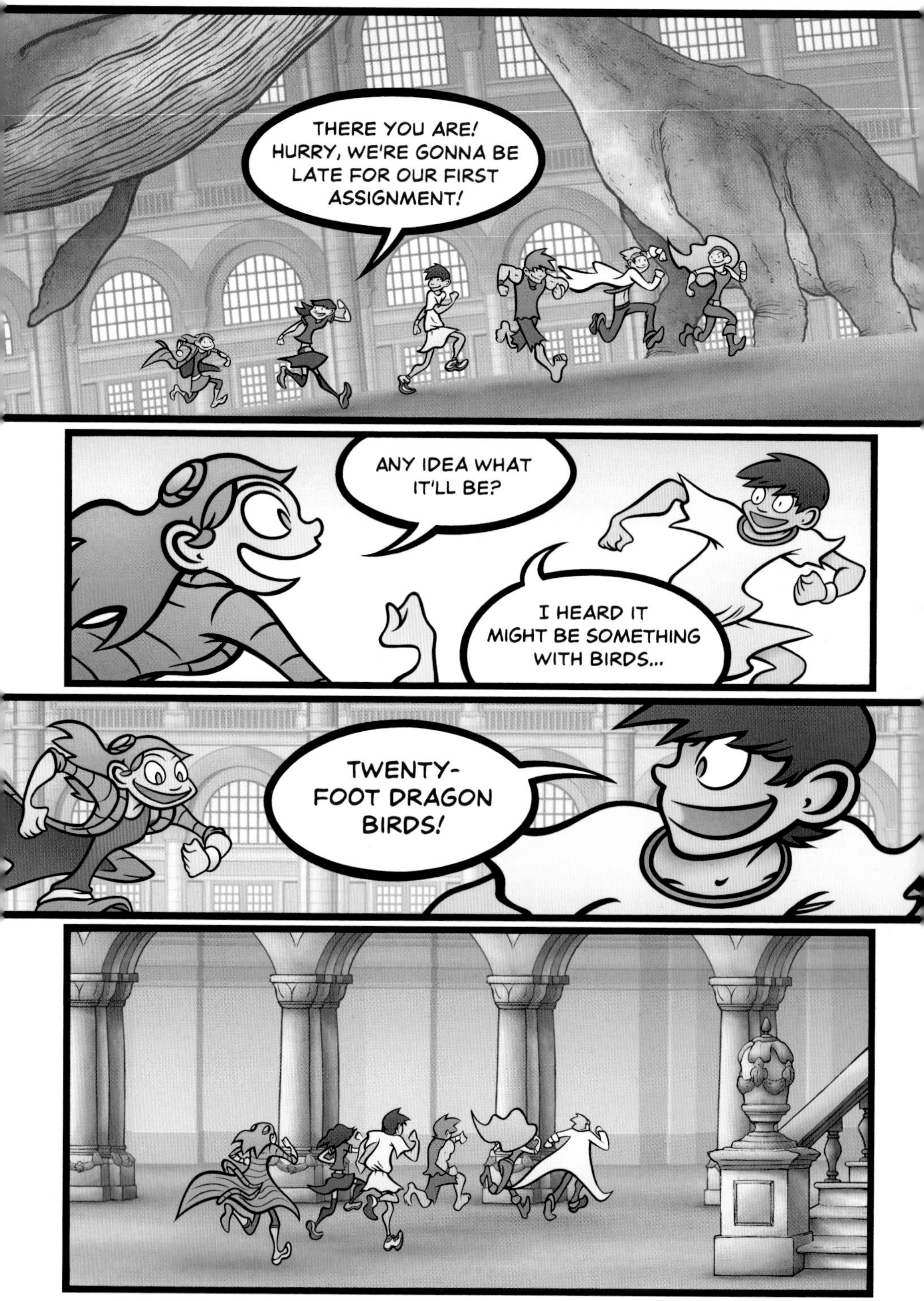
THERE YOU ARE! HURRY, WE'RE GONNA BE LATE FOR OUR FIRST ASSIGNMENT!
ANY IDEA WHAT IT'LL BE?
I HEARD IT MIGHT BE SOMETHING WITH BIRDS...
TWENTY-FOOT DRAGON BIRDS!

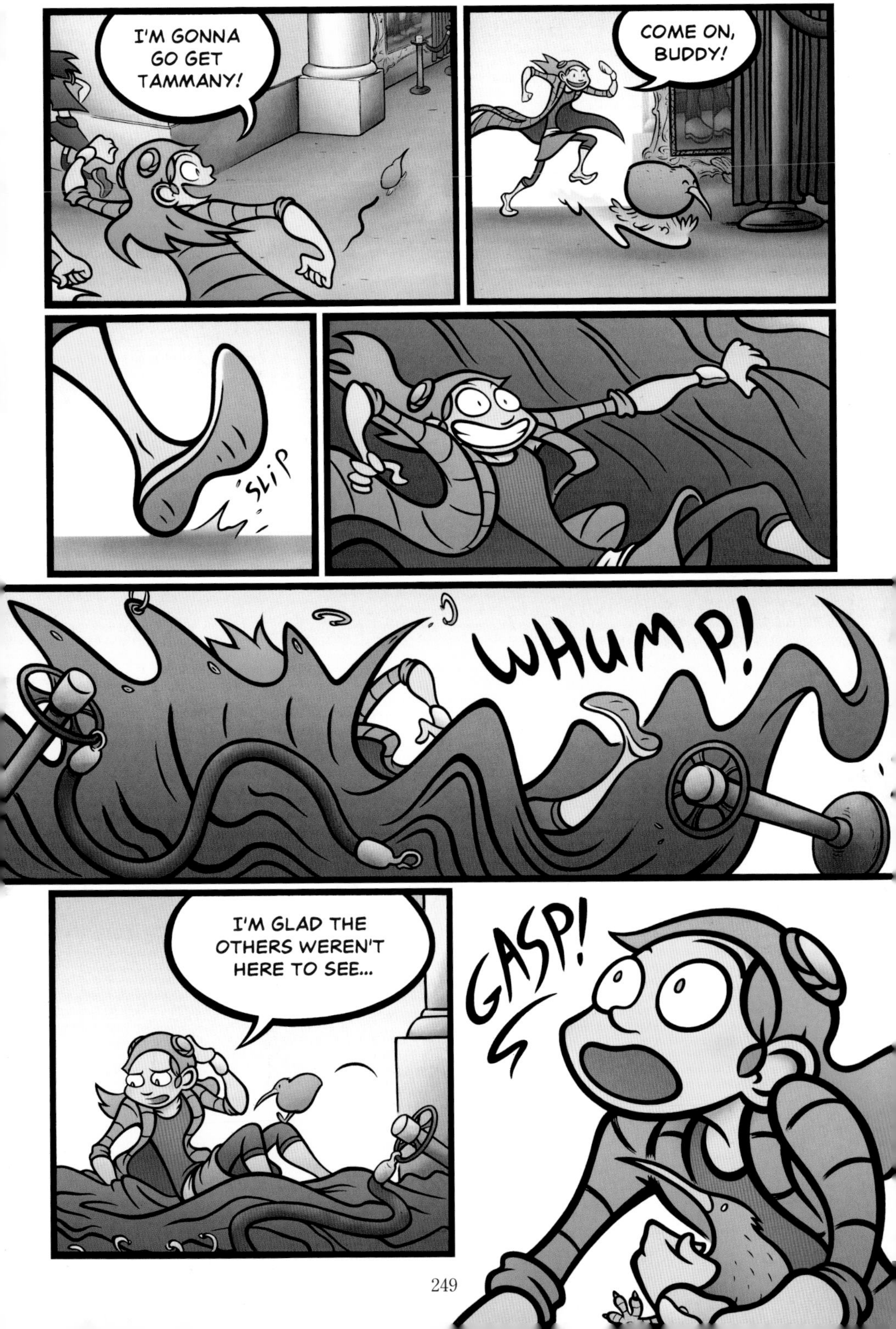
I'M GONNA GO GET TAMMANY!
COME ON, BUDDY!
SLIP
WHUMP!
I'M GLAD THE OTHERS WEREN'T HERE TO SEE...
GASP!

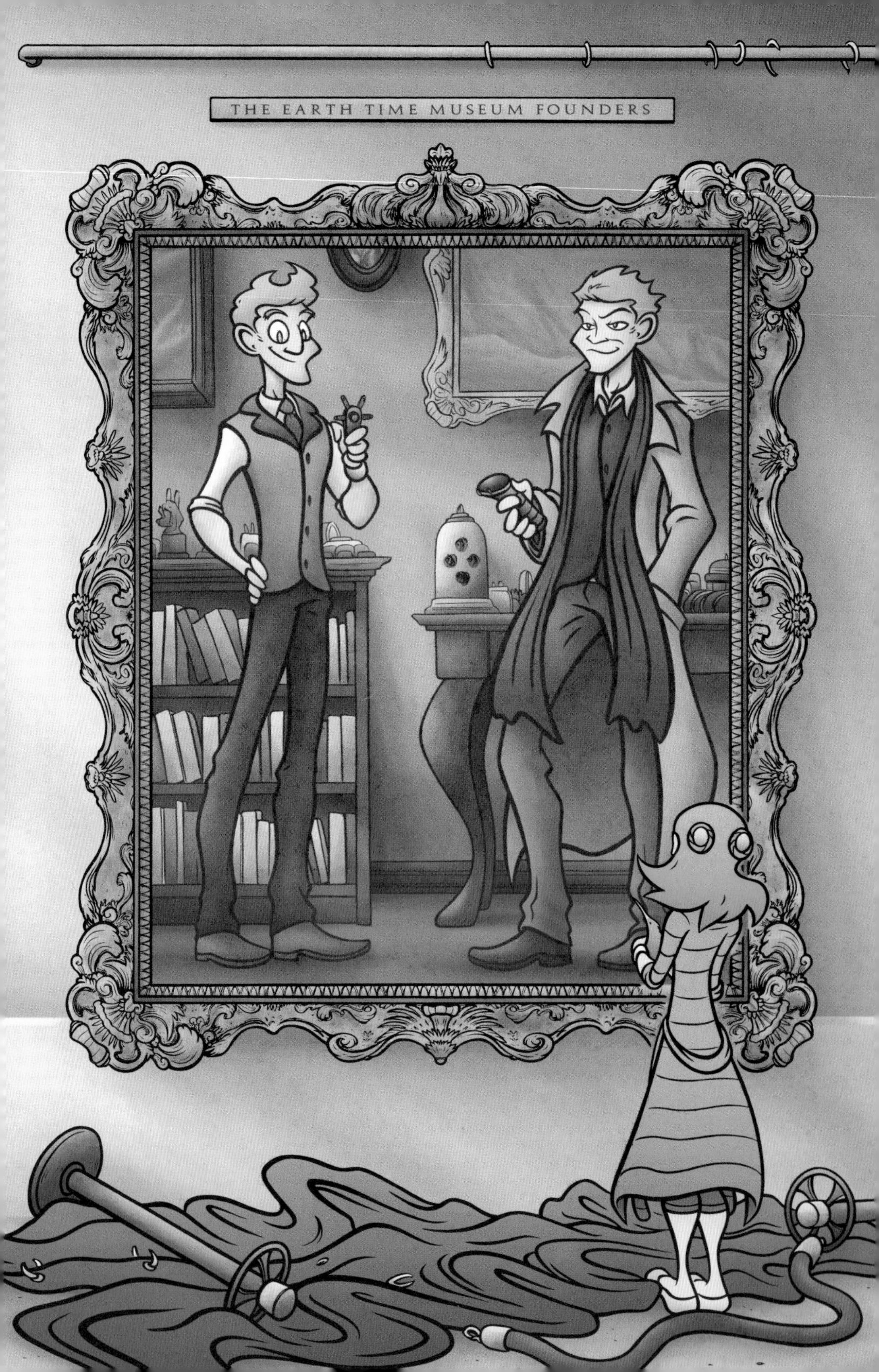
THE EARTH TIME MUSEUM FOUNDERS

THE TIME MUSEUM

Continues in

Book Two!

First Second
New York

Published by First Second
First Second is an imprint of Roaring Brook Press,
a division of Holtzbrinck Publishing Holdings Limited Partnership
175 Fifth Avenue, New York, New York 10010

Library of Congress Control Number: 2016938732

ISBN: 978-1-59643-849-1

Our books may be purchased in bulk for promotional, educational,
or business use. Please contact your local bookseller or the Macmillan
Corporate and Premium Sales Department at (800) 221-7945 ext. 5442
or by email at MacmillanSpecialMarkets@macmillan.com.

First edition 2017

Book design by Danielle Ceccolini

Printed in China by Toppan Leefung Printing Ltd., Dongguan City, Guangdong Province

10 9 8 7 6 5 4 3 2 1

Penciled on Strathmore Bristol paper with a drafting lead holder and HB drawing leads.
Inked in Winsor & Newton black India ink with several Series 7 sable brushes (size 0)
and colored digitally in Photoshop.